"It's NOT the Heat, it's the Humidity, STUPID!"

(Growing up in the nation's most energetic, eclectic, and yes, expensive county...Palm Beach)

MIKE FLEMING

authorHOUSE®

AuthorHouse™
1663 Liberty Drive
Bloomington, IN 47403
www.authorhouse.com
Phone: 833-262-8899

Published by AuthorHouse 09/23/2022

ISBN: 978-1-6655-7157-9 (sc)
ISBN: 978-1-6655-7156-2 (hc)
ISBN: 978-1-6655-7158-6 (e)

Library of Congress Control Number: 2022917694

Print information available on the last page.

This book is printed on acid-free paper.

CONTENTS

INTRODUCTION

When I retired from the Palm Beach County School District after thirty-seven years as a high school classroom teacher, coach, athletic director, and department chairman, I needed to start a new chapter. Teaching was great in so many ways, which I will hopefully express with the passion the profession deserves as I put pen to paper. I cannot just go golfing or fishing every day. For some that works, but not for me. I have written before. I have made contributions to nonfiction US history textbooks. It is cool to see your name and school in the credits, I will admit. I wrote a crime-themed thriller set in West Palm Beach and the Bahamas that apparently did not thrill my potential editors. It did not help that my connection to the publishing world died in a seaplane crash. I was truly fortunate to have taken a creative writing class as a senior at the University of Mississippi, more affectionately known as Ole Miss. I have a deep love for literature because of the many great writers from the area, such as Nobel Prizewinner William Faulkner. It is such a treat to study the man's work at a class held in his house, in his study. The great Eudora Welty is a Mississippian, and along with the ultra-talented author and editor Willie Morris they were my creative writing teachers in addition to some guest instructors. Yes, I met Harper Lee. This class inspired some great writers, such as best-selling authors John Grisham and Donna Tartt, and the underrated and under-read Larry Brown and Barry Hannah. I thought that with *It's Not the Heat; It's the Humidity, Stupid!* I would give it another shot and write about what I know—and I know Palm Beach County.

Palm Beach County, located in the southeast corner of Florida, is diverse and unique in so many ways that the subject matter can be overwhelming. What I decided to do was to write about the experiences of me, my family, my friends, and my community. Most of the names have been changed, and some of the characters are a blend of multiple people. I witnessed most of the events described herein firsthand, while a couple of the others are stories of the locals.

Most outsiders see Palm Beach County from the immediate coastline west and in a few miles and really have no idea how big and diverse it really is. Palm Beach County has an area that is larger than that of two states (Rhode Island and Delaware). One can drive all day from the North County line in Tequesta south to Boca Raton, then west to Canal Point, to Belle Glade and Pahokee in the agricultural west, and back east again and have driven all day. Blink on I-95 and you'll miss Delaware, for purposes of comparison. Also, Palm Beach County is very diverse in its makeup. It is one of the wealthiest communities in the world with its mansions, millionaires, five-star hotels, and exclusive stores and clubs, and is home to two presidents (JFK and Donald Trump). The South County has been described as the "sixth borough" as so many transplanted northeasterners, especially from New York City, inhabit the area from Boynton Beach–Delray Beach to Boca Raton. Jerry Seinfeld had fun with this area in his eponymous popular TV sitcom by renaming the retirement community "Del Boca."

Going west from Palm Beach, you travel through the central communities of Rivera Beach, West Palm Beach, and Lake Worth Beach. Officials added the word *Beach* to the name just recently. It's still Lake Worth. West Palm Beach was started 125 years ago as a "city of servants." It is the county seat and now a semimajor city with all its potential and, yes, big-city problems. Leaving West Palm Beach, you will drive through the sprawling suburbia that is known as the western communities, which area is home to one of the leading equestrian communities with million-dollar barns, paddocks, and horse training and competition sites. These were at one time agricultural fields with peppers, strawberries, and sweet corn. Continuing west, you pass acre upon acre of rich farmland where winter vegetables and sugar are grown. The soil is the gold here. The towns of Belle Glade and Pahokee are rich with pride but short on money and services. Poverty and crime are everywhere, but so is young athletic talent. The National Football League is filled with stars who hail from this impoverished area. They boast about their hometowns with pride.

Going north, you'll find the communities that make up the North County. Palm Beach Gardens was started by billionaire John D. MacArthur. "Mr. Mac" made his money in the insurance industry of Chicago and, like the true father of the county, Henry Flagler, came south with a vision and with a love for the weather. Mr. MacArthur built his community around the game of golf, where it still flourishes today. So many of the top golfers call the North County home, including the two best: Jack Nicklaus and Tiger Woods (the latter lives in southern Martin County at Jupiter Island). Jupiter used to be a small agricultural and fishing town. It is famous for its lighthouse, which was surveyed by a young Robert E. Lee and built by George Meade. These two men would meet again at Gettysburg. The Interstate Highway Act changed the North County as I-95 was finally complete by the late 1970s and early 1980s. This led to the development of North County suburbia as a new group of commuters would settle in the Jupiter area. The village of Tequesta borders the county line with Martin County. Once a town filled with engineers who worked for Pratt & Whitney (doing jet engine research and development), RCA electronics, and various supplemental firms, Tequesta changed when Pratt was bought by United Technologies and moved to Connecticut and when RCA moved to Asia. In the past twenty years, people, both retirees and suburbanites, have rediscovered Tequesta.

The variety of the towns and cities in Palm Beach County is matched only by the variety of people who call it home. There are the old Florida crackers, generational locals who wear that badge with pride, who are retirees from the North and especially the Northeast. Their numbers are getting smaller every year. There are fewer and fewer barbecue restaurants and more Italian food and bagel establishments, which is direct proof of the change. When Fidel Castro overthrew the government of Cuba, many Cubans escaped their homeland and came to South Florida, mostly Miami. But many came up to Palm Beach County. Spanish is the primary language spoken in many neighborhoods here now. Many residents of Cuban descent are now of the third generation and have risen to prominence in law, medicine, and education and have intermarried with the locals. Haiti, an extremely poor island nation, is another source of immigration to the county. Language barriers, economic competition, and poor primary education have hindered these immigrants' attainment of, but have not stopped their journey toward, the American dream. Recent arrivals have come to the United States in search of the promise expressed by the O-word *opportunity.* These people come here looking for a chance and have an incredible work ethic. Places such as Guatemala, Mexico, and Honduras are the areas they used to come home. Now it is Palm Beach County.

There has always been a vibrant African American community who have also called this diverse area home. For years, black communities had been victims of Jim Crow segregationist policies, and today many are suffering from the same problems that other areas of the United States are experiencing. Crime, drugs, and violence hurt many of these communities, yet many Palm Beach County African Americans have been part of the huge movement to the middle class and toward success. There are smaller immigrant groups such as the Finnish in the Lake Worth area, along with Canadians, who have come in search of warmer climates, lower taxes, and more readily available health care. Other immigrants include wealthy people from South America escaping political turmoil, and Europeans, who also come looking for that elusive, but available, opportunity.

This is Palm Beach County in all its beauty and with all its warts.

CHAPTER

1

The Story of John and Charlene Finch

The story about one Nicholas Finch, or Nick, begins in upstate South Carolina, in the town of Spartanburg. His father, John Wendall Finch, was the tenth of eleven children born to Harold and Marion Finch. J.W., as he would come to be called, grew up on the biggest dairy farm in all of South Carolina. Finch ice cream, cheese, butter, and of course milk could be found throughout the "Gamecock" state. All the brothers and sisters worked daily chores on the farm. The girls cooked and did housework, while the boys worked the dairy. Dairy farming chores needed to be done every day, and twice a day at that, since milk cows do not comprehend holidays such as Easter and Christmas. They do not care about the heat, the cold, the rain, or anything else. On the Finch farm, they had to be fed, led from the barn twice a day, and milked twice a day. Milk then had to be taken to the dairy plant for processing and delivery.

When J.W.'s older brothers and sisters grew up, they married and were given some land and cows. From this, they proceeded to start their own farms. J.W. and his younger sister Millie swore they would be out of there as soon as possible. They both did well in school. J.W. was exceptionally good at math and athletics, and Millie was an attractive young woman who loved the classics of literature. Millie had no thoughts of being a farmer's wife. She would go to Furman University in Greenville and become an English teacher. She married the shop teacher and baseball coach. And their daughter, Kelly, was an early family celebrity, having been chosen to be a Gerber baby bottle model. This was the start for Kelly, who would later be named Miss South Carolina and become second runner-up to the Miss America title, with the woman who won the crown having come from Mississippi. A Clemson graduate who became a young reporter and anchor for the NBC affiliate in Charleston, Kelly would marry a local heart surgeon, retire from TV work, and become a leading charity icon. When Kelly would visit her uncle J.W. in Florida, it became quite clear to her why friends and teammates of her cousin Nick would just happen to stop by. They were hunting dogs following a scent and in pursuit. J.W. laughed about this all the time. Those who came seeking got nowhere.

Charlene Elizabeth Smith was the same age as J.W., but she lived about five hundred miles away. A townie of Avon Park, Florida, she was the daughter of a fruit company plant manager and contractor, Pete Smith. Pete married a local woman named Sabrina Jones.

Avon Park was a small town, then known for its railroad depot where citrus and beef cattle would be shipped out. Much like her future husband, Charlene was counting the days before she could move up and out, seeking bigger and better things. Her desire only increased after her dad died of cancer when she was just thirteen. She missed him very much and did not care for her mother's newfound experiences of courtship. Charlene would stay in her room for hours listening to the radio, reading, and studying. She too was a good student, especially in the sciences. After her graduation, she quickly moved to Tampa and started studying for her nurse's license. She believed the profession would provide a decent wage, clean work, and a chance to travel.

Everything changed for both families when, on that fateful day of infamy, December 7, 1941, the United States was plunged into war. J.W.'s older brothers quickly enlisted. Farmers were considered essential, so he stayed on the farm until 1943. When he turned twenty-one, he enlisted in the army as a paratrooper. He was assigned to the famous Eighty-Second Airborne Division and was shipped off to Fort Bragg for jump school. His leadership skills were noticed, and he was quickly made a corporal. Then it was off to England. While in England, he was awarded his sergeant stripes. Things were happening at a dizzying pace.

Rumors were flying all over England about an invasion of France. On June 6, 1944, the Allies hit the beaches of Normandy. D-Day was on. J.W. would not be there, but he would parachute in three days later, on June 9. Upon his landing in Europe, he quickly called the command trailer, where a colonel would, in a noticeably short ceremony, promote Sergeant Finch to Captain Finch. The colonel would then tell Finch to report to his new company. Having gone from an NCO past lieutenant and right on to captain, J.W. Finch was stunned by the promotion. The colonel told him that a huge number of officers had been killed on the beaches of Normandy as the German snipers had targeted them. The army needed new, fresh leadership, and J.W. was the man. Overwhelmed and in a fog, Captain John Finch found his new command in a small French village. His head was spinning.

He would call the men he commanded the finest men he had ever known. J.W. would share little about his war experiences, and it was not until he was on his deathbed that he revealed the whole story. He shared his experience with military life with his son Nick, and Nick only. He considered his service to have been an honorable job that he did and completed, and then came home.

Charlene Smith graduated at the top of her nursing class at Tampa General Hospital. There was a war now, and the leadership knew that nurses would be needed. They would go all over the world to fulfill their assignments. This was what Charlene had dreamed of. She would finally be out of Florida and was ready to explore her future. Her class load was doubled, and everyone could sense there was a mandate to get the Nurse Corps up and running. Charlene was now Lieutenant Smith and was off to Columbia, South Carolina, and US Army base Fort Jackson.

From there, she could end up anywhere, the Pacific, Europe, or Asia—just anywhere that was not Avon Park, Florida. At Fort Jackson, she would serve with the finest-quality nurses she would ever have the pleasure to call colleagues. There were nurses back from England, Italy, and the Pacific campaign, and even two who had survived Pearl Harbor. Fort Jackson nurses had two duties. One was to tend to and mend soldiers who had been injured in local training. The other was to work with discharging and returning soldiers. The nurses would give them the once-over before signing off on their last day in the service. Was it exotic and exciting? No, but it was fulfilling. Charlene was able to notice the difference between the men who had not been in combat and the ones who were coming home for good. The latter were happy but reserved, proud but humbled, and they wished the new recruits good luck and told them to stay safe. Charlene was amazed by their dignity.

As J.W. and his men fought, cried, and laughed their way across France, they thought there could not be much more of the war left, at least in Europe. Paris had been liberated, as had Italy. As the weather got colder, they were ordered north to Belgium for what would come to be known as the Battle of the Bulge. This would be the bloodiest battle of the war, as a desperate Germany threw everything it had at the American lines. The line would bulge but not break, thanks to the bravery of the US military. They held on, but at an awful cost. J.W. lost five of his men and wrote letters home to their families. Then, during the early evening of December 23, J.W. put himself against a wall of a bombed-out building attempting to get a few minutes of sleep.

Suddenly, he awoke, or thought he had, as he heard the singing of angels. J.W. thought we was dead! He had "{bought the farm". *So, this is what happens when you die,* he thought. At least there was no pain. His family, his dreams, and his ambitions were gone. But he was cold. He picked up some snow and threw it on his face. He felt the frost. But then, what about the angels? J.W. turned and investigated the mangled and bombed-out building. It was a church, or what was left of one, and there was a youth choir, small boys, singing inside. They were rehearsing Christmas carols for the upcoming Midnight Mass. He realized then that he was not dead. Shaken, J.W. Finch went on a quiet and lonely walk by himself. He decided that when, not if, he got out of this war, he would never be cold again. He was going to go to Florida and never milk another cow. He promised himself just that on that cold December day in 1944. He would live and move to Florida.

It was springtime in the South, and the trees became green again, flowers began to bloom, and people started going out for evening drives once more. Columbia, South Carolina, was no exception. It was the state capital and home to both the University of South Carolina and Fort Jackson. Captain John Finch arrived at the fort in late May of 1945.

He was worried that he would get orders to head for Japan and assist with the invasion. Training had already begun in Germany when the mood suddenly changed. So, it was back to the States. *I guess the Marines will handle the*

Japanese, J.W. thought. And that was simply fine by him; he had seen enough. It was time for him to move on with his life. He had fulfilled his obligation to Uncle Sam, and five outstanding young men under his command would not get to enjoy the fruits of their labor. They had freed a continent gone mad and had done it with honor. They were buried in Belgium. Years later, when Charlene proposed a possible vacation to Europe, J.W. looked at his wife as if she were crazy.

He explained that he had already vacationed in Europe and said that the Europeans were not the greatest of hosts. No, thank you. Everything was old there, the cities, the towns, the churches, and especially the memories. The Finch family would never go camping either. As J.W. explained, "Why would I want to sleep outdoors when perfectly good indoor lodging is so close?" Nick figured it out. J.W. had camped, and it was called World War II. John Finch built big walls around his memories of the war and very seldom were people allowed inside those walls.

Captain John Finch knew Columbia very well growing up; it was about a thirty-minute ride away from Spartanburg. When he sat down for the first time at the officers' mess hall, a large grin appeared on his face when a bottle of Finch's Fine Milk was placed on their table. He was home, but not for long. After three days of debriefing meetings, it was time for a quick physical that consisted of a few questions and a check of vitals such as blood pressure and heart rate. After that, he would be issued his "ruptured duck," which is military jargon for one's last paycheck and discharge papers. The line was much shorter for the officers when Captain Finch heard his name called out for the first time by the future love of his life, Charlene Finch. Lieutenant Smith had had enough of flirting and come-ons. It came with the territory.

John Finch did not say much as the young nurse took his blood pressure and asked a small battery of questions about possible injuries and his state of mind. Instead, he just kept grinning—not smiling, but grinning, to the point where Smith asked what it was all about. "I would love to take you out, if you would like?"

The ease of the request surprised both. What was even more surprising, Nurse Charlene Smith replied, "Sure, I'd love to."

Romance and love quickly overtook the two of them. Within a month, both knew they had found their soul mates. They decided to elope, and it was off to Charleston for a quick Episcopal wedding. Lieutenant Smith had requested her discharge now that she was married. The army agreed, if she would remain on standby in case she was needed again. She was called back from standby in 1950—sent to San Francisco after the outbreak of the Korean War. J.W. was not happy and made a few phone calls to his connections. Nurse Finch was sent back home.

At first, Charlene was horrified that the young couple would be moving to Florida. J.W. had a connection with Morrison Air Force Base in West Palm Beach. The John W. Finch Painting and Decorating Company was born, and the first contract was to paint the military housing units surrounding the base. It was good work, and the government paid on time. The company expanded to paint some of the hotels and mansions on Palm Beach. Charlene Finch plied her trade at St. Mary's Hospital in West Palm Beach, in the emergency room. She liked Florida, where the young couple had settled down, bought a house with the GI Bill, and started a baby boomer family. The Finch family grew fast, as did Palm Beach County. First there would be J.W. Jr., followed by three straight girls thirteen months apart: Julia Elizabeth, Trisha Elizabeth, and Addison "Addie" Elizabeth. All the Finch family kids were born in December or January. Mr. and Mrs. Finch apparently celebrated springtime in their own way: by making babies.

The Finches settled in the south end of West Palm Beach, and the children made their way through the school system. John and Charlene, and reluctantly the children, made their way to the Palm Beach Episcopal church called Bethesda-by-the-Sea. Charlene attended many times straight from the hospital in her white nurse's uniform and cap. J.W. was proud of those occasions. Many of the parishioners were also happy to see their favorite nurse as Charlene had often taken care of many of them and their children. Many of these trips were made to the ER with the highest degree of secrecy; Charlene Finch never shared individuals' names or predicaments. Very ethical, she was.

J.W. Jr. was in flight school for the navy, and the girls were at the local high school, Forest Hill, in grades nine, ten, and twelve. Something was wrong with Charlene's body; she could sense it. She was forty now. Could it be early menopause—"the change"? Could it be worse, like some sort of female cancer? Something was off, and she knew it. Now no one from the Finch family ever had gone to go see a doctor with a traditional appointment. After all, they had an RN in the house—or they could simply swing by the hospital and have whatever doctor who was making rounds check them out. This was different. She contacted their family doctor and friend Dr. Ira Kimball. Now, Doctor Kimball, who was teased constantly for having the same name as a fictional TV doctor, was also a member of the Masonic Order and the Shriners with J.W. Ira's wife Sandy, a former nurse, was a member of the Eastern Star. These organizations were fun, and they gave back to their communities—kind of an adult version of a fraternity and sorority.

Dr. Kimball ordered a battery of tests for Charlene. J.W. had no idea about the appointments. The following spring Friday, J.W. shut down the office early after having delivered paychecks to his painters, who then had gone to play nine holes of golf at the West Palm Beach Country Club. Nervously, Charlene kept looking at a quizzical Dr. Kimball. He closed the folder in his hands and closed both doors to the room. *This cannot be,* she thought. He asked her if she was ready for the life-changing diagnosis. She nodded. "Well, Charlene Finch, my friend, you and J.W. have killed the rabbit." Stunned, Charlene asked if, he was sure. He was.

How could this have happened? Well, she knew how it had happened. Now how was J.W. going to take the news? He was counting the days until the girls would be leaving the house. Charlene drove straight to the golf course.

When Charlene sat down and waited for her husband's foursome to finish, the bartender asked if she would like either a whiskey sour or a glass of beer. These were her drinks of choice when she did drink. The bartender knew the Finches from the Masonic dances at the country club. She heard herself say yes, but quickly changed her order to a lemonade.

J.W. walked into the bar, all happy as he had won about twenty dollars in golfing bets. Suddenly he saw his wife; she had a look of genuine concern on her face. He went immediately to her and asked, "What is wrong?" She replied she had gone to Ira Kimball both last week and again today. Suddenly, the woman J.W. loved was looking scared. He did not know what to do except to ask how the appointments had gone. She explained she was not going through "the change" and didn't have cancer. Well, then, what was it?

She leaned forward so nobody could eavesdrop. This was private, and she had no idea how J.W. would react. She whispered, "I am pregnant."

J.W., stunned, backed up, took a seat, and looked toward the golf course and then at his golfing buddies laughing up a storm in the far corner of the bar. Charlene thought, *this is not going well.* John Finch slowly turned around and looked at the love his life. On his face was that grin she had seen on their first meeting at Fort Jackson, South Carolina. He hollered out, "Oh, hell yeah, I am going to be a dad again!"

Some nine months later, Nicholas John Finch was born at Good Samaritan Hospital on an unseasonably cold January day. The Finch family was complete.

CHAPTER 2

J.W.'s Atticus Moment, and Growing Up with Segregation, Palm Beach Style

In the 1950s and 1960s, Palm Beach County was segregated by race—not by law, but by custom. It was not in-your-face segregation like in the Deep South states with separate facilities in just about every public institution. In 1954, the United States Supreme Court reversed the 1896 decision of *Plessy v. Ferguson* that created the two separate societies with the doctrine of separate but equal. This was the cancer that remained even after the Civil War—an uneasy but accepted lifestyle. Then in 1954, the landmark case of *Brown v. the Board of Education of Topeka, Kansas,* reversed forced segregation for US schools with the hope that desegregation would peacefully spread to other social institutions, especially in the South. The South resisted in places such as Little Rock and their Central High School;

and Oxford, Mississippi, with the University of Mississippi (Ole Miss) and the University of Alabama, with Governor George Wallace promising to block the schoolhouse door. With the power of the federal government, the Justice Department, and even the United States military behind the effort, schools reluctantly began the process of integration. Private schools opened and flourished throughout the region. Palm Beach County stayed segregated. In fact, the last two districts to be integrated in the United States, and that by court order, were Palm Beach County and the Greater Boston School District. In Boston, it did not go well. Buses were rocked, students were met with hostility, and the locals even burned down the birthplace of John F. Kennedy. Palm Beach would have trouble, but nothing like its "enlightened" friend from Massachusetts.

With the approval of the federal government, Palm Beach began its journey to integration by taking slow steps. High schools were merged, with compromises made on new names, mascots, and colors. Simply for logistical reasons, some schools were bypassed and didn't see any such changes. Nick's future high school was one of these. Forest Hill, located in the south end of the city, only experienced minor busing from a small black section of West Palm Beach. The school was getting a minority boost from the large contingent of recently arrived Cuban immigrants. The flagship school of Palm Beach High, with its famous alumni, such as Hollywood superstar Burt Reynolds, would combine with an athletic powerhouse, the black school of Roosevelt High, and become Twin Lakes. Yes, it was a powder keg, but the teachers and students made it work. It also helped that the school's basketball team eventually became a powerhouse and the team helped unify the school. People like winners.

To the north, Kennedy High, the black school, and Riviera Beach High, the white school, combined to create Suncoast High School. The new school of Palm Beach Gardens and Jupiter for the most part was ignored. In the South County, Carver High combined with Seacrest High to become Atlantic High, home of the Eagles. Boca Raton had not yet experienced its massive growth, which would occur in the eighties, and therefore remained intact. Out west, Lake Shore, the African American school, joined with Belle Glade High to become the new Glades Central High School. Most white students transferred immediately to new private and segregated schools that were established in response to the court order. Most of this did not affect a young Nick Finch as he was entering the third grade at the all-white South Olive Elementary located in the south end of West Palm Beach.

This was not to say there were not problems. Like most of the United States, Palm Beach County suffered an awful year in 1968. The six-year-old was just beginning to watch TV shows other than *Walt Disney's Wonderful World of Color* and *Mutual of Omaha's Wild Kingdom.* He observed his concerned parents when they watched the nightly news reporting on events such as the Tet Offensive in that far-off war in a place in Asia called Vietnam. He could hear J.W. mumble about its being time to bring those boys back home. Then came the terrible night of April 4, in Memphis, when Dr. Martin Luther King Jr. was assassinated. Many of the nation's cities burned with rage. West Palm Beach did not. Chief of Police Billy Barnhill, a former FBI agent who never wore a traditional policeman's uniform but wore a heavily starched fresh white suit with pressed slacks, immediately ordered a state of emergency, implemented a dusk-to-dawn curfew, and let it be known that if one were to be found out after dark, one should expect to be shot by West Palm's finest. Chief Barnhill was also a neighbor to the Finches, living just four houses down the street. The problem was, how was Charlene going to get to work at the hospital amid potential unrest?

Charlene Finch was the chief nurse in charge of the emergency room, and of course most of the action occurred at night, when she worked. She loved her job. She clocked in at ten o'clock every night and came home at mornings around six. Her schedule ran from Sunday through Thursday. Her practice would allow her to be home when the kids got up in the morning and to be there to say good night to them in the evening. It worked for the Finches. It had to. Her paycheck was particularly important to the household finances. The schedule also allowed J.W. and Charlene to enjoy their weekends together. Every night at St. Mary's was different, and it was a place where Charlene could make a difference. She loved her career.

J.W. got off the phone with the chief. They had formed a plan. Around nine thirty, a police squad car pulled up in the front of the Finch house. From his bedroom window, young Nick watched as his mother kissed her husband on the cheek, left the house, and climbed into the squad car. Young Nick raced from his room to the front door and sprinted to his dad. He was confused. Why were the police taking his mom away? His mom waved goodbye as the police car sped away. J.W. looked at his young son and, in his quiet, unassuming, but firm voice explained that everything was all right and Mom was getting a special ride to work just to make sure she would be safe. Nick smiled as his dad tucked him back into bed.

The rest of 1968 was one awful event after another. Senator Robert Kennedy, who was running for president after his older brother John had held the office, was assassinated in Los Angeles. The Democratic National Convention seemed like one continuous fistfight between young protestors and the Chicago police. But there was one bright spot that year. The Finches drove up to the Cape to watch the liftoff of the Saturn moon rocket *Apollo 8*, which was taking three American astronauts up to the moon. Every week, students at every level of the Florida school system studied the space program and NASA. Florida played a major role in US space exploration and was proud of it. Nick learned about the space program through a series of specially printed youth magazines written by Charles Schultz and featuring the United States' favorite beagle, Snoopy, as the lead astronaut. Now Nick and his family watched with pride as the giant rocket took off. The ground shook and there was a loud boom, then the giant rocket became smaller and smaller as it rose into the sky and disappeared, traveling to the moon. A few days later, the family huddled around the living room TV and listened to the astronauts read from the Bible as they circled the moon. It was Christmas Eve 1968.

When Nick was in third grade, in 1972, Palm Beach County began phase one of court-ordered integration with a gradual easing-in process. That year most new teachers out of college would be assigned to schools with students of a race other than their own. Veteran teachers could volunteer for a special transfer that included a thousand-dollar bonus and could have their own children follow them to the same school they had transferred to. Mrs. Edna Williams was a lifelong educator and a proud churchgoing woman who had already raised her family. Her children followed her into the field of education and now were teachers too, one in Washington, DC, and the other a young promising professor at the historically black college in Florida known as Florida A&M, more popularly called FAMU. Mrs. Williams's husband William was also a World War II veteran and was a mechanic at the local Ford dealership. Edna was a proud graduate of the famous Tuskegee Institute in Alabama, the school that Booker T. Washington had founded. She was an English major. She loved the classics. Her English delivery was perfect, and even though she had taught high school for most of her career, she was up to the challenge of teaching third graders at an all-white elementary school. She would have to be, as there was a group of parents who were skeptical, especially the well-connected stay-at-home housewives who were part of the local tennis club.

After two or three weeks, it reached a point where just about all of Mrs. Williams's students didn't even notice her skin color. She was their teacher and they liked her. They loved that she allowed them to pick their own teams for dodgeball as she sat under a tree and read Zora Neale Hurston. They loved story time, when she would pick up a book and make the story come alive with her perfect delivery and pitch. She would have the class moaning when story time was over. They wanted more. She allowed the class to use a buddy system to practice reading and writing. The slower students were paired up with the more accomplished students. She had been forced to use this strategy because the schools where she had taught many times did not have enough books.

This is not said some of her quirks did not raise eyebrows and, on occasion, cause her class to snicker. Many times, when addressing the class before lunch, she would break out a chicken drumstick and start her meal early while never missing a beat of instruction, book in one hand and a drumstick in the other. Real talent. Also, she seemed to be always cleaning her ears. That is not usual, but her method was, well, unique. She used the tips of wooden kitchen matches. When she was satisfied with her cleaning efforts, she would inspect the used match and then discard it in the trash can. By the end of the day there would be anywhere from five to ten matches in the can.

To the South Olive Women's Tennis Association, the integration experiment was not working. Two students withdrew and enrolled in the private Catholic school, Saint Juliana—and these students were not even Catholic. The queen bee of the tennis women was a housewife by the name of Dottie Simpson. She was a sorority queen from the University of Alabama, where she had met her future husband, Jack Simpson. Dottie's one goal for going to college had been to get her "Mrs." degree. This was not a master's degree but meant finding the perfect future husband, who of course had to be successful. Jack Simpson was just the guy. Quickly moving up in the banking world of Palm Beach, he was named president of the "Yellow Bank," First National Bank of Palm Beach. This bank was started by none other than the true founder of Florida. No, not Ponce de León, and not Andrew Jackson, but the cofounder of Standard Oil and baron of the Florida East Coast Railroad, the one and only Henry M. Flagler. Henry Flagler, and to a lesser extent Henry Plant on Florida's west coast, and later Walt Disney in the Orlando area, would change Florida. Jet travel and air-conditioning and their visions for Florida would be up and running. New and old money both still needed the same thing, banking services, and First National Bank of Palm Beach provided the answer. The Finches did their modest banking there. The Finch Painting Company every year painted the building in its distinctive bright yellow color.

The tennis moms met with the principal of South Olive, a statuesque blonde woman six feet in height with an hourglass figure, Mrs. Virginia Fox. Mrs. Fox was a Korean War widow and had not remarried. Her private life remained just that, private. J.W. knew that the principal dated, but only older wealthy Palm Beach men—and discreetly. Mrs. Fox was a genuinely nice woman, but that is not say she was lax in discipline, as she would swing a mean paddle when needed. Florida still practiced corporal punishment. No longer did teachers administer the punishment; it would have to be dealt by an administrator. Mrs. Fox always offered an alternate sentence. Students would be given a choice of three "licks" from a wooden paddle or a three-minute phone call to their parents. Every one of them took the whipping. It would be much worse at home.

There was one student, a new one, who refused the paddling and told Mrs. Fox to go ahead and call his home. Nobody would be touching him. This student had recently moved to Palm Beach from Manhattan. Nick and the others were stunned. The next day the boy came back to school and bragged that nothing had happened to him. Years later, this same student, who was now a young man, had been arrested and convicted of grand theft auto. When the judge was about to sentence the twenty-one-year-old first-time offender, the young man arrogantly answered the judge's questions with the same response he used every time: "Whatever, man, whatever." The disrespected judge responded with the maximum sentence, completely unusual for a first-time offender who was being represented by a top-shelf defense attorney from New York. The young man got ten years! The typical sentence ranged from probation to less than two years, and he got ten. Maybe if he had taken the whipping when he was in elementary school, things would have turned out differently in the future? Probably not.

The bee's nest was now in Mrs. Fox's office, and they did not request but demanded a change of teachers for their precious children. The school principal took notes, or at least pretended to, and seldom looked up. When the meeting was over, she looked directly at Dottie Simpson and asked if that was what most of the parents wanted.

Dottie's answer was that she was confident it was. Mrs. Fox would call for a parent–principal meeting at seven o'clock the next evening in the third-grade classroom so that all the parents, including those who worked, could attend. Unsure how long the meeting would last, Charlene went to the meeting in her white nursing uniform. J.W. found a seat next to local football legend and high school coach Jake Peterson and his wife, a guidance counselor at Conniston Junior High, Angela. The Finches and Pattersons would remain friends throughout their lives. Both men had the highest respect for each other. The wives also had mutual respect since they were both a rare breed in that both worked. Nick and the Patterson son, Jerry, would be teammates throughout their school athletic careers. Mrs. Williams would not be at the meeting. Would it be fair or an academic to appear for a social lynch mob? The bees launched into their complaints, especially about the eating and the personal hygiene practices of their children's teacher. Dottie approved with smiles, grins, and nods. She did not say anything. She didn't have to. After all, she was the Queen; she gave the well-rehearsed orders, and the worker bees did the lifting.

Jack Simpson arrived a little late and with a touch of scotch on his breath, so he stayed in the back of the classroom and gazed at the class decorations. Finally, Mrs. Fox got up and looked right at J.W. Finch and football coach Jake Peterson and asked the fathers if they had anything to add. J.W. looked over at Jake and got up. The two had not spoken, but it was clear they were on the same page. This was a ridiculous waste of time and energy and was beneath their dignity. John Finch looked straight at the principal and then directly at Dottie Simpson and stated clearly, "I am very embarrassed for our children if this is how the adults acts. And let it be very clear that Nick Finch will be staying in the class." Charlene Finch noticed the death stares of Dottie Simpson directed at her husband. She stared right back at her. Charlene Finch's angry stare could melt the North Pole, and she was giving right back to the queen bee. The worker bees fidgeted nervously and gazed down at their feet on the floor.

Coach Jake Peterson took J.W.'s place, now standing as John Finch had returned to his seat. The three-time All-American football star from Florida State who'd had a small professional career with the NFL's Detroit Lions spoke. He stated in his locker-room voice, which at first was somewhat quiet and measured but which got louder as he spoke, that Jerry would be staying in the class and that this whole episode was embarrassing.

Paper was passed out, and the parents were instructed to write "stay" or "transfer" on the paper, along with the student's name, indicating their choice. Mrs. Fox would approve the transfers. Of the twenty-six kids in class, only two of their parents asked for a transfer. Even the bees turned on their Queen. Only Annie Simpson, the princess bee, and the newly arrived New York student requested, and were granted, transfers.

There was some fallout from the whole fiasco. The students noticed that Mrs. Williams now ate at her desk and refrained from cleaning her ears in front of the class. Nick and Jerry quickly became the teacher's pets as news of the meeting worked its way back to Mrs. Williams. Mrs. Edna Williams would retire at the end of the academic year with no regrets whatsoever. First National Bank of Palm Beach canceled its yearly painting contract with Finch Painting and Decorating. The Finches withdrew their modest savings, closed out their account, and moved their money to Fidelity Federal Savings and Loan. Jack Simpson had his assistant tell J.W. that they were going in a different direction regarding the upkeep of the building. He hid in his office with drink in hand. Dottie Simpson would never speak to Charlene again, whether it was at church or at the grocery store. The South Olive Women's Tennis Association broke up and disbanded. Only singles matches would be played for now.

Four years later, when Nick was in middle school, the assignment given was to read and write a book report on *To Kill a Mockingbird* by Harper Lee. Nick had noticed his all-time favorite teacher, Mrs. Williams, would read the book sitting under a tree during recess. He asked if he could read it or maybe if it could be the book for story time. Mrs. Williams smiled and said they were not ready for it yet, but they were close. When Nick Finch finished the book, he followed it up by watching the movie. It upset him until he watched his father pull into the driveway, and then he realized that John Finch had delivered his Atticus moment for him, for his friends, and for his all-time favorite teacher. John Finch was Gregory Peck in his son's eyes. And that was simply fine with J.W.

CHAPTER

3

The High School Years—Paddling, Parties, and Proms

Elementary school culminated in a train trip to our nation's capital, Washington, DC, with all the safety patrol guards from the elementary schools throughout the district. This was the yearly reward for being an expanded-duty school monitor, whose turf included not only the school grounds and hallways, but also the adjoining streets, and performing the task of helping the young students to cross the streets. For the most part it was uneventful as duties were rotated, but it always seemed the boys got the street posts and the girls got the school hallways. Without saying it, the administration knew common sense and safety was important not only for the study body at large but also for the patrols themselves. The only drawback was that being a school monitor added an extra hour to the school day, a half hour before and another thirty minutes after school. The bright orange belt that wrapped over the shoulder with the attached badge gave the young men and women extra responsibility and privileges. There would be an adult teacher and administrator who oversaw the program, and the patrols would be like military ranks, officers only, with the student leader being a major, followed by two captains, with the rest being lieutenants. No unlisted men were allowed, as this was a special unit. They even had inspections that included being graded on dress and grooming. Nick was always a lieutenant, and that was OK with him. Four highlights of this trip to DC were the train ride itself; being away from home without Mom and Dad; having a huge picture of the county's student patrol taken on the Capitol's steps; and getting a very brief glimpse of a drive-in that was observed by the passengers as the train passed through a Georgia town, the screen showing a full-blown triple-X porn movie. It took a good hour for the chaperones to settle the district's majors, captains, and lieutenants after they had viewed hairy adults climbing all over each other!

Leaving South Olive Elementary in the past meant going on to Conniston Middle School for the junior high years. Not anymore, as a select few from an area twenty blocks or so in size at the south end of West Palm Beach, from Forest Hill Boulevard south to West Palm Beach Canal, which was on the border of Lake Worth and West Palm Beach—about fifty students—would be bused to the island of Palm Beach. You see, court-mandated integration had continued. Well, kind of. The town of Palm Beach and its citizens, and taxpayers, as they were quick to remind elected officials, worked out a compromise. Instead of inner-city youths, white middle-class students from working-class families would be used to fulfill the busing requirements. The Finch's were pleased with the new assignment as Palm Beach Public Middle School had only about two hundred students and sported a top-notch faculty. It was like a free private school.

Nick really enjoyed his two years as a Palm Beach Comet, earning good grades and learning a lot for a young teenager going through some uncomfortable changes, both physical and mental. Such is the life of a middle schooler. Most of Nick's childhood friends were with him on the bus ride down Flagler Drive and the Intracoastal Waterway; over Southern Boulevard, or the "south bridge"; past the mansion known as Mar-a-Lago, and recently the Southern White House; and along South Ocean Boulevard with its picturesque views of the ocean on one side and million-dollar mansions on the other. Not a bad drive even if you were on a "yellow dog." Once the buses unloaded, the students, unlike many of the adults of the time, got along simply fine. Nick and the south end kids quickly found out the Palm Beach students had the same wants, desires, and passions as they did. They were both attracted to the opposite sex. In fact, the Palm Beach girls took a liking to the new kids, and the South Olive girls really liked the preppy surfer dudes of Palm Beach. They both shared a passion for sports. Surprising to many was just how competitive the tiny island school was on the football and baseball fields and the basketball and tennis courts. Despite having only about a hundred boys in the entire school and only one African American male, who was a teacher's son and didn't play sports but was an outstanding singer in the choir, they posted winning records in every sport and won the county championship for both baseball and tennis.

Most of the Palm Beach students would leave their only public-school experience and head off to boarding schools up north, military schools in the south, or local private schools in the area, such as Saint Andrew's in Boca Raton or the Catholic school in West Palm, Cardinal Newman High School. When they would meet up during their high school years, their previously temporary friendships would be reignited with hugs and laughter as they told stories about their past in junior high. They truly made it work. Imagine that the kids "got it" Now if only the adults could.

It was 1975 and time to go to high school, so that meant heading home and leaving "Fantasy Island." So long, Palm Beach. It was nice to get to know you.

Forest Hill High School was in the south end of West Palm Beach, located right next to the West Palm Beach Country Club. It was a baby boomer school that had been built to accommodate the massive growth of Palm Beach County, which was thanks to both natural childbirth and transplants moving into the area. The school, for various reasons, missed out on the trials and tribulations of forced busing and integration. The makeup of the study body mirrored that of the staff and faculty. Ninety percent of the school was white, of upper-, middle-, and lower-class backgrounds; 5 percent were Hispanic, but really that group was nearly all Cuban expatriates who had fled Castro's communist regime; and about 5 percent were black from the inner-city section of West Palm Beach, one of the neighborhoods of which was ironically named "Pleasant City".

Nicolas was the fifth Finch to attend Forest Hill. Most of the faculty and staff knew both John and Charlene. There was a small-town feeling to the school despite its being in a medium-size city. With connections to Coach Patterson and his son, Jerry, Nick had spent Friday evenings on the sidelines while in middle school as a ball boy for the football team. He had an advantage that many of the other incoming freshman did not enjoy in that he already knew many of teachers. While it was indeed an advantage, it could also be a real pain in the ass—literally, as he would find out. Because of growth and limited space, upperclassmen could opt in to a zero hour, which was an academic class that would start at six thirty in the morning rather than the traditional start time of seven thirty, which was when the entire school would start. Junior and seniors who opted in had to have their own transportation to and from school, but they were rewarded with an early dismissal and no afternoon classes. Almost all opted in.

The last class of the day for Nick and his friends was fourth hour. It would end just a little after eleven o'clock in the morning, and then they were out of there. Whether they went to lunch, went home, or went to work, as some did, it was freedom. Nick and some of his close friends had chemistry for fourth hour. Unlike his mother, Nick hated the sciences and his math classes. He was not above taking "short cuts" to help his boost grades in these classes. As much as he despised these courses, he loved social studies, especially US history, and English classes. His father loved US history, and of course Mrs. Edna Williams, his third-grade teacher, had inspired him to love English, especially American literature. As a reward for his love of US history, Nick was awarded an appointment to "Boys State," which was a weeklong mock government made up of students from across the state, was sponsored by the local American Legion posts, and convened in Tallahassee. They would elect their own officials, propose laws, vote, and debate. They met the governor and other elected officials of the state for photo ops. Nick enjoyed the experience, but he also realized that politics was not for him. What he did observe were some overly ambitious honorees who loved participating and could be ruthless. They later would end up running for elected office. Some would win, many would lose, and some went to prison for white-collar crimes.

Chemistry class was just awful. It was painful and it was torture watching the clock slowly tick before dismissal. The teacher's name was John Costello, an elderly man who was clearly out of gas. He bragged he made more money and got more respect selling washers and dryers at Sears in the Palm Beach Mall than he did teaching. He taught for his pension and his health insurance. He would need that insurance since Mr. Costello was a chain smoker. Smoking officially was not allowed on campus but there were spots both students and faculty could sneak a "heater" in during the day. Obviously, the restrooms and the student parking lot for the kids worked fine. For the staff there was the custodian's office, the boiler room, and faculty parking lot.

Mr. Costello could not wait until lunch or the planning period for he needed to smoke, and he smoked a lot. The chemistry teacher would instruct about ten or so minutes and either put an assignment on the board or hand out a work sheet that corresponded with the daily lesson. Four or five would do the work and rest would copy it. Mr. Costello never noticed or cared for he was outside his locked classroom and down the outside exposed hallway firing one up. He locked the door so nobody would leave early. Or so he thought. Like many South Florida schools of the time built in a moderate climate, all hallways were open air. It saved on air conditioning, allowed for easy traffic flow, and one might be able to sneak a smoke in and blow the smoke into nature without being reprimanded as unprofessional. Five of Nick's friends were in this class also, and they, too, hated it: Jerry Patterson, the head coach's son, who was a math whiz; Scott Clark, a towering figure who played both football and basketball at a high level; Tommy Coughlin, a surfer and beach bum who excelled in industrial arts classes like drafting and shop; Brian Parker, a star football player who was also a senior but only recently had started to challenge himself academically as football scholarship offers began to interest him; and a fairly new student who moved had moved to Palm Beach from the Florida west coast town of Naples, Ray Wade. Ray was a country club kid who excelled in such sports as golf and tennis. He was scratch in golf and nationally ranked in tennis. He also had a wild and crazy side, to borrow a phrase from a *Saturday Night Live* routine featuring Steve

Martin and Dan Aykroyd. Ray Wade quickly fit in with the group, and he had an escape plan.

Ray had observed that Mr. Costello left the class every day at a quarter to eleven and locked the door from both the inside and outside so nobody could leave. This was a violation of many codes, but nobody would tell their parents because it made cheating in the class very easy to do. Everyone got As. Only about five of the twenty students assigned to the class learned any chemistry. Nick would later joke that the only elements he knew were "Earth, Wind, and Fire" And that was fine with him.

Located on the second floor, the chemistry class was held in a corner room with an entire north wall of windows, except one had been removed for the installation of an air conditioner. Below one of the windows was a small ledge just above the first floor that served as a concrete canopy over the side entrance and bus loop drive-through, where the bused students would arrive and exit. The plan was for the five boys to climb out the window, hop down to the canopy, and jump and roll on the grassy area next to hall much like paratroopers land. From there they would be out of there, escaped inmates, as they fancied themselves. Why not? What could go wrong? The rest of class was sworn to secrecy as the five followed the plan exactly. And it worked. They were free and off to lunch twenty-five minutes or so early. The problem was that soon they got greedy and began to escape not only on occasion but daily. They were spoiled by their success and had gotten lazy. There would be a problem and a price to pay.

Neighbors from the school across the street watched in horror the first time they had seen the students jump from the second floor. They thought there must be a fire or a gas leak, but now the practice had become a daily event. The neighbors shook their heads and laughed, wondering what in the world was going on at that school. One of the observers, having seen enough, contacted the principal directly. Mr. Jamison, the school's principal, was livid and went directly across the hall to his assistant principals in charge of boys. They were called deans. Dean Whitiker was a southern gentleman with distinctive southern drawl who chewed tobacco throughout the day. The other, Dean Mitchell Bradley, was black and was a giant of a man. Educated at the old Roosevelt High and having been a two-sport star, football, and basketball, at FAMU, he was about six foot six and two hundred seventy pounds with a contagious laugh. The students at Forest Hill never saw color, and they hoped never to see him angry.

One day, according to the principal's plan, the deans were hiding the best they could behind some bushes, and sure enough down came the boys. The adults emerged with large grins. The boys were caught and were marched down to the dean's office. First Mr. Jamison came in and hollered and screamed at the boys, saying that in forty years of education he had never seen such disrespect. The convicts remained quiet and stared at their shoes, doing everything they could to keep from bursting out into laughter. The principal left the office, and now things got serious. Dean Whitiker pulled out a bag of Red Man chewing tobacco, put in a load, opened his desk drawer, and brought out a small gold-colored spittoon. He never stopped grinning. Dean Bradley clasped his gigantic hands behind his head and leaned back in his chair. Finally, the silence was broken. Dean Bradley would be the judge, jury, and executioner. He asked the boys what they thought he should do, and Raymond Wade responded quickly with, "Give us a warning, and we promise never to do it again." No, that was not going to happen, but at least Ray had tried. Mr. Bradley finally spoke and handed down the sentence. The boys were given a choice. He could call their fathers and explain what had happened and put the discipline referrals in their permanent files, or they could each take three licks of the paddle. Scott Clark raised his hand and said, "I cannot speak for the rest, but I believe they do as I do. Please put that phone down and whip me. Please do not call my dad." The rest immediately concurred. The three got up and put their hands on either the desk or the chair in front of them. Dean Bradley got out his paddle, which had some Greek letters on it, apparently the fraternity he had belonged to as a student at FAMU. There were holes drilled through the paddle to decrease the amount of drag when swung. This would not be Mrs. Fox swinging a small ping-pong paddle, but a full-grown former college athlete doing the deed.

The first whack took each boy's breath away; the second caused the blood to shoot straight from their buttocks to Lord knows where; and the third, well, they were already numb. It was still better than the phone call, but it hurt like hell. Then they were excused to go. One more thing: Dean Bradley took the referrals, tore them in half, and put them in the trash can. There would be no record of the offense or the punishment. It took a good five minutes for the boys to start talking. Nick spoke first: "I don't know about you guys, but my ass is on fire." Ray Wade had never experienced corporal punishment of any kind, either at home or at school. He looked at his new friends in puzzlement and said, "Just think, guys, there are weird people who enjoy that shit. I think they call it S&M." The group went to lunch but did not sit down. They couldn't. Mr. Costello retired at the end of the school year. J.W. never knew of the "great escape" or the "trial and execution of Nicholas Finch." And it was better that way. Much better.

Forest Hill was a very social school with meetups at popular pizza restaurants, a local drive-in called the "SkyDrome", the beach, and later even a topless doughnut shop. Also, there were other places like the shell pits west of town, which was littered with alligators and such. Today that is Okeeheelee Park. Wellington had yet to be built. Rock concerts were held at the local West Palm Beach Auditorium, nicknamed the "leaky teepee" because the cone-shaped roof always leaked when it rained, and down south in Hollywood at the Sportatorium, a horrible building that originally had been a blimp hangar for Goodyear. One of Nick's favorite experiences was seeing the southern rock band Lynyrd Skynyrd play there before the airplane crash that claimed the lives of two of its members and one of its backup singers. Starting in late January and going through to the end of March, the Atlanta Braves and the Montreal Expos called West Palm Beach home, as this was where they did their spring training. In West Palm Beach, there was plenty to do, and for the most part the weather accommodated the plans. There was one more thing Forest Hill Falcons could do well: party.

The drinking age in Florida was only eighteen at the time, but for certain stores and clerks that meant sixteen if discretion was used. There were plenty of venues available for such parties, such as the Double Roads beach area up in Jupiter or the shell pits. The best was someone's house when their parents were away. With the chief of police living just a few houses away, the Finch house was open to only small-invitation parties of a few couples. J.W. and Charlene did leave frequently for Masonic and Shriner functions, so that was when the Finch "bed-and-breakfast" had vacancies. For the most part, word would spread of a party at someone's house the upcoming weekend. Some of these parties were free, whereas others had a cover charge. Beer on tap was the beverage of choice, with some of the girls selecting such fine wines as Boone's Farm and "Mad Dog 20/20". It just so happened that the Wade'mom would be out of town one April weekend and Ray was to stay home and watch his sophomore-age sister Karen. A pool party was planned for the afternoon. The Wade house was in one of West Palm's original western suburbs, Lake Clarke Shores, a freshwater lake community that was now in the middle of the city and was very desirable among the upper middle class.

That spring Saturday was hot, so the pool was in action, which was great for bikini watching. The beer flowed, and Ray's little sister Karen and her friends seemed to be up to the task of drinking and partying like her brother's senior friends. Drinking games and chugging challenges kept most of the boys busy. Many were in the pool cooling off, while some played throw and fetch with the Parkers' big Chesapeake Bay retriever named Lord Baltimore, "Balty" for short. Brain Parker, having to use the restroom and relieve himself, worked his way into the house and noticed there were lines in front of two of restrooms with young women who did not want to sneak off into the bushes like most of the guys did. Ray had found the master bedroom bathroom, where he sat down on the toilet and went from both ends. So that is why he gone inside. After washing his hands and checking out his hair and tan, he left the bathroom and walked by the king-size bed that was covered with a bright Lilly Pulitzer comforter. He also noticed that one of the lights in the bedside table lamp was flickering. As he went over to turn it off, he noticed that the bottom drawer was slightly open. He decided to take a peek. What he found inside both shocked and amused him. Located in the bottom drawer of the nightstand on apparently Mrs. Wade's side of the bed was a ten-inch-long, two-inch-wide rubber sex toy! In those days, they were called dildos, and lo and behold, Mrs. Wade had one and it was black. Wow. Suddenly, a wide grin spread across the football star's face. He lifted the dildo from the drawer and smelled it. The fragrance was like that of a new rubber band, but a big, stiff rubber band. He then put the toy inside his shirt and went back outside to the party.

Nick, noticing Brian's big grin, walked over, and asked what was up. "Watch this," Brian responded. The senior got the big dog's attention and commanded, "Fetch."

He threw the large rubber sex toy into the pool. From a distance it looked like a large stick. Balty responded like a retriever of his breeding would do and leaped into the pool and retrieved the prize. Brian and Nick walked over to a group of girls they knew well as Balty came over to the group, wanting to do it again. Brian took the training device from the dog and asked if any of the girls wanted to give it a throw. Two of the girls immediately reached for the toy without really noticing its design and began playing tug-of-war to see who would be rewarded with the task. Nick and Brian burst into sidesplitting laughter. The girls seemed puzzled, but then one of them realized just what they were fighting for. Suddenly the two looked at each other and immediately dropped Mrs. Wade's "private lover." The two girls released a torrent of profanity that got everyone's attention. Laughter spread throughout the gathering.

Ray Wade emerged from the kitchen with some more cups and asked what all the commotion was about. He saw the source of the profanity and laughter and simply asked, "What the hell?"

Surfer Tommy Coughlin flipped his long blond hair and said, "The girls are fighting over your mom's toys." Tommy continued, explaining that his own mom supplemented her income she earned from being bookkeeper for the family upholstery business by hosting sex toy parties. She learned the premise from her mom and grandmother, who were both Avon representatives. She thought it was cool. Ray shook his head and replied, "Whatever." he returned to the house grinning. Later he would do the retrieving and put back the toy in its home. He noticed there were some bite and ding marks on it. The boys would always in the future greet Mrs. Wade with wide smiles and grins. *What polite young men,* she would think.

Nick and his friends got ready to finish up their memorable high school years with certain senior events such as the annual Disney Grad Night, an all-night party at the Magic Kingdom for seniors throughout the state. It was fun. The entertainment was provided by KC and the Sunshine Band. And then there was prom.

Prom at Forest Hill was unlike many across the country, as Nick would find out from his new college friends when they recollected their proms. They were extremely impressed and envious of what the Forest Hill kids did for their prom. For starters, their prom was not held in the high school gym or at a local lodge or hotel. The Forest Hill prom was held at Whitehall, the Henry Morrison Flagler mansion, located on the island of Palm Beach.

After leaving his partnership with John D. Rockefeller and the Standard Oil Corporation of Cleveland, Ohio, Mr. Flagler moved to Florida. Originally, he settled in St. Augustine, but then decided to move farther south to Palm Beach. With oil money, vision, and a keen sense of business strategy, he built South Florida, specifically, Palm Beach. He would construct a railroad that would cross the seas, doing what was impossible, extending his own Florida East Coast Railroad past Miami and connecting a series of train bridges ending at the southernmost location of the continental United States, Key West. He later built the largest hotel in the world next to his mansion, called the

Royal Poinciana, which even had its own power station. The hotel would later burn to the ground. Next, he would build the beautiful Breakers Hotel, which still stands and flourishes today. For himself and his wife, Flagler would build a Gilded Age home to rival any in the nation, from Hearst Castle in California to the Biltmore of North Carolina. Whitehall was that type of gift.

Forest Hill boys would rent tuxedos and buy corsages. The girls would buy gowns and do their hair up for the big night. Expensive restaurant reservations would be made, and hotel rooms would be booked. In some cases, limousines would be rented for the evening. The mid-May date was put on the calendar. This would be their last event before they all went off to college, and they were going to do it right. Nick was dating a college freshman at the University of Florida who had graduated from Forest Hill a year earlier. Annie was now home from Gainesville and was not crazy about it. She liked going out with Nick, but she had been spoiled by college life. The boys proposed their plans to their parents first, who thought the idea was neat. Even the more "mature" Annie thought it was cool. The boys booked round-trip tickets on an hourly commuter plane to Paradise Island in the Bahamas. Most of the travelers went there for its nonstop casino gambling action. This group decided they may, after getting dressed up in their tuxes, stop by the casino and do their best James Bond imitation. What they would end up doing would be to book private beach and poolside bungalows, drink tropical cocktails, and eat fresh seafood including conch and grouper. Then they would make themselves up and take the return trip (the cost of the round-trip tickets was only seventy-five dollars) to Palm Beach International Airport, then fly over to Whitehall. The airline representatives thought the idea was unique and were really impressed when the group came back on the return flight in formal wear. It was much different from their own prom memories. After pictures, and one long slow dance by exhausted teenagers that was really a five-minute circular hug, it was off to the local Palm Beach Island Hilton for the postparty and hopefully some romance. Around midnight there was a commotion in the parking lot with about fifteen squad cars with lights on and a police helicopter hovering over the hotel.

Nick came out onto the balcony to observe and began to wonder what idiot classmate something had done stupid to bring on such action. He instructed Annie to turn off the room lights so as not to bring any attention to the balcony. Annie came out and joined Nick with a blanket covering her. She stated, "This is why I hate high school stuff; this would never happen at UF." Oh no, a police wagon or van, known simply as a paddy wagon, pulled up outside the lobby doors and about fifteen adults were being marched out in handcuffs. These were not prom attendees … but yes there were! They were faculty chaperones being hauled off to jail. Apparently, the teachers had had a post prom party themselves and had a novelty slot machine in the party room. The Palm Beach police had been tipped off that a high-stakes illegal gambling outfit was being run out of a local hotel. They raided the "casino" using SWAT members, K-9 units, and air patrol. The police boat was trolling offshore just in case. A reporter from the Palm

Beach newspaper had been invited to go in on the big bust. Instead, fifteen teachers were arrested over a novelty slot machine that did not even work.

The next morning the headline read, "Teachers Arrested in Mob Gambling Syndicate." Nick wondered if they would get a choice of a phone call home or three licks from a paddle like what happened to them. Quickly the case unraveled, and the teachers each received anywhere from ten to twenty thousand dollars after winning a lawsuit against the town. The teachers hit the jackpot and the town crapped out. What a prom. But now it was time to get ready to leave home and go off to college.

CHAPTER 4

It's Time for an Audible, or a Change in the Playbook of Life

Many say that American football came of age in 1958 when the entire nation watched as the Baltimore Colts defeated the New York Giants in overtime on the new mass communication device, the TV. Television was perfect for football as the game was timed and the field was perfectly gridded out with a total length of one hundred twenty yards and with a width of just over fifty yards. Four or so cameras with a play-by-play announcer and an "expert" commentator and you had three to four hours of entertainment right in your suburban baby boomer ranch-style home. There was enough stoppage in play for commercials advertising cars, beer, and cigarettes. The truth is that the South had already fallen in love with the sport in the early part of the century. Poor and with no professional teams, the southern states adopted their college teams as their heroes. To an extent, this tradition continues today. As the game progressed, new schemes and strategies emerged. One of these was the idea of calling the play at the line of scrimmage by using a set of coded numbers and colors chosen by the quarterback. If the quarterback "did not like what he saw", in the opposing defense, he would bark out a new secret command to switch to a different play. In a similar vein, Nick Finch would be forced at the end of his college days to call for an audible. Such is life.

Nick, like his mother, Charlene, wanted out of Florida. College would provide his exit route. The youngest Finch was in the process of exploring colleges when he sat for his ACT college entrance exam one winter morning at the local junior college. He felt fairly good about the test once he'd left the building, but he had no idea just how good he had done until about three weeks later, when he opened the envelope addressed to him with his test scores. He had crushed it, getting a 33 out of a possible 36! This put him in the top 5–10 percent of students from all over the country. His parents were pleased and proud, but Nick would not know just how proud they were until people later told him that J.W. and Charlene would tell anyone and everyone they ran into, whether they knew them or not, of their youngest son's ACT results. His sisters got very tired of the news.

Doors were opening all over the place. Nick was receiving information from colleges, each indicating why it the perfect choice for the young Floridian. Most of his friends would be attending either the University of Florida in Gainesville or Florida State University in Tallahassee. Both were known as party schools, and they offered in-state tuition, which was a great savings for middle-class families such as the Finch's. The other major institution, the University of Miami, was private and attracted mostly northeastern students who wanted to go to "Suntan U" and could afford it. Nobody in Nick's class would go to the "U". Nick did his own research. Among his criteria were that the school had to be in the South, embrace sports, have pretty coeds, and have good English and history departments, and pony up some scholarship money. And it could not be in Florida.

Nick flirted with the idea of one of the service academies. The big three of West Point, the United States Naval Academy, and the United States Air Force Academy had been in contact with his guidance counselor once the ACT scores were reported. J.W. was against the idea, but it was his son's decision. He told Nick, "Your mother and I served, so you do not have to." Still, it did intrigue Nick, until he saw a documentary on PBS one night on the life of a freshman or plebe. Shaved heads and people screaming at the young cadets and midshipmen quickly changed his view on a possible appointment. There was also a lack of female enrollment. Somebody else could take his place and keep the nation safe.

After going through the brochures and catalogs, Nick decided to check out the University of Georgia in Athens, the University of North Carolina in Chapel Hill, and the University of Mississippi, known more affectionately as Ole Miss, in Oxford. He also proposed the idea of attending the University of Southern California in Los Angeles after watching the Rose Bowl on New Year's Day with the constant TV sideline shots of the drop-dead gorgeous USC cheerleaders. The proposal was quickly shot down by both parents replying simply and directly, and in unison, "No." No explanations were given and no discussion ensued, just a no. The idea was never broached again.

The Finch's, mom, dad, and son packed up the family sedan and headed off for a tour of the three finalist colleges. Nick's brother and sisters had gone off to school, at least attempted higher education. His older brother was in Navy ROTC and would become a pilot until blood pressure grounded him. He left the service very bitter. Nick's older sister married a successful Cornell grad and settled into the life of a suburban housewife with cocktail parties. No work for her. The other two did graduate from college, Trisha from the awfully expensive Boston College with a degree in the new field of computer science and would move up in the corporate world with Hewlett-Packard. Addie graduated from Florida with a degree in political science and would become involved in local politics in Raleigh, North Carolina, later marrying a research engineer who worked with various firms within the triangle of Raleigh, Durham, and Chapel Hill. Now it was Nick's turn.

As the car went up the Florida Turnpike, the north–south toll highway, it passed right by Gainesville on its way to Athens, Georgia. Everyone was impressed by what they saw on the tour, especially the manicured hedges at Sanford Stadium. Nick liked the nightlife, especially the music scene. There was an unusual new wave group playing that evening who apparently called Athens home. They were the B-52's, and they did a twenty-minute live version of "Rock Lobster." Now that was cool. Next it was through South Carolina with a stop by at family dairy in Spartanburg. J.W. hated going back there, but they did stop by and see the once huge dairy now divided into four smaller dairies, one for each brother. There was an incident at Nick's uncle Tommy's house when the small family dog, a dachshund named Shultzee, without being provoked, bit Nick on the back of the leg. It was a flesh wound, but it did draw blood. Charlene cleaned the wound and determined it would not need stitches. Shultzee might have, though. J.W. witnessed the sneak attack by the small canine and, without warning, ran over to the side of the living room where the small dog was and kicked so hard, the dog looked like a football that had just been kicked for an extra point—but instead of clearing the goalposts, the dachshund cleared the rabbit ear antenna that was perched atop the TV. The dog hit the back of the wall, shook his head, dazed, and confused, and ran into the arms of Aunt Margret. The visit ended then.

Chapel Hill was beautiful and stately. Franklin Street, the entertainment district, was jumping. The highlight of the tour was seeing Carmichael Auditorium, where the powerhouse Tar Heels played basketball. Now that was neat. Leaving North Carolina, the Finch's traveled the width of Tennessee, which seemed as wide as Florida was long. They went right by Knoxville and UT and through Nashville, which is home to Vanderbilt. Vanderbilt is private and awfully expensive, so becoming a Commodore was not an option. The Finch's took a left in Memphis and headed south on I-55 to Oxford. This would be the final stop on the college tour, for so many reasons.

Upon reaching the beautiful college town of Oxford, Mississippi, almost instantly and instinctively they knew they had arrived. Charlene and J.W. loved the beauty and charm that Oxford offered. Almost everyone answered questions with a "Yes, sir" or a "No, sir." Doors were opened and chairs were pulled out for the women, and meals did not start until there was a holding of hands and a family prayer led by the oldest male. It intrigued Nick, but it took his parents back to their youth and upbringing. Oxford was where time stood still, where it was still 1955. The Finches liked that. Nick Finch really liked the fact that even though Ole Miss was ranked in the dead middle of almost all academic ranking rubrics, it scored in the top ten in both literature and history. This was the home of arguably the United States' greatest author, the Nobel Prizewinning William Faulkner. Later, one of Nick's academic highlights was taking a class called Faulknerian literature at the author's majestic home, Rowan Oak. His history professor and adviser, Frank Shelby, would later achieve rock star status because of his significant role in the PBS documentary on the Civil War. Nick would never take for granted how lucky he was to have had those academic experiences. And there were three more boxes that he could check. Ole Miss would offer a generous financial aid package because of Nick's ACT test score and what they called his unlimited potential. Basically, the Finch's would be allowed to pay in-state tuition rather the double out-of-state fees. Nice. Next, the Rebels played in the sports-crazy Southeastern Conference, the SEC, with all its passion, energy, and tradition. He could not wait for football season. And finally, there were the coeds. Nick had grown up in a "talent rich" environment of beautiful beach girls. This was different. These young women dressed up to go to the gym or to take a jog. Their hair and makeup were always perfect, and their southern drawl was intoxicating. And there were so many! They would walk in groups, usually fellow sorority sisters, around campus, around the open park in the center of campus called The Grove, or around the restaurants, shops, and bars that made up Oxford Square. That last and important box now had a check in it. The Florida kid was headed to the Deep South for college and he could not wait, except he had to work for his dad's company that summer to earn some spending money. It was off to the Breakers Hotel for Nick to paint and pressure-clean the Finch Company's biggest client and cash cow, and then change into dark clothes and umpire little league baseball games in exchange for twenty dollars, a Coke, and a hot dog. He was ready to go.

When John and Charlene dropped off their last child in Oxford that late summer day, Nick noticed there were tears in his mother's eyes. He had never seen her cry. Ever. Nursing, with her nightly witnessing of pain, death, and heartbreak, had hardened her. There were times when Nick thought his mom could be plain callous, such as when describing her night of work as "having three die on me last night." When Nick would call her on this sort of language, she would simply say something to effect of people's need to make better personal choices, such as hanging out with better people, refraining from playing with guns, or refusing to ever ride a motorcycle. She called motorcyclists "organ donors." What was happening now was different, though; she was saying goodbye to her last child as a boy, and now he would become a man. J.W. was ecstatic as the house was finally empty. He would celebrate by taking that same I-55 South, but to the Big Easy, New Orleans. Soon after returning to West Palm Beach, J.W. and Charlene would put the house on the market and move to an oceanfront condo on Singer Island. They would shake hands with Nick and shortly thereafter drive off to their new lives. Nick also had a new life in front of him.

Nick Finch quickly adjusted even though he knew no one at Ole Miss. He quickly made friends in his dorm and during fraternity rush, where he heard all the fraternities giving their best sales pitches, much like car salesmen, for why Nick would be a perfect brother for life. They were impressed with his academic record, by the fact that he had been involved in high school athletics, and with the idea that he could help them with intramurals. And he offered them great potential for spring break as a new member close to both Fort Lauderdale and Daytona Beach.

Nick made his final choice, and he hoped that the fraternity would select him as well. He would now be a pledge for Alpha Kappa Alpha, or "Ally Cat." They welcomed him by throwing an ice-cold bucket of water on him while he was sleeping in his dorm. He pretended that the action was cool, but he really thought of it as a junior high sleepaway camp prank and very immature.

Nick would declare history as his major and political science as his minor. There would a lot of English classes. He would take the minimum number of science and math courses, which was a total of fifteen hours—five classes. He chose college algebra, geology, astronomy, and one biology class that almost derailed him. Nick had taken biology as a senior in high school and figured a freshman-level class could not be that hard. Wrong. He had not taken the time to read the small print as that class was for premed majors. It would be the biggest class he ever took with seventy-five classmates, seventy-four of whom were freshmen. He studied more for that class than he did for any other course he took. Hell, he studied more for that biology class than for all his other classes put together. His final grade was a C, and he was damn proud of that C. He was average, and that was fine with him. He was one of only eighteen of the seventy-five who passed the class. The rest failed, stopped coming, or dropped the class and changed their majors. One student in the middle of a test got up and proclaimed to his classmates and the professor he was, "going to take his "F" like a man and fuck it." He slammed his test and paper on the front desk and walked out proudly with his head held high. Nick grinned ant thought this was very cool and went back to his own exam. That student would never reappear in that class. This would be his only C in four years of college. Nick Finch would graduate with honors.

The rest of his classes honestly were not that challenging. He had a good study habit of immediately reviewing the day's lessons, finding a quiet place to study (the law school building), using fraternity files to look over past tests, and most importantly being very energized by the subject matter or the professor's teaching style and manner. In short, school came easy to him. Being a history major required twelve hours, or four classes, of economics. This concerned Nick since there would be math and graphing. And the instructor was Dr. Woodfield Richardson. Dr. Richardson was the only professor who taught these versions of micro- and macroeconomics. He was tenured, and he intimidated many students. The old line was that students should roll out when he rolled in. You see, Dr. Richardson had lost both his legs in a logging accident as a teenager. His legs were gone, but not his mind. He graduated from Vanderbilt and later from Harvard. Nick took a liking to him and the professor to him. Nick would wheel him to and from the classroom to his office, or to his specially outfitted car. It can't hurt to "brown nose" a little bit.

The grading system for Richardson's class was unique with just three graded assignments averaged equally to determine the final grade. There would be a final, a midterm, and an at-large question the individual would deliver orally to the entire class. At the end of each class session, the econ professor would write three questions on the overhead for the class to copy. At the beginning of the next session, Dr. Richardson would spin a large bingo hopper and pull out three names of students enrolled in the class. The named students would have to rise and give their answers, possibly including drawing a graph on the overhead. Once a student's name was called, he or she would never be called again. The good professor stated publicly that since most were business majors, they would be asked direct questions by their bosses or clients and they had better be ready each day. He looked right at Nick Finch, who was smiling. Richardson said he had no idea what a history major would be asked or by whom. It was good-natured ribbing. Students who had prepared to be called either expressed their ecstasy if called or groaned when they were passed over. Ohers prayed out loud not to be called because they were not ready. If they were called and at least attempted an answer, they would get anywhere from a D+ to a C−. That could be overcome. Not being there would result in a zero. No recoveries there. It was a unique way to teach and probably did help the future business executives and lawyers who made up 95 percent of the class. Dr. Richardson made sure that his history major was never called. It hadn't been a bad choice to brownnose after all.

Nick Finch went home for the first time at Thanksgiving. He could not wait to see his high school buddies and see how things were going for them, if they had gone Greek, and if so, what fraternity, and what the young women were like at their schools. They met up at the last high school football game of the season, all sporting T-shirts with college logos and Greek letters. They saw many of their former teachers and coaches. They exchanged stories about the new experiences they had had as college men. By the third quarter, Nick Finch was bored and wanted to go back to Oxford. Oxford, Mississippi, was his new home, and his address was the Ally Cat House on the Ole Miss campus.

Living in a large fraternity house was an experience. Fifty-plus college-age men living two to a room—except officers, who had private suites—ate, studied sort of, and partied there. They shared experiences and learned about coping with different personalities, crises, and friendships. They also learned outside-the-box coping skills. Early risers got hot water for their showers, as well as the best of the sausage biscuit breakfast sandwiches. Nick always chose the earliest classes available because of the hot water and the food, and he wanted his afternoons free to do with as he wished.

There was always somebody willing to party if you looked hard enough. About twenty of Nick's pledge brothers dropped out or transferred because of too much partying. In Oxford, this is called "falling into the velvet ditch." It was kind of a soft landing onto a rough patch in life. Some climbed out of the velvet ditch. Others did not. There were drugs, but not out in the open like at some of the western or northern colleges and at FSU and UF. It was more discreet. Nick was from the drug capital of the United States, South Florida. Drugs, especially cocaine, came through from Central America in such great quantities that drugs trailed behind only citrus as the number one crop. TV shows such as *Miami Vice* and movies such as *Scarface* glamourized the issue. Despite Nick's background, he never more than dabbled with drugs. He felt marijuana, also known as weed, ganja, or pot, just made him lazy and hungry. He needed no help in those areas.

Nick Finch and some his closest new friends liked happy hour at the local watering holes, such as the Gin and the

Warehouse, which offered cheap beer and bourbon and the chance to "fall in love" on a Friday—and then rinse and repeat the next Friday. He also traveled throughout the Deep South, going with friends to their homes as a guest. He always answered questions with politeness and made his bed every morning. He would strip the bed on his last morning. Manners were important; Charlene had raised him right. He was always invited back. Arkansas, Louisiana, Tennessee, and Alabama became destinations for a weekend getaway. He absorbed the local cultures and customs and attended many a Baptist and Methodist church service, which were quite different from the Episcopal services of his upbringing.

When a Pike alumnus donated a used Winnebago motor home, it was off to away football games to watch the Rebels play and check out the local landscape, that is, the home team's nightlife. Nick traveled to the 'villes—Fayetteville, Knoxville, Starkville, and Gainesville. He also went on what was like a trip to a foreign country, namely, Baton Rouge on a Saturday night for an Ole Miss–LSU game. Now that was a different culture, and he was amused and amazed at the same time by all the passion, pageantry, and pride exhibited down on the bayou. It was completely different from the starched preppy button-down shirt and blue blazer look that Ole Miss men sported at their games. Memories were made that would never be forgotten, and some were relegated to the realm of secrecy forever.

Nick had a fraternity brother from the Cincinnati area named Jerry Doyle who was a nationally ranked player on the men's tennis team. There was only one thing that people admired about Jerry Doyle more than his blistering serve, and that was his long blond hair. He would sport a headband or a baseball cap turned backward and was constantly removing his headwear to readjust his blond locks. Coeds were jealous of his hair. Jerry did not use shampoo, he used "product" that he specially ordered. He showered much longer than the allotted three minutes because of all the product and the time required for washing, conditioning, and rinsing. Many times, the hot water supply was depleted after he had showered. This was beginning to annoy some of the brothers. A clandestine meeting was called by Nick's roommate Tom. In attendance were Nick and Tom along with four others. They all complained about the grooming habits of Jerry Doyle. Nick was half listening as he was also half studying. Multitasking is such a gift. Suddenly, Big Tom, as he was known because of his six-toot-four, two-hundred-fifty-pound frame, got up and opened a gym bag that he had gotten for having played football for the Rebs, until a terrible shoulder injury ended his football career. He unzipped the bag and pulled out what looked like a bottle of shampoo. Not product, but shampoo. A closer look showed it was not product or shampoo, but a women's hair removal solution called Nair. The plan was to cut Jerry Doyle's product with the Nair.

Tom left the room and returned shortly with a bottle of product on whose label was printed a fancy French name that no one in the room could pronounce. On the side of the bottle, it was announced in bold English that the contents were a product of France, with a small French flag beneath. Tom poured about half of it out and put it into his Head and Shoulders bottle—after all, it shouldn't be wasted. All the guys let out a good chuckle. That half was replaced by the Nair, with the bottle returned to the tennis player's room. Now the waiting game was to begin.

For the first few days it seemed there was no effect. To keep things normal, the boys hollered at Jerry for taking too much time in the shower and using up all the hot water. Before one night out on the town, Nick noticed Jerry examining his scalp in the mirror above the row of sinks. Nick asked what was wrong. Jerry replied, "I'm not sure, but I feel I am losing some hair." He then examined his brush and shook his head. He was perplexed. About three days later he knocked and came into Nick's room and asked if they could talk. Jerry Doyle looked very worried and even scared. There were now patches of his long blond hair gone. That would explain why he now never took off his baseball cap. He explained that he had gone to a doctor, who ordered blood tests and the results were negative, but there had to be something wrong. His parents were on the way down from Cincinnati and had scheduled another doctor's appointment, this one with a cancer specialist in Memphis. Things were spinning out of control. Now it was Nick who was worried. Later that night Nick called for an emergency meeting of the "barbershop five." He explained what Jerry was going through, mentioned that Jerry's parents were coming, and discussed everything else about the situation. The group swore to lifelong secrecy. As one relayed, they were to bury the issue then bury the shovel.

Nick had another plan. In one of his psychology classes, he learned that stress could actually make people become physically sick. Jerry was now losing weight, and his cocky smile was gone, having been replaced by a look of horror. He was dying, at least that's what he thought. Nick reached out like a good fraternity brother would do. He asked the scared young man if he was having woman problems. No, that was not it. How about school? Any classes kicking his ass? Yes, was the answer, and it was an answer many of the business majors there would have given. Managerial Accounting taught by Dr. Albert Leigh. That one class had turned many a business major into a marketing major or a math teacher. *Well, now we know.* "Have you scheduled an appointment with him?" Nick asked. "No, I can't, because I always have practice, or we have matches."

The Memphis doctor ordered more tests. A day later, Nick suggested that Jerry meet with his adviser and the athletic department and request a schedule change. At least take the class in the fall when the tennis player would have more study time. Jerry Doyle was going to do just that. Also, Nick suggested that maybe Jerry should change his "product"— "You know, "start over fresh and new."

"Absolutely," Jerry agreed. Soon thereafter, the hair loss subsided. In fact, his hair started growing back. The new clinical reports came back clean. The smile and the long showers returned, but with Breck Gold Formula shampoo, imported from Jerry Doyle's hometown of Cincinnati and made by the Proctor & Gamble Company. Jerry Doyle was now in full recovery, and he had the Florida kid to thank for the advice. To this day when there is a TV commercial for a hair removal product, Nick Finch grins but never shares the reason for that grin. He and four others know.

Weather and the real four seasons are something that Nick Finch had never experienced growing up in South Florida. South Florida never really has a fall or autumn season, depending on whom you talk to and where they were raised. After all, it had only snowed once according to the record. That day was January 19, 1977, a day that is frozen in the memory of all the locals. Nick was a freshman in high school when he awoke and saw his dad at the kitchen table reading the morning edition of the *Palm Beach Post*. Later in the afternoon, J.W. would read the *Evening Times*. In those days, daily newspapers were popular, in fact so popular that each day there were two editions. Today the newspaper industry is on life support. J.W. grinned as he looked at his young son and asked him to go outside and see if he noticed anything, then come back. Nick, still half asleep, did as directed and went outside, where he saw white flakes falling from the sky. Was this sugarcane residue caused by the burning of the sugarcane stalks, which usually occurred in February and caused lots of breathing problems for his mom, Charlene, given her asthma—or was it really snow? He saw his breath in the air, caused by the cold weather, and determined, after brushing some of the fresh snowpack off his dad's Bronco, that it was snow! Real snow. And it was falling in West Palm Beach, Florida, on this date, January 19, 1977!

Nick's mom was still at work at St. Mary's. Did she know? When asked about this, J.W. responded yes with a laugh. Nick asked if he could call his sister Trisha, who was a senior at Boston College and was herself buried knee-deep in snow. He woke her with the earliness of the phone call, screeching about how it was snowing. She listened and told her little brother to go back to bed because he was "sleepwalking." After she hung up and thought about it for a minute, she called home, to the hospital, knowing her mom would be there, and shared her concern about her little brother's mental stability or drug abuse. Charlene, after she stopped laughing, explained that it was indeed snowing here. It did not stick, but it was snowing. The locals would never forget that day. The next day, the twentieth, the schools were given a snow day, not because of the snow, but because of the power overload from the electric space heaters being on full blast and Florida Power & Light having trouble keeping up with the demand. Closing the schools would help. The temperature got down to twenty-eight degrees that night. As a sidenote, the Finches did not have a working heater in their house. J.W. always stated that no matter what the thermometer said, it was not that cold, and he knew cold from his stint in Europe. They did have a fireplace though, and anything went into it if it produced a flame and some heat. Palm tree fronds, leaves, and even garbage went into the fireplace. The chimney outside looked like a Pittsburgh steel factory smokestack as the smoke was very thick and black. It even smelled weird.

Spring started early in South Florida, and the weather was fantastic. Not hot, not cold, and even less humidity and rain. There is a reason Major League Baseball teams call Florida home in the spring. Summer, simply put, is brutal. The term "long hot summer" could have been coined to describe Florida. Most of the country is hot in the summer months, but here the heat extends into September and October. There is a reason that the peak of hurricane season is September 13. The term "endless summer" to most locals is not the title of a surf movie but a way of life.

Nick found himself falling in love with cool, crisp autumn mornings with the brilliance of the leaves in and around Oxford. The pumpkin patches, the spiked apple cider, and the wearing out of sweaters with a polo shirt underneath and collar up while attending a football game was new to, and appreciated by, the Floridian. Winter, on the other hand, as he soon learned, was very overrated: short days, freezing rain, snowed only five or six days a year, and it never really stuck, muddiness, and a look of despair and death. It got dark around five, and the leaves had all lost their colorful foliage. Instead, it was gray all day, followed by cold nights. Indoor activities now were the games of choice: shooting pool, playing cards, bowling. And maybe some female companionship would keep Nick warm. He never really learned how to shoot a good game of stick; card playing bored him and took too long; and bowling, except for beer frames, was something he had never really taken a liking to. He was always up for companionship to keep warm. Ah yes, indoor sports.

Spring in Oxford was fantastic as he experienced spring fever for the first time. Time for a jog, a game of golf, to wash the car, to go up to the local lake, and to lie out and get some color. After all, spring break was coming up soon, and at least two capfuls of fraternity brothers would be the guests of the Finches. It was time for Nick to repay them for his weekend trips to their hometowns. J.W. loved the visitors as he listened to their stories about college life. The boys loved the location, which was oceanfront on the twenty-first floor of a condominium building known as the TradeWinds. Also, they were only about a forty-five-minute drive from the Fort Lauderdale Strip. And there was plenty of hot water!

The books were going quite well for the Florida junior as he had begun to slow down on his socializing and nightlife. He knew that a history degree brought with it only two real opportunities, teach or go to law school. He had had his share of campus romance, lots of it in fact, but now was dating only one young woman, Leslie McMahon, who was from the Mississippi Gulf Coast town of Gulfport. Tommy had set Nick up with Leslie. Nick liked people from the coastal towns such as Pascagoula, Biloxi, Gulfport, and Pass Christian. They knew what actual fresh seafood was, they were familiar with palm trees, and they had experienced killer hurricanes like Camille and Frederick.

Leslie was the daughter of a nurse—that was a plus—and a hospital administrator. She was almost as tall as Nick was, five foot ten. His friends asked what it was like to look up to his date. Leslie overheard the sarcastic comments one evening and after that wore only flats. Nick was appreciative. Leslie McMahon was an accomplished pianist and was third runner-up in the Miss Mississippi beauty pageant held in Vicksburg. Nick had gone and cheered on his girlfriend but was mostly amused by the people-watching. The coaches, stylists, and stage moms were beyond description. Maybe that is why they are now the subject of reality TV shows. Bizarre.

Leslie was always over at Nick's apartment since he had left the fraternity house. His three roommates enjoyed her company, and she was great at baking. Nick and Leslie went to games together, to the movies, and down to New Orleans for a Rolling Stones concert. Nick thought he had better see them now because they were not getting any younger. Little did he know that he would see Mick, Keith, and the other members almost forty years later in Miami with his grown children.

Leslie and Nick took the *City of New Orleans* train to Baton Rouge to see the Police—the pop group, not the squad—and the all-women group the Go-Go's. Each introduced their significant other to their respective parents. Apparently, they had passed that test. Their relationship was good, very good indeed, but not great. Nick could not explain why it wasn't great. Little did he know that when speaking to her sorority sisters, Leslie called her relationship with him "comfortable." The couple now could sense a lack of the spark they once had. Both wanted to end the relationship, but on positive terms. They really liked each other, but it was not quite love. Finally, one night at dinner, the matter was discussed, and they both laughed, giggled, and cried. They agreed to go as dates to each's upcoming spring formal.

Later, Leslie married a top doctor in the Jacksonville area, settled down, had three children, divorced, moved back to Gulfport, returned to nursing, and got remarried. She was finally happy. In the future, she and Nick would stay in touch and smile at each other when in social settings. No bad blood there.

Nick entered his senior and final year of undergraduate school, and other than that horrible biology class, he was breezing through his academics. He signed up for a special tutoring class that met every Sunday at the local junior college to prepare for the test for entry into law school, the LSAT. Nick Finch had thought about it, and law school it would be. He was not particularly sure why he had made this choice, but he did like the money that lawyers were reported to make. He could read and write as well as any English major, and with his history background, precedents did not worry him. Still, he did not want to embarrass himself, so he took the tutoring class. Every Sunday the class met with about thirty students, mostly from Ole Miss but some from Memphis State. Three Ole Miss law school professors taught the class, moonlighting to supplement their incomes. For fifteen weeks, Nick went and listened and, hopefully, learned.

When the day of the exam arrived, he found that it would be administered and proctored at Lamar Hall, the Ole Miss law school building. When at last the proctors ordered, "Stop and put your pencils down," Nick could relax. He thought the test was tough but fair. Hell, it was easier than biology. A month later he received his scores, and once again they were off the charts. Apparently standardized tests were not that hard for Mr. Nicholas Finch, future barrister, and esquire. Or something like that.

During his senior year, to make some extra money, Nick tended bar at the Gin, Oxford's most popular watering hole. J.W. had always told him to do something he was good at, and, well, he was good at going to bars. Two of his fraternity brothers were bouncers. Nick would help, once the lights came on, to shut down the bar and clean up. He would empty trash cans, sweep the floor, and restock the refrigerators. The owner of the Gin was a local attorney named Watson White. Mr. White was impressed by Nick's volunteerism and work ethic. He also had spotted the young future lawyer at St. Peter's Episcopal Church for church services. Nick Finch, unlike most of his college friends, seldom missed a church service. Upon leaving, he would feel refreshed and full. You see, besides the spirituality of Communion, there was a post service home-cooked meal provided by the Episcopal churchwomen and altar guild. Meat loaf or fried chicken with all the sides sure beat anything he could cook, or fast food.

One evening at the bar, Mr. White stopped by the table where Nick was sitting sharing a pitcher of beer with some of his friends and asked him to follow him to his office. Watson White shared his impressions of Nick and asked him about his life and future. Nick shared freely about his family, his upbringing, and what he imagined lay ahead for him. Watson White stood up and offered Nick a job as a bartender at the Gin. These jobs were coveted. Minimum wage and all tips would be shared evenly, and the tips were good. Weekend evenings, there would a line and a cover charge. Outstanding bands would play live and would be enjoyed by all. Some actually had a Top 40 hit or two. Nick accepted the job. He began to bring in about three hundred dollars a week in cash for about fifteen to twenty hours of work. Life was good.

Nick had noticed Patricia Marks was also an Episcopalian and attended the same church services he went to. If a lot of people knew Nick Finch, everyone knew Patty Marks. A leading sorority Delta Delta Delta, or Tri Delt, she was a legacy whose mother was a finalist for Miss America. Carol James, later Marks, Patricia's mother, also knew of the "Mrs." degree strategy as she had married a law student who would join his daddy's practice and then enter politics. Robert Marks would be the United States congressman for the area around the state capital, Jackson. They were part of the elite of Mississippi. Patty was intrigued by the Florida bartending Pike. She asked around and found that his parents lived on the beach and went to the famous Breakers Hotel frequently. They did, but it was for work. Nick found himself attracted to both Patty and her ever-present roommate Tammy. The two would stop by the Gin during the slow hours after lunch, but before happy hour and always order two glasses of wine, one white and one red. Nick teased Patty, saying she was taking Communion early. Patty giggled and smiled, then would leave to freshen up.

One day, Tammy, when Patty was away, shared with Nick that the congressman's daughter really wanted to go out with him. That answered a question that had been dogging him: not if he would ask one of them out, but which one he was going to ask out, either Patty Marks or Tammy. His old girlfriend Leslie would shake her head when she would see Nick and Patty together. She did not like Patty at all. Beauty pageant rivalry or something. Immediately, Patty would reach for Nick's hand to hold it as if to say, *back off. You had your chance. Now he's mine.* Nick hated all forms of public affection, such as holding hands or having a date sitting right next to him if he were driving a truck or car with a bench seat. Public affection was a no-no and considered trashy by Charlene. Nick had never seen his parents ever hold hands, much less kiss, in public. Those were private expressions of affection.

The Marks' took a liking to Nick. And the fact that he would be going to law school and was an Episcopalian, well, that was the cherry on top of the ice-cream sundae. Patty Marks would eventually get her Mrs. degree, much to the satisfaction of her mama Carol. Patty always took summer school classes and never, ever had a real job. She graduated with her degree in home economics in three and a half years and returned to Jackson, where she assisted a family friend with her catering business. Nick was looking at law schools now, and with his 3.85 GPA and his top LSAT scores, offers came in—and with financial aid. The Mark's really pushed for him to stay in Oxford, saying that he could stay in their in-town condo for free, adding that if those who graduated from Ole Miss law school were exempt from the bar exam. That would explain how Robert Marks was able to practice law in Mississippi yet had never set foot in a courtroom or, for that matter, really did anything connected to his degree. Nick thought of him as a simple court jester of a man. Simple, very simple, but he got reelected to the House of Representatives time and time. "Make your mark with Marks" was what it said on the bumper stickers and billboards. Nick never put one on his car. He said it was a family rule as his car was a company car. The explanation worked. Among the offers, UNC–Chapel Hill had come back, as they had four years earlier, with a full ride. Nick wanted to go there, and he would eventually do so. This would not go over well with the mother or the daughter. They liked form and order, and this was not part of the plan. Things began to be quite cold and frosty between Patty and Nick. Meanwhile, Tammy was now coming into the Gin alone for afternoon chitchat with Nick. She was an accounting major from Atlanta, very bright and quite beautiful. The two grew closer and closer. After all, Tammy most likely would be their maid of honor. And he and she were, "just friends."

One evening there was a line with a cover charge to get into the Gin when one of the bouncers, Tommy, motioned for Nick to go to the back emergency exit. Nick went and found Tammy. She had been crying as her boyfriend, whom she had dated since her senior year of high school in Atlanta, Angus Wallace, had broken up with her. He needed space and was soon going backpacking across Europe. Nick let her in and had her sit in the office, saying he would be back to check on her. Ten minutes later, Tammy Barkley emerged from the office. She had, as it is said, cleaned up really well. Gone were the tears. She took a seat right by where Nick was bartending, and he asked her if she wanted a white wine. "Hell no, I want a shot of whiskey, and I want it now!"

Soon it was closing time. Nick said he would lock up. The rest of staff smiled as Tammy stayed behind. She would not be driving anywhere. Nick counted the receipts and recorded the night's business, then took the cash and put it in a safe underneath one of the freezers in the back. Tammy came back to the office, where they were alone. She asked what he really thought about her roommate, Patty's "bitchy" mom, and their future. Nick was honest, telling her that the relationship was going south and doing so really fast. Tammy suddenly sat on Nick's lap in the wooden swivel office chair and planted him with an open-mouthed kiss, giving him some tongue. Nick Finch was taken aback, but just for a moment, then responded with his best effort. He had always been told he was a great kisser, probably because his older sisters had tutored him on what a girl liked, which was the three S's: smooth, soft, and slow. Tammy stopped for an instant, not to reconsider what she was doing, but to share that Patty had told her what a good kisser Nick was. And it was true. He smiled and went right back to what they were doing. The passion continued right there in the office until both were spent and exhausted. Surprisingly, neither felt guilty, which was probably wrong, but they would be graduating soon and leaving Oxford single. Actually, they were relieved.

Nick called Patty the next day to officially break it off. Carol, the mom, called him almost immediately and between the screaming and profanity, told the future lawyer that she hoped he would die in a fiery crash on his drive to North Carolina. Nick hung up and looked over to his bed, where Tammy was waiting and laughing as she had heard Carol's angry voice from across the room. Patty would later find out about Nick and Tammy's dalliance from a nosy sorority sister. The two would never speak again. Patty would later marry another law student who was by many accounts obese and goofy, but obedient. He would fit in perfectly with the Marks family. The congressman would be caught by an FBI sting operation taking bribes for natural gas leases on public land, after which he would be forced to surrender his law license and was sentenced to six months at Eglin Air Force Base prison in the Florida Panhandle. Tammy would marry and start a family of her own yet continue to work as a partner in a top-ranked Atlanta accounting firm. She wanted never to go Europe. Everyone had heard Angus had been beaten up in a punk rock pub in London. Karma. Nick had changed his choice of who and where, as he would make a huge change of plans. Just a few days before the graduation ceremony was to take place in the Grove, his mother, Charlene, would call, and Nick would make a life-changing audible.

CHAPTER 5

Growing Up in A Hurry

Nick had grown apart from his parents, not on purpose, but because he was changing and growing up. He still called on Sunday afternoons, and their discussions seldom veered away from the usual script. He discussed the morning's church service and sermon. Sometimes he spoke on the subjects as if he had been in attendance that morning, which many times he had not. Was that wrong? This pleased his parents, and after all, one is supposed to honor one's father and mother. He talked sports with J.W. and dating with Charlene. They used to talk three times a week, but now it was down to one three-minute phone call. With just one week before graduation, Nick needed to find out how many rooms he would need to reserve for his family for the upcoming commencement ceremony. He called home this time, not on Sunday, but on a Wednesday afternoon, figuring it would be quick and he would just get his mom. After all, she was the travel agent of the family. Turns out it would be a call that would rock Nicholas Finch to his core and change his life forever.

Charlene was startled when the phone rang that afternoon. The phone seldom rang at this point in her life with all her children grown and out of the house or now, the condo. Her kids, like Nick did, all called on Sunday, and this was a time period when Spam meant mystery meat, not unwanted phone solicitations that seemed to badger one at the worst of times. Charlene answered, thinking maybe it was the hospital with a change of schedule, but it was her baby boy, now young man, Nick. He asked what his parents' plans were for the upcoming graduation, how many rooms they would need for the family, where he should make dinner reservations, and if they were going to be driving or flying, the latter of which would require a trip to the Memphis airport. Nick waited as there was a long pause. When his mom finally spoke, it was in a low tone as if she did not want to waken anyone who might be asleep. Nick's dad was indeed asleep, home from work, on the couch. Charlene, with her voice cracking, said, "Son, we are sorry, but we will not be coming up there." At first Nick was not pleased as he wanted to share the special moment with the people who to him were the most special in the world.

His response was quick and terse: "Really?"

Then Charlene's voice began to crumble. Something was wrong, very wrong.

"Nick, your father is sick, and the trip would be too much for him."

Too much for him? Honestly, Nick had never seen his father sick in his life, not even with the common cold. "What could it be?" he asked. The answer was cancer. Now Nick was the one who got quiet. He composed himself and asked, "How bad is it?"

Charlene took a deep breath and replied in a strong voice, "Bad. Really bad."

"How bad is really bad?"

Charlene, beginning to sob, said it was terminal and that the husband she loved so much and the father of her five children had been given six months, maybe, to live. Nick became noticeably quiet and asked about treatments and the strategy they were employing. Charlene stated they had exhausted all the local help and had just returned from a midweek trip to Houston and the MD Anderson Cancer Clinic. They all had given the same prognosis. Six months and maybe a miracle, but the treatment would be brutal, with chemotherapy and radiation as the prescribed treatments. Then Nick heard a request he had never heard before from the strongest woman, for that matter the strongest person, he had ever known: "Son, I need help. Please come home as soon as you can. Please."

"I will, Mom."

Nick left his apartment and walked to a nearby wooded area, where he sat against a big oak tree and looked up at the blue sky or was it heaven. He broke down and sobbed as never before in his life. His body convulsed and shook, and tears flowed down his face and dripped onto his blue jeans.

Nick was not quite sure how long he stayed in those woods, but when he returned to his apartment, his roommate Tommy was there. Tammy, in her new green Monte Carlo, pulled up in front of their duplex just as Nick emerged. They both looked at Nick and then at each other. Nick looked at them and just blurted out, "My dad has cancer and has been given just six goddamn months to live."

Nick Finch found himself crying again. Tommy turned around and went inside up to his bedroom, where he shut and locked the door. This brought back bad memories for him as his biological mother had died from breast cancer when he was just seven years old. He really liked his stepmother, but he loved his mama, and now a similar thing was happening to his best friend. Unfortunately, he could relate. Tommy, who had met J.W. six or seven times and really liked the man, found himself tearing up. He fell to his knees and said a prayer, not for his friend's father, but for his friend, because he knew what the next few months would be like.

Tammy, like Nick, knew their days as a couple were coming to an end. She would be pursuing her MBA at the University of Georgia in the fall, while Nick would be going to North Carolina for law school. She put her arms around the man whom she secretly had married hundreds of times in her dreams. That was not to be, but she had to be there for him now. And she would be.

Nick had a lot to do in a short amount of time. He gave away his furniture, paid up his final bills, and said goodbye to the many friends who were wishing him well and good luck at Chapel Hill. The ones who knew about his father's condition offered their thoughts and prayers. He had to go to graduation—the university made it a requirement—but if Nick were to push it, he probably could get a waiver. But he could not get a waiver from his parents. They demanded he walk across that stage.

Nick remembers so very little of the commencement program. The guest speaker was Senator Edward Kennedy, who spoke about how his brothers President John and Attorney General Bobby, and Ole Miss, would always be tied together because of the federal action his brothers initiated to integrate Ole Miss in a historic event known as the Meredith Crisis. Nick Finch could care less about what the senator, who had presidential ambitions, was talking about, and instead focused on James Meredith, who himself who was a guest on the stage. Nick had learned about all the shameful indignities Meredith had had to endure, and now the man was a guest seated right next to the university chancellor. Nick thought, *now there's an example of dignity.* The man was all class. Nick's thoughts were few and far between as he waited to hear his named called so he could get up, receive his diploma, and return to his seat. The students were now graduates of the University of Mississippi, but they were reminded no one ever leaves Ole Miss. Also, one more thing: they were requested to become active members of the Alumni Association and pay their dues. Whatever.

Once it was over, Nick quickly left the ceremony, got into his Ford Fairmont, which he called the "Dullmont" because of just how plain and boring the company car was, and proceeded to drive home. What would he find? What would he say? So many questions danced through his head on the twelve-hour drive.

He arrived at the TradeWinds condo on Singer Island and punched in the four-digit security code that unlocked the entrance door. It was an end to, at that time, the longest twelve hours of his life. It was four in the morning when he opened the door slowly so as not to wake his parents. Instead, he found his father sitting at the kitchen counter by himself with just the ceiling kitchen light on, drinking a cup of coffee and smoking a cigarette. The ashtray was full of butts. Nick dropped his duffel bag on the floor and looked at J.W. Finch, his father, his hero, and did not recognize him.

Nick walked for a step or two, then ran across the room, not to shake hands, but to hug his father. The Finch's were not hugging people. Handshakes were just fine with this family. Nick hugged his father longer than he had hugged anybody in his whole life. He started to cry.

"Now, now, that's enough," J.W. said as the embrace subsided. Now Nick could actually look at his dad. He would not have recognized him if had simply seen him on the street. J.W. had aged twenty years or so. He did not look his real age of sixty, but more like a seventy-five-year-old grandfather. His formerly black hair, what was left of it, was now an ash white. Patches of hair were missing. He was thin, and his skin was pasty, a grayish white like the color of wall spackle. He had lost some twenty pounds, and his clothes hung on him as if on a clothesline. J.W. Finch had always been a dapperly dressed man. He ironed his own slacks and shirts, got his hair cut every Saturday, and made sure his shoes were shined. And he was clean-shaven, allowing no facial hair. Now he looked like a survivor of a World War II prison camp—death warmed over. He looked at his startled son and welcomed him home, saying how proud he was of him.

Charlene emerged from the bedroom, having heard some commotion, and there was Nick. She let out a short cry of joy and went and hugged her son. She had aged too, even though she had cut back on her hours at the hospital. She felt now that she never left work as their condo was a hospital unto itself. Nick noticed the rows of pills on the kitchen counter. In the refrigerator, there were bottles of different medicines and potions. She had planned on retiring next year, but now she wasn't sure.

J.W. excused himself and went to the bathroom, where he closed the door. For the next ten minutes Nick could hear his father hack, cough, and vomit uncontrollably. Charlene informed Nick that this was one of side effects of the cancer-fighting drugs that he was on. Nick asked when they had found out and why only now, they were sharing the news with him. They had found out when J.W. went in to see Dr. Kimball for a physical because, as he stated, he felt off. Cancer was discovered. It started with the esophagus and spread throughout the core of his body, including his liver and pancreas. In short, J.W. was full of cancer and it was inoperable. The cause was a combination of chain-smoking and genetics as both J.W.'s parents had died of cancer. They had not informed Nick because they did not want to worry him. He had things to do, and there was nothing he could do anyhow. That was Nick's parents, staring death in the face and being more worried about upsetting their college son's lifestyle. His mother held has hand as the sound of J.W.'s vomiting continued to ring out from the bathroom. She said, "Thank God you are home. I need help."

"I am here, Mom. I am here for you. What do you want me to do?"

Nick Finch was in a fog like never before. He was still stunned by the recent turn of events. One day everything was sunshine and lollipops, and now he was witnessing firsthand how people both suffer and die. But this suffering and dying was his father's, and he was sad, angry, and confused at the same time. He didn't know if he was coming or going. It was mid-May now, and he began to settle into a strange routine. His mom would return home from the hospital anywhere between six and seven in the morning. Nick had noticed she no longer was wearing her white nurse's dress, with the white stockings and cap, that sported several emblems, including her lieutenant bars, a cross, and her Eastern Star pin. For years, Nick remembered going into his parents' bathroom and seeing white stockings hanging across the shower rod, while Charlene would be at the kitchen table shining up shoes with a white chalky substance from a sponge bottle while simultaneously challenging herself with the daily crossword puzzle. A cup of coffee, black, would be sitting next to a paper plate with an English muffin smeared with smooth peanut butter. This was how she would wind down after a night in the ER at St. Mary's. This routine was as reliable as the summer heat in Florida. It just was. Now Charlene

Finch, chief emergency room nurse, was sporting white pantsuits. She drew the line there. It had to be white; colored scrubs, the new in thing, would not do for her. She cut her hair short and stylish and even gave her cap a night off now and then. She still had her scope and multicolored pen for charting. Some things never change. She would arrive home, and J.W. would be up, sitting at the table, working on both his coffee and his cigarette nonstop. This also was routine, except now he waited even more anxiously for his wife. He realized his days were numbered. In the past they would give each other a quick kiss, then it was off to bed for Charlene and off to the shop for a day's work for J.W. Now Charlene was still on the clock as her rounds were at home, taking care of her dying husband. She brought out a glass of water and a whole battery of pills and medications. She made sure he took them all. Once she had caught him secretly washing some down the sink. On cue, ten minutes later, J.W. would be in the bathroom vomiting and hacking away. Now Nick would step in and take his father to the shower and get it set up and ready. After the shower, he would hand him a towel as J.W. slipped on a bathrobe that looked at least two sizes too big. Nick then would pull out the shaving cream and a disposable plastic razor and shave his father. From there he would help his dad pick out the clothes for the day. Last, he would comb his hair, and J.W. would pick out a ball cap to cover his depleted hairline. Usually, it was an Atlanta Braves cap. One day J.W. looked at his son and said simply, "I am so sorry for this. You didn't deserve this."

Nick looked at his once proud father, who now was clearly broken, and replied softly, "No, Dad, you didn't deserve this. I owe you so much. And I am glad I could help you and Mom." J. W. smiled—the first time he had done so in a long time. From there it was down the elevator to the Bronco. Nick would drive to the Howard Johnson's restaurant located on the corner of Dixie Highway and Belvedere Road. It was the ritual of having morning coffee and conversation with the other contractors and suppliers. About eight of them met there almost every day. They laughed, joked, and shared business opportunities with each other. There was an electrical engineering firm, Donaldson Electric, led by "Shorty" Donaldson, and an air-conditioning company named Sundance AC, the founder and president of which was John C. Newman, who would be there too. Also on hand were the suppliers to the contractors, mostly hardware store owners. This was before the emergence of Home Depot and Lowe's. The men traded stories, but now J.W. had taken a back seat and no longer led the conversation. Now he mostly just listened. One time, J.W. left his hat in the restaurant, and Nick went back into retrieve it. The men looked at the boy, who now was a man, they had known their entire lives, having watched him grow up before their eyes. Now they had trouble looking him in the eye.

As Nick turned around, "Shorty" Donaldson spoke up: "Son, we hate seeing your father like this. We love him like a brother."

Nick nodded with approval. As he approached the door, Mr. Newman spoke up: "Son, he is so proud of you. He loves you so much. I think you needed to know that." Nick nodded again, and his lips formed into a small smile as he made his way back to the Bronco. From there it was to the office/shop. The front half of the building was three offices with a water dispenser, a coffeepot, and a drafting table. Seated at the front of the office was a local high school girl whose job it was to answer the phone, take messages, and do some light typing. John Finch would reach out to his friend Bobby Newcombe, the principal of Forest Hill, for such a girl every year. Bobby would send only the best and most reliable. J.W. rewarded them with double the minimum wage and a gas account at the local Mobil station. This system had worked for many years; why should he change now? The back of the office was a supply shop with gallons of paint, ladders, compressors, and drop cloths. It was anchored by a four-stall garage. By noon J.W. was exhausted, and Nick would drive him home for his afternoon nap. Occasionally the routine changed if there was a doctor's appointment or a trip to the accountant's or lawyer's office. John Finch was trying to sell his company, and he wanted it sold by the time he moved on. This schedule would continue for the remainder of the summer. It was emotionally grueling, but it did help Nick's mother. And Nick found himself getting closer and closer to the most important event he would ever experience that is until he started his own family.

Nick had contacted the law school at UNC and told them of his home situation. They were great and granted him a deferment until January. They gave him a list of books he would need to read before he enrolled. He was very thankful for the respect they afforded him at this difficult time.

Nick was picking some baseball games to umpire, but he was getting restless. He remembered what his college history professors had told him he could do with that bachelor's degree in history: go to law school or teach. Law school was on the back burner and was going to be delayed. A wonderful new organization, with the concept being in its infant stage, was now in charge of the daily care of John Finch: Hospice, whose motto was something to the effect of "Comfort and not the false hope of a cure." Nick found these people to be remarkable. They could be patient with the patient yet do it with humor. They said just the right thing at the right time. They made Nick look like the amateur he was. The concept of hospice had been introduced in Scandinavia. Charlene had seen their work firsthand as they built their campus right behind St. Mary's: a thirty-bed facility stocked with caring individuals, comfortable home-style furnishings, and plenty of painkillers. J.W. was not there yet, but two hospice people came every morning now Monday through Friday and provided the care he needed. Nick thought these people could pass right by Saint Peter and go straight into heaven as their wings were already there and waiting. Anybody who cares for and deals with the terminally ill is truly gifted. The help of the hospice workers also allowed Nick to go out and find a job. He did not know that the job he chose was one he would hold for close to forty years.

Nick gingerly approached his parents with the idea of staying on to continue to help, even though hospice was now doing the lion's share of taking care of his father. He went about raising the idea after church. For years, the Finch's had gone to Palm Beach and worshipped at Bethesda-by-the-Sea Episcopal Church. Many times, Charlene would meet the family in her nurse's uniform after a shift. Nick's three sisters had all gotten married there the first time around. Their subsequent marriages would take place either at the county clerk's office or in Las Vegas. After church, the family, and later the just the three of them, would head to Greene's Pharmacy for a sit-down breakfast. The place was right out of the 1950s with a lunch counter, hand-dipped ice cream, and fresh milkshakes. Local legend has it that JFK would read the paper seated at that very lunch counter and wait for his mother to finish Mass at the Catholic church across the street, St. Edward.

Charlene went in first and landed a coveted table as Nick helped his father shuffle in and take his seat. J.W. was out of breath. Everyone the man knew would glance over and give an uncomfortable head nod or wave of the hand. From the Palm Beach police at the counter to the millionaires reading the *New York Times* or the *Wall Street Journal*, everyone seemed to know the Finch family. The parents listened to Nick as he explained he wanted to help and, more importantly, wanted to spend time with his father and play catch-up after the four years he had been away at college. Without saying it, he was disgusted by his brother's and sisters' lack of participation. Charlene would cover for them, saying their lives were busy and complicated. Nick would roll his eyes. J.W. said nothing. And there was one more thing: Nick told them of his law school deferment and said he thought he would give teaching history a shot, and maybe even coach. He loved history and he loved sports, and he refused to feel like a freeloader at the condo. They nodded in agreement, saying it was fine with them if that was what he wanted to do.

Robert Newcombe Jr. was the principal of Forest Hill, having been appointed by the school board just two weeks after Nick had graduated from that same school. Robert—or Bobby or Coach, as the people who knew him—had grown up in West Palm Beach. He was the son of a World War I hero who had been gassed in the Great War as a doughboy serving in France. His burned-out lungs and windpipe made the man wheeze and gasp for air. His voice was barely audible. Nick vaguely remembered meeting Principal Newcombe at the local barbershop where J.W. and Nick went every Saturday morning to get their hair cut, along with the same regulars such as the Newcombe men. One day the young Nick just up and asked his dad why that old man wheezed and what was wrong with him. J.W. told him the man was a hero who had gotten hurt in the Great War. Nick asked if it was like the war J.W. had fought in, and J.W. said all wars were bad. Then he turned up the radio as a cue to his son to ask no more questions. Barbershop time was actually kind of neat. After his haircut, Nick would receive a quarter and go next door to the convenience store to buy a pack of baseball cards. The men would inquire who was in his pack and comment on the players on Nick's cards and their favorite players when they were young. They did this while taking their attention away from the TV that was resting on the small table. Florida Championship Wrestling would be on, with Gordon Sole providing punch-by-punch analysis of the "Pier Six brawl" that was going on or talking about how total chaos had taken over—but remember to tune in Monday night when wrestling moved to the West Palm Beach Auditorium. Nick loved the action, and later he and his friends went to the live show at the "leaky teepee." Nick was also realizing a lesson that J.W. had shared with him after a barbershop trip: men do not gossip, women do. Men tended to bullshit. What was the difference then? J.W. smiled and said, "Not a goddamn thing." The barbershop was where Bobby Newcombe and Nick's dad had become friends. They had a lot in common. Both were self-made men who were respected. Both were veterans. The young Bobby enlisted as a marine and saw considerable combat in such famous battles as Iwo Jima and Okinawa. He later would be part of the occupation force in Japan. When he returned, he took advantage of the GI Bill and went to Stetson College in Deland, Florida, where he played football. He married his college sweetheart, a sorority beauty queen from Palatka. After the war, he returned home and went into education as a schoolteacher and coach at Palm Beach High. He would later open two new schools, Forest Hill, and Palm Beach Gardens High School. Nick did not know that J.W. had contacted Bobby about Nick's becoming a teacher until his dad emerged from one of his vomiting sessions and told him Mr. Newcombe wanted to see him right now at his house in Lake Clarke Shores. Nick went in and changed into a button-down shirt and a red, white, and blue striped tie. J.W. suggested, meaning he ordered, that Nick take a set of work clothes to change into.

Nick pulled into drive of the lakefront house of Robert Newcombe Jr. Suddenly, the man himself emerged from the side of the house, sweating up a storm and shielded by what had to be the largest straw hat ever made. He walked over and shook the young man's hand. Having decided it was break time from his trimming of the hedges, he sat down right under the large banyan tree, which provided shade. He opened a small Igloo Playmate cooler and took out a can of lemonade. He offered Nick one. Bobby Newcombe never drank alcohol as he was a deacon at the First Baptist Church of West Palm Beach, the area's first megachurch. He asked how his friend J.W. was doing and, like many, wanted the son to know that he was in their thoughts and prayers. In fact, he informed Nick that J.W. was on the prayer list at First Baptist. He shook his head and stated firmly, "Your daddy is one the finest men I have ever known. I want you to know that." Nick smiled and acknowledged the compliment. Next, Robert Newcombe looked at the prospect and said, "So, you want to teach and coach, do you?"

The most informal interview of all time continued. Nick excused himself and changed into the work clothes, then grabbed a pair of shrub clippers and worked side by side with the man who would be the first boss he'd had who was not his dad. When the clippings had been raked and bagged, Bobby Newcombe and Nick Finch were drenched in sweat, and this time Nick accepted the lemonade. As Nick made his way back to his car, contemplating what had just happened, Bobby Newcombe told him to come by the school first thing Monday morning to sign some papers and get to know the football staff because football practice was just a week away. Nick looked back at the smiling principal, who waved and said the parting words, "Welcome home, son. Welcome home."

A wise writer once said that you can never go home again. Well, Nick Finch was going to test out that theory. Not only was he living at home, but also, he was now going to back to his high school to teach and coach.

The hospice workers appeared as Nick's mom was emerging from the bedroom and as he was walking out. J.W. was already up and working on both his coffee and cigarette, having already gone through one prolonged vomiting and heaving session in private. Nick had recently taken J.W. to one of his checkups, and the doctor requested one last time that Nick persuade his father to quit smoking. Nick hated the habit for many reasons, especially now as it was the primary cause of his dad's impending death and because of what it was silently doing to his asthmatic mother, but to take one of the last pleasures away from the man he loved? He would have none of it. It was J.W.'s pacifier, and he would just refuse to quit anyway. J.W. had told Nick once never to get started smoking. His sisters did smoke. J.W. explained he had started while at war because it calmed him down and reminded him of home and all he would return to if he could survive the madness. It made sense to Nick, who realized that the cigarettes were doing the same thing all over again, but instead of the Germans trying to kill his dad, it was cancer. Cancer would do what the Nazis could not. The smoking would comfort J.W., so how could Nick ever confront his dad with Dr. Kimball's request? All Nick could do was to turn around; glare at the medical professional he had known his all life, not as the young boy he used to be, but now as the man of the house; and reply, "Really, Doctor? Really?" The doctor realized a couple of things immediately: the cigarettes were staying, as they were as important as the painkillers, and Nick Finch had grown up and the Finch household would be fine. The torch had been passed.

Nick pulled into the visitors' parking lot in front of Forest Hill High School, which was not on Forest Hill Boulevard but on Parker Avenue. He went to the main office, which was right across the hallway from the dean's office, where he and his friends had accepted their corporal punishment a few years earlier. The painful memory brought a grin to his face. Before he could open the door to the main office, Dean Mitchell Bradley, the administrator of the "Board of Education", and his sidekick Dean Whitiker walked out of their office. They were both roaring with laughter as they came over to welcome one of their own back. They explained they had been told at the Monday morning staff meeting of Nick's hiring. They asked about his dad and said that if J.W. ever needed anything, Nick should just ask and they would be there. He was home as he shook his head and smiled. He entered the main office and saw the same two secretaries, Mrs. Manzell and Miss Howard, still worked there. It was as if they were frozen in time and had not moved from their desks in four years. They leaped from their chairs, made it around the long counter that divided the room in half, and passed the vintage public address system complete with a large silver metal microphone and switchboard. They gave Nick a first-class welcome, their exuberance notifying Principal Robert Newcombe's private secretary that the newest member of the faculty had arrived. Mrs. Judy Ryles walked down the private hallway and introduced herself to the new history teacher. Mrs. Ryles had followed Bobby from Palm Beach Gardens High School, which they had opened about seven years ago. Many principals brought staff with them when they transferred, for various reasons, but especially because they valued the loyalty—there was no one more important to a principal than a loyal secretary. Years later when Nick was studying for his master's degree in educational supervision and administration, a wise former principal explained to him that the three most important people were, in order, students, a principal's secretary, and the head custodian. Everyone else was expendable. He was right.

Mrs. Ryles introduced herself and asked the young teacher to take a seat by her outside the principal's office, whose door was closed. Nick could vaguely hear conversation and laughter through the paneled walls. Mrs. Ryles notified Principal Newcombe by phone that the new teacher and coach was here. About thirty seconds later, Bobby Newcombe opened the door and hollered, "Coach Finch, get the hell in here."

Mrs. Ryles grinned. "He'll see you now. And welcome."

Nick Finch walked into the office and saw the principal, family friend, former head football coach, athletic director, Marine Corps World War II veteran, and apparently yard maintenance man extending his hand for a warm, firm handshake. Also inside the room were the superintendent of the Palm Beach School District Dr. Michael Thomas and Assistant Superintendent Richard Stockman. They also extended their hands for a formal welcome. Nick took the seated to which he was pointed. On the walls were framed pictures from the newspaper, one with football players, who were all white and with crew cuts, carrying their coach on their shoulders, celebrating a big win; a couple of wooden plaques; a marine insignia; some framed oversized military coins; and finally, a big picture of the principal with local movie star Burt Reynolds, their arms around each other, on the set of *The Longest Yard. Now that is cool,* Nick thought.

Principal Newcombe wanted his newest teacher to meet the men who had, say, sidestepped protocol to hire him. Newcombe explained there was actually a hiring freeze and principals were forced to hire teachers from a group that had been excessed from other schools first—and then and only then could they bring in people of their own choosing. What was about to be said would stay in the office, and there was to be no written record of the meeting. "Absolutely," Nick affirmed. Nick had never met the superintendent and, for that matter, hadn't ever heard of him, but he did know Mr. Stockman from church.

Mr. Stockman was as round as he was tall, but surprisingly he was a good athlete. Nick had seen him play golf with his father and had seen him move like a floating feather in the annual church Christmas play as the talking donkey. He was the star and stole the show every year. J.

W. would have nothing to do with the play other than to attend. He was not going to volunteer to make an ass out of himself, literally. Nick once played the innkeeper to please his mother and ushered Joseph and Mary out to the stable.

Imagine a keg of beer with legs and arms; that's what Rich Stockman looked like. Dr. Thomas was tall and was wearing a fine suit and tie with perfect hair. He looked more like a senator or the male lead in a soap opera than a former junior high math teacher and basketball coach, which he was. Mr. Newcombe explained to Nick how these men had stuck their necks out by allowing him to bring on the new teacher. They readjusted the minutes of the previous school board meeting to slip Nick's name into the official record under "emergency hiring," and he was to be given full-time, not interim, status. That meant a little more extra pay, sick days, and insurance benefits, and later, much later, it would allow him to retire a year earlier. They laughed, saying he would be the only one left alive, but he thanked them for that extra retirement date. He nodded thank-you, but for what, he did not know. Thirty-seven years later he would posthumously thank them.

They all shook hands again, then Nick was asked to leave and sign some papers, being told to ignore the preprinted date on them. He noticed the papers said August 1, 1983, rather than the actual date, which was now August 14, 1983. No problem. He was now an official employee of the State of Florida, the County of Palm Beach, and Forest Hill High School.

CHAPTER 6

Those Who Can't …

The old saying of "Those who can't, teach, and those who can teach, teach teachers" was front and center as Nick was required to go to a three-day workshop sponsored by the district for all new teachers to Palm Beach County. They were to be taught the protocols and procedures and everything that would be expected of them, and hopefully be given some insight into what they were about to dive into. The workshop was to be conducted at a nearby high school named John I. Leonard Media Center, which was in suburban Lake Worth. The term *workshop* always amused Nick as he thought workshops were places where people built actual products like birdhouses and picture frames, places like the one where Santa and his elves made Christmas toys for all the good little boys and girls. Also, it wasn't that long ago when Nick went to the school library which he deduced was renamed for some reason as a "media center." Nick looked over the one hundred fifty plus new teachers to see what his peers would look like. It was definitely a cross section of society in attendance. Old, young, middle aged; men, women, and others he wasn't so sure; black, white, Asian, and Hispanic; tall and short; well-dressed and scruffy; skinny and fat; tan and pasty; long hair and short hair; attractive and—well, you get the picture. A placard with a school name was placed at each round table. You were to sit at your school's table apparently. Nick looked at the names of all the schools. Some, he had never heard of. There had been a population explosion, especially in the South County, and the high schools Santaluces in Lantana and Spanish River in Boca Raton had been added to the mix. Soon there would be many more added as Palm Beach County experienced unforeseen rapid growth.

The superintendent welcomed the group. As Dr. Thomas explained, the attendees were the most important of all the employees he would be overseeing. This was not what Nick had been told. He remembered it was the principal's secretary and the head custodian, but whatever: it was nice even if not true. This would be the same introduction that the good doctor would give every year to the new teachers. It was well rehearsed—tried and true. "If it ain't broke …" Next to speech was a different group of well-dressed district administrators, most of whom, Nick later would conclude, would be unable to find their asses even with a road map and compass. They'd been kicked upstairs and were taken care of for some reason. Nick and the people at his table represented the same cross section prevalent in the whole room. There would be five new teachers to the district for Forest Hill. In the past few years, while Nick had been away at college, the school had added an extra one thousand students from a brand-new planned suburban community named Wellington. The main east–west road through Wellington was Forest Hill Boulevard, which was a straight shot to their new school. That straight shot was a good ten miles of high-speed travel and could be dangerous, especially if the student were driving himself and was late to class. There would be tragedies.

The four new Falcons introduced themselves to each other and quickly drowned out the pleasantries from the speaker at the podium giving the welcome and making introductions. They were each given a folder of the activities and different examples of the official district paperwork they would be using, with the admonishment that if they were to fail to use it correctly, it could be grounds for dismissal. Nick would later learn it would take a lot more than an uncrossed *t* or undotted *i* to be sent packing.

The other four new teachers seemed interesting. There was an older man from New York City who had come to Palm Beach for a better and safer quality of life than the Big Apple was giving him. He would be teaching English and coaching basketball. His name was Hank Gibbs. He and Nick would work together for some thirty years at two different schools and in different roles. Today was the first day of their unofficial and unspoken mentor–pupil relationship. The other three new teachers were females. Amy George would be teaching English. She was quite attractive. The math department had brought in a thirty-something Kentuckian named Carolyn Sessions and a true flower child caught in a sixties time warp named Daisy Phillips for what else but art. There was one administrator Nick caught falling asleep more than once who had the important job of pulling the winning ticket showing the name of the person who would win the lottery and be given a twenty-dollar gift certificate to the Palm Beach Mall. It would be the one time the speaker would have the full attention of a captive audience.

Following would be instructional films of how to do things and what not to do, instructional videos that always would be proceeded by a loud, rude call from the audience of "Can't hear!" Nick learned early that teachers did exactly what they would not allow their own students to do, carrying on private conversations, not listening, doodling, passing notes, and even sleeping. This behavior would continue but would get worse after the introduction of the cell phone. They could be a rough audience, one that even the most seasoned stand-up comic would avoid.

It was the Friday before the staff was to report for the first day of duty, which was one week before the students would arrive. The administration would have one more meeting for the new teachers, but this time at the school and with the immediate staff with whom they would work daily, not the district administrators, with whom they would have little or no interaction. The meeting was scheduled to take place in the media center beginning at eight o'clock and would run to noon, and then the new teachers would be treated to lunch next door at the West Palm Beach Country Club, which backed right up to school on the south side.

This was the same venue where Charlene had broken the news to J.W. about her pregnancy when she had found out she was carrying Nick. Oh, the irony.

At two o'clock there would be a football coaching meeting in the coaches' office, located in the gym, for introductions and a practice schedule, followed by a less formal meeting down the street for beer and chicken wings.

At the new teachers' meeting, Principal Newcombe spoke first. He welcomed his new teachers and introduced them to his assistant principals. Nick knew four of the eight from his days as a student, one of whom had been his algebra teacher, Air Force Reserve major Derek Lyons. Mr. Lyons would at times be forced to take time off from school to attend to his military duties, but with Bobby Newcombe in charge, his absences were never a problem. The guidance staff had turned over, but Mrs. Peterson had come over from the middle school and was now on the same staff as her husband, who had stepped down as head football coach but still taught drafting. Throughout Nick's time at Forest Hill, there would be no fewer than five married couples working together at the school. He thought this was strange as he could never imagine his mom and dad working together or, later, he and his wife working side by side in the same building. No way, at least not for him. Then the real personnel were introduced, the nuts and bolts of the school, including the head custodian Mike Gonzalez, the secretarial pool, the school nurse, and the data processor.

On the way to the country club, the administrators each sidled up to the new teachers for some private talk while they walked. Nick got Mr. Lyons, who really only wanted to talk about were some of Nick's past female classmates, including what they were doing now and how they looked; his fraternity life at Ole Miss; and if the young women there were as as he had always been told they were.

After lunch at their specially decorated table complete with ceramic red apples that said something to the effect of "We love our teachers!" the group was free to go home and get ready for Monday, all except Nick, who had a football meeting at two o'clock in the coaches' office in the gym. Nick stopped by the main office and signed for his keys; there were a lot of keys. Nick would float and use four different classrooms as there were more teachers than classrooms. He was given a key for the social studies workroom/lounge, a key to the gym, a key to the locker room, and finally one to the gate for entry into and out of the school grounds. Altogether Nick would have close to ten keys. He would need a new ring, and it would have to be big and strong. He would learn to attach the ring to his belt as he learned the keys would destroy his pants pockets.

Nick arrived about ten minutes before the scheduled meeting. He had learned from his father that actually arriving on time meant you were in reality late or tardy. He knocked and heard a loud reply: "It's open." Three coaches and the athletic director were already in the office.

The head football coach, Tim Applewood, was there busily writing what would be a duty roster of non-coaching-related activities such as locker-room security, bus supervision, taping of players, equipment room maintenance, and discipline/punishment practice. Coach

Applewood was from Cleveland and had been a three-year starter at Ohio State under the legendary Woody Hayes. He would become the topic of a trivia question: "Who was the tailback before two-time Heisman Trophy–winning Archie Griffin?" He had a short stint with the Cleveland Browns, but bad knees ended his NFL dream. His coaching had turned Forest Hill into a respectable program from the disaster it had been just recently. Nick had kept up with the scores while away at college.

Seated at the desk closest to the door was the defensive coach, Larry Timmons. Coach Timmons had gone to Lake Worth High School and then went on to play as a guard at FSU under the legendary Bobby Bowden. Larry was exceptionally good at coaching defense. He also gambled like he lived in Las Vegas. He literally doubled his salary, according to him, betting on athletic contests, the dog races, the horse races, and a game imported from Cuba called jai alai. Larry's mood each Monday was a direct reflection of his success or failure at the games of risk of the past weekend. Moody and pissy meant he had hit a bad streak. A constant grin and smile signaled success with the bookies or at the window. This gauge of his mood was more reliable than the sun rising in the east.

At the other desk was a large black man who immediately got up and extended to him what had to be the largest palm Nick had ever seen. His name was short and simple: Mack Lee. Mack was a gentle, complicated, sensitive man. He had known the principal longer than anyone there except for Nick. A young Mack Lee had been part of the first integrated class at the new Palm Beach Gardens High

School, which Bobby Newcombe had opened. The two had developed a strange-for-its-time father–son relationship. Now such a thing is not uncommon between male teacher/coaches and their male students, especially players who played for them. With so many single-parent households headed by women and lacking a male figure, many times a teacher or coach steps in and steps up to do the right thing. Bobby Newcombe did that, also crossing race lines at a time when many would not do so. But those people were no Bobby Newcombe. When it was time for college, the principal personally made sure that Mack Lee would not be left behind. He arranged a full ride to Georgetown College, not the basketball school in Washington, DC, but the school in the middle of horse country in Kentucky. Georgetown was private and all white. Mack Lee would break the race barrier there and would become so popular that he would be voted by the student body as the "Most Popular Senior" at the school. He was a dominant football player and was offered a tryout with the Cincinnati Bengals, which he turned down. He graduated with honors and with two degrees, one in mathematics education and the other in philosophy. At Forest Hill he taught upper-level math and could be caught in the teachers' lounge reading not his playbook or practice schedule, but Homer, Gandhi, or the Bible.

The remaining person in the room was the athletic director, Jake Carpenter. Coach Carpenter had graduated from FSU in the late fifties and had been a teammate of local hero Burt Reynolds. There was one big difference between them though: Burt Reynolds was hurt a lot of the time and did not play much, whereas Jake Carpenter was a three-year starter. Originally from Chicago's north side, Jake's dream of playing for Notre Dame never materialized, so he went to Tallahassee. After his time on the gridiron, he did two years in the army, mostly in the occupation and rebuilding of Japan, and then returned to, Florida where he went into athletic administration. Coach Carpenter had a booming voice; at one time in the service, he served as a basic training instructor. He had the voice for it. He extended his hand toward Nick and said, "Welcome back, Coach Finch." It was the first time anyone had addressed him as Coach Finch. Nick liked it.

Certain states and areas are famous for their high school sports. Kentucky and Indiana, for example, are known for basketball. The same is true of some cities where basketball begins on the playground, then players move on to play in high school, at college, and for some, in the NBA. Ice hockey is played mostly in upstate New York, New England, and the upper Midwest. The Midwest and Great Plains are known for wrestling. In general, in the South the sport of choice is high school football, but in Florida, because of the weather and facilities, it is both football and baseball. Same with California. Football season starts two weeks or so after the last game of the year, with weight training and conditioning, unless the athlete is playing a winter or spring sport. In mid-August, actual practice begins with the customary two-a-day, meaning two practices a day. The morning session usually involves conditioning and drills, followed by a cool-down lunch period, then an afternoon session with actual strategies, game planning, and scrimmaging. The days are hot and long. The humidity is brutal, with both coaches and players privately praying for a thunderstorm so the practice will be moved into the air-conditioned gym.

Head Coach Applewood was the one to hand out a handwritten practice schedule to the coaches. It was kind of a lesson plan for football practice rather than classroom instruction. Included on the schedule was each coach's extra duty. Nick Finch would be assigned to take the kickers, punters, snappers, and holders-out through prepractice drills. It could have been worse, such as locker-room duty, but that was usually assigned to the biggest and scariest coaches to make sure no nonsense, horseplay, or thievery took place. The AD, Coach Carpenter, gave his new coach and Forest Hill alumnus five white practice T-shirts with the Forest Hill Falcon logo at top right on the chest, three polyester biking-style coaching shorts, and one Forest Hill cap. The coach had to supply his own socks. Coach Applewood was strict about his coaches being dressed in uniform.

The players met in the gym after getting dressed in the locker room. Almost all of them were returning lettermen and upperclassmen. Freshmen would come out after the first day of school. The players took seats on the gym bleachers as Coach Applewood called roll. After completing this, he introduced the staff, most of whom the players already knew, then named his new offensive coach, Coach Nick Finch. The players applauded as they looked at their new coach, who was only three or four years older than some of them. In fact, many already knew Nick as he was friends with their older brothers and sisters. Then it was announced with a booming voice and a whistle that it was time to go to work. The football season had begun.

When fall sports such as football started, that meant school was right around the corner. In Florida, school opened in mid-August, unlike up north, where Labor Day meant the unofficial end of summer and the beginning of the school year and autumn. Some could argue in Florida that there was never an end to the summer and that Labor Day was just another day for barbecue and a trip to the beach. Relocated families from the Northeast had a hard time adjusting to the earlier beginning of the school year, but as the locals would tell them, it was better to be indoors in the air-conditioning at the end of summer then be out early to prepare for the early summer hurricane season. Locals have always said it is not the heat but the humidity that will sap the life out you—and the humidity seemed to be worse in September than in any other month of the year. It isn't clear if this is true, but it probably is given the length of the Florida summer. Up north people begin breaking out their sweaters and raking leaves in September, whereas in South Florida they are sweating and cussing the heat. They will tell you the heat does not break until Halloween. They are almost always right.

Football practice was exciting, but it also would drain the energy right out of the hardiest of people. Nick was amazed that some of the older coaches hung right in there with him, a twenty-one-year-old first-year coach. On returning from one especially hot and exhausting practice, Nick Finch pulled into his parents' condo and, instead of taking the elevator to the twenty-first floor, went straight to the condo's outdoor swimming pool. He walked right down the steps in the shallow end and kept walking until the water was over his head. He stayed exactly in that position and did not move until he ran out of breath. In full coaching garb, shorts, shirt, shoes, socks, cap, and whistle, he had not stopped to at least attempt to take his shirt and shoes off. Nope, it was a full-body bath. Some of the senior citizens who were poolside witnessed the spectacle in amazement. They were busy swapping often-told stories of their younger days while working on a tropical cocktail, a can of beer, or a plastic glass of wine (no real glass was allowed in the pool area).

Nick emerged on the ladder at the deep end of the pool, got out, turned around, and headed for the lobby elevator. He nodded at the happy hour crew, who were speechless. All he said was, "Hot today. Good night." The witnesses nodded in agreement. When Nick reached his parents' place, J.W. looked up at his son and pulled down the oxygen mask, which he was now using to help with his labored breathing and asked if it had rained at practice. "Nope, I went for a swim." After that reply, Nick went to take an official shower, after which he had a quick bite to eat and went to bed. It was still daylight, but he was worn out. He would not awake until the alarm clock went off at five thirty the next morning.

Nick had put his pair of shorts, shirt, socks, and shoes on the patio to dry out in the constant ocean breeze. After dressing, he gave his dying dad a quick kiss and went back to the school for more football. Secretly, Nick and others were anxiously waiting for school to start so then football would be only part of the daily routine rather the all-day ordeal it had become.

Later that week, Nick saw in the TradeWinds condo residents' newsletter that there was a directive from the association board: people using the swimming pool must be in proper swim attire. Nick knew what they meant and why this was now a rule. He called it the "Nick rule."

The week before the opening of school, student football practice was scaled back to allow coaches to attend various meetings on campus. Nick Finch welcomed the change, the break from the gridiron, and the air-conditioning. There was a general faculty meeting held in the chorus room, which had risers that gave it a college lecture hall feeling. New members were introduced for a once-over by the veterans. At the end of the week, Friday, they would meet there again for final nuts and bolts and words of encouragement. Throughout the week there would department meetings, club meetings, athletic meetings, and meetings to plan upcoming meetings. Nick was asked to sponsor the Kiwanis Club, a service club for the students where about twenty kids did all the work and the rest made sure they spelled the name correctly on their college résumés. The sponsorship paid five hundred dollars, which Nick could use. He had not been paid yet and was wondering what his take-home pay would be. There was pressure talk from the union representative on campus, a man with a ponytail and earring who taught freshmen English and helped with school drama productions. Nick listened politely but said, "Thanks, but no, thanks." The union representative told him it was a decision he would come to regret, adding that the door would always be open for anyone who wanted to join the cause. Nick had experienced firsthand his father's dealings with trade unions, and although the stories were one-sided, he could not see himself as a union member, but he understood those who did end up joining.

Nick got the schedule of classes he would be teaching, three units of junior US history and two senior-level US government classes. His planning period would be fifth hour. Some of the veterans in the social studies department nodded in approval upon seeing the course load but rolled their eyes at the planning period. Fifth hour planning meant cafeteria duty, which meant lunch supervision. At the Friday faculty meeting, the duty roster was handed out, and Nick, sure enough, had cafeteria duty. He was to walk up and down between the tables and make sure the students picked up after themselves. It turned out to be not as bad as Nick had thought it would be as football players knew where they could find at least one of their coaches—in the cafeteria. The rest of the coaching staff was always holed up in the football office, segregated by choice away from everyone else. Nick also he remembered that he would be a floater, using four different classrooms throughout the day, as there were more teachers and students than classrooms at the school, which had been built in the segregated fifties. When Nick finally moved up in seniority floor and earned his own classroom, he would cherish his classroom as much as any house he would own. After three years as a gypsy, he would finally have roots and could decorate as he saw fit. He also would welcome any new floating teacher with open arms as he had learned firsthand how difficult it was and how some colleagues could be flat-out rude to floaters. He never forgot who had treated him professionally and had who made an already difficult situation worse. He had a long memory, and as it is said, paybacks are a bitch. He would have his day to repay his former "landlords."

The first day of school is always a day of nervousness for everyone. Administrators are worried about the opening; teachers are worried about their classes; parents are seeing their children grow up and remembering their own high school days; and students are experiencing off-the-charts anxiety. The seniors want to act cool but are hiding their insecurities. Juniors are realizing this is the year to either fish or cut bait. Sophomores, who once thought they understood everything, are quickly coming to realize they do not. And the freshmen are just plain scared to death. There are few life-or-death days like the first day of school. The nervous energy is everywhere. You can almost see it.

Nick was right there. He had had trouble sleeping and did not even have to turn his alarm clock off as he was awake staring at it. He showered and shaved, then dressed in his starched college button-down shirt with a red, white, and blue (school colors) striped tie, khaki pants, and penny loafers. His choice of dress could not have been any more timeless. Mr. Newcombe had stressed that he should dress up every day so as to look more mature to distinguish himself from his students, who were close in age to him. Nick Finch would wear a tie almost every day for the rest of his career, except on Fridays, when he would wear a school emblem golf shirt.

First bell was at a quarter after seven, so Nick showed up for his first day at six thirty. He noticed the faculty parking lot was already half full. He drove by and saw Bobby Newcombe waving and pretending to shoot at his staff members as they arrived for work. If Bobby Newcombe shot you with his imaginary pistol, an index finger pointed at you, that meant you were in good shape. You wanted to be shot by the boss. The principal shot Nick and welcomed him with, "Good morning, Coach Finch."

Nick responded, "Thank you, Coach Newcombe." Bobby Newcombe may have been the principal, and indeed that was his official title, but he loved being addressed as a "Coach." Many times, he would hold court, so to speak, and seldom tell stories about administrating a school. No, the experiences he would share were of his coaching days. Nick's dad was the one who had told him, on the day of his unofficial interview doing yard work with his new boss, that Bobby loved being called Coach Newcombe. Nick never forgot that bit of advice. Hearing Nick refer to him that way always brought a smile to Principal Newcombe's face. Smiles are good. Nick would also learn that a frown from Bobby Newcombe could be very unpleasant. Not good at all.

The day and the time had arrived; school had started. Nick had a few advantages that most first-year teachers did not enjoy in that he had been seated in those very desks just four years ago, he knew most of the staff, he had gotten to know the football players, and he knew some of his students as they were his friends' brothers and sisters or were from the old neighborhood. The seventies sitcom *Welcome Back,*

Kotter, was now *Welcome Back, Finch*. Finch stood outside his door and welcomed each student into his classroom. There was no class size amendment at that time, and when the last kid had arrived, the final count was thirty-six. The classroom had thirty-five desks, so one student sat at the teacher's desk, which did not make the teacher who usually taught in that room very happy. She saw to it another desk would be moved into the room ASAP. That meant the next day. It was her desk and nobody else's. Very territorial. Her room was always locked. Also locked up were the classroom tools including tape, pencils, and stapler. Nick would have to bring his own. No renter's bill of rights for Nick Finch. Nick fumbled through some of the names as he attempted taking roll for the first time. Some names were easy, some not, but each told a story—and that would be the theme of the first assignment he'd give his students.

An icebreaker assignment is one that can used to introduce a person, a group, an objective, or basically anything new. Its purpose is to relax the audience. Nick had learned what he thought would be the perfect icebreaker from, what else, a psychology class he had taken at Ole Miss. He learned that psychology classes were usually fun and not that academically challenging at the undergraduate level. The professors could be a little different, but they were very motivated by their work. And their joy spilled over into their classes, which were enjoyable and not academically taxing. One such teacher on the first day had the students write their full names, first, middle, and last, on index cards, then he shuffled the cards and called out one of the names from among the ten selected students in the front. The rest of the class would vote for which of the standing students belonged to that name. The purpose of the exercise was to introduce the concept of preconceived notions. It was easy to pick out the Skip's, Tripp's, the Babse's and the Muffy's as they tended to be straight from Fraternity and Sorority Row, as well as the students who had ethnic names, since 95 percent of the class was southern and lily white, but it was much more difficult with run-of-the-mill names like John and Beth. You could not vote if you knew the person. Nick always thought back fondly on this assignment, which he modified for his first day of class. After introducing himself to the class and talking a bit about what he expected, he handed out the homework assignment. The class groaned: *Really? Homework on the first day?* The young teacher asked the students to write down their entire names, first, middle, and last, and why their parents had selected the name. He explained, "We all have a history, and it begins with our names." He also asked them to include their ethnic background, if known. Nick had taken a class on historical research where he'd had to research his ethnic and national origins, which ended up being exactly what he had been told by his parents and grandparents. He was 75 percent English and 25 percent Welsh. Today, a popular hobby for many is to pay for a blood test to get such a personal history. Nicholas John Finch later ordered such a test and found out the blood test results matched the family story almost exactly. The last part of the assignment asked for any anecdotes and family folklore the students wished to share. Nick would share that his paternal grandfather, who had been the largest dairy farmer in South Carolina, was also probably the largest moonshiner in the Gamecock state. The boys in the class roared in approval of his family's way of supplementing their income. Also, there was no royalty in Nick's blood, but his paternal great-great-great-great-great-great-great-grandfather had been a horse thief in London and was given a choice between a public beating followed by a hanging or moving to the New World. He obviously chose the latter, arriving in Charles Town in 1690. (Charles Town, named after King Charles, would later be renamed Charleston, after the Revolution.) Again, the boys liked that Mr. Finch's family were the car thieves of their day. Nick had been named after his dad's favorite older brother, his uncle, which was also the middle name after his father. He also mentioned that almost every female in his family tree on both sides had the name Elizabeth somewhere in their formal name—his sisters, mother, both his grandmothers, and many of his cousins. Now the students knew something about their teacher.

Nick also placed a shortened syllabus and course outline on the back side of the homework sheet, along with a line for the parent to sign to acknowledge he or she had reviewed the sheet. He also hoped the assignment would fire up some family conversation about each family's own personal history. Most of the time it did. Nick Finch would use this assignment throughout his career, whether at the high school level or in some of the college classes he would later teach. "If it ain't broke, don't fix it." Lastly, at the bottom of the page, were his class rules. After looking at some of his colleagues' rules, he concluded that some looked like a criminal law book with offenses and consequences for just about everything one could imagine, no matter the seriousness of the infraction. Nick thought long and hard and kept coming back to what his father expected both at home and at work. The three P's would work just fine for him. These would also follow him throughout his career at all levels. He would try, not always successfully, to implement them with his own children. The P's were *prompt*, *polite*, and *prepared*.

They were simple, and they worked. They were more than a classroom directive but were a life lesson. If you were on time, mannered, and ready to go for whatever lay ahead, you should do just fine with whatever your teacher, your boss, or your family had in store for you that day. It worked and still works.

The names Nick would come into contact with throughout his career were fascinating, confusing, and at times amusing. He would teach the color-coded names such as Holly Green, Crystal Blue, and Red Wood. He would have a holiday name in Mary Christmas, a dinosaur in Terrence Dactil (Terry Dactil), and religious leaders and founders in names such as Jesus, Moses, Abraham, and Muhammad, as well as the names of the Four Gospel writers, Matthew, Mark, Luke, and John. Later he would notice more and more hyphenated names. There was one name he simply could not believe when he came across it on a first day a few years later. He thought it was practical joke being played on him by the data processor and others, their hoping that when he pronounced, it would cause the students to laugh and him to be embarrassed. When he got to the name, he stalled and looked it over a few times in astonishment. *This can't be,* he thought. *This must be a joke.* He decided to call the prospective student by her surname, which was Young. "Miss Young?"

"Here." A young woman raised her hand, acknowledging that her name had just been called. Nick then asked how he was to pronounce her first name. Nick would always have trouble with Spanish names as he could never roll the *r* correctly. He would always apologize and explain it wasn't his fault, citing his southern upbringing. Self-deprecating humor always seemed to work, and it never really bothered the Latino students he taught. This name was completely different though. After Nick had asked her to pronounce it, and the girl, seated in the first desk of the middle row, said, "Sha-thead." Nick looked at the pleasant young student with a last name of Young and a first name of Sha-thead, with her beautiful smile and her hand raised as high as it would possibly go. He looked over the name a few times and realized it worked and that the pronunciation justified the spelling. Well, kind of. The spelling of Miss Young's name on the attendance sheet was Shithead Young. Miss Young, as he would usually address her, as he did with most of students, using the proper gender prefix and the surname to show them that he saw them as young adults, quickly became one of Nick Finch's favorite students. Today Nick cannot understand the movement to eliminate gender-specific pronouns.

With straight A's in both conduct and attendance, with a contagious smile and personality, Miss Young was easy to like. When Nick shared the story of her name with other people, he saw a complete spectrum of reactions from humor to horror. All agreed that places such as employment offices, interview rooms, and the DMV could present a troubling moment if the person in charge was not delicate in the introduction process. Shathead Young is an outstanding lawyer today, representing people who cannot afford representation. It is not the person's name but what the person is. Shithead Young is a winner.

CHAPTER 7

Remember, Reflect, and Respect because It is Time to Say Goodbye

Principal Newcombe's voice buzzed into Nick Finch's classroom via the PA speaker located next to the US flag at the top and in the middle of the wall behind the teacher's desk, interrupting the young teacher's lesson on the final movement west post–Civil War, complete with pioneers, the Indian Wars, the gold rush, and the building of the Transcontinental Railroad. The interruption startled Nick. Seldom did the principal use the PA system; instead, one of the secretaries or the appropriate assistant principal would deliver the command or relay the relevant information. Most of the time the PA was used for the dismissal of a student, asking him or her to come sign out for whatever reason, but this time it was the boss communicating directly with Nick. "Coach Finch, please get your belongings and come and sign out. You will be going home. Your family needs you." Toward the end, Nick could hear a slight cracking of the voice of the former combat Marine as he was delivering the command. Almost immediately a substitute teacher opened the door and entered the room. Now almost any other time if the principal had summoned a teacher over the intercom, it would be met by laughs and warnings about how much trouble the teacher was in. This time the class was dead silent. They knew what this was about because Nick Finch had updated them from time to time about the deteriorating health of his father, anticipating the time when he would have to miss a few days, and had told them it would mean a lot to him if they would refrain from driving the substitute crazy. They had been known to treat substitute teachers as prisoners of war and to terrorize them as captured prey. They assured him they would not treat the substitute this way if Nick had to be out for a while to care for his father. That would happen on other teachers' watches, but not Coach Finch's. Just as they had promised him, they kept their promise. Also, many of the students' parents personally knew the man they called J.W., so the students could update their parents on the condition of the dying man. No problems here.

Nick fumbled with the leather satchel he used as a briefcase. It was his father's, who had given it to him on his first day of work. Nick cherished the worn old leather satchel and still has it to this day. He had always looked at it as if his dad were accompanying him to work. Suddenly, one little girl, a student from the first row, jumped up, ran to Mr. Finch, and hugged him, fighting back tears.

She had lost her father just a few months earlier in a car accident on a dangerous stretch of road known as Twenty mile Bend out in the western part of the county where the farm community meets the Everglades. The young teacher had attended the funeral service for his student's father out of respect, but it was he who was given respect by so many for having made this small gesture, as word made its way back to many about how the young coach "had done the right thing" by attending the mourning family's ceremony to say goodbye to their husband and father. Nick Finch always attended these funerals with his family as it was a teachable moment, showing his kids how they were to dress and act and what dish to bring to share with the grieving family. He would be surprised to discover many of his friends had stayed home and shielded themselves from the painful day. Not so for the Finch's. Nick was glad that he knew the proper protocol for such an event. But today this was different, much different: this was his dad.

The principal was waiting by Nick's car. He mumbled something to the effect that they were all there for him, his Forest Hill family. Nick nodded in gratitude as everything was beginning to blur. The last thing he remembered as he left the faculty parking lot was Principal Robert Newcombe, no, Coach Newcombe, pulling out his imaginary pistol, using his extended index finger as the barrel, and pretending to shoot the young teacher, who was also the son of his dear friend. Nick would drive to St. Mary's Hospital with so many thoughts and memories rushing through his mind that it had a numbing effect. He knew he had to get it together for his mother's sake.

He took a deep breath when he arrived at the place, he had been so many times before to meet, deliver, or pick up his mother: her place of work. Yes, he would be meeting her and his brother and sisters there, but he would also be saying goodbye to the strongest man he would ever know, and he knew it. He wasn't sure if he could do it, yet he had to. If anything, his dad had taught him to rise to the occasion amid a crisis and be strong for others. This would be one of those times.

Two weeks earlier Nick had driven his parents to the family lawyer for a sit-down meeting. It was an afternoon. Nick stayed in the lobby and graded papers and stood up immediately when they emerged from the office about an hour later to shake hands with attorney. Nick had been looking around at the office, located on the sixth floor of the Comeau Building in downtown West Palm Beach. The structure was one of the original "skyscrapers" of the formerly young bustling city. Now it was known as a historical site and, being art deco in design, once again was in demand and trendy. Nick at one time put down the papers he was grading, the assigned essay being "Promises Kept and Promises Broken of Reconstruction," and looked around at the office. He thought this could be his life. Fancy downtown barrister in an art deco office building with all the trappings, such as a fancy suit, a real briefcase, a personal secretary, and a very enjoyable salary—things that teaching did not provide. Oh, how so close he once was. He figured by now he would be in the middle of his law school years at Chapel Hill, but instead he was grading papers with a paycheck not all that much higher than minimum wage and witnessing firsthand how the terminally ill die. Quickly realizing how counterproductive this line of thinking was, he shook his head and went back to grading a student's paper discussing the Thirteenth, Fourteenth, and Fifteenth Amendments to the US Constitution.

Nick raced to the office doorway, took his father's hand, and steadied him as he shuffled from there to the doorway that led to the elevator. No one said a word. When the family reached the lobby, Nick raced to the pay-by-the-hour parking lot, where he paid the attendant and retrieved his mother's car. J.W. no longer drove and found it almost impossible to climb up into the high truck cab, but he could slide into Charlene's Lincoln Continental. J.W. sat in the front while Charlene was in the back. The radio was silent, as were the first five minutes of the journey home.

About five minutes away from their destination, the condo on Singer Island, J.W. spoke, saying something to the effect of Nick's having to promise him to take of his mother in the future. "Absolutely," Nick replied, thinking this request had come out of the blue. After all, Charlene Finch was the strongest, most independent person he had ever known, and she was right in the back seat. If she were ever stranded on a deserted island, she would not only survive but also thrive. But this turned out to be the icebreaker the patriarch needed to begin discussing the meeting with the lawyer and his plans for the near future. J.W. stated that he had sold the company to a friendly competitor and thought he had been lowballed because he was dying. The company was worth more, but he was not in a good position to negotiate. The Bronco he drove would go to his brother, who was a building contractor in Arizona. J.W. would need Nick's immediate help, along with Charlene's, as they would be cleaning out his office, which included removing his personal belongings and mementos, that upcoming Saturday when nobody else would be there. The new occupants were wasting no time and wanted to be in that Monday. He explained the condo had been paid for in cash, so Nick didn't have to worry about that, adding that he could stay if he needed to. Nick had been wanting to move out for some time now, but he realized this was an impossibility for the foreseeable future. There were worse places to live than oceanfront and with all the amenities, even if the average age of the residents was, he figured, seventy-five. The last thing J.W. said was that he and Nick's mother named him executor of the will, meaning he would be in charge and oversee everything, including the funeral, the expenses, and all the final legal matters. Nick questioned their choice. After all, he was still only a month away from his twenty-second birthday. J.W. told him that Nick knew the situation better than his brother or his sisters and reminded him of the fact that he lived local, whereas his brother was in Arizona and his sisters were in Tampa, Texas, and North Carolina. J.W. added that Nick was single and therefore did not bring into the equation in-laws and the potential for meddling. Nick did not understand this, but he sure would find out when his mother died some ten years later. You can pick your friends, but not your family, including your extended family, who were especially problematic. Nick, too, thought the company J.W. had worked so hard to make successful and respected would have been worth more. He never saw his parents struggle economically, but then again; they had never lived beyond their means. They paid for Nick's college and his three sisters' weddings, at least their first ones. Charlene got a new car every two years. Charlene worked and many times took a double shift and always signed up for holiday duty as that paid her time and a half. During the "Carter Recession", her nursing paycheck helped a lot as many people put off painting their homes or offices for another year or until the economy picked up. J.W. had told Nick that teaching and nursing were both recession-proof, and he was right.

With all the legal matters put together and tied with a tight bow, it was now a waiting game for what was coming up fast—not if, but when.

In the past when Nick had gone to the hospital, he'd always used the emergency room entrance as the ER was where his mother would always be. Throughout the years, he had gotten to know many of her colleagues and recently the security guard, who had been replaced by a West Palm police officer whose duty it was to add security and provide protection for a place that could quickly get out of control. It was a sign of the times. Why should Nick change his habits now, he wondered, as he left his car and walked right by his mother's, which was parked in the same spot almost every time, one marked "Reserved: Nurse Staff." Few things could upset her more than somebody parking in her place. Her place of work might not give her the raise she deserved, but they could give her a special place to park—and, by God, that was hers.

Once Nick had walked through the double automatic doors, his mother met him. She was still in uniform as she had worked all night. During her breaks she would go upstairs to her husband's room, where he was dying. She looked at her son and explained his brother and sisters were upstairs and waiting for them. Nothing was said in the elevator. The room was located right by the waiting area, as requested by Charlene—more of a demand—as she wanted enough space for her family to be comfortable yet still close to their father. Nick's sisters looked up when their little brother emerged from the elevator with their mother. Charlene quickly and quietly grabbed Nick's hand and held it. She had never, ever in her life had done such a thing. She needed her baby boy, who now was a man, to be there for her. He was there for her. He squeezed right back.

The two entered the waiting area that was right outside J.W.'s room. The head nurse of the floor, a woman by the name of Gloria Sontage, was waiting for her. Nick had known Mrs. Sontage his whole life. She gave a hug to her friend and looked at the young man standing beside her. "Char, I am so glad you made it here. The end is near. In fact, the doctor is getting a head start and has begun the paperwork for J.W.'s death certificate." Wow, that was like a punch in the face. And so much for bedside manner. Charlene nodded and basically gave out floor orders as she had done her entire career as a nurse, except now it was for her family. She would go in first and alone, followed by her oldest son, J.W. Jr., and then the girls, who could decide if they wanted to go in solo or as a group. They had grown up together with only a grade separating them. Nick would go last and ask his father for any last requests.

J.W. Jr. shook his little brother's hand. There was a quick acknowledgment between the two that lasted all of five seconds before the eldest Finch child, a grown man with his own family, went into the dying man's room. Little was said between the two brothers as there was little to say. They were not close as they were separated by nineteen years. There was no animosity, but then again there was little brotherly love. When John Finch Jr. came back, he was visibly shaken. He kissed his mom and went straight to the elevator, then it was off to the shop to pick up the Bronco before heading straight off to Arizona. He would miss the funeral; having told his mother he just could not do it. She nodded with approval. Nick could not understand, thinking it was disrespectful, but Charlene later would explain that people mourn in different ways and one should never critique another's actions, public or private, when it came to death. It made sense, as things always seemed to when his mother explained a situation that needed explaining.

Nick's three sisters were next, staggering their entries by five minutes so each could have private time with their father, and then they had a concluding group meeting with J.W. At first, they were taken aback when they saw their little brother all grown up and dressed in a shirt and tie. All three had shared babysitting duties growing up for the child they occasionally called the "mistake" or an "oops." Once when Charlene had overheard the snarky comment, she was quick to act and was all over one of her daughters, right in her face, issuing a stern warning that she had better never hear such talk ever again. Seldom had Nick seen her so mad. He could not understand the outburst. He could not even remember which sister it was who'd had the lapse in judgment and hadn't realized that her mother was within earshot. Later he would come to understand. He understood both sides of the story because of how the household changed once the baby of the family had arrived. As was the case with Nick's brother, his sisters were not close with him. Nick remembered tagging along when one of his sisters wanted to see a movie but did not want to be alone with her date. Each time this happened, the sister would explain to the disappointed suitor, "I have to bring my little brother along." Nick went along with his sisters to Putt-Putt golf, the beach, and movies more than once. As a naive young boy, he saw the controversial movie "*The Graduate*". He did not understand the plotline, but he did recognize some of the music from the car radio as his sisters would play it as they raced around West Palm. J.W. and Charlene were none too happy to learn their seven-year-old young son had watched Mrs. Robinson seduce Benjamin.

The sisters came out of J.W.'s hospital room together, hugging and sobbing. There is something about a father and his daughters that is hard to explain, but it is a different relationship from the one between a father and his son, a mother and her daughter, or a boy and his mama. Sigmund Freud would have theories about this, as would others, but there is something to it.

It now was Nick's time for his final goodbyes. The time period between his exit from the elevator, the hugs and handshakes from his siblings, and then to his seat had, in his mind, run a million miles an hour. It was like playing a 45 record at 78 speed. His memories of his father and his interactions with him were coming back to him at warp speed. He remembered his father being the perfect fan parent before, during, and after his games, never criticizing, but never overpraising an effort. Nick would learn through years of coaching high school athletics that this was rare. Some parents would rip into their sons or daughters immediately after a contest, while others would lay the blame at the feet of the coaches or teammates. Then there were those who, even worse, never went to a game. J.W. never missed a game, and many a time his wife, Charlene, was seated right next to him in her uniform. He was always good for a hot dog and a Coke and would sneak under the bleachers for a smoke, but he was always there. Nick appreciated that now more than ever. He remembered that his father had also been his boss for most of his life. Nick had started to work at the shop around the age of eight, straightening up, sweeping, and doing minimal chores on Saturday for a few dollars. Throughout high school, with one disastrous exception, he had been part of the Finch Painting and Decorating Company. Nick would wear the required white uniform and, as part of his first position, pressure-clean all the exterior areas that were about to be painted. Very boring and mindless work, but it paid well, and on a hot summer day it was actually kind of cooling. He would work his way up the company ladder, so to speak, doing prep work like patching, sanding, and taping while spreading out the drop cloths. This wasn't bad either, but it was also boring, although for the most part it was indoors and air-conditioned. He learned there was an art form used by the master craftsmen, whom the union called journeymen. After a while, he too took hold of a brush and roller under the watchful eye of his dad and the superintendent or foreman, a man named Sam Bonino, and painted. Lastly, he learned the tricks of a compressor, an airless spray machine, and other power painting tools. He could now operate a power scaffold and a bucket truck extender. His paychecks were more than what he earned as a first-year teacher. Nick's first contract for the 1983–1984 school year was $13,900, and with a few supplements his pay came to around $15,000. He had to live at home.

Work did bring with it some family conflicts. Once Nick was on a scaffold scraping, prepping, and painting windows on the old Southern Bell building on Dixie Highway. When a row of windows was completed, he would go to control handle at the end and pull it a little so that the motor would engage and lower the scaffolding a story, until the next floor of unpainted windows appeared. Nick was working alone on this project, and the offices had been closed while the painting took place. After Nick had finished a floor, he went to the control handle and engaged it. Suddenly, the entire scaffolding flung itself downward about five feet, but on side only. Nick grabbed the rope railing and hung on for what seemed like an eternity but was only a second or two. The gallon of white high-gloss exterior enamel spilled over the planks and down onto the dark brick siding. The sudden movement had also tripped the breaker, so there was no way to reengage the system. Nick was rattled and scared but soon got it back together and tried, to no avail, to move the scaffolding. After that failed attempt, he began to bang on the windows, but he soon realized that the staff had been relocated for the painting project. Nobody was home. He sat down and tied a free rope around his waist just in case the scaffolding were to give way totally and for good, crashing six stories down to the parking lot.

He waited and waited for his father to swing by the jobsite at a quarter after two o'clock as he did every afternoon. Sure enough, the Bronco arrived. J.W. looked up and saw his son and knew exactly what had happened. It was rare, but it had happened before, although not with his son. He raced up to the roof and switched the breaker. Nick then hit the control handle to even up the planks. J.W. raced to the empty office and opened a window. Nick climbed through the opening. He was on a solid floor and relieved beyond description. J.W. asked his rattled son if he was OK. He was. There was a problem in that the paint that had spilled left a four-foot trail on the side of the brick exterior. There was some spillage on the parking lot asphalt too. It looked like a modern Jackson Pollock mural. The spilled paint was now mostly dry.

Nick and his dad went downstairs and out to the truck. J.W. kept looking at the wall as he took out some different colors of paint and mixed them together until they were a perfect match for the dark brick that had been there since the 1920s. Nick took the new paint and arranged the scaffolding right where the now dried spill had done its damage. He quickly painted over it. The next day his father would bring some asphalt sealer and "erase" the spill from the parking lot. Nick would never again be at that work site, nor would he ever again be on a scaffold. Charlene made sure of that. Nobody outside the family ever knew of the incident. To this day when it rains, the old Southern Bell building, which is now an upscale apartment building for downtown lawyers and bankers and houses the in "crowd", there is a definite change of appearance when the water beads off the painted brick. Nick smiles every time he sees that.

The time came when Nick was tired of the painting business and wanted to prove he could work somewhere else with better hours, so he got a job at Deepwater Fish and Lobster Purveyors. This was a restaurant supply company that supplied all the local restaurants with fresh fish, scallops, lobster, shrimp, clams, and oysters. How fresh the supply was, was debatable. Nick had to report to the factorylike building on Florida Avenue in the trade and warehouse section of West Palm by four o'clock in the morning, but he was done work by noon, which left plenty of beach time. Nick was fifteen at the time, and the beach meant girls in bikinis. That was better than pressure cleaning till five thirty.

Nick arrived and was immediately given a pair of used large rubber boots to wear. In the next fifteen minutes or so, about ten commercial fishermen arrived with their catches of snapper, grouper, pompano, mackerel, king, and bluefish. Nick and four others would help unload the catch from the pickup trucks and take the fish into the cutting and cleaning room, where six men with rubber boots and rubber aprons were stationed at a large table with constantly running fresh water. These men would gut, clean, and fillet the fish. At the end of the table was a "challenged" man by the nickname of Bobby Box. That was not his real surname but described his occupation. It was Bobby's job to take the fillets, wrap them in cellophane, place them in a box, seal the box, and take a marker and write one big letter representing the type of fish inside that was to be wholesaled to the local eateries. *G* was for grouper, *S* was for snapper, and so on. Shark was also filleted and then cut with sharp cookie cutters into small round pieces and boxed with a mark of *SC*, which stood for scallops, which of course the shark was not. The tourists would never know!

After a substantial number of boxes were ready, Nick would deliver the boxes to the freezer and stack them. Each type had its own shelf, much like in a store or even a library. Each species had its own place in the freezer room. Each of the four unloaders took turns leaving the freezer either to deliver a needed product or to retrieve a completed box from Bobby. The hard part was the constant change in temperature from ninety degrees to twenty-eight degrees and back again. The workers were always sniffling. They took turns climbing on the top of the middle shelf and warming up next to the uncovered light bulb.

Nick soon realized the mistake he had made. No beach or bikini was worth this. The other three knew that the newbie was a one-day wonder. They had seen it before.

Nick had told them it was a pleasure, but he would not be coming back. Soon there was an exchange of money as apparently the freezer staff had wagered whether he would make it and be back the next day or if he would quit. Before he left, they asked him to make room under his jeans and stretch out his socks. They told him to leave off his shoes. Nick was perplexed. They explained he was to get his "parting gifts," as they stuffed every available space on his body with lobster tails, compliments of Deepwater Fish.

J.W. was waiting outside in the Bronco to take Nick home. He got in the truck, and his dad sped off, driving all of two blocks before he stopped and told Nick he would have to walk home. He made an off-color remark, saying that Nick "smelled like a New Orleans whorehouse at low tide," whatever that meant. Nick would walk the mile or so home followed by a parade of cats. He wasn't sure if they were a pride, a herd, a litter, or what, but by the time he arrived at the house, there were at least twenty behind him. J.W. greeted him with soap, shampoo, and a fresh cut lemon for an outdoor shower. The next day Nick would back in his painter's whites, but they would have grilled lobster for dinner.

Nick grinned at those stories, but there were two others that crept in from his memory bank that were not so good. When Nick was about ten, the family had visited his aunt, his uncle, and his cousins. The family was from Charlene's side—her only sibling, a brother. The families were not particularly close as Charlene was twelve years her little brother's senior. The aunt was from upstate New York—a social worker and very liberal. It was just not a good mix between the families, so visits were infrequent. The one good thing was that in this family Nick had two cousins similar in age, with the girl Elizabeth, or Beth, being just a year older and the boy, Sean, being a year younger.

At their Sarasota house, the boys went out a played like ten-year-olds do, but suddenly Sean pulled out a pack of matches and began to light some pine needles. Nick watched with fascination as he knew that playing with matches was a no-no, which was constantly repeated by Smokey Bear in the public service commercials on TV. Florida is not as bad as, say, California, but it does have a wildfire season. Not only was Nick watching, but so were J.W. and his brother-in-law. The grown man called for the boys, who quickly hid the matches. J.W. looked at Nick straight in the eye as he bent over and asked a simple question: "Were you boys playing with matches?"

Technically Nick was not, but he was there and watching his cousin do so. He looked down at his shoes and mumbled, "Yes, sir." He was directed to go immediately to the car and wait there without passing go.

Sean blurted out, "Nope, not me. It was Nicky." Now the two men had watched the same exact episode. Sean was excused to go play, and Nick took a spanking, not a hard one, but a spanking, nonetheless. He knew better than to play with matches, and yet he kind of did play with some, and for that he took the spanking. It was not too bad. No belt or paddle, and it was on the outside of the jeans. Still, Sean got away with it and he was the one who'd mostly committed the infraction.

J.W. knew how unfair this was. He walked over to his wife and said, "We are leaving now." Charlene had not been informed of anything about the incident. She would later be informed, and she was angry, not at Nick, in whom she was disappointed in him, but at her husband's brand of justice. But mostly she was pissed off at her brother. It would be a long time before the families got together again.

The other painful memory was much more severe. Nick was sixteen years old and playing American Legion baseball in the summer about four to six days a week. The team was made up of seniors and some junior college freshmen from the area and was incredibly competitive. It was also exhausting after painting and such all day and then playing baseball. It made for a long day. Ironically, seeing as it was the local American Legion that sponsored the team, some the members would ask Nick to ask his father to join their organization. "No way" was J.W.'s simple reply. One time after a day of teaching and sharing stories with his dying father, Nick asked him why he had never joined the Legion. J.W. explained he did not have the time and, plus, he was already a Freemason and a Shriner. He paused for a moment and gave the real answer: "Those men, Son, served far away from the killing and dying, yet they sit on those same damn barstools every day and talk like they are George Patton himself. I can't be around that when I think of the good men who did serve in combat and didn't come home. I am afraid of what I might say." Nick finally understood. Many of J.W.'s brothers were still in Europe and would be there forever.

Late one night after a game and pizza, Nick arrived home after midnight. His mom was at work, and his dad was listening to the Atlanta Braves on the radio, who were losing again to the Los Angeles Dodgers on the West Coast. The conversation was like it was most of the time: short and to the point. No work tomorrow for Nick the painter as the economy had really slowed down and J.W. needed to pay his men who had families and mortgages rather than his own son, but he did want that grass cut tomorrow. If Nick was not working, he could do some chores. Nick grunted in acknowledgment and went to bed.

Nick finally climbed out of bed and looked at the clock at eleven thirty. He made his way to the kitchen, where his mom was still in her nursing uniform after having pulled a double shift. They could use the money. She looked up from her newspaper crossword puzzle and the kitchen clock and said something to the effect of, "Your father wants that grass cut." Nick, still half asleep and shirtless, wearing only gym shorts and nothing on his feet, blurted out loudly, "You know, I am getting God Damn tired of doing all the work around here!" It was a mistake he would regret for the rest of his life. Little did he know that his father was home for an early lunch and to talk to his wife about various matters. J.W. came flying out into the kitchen, looking like Nick had never seen him look before. He had wild eyes and seemed to be possessed. He threw a right-handed closed-first punch that hit Nick square on the jaw. J.W. had boxed in the army and had been told by more than one person how tough his father was. Nick Finch found out that summer morning as he flew across what was called the

Florida room, the local's name for a family room. He came to land in a dirty fireplace, stunned and woozy. J.W. now stood over him, towering, his posture seeming to indicate that this was not the end, but just the beginning of a first-class ass whipping.

Charlene screamed at her husband and leapt from her seat at the kitchen table, grabbing J.W. by the arm. He was still staring down at his son and said through a clenched jaw, "So, you do all the work around here and think you have the right to raise your voice to your mother, the woman I love and whose paycheck is going to allow you to go to college? How dare you?" Suddenly, J.W. turned around and walked out the front door. He got into his Bronco and sped off without saying another word. Charlene looked at Nick's jaw and the dings on his back and the on back of his head from landing in the fireplace. He was all right. She had seen worse every night at St. Mary's. Nothing was spoken. Nick realized he had gone too far, way too far, but his father's having come that close to knocking him out was also going too far.

Charlene came back to Nick with an ice pack for the back of his head and another for his jaw. After five minutes of complete silence, Nick Finch got up, went out to the carport, cranked up the lawn mower, and cut the grass shirtless and barefoot. His emotions ranged from *He can't do this to me* to *What have I just done?* Charlene called in to say she would be missing the early part of her double shift. She wanted to be home when the two met up again.

There was no game that night, nor was there much said between Nick and J.W. For the next three days or so, the silence was so thick that you could cut it with a knife. Later that week, Nick looked up in the stands of his Legion game, which was being played at the spring training home of the Atlanta Braves and Montreal Expos, West Palm Beach's Municipal Stadium, and saw his dad there and in attendance. The healing had begun. They both regretted that day for the rest of their lives.

Nick passed his sobbing sisters and walked into the dark room. There were some cards, along with some candy, which Charlene called "nurse bait." If the family let it be known that the candy was there to share, then the nurses on the night shift would swing by throughout the night and, while taking a piece of candy, decide to check on the patient. It worked every time. Nick would not forget that tidbit. Nick went right up to his father, the man he loved and respected very much, and saw a beaten-down and broken man who wanted to be "called home". But his eyes, those blue eyes, were very sharp and focused and looking right at Nick. They would get right to it as the beeping sound of the machine kept rhythm in the background. It was constant and surprisingly not annoying. J.W. started by saying that he was ready to go, either on the escalator up or in the mine shaft down. He hoped he would be going up to see Saint Peter. Nick smiled at the dark humor. Nick then asked the important question his mother had requested he ask: "Dad, what do you want in the box with you?" J.W. was quick on the response with a command: he wanted a closed casket because nobody was going see him looking like this. "What else do you want, your Army medals?"

Once again, the response was quick and to the point, even though the voice was very quiet: "Hell no, Son. That was a job I did, and when I finished up, I swore I would never look back." Then the final request was whispered. John Finch wanted the picture that was beside his bed at home, the one of him and his wife at what looked to be a New Year's party, and he wanted it placed over his heart facedown. He looked at his youngest child and said, "I love that woman so much. And you know what she did? She made me a better person. I love her for that. I hope you meet someone who has the qualities your mother possesses." The response floored Nick as he took a seat next to his father. He knew J.W. loved Charlene, but in the Finch house love was private and not publicly spoken of. Nick had never even seen his parents hold hands. The request was so genuine and heartfelt that Nick found himself choking up. "Now, now, stop that," the dying man requested. Nick composed himself and asked if there was anything else. After a short pause, J.W. said he wanted his Shriners fez next to him and his Mason's ring on. That would be it. He then looked at his baby boy, who now was the man of the house, and said, "Son, I am so very proud of you. I know I don't say it enough, but I really am."

"I love you, Dad; I love you so much. And don't worry, I'll take care of Mom." J.W. managed a smile. Then Nick, thinking of something he had been wrestling with, told his dad he had something to share with him. "Dad, I am not going to go to law school. I really like teaching, and I want to be a teacher."

John Finch looked up to his son and with those big, beautiful eyes, the one feature of his face the cancer hadn't been able to change; motioned that he move in real close as his voice was getting weaker and weaker; and said, "Son, you have made me very happy. I will die a contented man knowing I am not responsible for putting another God Damn lawyer in this world." John Finch then cracked a grin and closed his eyes. The beeping stopped on the machine and was replaced by a constant low whining sound. J.W. Finch had flatlined—he was dead—and the last words he'd spoken while on this earth would remain with an immensely proud teacher, Nicholas John Finch, for the rest of his career. Moments later, Mrs. Sontage arrived and began to close things down.

Nick walked out into the waiting room and, with a composed voice, said, "Dad is gone." His sisters cried and hugged each other. All those at the nurses' station on the floor, along with other hospital personnel, came and gave hugs and offered condolences to their friend and colleague.

Charlene remained stoic, biting her lower lip. Nick walked up to his mother. She had one question for her son: "What did he say to you?"

Nick looked his mother right in the eye and said with his voice cracking, "Mom, he loved you so much and he wanted you to know that." She nodded her head, walked to the elevator, got in, and went back to the ER to complete her double shift. Nick never shared J.W.'s actual last words. That was evidence of the bond between the father and son who loved each other very much and understood each other very well yet seldom said it. They did not have to; they each knew it.

There was a quick turnaround with a short but sweet service at the Episcopal church on Palm Beach Island. From there it was to Hillcrest cemetery, which was visible from the second floor of the A wing of the high school. In coming days, Nick would occasionally walk over there and spot the flag flying in the middle of his father's resting place. He'd say a quick prayer and mumble something to the effect that he was still teaching and loving it, then smile and walk back to class. At the funeral home, Nick had had to sign off on the fact that John Finch was actually in the coffin. He'd also made sure the framed picture was over his father's heart, that the fez was beside him, and that his ring was on. The box was closed and was delivered to the cemetery, where a hole had been dug.

People, lots of people, surrounded the site. Family, friends, coworkers, competitors, people from St. Mary's, and some Nick had never seen before. The pallbearers were made up of Nick's friends, as they too loved the man, but were also there for their friend during this difficult time. Nick did notice the biggest flower arrangement had come from Forest Hill High. He smiled because his "work family" had remembered. Just as he did so, the football coaching staff—heck, the entire faculty, it seemed—along with a lot of his players and students, emerged to pay their final respects. Leading the contingent was Mr. Robert Newcombe, who came up to the young teacher and coach choked up, unable to say even a word. He just waved and hugged Charlene, then got into his truck with his wife and left. It was touching.

There would be no formal wake as the family was exhausted. Everyone understood. Nick was the last to leave, or so he thought. Driving along the road, he found himself turning around to have one more private moment with his father. When he arrived back at the gravesite, he stopped a distance away as there was another private service going on. As he looked, he quickly realized it was the local Masonic Order giving the last rites. This was for Masons and Masons only. Nick respected the rituals they were going performing. He'd always been fascinated, not by his father's membership, but by the actual history of the Freemasons. After all, many of the Founding Fathers had been Free Masons, including George Washington. The cornerstone of the US Capitol features the Masonic emblem, and General Sherman refrained from burning the Mississippi State Capitol to the ground because it doubled as a Masonic lodge. So here was Nick Finch, the US History teacher, fascinated by the discipline and order shown by these men. Nick, the son of J.W., realized something right then and there: yes, the Founding Fathers of the nation were Masons, and so was his own founding father.

CHAPTER

8

I Love The Eighties

Much later in life, when Nick found himself in a higher tax bracket, he could afford some nicer things in life such special options on high-end automobiles, for example, satellite radio. The greatest part of this high-tech entertainment system was, in addition to having few or no commercials, the selection of music from which one could choose. You name it, there was a channel for you. Nick was particularly fond of the channels that played only the music of a particular decade. Channel 5 played music from the fifties; channel 6, the sixties; and channel 7, the seventies. You get the picture. Now every generation feels its music is the best because there is always one song or one artist who can take you right back to a special time. J.W. and Charlene loved the big band music of the war years and early fifties. Whenever Frank Sinatra and the very cool Dean Martin came on the radio, J.W. would pipe in, "Now that's music." That music had gotten them through World War II and the early years of their marriage. Nick even agreed there was something about Dean Martin; he had "it". Anyone who could sing a song about seducing a young date during the Christmas season, or about having fun with a pizza pie, was just flat-out cool. People who'd grown up in the fifties could describe their decade of music with just one name: Elvis, the boy from Tupelo, Mississippi, and then from Memphis, who was and will always be the King of Rock and Roll. Now Nick had gotten to know the music from the late sixties from his drives with his older sisters. He still listened to music from that era quite often. The children of the sixties are tough to beat when it comes to music. From the British Invasion of the Beatles and the Rolling Stones to the streets of Detroit and Motown, up to Woodstock and the folk music and protest songs, the music of their generation is a cultural phenomenon. Then came the seventies, which was a buffet of music. During one stretch, people would be listening to Led Zeppelin; then it was on to Lynyrd Skynyrd; and then came disco and doing the "Hustle"—even some early punk. Variety marked seventies music, which Nick listened to every Saturday at Clark Beach in Palm Beach while soaking up the rays and listening to Casey Kasem and *American Top 40* on an overweight "boom box". The local FM radio station, WRMF-98, broadcast Casey and his "long-distance" dedications, plus the neat insider's info on the featured artist. Nick Finch listened to all these, and to specialty stations playing jazz, easy listening, and any spotlighted artists, but he would always come back to channel 8, whose call jingle was "I Love the Eighties!" Nick did just that: he loved the eighties. This was the music of his college years and the early years of his life of being single and teaching in one of the party capitals of the country: Palm Beach. He could be "Hungry like the Wolf" one moment and then," Walking on Sunshine" right after. Nick could "Celebrate Good Times" and then listen to the moving tribute by U-2 for Dr. Martin Luther King in "Pride." All these songs took him back to the Ally House at Ole Miss; Bradley's Bar on Palm Beach; the Greenhouse, either the one on Singer Island or the one in West Palm; Gainesville, where he'd taken road trips to watch an SEC football game; or the US Caribbean and the quirky town of Key West. Music transports everyone by giving rise to private memories and the accompanying emotions.

Each day teaching was getting easier, but not easy, for Nick Finch. It really helped that he knew his subject matter and loved the story of the United States. It showed—and the kids really enjoyed coming to his class. This was a time before high-tech invaded the classroom. There were no individual PCs, which would come later in the nineties. Technology was knocking on the door, so to speak, but was still on the outside looking in. Instead, the technology a teacher used in this era was a good handheld calculator for figuring out final grades, which were recorded in pencil in a blue gradebook, and an archaic but very useful contraption called the E-Z Grader, which was a sturdy 4 × 8 tool from the top of which you selected the number of questions asked and then were given a horizontal listing of final scores determined by the number of questions missed, scaled down in order. The scale easily slid back and forth horizontally, and there was a front and a back, with the number of questions ranging from six to ninety-five. For the mathematically challenged social studies teacher, this tool would be part of Nick Finch's teacher's desk until the day he retired.

The most important tool was the same as it had been for hundreds of years, heck, maybe going as far back as the Greeks, and that was the pencil, specifically, the no. 2 pencil, which was used for recording grades in the blue gradebook, which grades could be changed with a few firm strokes of an eraser, and for filling in bubbles on scanner sheets for daily attendance, final grades, and conduct. Not exactly IBM-generated educational software, but it worked. Announcements still came on the PA and were delivered by class officers and followed by official warnings: "Look out for …" and "I need to see the following …." These official announcements many times would bring a chuckle and even a burst of laughter from all who listened.

Dean Whitiker had a slow, strong southern drawl that could match that of any Hollywood actor portraying a redneck sheriff. If you listened closely enough, you could make out the delay between the calling of names and a quick spitting of chewing tobacco juice into the spittoon that followed the North Carolina native everywhere indoors. Outdoors—well, nature was provided with an organic watering with the assistant principal discreetly spitting when no one was looking, especially in female company. There was not one racist bone in his body, as he explained where he had grown up, everyone was poor, black, and white, and the Korean War had proven to him that all blood was red, not white, or black. Still, Dean Whitiker was very descriptive with appearances when calling out the names of students who needed to report to the Dean's office for anything from discipline to early dismissal notes and dropped-off lunches. More than once he would call for, "Roger Brown, not the black eleventh grade Roger Brown, but the short, fat, white ninth grade one." There would be no mix-ups, and the correct Roger Brown would make it to the office. No one thought this method was inappropriate except maybe one hefty freshman boy. Spanish names also could be challenging to Dean Whitiker, and like many southerners, the way he rolled his *r*'s would cause the Hispanic staff members and students at the school to shake their heads.

One day Nick found himself laughing so hard that he had to walk outside his room to regain his composure. And when he went outside, he found he was not alone. There were at least three other teachers shaking their heads and laughing in amazement. The vice principal had called for a student named Jesus Rodriquez, but he'd pronounced the first name in English, so it came out as if he were speaking the name of the Son of God himself: Jeezus. Making it worse was the surname, which escaped as "Rod-ra-gize". Jeezus Rodragize apparently needed to come to the office for something. Another day a fellow administrator announced that parking decals were now being sold in the Dean's ffice on a "come serve, come first basis while they lasted." It was obvious what was meant to be delivered was "first come, first served." It had to be a simple mistake, but the following day she repeated the same command of "come serve, come first." There was a change in announcers for the third day. Such is announcement humor. Later, announcements would be replaced by student-generated TV newscasts, which were rather good, yet at times veteran teachers yearned for the PA announcements that would take a left turn and provide some good-spirited humor, that is, before society became politically correct. Dean Whitiker would not survive in today's ultrasensitive culture.

As Nick became more and more comfortable teaching, he also became more comfortable with his fellow teachers, many of whom had been his former teachers. He also became aware of the different cliques that had been unofficially formed by the staff. People seemed to naturally separate themselves into the traditional groups and subgroups based on age, gender, race, subject area they taught, and family and marriage status. There were other dividing lines, such as college background, favorite and sports teams, support or not for the fine arts, dress, and appearance, and a new one to Nick, sexual orientation. Nick, although not gay in the least, could care less about who saw whom in their free time, but the fact that some of the teachers were gay did cause some friction among the older faculty members. Even the ones who were gay still preferred remaining in the closet, so to speak. Some of Nick's former teachers whose sexual preference he'd had no idea about brought about a reaction like, "Well, I had no idea." Then there were the teachers who he presumed were straitlaced and who moonlighted as preachers or deacons, only to find out they could drink with the best of any lumberjack or sailor and cuss just as much. It was a fascinating dynamic of more than one hundred professionals working in close proximity and mostly working toward one goal: the success of the students whose learning they had been entrusted with. Nick concluded that the closest thing to his work environment was his mom's at the hospital. He naturally gravitated toward his fellow coaches, other social studies teachers, and his former instructors.

Coaches get to know their fellow coaches' personalities, wants, desires, and struggles better than anyone else. When the Penn State Jerry Sandusky scandal rocked the college football world, Nick never believed that Head Coach Joe Paterno had no knowledge or at the very least any suspicion of the horrible incidents of child molestation that were occurring up at State College, Pennsylvania. One really gets to know everything about the guys with whom one spends every day after school in the heat and rain, Friday night under the lights, and first thing every Saturday morning to review previous matches and preview those that are upcoming. The young offensive coach saw his head coach and boss Tim Applewood carry his love for Ohio State and Woody Hayes right on his shoulder. It got to the point that the rest of staff learned to dislike the Buckeyes and hoped they would lose every Saturday, so then they'd get to hear every possible excuse for why it had happened.

Tim Applewood was an exceptionally good man and placed his family as his top priority. That was why it was so difficult to watch his family come apart at the seams.

Tim's marriage crumbled with rumors of infidelity, and the children rebelled against their father as they took sides in the fighting, the separation that followed, and finally the divorce. Tim Applewood was a strong and devout Roman Catholic who believed divorce was a near-fatal decision. The whole episode was painful to observe, but what was remarkable was that Coach Applewood seldom allowed his problems to interfere with his coaching duties. Unless one had been in the coaches' office and overheard the emotional phone calls to family members and the speaking in hushed tones to the lawyers, one would have had no clue of Coach Applewood's home situation. Rarely can a person separate a tough home life from work, but Tim Applewood did a hell of a job of doing just that. Nick Finch made a mental note that years later when he started his own family, he would step down from coaching.

The defensive coach, who also taught weight training, was Larry Timmons. Larry and Nick gravitated toward each other as there was only a five-year difference in their ages, both were single, both had grown up in Palm Beach County, and both had played locally. Coach Timmons was an undersized high school linebacker who had ended up playing on the offensive line at a high level at Florida State. Larry Timmons, unlike Coach Applewood, was overly critical of his alma mater. He would holler and cuss at the Seminoles as much as he would at their opponent or those officiating. Nick observed that Larry Timmons really got into watching all teams play college football as if it were a matter of life or death or he had money riding on the outcome. In fact, it was because he had money riding on the games. Lots of it. The coach's disposition and mood would vary widely depending on how well or poorly the teams he'd wagered on had done. He would place every type of bet: final score, over-under, total points, and exotic. All types of gambling were in Larry Timmons's playbook. Inside his gradebook, the local dog track parimutuel book was placed in front of the students' names and grades. To an outsider, it looked as if the physical educational teacher was investigating his students' progress and was doing so all period while the kids lifted weights. If only they knew. More than once, the coach would send a student who was enrolled in the work experience program to stop by the track and place a bet for him. For that favor, Larry Timmons would buy lunch for the student, which was usually the local favorite, a Russo's submarine sandwich. The student got lunch and the coach had his bet placed. Not ethical, but everyone won, so to speak. That professional gamble was worth it.

Math teachers, Nick found to be an interesting breed. As Principal Bobby Newcombe said, although it was a stereotype, English teachers should be seen grading essays, social studies teachers should be reading the most newly released books on the subject they taught, and math instructors should be in their classrooms before school, at lunch, and after school giving extra tutoring instruction. There is some truth to his observation. Coach Mack Lee could always be found before, during, and after school providing extra math help for his students. If it meant he would be late to football practice, oh well. Did it upset Coach Appleman? At times, but Coach Lee knew that the principal would much rather have him working with a struggling student given the standardized tests that were mandated by both the district and the state. These tests, although somewhat defensible in theory, caused incredible tension and anxiety among the students. Players could be coached on either how to hit the blocking sled or how to pass their required tests and graduate. Coach Lee always chose graduation. An interesting and private man, Mack Lee would have incredible conversations with Nick, the topics ranging from the advantages of the wing-T offense for high school football to the theories of Plato. Nick Finch surmised that Mack had the highest IQ of any coaches on the football staff. He would later find he was correct.

Mack Lee kept his off-campus life to himself and let very few inside his world. Having grown up in the slums of Riviera Beach, breaking the color line in both high school and college, excelling on the football field and on the track as a shot putter and discus thrower, graduating with top honors and being voted most likely to succeed in both high school and college, he had a lot to brag about. He never did brag, though. It took others who knew Mack to share these accomplishments with his peers.

One day the giant of a man did ask the first-year coach for help with a small writing assignment. Nick Finch, feeling honored and privileged, readily agreed. It was a small paragraph that used abbreviations. Coach Lee asked for an appraisal and any suggestions to make it wittier. Nick read it and then reread it, and suddenly it dawned on him: it was a personal solicitation for the classified section of the *"Palm Beach Post"* newspaper. Mack was looking for a date.

Nick turned around and looked back at his friend with the widest grin and was met by a finger across the mouth of Coach Lee: *Be quiet; this is a secret.* Nick changed a few things, and Coach Lee loved the editing his new friend had done. Nick promised secrecy.

With the suspense killing him, about a week later Nick worked up the nerve to ask how their collaboration had worked out. A giant smile emerged on Mack's face as he quietly produced a sheet of paper with twenty-plus phone numbers with stars and checkmarks next to them. Nick walked away, amused, as he heard another request for some more pointers for the next posting. "Absolutely, would love to" was his response as he walked, grinning, planning his next choice of words for the "Love Connection." world. The *"Post"* was the eighties version of today's online single dating and hookup sites. The *"Post"* was the Tinder of its time.

Speaking of dating, Nick himself was still happily single and looking for the right person, but he didn't want to be tied down. He could not imagine himself with one woman exclusively for the rest of his life. At least not yet. His father had always warned him about crapping where you sleep—in other words, do not bring romance to the workplace. Nick saw that more as a suggestion and not a law written in stone. During faculty meetings he was attracted and drawn to the young English teacher he had met in preschool training, Miss Amy George. Attractive, from Delray Beach, and a graduate of Atlantic High who then went on to the University of Florida, she did check a lot of boxes. Add to this the fact that she was damn good-looking, and

Nick decided to make his move. He found out when her planning period was and made sure he dropped into the teachers' lounge, rather than going to the coaches' office, to increase his chances of "running into her". It paid off. Both seemed to hit the vending machine around the same time every day with a chance to buy a Classic Coke, a New Coke, or a Tab. Amy always grabbed a Tab and a packet of cheese crackers, while Nick got the "Real Thing," Coca-Cola Classic. Then they would commandeer an empty table and each pull out a stack of ungraded papers. Most of the time the papers never got graded as the two made small talk about college experiences and their own personal lives. It was singles bar talk, but at work and without the alcohol.

The lounge itself was a world unto its own. Most schools today no longer have a teachers' lounge as the new and improved plans have all but eliminated them at the request of administration. The higher-ups saw these lounges as dens of discontent, rebellion, and insurrection. To a point, they were correct in their assessment as union leaders used such rooms as field offices for recruitment and strategy sessions. But there was more. No matter what time of day it was, you could find a colleague on the phone pleading his case for keeping the water or electricity on, saying, "The check is in the mail, swear to God." There were one or two teachers always sound asleep on a disgusting worn-out donated sofa or who plain had their heads down on the worktable, looking and acting like the students they had just left. There were various reasons for this behavior, such as working the night shift at a second job, having a hectic home life requiring the juggling of parenthood and work, or having spent a late night on the town.

Profanity could be heard when the vending machines malfunctioned and took a hard-earned fifty cents away from a thirsty or hungry teacher, who then would place a sticker with his or her name on the machine with a few words about how it had taken his or her money. The custodians would simply take the stickers off at the end of every day. No money was ever refunded, but there would be a sign placed on the front of the machine reading, No Refunds: Use at Your Own Risk. This was protested by way of a strongly worded objection from the union. See, they did do some things to help the workingman.

It was early October when Nick asked if Amy if she had gone to a football game yet and how the game against her alma mater, Atlantic High School, had gone. This Friday would be the perfect time, he said, if she would like to accompany him to a postgame party at a local pizza parlor that had a private room reserved for the coaching staff and family. Her answer was an immediate "yes" even before Nick finished up the proposal.

As usual, Atlantic, a perennial powerhouse, beat the surprisingly good Forest Hill team. As Nick left the gym, he saw Amy waiting by his new car. He had opened a savings account at the teachers' credit union, and one of the first things he'd done was to trade in his old Ford company car and buy a VW Cabriolet convertible. Some of his friends teased him about its being a "chick" car. Nick would agree with them, adding that chicks loved his car. It was a magnet, especially with that kick-ass AM/FM cassette sound system. Put the top down with the music blaring and he would get noticed. More than once, Amy had acknowledged how much she loved his car.

Other faculty members had noticed the blossoming fall romance between the young teachers and, without warning or notice, gave their opinions, which ranged from "Don't do it; stay unattached" to "Start shopping for rings." Funny thing is, both he and Amy seemed to get the same advice from the same people, but always when they were alone. They laughed, they rolled their eyes, and they went on dating till almost Christmas break. They had a good time together and had so much in common that many assumed it was just a matter of time before they tied the knot. Nope. They had two things that would doom any long-range plans. One was that Nick began to fall in love with teaching more than he loved Amy George. As each day passed, he found himself more comfortable in the classroom than he did when he was alone with her. The opposite was true for her. As each day passed, she found herself disliking her job more and more and began to look for escape options.

One day, shortly after returning from the Thanksgiving break, Nick saw her in the main office before school. Amy George was never an early riser or one of the early arrivals. In fact, most of the time she came on campus about the same time as the students did. Nick was always at least forty-five minutes early. He was hanging around the office as she emerged from Bobby Newcombe's office and walked by an awaiting Nick very quickly. She whispered the fateful words in his ear: "We've got to talk." He looked back at his boss, who pulled his imaginary pistol from his holster and shot his young history teacher. Whew, at least Nick wasn't in trouble.

When the two met a few hours later in the lounge during their planning period, Amy changed the venue for the discussion to someplace outside the room, away from all the ears and eyes in there. Nick was wondering what this could be about. Possible topics had raced through his mind all morning. Was she in some kind of trouble and that was why the principal had wanted to see her? Was it something he had done or said? Was she pregnant? Oh God, please, no. Was it the fact that his mom, Charlene, had given her the cold shoulder when meeting her on multiple occasions when they were all together? Amy was very perceptive and was able to discern Charlene Finch's thoughts about her. Mrs. Finch was polite, but she was also quite cold and distant toward Amy. Nick noticed, but he ignored his mother's attitude as it always seemed she never approved of any of Nick's girlfriends. She was a very tough judge and critic of his love life. So, what could it be?

Zero hour had arrived. It was about eleven o'clock in the morning when Amy and Nick went for "the walk." The first thing that Nick needed to know, she said, was that it wasn't him, but was her, and she wanted to remain friends. She really liked him, but she needed to go in a different direction. He thought just then that she would make a good coach, especially when it came to cut time and final selections for the team, which required an "I am sorry, really sorry, but I can't keep you on the team."

Nick was getting cut. Oh, OK, but why? He thought maybe it was because he was comfortable with Amy but was not in love with her. That being the case, their breaking up was not unexpected, except he thought he would be the one doing the cutting. She explained to him that she had begun to really hate teaching and had noticed how much he enjoyed it, so they couldn't share the same love of the classroom. Her personal answer was what Nick had recently passed on: law school. She was resigning from her teaching position effective at the Christmas break and would start at Nova Southeastern Law School in January. She then went on to speak highly of the virtues of Nick Finch, saying that somebody was going to be so lucky to become his wife. He had helped her through a difficult time and had made her laugh and feel wanted again, she said. Nick basically mentioned the same qualities about Amy, saying that she was very bright and engaging and had taught him to like and accept new things such as foreign movies. That was a lie though, as he hated those movies, especially if they were French. He also told her that she was the ultimate "arm candy" in that she was very attractive when they went out. Amy loved that and began to cry. Nick told her he meant everything he said and wished her good luck, adding that the field of law was getting an "outstanding addition" and that the field of education was losing out.

Amy's response was short and to the point: "Not as long Nick Finch stays in the classroom." She gave him a peck on the cheek and walked back up to her classroom. She then turned around and asked her new ex-boyfriend, "Why does your mom hate me?"

Nick shook his head and replied, "She doesn't hate you. She's just protective of me, I guess."

Every now and then Nick would read about Amy as a lead counsel in some sort of lawsuit. Sometimes she was representing the defendant, other times, the plaintiff. Her attractive looks garnered the attention of many, including local television stations, who interviewed her as an expert who was able to give insight into what was really going on in some trial. Every now and then he would catch her on national cable news programs giving her critiques and opinions on some aspect of a local trial that was making national news. She also caught the eye of a highly successful partner in a powerful downtown personal injury law firm by the name of Garrett Lantsky of the often-advertised firm of Weinstein, Blumberg, and Lantsky. Their slogan was "We Win because We Care." And their phone number was plastered across the bottom of TV screens and on highway billboards: R-U-HURTN, which is 784-8786, with the addition that they were available 24/7/365. Nick would grin, shake his head, and mumble something like, "Good for her." Some thirty years later, Amy Lantsky became a circuit court judge deciding and officiating all kinds of cases.

One day, Nick Finch went to his mailbox and found he had a summons for jury duty. He knew that as a history and government teacher, he should welcome the chance to be part of the solution and not the problem and do his civic duty of reporting and serving in the legal process. The problem, Nick found, was that he had been called five times and some of his colleagues had never been called.

Why couldn't he have the same luck with the lottery? After working on lesson plans for a substitute, he would have to report downtown to the courthouse with a hundred or so other "lucky" winners. Then, when and if his name was called, he would report to a courtroom and be instructed by a bailiff to wait outside and remain respectful. There were times when, unfortunately, Nick would see some of his ex-students and even some of his friends and acquaintances shuffle by in orange jumpsuits, their ankles shackled together, on their way to some sort of procedure like an arraignment. Occasionally they would spot their ex-teacher or past friend and either wave or nod, or in some cases blurt out a big hello from the other side of society. Nick would always acknowledge their presence and try not to judge. That would be the job of Judge Lantsky. Nick also found he was never, ever seated on a jury. He would be dismissed—what so many of his peers were praying for. They did not want to sit on a jury that paid them well below minimum wage for their service. For many, jury duty presented an economic hardship, causing them to lose valuable working hours and pay. Nick had seen people plead their cases for why they could not fulfill their duties. Sometimes they were excused, other times, not.

One time, for a low-level drug selling charge against a youth, he saw two such incidents occur right in front of him during the void dire, which means jury selection. The defendant in the case looked all of eighteen years old and was sloppily dressed. He was black, defended by a public defender who had to be a very recent graduate of law school and looked only a few years older than her court-appointed client. One gentleman, in his US Post Office shirt and shorts, sporting a long-braided ponytail, raised his hand and explained why could in no way be impartial. He explained that he was a Vietnam War veteran and that grass, as he called marijuana, had gotten him through that awful war. He got high every night so he did not return to Vietnam in his nightmares. He described the defendant as an angel of mercy who provided needed medicine for some. The prosecution immediately dismissed the mailman, who parted with a "good luck" to the defense team. Another rough-looking, unkempt man raised his hand and quite simply said he hated blacks. But instead of using *black*, *colored*, or *African American*, he used the dreaded N-word. The defense excused him immediately. Nick could not tell if he had done that intentionally to be dismissed or if he really was the racist bigot that his diction portrayed him as. Nick shook his head in amazement as he waited for the final cut list, and once again he had not made the team. Friends of his who were lawyers said that being a white male and educated was usually a good reason for being excused. Such is our legal system.

This was the fifth time Nick Finch had been summoned, and by now he was an old pro at it. Always the bridesmaid, he was invited but never got the ring—in this case, the chance to sit on a jury. He was almost fifty now and was prepared, having brought his copy of the new James Patterson thriller to pass the time. He also noticed that in the past he always recognized someone he'd grown up with who also had been called. He looked around while listening intensely to the roll call and the swearing in. He knew only that seeing someone he knew was becoming more and more unlikely. With the population explosion of the recent years, and with the size of Palm Beach County, the odds were against being familiar with any of the other candidates. He settled in and had to have his name called twice before he realized it was him. Then he was to follow the bailiff to the elevator and remain silent. He and thirty or so fellow residents of the county had been called for a civil lawsuit between a resident and the homeowner's association, or HOA, of an over-fifty-five community located in West Boynton Beach. It had something to do with the HOA's having failed to notify the residents of possible alligator attacks and protect them as of there had been a gator attack on a miniature poodle. The French dog became an appetizer for the hungry reptile, but this was no ordinary dog: this was Pierre. Pierre was an award-winning canine with a long pedigree. He not only provided a comfort and security to his owner's family but also was considered a family member. In addition, he was a partial breadwinner as he was accomplished in the field of breeding. Pierre was a stud, and now that he was gone, somebody had to pay.

Nick did his best to hide his sarcastic smile as the plaintiff's lawyers explained the heartbreak and financial loss to the family. The defense countered with, "This is Florida, and as heartbreaking as the incident is, this is a case of natural selection." The judge, who had not looked up, seemed to be bored and was doodling on some scratch paper. As a veteran teacher, Nick knew when one of his students was not interested in the lesson, so it was apparent to him that the judge was not interested. Seated high on the bench, the judge gave instructions for the jury selection process and asked if anyone knew any of the people connected with the case, and if so to raise their hands and explain themselves. Nick could not believe it, it was the Honorable Amy Lantsky, or as he remembered, the young English teacher Amy George. They went down the row back in the gallery section of the courtroom. Nick could not imagine there would be a big crowd of spectators or TV cameras for this trial. Two people complained about the economic hardship that sitting on the jury would them. Another stated that she was the caretaker of her elderly mom. One man claimed he was a licensed trapper who was on call to remove nuisance gators from human-inhabited areas, like in this case. They were all excused. Then Nick raised his hand, and the judge called on him. "Yes, Judge, I do know someone involved in this case: you."

The judge quickly looked up as both tables of counsel turned around to peer at the man claiming he knew the person on the bench. Judge Lantsky put on her glasses, looked right at the possible jurist, and banged her gavel. Almost screeching, she said, "My God, Nick Finch, is that really you?"

Nick could not resist the answer: "Guilty. And would you like me to explain to the entire courtroom how well I know you?" The judge then dismissed the courtroom for lunch and told them to report back at one thirty to finish the selection process. Nick was excused but was ordered to chambers. The little old woman seated next to him just had to know what Nick and Amy's past relationship was. He whispered that he used to be her paid escort, a gigolo, so to speak, and winked at the old woman, who smiled and winked right back.

As the prospective jurists left, Nick approached the bench. The judge emerged from up on high, came around in robes and all, and gave her former boyfriend a hug and a kiss on the cheek. Both sets of lawyers looked at each other in amazement. Amy and Nick were now both veterans in their respective professions, but memories quickly took them back to their early twenties—teachers' lounges, classrooms, VW convertibles, and what-ifs. After a lunch together, they made a promise to get together again. They never would, but that was OK with both of them. Their memories brought back smiles, and so often in their worlds, smiles were hard to come by. Nick Finch was finally glad he had jury duty.

CHAPTER

9

It's Summer: So Much to Do, So Many to See, and So Little Money to Do It with—and It's So Damn Hot!

There was an immensely popular romantic comedy TV show in the 1980s called "Moonlighting". The show had very popular well tested and trusted plot line with predictable character developments and yet it achieved high ratings perhaps due to the fantastic chemistry of the two stars. Bruce Willis one-time bartender with a wicked grin, a quick wit, and an everyman appeal that was cast next to a beauty queen from Memphis that could play saint and sinner depending on the situation named Cybill Shepherd. It worked, and the American public loved it. There is another type of "moonlighting" however that was not fantasyland from Hollywood and that is a second job to make ends meet. To pay the bills and some extra spending money in one's pocket became the objective. Nick Finch quickly found out that his teaching salary demanded an extra income, especially if he wanted to move out of his mom's condo. The search was quick and successful as he would hold down these two "jobs" for more than ten years. They enabled him to get his own place, travel, date, and pay for graduate school.

Nick was referred to by two colleagues as the new guy. He would be the third swim instructor and lifeguard for the Village of Wellington. The village had exploded in terms of growth and was a typical high-end suburban enclave. Home prices ranged from some the middle class could afford to others affordable only by the extremely wealthy, and the village placed an emphasis on its equestrian community and activities. Polo, not the clothing brand but the sport, became a passion and fascination for Wellington residents. There was the equestrian group who dressed the part for competitions, jumping over rails and tiny man-made water hazards. Nick was impressed by the athleticism of these athletes. They were different from the traditional football, baseball, and basketball players he knew when he was either a participant or a coach. He respected the speed of the horses and the danger these athletes encountered atop a two-thousand-pound animal. Injuries here could be severe, very severe, and Nick respected that. Nick also quickly recognized that these sports also brought very attractive spectators. He liked that. These residents demanded of their newly chartered local government on-time garbage collection, police and fire safety, and a recreation program for their children.

The Parks and Recreation director for the Village of Wellington was a Midwesterner from Indiana, where he had played college football at Butler. His name was Tom Grabowski. He was perfect for the job, not because of his knowledge of sports, but because of his disarming smile, calm voice, and giant frame of six foot seven. When very upset, residents came into his portable trailer, which he used for an office while construction continued his new recreation center. Tom would calm them down by saying, "Let's sit down. Pull up chair and talk to me. I just know we can work this out."

Most of the time this worked just fine, but on occasion he would be forced to use his massive size to intimidate the outraged "I pay your salary, buster" Wellingtonian. In ten summers, Nick never saw him must use a strategy number three. Nick and Tom hit it off immediately during an interview that took place over lunch and a couple of beers. Nick showed documentation indicating he was a certified swim instructor, along with his lifeguard credentials. Add to this the fact that about one-third of his students and players lived in Wellington, and he was a natural fit. He was hired for a whopping ten dollars an hour for the forty-hour workweek and fifteen dollars for weekends and holidays if he opted in. Not bad for the mid-1980s.

Working with Nick, and on his recommendation, were two other Forest Hill teachers and coaches. One of these was Carl James, former letter winner in swimming from the University of Florida and the school's swim coach.

Coach James was also an excellent language arts teacher, which was the new name for an English teacher. Because of overcrowding, Coach James's team taught with Hank Gibbs, the new transplant from New York. Although quite different in personality and delivery, their style of teaching and their ability to work together was magic. Nick found himself more than once slipping into an open seat in the back of their classroom to take it all in—the delivery, the instruction, and best of all, the humor. Nick found himself wishing they had taught him high school English; they were that good.

Carl James was a wild man outside the pool or classroom. He drank hard and partied even harder. For Hank Gibbs, everything revolved around his family. Carl James was married in the legal sense but not a particularly good husband. He was the kind of guy you liked to hang out with but whom you would never let your sister date. Hank Gibbs was the kind of guy you'd ask if he had a brother, you could set your sister up with.

The other summer swim instructor was the wrestling coach and fitness freak named Charlie Erickison. Coach Erickison had been an All-American wrestler for the University of Iowa. On the mat he was the real deal, and twice he'd been invited to the Olympic trials, where he was runner-up. In fact, he had some obscene overall wrestling record of 180–5. Charlie actually did not know his record, but Nick saw it in a newspaper article that was framed and on Charlie's wall at his townhouse. Coach Erickison was a health teacher who would relate the ideas of a healthier life and lifestyle to his class. Unlike some health and PE teachers who had been hired because of their coaching or athletic résumés, Charlie really got into his subject area. He set up workout programs, suggested diets, and preached the importance of mental health. He was a man who taught by example: he was in perfect shape, muscle on top of muscle; ate a lunch of fruit and vegetables; and spent break time swimming laps in the pool. At lunch, while Carl James was hitting on a joint or slamming a beer, followed by mouthwash or gum, Charlie Erickison rode his competition ten-speed bike along a ten-mile loop.

The mothers who brought their children for the morning swim lessons or back to the pool for the afternoon free swim would sit, stare, and gossip with each other about the former wrestler. Nick watched their conversations from afar with amazement as he sat in his elevated lifeguard chair. Charlie Erickison was happily married to an Iowa farm girl who was the epitome of the "girl next door". He never noticed or acknowledged the stay-at-home moms' fantasy sessions because he was married and that would interfere with workout time. So, Nick Finch found himself sandwiched in between a borderline genius with some serious addiction problems and a wrestling god whom the Greeks would have been proud of. Nick loved it and took it all in. And he got paid.

Another set of teachers who also coached set him up with another opportunity for some more money, but year-round: valet parking cars on the island of Palm Beach. Perry Hahn and Frank Fletcher both taught at Twin Lakes High School and coached various sports, but they also knew the Finch family. On the rare occasion when J.W. And

Charlene had a "date night", they would go out to dinner either at the Riverhouse on the Intracoastal Waterway in Palm Beach Gardens or at Nando's Restaurant on Royal Palm Way on the island. These events usually meant no children and were reserved for occasions such as birthdays and anniversaries. Perry and Frank were fixtures as the valets at Nando's. They were in many ways as important as the maître d' or the chef. Theirs were the first faces seen by the patrons who were beginning their nights on the town, and then theirs were the last faces they would see after a five-star dinner, probably of shrimp scampi, the restaurant's signature dish. The problem was that Perry and Frank were not getting any younger—age was catching up with them—and they wanted some relief so they could have some time of their own. They needed a relief pitcher, so to speak, a third valet to work weekends during the peak season or to fill in when one of the two needed a night off. Nick was the perfect fill-in. He was compatible with the two founders and only employees of "Island Valet Services". He would work for cash, and he could sprint to get the patrons' cars, as the look of personal hustle was a key component of receiving a large tip. Sprinting for the car was as important as opening and closing the car door. It showed the customer that the valet cared and that their time and car were both very important. Another perk, which was not underrated in Nick's eyes, was that at a certain time in the evening a valet could walk to the back of the restaurant and get the same five-star dinner that the patrons were paying top price for. It would be waiting for you at no charge. Nada. Nothing. For one certain young bachelor living alone, this perk was right up there with the generous tips. For ten years, Nick Finch would answer the call of his two valet partners whenever they needed their trusty third. The money was good, and the food was even better.

Many of Nick's boyhood friends were also finding their way back to Palm Beach County after their stints in college. Scott Clark returned as a PE teacher and coach at Suncoast High School in Riviera Beach, where he got married and quickly started a family. Raymond Wade came back from the University of Florida with two degrees, one in history and the other in Spanish. Also, his graduation had caused the UF administration to sigh in relief as the young Mr. Wade left Gainesville on social probation status, which had been ordered by West Palm Beach native and school president Dr. Marshall Criser. The former tennis and golf standout went on to become a legend whose, stories of whose antisocial behavior continue to this day.

When Ray was doing his internship, more commonly known as one's practice teaching, at nearby Ocala Vanguard High School, the young unaccredited teacher who was broke and had a near-empty gas tank took matters into his own hands and used a "Georgia credit card" to fuel up from the principal's van—slang for using a hose to siphon gas from the van and into his fuel-guzzling, but classic, 1969 convertible Chevy Impala. He was caught by the principal, who was leaving for a hunting trip to South Georgia. The principal took the promising young teacher into his office for a talk. Consequences could have been bad with dismissal from the teaching program, suspension from

UF, or even arrest. At the end of the meeting, the principal took the history teacher down to the work shed where gasoline was stored for the lawn maintenance equipment and filled up his car. Both left laughing and shaking their heads. Raymond Wade had the ability to sway negative situations and turn them into what later would become humorous folklore accounts.

Another incident brought Ray face-to-face with an upset college president. One of Wade's fraternity brothers was "Albert the Alligator, the school mascot who paraded around in costume at athletic events entertaining the crowd while trying to get the hometown fans to show their spirit and help the Gators on to victory. Ray's frat brother had come down with the flu, most likely the "whiskey flu," which included symptoms such as vomiting, fatigue, and a splitting headache—the same as a traditional Saturday morning hangover. Imagine that. The brother asked Ray if he would substitute for him but asked him not to take off the headgear or talk, because then the switch would be discovered. With a wide grin, Ray agreed to the task. It was a twelve-noon kickoff time for the Auburn game, and it was blistering hot out, especially on the artificial turf that covered Florida Field. It was even hotter, much hotter, in the reptile costume. At first Ray was up to the challenge as he walked around the field-level side seats and posed for pictures with the home team fans. Little fans especially loved Albert, and their parents loved taking pictures of the next generation of Gators. Many of those snapshots became Christmas cards. As it got closer to kickoff, Ray was reunited with the Gator cheerleaders and was introduced to the Auburn cheer squad for a traditional picture of the two teams united in goodwill and sportsmanship. As both teams crowded close together, "Albert" found it a great opportunity to let his paws explore female Auburn Tigers cheerleaders' backsides. The picture was snapped. You can see the startled look on the face of the blonde-haired cheerleader who was stationed right in front of the rowdy reptile. Her expression of shock and surprise at having been startled did not match the expressions on the faces of anyone else in the two squads combined. That picture hangs today on the wall of Raymond Wade's classroom, but only a few know the whole story.

Later in the game, the heat and the humidity were beginning to take its toll on Ray. For the traditional Mr. "Two Bits" routine, a Florida football tradition, Ray was seen on the team bench in a pose that could only be described as one of surrender. The heat had won, and this was no longer any fun at all. As he got up, he felt a little dizzy and nauseous. He started walking toward some shade, when a mother and her little Gator pleaded with Albert for a picture. Albert ignored them as he continued to slither away. The little boy began to cry, and then the mom turned mean and being hollering profanities at her formerly favorite mascot. Ray Wade stopped dead in his tracks and walked over to the two, who each took a side and began to pose. Apparently, the husband, with camera in hand, readied to take the picture. Then things got ugly. Ray Wade turned to the mother and, with his hands—er, webbed forefeet—pulled his alligator jaws apart and vomited all over the horrified woman, with nearby fans having witnessed the event. She was frozen and stunned as the mascot turned around and began to walk away. Then he turned around as said, "There's your goddamn picture!" Albert kept walking until he reached an exit sign, then he walked out of the stadium and through the parking lot, where costume and all, he entered a city/university mass transit bus and rode away. There was still a full quarter of football left, but this game would have to finish without the beloved mascot, who was back at the fraternity house slamming a beer when the final whistle blew. The president and the AD were not happy. Oh well.

Brian Parker had left undergraduate school with a degree in business administration. Brian was a late bloomer in terms of the academic game and spent most of his high school years playing high-level football and chasing bikini-clads girls at Clarke Beach, also at a high level. Then he got serious with academics and became an honor roll student, then it was on to law school at the University of Miami. Miami, which had the nickname of "Suntan U" for undergraduate studies, is top ranked for its graduate programs in areas such as marine studies, medicine, and law. It is also a private school and very expensive. Brian found himself taking more and more student loans and piling up more debt, which would hound him his first years after passing the bar. One semester, unbeknownst to Nick, J.W. and Charlene helped with his tuition. Brian Parker, who'd grown up without a real father figure, gravitated to his coaches and J.W. Finch to substitute as his dad. Nick even noticed at J.W.'s funeral, where Brian was a pallbearer, that

Brian seemed much more upset than others in attendance. He knew why.

Brian Parker was finishing up his studies in Coral Gables, and that included practice trials called Moot Court. The future barristers needed volunteers to play witnesses in the fictional trials that were based on real-life courtroom experiences. Nick was always willing to help as it kind of showed him of what could have been had he decided to attend law school. It also allowed him to act out a secret fantasy to be a real stage actor. And the fact that the practice trials were also filmed allowed him to say he was a film or TV actor. Fantasies are free. A generous grant from a prestigious criminal defense firm from Miami–Dade County that specialized in defending the Colombian cocaine cartels paid for the expenses the university incurred in their mock trial program. It also paid the volunteers a thank-you stipend of fifty dollars. Nick found himself playing everything from a drug dealer to a dishonest car dealership owner in the courtroom, and he really got into his roles. Brian's classmates often pleaded with the former football star to bring down his teacher friend from West Palm, and Nick almost always said yes. He did, however, draw a line by refusing to play a drag queen. Nope, not him. He had his limits.

Nick learned a lot from these trips down to the University of Miami. He realized that he had made the right decision not to go to law school. Brian Parker had opened his eyes to the cutthroat nature of the profession. Before, during, and after the practice trials, the students would get together to discuss the trials, their roles, the possible outcomes, and the papers that were to follow. Nick found most of Brian's peers to be ambitious but quite nice. Brian quickly brought him up to speed when he said, "All of them are nice to your face, but behind your back, they stab you, skin you, and then sell your body parts to a Mexican clinic." They would steal or hide research books, erase other people's names for professor meetings or job interviews, and do just about any other horrible thing they could think and all the while smiling at you. He explained there were too many lawyers and the competition was brutal, so it was easier to eliminate the competition early in the game, or else be fighting them for the same office space in the real world.

Not all Nick's classmates were jerks. One of the good guys was a top corporate lawyer's son, Tom Westin. The Westin fortune had been made first defending Big Tobacco, then going after the same cigarette companies as a plaintiff. The switch of teams allowed the Westins to live on a compound in the Miami Lakes section of North Miami. It was gated and very wealthy. Legendary football coach Don Shula was a neighbor. Tom wanted nothing to do with civil law as he preferred criminal law, and not defense but prosecution. His older brother was an FBI agent and worked the dangerous War on Drugs task force in South Florida. After one such mock trial, Nick was invited back to the compound where there was to be a big pool party.

At the party, Nick Finch was introduced to the brand-new sport of "wheelchair swimming". Now, in recent years many new opportunities had been introduced and offered to those who for too long had been denied the joy of sports and competition. Special Olympics and wheelchair basketball come to mind, as do specially designed chairs that allowed paralyzed athletes to participate in marathons and downhill skiing. Wheelchair swimming was brand new when it was introduced at the Westin compound that spring Saturday in 1984.

There were about one hundred partygoers already there when Brian and Nick went through the two security gates, one manned, the other requiring a passcode. Almost everyone there was out by the pool, on the dock, or lakeside, enjoying the beautiful spring day. The menu included a whole spit-roasted pig cooked with special Cuban *mojo* seasoning, all the sides, and most importantly countless coolers filled with beer, along with an open bar with a bartender dressed in a Hawaiian-print shirt. Most, especially the young women, were drinking a South Florida favorite, the rumrunner. The whole scene looked as if it were part of the hit TV show *Magnum P.I.*

As the two West Palm guys began to mingle, they both noticed a man by the pool in a wheelchair. Brian asked Tom about the misfortunate guest. As Tom explained, he was a longtime family friend who drank too much, and one night it had caught up with him as he wrapped his Porsche around a palm tree when returning from the Bartenders' Bash, a yearly drunk fest in Key Largo, and was thrown from the car, which busted up his spine. He now was confined to the wheelchair, having lost the use of his legs. *Poor bastard,* the two thought as they went back to scoping out the talent. And there was a lot of talent there. Soon there was some gasping and a scream from the area around the pool where the wheelchair victim was stationed. Tom had joined his Palm Beach County friends at the outdoor authentic tiki bar—authentic in that real Seminoles had built it and thus there was no taxes and no governmental intrusion such as inspections or permits needed. It was the government's "gift" to the tribe. We can take your land, but we will allow you to build our bars so we can drink "fire water." It was a head-scratcher, but in the end the Seminoles put tiki bar construction on the back burner as they opened million-dollar enterprises focused on the casino industry. Who is winning now?

What was happening poolside was that the "poor bastard" in the wheelchair was now drunk and was being belligerent to the young women who passed his way. He grabbed their backsides, pretending he could not hear so the young women would bend over, and then would grab their breasts or spray them with his drink from his straw. He was obnoxious, crude, and rude, and his behavior was becoming boorish. Tom's older brother came over and whispered something in his ear while pointing in the direction of the pool and the wheelchair drunk. Suddenly, a young woman screamed out loudly as her top fell off. The man had used his workable hands to untie the back of her halter top, which proceeded to fall completely off. Shocked and embarrassed, she grabbed her top off the pool deck and ran into the house. Tom and his brother, having seen enough, sprinted at full speed toward the serial groper. Suddenly, the wide grin disappeared as the young man felt his wheelchair moving at a high rate of speed right off the coping and into the deep end of the massive pool. The partygoers were stunned. The man, for safety reasons, had been strapped down to the chair to keep him from falling off or out, and now he found himself at the bottom of the pool, staring up at the brothers who had put him there. He didn't move. He couldn't.

Nick and Brian were right behind. After all, Nick was now a lifeguard. They looked at the brothers and asked them what they were going to do. "Let him sit there a second or more so maybe he learns his lesson." After what seemed like an eternity, but was just a few seconds, the brothers jumped into the pool and wheeled the "diver" to the shallow end, where others helped to lift the man and his chair out of the pool. He was drenched and speechless as his caretaker wheeled him into the house for a change of clothes.

About half an hour later, he emerged, wearing some of Tom's University of Miami sweatpants and a T-shirt. He did not say anything except to ask the bartender for a Coke as the brothers came over to him. All he had to say was, "Wheelchair swimming will not be an Olympic sport." The crowd roared with laughter, and the smile returned to the man's face. All was good. That was the one and only wheelchair swimming performance, and Nick and Brian had witnessed it.

Nick now was in a routine of teaching, coaching, lifeguarding, parking cars, and still looking for the right woman to share his life with. Being a coach and everything, he conducted tryouts—a lot of tryouts. His old college girlfriend Patricia Marks tried to restart something with him by leaving a message on Charlene's answering machine saying, "I miss you so much," which was followed by a small clip of the eighties song "There's Always Something There to Remind Me" by the British group Naked Eyes. Apparently, Patty thought he still lived with his mom. After church that week and breakfast at Greene's Pharmacy, Nick took his mother back to her condo. Charlene asked him to hit the play button on her answering machine, which was blinking with a red light. He hit play and quickly recognized the voice. He did not know for whom he was more embarrassed, himself or Patty. Charlene mentioned something about someone having the maturity of a junior high girl, and that was that. Nick never returned the call. About twenty years later, he and Patty would run into each other in the Grove before an Ole Miss football game, both with their families beside them. It was awkward when Nick broke the silence by extending his hand to Patty's husband, who reluctantly returned the gesture. Patty followed by giving Nick a quick, nonthreatening kiss on the cheek, but still this was enough to produce a small frown from Nick's wife. Nick, looking over at the small boy wearing a replica Eli Manning jersey, extended his hand and asked him his name.

Patty quickly took the cue: "This is my son Nicholas John. We call him N.J."

There was an uncomfortable two seconds of silence, then Nick's wife responded with something to the effect of, "It has been so nice to finally meet you, but we have to go." Nick could not believe she had named her first son with his name and, even more, that her had husband agreed to it. Wow. *Kind of a backhanded legacy,* he thought with a grin. For the rest of the day, Nick grinned like the cat who ate the canary.

National politics in the eighties was dominated by Ronald Reagan. The former actor and governor of California won both presidential elections in a landslide. The economy roared, there was peace, and the Berlin Wall came down. Reagan's ability to talk to the American people and not down to them was very refreshing after the disastrous presidencies of the seventies. His style led J.W. to become a Republican before he died, formerly having been an up-till-then lifelong Southern Democrat. As a history and government teacher, Nick followed politics much more closely than his friends did, and he always believed that the president's style would have made him a great teacher. Folksy topflight communication skills with an added sense of humor have been proven to work in the classroom. Ronald Reagan would have made a great teacher and coach. After all, he was a lifeguard and former football player. Nick observed politics from afar except for one memorable night on Palm Beach Island. He was closing the valet service at Nando's by himself, waiting for the last customers to pay their restaurant bills and either head out for some more fun on the town or head home for maybe a different kind of fun. Just as the last patron was squaring up, Raymond Wade pulled up in the "Von Guzzler"—the nickname for the classic Impala from his college days that he still drove and that was legendary for its gas consumption—and asked Nick if he was up for one or two or ten drinks. Ray was a full-time scuba dive instructor, a guide, and a licensed boat captain. His job duties ranged from giving lessons and certifying potential divers in the sport of open water scuba diving, to driving the dive boat out for open water dives, to selling the needed equipment in the showroom of the dive complex. It was a perfect job for the free-spirited, bilingual, intelligent, but at times very immature young man. The profession did not pay very much, so Ray supplemented his income by giving tennis lessons or hustling some matches with tennis players who thought the tan shirtless and shoeless man would be an easy mark for a quick twenty dollars. Little did they realize Raymond Wade at one time in his youth had been ranked among the top fifty sixteen-and-under players in the country. Ray would put his beer down by the back fence and proceed barefooted to beat his challenger 40–love in about two minutes. He now had his happy hour money. Add in the fact that he lived at the dive house for free with a cot in the back storage area or sometimes even on the boat itself, and it was perfect. Ray knew this was not a lifelong career, but it did delay his entrance into the real world. Nick agreed to meet Ray at Maurice's, an Italian restaurant around the corner. What happened next causes people new to the story to laugh and shake their heads.

As the last customers left the Italian restaurant, the owners shifted gears and took out leftovers, such as pizza, and put them on a heated buffet table to serve the restaurant crews from the nearby eateries, also offering them late-night drinks and conversation. The other late-night watering hole for the car parkers, bartenders, waiters, and cocktail waitresses was the Mandurian in North Palm Beach. A Chinese restaurant, it too would put out a food buffet, but with egg rolls and spareribs. Both were good places to unwind, relax, and occasionally find a little companionship. Also, the Mandurian had live music, a one-man piano entertainer named Darryl Chambers, who was the local version of Billy Joel. Today, Maurice's is a high-end steak house named "The Meat Market" Occasionally, Nick will go there, and when he does, he smiles broadly when remembering the mid-1980s winter night that he and Ray shared with one of the most powerful men in the nation, the senior senator from the Commonwealth of Massachusetts named Edward Kennedy.

The Kennedy family were fixtures on the island. The "Winter White House" was there during the presidency of John F. Kennedy. There was, and still is, a bomb shelter on Peanut Island, an elevated sand and pine tree island that is in the Intracoastal Waterway sandwiched right between the north end of Palm Beach and the south end of Singer Island and the Lake Worth inlet to the Atlantic Ocean. It had been built for the president's protection. After all, the Cold War was on at the time, and there was that little situation called the Cuban Missile Crisis. Today tours are given offering insight into the dangerous world of the Cold War era. Joe Kennedy, the father, had his compound built directly on the ocean, sprawling on the north end of the island. The family wintered there every year as the Kennedys were fixtures at St. Edward Catholic Church and large contributors to St. Mary's Hospital. First Lady Jackie Kennedy brought style and chic along with her class and beauty, but there was a dark side. The Kennedys also brought their recklessness and wide-open lifestyle to an island that loved to party, but they did so in private and behind closed doors. More than once, Nick had parked the cars of the rich and famous with men doing cocaine in their automobiles, half dressed and without their spouses. He would smile as he opened their car doors and many times discreetly and tactfully notify the man of that his trousers were unzipped, that he had white residue under his nose, or that his "date" was exposed. The patrons truly appreciated the extra attention their valet gave them; there would be a twenty-dollar tip for his discretion.

There was David Kennedy's death by overdose and the subsequent cover-up, and later the William Kennedy Smith ordeal. These tragedies surprised no one as such things happened to a lot of Palm Beechers, but since their last name was not Kennedy, it never, or seldom, ended up in the papers or on the evening news.

Nick was closing alone that night. He put the folding table and chair away behind the front door of the restaurant and said goodbye to the inside staff, who were sweeping and cleaning up. Nick waved to Joseph, the maître d', and looked at the wad of money he had made, mostly ones, but some fives, some tens, and two twenty-dollar bills. He also had a can full of coins, mostly Canadian, as the neighbors to the north were notoriously terrible tippers and many times would promise to "get you next time" or else give coins embossed with an image of the Queen or a beaver. Nick and the others would glare and proceed to put the coins in a large empty tomato sauce can, and at the end of the season they would take the coins to First National Bank of Palm Beach, more commonly known as the "Yellow Bank," and cash them in as the bank had a currency exchange desk. The full bucket of coins would amount to less than fifty dollars for three to four months of parking. The boys then would take their money and buy a couple of cases of Molson beer, their favorite import from north of the border.

Maurice's was mostly empty, but there were a few people, mostly from the restaurant industry, at the bar. Nick recognized Raymond Wade seated toward the end of the bar close to the buffet offerings and right by the entrance to the main dining room, which was closed and dark, and the entrance to the restrooms. Ray's blond hair was a little disheveled after two scuba diving excursions that day, one in the afternoon and one being a rare evening dive. There was a full moon. He was busy talking in fluent Spanish to one of the busboys. Nick was envious of Ray's ability to converse fluidly in Spanish. Like a fool, Nick had taken French, and as he would later find out, it would never, ever help him in life.

The tanned dive instructor / tennis pro was drinking a rum and Coke, his beverage of choice, as Nick ordered his usual, a Jim Beam and water. Ray nodded to Nick to indicate he should look over at the last booth in the row that was stationed next to the wall and windows and at the cars that were parked on Bradley Place, the road on which Maurice's was located. Sure enough, Senator Edward Kennedy was seated with what seemed to be two middle-aged women who were dressed as if they were still eighteen. Their English was broken, and Nick recognized it was French, most likely French Canadian mixed with

English. The two conversed with each other in French and, when needed, spoke to their waitstaff or the senator in broken English. It was readily apparent that the two women were buzzed, but the onetime presidential candidate was plastered. At times he would lay his head on the table like an uninterested student will do in school or would tilt his head way back and stare at the ceiling. Rudolph had nothing on him as his nose was a glowing bright red. Although it was chilly outside by South Florida standards, in the mid-fifties, Mr. Kennedy was sweating profusely. Nick not only recognized the highest-ranking member of arguably the most famous family in the United States, but also remembered that the "Lion of the Senate" had spoken at his commencement ceremony upon his graduation from Ole Miss. Nick shook his head and thought, *someone needs to call a cab or something,* when he looked back at Ray, who was wearing a devilish grin. He was up to something, maybe an Albert the Alligator prank.

Located on the bar were two imitation silver chalices. One was full of beer nuts or peanuts; the other, small goldfish crackers. Ray looked at Nick and said, "Watch this." He then took one of the small peanuts and, without anyone noticing, flicked it in the direction of the senator. Kennedy's two friends didn't see him do so as they were busy with their scotch and private conversation. The peanut hit its mark perfectly, right in the back of Kennedy's head. Startled, he looked around and then went back to using his swizzle stick to stir his drink. Ray reloaded and fired again, and again the peanut hit its target perfectly.

This time the senator hollered, in his New England accent, "Goddamn it, I am getting hit by something!" The women turned their attention to their friend and reassured him that nothing was hitting him, then quickly returned to the topic they were discussing together. Nick was really enjoying this despite the possibility that he and Ray could get in real trouble. There must be some law against throwing snacks at famous people. Ray waited about thirty seconds before he reloaded and took aim to launch his third mortar round. Perfect, right-on target. This artillery marksman was really good. Now the senator was sure of it: he was getting hit by something and by someone. "Teddy" attempted to get up, but he stumbled a bit, swaying back and forth, and looked over the patrons. Nick and Ray immediately went to a fake in-depth conversation. And it worked; they were not called out. There it was a two-minute delay or so before the next volley would be loaded and fired. Once again, "bulls- eye". The senator had had enough of this disrespect and harassment. He hollered out some profanity and remarked he was going to the "shitter," adding that when he got back, his two friends had better be ready to go. He stumbled his way to what he thought were the restrooms but instead were drawn curtains that led to the main dining room. Right at the entrance were about fifty champagne standards set up for the next night. The ranking member of the Judicial Committee plowed right into them as if he were a bowling ball blowing through pins in an alley. "*Strike*". The pins, or standards, crashed, as did the senator. His friends quickly got up and retrieved their partner, and the three made their way to the exit.

Moments later, a man came in and flipped a fifty-dollar bill to cover the expenses, and Kennedy's limo quickly sped away. It was an amazing thirty minutes that would live on in folklore forever.

Nick was still single, very single, but still on the hunt for Mrs. Right. He realized not only did she have to satisfy his requirements, but also, she had to pass the Charlene Finch test, and that would be tough. Also, she had to be able to fit in with his tight circle of friends and their significant others. This was a tough task indeed. A popular happy hour hangout during those times was TGIF, or Fridays, on Village Boulevard in a new planned community in West Palm Beach. The area was quickly built and was sandwiched between the I-95 exits of Forty-Fifth Street and Palm Beach Lakes, which made it perfect for commuters going either north or south or into the city. Mostly young professionals flocked to the new community, which was quickly taken over by such places as Bennigan's Tavern, Hooters, and the Raindancer Steak House. All were quite popular but the "in place" was TGI Fridays. It was festive and fun, and it had great bar food such as wings and potato skins. It was also a great place to meet members of the opposite sex.

Nancy Foster was a graduate of Palm Beach Junior College, School of Dental Hygiene, and was employed by a dentist by the name of Dr. Jack Wilkes. Jack was the Finch family dentist, who was a local and had used the GI Bill to pay for dental school at West Virginia University. J.W. used to tease him by asking how they found patients to work on in West Virginia who had teeth. Jack Wilkes responded with, "I tried to go to the University of South Carolina, but they had no dental program, and in fact there were no dentists in the entire state." There, right back at you. Nancy was a freshman in high school when Nick was a freshman in college, and the two had never known each other until Nick went in for a teeth cleaning and checkup. He was quite impressed with the young woman who explored his mouth and flossed him. They made small talk. As he was turning to leave after paying his bill, she alerted him to the fact that she and her friends always went to TGI Fridays after she closed the office on Friday afternoons. Information noted and processed.

Sure enough, Nancy was at bar the next Friday, surrounded by four or five other young women, all in hospital scrubs. Nick would learn they all had gotten to know each other while at PBJC, and they worked at various dental offices. When Nick approached the group, the others shut up and listened to the young teacher and coach as though they had been prepped on who he was and what he looked like. They seemed to approve of Nancy's prospective suitor. He knew this because when she got up to refresh herself with a friend on a trip to the restroom, the remaining friends quickly told him how their friend was interested in him, how great of a friend she was, and what a great couple they would make. The conversation ended as quickly as it had started once Nancy Foster returned. Then she and Nick made time for each other. She turned away from her friends and concentrated on the prospect in front of her. A little while later she announced she had to leave as her friends had promised a girls' night dinner together. She leaned over and gave Nick a quick kiss on the cheek and, while shaking his hand goodbye, slipped him a small bit of a cocktail napkin with her number on it. Nick grinned and called her later that Tuesday. After all, you cannot be too interested. So was the mating call of the young.

Nick found out during the introductory phone call that Nancy was also a beauty queen, having won the title of Miss Sweet Corn Festival and, even more impressive, Miss South Florida Fair. That title would enable her to compete in the Miss Florida Pageant, the winner of which would move on to the Miss America pageant in Atlantic City. Nancy sure had the looks for it. She was the typical blonde-haired, blue-eyed beach girl. She looked as if she could model beach products, and she did later, winning Miss Hawaiian Tropic for Florida, for which she was given a new Mustang convertible. She played the piano for the skill portion of the competition. Nick had no musical abilities, but he knew that to call Nancy a piano player was to be unfair to piano players. She was average at best, but with that smile and her perfect teeth, one could overlook the fact that her musical ability was not up to par. Nick also noticed conversation became strained if the topic was not something within her comfort zone, which was pop culture, for example, Madonna or Prince; aerobics; or the latest of the *General Hospital* saga, which now she had to read in fan magazines since her full schedule of work prohibited viewings. The introduction of the VCR was right around the corner, and it could not come soon enough, because she just could not figure out her Betamax—and just what was happening to Luke and Laura? Nick Finch was quite sure that Nancy would not become Nancy Finch, but for now she would do fine. She was really cute. No, she was really pretty.

Nancy wasn't exactly thrilled with the idea of a long-term relationship with a teacher. She never really liked school, and most of her teachers, and the fact they earned hardly any more than she did, were boxes left unchecked, but she was attracted, if only temporarily, to this teacher, coach, lifeguard, and VW convertible–driving car parker. They had fun together.

They went to movies. They went to concerts. Yes, they saw Prince at the Orange Bowl in Miami, and surprisingly Nick was impressed with the show. They partied like it was 1999. Nancy would swing by at night when Nick was parking cars, and Joseph would invite her in for a drink at the bar, where she waited for Nick to close. More than once, gentlemen at the bar would make their best run at her. She would be polite and then turn her back in midconversation to let them know she was not interested. Occasionally she would go to one of Nick's games and would sit next to Charlene, who loved to go to the games her son was coaching. Nick would notice that his mother was intensely watching the contest, whereas Nancy was watching the cheerleaders and their routines. There seemed to be little conversation between the two. Nick's mom would always leave early to beat the traffic and give a small wave goodbye as she left the stadium. Nancy watched the clock and counted down to 00:00. Many times, she would not even know the final score. She hated going to those games, but she really liked being with Nick, so it was worth it.

What Nick really enjoyed, other than the mutual sexual favors, was the fact that on Fridays Nancy oversaw the closing and locking up of the office. She would change out of her scrubs there and do a once-around, then she and Nick would be off to do whatever they had scheduled. One time as Nancy was checking all around the office, Nick was seated in an examination chair and noticed a tank with a mask and hose attached to it. On the tank, "Nitric Oxide"—laughing gas—was printed. A thought came racing into his mind. Nancy came into the room and said, "We're ready to go." Not so fast. Nick motioned over to the tank. At once, they began nodding and grinning in unison. Nancy untangled the hose, placed the mask over Nick's mouth, and turned the valve on. He quickly took two or three inhalations, or "hits" then she did the same. They paused and then broke into laughter. One more round was followed by more laughter as they made their way to Village Boulevard and TGI Fridays. Once there, they hooked up with their common friends. They continued to laugh and giggle. Their peers even remarked on what a happy couple they made, always smiling, and laughing when they were together.

This was now their pre–Friday date routine. One time after a few hits, Nick, after a little persuading, got Nancy to join him on the dental chair for a little lovemaking. Like canoeing, it was a bad idea. Extremely uncomfortable. Novel idea, but bad results. Canoeing sounds like a good idea, but powerboats are much more comfortable and enjoyable. So are beds.

After church one Sunday, while eating at Greene's Pharmacy, Charlene out of nowhere just blurted out, "I really hope you are not thinking seriously about Nancy." There, she had said it, but she had been thinking about it for a couple of months. Nick put down his fork and just stared at his mom. He knew there was no real long-term future for the two, but it was not his mother's place to express her opinion on the matter. The waitress at the counter of Greene's stopped refilling Charlene's coffee as she wanted to hear the young man's reply.

"Really, Mom? Really?" He followed up with, "You don't even know her or give her a chance." Charlene knew she had crossed the line, but she was worried about her baby boy without structure or being settled down before she left the earth to join J.W. She thought about it constantly and it worried her. Nick shook his head, the unspoken being, "*no you didn't*". He explained that it was none of her business, but deep down he knew it was her business because something as important as his marriage had to be given his mother's approval. He stated how much fun he and Nancy had together, and he finished up by saying that she was smoking hot. There, now he'd said it. He knew his mother was right, but he could not surrender so easily.

Charlene now lowered her voice as she moved closer and said, "I agree, she is very pretty, and I guess fairly nice, but tell me, can she spell the word *cat*?" Not to let it go, she continued with, "I will spot her the *c* and the *t* if that would help."

Nick stared right at his mother with the same stare she had used her whole life, both personally and professionally, to disarm and intimidate the selected target. Nick had learned from the best, his mom. He occasionally used the strategy with unruly students in class, and it always worked. "Time to go." He put down enough money for both the bill and the tip. There was little spoken on the ride back to Singer Island. Both had learned of new boundaries formed that day, and the topic was never brought up again. Two weeks later both Nancy and Nick came to the mutual conclusion it was time to see other people while they were still on friendly terms. To this day when goes to the dentist's office, he asks if laughing gas will be used during his visit. When he is told no, he still smiles and thinks back. Charlene Finch was now relieved.

As any truthful teacher will tell you, the best part of teaching is the time off in the summer months of June, July, and half of August. The advantages of that perk are closely followed by the two-plus weeks during the Christmas season a full week in the spring. Truth be told, teachers work 180 days, as that is the number of days when school is in session with students. The vacation time can be used for important things such as attending educational seminars; continuing one's professional development, for example, by attending graduate school; or traveling to enhance one's life experience, then telling stories about it to help "sell" a lesson to one's students. Also, time off can be an opportunity to make some extra money with part-time work, like Nick was doing. He worked lifeguarding, teaching swimming lessons, riding on a UPS truck to deliver Christmas packages, working toward his master's degree, and traveling. The pay wasn't great, but the benefits were top-notch. He made money, got his master's degree, and traveled to all kinds of places, making memories to last a lifetime.

One such trip was a boys' trip to the "US Caribbean," the Florida Keys. The real Caribbean was out of their league as far as cost and the hassle of passports and travel. The Keys delivered a fine vacation at an affordable price, no documentation needed, and traveling there meant putting the top down and hitting the Overseas Highway, taking it to the Southernmost point in the United States", Key West.

This journey meant packing all the essentials for the trip: toll road money; a cooler filled with all the beverages; one suitcase with college T-shirts (which were great for starting conversations with others, hopefully pretty young women who were familiar with your undergraduate school), Hawaiian print shirts, plenty of shorts, and bathing trunks; and a case of the proper cassettes for pleasant tunes. No blazers, trousers, neckties, or dress shoes needed. A good pair of flip-flops sufficed for footwear. The drive down to Key West is breathtaking, and the highway is really Henry M. Flagler's legacy, as he proved he could do the impossible by building a rail line over open ocean to the trade port city. This would lead to a highway that used the same engineering principles. The terrible hurricane of 1933 wiped out the train route, and after all, the automobile was now the American family's choice for travel. It's off to Key West and they would be damn lucky to get back to Palm Beach without an arrest record.

After getting through the urban sprawl of Broward County and Ft. Lauderdale followed by Miami-Dade

County you made your first turn in Homestead which is really last exit before virtually and literally when leaving the mainland. This poor town would be wiped out in the early 1990's by Cat 5 Hurricane Andrew. The town is still in recovery mode. The Air Force base for most part has closed. The Cleveland Indians baseball team intended to have spring training in Homestead, but after the destruction, they reconsidered and moved to Arizona. But NASCAR took over the training facility to hold their end-of-the-year racing championship there. NASCAR and Homestead are a good fit. Homestead is a tough place where bikers perhaps outnumber SUV owners. This is especially true on weekends, when packs of motorcycle enthusiasts head south down the peninsula for the beautiful ride.

Those who are familiar with the drive usually turn at Card Sound for a shortcut to Key Largo, which means a must-stop at the watering hole known as Alligator Jack's that is located before the toll bridge. Good food, good drink, good music, and great people-watching, it is a great first stop on the journey. From there you pay a toll of a dollar, cash only, to cross over the Card Sound Bridge. The toll collector does not look in any way to be an employee of any state or local authority as he is usually in baggie shorts, a tank top, and flip-flops, with an earring in place. If you have ever seen the movie "Captain Ron", you will notice the man keeping watch by the gate is usually a spitting image of Kurt Russell's character in that very underrated comedy. On the other side of the bridge, you must make a turn either left or right as the road ends. Make a left and you would be entering the Ocean Reef Club. You must be a member or be invited as the club is very exclusive. For that reason, it was not on the boys' itinerary. Years later when Nick entered a different tax bracket, he would have the opportunity to stay at the resort. He always mentioned it was a lottery dividend in that if he won the official game of chance, one of the first luxuries he would buy would be a membership to the Ocean Reef Club. It was and is that beautiful. Making a right takes you eventually back to US 1, also known as the Overseas Highway. You rejoin at a fork in the road that houses a Circle K convenience store, or as Floridians call them, "Stop-and-Robs." It is a tremendous location for refueling, refilling, and refreshing. Circle K probably sells more ice there than anywhere else. Coolers must be restocked, and fresh fish or lobster must be iced down.

The next stop was the Holiday Isle Tiki Bar and Motel in Islamorada for a famous rumrunner frozen drink, a quick walk around the complex, and maybe a quick dip in the swimming pool to refresh before heading down to Key West. Swim at your own risk, because only the Lord knows what bio-organism is living in that pool. Then again, there is always a layer of oil to rival any environmental oil spill either in Louisiana or Alaska. Here I'm referring to Johnson's baby oil, which was the "sunscreen" of choice in the 1980s. Heck, it afforded no sun protection and, in fact, acted as an accelerant, or else as an oil to fry foods in, except it fried the young women who were poolside. If you listened closely, you could almost hear their skin frying. Today many of that generation now suffer from what is nicknamed "Florida Cancer." Nick goes to the dermatologist at least three times a year and always leaves with some area frozen off. Two times he had places on his face cut out, followed by plastic surgery to help conceal the scars. Such is the price that must be paid to live in the Sunshine State. Oh well.

Next stop was the Buccaneer Lounge and Motel located in Marathon, or the unofficial halfway point. A few years later Nick had been invited to this place to help judge a "beauty contest" that was really a wet T-shirt spectacle. A former fraternity brother's family owned a string of radio stations, one of which was "Whale 106", in Marathon, and he served as the DJ while trying to find his way in the real world. Nick questioned the purpose of the employment assignment, knowing that most people went to the Keys to escape the real world and certainly not to "find themselves." Even Ernest Hemingway realized this. Nick's new, fictional title was Palm Beach talent scout for the Burt Reynolds detective show *B. L. Stryker.* Morally it went downhill from there.

Crossing one of the United States' great engineering achievements, the Seven Mile Bridge, still causes Nick to feel amazement and pride. The bridge also marks the downhill stretch to Key West.

Key West, Nick believed, was and is the United States' most eclectic city—more so than New Orleans or San Francisco, which cities can be expensive and dangerous. For years Key West was a trade port town with all the types of people and professions who make a living in trade and shipping. Also, shipwrecks and salvaging from another person's loss could be profitable. It helped lead to a legal specialization in maritime law. The University of Miami is a leader in that field. Treasure hunter Mel Fisher, his family, and his staff searched the areas around the Keys for treasure. He was quite successful, in fact, so successful that there is a museum that sports his name with relics and stories of their adventure. The jury is out as to his character—hunter or thief? It depends on who you talk to. The town once elected a drift boat charter captain and bar owner who went by the name of Captain Tony, whose philosophy on life was, "All you need in life is a tremendous sex drive and a great ego. Brains don't mean shit." It is believed that Jimmy Buffett's song "A Pirate Looks at Forty" is about him. And he was actually elected mayor. The town is filled with people escaping problems they cannot seem to shake off: bad marriages, high alimony payments, and other curveballs of life. Key West is their sanctuary. Conchs, as they are known, are usually addressed on a first-name basis only because not only are they very friendly but also surnames can be traced back to the mainland—and they do not want that.

The modern Key West is now spotted with bars and restaurants. The once thriving shrimping industry is nearly gone. The Navy and Coast Guard have their footprints all over the area. Not a bad duty to be stationed at. It sure beats the hell out of breaking ice in the winter on the Great Lakes or the Saint Lawrence River. Cruise boats will make excursion trips ashore as tourists come to the key to hunt for bargains, such as low-cost T-shirts or oversized shells that make good ashtrays, or for a quick ride on the Conch Train to get a tour around the island. Sophisticates will go to the

Hemingway House and the Truman Complex, which was the original Winter White House; the unsophisticated will go to the strip clubs in which Eastern European women will dance and provide adult recreation in between cigarette breaks. Key West has a large Cuban contingent because of its proximity to Cuba, which is less than ninety miles away, with Key West being the place of the first footfalls on US soil for Cuban immigrants who are able to cross the dangerous Florida Straits. The "wet foot, dry foot" policy states if they can land on US soil, they can stay. Many have done so, and unfortunately many have tried but did not make it. Such is the price for freedom and escape from dictatorial communism. Also, the southernmost point of Key West is the place where many among the LBGTQ community make their home. Restaurant and bar owners will tell you such people make perfect employees. Neat, clean, punctual, and hardworking, they perform many of the service jobs. There are festivals all the time in Key West, everything from a Hemingway look-alike contest to Fantasy Fest, for which clothing is optional. Check the events calendar because there seems to be one every weekend. They dare hurricanes to shut them down. Tough and fun are the characteristics of the Conchs. For Nick and his friends, Key West was a great place to visit and escape to, but he could never live there. Not him.

When the boys arrived, they checked into their motel rooms. Later in life, when they were more financially secure, they would stay at the Pier House or the Casa Marina, high-end lodging with prime locations, but for now "America's Innkeeper," the Holiday Inn, would do just fine. After unpacking and taking a quick rest, it was time to do the "Duvall Crawl," which meant hopping between the numerous bars on the main street of Key West, famous places like Sloppy Joes, which is said to be Hemingway's old haunt; the Bull; the World's Smallest Bar, which is basically a small covered table but is very "Key West", Irish Kevin's, for both music and comedy; and the Boar's Head Saloon. Then there are others that are not so famous. Just multiply by three and maybe you'll get the number of bars offering the opportunity for a good time on this one street. It's a toss-up between Duvall Street and New Orleans' Bourbon Street for the gold medal of carousing and debauchery. Plenty of sin and depravity at both addresses.

In the group was Nick, Ray Wade, Brian Parker, Carl James, Charlie Erickison, Bobby Westin of Miami, and three others, one of whom was Jay Burbank, the nephew of the president of University of Florida. His father, Jay Burbank Sr., was a partner in the prestigious law firm of Harrimen and Burbank. No one was sure if Jay ever really graduated from the University of Florida or, if so, with what degree. He sure as hell was not a lawyer. "Fun guy" and "trust fund baby" are the terms that best describe Jay Jr. Another on the trip was Mike Yardley, who had gone to fire school and was a fireman until, years later, some difficulties with decision-making forced him to resign, after which he started a lawn maintenance company. Wild and out of control were just some of his personality traits. Rounding out the group was "Tall Boy" Donaldson, the son of contractor "Shorty" Donaldson. The former apparently got his nickname in college because of his love for tall boy beers, which helped him study and graduate from a demanding degree program in accounting. Good thing there was no driving as all street traveling was done on foot.

After two days of eating and drinking, the group had reached their last night before the trip back home to Palm Beach, which would be nonstop. They were tired and running out of money. They elected to finish up on the rooftop bar at the prestigious Pier House, which is located at the end of Duvall Street. Go to the Sunset Festival located in the dock area at when? Sunset. There you can see a man herding cats; fire-eaters; a tin man; acrobats; and other such talented people who are paid by the tips they receive. Don't laugh: Nick got the opportunity to talk to one the performers and learned that he was paying his daughter's Ivy League tuition with the cash he made nightly from performing an hour or so for the tourists. Income taxes are more of a suggestion than a law in Key West. An IRS agent would be very unpopular here. If he were to try to audit some of the locals, he may find it difficult to leave the town of his own free will. It could be dangerous.

After the performances, the boys went up the three flights of stairs to the rooftop bar and found a table, then proceeded to order some peel-and-eat shrimp and a variety of alcoholic beverages. Some of them were beered out and switched to liquor, while others still ordered frozen drinks. They ate and drank a lot and listened to what must have been the fifth Jimmy Buffett cover singer and guitarist. This one was surprisingly good. They sang along, laughed, and insulted each other as friends do. The surrounding customers from Michigan liked them and, at one time, sent over a round of drinks. They took turns putting cash in the singer's tip bucket in appreciation of his talent. All they had to do was make sure they had enough for gas and turnpike toll money for the return trip.

Now their waiter was a different story. Todd was the name printed on his name tag, which was pinned to his shirt, and Todd did not like his assignment waiting on the table of the young men from Palm Beach County and the one third-year law student from Dade County. Todd was also very effeminate and openly gay. He swished when he walked back to the bar for another order. He was condescending not only to their group but also to the Michiganders. Todd just did not want to be there that night. Personal problems, who knows what, but he sure as hell did not like his life that night. It would get worse for Todd. Much worse. Brian Parker waved for their server to come over to their table. A look of disgust came over Todd's face. *What do they want now? Can't they just go to whatever place they call home?* He gave a large shrug, followed by "What now?"

Brian responded with, "Check, please." *Finally,* Todd thought, *they are leaving.* Ray Wade was getting a little annoyed by his service and mumbled something under his breath that apparently was not very nice. Todd noticed once the group from Michigan exploded in laughter. It seemed Todd was spending a lot of time and energy, using a calculator and everything, on figuring the final bill. He returned with the check, which Tall Boy Donaldson took, as he always did. He was a certified public accountant and had the ability to calculate what everyone owed down to the penny. At times this would annoy Nick because he remembered his time bartending and now parking cars, when he observed that other than Canadians, accountants were the worst tippers.

Tall Boy was having trouble calculating the totals, and he was practically sober. Nick looked over at him and asked, "What's wrong?"

The CPA looked over the bill for the third time and said, "This doesn't add up. He is double charging us. He is ripping us off."

Raymond Wade, who was drunk, said, "We'll see about this." Todd came back with one hand on his hip, the kind of posture your mother assumes when she is annoyed. Tall Boy explained that the bill was wrong and Todd needed to fix it.

Todd took a stand now and replied, "Nope, that is your final bill. Now pay up!" Ray Wade had slipped behind the apron-wearing server and put him in a bear hug restraint. Todd was shocked and said in a disconcerted voice, "What's going on here?" On cue, Mike Yardley grabbed Todd's ankles, and the two began to roll the disbelieving employee back and forth as if he were on a farm and his cousins, after swinging him back and forth, were about to let go and launch him into a bale of hay. Close—and it would not be hay. The abductors were now counting "One, two, and three." They let Todd go right over the railing. He sailed down three stories into the tarpon pool that backed up to the hotel and restaurants of the Pier House. Diners in the casual second-floor restaurant spotted the staff member flying by, and the fine dining patrons on the first floor also noticed in a blink of an eye someone or something crashing down and making a large splash. The Grosse Point group were laughing at first, then let out a concerned screech. Nick could not believe what he was witnessing. He thought for sure his friends would have let Todd go. They let him go all right, right over the railing. Nick looked over the railing and saw the face of fright and the waiter's arms and legs flailing as he sped toward his final landing spot in the water. His apron was flapping back and forth as tickets flew out of it. It looked exactly like a scene from an Alfred Hitchcock movie, with Todd playing the part of a victim being thrown off the roof a building.

Quickly, Nick and Tall Boy said something right out of *Animal House*: "We're out of here!"

Brian Parker sagely added, "Split up, blend in on Duvall Street, buy new T-shirts, put them on, ditch what you are wearing now, and meet back at the Holiday Inn."

Sounded like a plan. The boys hit the side stairs and did just as suggested. One by one, they made it back to their rooms. They had noticed an increased police presence, but maybe they were just paranoid. The two future lawyers explained that what they had done was called assault and defrauding an innkeeper, which were both felonies. That was not good, but one is only guilty if caught and prosecuted. Thankfully, they had not been caught. The next morning, bright and early, they were on the road back to Palm Beach County. They had escaped justice. About halfway home, Nick wondered out loud what had happened when Todd got home and his partner asked him, "How was work?" The travelers all let out a hearty laugh. Todd, the Michigan tourists, patrons of the restaurant, and the boys would have a story to remember and share.

As summer was winding down, Nick decided to transfer his graduate credits in educational leadership from Florida Atlantic University in Boca Raton to Nova Southeastern University, the main campus of which was in Fort Lauderdale, but there was a satellite campus in West Palm Beach with classes at night and on Saturdays at Conniston Middle School. There were advantages and disadvantages to both programs. FAU was a state school and much more affordable and had a better reputation outside South Florida. In addition, it was a real school on a real campus with tenured professors. The downside was that the classes were in Boca and were scheduled at impractical times for a full-time teacher and coach. The tenured professors had a penchant for being more theory based and not reality based, and honestly, they were kind of lazy. Nova, on the other hand, hired local principals and administrators from the district as adjunct professors. Not only did they have real life-experience to share, that is, what they went through daily, but also the classes served as an opportunity for students to show their skills and gain insight into their potential future bosses. Kind of an eighteen-week interview. Also, both the teacher and the students were tired after working all day, so there was little homework. In short, the choice boiled down to reality versus theory. Also, the campus was only about two miles from Forest Hill High. The negative aspects were that many on the outside saw Nova as a diploma mill: pay your tuition, show up, and in about a year have your master's. Not all true, but then again not all false either. The biggest drawback was the cost. Nova is a private school and is not cheap; at the time it cost about three times more than FAU. Nick thought, *Thank goodness for the valet service, the Christmas deliveries, and the lifeguarding and swim lessons.* Also, there was a small stipend for club sponsorships and coaching. He could make it work, but he felt an ouch when he wrote that check. One last thing: Nova required a modified master's thesis or final paper based both on research and implementation of a program that was to be signed off by an administrator from one's school of choice. Nova it was.

Meeting every Saturday morning for graduate school class was tough, especially if class followed a Friday football game or a night of running back and forth to retrieve cars for the customers at Nando's. Nick had a calendar in his apartment on which he drew an *X* for every completed Saturday class, much like prisoners mark off their days of incarceration. The class would start at eight o'clock sharp at the middle school and would have one break, which many used to grab a smoke. Lunch was a treat, and that ran from noon to one o'clock. Conniston Middle School is in south central West Palm and is dominated by working-class Cubans. One perk of the neighborhood is the availability of Cuban cuisine, which Nick loved. Across the street was a Cuban bakery with the best pastries that could be had, and across Southern Boulevard, south of the campus, was a large Publix supermarket. The locals called it "Cuplix" instead of Publix. In that store they had a deli that served fresh sandwiches, which to Nick meant a Cuban sandwich: ham, mojo pork, cheese, pickles, and mustard on a honey pressed roll. So good. Class itself was interesting with teachers who were in the same trenches as the students. They shared what was going on at their institutions, and the students reciprocated with their own stories. There was a lot of discussion and not much writing. Nick liked that.

Nick also observed that teachers continued to make the worst students as far as behavior went. They talked, were late or tardy, and came up with all kinds of excuses for why their papers were not ready to turn in, asking if they could have some extra time to finish up. They cheated on tests and sometimes skipped out after lunch. They did everything they complained that their own students did. Nick kept to himself mostly and tried to get as much grad schoolwork done there as he could because he was so busy after school with his own responsibilities. For the most part, it worked out well. The instructors sought him out for information about the previous night's game, for gossip about life at Forest Hill, or to chat, which was kind of an unofficial interview. Nick liked these people, and they liked him. Everyone loves a local boy who makes good and comes home and contributes. Nick was not sure if he wanted to be an administrator, but a couple of thousand extra dollars a year would sure help.

Some of Nick's friends slowly left the cruising circuit, which meant "looking for love in all the wrong places"—lyrics that Mickey Gilley immortalized in the movie *Urban Cowboy*. They were beginning to find their respective significant others. Nick Finch was so busy with coaching, moonlighting, and grad school that he had little time for formal romance. He had plenty of hookups with cocktail waitresses or female bartenders after a night of parking cars. They usually made it work when their children were with their respective ex-husbands that weekend. The thought of becoming a father gave Nick chills and being a dad to someone else's child was something he could not fathom, at least not yet. He did admire how these women made it work. Many regarded the restaurant profession, whatever it was, as a second job. They hurried back and forth, shuttling their children to and from school activities, then to the babysitter or a family member who was helping, and then went to their second job—day after day. They were remarkable. Nick found himself disgusted when he whined about how tough he had it with teaching, parking cars, and going to grad school. So, what if these women got a little love and affection? They sure as hell deserved it. And who was he to judge? Plus, the physical benefits were pretty good, and he learned some tricks from the more experienced women in terms of what they liked and when they liked it. He took mental notes. As a coach, one is trained never to stop learning or trying something new. Same with lovemaking. Practice does improve performance. Every coach will tell you that. Nick learned by watching these single moms, and he tried not to judge people because he had no idea what their home lives were like. When and if he got married and started a family, he sure as hell was going to do everything, he could and make it work.

Late one spring day, Jay Burbank said he needed to see Nick as soon as possible. It was 1987. Nick had found himself in a routine and needed something or someone to help him snap out of it. Jay, the trust fund baby, swung by the restaurant and parked his own car down the street a bit, then came up and took an empty folding chair next to Nick. Jay had pretty much disappeared from the gang as he was in a serious relationship with a rich and attractive young nurse by the name of Jane Campbell. Jane also had gone to the University of Florida and was also a trust fund baby whose self-made parents required her to hold a full-time job and earn a degree if she wished to continue receiving her stipend. Nick thought it was both cool and extremely smart, the plan they had set up for their daughter. The Campbells had made their initial fortune in cattle ranching. Many do not realize that Florida trails only Texas in beef production. The Campbells had large working ranches throughout the state. From there they branched out to phosphate mining, insurance, and banking. Mr. Campbell wore a big hat, but with the land and the money to fill it. Jane was given a large bonus and new car for a graduation present, and a clause in her trust stipulated that her parents would match her salary. On June 1 there would be a deposit in her name at the Campbell Bank in Okeechobee, then another on January 1. There were provisions regarding the type of job she could hold. For example, because she was a nurse, she was given more money. If she worked for the family business, she would be given less. The Campbells had made their money themselves and wanted their children to do the same, but they also wished to give them a hand, especially early in life, the is struggling years, so to speak.

Jay was quick to get to the point. He showed Nick the engagement ring he had purchased at Michael's Jewelry Store on Clematis in downtown West Palm. The ring was impressive. Next, he asked Nick if he would be a part of the wedding, adding that he would be honored if Nick would agree to be his best man. Nick's reply was quick and to the point: "Absolutely. Just tell me when and where." The wedding was scheduled for late summer in St. Augustine at Henry Flagler's old church. This was at least the sixth wedding Nick had been a part of. College fraternity brothers were the first group to get married. Nick loved going back to Mississippi for these events. And given that most of the guests were young and single—well, let's just say that a fun time was almost guaranteed with the young men dressed up in tuxes and the young women in evening wear. And the great music and open bar put almost everyone in the mood for some loving. Nick even noticed older guests had their fins up, so to speak. Weddings also meant engagement parties, where both sides lined up the talent. Also, there would be rehearsal dinners and, of course, bachelor and bachelorette parties.

Nick came up with a unique idea for Jay's party. He hated strip clubs, seeing them as demeaning and a complete rip-off. He also thought of his three sisters and just could not imagine one of them being up on that stage. Instead, Nick worked with a travel agent to get a group rate and arranged van transportation from West Palm to Port Everglades and back for a one-day Sea Escape Bahamas cruise. The fee would include a sit-down dinner, tickets to a show, unlimited gambling, and adjoining staterooms. Everyone loved the idea for the party, which would be great and classy, unlike the strip club scene. There was also a large group of travel agents booked for the same church, and both sides got to know each other before the end of the night. Some guys made some money at blackjack. Most lost money but still had fun. All in all, it was a great time, and everyone agreed that what happened on the ship would stay on the ship.

The following week, it was up to St. Augustine for the wedding. Apparently, this was not a Saturday only event but a full week of activities in "America's Oldest City". The entire top floor of the ocean-side hotel was booked for the groom, the best man, and the groomsmen. There was one room at the end of the floor that was manned by a twenty-four-hour assistant, or valet, with a well-stocked refrigerator and bar. He was there to assist and provide anything the gentlemen might need. If it was not there, he could get it. The parents tipped the two men generously for their service. One of the groomsmen privately asked where he could get some weed, and lo and behold, an hour later there was a knock on the door and an envelope slid under it that had about ten perfectly rolled joints for his recreational pleasure. Such is the life of the Florida elite. This group was much different from the Palm Beach elite as this group was almost always homegrown and self-made, in this case through the legal system and the agribusiness empire, which is how the Burbank's and the Campbell's had amassed their fortunes. Palm Beechers made their fortunes usually up north, most likely New York, or they inherited it "old money". Florida elite kept themselves to a small circle that included business leaders, politicians, and those in the education field. It is no wonder that so many of Florida's college presidents' former occupations were in private business, law, or public service. It is still that way today. They get together at private and public events and especially enjoy the merging of the families through marriage, including all the pomp and circumstance that surrounds such an event. Jay's wedding was no different.

The bride and her bridesmaids would be sequestered in the private residence of a wealthy family located close to Flagler College. The first time the two parties would get together would be at the rehearsal at the church and the dinner to follow. Most of the week for the guys included pool and beach time to work on the suntans they would need to accent their tuxedos; golf; tennis; and fishing. It was like an all-expenses-paid vacation. Sweet. The only thing expected of them was to show up on time at the proper venue and be sober. Once the "I dos" are proclaimed, let the party begin. The hotel party room at the end of the hall was great, and they took advantage to the point that Nick started to decline invitations to engage in debauchery. He needed to work on his best man's toast, which he would deliver to the guests and wedding party. He loved to speak in public as he did it every day, but also, he would read scripture at church and emcee different events. Public speaking did not frighten him as it did so many. He read that the number one fear for high school students was public speaking; second on the list was death.

Nick surmised that his own students would rather die than speak in front of a crowd. He could not understand that. He would assign oral reports and work with his kids on strategies for overcoming their fears, and for the most part he was successful. Watching them overcome their fear from the back of the room, where he was sporting a wide, convincing "you can do it" smile, was the strategy that he almost always found to be successful. When they finished with something like Lincoln's Gettysburg Address, he would cue the class to deliver a round of applause, accompanied by the wink of an eye. A smile of relief from the presenter almost always followed. This speech would no different, except some of the guests were old enough to have been at Gettysburg when Lincoln delivered his famous speech, and some were almost as famous. Nick had better be ready.

The formal wedding went off without a hitch as everything was tight and on time. The wedding parties looked fabulous in their formal wear: classic black tie for the men and powder blue for the women. After the ceremony and photograph session, the wedding party boarded a luxury yacht and took the short trip to the St. Augustine–De Leon Yacht and Fishing Club for the reception. To kick off the party, the father of the bride had special water poured into the wedding party's champagne glasses for an introductory toast. He notified the guests that the water had come from Ponce de León's secret Fountain of Youth and that the drink would keep the couple young at heart throughout their marriage. Two things about this little event: Nick saw the waitstaff pour Zephyr Hills bottled water into the pitcher that had the markings of Spanish colonial royalty engraved on the sides, and the marriage of Jane and Jay Campbell would last less than ten years. Oh well.

Food and drink followed, and there was an unlimited supply of both. The band played everything from Frank Sinatra to Billy Idol.

Soon everybody was whisked back to their seats as it was time for the best man's toast. Nick was working on a good buzz as he made his way back to the dais or head table for his performance. He had in his pocket a small note card with cues for what to say and whom to thank, mixed in with a jab or two. As he walked up, an old friend and neighbor gave him a small shot glass of liquid courage, otherwise known as tequila. Richard Henry was also a trust fund baby, and he needed to be one because his life was always on the edge as he went in search of the perfect party with a drink in his hand and a nose for the best cocaine. Nick looked at Richard, thanked him, and slugged down the Mexican import.

Suddenly things began to change. The room became a little fuzzy; Nick started walking as if he were wearing large clown shoes; and his tongue felt ten feet wide. He got to his destination; pulled out his note card, which made no sense at all now; and gazed at the guests, who were awaiting his humor and pearls of wisdom. These never came. The impressive list of guests was a who's who of Florida. Staring at him was governor and former mayor of Tampa Bob Martinez; former governor and senator Bob Graham, bright red nose, and all; UF president Marshall Criser; and "Walkin' Lawton" himself, Lawton Childs.

Brian Parker, also a groomsman, noticed the snafu and whispered in Nick's ear, asking if everything was OK. Nick turned, looked at him, nodded, kind of grinned, raised his glass to the awaiting wedding party and invitees, and stated firmly and loudly, "Hey, how about it!" He then took a swig of the champagne.

The crowd, stunned, composed themselves and responded in unison, "Hey, how about it!" The worst ever best man's toast was over. In a way, it became legend as to this day all the guys and many of the guests who were in attendance that evening will give the same toast at all their special occasions. It is usually followed by the backstory of said speech.

It was Nick's time to get on with his life, terrible toast notwithstanding.

CHAPTER

10

Growing Up and Maturing is Very Hard, Especially in South Florida—Just Ask The Locals

A popular offbeat TV show during this time was "Pee-wee's Playhouse" which was a takeoff on 1950s children's TV programming, with a lifelong childlike man much in the spirit of Peter Pan. A popular cultlike movie was made from the series, called "*Pee-wee's Big Adventure*," starring a Floridian by the name of Paul Ruebens. Never grow up and stay innocent and look at life through the lens of a 13-year-old. Forever. Fight off the temptation of growing up and continue to live for the weekend. Today this generation that is Nick Finch's is extremely critical of millennials and generation X, Y, or Z or whatever in vogue letter tag they attach to the young professionals of today.

If they look close at themselves and remembered their lifestyle choices when they were in their twenties, they might be surprised to see they were basically living like the ones they critique now. It is hard to grow up and take on adult responsibilities and interpersonal relationships such as marriage and parenthood, all while growing in one's profession and making responsible decisions. All that means no more keg headstands, last-minute road trips, or one-night romances. Say it's not so. The horror. I must grow up! Many accept the challenge; some move on and then later take on the challenge; while a few never grow up and embrace the Pee-wee lifestyle that is adolescence forever. But most find the in-between time a trial-and-error period. Such was the case for Nick Finch. What made it hard for him to grow up was that the South Florida environment he was living in catered to both retirees and single twenty-somethings and left out most of the population.

Teaching was always challenging, but Nick found it was getting easier. Every day he was more comfortable in the classroom. Grad school was getting to be a chore, attending class every Saturday and on Tuesday and Thursday evenings, making it tough to juggle his work coaching, parking cars, and teaching. He also had to check in on his mom at least nightly by way of phone, and he made a point of stopping by on the weekend as the two still went to church together every Sunday, followed by breakfast. Growing up, he had learned to tune out parts of the church service, especially long-winded sermons, and swore that once he was on his own, first at college and then when he returned home, he would exercise his God-given right to say no to organized religion. He never did.

While at Ole Miss, Nick attended the Sunday evening service for college students only. It didn't hurt that they provided a home-cooked supper after the service, which meant meat loaf, roast beef, or fried chicken and all the fixings. This was a great perk and was welcome relief from his usual diet of pizza for breakfast, nothing for lunch, and wings and beer for dinner. One of the things that reinforced religion for Nick was a class he took called Religion in the South. The course description matched up with the reality of the class, which many times is not the case. There were some twenty students in the class, juniors and seniors, whose majors were sociology, social work, health care, and psychology—and for Nick, history. The class was divided up into traveling groups of four or five by a blind lottery drawing, and then each group had to set up a meeting with the clergy of the church they would visit, interview the staff about the nuts and bolts of their faith and their congregation, and then attend a Sunday service. After the visitation, the students would present to their classmates a report of whom they had seen, what they had seen, and their overall impression of the experience. As the course would go on, they would have the component of comparing earlier-visited churches to their most recent visitation.

Nick was fascinated by the many ways and methods of teaching and preaching the Good Word. He found that for certain Protestant faiths, Sunday was not a day of rest but of intense worship, singing, stewardship, and eating. He and his classmates were always welcomed and appreciated. He marveled at the deep devotion that black congregations demonstrated. Despite all the societal setbacks they had endured, the church was a refuge full of love and compassion.

On one Sunday, Nick was witnessing a remarkable development in one of the more prestigious churches in Oxford that would have made local legend William Faulkner proud. The pastor of the church was finishing up his sermon about God's being the only true judge of character and the admonishment: "He who is without sin, cast the first stone." As he finished, he looked out at the assembled congregation and gave a full and complete confession that would have made any Roman Catholic, whose faith includes both public and private confession, blush. The tan, well-dressed minister with the perfect hair who very much resembled the young Palm Beach native George Hamilton took a deep breath. After a moment or two, he composed himself and continued. Nick, who was doodling on the service leaflet, sat up and took notice of the event that followed, one that is still talked about by the locals of the Oxford community. The preacher looked out at his flock and started out by confessing that he had broken his marriage vows, not once but many times. Nick was witnessing in person an event like those that seemed to be happening all the time on TV with the likes of Jim and Tammy Faye Bakker and Jimmy Swaggart. The minister continued, saying that he had fallen in love with the church bookkeeper and they could no longer hold back their feelings for each other. Then the remarkable part was delivered, if the foregoing alone hadn't been not enough.

He scolded and lectured his listeners, "And I know a lot of you think you know it all. You do not. I have heard the whispers and the nasty little things you say under your breath as if I cannot hear them. Well, let me tell you, there are five other women here today whom I have also sinned with in a carnal way. So, gentlemen, look and wonder if your wife is one of them. Now, I am out of here!"

The audience shocked let out a loud gasp. One well-dressed gentleman hollered out, "Good Lord, what is wrong with you, man?"

The preacher was now at the side door of the massive sanctuary. He turned and looked back at the stunned congregation, then shouted, "See you later. And praise the Lord!" With that he jumped into a waiting car with his new love interest and sped away, never to return. Wow. An earlier group was jealous that Nick and his group had witnessed firsthand the talk of the town. When they had gone to visit that church, they thought they had seen everything when the same preacher warned his congregation, he was going to post on the church door all the members who subscribed to such filthy magazines as *Playboy* and *Penthouse.* The congregants had one week to cancel, or he would post the list that had been provided to him by the local postmaster. What a place of faith. And wow again.

Nick's Sundays with Charlene were a nice break from a very hectic week. She also lightened up on the interrogations about his love life, which in the past had dominated the first few moments of their meetings. She now had a church group nicknamed the Widows' Club, and they often socialized together. They would book trips together to Las Vegas that Larry Timmons helped plan. They also went on an Alaskan cruise and a two-week trip to Europe. Charlene was going to see places that she had put off seeing because of marriage, family, and work commitments. Good for her. There were a couple of gentleman callers whom Charlene quickly dismissed, politely explaining that she was happy and content, having been blessed by many years with a loving husband, and nothing was going to spoil those memories. Her sister-in-law, J.W.'s sister, brought her husband everywhere with her, which would not have been unusual except he had been dead for ten years. You see, it was her husband's ashes, in an urn, that she took everywhere—church, social events, and reunions. That is devoted love.

When Nick got the time, he would go to the favorite late-night hangout on Palm Beach named E. R. Bradley's. The bar was named after a larger-than-life gambling legend who split his time between his casino here and the ponies, wherever they were racing. Gambling was, of course, illegal in Palm Beach County, but that was more a suggestion than a law. Punchboards were found in many of the small stores and barbershops, where for one dollar you could punch out a potential prize. Much like with today's lottery, there were just enough winners to keep people coming back for another chance. Miami had both jai alai and the famous Hialeah horse racing track. The county would follow up by allowing the Palm Beach Kennel Club to be built for dog racing. That establishment was owned and operated by the famous Rooney family of Pittsburgh Steelers fame. Also, the West Palm Beach Jai Alai Fronton opened on

Forty-Fifth Street. Later, after it closed, the building was purchased by the famous boxing promoter Don King. It is still there, but it's vacant, although there is a train stop at that location. E. R. Bradley's was nearly a perfect place to go. It was safe and clean, and captured the interest of a young and attractive clientele. A neat little novelty they had there was a large block of ice that was molded into what looked like a four-foot miniature ski jumping venue. There were no skiers, but for the price of a shot of liquor, usually vodka, tequila, or Jack Daniel's, the patron would place his or her mouth at the foot of the man-made slope, and the beautiful slope operator, in costume, would poor the liquid from the top of the ice sculpture into the waiting customer's mouth. Sanitary? No. But fun? Yes.

One Saturday night, Nick had brought a change of clothes, a toothbrush, and some mouthwash and cleaned up at quitting time in Nando's bathroom. It was maybe a mile to Bradley's, where he would meet up with some of his friends for a drink or two. He had a large wad of bills, mostly ones, so he put a twenty on each side of his clip of cash. To the unknowing, it looked as if Nick was loaded with money, when in reality he had about seventy-five dollars on him.

That one particular evening at Bradley's, Nick met a young woman who would really expand his horizons in terms of travel and experiences. There was a group of three attractive young women seated at the bar in near proximity to the "shot slope". Nick was there, along with first-year assistant state attorney Brian Parker, who had graduated from Miami Law and now had entered the world of jurisprudence. Nick bellied up to the bar and ordered a bourbon and water, when one of the attractive women started up a conversation with him. He learned that her name was Michelle Mitchel, but her close friends called her Mitch. She was down from New York City, staying at her parents' place in an exceedingly high-rent district of the south-central beach area known as Gulf Stream. Michelle had felt the need to get out of the cold, dark city for a while, and her parents invited her and her friends down for the long Presidents' Day weekend. She now was neglecting her guests and focusing on the young man next to her. She mentioned something about the combination of drink choice and slight southern accent, saying that he must have been from the South. He concurred but corrected her, saying that if she thought he was southern, she needed to meet some of his fraternity brothers or South Carolina cousins. Nick learned that Michelle had graduated from Smith College, worked for NBC at Rockefeller Plaza, and lived in a Midtown apartment within walking distance to work. She had grown up Greenwich, Connecticut, and went to a private all-girls' prep school, where she had played tennis and field hockey.

Pretty soon the two were deep in a private conversation and ignoring both sets of guests. When the bar flicked its lights on and off, notifying the patrons it was time to go, Nick walked Michelle to her car. Her two friends had gone ahead to give the two a few moments alone. He leaned forward to give her a quick kiss on the cheek as a gentleman would do, and immediately she took charge, took his face in her soft hands, and changed the polite peck to a full-blown lip-on-lip kiss with an exchange of tongues that lasted a good minute. The two exchanged phone numbers and promised to keep in touch. To Nick's surprise, the next day, Sunday, he answered his phone and found Michelle was on the other end. She had reached out to him first, which was a first for him. According to how he had grown up, the man always initiated the first contact.

Nick and Michelle talked, laughed, and shared a really fun conversation. Unfortunately, she had to fly out of Palm Beach International Airport (PBIA) first thing the next morning, but she made it clear that she hoped this would not be the last time the two would talk, adding that they needed to make it a real date when she came back for the Easter season. There was something about her, other than her incredibly good looks, that Nick really liked. She was confident without being obnoxious. Immediately after the phone call ended, Nick went back to writing a paper for grad school for a class he was taking called Educational Finance. Yes, the class was as bad as its title, but it was a mandatory course teaching students how to find out the source and the implementation of a school's and a district's funding. When he finished the paper, he decided to change the narrative on this potential new relationship with this New York woman just a little. He picked up the phone and called her New York number, knowing good and well she would not be there yet. Sure enough, an answering machine clicked on. He left a message expressing how much he had enjoyed meeting her and talking to her, adding that he was eagerly awaiting her return to South Florida. He hoped that when she put down her bags and checked her messages, she would hear his voice on the machine.

On Monday night, Nick's home phone rang. It was Michelle on the other end, saying that it had made her day to have heard from him. Nick grinned as he realized his plan had worked. After that, they made a point of trying to talk to each other when their schedules allowed. From then on, there always seemed to be a blinking light on his machine when he got back from school. It was nice. Even better, Michelle had informed him that she could not wait until Easter; she had booked a round-trip ticket to Palm Beach in two weeks. There would be no car parking that weekend for Nick as he cleared his schedule for her and allowed for nothing else. He found himself shaking his head, feeling like he was back in high school with the phone calls and pleasant conversations the two had together.

Once Michelle was in town, Nick took her to Nando's, and for once he was a patron and not the valet. They also went to the beach and walked down Worth Avenue together, window-shopping. He met her parents, who were polite and standoffish, the mom more so than the dad, who was always either going to or coming back from the tennis courts. Mom looked as if she could be related to Lilly Pulitzer with her print outfits. Neither wore their sweaters but put them over their shoulders, tying the arms together at the collarbone. Nick had noticed more and more that this must have been an "up north thing."

Michelle had told her parents that Nick had agreed to take her to the airport Sunday afternoon for her return to New York and NBC. She gave her mom and dad a kiss on the cheek and got into Nick's new car. It was preowned, but it was new to him. He had traded in his VW convertible and had bought a jet-black Nissan 300Z with a T-top and state-of-the-art AM/FM cassette stereo. As the two entered I-95 headed for PBIA, Michelle was grinning from ear to ear. She said, "I lied to my parents. My flight is tomorrow. Let's go to your place instead." Nick immediately exited the interstate. For the next twenty-four hours, they holed up in his apartment. He even called in to say that he would be missing Monday and got a substitute to show a movie. He would be busy.

Nick made sure that after he dropped Michelle off at the airport he called and left a message on her answering machine. He was proud of that initial strategy and of how well it worked. Now it was his turn. Later that week, as they were talking on the phone, he suggested that he return the favor and make it up to the Big Apple. Her response was to shriek loudly and say yes. Now, Nick Finch did not have the disposable cash that apparently Michelle had, but he went over to PBIA the next Thursday morning, as he would take both Thursday and Friday off, and bought a round-trip ticket on a low-cost airline that went by the name of People's Express. It was like a Greyhound bus but in the air. You boarded and then paid for your ticket with your credit card as the flight attendant brought a handheld charge plate, sliding the bar on the machine back and forth to get a carbon copy of the charge card on the sales slip.

The trip would not be glamourous, but it was affordable. After landing at the Newark airport, he took a cab to Rockefeller Plaza, where he would meet up with Michelle at the outdoor restaurant next to the ice rink. They shared a quick kiss, then she turned him around to wave to the people looking out their windows at their colleague's new boyfriend from Florida. She gave him directions to her apartment five blocks away and handed him a key that she had had made for him. They would meet up immediately after she got off work, when she had a big surprise for him.

It was only noon when Nick, by himself, walked up the three floors of stairs to apartment 3B and opened the door. He walked in, put down the one bag he had brought with him, and removed his blazer. Nick would always travel with a blazer when flying, not only for the sharp look but also for the four extra pockets it afforded. He looked around and found the apartment neat and clean with plenty of family pictures, magazines like *Cosmopolitan*, and some Playbill programs from Broadway plays Michelle had attended. Her answering machine was blinking, and it took all the willpower he had not to listen to the message. There was another thing: the place was small, very small. He couldn't find the bedroom because there wasn't one. He learned that she had an uncomfortable Murphy bed that pulled down from the wall, so the living room would immediately become the bedroom. The refrigerator was not much bigger than the one he had had in his fraternity house bedroom. There was one small sink, and the bathroom and shower space was not much bigger than a phone booth. There was a new bottle of Jim Beam with a big heart and a welcome message on some scratch paper. "Enjoy. I will be home ASAP" was written on the paper.

Nick had showered the best he could in the limited space of the bathroom. He found a little room for his shave kit. He put on some jeans, a white button-down starched shirt, sockless penny loafers, and his blazer and went out for a walk. Time to explore the neighborhood. It was kind of cool with little restaurants, pizzerias, bars, and shops. He also he noticed it got dark a lot earlier in New York than it did back home. It was also very loud and crowded. Nearly everyone looked to be in a hurry, as if they were running late to something important. After a walk of about three blocks, he popped into a small alley-like bar that had a TV playing, was decorated with framed newspaper headlines of the past, and had a long dark oak or mahogany bar that fronted a mirrored wall with bottles of liquor organized according to brand and type. At the bar there were three or four groups of two separated by an empty seat. Nick took a seat by himself at the end of the bar next to the entrance, when a large round man with a white apron came over and, in a thick New York accent, inquired, "What will it be, buddy?" Nick answered that he would like a Jim Beam and water. Suddenly, the entire bar of about ten people looked at the new customer as if there was some sort of embarrassing defect to his body. The bartender nodded and, with a quizzical look, asked, "You are not from here. So where are you from?" Before Nick could answer, the patrons started a game that had turned their attention away from the TV, which was showing *The Price Is Right.* Bob Barker and the pretty models were no longer important; what was important was finding out where in the hell this guy was from. Next, Nick saw everyone throwing down five dollars, openly betting on the stranger's origin. Before Nick could answer, the bartender brought his index finger to his mouth to tell him to be quiet so as let the wagering continue. The groups quickly discussed their wagers and wrote them down on a piece of paper. Then the bartender gave Nick permission to speak. He said firmly and loudly, as he had to compete with the studio announcer on the TV, which was blasting, saying, "Come on down. You are the next contestant on *The Price Is Right*."

"Florida. Palm Beach." There was one winner, while the others openly complained about the authenticity and believability of the answer. Nick grinned at the new sport, Tourist Origins. He found out the other guesses they had written down were South Carolina, Alabama, and New Orleans—not Louisiana, but New Orleans. They waved him down to join them, making introduction. Some shook hands with Nick, while others nodded in approval. Then the betting continued. Who would win the final showcase or the last bid on today's episode of *The Price Is Right*? Nick paid his tab and headed back out as now it was getting dark and cold and he wanted to be back to Michelle's apartment before she arrived after her day of work. He beat her by ten minutes. As she explained, her boss had let her leave early since her new boyfriend was in town visiting.

When Michelle arrived back at her place, Nick was stunned by her appearance. She looked very professional and mature with a plaid skirt, matching sweater, and high leather boots. She took Nick's breath away. All he could get out was, "Wow!"

She explained she had been caught a few times that day by her immediate boss and some of her coworkers staring blankly at the clock and doodling nonsense on any piece of paper nearby. She said she used to do the same thing in high school and again at Smith College when taking history classes. Nick reminded his new girlfriend that he was a history teacher, adding that she would not be wasting her time in his class. She asked him where exactly he would have her sit if she were his student, then walked across the room and sat directly on Nick's lap. They kissed. He explained that this behavior would mean she would have detention with him after school. Continuing to playact, she, doing her best Valley girl impersonation, stated much more like a Californian than a northeasterner, "Well, if I have to. I mean, I guess, for sure, Mr. Finch." She then rolled her eyes with an expression of *This is such a waste of my valuable time.* Nick could not stop laughing. It was cute and fun. Moon Unit Zappa had nothing on Michelle Mitchell. It was a lot of things, but sexy was at the top of the list.

Soon, Michelle took Nick to a local bistro for dinner and told him not to order too much as they would have dessert at a different location that was famous for its cheesecake. They laughed and talked throughout the night. It came quite easy to both. Nick finally learned what Michelle did other than working for NBC. She was an account executive and was qualified for the job with her impressive college degree and the connections of her Madison Avenue advertising mogul father. Nick learned she made almost three times as much as he did. He was impressed and not jealous at all. He also learned she paid three times as much for her storage unit of an apartment as Nick did for a two-bedroom, one bedroom of which he had converted into a study, with amenities such as a pool, car washing station, and fitness room. Michelle really had only one room that was divided by partitions and curtains. She explained that the key was her location and the fact that she could walk to work safely and not have to ride the subway or hail an expensive cab. Both modes of transportation could also be creepy, she said.

At dinner she broke out her surprise, Nick's reward for having flown up to see her: tickets to *Saturday Night Live*.

Arriving at NBC Studios, which hosted *SNL*, at a quarter to eleven, they found the crew was busy cleaning up from their dress rehearsal in front of a live audience also, but with two extra skits. The audience's response would determine which skits would make the final cut for the show the entire nation would watch. The night's musical performers, along with the house band, were also running their numbers and doing sound checks. Nick was fascinated by the whole setup and teardown and by the organized chaos that seemed to follow a plan. It reminded him of the pregame procedures for a football game—offense, defense, special teams, cheerleaders, and of course the band.

For *SNL*, this was the time for round two after the groundbreaking original history-making cast of Chevy Chase, John Belushi, Dan Aykroyd, Gilda Radner, and the other, whose footprints remain to this day. This new cast was also very impressive, with comics such as Dana Garvey, Eddie Murphy, Jon Lovitz, and Dennis Miller, who did the news. There was excitement in the air as the NBC stage crew went over the ground rules with the audience. They were there to laugh and provide support but not be part of the show. Fair enough. Nick also noticed just how small the actual theater was. He looked and surmised there were no more than one hundred people in attendance.

This is going to be cool, he thought. And it got better when Michelle produced two tickets to the after-show cast party. One of the perks of working at NBC and a having a high-powered advertising executive for a father who in a way paid for everything. What were two tickets to an NBC show? The show's guest host was an A-list Hollywood movie star who by his own account was scared to death because, as he explained, he was not an actor but a movie star, and there is a big difference. Actors work on stage with a live audience, whereas movie stars are on sound stages or on location, and almost all scenes can be done over. Not so onstage or live TV. News got back to Michelle that the star was so overcome with anxiety that he had locked himself in his dressing room until somebody brought him some weed to calm his nerves. Nick shook his head in disbelief and waited for the inevitable disaster that was about to happen. It never happened. Was it the "pregame meal," or had the star risen to the occasion? No matter what it was, it worked.

After the show, Nick and Michelle made their way to the cast party, where, sure enough, the star was busy hitting a bong. Nick noticed it was not unlike a postgame locker room. The cast members all had different reactions to the performance. Some liked the show, while others were hard on themselves. Some of the most well-known comics who made up the cast were very withdrawn. The English punk band that had played two songs—what was loud noise—came in with their entourage of young women and men with noticeably big arms and tight shirts, even though NBC provided tight security with off-duty NYPD officers, who had been reminded that whatever happened at the party should stay at the party. No page 6 material should emerge. Ever. Still, the band had brought their own security.

Michelle and Nick were welcomed by the entertainment host, who whispered something in Michelle's ear. Nick did not like that, but Michelle assured him it was nothing, adding that she would explain at the first opportunity once they were alone. He later learned that the host had reminded Michelle that Nick was not to have a camera or other recording device and that the two of them should speak to the stars only if they were spoken to.

Honestly, the party was dull as the cast was coming down from a performance high. Many left early. Nick and Michelle did not stay till the end as both were getting tired and Nick had a midmorning flight back to Palm Beach from Newark. They thanked the host and returned to Michelle's apartment for some alone time.

Two more times Nick would return to New York, and Michelle came south on three different occasions. It was becoming more and more difficult for Nick because of the travel and the missed work, never mind his grad school responsibilities. They both began to realize that maybe this was not meant to be. Charlene, the biggest critic of Nick's love life, liked Michelle, but with reservations that, of course, she shared with her son. She said that long-distance relationships were impossible and that the fact the two came from completely different family backgrounds would make things difficult. She also said she could never see Nick living in the city. She was right of course, as always, but Nick himself had already seen the end in sight. A trip to the Mitchell family home in Connecticut would prove that his mom was spot on.

Nick and Michelle had been invited to Greenwich so Nick could meet her family and friends. Quickly, Mrs. Mitchell made it clear to invitees to the wine and cocktail party that Nick Finch was from West Palm Beach and not Palm Beach but apparently came from a good, hardworking family. Whatever that meant. He met Michelle's ex-boyfriend, who had been giving Nick the "stink eye" all evening. Nick was taken aback by the introduction given by Michelle's mother and the stare he was getting from Trey, who had saddled up to the bar and was making conversation with Mr. Mitchell. Having had enough of this, Nick walked right over to Trey and extended his hand to the Harvard grad. Trey looked at the extended hand, shook it, and turned back around, mumbling something about staying among those of one's own social class, adding something about Nick's southern roots. Mr. Mitchell, who had witnessed the whole spectacle, got nervous and excused himself to go see if his wife needed a hand in the kitchen. That was a bullshit reason; Nick doubted Mrs. Mitchell even knew where the kitchen was. Michelle had witnessed the entire exchange and came running to her boyfriend's rescue. She also realized that there was not much left in the tank between her and Nick, but she did love him, kind of, and what she had seen was deplorable. Nick was not sure if he was going to dole out a southern ass whipping or laugh it off as being the desperate act of a spoiled and entitled prick who could not come to grips with the fact that he had lost out to a southern schoolteacher. Plus, Trey was in uniform, wearing his sweater over his shoulders and the collar of his polo shirt up like every other male there that night.

Michelle took her boyfriend's hand and requested that he accompany her outside for a breath of fresh air. As she turned around to leave, she left an impression on Trey when she ground the heel of her shoe right into his foot. He let out a pathetic whimper and said something sarcastic while she was exiting, using the word *bitch*. Nick and Michelle walked out to the barn, or stable as they called it, where the equestrian ponies were kept. She kept apologizing for everything that had occurred during the evening. At least five times she told Nick he was better than anyone at the party.

The next morning, Nick got up first, having slept in the guest room. He showered and made his way to the kitchen, where Mrs. Mitchell was seated reading the Leisure and Travel section of the *New York Times*. Nick sat down and declined the cup of coffee that he'd been offered by one of the help. Nick never drank coffee. He thought it looked like brackish canal water and had never acquired a taste for the beverage that his parents would inhale all day long.

After an awkward extended silence between them, Mrs. Mitchell peered from behind her paper and blurted out, "You know, this will never work out. The two of you,

I mean. It's cute that you make her happy, but you two are too different in the important ways that make for a successful partnership of marriage."

Partnership of marriage? What the hell does that mean? Nick knew that he was not society page material, which is what the Mitchells wanted for their daughter. Nick, saying not a word, excused himself from the kitchen table and went for a jog to clear his head. When he got back, Michelle was waiting for him on the front porch. She told him that she was sick and tired of being home and wanted to head back to the city. She suggested they leave. As they got into the Jeep Wagoneer that would take them to the train, Mr. Mitchell, able to sense the tension among his family, got ready to put the SUV in gear and head to the depot.

Mrs. Mitchell seemed to appear out of nowhere to wish them safe travels back to the city and, for Nick, back to Florida. She leaned forward and whispered into Nick's ear, "Remember what we discussed. It will never work." Michelle knew this could not be good. She gave her mother the death stare.

Nick returned a whisper to the mother: "Mrs. Mitchell, I think we have to get married because Michelle thinks she is pregnant."

The mom stumbled back, shook her head in disbelief, and returned her daughter's death stare. She followed up with, "How could you, Michelle? How in God's name could you let this happen?"

The car was now coming up on the train station. Michelle quietly asked what Nick had told her mother.

Nick pulled her to the side to reply, after checking to make sure her father could not hear him. "I told her you were pregnant and we have to get married."

Michelle looked right at her soon-to-be ex-boyfriend and cracked the biggest smile. She hollered out, "Yes, I love it!" and continued laughing. Even her dad mentioned that he loved it when his daughter laughed. Somehow Nick was able to pull that emotion out of her, and for that her father thanked him. Nick nodded in agreement. If only he knew the reason for the laughter.

The two rode in virtual silence on the train from Connecticut into the city. Nick worked on a paper about curriculum development, while Michelle opened her impressive briefcase and began to work on accounts. Almost all the passengers were quiet, reading, working, or just staring out the window. The two looked like the ultimate preppy couple as they worked away, half concentrating on their tasks while contemplating their future together. Both, without saying it, knew it was the end of the line for their relationship. Nick thought about if he could teach in NYC or even in Connecticut or New Jersey, and he knew he just could not do it. Michelle's brain raced back and forth, wondering if she could possibly in South Florida and likely concluding, *No way. I love my career and the all the city has to offer.* One thing she was sure of though: her mother would not plan out or dictate her life. Not now, not ever.

This would be it for the young couple, and it hurt. It was not devastating. Actually, it was kind of funny for Nick and Michelle, thinking of the horror that Mrs. Mitchell was going through in her luxurious suburban home. That unwitnessed scene brought a smile to both their faces, but especially Michelle's, who could not wait to share it with her friends and coworkers. She kept that episode close to her heart. And it did have a lasting effect on her mom as she never again interfered with her daughter's love life.

It was noonish when they arrived back in Midtown. They decided to go over to Central Park for a walk and a talk. It was a late spring day, and the weather was breathtaking. Many people were out to enjoy it as they knew it could change in an instant. Both Nick and Michelle knew it was the end. They found a park bench and sat down to speak about the elephant in the room. They really liked each other and maybe even loved each other. Who knew, as that final commitment was territory neither had ever traveled before. Michelle and Nick each talked about the obvious. She had a six-figure salary and a bright future in the broadcasting business, and she loved her tiny apartment, the location, and all the choices. Nick was a Florida boy, born and bred; he loved teaching; and he knew deep down it was his responsibility to take care of his widowed mom. They also discussed but dismissed the idea of keeping what they had going in terms of their long-distance relationship. They agreed to a clean break, but Michelle was going to keep her mom guessing for a while as a lesson to her. She thought about, but decided against, getting a little bump from the props and wardrobe department at NBC to increase her mom's anxiety. And in fact, when they got back to her place after the train trip, Michelle's answering machine had four messages on it from her mother. "We've got to talk" was the first one. The second one was the same, except the word *please* was added at the end.

The last two were hang-ups. Nick thought that perhaps the joke had been too much, but Michelle's response was quick and to the point: "Hell no!"

As Nick and Michelle were simultaneously finishing up their walk and their relationship, still smiling and holding hands, a mime in costume jumped right in front of them and began to do his entire act for them. Nick forced a smile and even nodded as a hint for the artist to move on. The mime would have nothing to do with it. To him this was his job, and the Central Park sidewalk was his stage. They saw it all. First, he was trapped in a box, then standing on a tightrope losing his balance, and then the wind began to blow him away. At first Nick was amused, but soon he was annoyed. Michelle stepped away to let her now ex-boyfriend take care of this. This was all new to the Floridian. If this guy were to try the same thing in certain South Florida areas, he would be looking for his teeth.

Nick asked him not once, but twice, to leave them alone. The actor's response was to mime a sad face, now with tears streaming down. Nick now questioned out loud, "What the hell is your problem? Go away." The whole scene was beginning to become a spectacle. Michelle whispered in Nick's ear to inform him of the proper protocol, which was to tip the actor for his craft. Nick looked at her, stunned. "Wait a minute. I am supposed to pay this annoying idiot so he will stop bothering us?" He rolled his eyes and thought about the "wheelchair swim" and how something like that would be appropriate right now. Then a brilliant idea came to his mind, not as good as the false pregnancy alarm from earlier that day, but close. Nick acknowledged the man, his craft, and his white and black costume with all the facial makeup, then smirked and moved his hand toward his back pocket very deliberately. The mime was about to earn his pay for his performance, or so he thought. The whole thing had now caught the attention of everyone close to the situation. Nick smiled at the performer as he reached toward his pocket, but his hand emerged with an invisible wallet, which he mimed to be opening. Then he completed his act by miming pulling out some invisible cash and handing it over to the awaiting performer. The nearby crowd roared with approval.

Immediately, the man in the black pants and face paint left character and spoke in for the first time. "Hey, buddy, go fuck yourself!" The audience applauded as Nick took a bow. The mime disappeared. To this day, Nick Finch rates that as one of his greatest feats. He made a mime not only talk but tell him to go forth and fornicate by himself. Success! The event does not have the staying power of the world's worst "Best man's toast", but it is in the team picture for so many reasons, not the least of which was the fact that it was part of the final goodbye to Michelle Mitchell. She still brings a smile to his face, and for all the right reasons. And he hopes she smiles when she thinks about him.

For Nick, it was back to the real world in many ways. He had a decided on the flight back that something had to give. He was stretched too thin, so something had to go. What ultimately went was coaching football. Nick had enjoyed his time coaching on the gridiron, and he did realize it had helped him to get his teaching job in the first place, but what with grad school, a possible career shift to administration, side jobs, his family duties, and a social life, this was the one thing he had some control over. He did the proper thing and went into Bobby Newcombe's office to let him know his decision and the reason for it. The principal asked him to shut the door behind him. Nick had noticed kind of a somber mood when he arrived, including what appeared to be a very upset secretary. Mrs. Ryles, the principal's secretary, just nodded and waved him in. She had a tissue and was using it to dab at her eyes as if to wipe away tears.

Mr. Newcombe was busy and with his back to Nick, taking some mementos and pictures off the wall. He turned around and looked to the young educator who, he privately told people, was one of his best hires and point-blank asked, "What's up?" Nick quickly dropped his resignation letter on the desk, in which he thanked everyone involved for the experience of coaching football and said how much he had learned and how much he loved the experience. He backed up the thoughts expressed in the letter by giving his boss a quick rundown of why he was leaving, something he had rehearsed. Even though he was very comfortable with Bobby Newcombe, who was his dad's good friend, he was still his boss. And Bobby could be intimidating. The principal, also a former football coach and athletic director, listened and agreed with the history teacher. He shared with Nick, who would be the first to know, apart from those who worked in the front office, that he would be retiring and not returning for the next school year. He made Nick swear to keep silent on the matter as he wanted to invite anyone who was interested to come over to the school tomorrow, when he would tell them of his decision in person. And seeing as it was summer break, he at least wanted the opportunity to say goodbye to his staff. He would also be sending out a letter later that day.

Nick, stunned, remained silent as he listened. When Bobby was finished, Nick went over to the man who had gone out on a limb and broken protocol to hire him and extended his hand for a farewell handshake. The former combat marine looked at the hand and, instead of shaking it, grabbed his young teacher in a bear hug, wished him luck, and told him how proud his dad would have been of him. Now it was Nick's turn to get teary-eyed. He left the office and asked for a tissue, which was already waiting in the extended hand of Mrs. Ryles. He left stunned. "What now?" and "Who now?" were the questions facing the school, the student body, the parents, and the staff.

Nick then went down to the coaches' office and offered the same resignation letter to Head Coach Applewood and Athletic Director Jake Carpenter. Both understood and accepted his decision as they were busy getting ready to welcome back the athletes for fall practice. As Nick left the office, Coach Carpenter asked him to join him in his office down the hall, which was adjacent to the gym. He once again thanked him for his service and asked if he would be open to other coaching assignments if any opened. Nick said he would always entertain opportunities, especially for the staff and students of his alma mater. Also, Coach

Carpenter wanted to know if nick would he be open to administrating and supervising home football, basketball, and baseball games. It would pay about twenty dollars an hour plus a free hot dog. Nick said sure if he was not parking cars on that night. As he left the AD's office, the same office that Bobby Newcombe once occupied for the first ten years of the school, Jake Carpenter had one more parting comment: "You know I will not be doing this forever, and I think you would be great in this office. Think about it." Nick said he would, thanking him again, and left.

Nick had always considered himself a teacher who coached and not a coach who taught. There was a difference, and that was always OK with him. For some of his colleagues, game time meant exactly that, game time. For Nick Finch, game time meant a rethinking of how the day's US history lesson would be taught and what it would be about. He had learned so much from coaching that teachers who never coached, or put on school plays or musicals, or worked with on competitive events such as debate and forensics would experience. There was much more to coaching than the actual contest—preparation; teamwork; professional development activities such as clinics; comradery; and the up close and personal contact that led to memories shared with the players—and those experiences made Nick a much better classroom teacher. If you are out every day after school in the heat, humidity, and rain, and when you experience, as the *Wide World of Sports* used to say, "the thrill of victory and the agony of defeat" and see the whole experience through the eyes of the young people and their supporters—parents, family, and friends—then you are part of the great educational experience that coaches and sponsors get to see. Nick would later say he could not remember all his students' names, but he never forgot a kid who had played for him. That about summed it up. He was very glad he had coached football, and although he hadn't realized it yet, he was not done with coaching or athletics. Far from it.

Nick had one experience common to younger teachers the year he had resigned from coaching football. It was an unusually cold December night when he agreed to help supervise a basketball game between Forest Hill and Lake Worth. The two neighboring schools were rivals in about every sport. Nick would hang out by the ticket sellers and ticket takers and would talk to the West Palm Beach police officers who had been hired to provide security and basically just be seen, but also, he simply loved the competition between the athletes. A couple of the basketball players had also played football, so Nick knew them from his days coaching offense. There was one outstanding athlete whom Nick would call the greatest athlete he had ever coached, Howard Tony.

Howard Tony could dominate a game, even a team sport such as football or basketball. A punishing hitter on the defensive side, he became an outstanding quarterback. He had to have the ball in his hand every play. In his senior year, he was Player of the Year and First Team All-State as he led the Falcons deep into the high school football playoffs. After the season ended late one Friday night in Sarasota, he was on the basketball court the next day for a Saturday hoops contest. Howard was a pleasant young man, which was impressive considering his upbringing and environment. He had never known his father, and his mother was a troubled young woman with too many responsibilities and too little money or opportunity to improve her or her sons' lives. The boys lived most of the time with their grandmother in her small shotgun shack of a house in Pleasant City. Do not be confused, as there was nothing pleasant about living in Pleasant City. It was inner-city urban decay at its worst. Crime and despair were rampant among the residents, yet just two miles away was one of the richest and most famous towns in all the world, Palm Beach. One would be hard-pressed to find such an in-your-face discrepancy between the living conditions in two other adjoining zip codes. On two occasions Nick was pulled over by the police when taking Howard home after a game or practice and was subject to the flashlight once-over of his Nissan 300Z sports car. The first time Nick took Howard home, his star athlete suggested that he drop him off at the top of the street for his own safety. Nick would have nothing of it, although honestly, he was a little scared. The next couple of times, the locals on the street corner who used to angrily stare him down now waved pleasantly at him. They realized the young white man was one of the good guys and Howard Tony's coach. The police, on the other hand, asked Nick if he was there to buy drugs, perhaps crack, which was destroying the inner cities of the United States. If not, was he there looking for prostitutes? This was kind of reverse racial profiling, and Nick did not like it at all. The first time he did all the things he'd been taught by J.W. to do when dealing with law enforcement: "Yes, sir" and "No, sir" responses, no quick movements, and keeping his hands always in sight. Although not needed, J.W. did add never to run from any overweight cops because, being unable to run, they would just go ahead and shoot you. Thankfully, Nick had never needed to follow this advice.

The first time Nick was stopped, it was by a young white cop, and the second time it was a black police officer, but they both asked the same questions as if from a playbook. Nick would tell them the same story, saying he was the passenger's coach at the high school and was taking him home after a game. They listened but gave Nick a look of suspicion before letting him go. There would be no third pullover as Nick called the chief of police and complained. He was never stopped again. Nick Finch now knew just a little what it must be like to be profiled as young African Americans are all the time. His experience was nowhere close to theirs, but he had gotten just a little taste of it, and it left a long-lasting sour taste in his mouth.

As the basketball contest was winding down, one of the police officers working the game was on his walkie-talkie and then made his way over to Nick and asked if they could step outside to talk. The cop asked Nick if he was the Forest Hill coach who at times was seen in Pleasant City taking some of the players home. Nick said yes and asked why he wanted to know. The police officer said he had some bad news: the home where Howard Tony stayed, his grandmother's, had an emergency medical call. It seemed that because of a lack of heat, Howard's grandmother had turned on her stove and opened the oven door to heat the place. Pretty soon she was overcome and died of asphyxiation—suffocated to death because of the gas. Family members and neighbors were already there. Nick agreed to break the news to Howard and to drive him to his house.

After the game, once Howard Tony had gone down to the locker room to change, Nick was waiting for him outside and said he needed to talk to him in private. The two walked into the coaches' office, where the game officials were changing and getting ready to leave. They complained about the cold as they left. Now Nick was with his star athlete alone. He had not had to break the news of a loved one's death since J.W. passed away. Nick took a deep breath and explained what had happened and why. The six-foot-four chiseled star athlete got very quiet, stood up, and walked out the back door of the gym. Nick followed, but at a distance of four or five steps to let Howard know he was there but also to give him space. Once outside, Howard looked up the heavens, let out a primal scream, and began to sob uncontrollably. He kept saying something to the effect of everyone around him dies. He asked about his little brother, and Nick assured him his brother was OK, at home with neighbors and friends. Howard wanted to go home immediately.

They drove to downtown West Palm Beach to the inner city where very few white people ever went. In fact, its nickname was the VFW, not Veterans of Foreign Wars, but "very few whites." When they arrived, there were fifteen or so people there. Howard's little brother came running up to him. Nobody could locate the boys' mother. Nick asked Howard if there was anything he could do, and to his surprise, Howard asked him to come inside and be with him. As Nick Finch walked into the small but tidy home, he felt if there were one hundred eyes on him. He nodded with respect as the local preacher came up and extended his hand to him. The two shared a traditional handshake, not the brother shake, so to speak. Nick looked at the residence, which was very neat and clean and yet so small. On the wall was a picture of Jesus, a picture of Martin Luther King Jr., and a framed clipping of Howard receiving the Player of the Year trophy in the *Palm Beach Post.* On the table was Howard's senior photograph in a black tie and tux. As the news spread, people began to emerge with both food and blankets. Nick looked and felt out of place and was uncomfortable. He looked over at Howard, who was holding his sleeping little brother against his chest. Nick nodded as if to say *My work here is done,* but Howard Tony requested, "Coach, please don't leave yet."

Nick cocked his head and, in a heartfelt way, replied, "Howard, I am here for you." The preacher smiled. Nick stayed for about an hour longer, until the mother arrived. She hugged her boys and thanked everyone. It was time for Nick to go, as now his work was done. As he made his way to the door and the small front porch, Howard, who had followed him out, reached out, hugged his coach, and thanked him for being there. Seldom do classroom teachers have experiences like this one, but coaches and sponsors do because they really get to know their players so much better than they get to know their students who sit at desks. The two still keep in touch.

There would be one more episode involving Howard Tony, this one occurring in late spring. Howard's grades were pretty good, but his SAT and ACT scores were not up to the standards set by the NCAA. Almost every major college in the United States was offering the star athlete a full scholarship, but it was not going to happen. Howard Tony would be going the junior college route on his way to a traditional university playing football, which would lead to a professional career in Canada, the NFL, and the Arena Football League. It would also lead him out of Pleasant City. Toward the end of the school year, a couple of teachers had sought Nick out to complain about Howard's behavior and conduct in class. Now the young athlete was not at the top of his class academically, but he was always polite and respectful to his teachers. This was completely out of character. Nick went to the government teacher during the last five minutes of class and asked if he could speak to Mr. Tony for a few minutes outside and alone. When the two were alone, Nick was blunt and to the point: "What's going on in your English and math classes? Those are good women who care about you, but they tell me you are rude and disrespectful to them and to your classmates. That's not you, not at all. What's going on?" The high school All-American, who towered over his former coach, mumbled something, and looked away. Nick then said, "What now? Don't mumble and look me in the eye. What is the problem?"

Howard looked at his coach and, after taking a deep breath, said, "I want to go to the prom, and I cannot afford to."

Nick, smiling from ear to ear, said, "That's it? You want to go to the prom? Well, heck, we can do that." A big smile appeared on the student's face. Nick took Howard down to Mr. Tux, where Howard was sized for a rental, including a top hat and cane—whatever the young man wanted, Nick paid for it. Then Nick set up a dinner for two at Nando's, who, once he had told the staff the young man's story, comped the meal, including the tip. Nick ended by parking his player's car the night of prom and got stiffed—no tip. Altogether, the evening cost Nick between one hundred fifty and two hundred dollars, but it was worth every cent to see that smile come back and later to watch Howard leave home and make something out of himself. He escaped and would not be a casualty.

About ten years later when Nick was watching a Forest Hill football game, there happened to be two giant black hands that came from behind and covered his eyes. Nick turned around to see his former star athlete, who was with his little son. They shook hands, and Howard left two hundred-dollar bills in Nick's hand. He wanted to repay his former teacher for his prom but, really, for everything. The two hugged, and Nick refused the money, saying Howard had repaid him with his college diploma. Those are the stories that bring a smile to Nick's face when he thinks about them. That is what it is all about.

Nick was finishing up his master's program at Nova University in the exact amount of time the institution had promised it would take: one year, which included forty Saturday classes from eight o'clock in the morning to four o'clock in the afternoon, even though seldom did the class last that late into the afternoon, and twelve Tuesday and Thursday evening sessions from six o'clock to nine o'clock. Some of the classes were very interesting, such as School Law, taught by the lead school board general counsel, which gave insights into current real-life situations at the national, state, and local level. The course had taught him how to identify a termination offense and included case studies with techniques for handling such an offense and determining the verdict. Maybe it was Nick's flirtation with a career in law that had caused him to be interested, or perhaps it was the fact that the teacher was also a practicing attorney, or maybe both, but it was his favorite course toward his degree in administration and supervision.

If School Law was the best, then Budget and Finance was the worst. Figuring out how to make a budget for a school and a district and finance it with the funds available was like undergoing a root canal. Nick did learn that almost every penny was spoken for and of how little a principal had in discretionary funds. Now he saw why school-based fundraisers were so important for things like awards ceremonies and banquets. He also understood why low-income schools struggled to host such events. It was not fair and remains inequitable.

Nick had two last hurdles to clear, one of which was to turn in a formal paper on a particular problem experienced by the school where he was worked, and the other of which was to complete and document some hands-on administration practice. The paper Nick chose to do was on attendance or truancy of second-semester seniors who come down with the terrible disease known as senioritis. The research was done on a system called ERIC, which was an educational research bank on microfilm and microfiche. The idea was to use new technology to robocall seniors at risk of senioritis, document his findings, and follow up. The kids quickly found the program annoying and troubling, and they hated it. Many would race home to erase the tape on the recorder or just unplug the machine. The kids' nickname for the program, called AT-Narc, was "AT&Snitch." Nick thought that was rather good. The practicum, as it was called, was kind of a "poor man's thesis". He presented it to his class at Nova and got a round of polite applause from his classmates and the instructor. Hurdle one cleared.

Then came time to learn the job firsthand by doing it. Unlike with a full-time intern, neither the district nor the school could afford to lose a teacher's class instruction for six full weeks. Nova and the district worked out a compromise, assigning Nick to a different assistant principal for one day a week for six weeks. This way, Nick's class would only suffer one day a week and the district would have to pay a substitute teacher not for an entire week, but just for one day. The prospective administrator would also have to attend all evening activities, sit in on parent conferences, and do all the things that real administrators hate to do, such as patrolling the cafeteria at lunch and overseeing detention. This would give the administrators a much-needed break from ball game supervision and the noise and confusion caused by fifteen hundred students trying to eat in less than forty-five minutes. Assistant principals loved interns.

Once the principal had signed off on this arrangement, there was a mandatory meeting and workshop with the district, and then it was time to apply for a job—a new career—in education. Nick Finch would learn that assistant principals were the hardest-working and most underappreciated staff members on a high school campus. Seldom did they see the successes or the good students, instead having to deal with situations that the public never learned of. Daily, they saw the dark underbelly of society and the damage that is done to our youth. Nick also learned that it would be best if every teacher were to shadow an assistant principal for a week to get a better understanding of what they go through, just like the APs should follow the principal, assistant coaches should check out the head coach's responsibilities, head coaches should try being an athletic director, and so on. The same principle might apply to almost all professions: if the subordinate were to learn what the supervisor did and if, maybe, the supervisor were to step back into the subordinate's role, then there might be a little more respect between them. But maybe not.

Nick quickly learned a couple of things very quickly. He learned he did not want to be an administrator. He learned most kids' issues and problems were the result of being around bad adults, some at home, some at work, and yes, some at school. He learned there were bad teachers who brought on their own problems and should not be around kids. He learned he loved the classroom, also learning he could control it. It was his kingdom. It was small, but it was his kingdom. Kind of like Luxembourg. He also learned he had to have all his coursework turned in and signed off on before July 1 so he could be grandfathered in and be paid at a rate commensurate with having his master's degree. After that, any bonus pay would have to come from working in-field, and there was no way he was going to go into administration. Too many bads: bad teachers, bad parents, bad policies, bad rules, bad hours, and occasionally bad kids. He now knew why there were so many miserable school administrators. The system beat them down. Nick learned to dread the days he was out of the classroom on his supervision assignments. He missed teaching his history classes. It took a while, but he was sure that he wanted to be a teacher, and this proved it.

After Bobby Newcombe's sudden retirement, the entire staff was in a tizzy about finding his replacement. The school had had only three principals in almost thirty years, and some of the faculty had worked under all three. Some people could handle the unknown, realizing that the choice of a new boss was out of their control, while others worried constantly. Still others worked their phones to check with their sources and try to find out who the new principal would be. The gamblers even set up a pool much like a March Madness NCAA basketball bracket grid.

Finally, a letter was sent to the staff members' summer addresses, which in Nick's case was still his apartment, unlike others, who had fled to the mountains of North Carolina for a break from the heat and humidity. Nick was still lifeguarding, teaching swim lessons, and parking cars.

Their new principal and boss would be Joe Peachstone. Mr. Peachstone, or "Peachy" to his friends, had been a science teacher, department chair, and assistant principal at a couple of high schools in the northern part of the district and was also a former baseball head coach. The coaches all let out a sigh of relief as some knew him personally and at least knew he would know what they did as coaches. Teachers liked the fact that he was a former classroom instructor, and the APs were thrilled that he had up close and personal experience with their daily schedule. Nick had never heard of Peachstone, but he knew the man's signature would be required before the deadline to receive the extra three grand in master's pay.

Joe Peachstone would turn out to be not only Nick's principal or boss, but also his mentor and friend. He would be there to give advice when asked, promote Nick, save his job by ignoring rules regarding seniority, trust him, play golf with him, take him as a committee member on recertification trips to other schools throughout the state, introduce him to top-shelf bourbon (and encourage him to move on from Jim Beam), and in short become a father figure, as Nick had lost his own dad with the passing of J.W. Joe Peachstone was the right man to appear at the right time for Nick Finch.

CHAPTER

11

Routine is Our Friend, Except in South Florida and in Teaching, Where There is No Routine but Managed Chaos

Nick thought that now he could settle in and get back into some sort of an organized routine of teaching, coaching, dating, and taking care of his mother. Not so fast, as there would hiccups in every area of his life, some of these good and some not so good, but all very memorable.

No longer was the administration assignment hanging over his head as he had told all the powers that be that he would not be headed in that direction. But he did finish up his postgraduation assignments and received his master's degree in educational administration and supervision, or M.Ed. He later noticed colleagues who would include their postnominals, whether on a business card or a formal paper. Nick would never do that as he personally found the practice to be an act of insecurity or pomposity. He never cared to call people who had earned their Doctor of Education "Doctor," even though they had the credentials to support such a practice. He thought doctors were the people who practiced medicine and prescribed medicine, not people who oversaw programs with titles such as "Assistant Superintendent for the North Area Elementary Schools in charge of nutrition and after-school activities for students in grades 3–5" and with last names beginning with letters *L* through *P*. Perhaps this was an exaggeration, but not much of one. If you literally have nothing to do, just go to any school district website and scroll through the list of programs and their leaders. You will be amazed. The amount of waste in terms of having a top-heavy bureaucracy is incredible and a head-scratcher. Many of these departments are headed by a Doctor of Education. Once entrenched in these jobs, these people are almost impossible to remove. They write their own evaluation criteria and get a next-level crony to sign off on them. On and on it goes. The system is set up to protect the incompetent and inept, who will do anything not to be reassigned to an actual school where there are living and breathing students. The horror! Many are former school site administrators who screwed up royally and who would be fired from almost any nongovernment job. Not with the district. Quickly, the leaders will create a new department in which to hide a friend with a salary of upward of one hundred thousand dollars a year and an expense card, and shortly the incident that got them in trouble will be forgotten and they will have survived. They quickly realize that the new job is great. It pays well, the hours are great, and there are no kids, parents, or faculty members to deal with. Then they realize it is up to them and their immediate supervisor, usually a close friend, to hold on to the new job, the title, and the salary. On and on it goes. They take care of their own, and they have long memories for those who buck the status quo.

Teacher evaluations are practically impossible to administer fairly, for many reasons. People in the real world who work with bottom-line numbers do not see why standardized test scores are ineffective as a workable rubric. This mindset is wrong on so many levels. With standardized tests, you are dealing with an uneven formula because of the human element, that is, each individual student. Every student is different and comes from an environment over which the teacher has no control. The teacher can do his or her best to control the learning situation, but that is for only fifty minutes or so a day and for one year only. Pre-class baggage is impossible to measure, and especially through a test with an answer sheet and the ever-present no. 2 pencil. To rely so thoroughly on standardized testing is easy and lazy for the state and the district. Give out the test, ship the completed test forms to a testing facility, calculate the scores, and attach the scores to a report bearing the teacher's name and class. There are examples of great teaching that are not measured by test formulas, such as a teacher who enables the success of a class full of non-English-speaking students, or one who works her ass off to ensure kids from the inner city and from broken families get a shot at a decent education—and the kids know it, even though they simply do not test well, through no fault of their own. Then there is the other side of the coin, such as a lazy, clock-watching, calendar-counting teacher who has a class full of self-motivated students who have stable parents who have provided them with extra help by hiring tutors and availing the kids of the latest technology. These kids' test scores are great, but not because they were inspired by their teachers. The evaluation-based testing system does not work, plain and simple.

There is another reason why these standardized tests are implemented in the classroom: money. People would be shocked if they were to see the price tag that corporations place on standardized testing and the amount charged to the various states and districts. The price is not only for the test themselves but also for the pretests or diagnostics used for lesson plans. Whole school calendars are arranged and rearranged around testing, and the amount of lost instructional time is astronomical. It is no wonder these firms hire legions of lobbyists to influence leadership in the district, the legislature, the bureaucracy, the governor, and the legislators in Washington, DC. It used to be that to make money in education, one would have to be a textbook salesperson. These people would arrive at a preschool with samples of the various books offered for each class and all the supplemental materials, such as workbooks and test booklets. Then school staff would see the same salesperson toward the end of the school year to re-up their order for the next year. Nick noticed these salespeople drove the latest and most expensive cars and tricked-out pickup trucks, usually with boat hitches. They also had great suntans. How is that possible? No longer. Textbooks went the way of the cassette and no longer appear at the top of the must-have column on a list of a school or district's necessities. Now it is software, technology, and testing supplies. That is where the money is. Those salespeople make the old textbook guys look like door-to-door encyclopedia salesmen. You do not even get to meet these people as they go straight to the top of the educational food chain with their sales pitches. And if you do need one, you make an email request on a website. Such is change.

Nick Finch actually enjoyed his yearly evaluation when an assigned administrator would come into his classroom, sit in the back, and observe the day's lesson. Nick was a confident, if not cocky, teacher, but he also took the time to make sure things were just right in terms of his presentation of the material and his classroom setting. Know your audience, and on that day his audience was not his classroom of students, but the principal or assistant principal assigned to give him his yearly competence report. Nick could tell when evaluation time was coming up as teachers, he saw, dressed up as if they were going to church, when every other day they looked like they were heading to Walmart. Nick himself always wore a starched button-down shirt and tie, except on Fridays, when he wore a school-themed sports shirt to support that night's athletic contest. Principal Newcombe had recommended in his first year that he dress older since he was so young, and he would continue the practice right up to his retirement. Year in and year out, students would vote Mr. Finch Best

Dressed Teacher. Other teachers, Nick would notice, as J.W. used to say, were as nervous as whores in church as the zero-hour approached. On his first formal evaluation, Nick would implement the concept of playing to one's audience.

Principals always did their first-year teacher evaluations themselves, but for the first part they already knew if their newbie was getting the job done by having made informal observations and had off-the-record talks with people he trusted in that department. Bobby Newcombe already knew Nick got it, but he still needed to complete the formal paperwork, so he scheduled his observation for a March morning before spring break in Nick's first year. Now, Nick Finch had known Bobby Newcombe his entire life as he was not only a family friend but also a close confidant of his father, J.W. The two men had both experienced the horrors of World War II, J.W. in Europe, and Bobby in the Pacific theater. Nick had his own battle strategy.

On the day of his performance, Mr. Robert Newcombe, principal of Forest Hill High School, took his seat in the back of Nick's classroom. The students noticed their visitor—they always did—and, as always, rose to the occasion. It was game time for everyone. No more practice as now it was kickoff. Nick called an audible, which in football talk means he changed the play at the line of scrimmage before the snap of the ball. Instead of going over the end of World War I and the problems with the Treaty of Versailles, boring, he shifted gears. This was where he was in his lesson plans, but he saw an opportunity for a touchdown, so called a different play at the line. "Today, class, we are going to discuss the terrible, brutal fighting in the Pacific during the Second World War." One student, a very bright one who loved the class and the subject, seemed puzzled and began to raise his hand to question the change, when he noticed all his classmates were giving him death stares and the student behind him kicked his desk. He then realized he had to get on the same page quickly. Or else. We must make Mr. Finch look good. He lowered his half-raised hand. Nick quickly talked about the start, mentioning Pearl Harbor and the island-hopping strategy of General MacArthur and Admiral Nimitz as the Americans closed the rope around Japan tighter and tighter toward victory. But standing in the way was the bloody battle for Imo Jima, or the "Island of Death." The island had to be taken by the United States Marine Corps. The few, the proud, would be asked to storm the beaches and raise the flag of victory. Bobby Newcombe would be one of those men.

As the lesson began, Mr. Newcombe was in the back of the room writing and scribbling on the formal observation form, but as the lesson went on, he dropped his pen and began to watch and listen like a student and participant. He did this until he could stand it no longer, then raised his hand. Nick acknowledged his "new" student and called on Mr. Newcombe who got up from his seat and walked to the front of the classroom, basically taking over the rest of the lesson. He gave a firsthand account of the battle from the viewpoint of a scared nineteen-year-old from West Palm Beach. He told of the valor and the heartbreak all around him; the story seemed to have been stored inside him for decades. The kids loved it. They inched closer and closer to the man who most had seen only as their principal and knew as the guy on the intercom in the morning. Now he was their history teacher, their neighbor, their grandfather, and yes, their hero.

The bell rang, ending the lesson, as tears welled in the old coach's eyes. The students stormed out of their seats, not to get to the door, but to go to the front of the classroom and hug the man they now felt they knew. After many years, Nick still feels this is one of the best lessons he ever taught, yet he taught so little of it. History came alive that day.

After school, Nick was called to the front office, where Principal Bobby Newcombe, briefcase in hand, was walking out to the administration parking lot to get in his car and go home. He wanted to thank his twenty-two-year-old history teacher for the joyous day he had experienced.

There was still a little quiver in his voice when he got to his small-size pickup truck and opened the door. He turned and thanked Nick one more time. As he slid into his truck, he smiled and looked at Nick, stating ironically, "Look here, now I drive a damn Nissan. Who would have thought I would ever buy something from Japan? Best vehicle I have ever owned." He drove off toward home and shared with his wife how his day had gone. About two weeks later Nick would have to go to see him again and sign his formal evaluation. It had the highest rating possible. The comments were so over the top that you would think Nick Finch was a cross between Aristotle, William Shakespeare, Thomas Jefferson, and Horace Mann, the "Father of American Education." Know your audience. Some people might think this was the wrong thing to do, but Nick would fight them over that. To this day, he believes that was the sort of real education that a standardized test will never be able to show. The students learned about a major event in US history by way of a firsthand account. There was 100 percent buy-in from the students. Nick bets they never will forget the day they learned about the Battle of Iwo Jima, not from their history teacher but from their principal. They will never forget the passion of the presentation. And as a sidenote, it reminded an administrator of his love of teaching. At the same time, he got to share one of the most important events of his life that had taken place at a time when he was not much older than his audience. Nick also thought Mr. Newcombe had gotten a few things off his chest—stories he had kept locked inside for almost forty years. The best thing was that these young people got it, loved it, and respected it. Everyone won that day. Nick's first formal evaluation would be his best. Every subsequent evaluation would be top-notch, but definitely not as memorable as the first one. It would be hard to match a first pitch in the major league resulting in a home run, but that is exactly what Nick Finch did with his lesson change, with his class, and most of all with his boss.

Nick began to make some minor changes to his life. First, he cut way back on his hours parking cars. Perry Hahn and Frank Fletcher were both winding down their teaching and coaching careers and wanted to cash in on every opportunity to make some extra money, especially since there were rumors that Mr. Nando was considering selling the building and shutting down the restaurant. Nick was now the relief for parking duties; when either one or both could not make it, he would step in. Football coaching was next, as that had to go. Nick picked up an extra three thousand dollars for having earned his master's, and now that he taught Advanced Placement United States History, he would receive a hundred-dollar incentive reward for every student who passed the AP exam with a score of 3, 4, or 5. He now taught two AP classes. Summer lifeguarding was also gone, replaced by adjunct teaching at the local junior college, Palm Beach Junior College (PBJC). Nick found himself teaching twice a week, on Tuesday and Thursday evenings, from six to nine, and one night a week during the summer term. His new postgraduate degree now made him a professor. Well, kind of. Maybe. Sort of. No, it did not.

Teaching at PBJC was a neat opportunity for Nick Finch. Apparently, a couple of the parents knew the president of Florida's oldest junior college and contacted him about the chance of hiring a young instructor whom their children had had at Forest Hill. Once Nick had earned his MEd degree and submitted it to Tallahassee and the Certification Office, his new certificate entitled him to teach grades 6–14 social science in the state of Florida. His previous certificate range was 8–12 social science. Many of Nick's close friends had attended PBJC, and some even graduated with their AA degrees. They took classes there for a variety of reasons, for example, to increase their GPAs for later admission to Florida State University or the University of Florid. Others were not ready to leave home and found it comfortable to attend PBJC, which was nearby. Some played sports there. A few, like Nancy Foster, went into fields that required only an AA degree, such as dental hygienist, and some took advantage of the very affordable tuition rate and the savings from living at home instead of paying room and board. What Nick found out was that PBJC was in many ways a grade 13 or grade 14, but in other ways it was continuing education and offered the experience of returning to college just for the academic enjoyment. Some students enrolled because they wanted to improve their lives. Nick taught many a single parent who worked all day and then, after making sure everything was OK at home, drove out to the Lake Worth campus for classes. He was amazed at their willpower and their drive to move up despite the curveballs life had thrown at them. Some looked frazzled and exhausted when they arrived, and some even dozed off. They were constantly checking their beepers, the communication device of choice in the late eighties / early nineties, for the status of their children at home. Nick would always stress to his history classes, whether at the high school level or the college level, the two greatest contributions the United States had made to Western civilization were the Constitution, or the greatest framework of organized government ever written down and followed, and free public education—not always fair and equal, but free. Americans did not invent democracy; the Greeks did. Our legal system is based on English common law, and our military is impressive, but what about Alexander the Great or the Roman Legions, or the Royal Navy and their remarkable accomplishments? But we the American people wrote down a set of laws and a framework that remains unrivaled, and here children of different races, different genders, and different socioeconomic statuses can attend school for free. With a great framework of laws and free school, the result was the great drawing card of the United States: opportunity, the "O" word that used to inspire, and continues to inspire, people to come to our shores. Education is a big part of the formula. For the five years Nick taught at the junior college, he taught a variety of subjects: US history, of course, but also sociology, political science, and Florida history. He enjoyed it, even. He would find himself daydreaming or zoning out after a long day of teaching high school and then climb right back into the instructor's chair for an evening session. The class makeup was as varied as South Florida's demographics: recent high school grads, college transfers and do-overs, day workers, and senior citizens who never wanted to stop learning. Every race, age, and lifestyle were represented.

Teaching at PBJC, which also went by a few nicknames, such as Peanut Butter and Jelly College; or UCLA, which stood for University of Congress and Lake Avenue; or insert the name of the high school from which you graduated and just add "West Campus," such as Forest Hill West Campus; or simply Grade 13—it did not matter—Nick liked the assignments, the interaction, and the money. It beat parking cars and giving swimming lessons. Soon Nick designed a system or format for instruction. He learned quickly he could not lecture the entire time, because then he would lose his students, and he was already tired from teaching all day. What he did was to go over the assigned reading topics from the previous session, give a lecture, give the class a chance to discuss, break for fifteen to twenty minutes, then return for group work and study, and three times a quarter give a small multiple-choice test with a choice of essay question. His high school exams, especially his Advanced Placement classes, were much more stringent and challenging than this, but once again, he followed the dictum of "know your audience." He took roll twice, once at the beginning of class and once after the break period when the class resumed. Attendance was always lower after the break. In terms of the format, Nick enjoyed two parts more than the rest. No, it was not the break period, during which he would join the students in casual conversation and learn about their lives—more on that later. He enjoyed the discussion portion as students bantered back and forth about the topic. And since so many were of a seasoned age, they could expand with firsthand or secondhand knowledge and accounts of the event and relate this directly to their classmates, many of whom were almost fifty years their junior. Nick also liked the group study time, watching this hodgepodge of students in a group setting discuss, debate, and strategize the upcoming assignments or tests.

There were other things that happened at PBJC that would never happen in his high school classes, such as his students just getting up and leaving or else sleeping in class. In high school, Nick saw sleeping as the ultimate sign of disrespect to him personally. It was like, *you are so boring and uninteresting that I might as well go to sleep.* When a student would fall asleep, he would drop a book or make a startlingly loud sound. In some cases, he would require the student to stand by his or her desk for the remainder of the period. He would tell his students that if they wanted to sleep, then they could do so like a horse, standing up. There was one student who could sleep standing up like a horse. Amazing. And occasionally Nick would wake a student and give him or her a pass to the clinic, figuring he or she must be sick. Most of the time sleeping in class was no longer a problem after a couple of kids found out firsthand how this action upset their history teacher.

At the college level, Nick ignored any students' sleeping, figuring, *God only knows what their day was like before class.* If it happened before the break, he made a point of talking to the sleeper, and if it happened after the break, he would wait for dismissal and talk to them if they so wished. If some were low on energy, his senior students were full of it, as if they had waited all day to discuss their views. They had watched their favorite soap opera or *The Price Is Right*, and now it was time for class—and they loved class.

Break time was needed by everyone at the night classes at PBJC. Nick thought of it as the final turn of a race—"Down the stretch they come," like in the final leg of the Kentucky Derby. He was tired and needed a Coke and a chance to get some fresh air. Students needed the time to check in and make sure everything was OK on the home front. Some checked out and left. One evening during break time in early February, Nick dismissed the class for their traditional time to get up and stretch or go for a walk, but basically to get out of class for at least fifteen minutes and get it together to return for the last hour or so. Nick would take the time to look over what he still needed to cover and would take a pack of "Nabs" from his briefcase, his nightly snack, "Nabs" being short for Nabisco peanut butter and crackers. He would take some change from his pocket and buy a Coca-Cola Classic, not New Coke, which was hideous, like a bad joke played upon the American public. No Tab either, as he wanted the caffeine that came with the original formula Coca-Cola, first mixed up by Dr. Pemberton of Atlanta in the late 1800s. Now that he was set, he would find a seat on a wall made of local coquina stone with a smooth-top surface. Opening both his Nabs and his Coke, he would admire the stars and pleasantly cool winter evening while drifting off into "no man's land".

One such evening, Nick found himself in a very relaxed frame of mind when he was startled by the pleasant sound of a young woman's voice asking if there was any room for her to sit by him. He looked up to find an extremely cute dark-haired, very young tan woman with a slight accent who was waiting for his half-awake response. "Sure, plenty of room." Nick had never seen the woman before; she surely was not in his class. She extended her hand and introduced herself as Maria Hernandez. She followed up her introduction with a question, asking Nick if he was a student or a professor. Nick grinned as this was the first time he had been referred as a professor. A small chuckle eased its way out of his mouth. "Professor? Ah, no. Teacher, yes."

Maria kept up the line of questioning, asking, "If you teach at the college level, then you are considered a professor, right?" Nick, still with that grin, said he wasn't sure, but if he was a professor, maybe he needed a pipe and a tweed jacket with leather elbow patches instead of the attire he'd been wearing since five thirty this morning—khakis and a blue button-down with a red, white, and blue striped tie, and on his feet, penny loafers with multiple scuff marks. That brought a grin from the inquisitive young woman. She would not let up. Her next question was what class he was teaching and how old he was. He replied that he was teaching a course called US History from 1877 to the Present in the classroom two doors down. He added that he had just turned twenty-five a couple of weeks ago. Miss Hernandez nodded, seemingly in approval.

Now it was Nick's turn. He asked much of the same about his inquisitor. What class was she taking? Where was she from? What high school did she graduate from? What was her major going to be? Maria Hernandez gave a quick autobiography. She was taking Abnormal Psychology in the adjacent room; she was from South Miami and had gone to a prestigious private school called Westminster Academy; she would be majoring in adolescent counseling; and she was a sophomore and soon would be graduating with her associate of arts degree in May, then would be attending Flagler College in St. Augustine both to continue her academic journey and extend her athletic pursuits as she was a scholarship golfer. She also added she was twenty-one. Wow.

Break time was almost over. Nick extended his hand to show that he had enjoyed meeting the pleasant and confident young woman, who responded with "The pleasure was all mine." Then they both got up and went back to their respective classrooms. Nick would always enter last to welcome his students back for the home stretch and to make a mental note of who made it back and who had called it night. Just as he was about to enter his room, he glanced down the hall and saw the brilliant simile with perfect teeth smiling back, and with a quick wave, Maria disappeared into her classroom.

Nick gathered himself and found himself wondering about what had just happened. One student raised his hand. Nick called on him, a longhaired surfer dude with the giant smile, who said in his best stoner voice, "Whoa, Mr. Finch, doing all right. Outstanding!" Nick shook his head in amusement and actually began to blush.

"Look, teach is blushing" came a female voice in the back of the room.

"Oh, so cute" another piped in.

Nick tried his best to restore order as he assigned something fun for the students to present in groups during the last ten minutes of class. He had the students call out numbers—one, two, three, and four in order—and then break into groups according to those numbers. The question he had the groups answer was how people could, without could directly asking, determine someone's ethnicity. He would use this assignment to discuss turn-of-the-century Ellis Island immigration. Name spelling, spoken language, and chosen religion could all be used. Then Nick would ask the students what their ethnicity was. He explained that if you were to line up ten young people next to one another and had to pick out the American, you had a one in ten chance of being right, even though Hollywood would have you think everyone was white with blue eyes and blondish hair. He mentioned that one method of determining ethnicity was to throw a soccer ball to the group of ten, and the American would almost always catch it, whereas the others would head it or kick it. The class nodded with approval as they had never thought of that, but they agreed that was exactly what would happen. Soccer was a global sport, although not as popular in the United States.

Nick looked at the clock and dismissed the class ten minutes early. He was tired, but also, he was intrigued by his new break buddy. He left campus grinning and now found himself really looking forward to next Thursday's class and especially break time.

Class the next Thursday night started with Mr. Finch lecturing and discussing the impact of and pushback against immigration in the early twentieth century. Then he turned to the Progressive Era, especially his personal favorite progressive, President Theodore Roosevelt, who legislated responsive reforms, Nick ending his lecture by discussing the storm clouds of war approaching Europe. The class would learn that this would be known as the Great War, now referred to as World War I. He administered a short twenty-question quiz, after which students exchanged tests, then Nick went over the answers and the reasons for them. The students were to write the total number of questions the person had answered wrong at the top of the paper and then pass them all forward. If the score was good, he recorded it; if not, he would double up on the next quiz. The testing format was definitely not like the SAT, ACT, GRE, MCAT, or LSAT, but it did allow the teacher discretion when recording grades. Nick did everything possible in the class to ensure the success of his students, who came twice a week for eighteen weeks the night course. He just asked the students not to take advantage of him, adding that if they had any problems, they should see him privately so they could work together to turn the problem into a success. The formula was simple: show up, try, and participate and you would be successful. When the students filled out their survey and instructor questionnaire at the end of the term, their responses were glowing. But now it was break time.

Nick took his "Nabs" and bought his Coke Classic, found a seat close to where he'd been sitting on Tuesday, and sat down. He shook his head as if to wake himself up and stop himself from acting like it was middle school and he was waiting around for a Missy or a Tiffany to show up at his locker. He looked out into the vastness of the dark skies, when suddenly the same pleasant, accented voice cut the night: "Hi, Teach. Any room here?"

Nick found himself giving a one-word response: "Absolutely." Maria Hernandez took her seat and popped open her Tab soft drink. She was wearing baggy old-school gray sweatpants and a matching gray hooded sweatshirt with the emblem that spelled out "Pacer Golf." She jumped right in, saying that she had done her research and found out that Nick was a teacher and coach at Forest Hill. She explained that in her psych class there were some local baseball players who knew of him. Nick responded that theirs was an uneven playing field and he hadn't been able to do the same research she had done. So, Maria Hernandez of South Miami gave a fifteen-minute version of her autobiography. She shared that she was of Cuban descent as her parents immigrated to Miami in 1962 to escape, as she explained it, that murderous bastard Fidel

Castro. Her father was a doctor and had to go to work in a hospital, not as a medical professional, but as a janitor, until his records could be obtained and he could pass the various Florida medical board examinations. He did pass and became prosperous and well known both in the Cuban community and in the medical field. She had two brothers, one of them two years older and at the University of Florida, and a little brother who was thirteen. She had chosen PBJC so that she could be close to her private golf coach, a pro who worked out of Delray Beach, which was just a little more than an hour's drive from her home.

Time was almost up for the break when Maria directly asked Nick, "Well, are you going to ask me?"

"Ask you what?" Maria smiled. My God, did she have a perfect smile, matched only by perfect teeth.

"Out?" Nick looked right back at the Cuban Princess and questioned, "You mean like on a date?"

Maria was in total control now. "Ah, yeah. Well? I will meet you back here after class if you are interested." She smiled and waved and walked back to her classroom, but with one more glance and a smile.

Nick went back to class in somewhat of a daze, like in junior high. His confidence and control had been taken from him. Two things that Nick Finch had a lot of were confidence and control, and now he was scrambling to regain them, not to mention some composure. *Is this, OK? I mean, she is a student, but not in my class, and there really isn't a major age difference.* When class ended twenty minutes or so early, as usual he waited until his students had all left before gathering up his old briefcase. Actually, it was more of a satchel, and Nick loved it because it had been his dad's. He had had it repaired and restitched a few times and still has it today. It is a legacy from his dad to him, and he will turn it over to his son someday. He opened and closed the door and was preparing to lock up when the night custodian explained he would handle securing the room as he still had to clean it. Nick thanked him and walked out. As he turned to look down the hall, sure enough he saw Maria waiting for him. He walked over to her, and she explained she had been hoping he would show up. Nick was still tongue-tied and had difficulty spitting out some words. Maria sensed this and handed the young "professor" a piece of paper with her name and number on it. She turned to walk away and turned back around, smiling. "Please call me either way." Nick nodded once again without saying a word. He would call the next afternoon, and they would talk for two hours.

The conversation between the two went splendidly as the two jabbed back and forth like boxers in the first round of a prize fight, feeling each other out and trying to learn as much as they could about each other without going in too fast. After what seemed to be just a few minutes but was almost two hours, Nick formally asked Maria out on a date. He suggested his go-to first date venue: Nando's on Palm Beach Island for dinner. Since Nick had worked so many evenings there, he was well known to the staff and was always treated on a first-name basis like a true VIP. This strategy had worked so well on his previous first dates, but unfortunately Maria declined as she had a golf tournament in Cocoa Beach on Friday and Saturday and would not be back until late Saturday evening, at which time she'd be wiped out. Nick understood, but with that Maria had regained the advantage. She said that Sunday afternoon would be open and could be a lot of fun. Nick was open to the idea after church with his mom. Maria asked if Nick would take her to the Waterway Cafe in Palm Beach Gardens on the Intracoastal Waterway for some music, dancing, food, and South Florida–style fun. Nick wanted to reply yes immediately, but he had some reservations, so he delayed answering. He was not a Sunday party guy, not for religious reasons, but because five thirty came quite early on a Monday morning. Also, he was not much of a dancer. He explained he was very "white," tight-hipped, self-consciousness, and downright uncomfortable on the dance floor. Denny Terrio of "Dance Fever" of the popular syndicated dance and music show on television, he was not. But there was another reason, an incident that had occurred about a month earlier at the Waterway, that made him reconsider and wonder whether anyone on the staff or any of the patrons would recognize him. He decided to take the gamble, thinking, *for Maria Hernandez, it's worth it.* At least he hoped so.

It was either the end of January or the beginning of February when Nick and some of his lifelong friends were spending an early Sunday afternoon on Ray Wade's new center-console Mako sport fishing boat named *The Mullet.* After a day of drinking, which started at nine o'clock in the morning, they decided to finish up at the Waterway with some reggae music, some rumrunners, and maybe, just maybe, some female companionship. At least there was the chance of it. Ray had inherited some money, in fact, a decent chunk of change, from a recently deceased uncle, and he'd used that money to register for, and take and pass, the test for his two-ton boat captain's license; become a dive boat instructor and captain; and buy his own boat, for which he rented in-our dry storage space at the PGA Marina located just north of the Waterway at the PGA Bridge. Basically, the marina was a big barn where a forklift would take one's boat out of the water, hold it while it was being hosed down, then place it inside the facility, out of the weather. The fact that it was all of two hundred yards from the Waterway made the Waterway Cafe the perfect end spot after a day out in the boat. On Sunday afternoons, the Waterway featured live reggae music for the diners' and drinkers' pleasure. Steel drums and rhythmic guitar riffs delighted the patrons without their having to go to Jamaica. Pleasant weather, waterfront scenery, tropical drinks, Bob Marley and UB40 tunes, and the beautiful people in their floral Sunday best: what could go wrong? Plenty.

As any local will tell you, besides a high-end car, say, a Porsche or Range Rover, or a Platinum American Express Card, the next best thing to attract the opposite sex is a boat. Well, on that Sunday Nick and his friends had the boat and a cooler full of beverages, and now a landing place to find and meet women. The Waterway Cafe was calling, and they were answering. The problem was that a lot of others had the same idea as the floating dock/bar was packed, as were all the boat slips. The only way to dock there was to somehow maneuver *The Mullet* between two of the boats and attempt to tie off to another boat, and maybe find an open cleat on the floating dock/bar. Not only was the boat traffic extremely thick around the docks, but also the Intracoastal was packed with what could be described as an unofficial boat parade. The increased boat wake made the task even more difficult, even for a certified two-ton boat captain. Nick even suggested maybe it was time to take the boat back to the marina and walk the two hundred or so yards back to the cafe. "Nonsense" was Captain Ray Wade's response. "Piece of cake."

There was one more environmental factor to consider in that the current running down the Intracoastal was, as they say, booking. That meant the current, or a river within a river, would add to the difficulty factor when docking. Ray was having a real problem with the whole plan and with executing the maneuvers required. Every time he got close, the current would grab hold of the boat and shift its location, or a large wake made by a passing boat would rock Ray's boat to the point that it made docking almost impossible. Ray's attempts were now drawing a crowd of drunk observers, who began to heckle the boat captain and his crew. They got louder and even more boisterous, laughing, and hurling insults at Captain Ray and his crew. Suddenly, that mischievous and playful grin came across Raymond Wade's face, and Nick knew something was about to happen. It did.

Ray began to trim his boat motor up so just the propeller remained below the waterline. The 115-horsepower Yamaha was idling, when suddenly Ray pushed down on the throttle and *The Mullet*'s motor, suddenly no longer used for moving the vessel, was now a giant, powerful hose as it sprayed down the patrons of the floating bar as if they had been doused with fire hoses. The entire, and I mean the entire bar was soaked from the shower of water that came over them. Screams and cussing could be heard. The band stopped playing "Red Red Wine" and looked out to see what the commotion was. There was a lot of finger-pointing and hollering at the captain and his crew.

Ray quickly lowered the motor fully below the waterline, then the center-console boat was off and running, making its escape down the Intracoastal, where the crew hid for a while in a secluded area and then quietly made it back to the marina for a quick removal and storage. This event was what made Nick nervous about returning to the scene of crime, so to speak. But again, he concluded it was worth the risk.

Years later, when Nick and Ray had become mature, as marriage and child-rearing will do to a person, the two were seated in the same boat after a day out on the water. They were tied up adjacent to the marina but on the north side, at an equally famous restaurant named the Riverhouse, when another incident occurred.

The Riverhouse was a high-end steak house with fresh seafood, impeccable service, and high prices to match. They also had a tiki bar located right by the seawall, where the patrons would have a predinner drink while waiting on their tables and for their names to be called. For many years this was Nick's favorite restaurant, as it was J.W.'s and his future in-laws'. It was that good. Nick and Ray were now approaching the big fifty when they experienced a mischievous blast from the past that would have made a young Nick and Ray proud and made their own children laugh.

The two were not going to have dinner but only a drink made at the outdoor bar and sit in the boat while waiting for space at the PGA Marina to become available. There seemed to be a three- or four-boat wait. As the two sat and waited, they reminisced, recalling the "great hose-down party" some twenty years earlier. They shook their heads and laughed at the memory, when suddenly there was some commotion coming from the marina. It seemed there was one boat holding up the collection process, and the captain was giving it to the dock attendant who doubled as the forklift driver, a pleasant young man who also owned a pool cleaning business and was a well-known surfer and free diver. Free divers were a fearless breed of adventurer as they would free dive down to depths greater than one hundred feet below the surface of the ocean with one breath and return safely to the surface. The young attendant was a laid-back pleasant type who already owned his own business. Although it was small, he owned it just the same, and brought home some extra coin working at the marina on weekends. Neither Ray nor Nick knew his real name as he went by his nickname: "Dive Man". In fact, his company's name was "Dive Man Pool Service and Cleaning". What Nick and Ray heard they did not like. A very loud man who was apparently the owner of an overpowered four-motor cigarette boat named *Empire Slayer* was giving it good to the Dive Man. The man was dressed in a wifebeater—the unfortunate nickname for a tank top—that was accented by enough gold chains to make Mr. T blush. He was in his late fifties or early sixties. His date was about twenty years his junior and was working her way back to his yellow Corvette Stingray convertible. It was obvious that her previous profession had been a dancer, and it was not ballet or jazz but the type of dance that revolved around a pole. She had enough plastic enhancement that if she ever were to sit by a reading lamp, she might melt. That is, if she could read. The man explained he would be gone for only half an hour or so and there was no need to lift his boat. He also made it clear that he, and only he, would tie his "ropes." Anyone who has spent any time around boats and docks will tell you they are called lines, not ropes. The fact he was tying his "ropes" to his cigarette boat, the type that had been made famous by the drug-dealing types in the hit show *Miami Vice*, and that he was dressing down one of the most likable people Nick and Ray knew showed the boys all they needed to see.

The two looked at each other and nodded. They got up from *The Mullet* and walked over to the marina as the "slayer" and his "artist" companion jumped into the Corvette. Before leaving, the man reminded Dive Man not to touch his "ropes". Dive Man shook his head. As Nick and Ray arrived, his disgusted look disappeared and a friendly welcoming smile spread across his face. Ray had one and only one question for the blond-haired, toned, and suntanned attendant: "He said not to touch his, um, ropes, right?" Dive Man nodded. Ray asked if the security cameras were on or if they were even working.

Dive Man laughed and responded, "They are for looks only. They do not work and have never worked."

"Good. And now if you would go back inside to the ship store or back into the barn for the next minute or two." Dive Man knew they were up to something and that they did want to get him to trouble for being an accomplice or something, so he did as Ray had requested. Raymond Wade then asked Nick to go back to the Riverhouse Tiki Bar and square up the tab, then crank up *The Mullet* and have it ready to go, pointed north toward Jupiter.

Nick responded with an "Aye, aye, Captain," and followed Ray's instructions. He jogged back to the tiki bar, paid up, started the boat up, and turned her around, ready to head north, just as Ray came running back and jumped in. Just then *Empire Slayer* floated right by at a high rate of speed and without any occupants, caught in that same swift current that had foiled Ray's docking attempt some twenty years earlier. What Ray Wade did was to untie the "ropes" and give the *Empire Slayer* a quick push out into the Intracoastal Waterway, and from there the current did its job. The cigarette boat was now rudderless, so to speak, as boats blew their horns and dodged the unmanned vessel. Fairly soon the boat crashed into a commercial dry dock, where it continued to crash and crash over and over, until two men from the repair office ran out and secured the runaway vessel.

The boys' work was now done, and it was time to head to Jupiter and through the inlet there, where they went through the turnaround and headed back south to the PGA Marina as if they were heading into port for the first time. When they docked a second time, Dive Man was waiting for them, shaking his head in amazement and most likely gratitude. Apparently, the owner had driven across PGA Boulevard Bridge to go to a liquor store, and when he was trying to return, he got stuck at the drawbridge, which then lived up to its local nickname of PGA—standing for "Please Go Around"—because it malfunctioned. The gentleman was stuck looking down the waterway and watching his boat continually crash until he could get down to it. It was his fault after all since he had tied his own ropes!

Now back to Nick's date with the golfer, Maria Hernandez. After quickly, very quickly, weighing the pros and cons of returning to the place of the spray shower, Nick agreed that he would pick her up at her apartment in downtown Delray Beach off Atlantic Avenue, very close to both the emerging nightlife and the ever-present beach. Her apartment actually was a cottage built behind the main house during the Florida land boom of the 1920s. Some people built these sorts of structures as in-law cottages, whereas others offered them to family members or only very close hired help. Today these cottages are sought after by the arts community and are rented out for a lot of money because of their location and the throwback style and architecture.

Wood floors and pecky cypress ceilings adorned Maria's small three-room, one-bedroom cottage. There were no modern amenities such as central air or heat and garbage disposal, and no modern appliances, but the place screamed charm. Nick wore some OP—Ocean Pacific—corduroy shorts with a floral-print shirt, with Topsiders for footwear, of course without socks. He also had with him his ever-present Ray-Ban aviator sunglasses with the wraparound elbows connected by a neck lanyard. He had also brought a used but stylish Ole Miss baseball cap. This was not for the sun but just in case he would need a disguise. He could pull it down low and add the sunglasses, and it might be a good cover, hiding his identity from anyone who might recognize him from the incident the month before. No one did, which was a relief. Maria asked him why he seemed a little uncomfortable as Nick kept surveying the staff and the patrons once they had arrived and were seated. He leveled with her, telling her the story. She broke out into full laughter and, once she had regained her composure, shared with Nick that she had heard about the incident from a friend who witnessed the spectacle from inside the restaurant. Who knew she was going out with a criminal legend?

After being seated inside, they ordered salads and some shrimp cocktails, along with drinks. Maria ordered a rum and Coke but was only served after she provided ID to the waitress. Nick rolled his eyes; he was going out with a young woman who had to prove she was of legal age to consume alcohol. He thought it was kind of cool, almost as if he were back in college again. Nick had a Red Stripe beer, an import from Jamaica. As they say, "When in Rome …" The two touched glasses, Nick his dark red bottle of beer and Maria and her tumbler with the lime floating on the top of her drink. She drank from her small red straw. The two shared stories of their upbringing. Nick was fascinated both by her story of her family's escape from communist Cuba and by her travels on the junior golf circuit. Maria was equally impressed with the true local and the teacher.

Soon the band cranked up and played some popular Bob Marley tunes, one of which was "Buffalo Soldiers." Maria knew all the lyrics but did not know the story behind the song. Nick, the history teacher, quickly added the sidebars, telling her the story of the African American horse soldiers hired by the United States Army, at a lower rate of pay than the white officers, whose mission it was to hunt down and kill Native Americans. The story horrified her but also enlightened her. She really began to like the history teacher and asked him to the dance floor. Nick shook his head twice but was still grinning and thinking, *if this girl only knew how poorly I dance, she would not be asking.* Maria reached the dance floor and kept motioning Nick to join her, index finger bent in such a way as to indicate, *Come here.* She was by far the most attractive woman in the place—and there were a lot of lookers there, as there were every Sunday at the Waterway Cafe. Nick reluctantly agreed and met his date on the floor, who immediately wrapped her arms around his neck while still swaying her hips in perfect rhythm to the island-flavored music. Nick took the unannounced cue and let Maria lead. It worked out just fine and, in fact, was a lot of fun. It is always fun when you're with the prettiest woman at the dance.

Approaching nine o'clock in the evening, both agreed it was time to wrap things up and call it a night. They continued talking away as Nick drove down Interstate 95 to Atlantic Avenue in his black T-top Nissan 300Z. Life was good. He drove past the house to the bright yellow cottage in the back, then got out and raced around to open the door for his date, whom he walked to her door, holding her hand the whole way. She was impressed by his manners. When they reached the door, Maria fumbled in her bag for her keys and, for the first time, seemed off her game and nervous about what would be coming next. Now Nick took his cue and played the gentleman. He leaned over and gave Maria a polite but lasting kiss on the cheek while whispering how much fun he'd had. Maria Hernandez, with her perfect tan, beautiful long jet-black hair, and cover-model-worthy teeth that accented her fantastic smile, looked back at Nick, pulled him closer, and gave him an impressively long first date sort of kiss that lingered for ten seconds. She opened her cottage door and went in, then locked the door behind her. Nick felt that this was a high school date and a college date all in one, and he liked it. When he got home and opened his apartment door, his phone was ringing. He answered it. It was Maria. They talked for a good thirty minutes.

For the next three months or so, Nick and Maria dated exclusively, even though both knew that there was no long-term future for them as a couple. Nick went to her golf tournaments while Maria spent quality time with her teacher boyfriend when classes or golf practice did not interfere. They really enjoyed their time together, including their dinner dates at Nando's, live stand-up comedy at the Carefree Theater, or just hanging out together. One late April Sunday, Maria invited Nick to a brunch down in Boca Raton as guests of her parents and family. When they entered the private room of the snazzy restaurant, Nick immediately felt every eye land on him. There was a stone-cold silence and a once-over that seemed to go on for minutes but was just a few seconds, then almost on cue conversation and laughter returned.

Maria introduced her "special friend" to her family. Her dad nodded with a smile, never taking his large cigar from his mouth. Nick had no clue what the talk was about but felt certain it was about him and Maria as the family spoke in what can only be described as excitable Spanish. There would be a glance and even a giggle from some of the female members of the party, while the males never seemed to look his way or even care about his presence. The entire time, from late morning to the early afternoon, people spoke only in Spanish. Even the waitstaff conversed in Spanish. The only English spoken was when Maria and Nick would whisper to each other.

On the way back to Delray, Nick apologized to his girlfriend for not having been able to join in on some of the conversation because he spoke no Spanish. He explained that one of his biggest regrets in college was having taken French and not Spanish. After a moment's pause, Maria looked over at him and confessed that her family was also fluent in English, but they preferred to speak their native language around him. She explained that indeed for the first half of the meal, the conversation was about him. They spoke in Spanish so they could talk freely about him without his being able to comprehend—kind of an open-air gossip session. Nick was silent for a few seconds and let that sink in. He felt it was rude and wrong but, in an offbeat way, strangely effective. "Well, how did it go?" he asked.

"You did fine, amigo" was the response, accompanied by a sarcastic laugh. As the ride was nearing its end, so was the spring fling relationship. Maria would be off to Flagler College to continue her studies and her amateur golf career. She would finish with her bachelor's degree in psychology and stop playing competitive golf after moving on to the University of Miami for both her master's and doctoral degrees in adolescent clinical psychology. She seldom picked up a golf club again but learned to play tennis. With her ability to be coached and her God-given athletic skills, she became an excellent tennis player. The two never saw each other or, for that matter never reached out to each other again. They both moved on. Dr. Maria Hernandez would start up her own practice of helping troubled youths overcome struggles such as depression, bipolar disorder, eating disorders, addiction, self-harm, and suicide prevention. Occasionally she would pop up on TV as a local expert when the news was covering some event or something else that dealt with teenage mental health. As a teacher and coach of teenagers, Nick Finch saw firsthand the problems adolescents faced daily, and these problems seemed to be much more prevalent than when he was a teenager growing up in West Palm Beach. He was thankful for people like Dr. Maria Hernandez-Domicci, as she now was married, and not to a fellow Cuban but to an orthopedic surgeon from Fort Lauderdale. Nick wondered if he spoke Spanish.

Many years later, Nick was still teaching, but now at Jupiter High School, in the north end of the county, when a colleague mentioned that he was from Miami and had graduated from Westminster Academy. He was about the same age as Maria. Nick asked him if he knew of a classmate by the name of Maria Hernandez who was a golfer. The fellow teacher, whose name was Mike Lombardi, smiled and said, "Hell yes, I know Maria! She was homecoming queen our senior year. She made the papers by showing up just in time at halftime, and not in a gown, but in a golf skirt, to have the sash and tiara placed on her. She had just left the Orange Bowl Junior Golf Tournament and then raced over to our game. Man was she smoking hot, and still is. How do you know her, Nick?"

Nick proudly responded as if he had just won the Orange Bowl Golf trophy: "We used to date, 'bout four or five months. Great girl." Mike Lombardi did not believe him and said their reunion was coming up, noting he would see her there. Nick asked Mike to say hi for him. About three weeks later, Nick got a call one Saturday evening. On the other end of the line, according to the caller ID, was Mike Lombardi, but it was actually a woman's voice that spoke—one that he recognized immediately. It was Maria. They talked for about ten minutes; it was a good talk, only positive memories, and laughs.

Then Maria handed the phone back to her classmate, who had only three words to say: "You lucky bastard!"

Nick was back to teaching full time, but he knew there was something missing, and it was missing from his professional life. He needed to coach again. He missed it. He missed the relationships and the competition. As the New Year started, he stopped by Coach Carpenter's office in the gym and popped his head in to ask for a minute of the veteran athletic director's time. He said he was open to coaching again and noted that administration was not for him. "Great minds think alike. You were on my to-do list because I want to offer you the head softball coaching job here. You know the team is good, and I and Principal Peachstone think you would be perfect for the job. Think about it and get back to me before the end of the week. Also, something else will be opening at the end of the year, but that is all I can say about it now, other than you would be perfect for that too."

"Why wait? Yes, I would love to coach the Lady Falcons," was Coach Finch's immediate, matter-of-fact response.

CHAPTER 12

It's Halftime, and at Halftime You Need to Make Adjustments

In any athletic event, there is usually a midway point in the contest. There is halftime for football and basketball; a turn is made after the ninth hole in golf; and at 13.1 miles you are halfway through a marathon. Life also features a halftime break, a time to reevaluate your position and your goals in life and for your work. Like a good coach or athlete, you adjust for the second half. Any person should do the same, whether it relates to your personal life or professional life. Nick was coming up on halftime in his teaching career and he needed to review where he had come from, where he was currently, and where he wanted to be going.

In the education field, there is a U-shaped curve as far as compensation goes. Starting salaries are high when compared to the salary of a teacher who has taught ten to fifteen years. The purpose of this is, of course, to attract new talent to the profession and be competitive with the other professions and trades. Late in one's career, the fruit ripens when it comes to pay. With step raises, and if one decides to enroll in DROP, the deferred retirement option program, one can double-dip, so to speak. One can retire up to five years ahead of one's actual date of leaving and receive a paycheck and all the benefits, all the while building up a nice nest egg that, when it matures, will amount to a nice six-figure bonus to enjoy. This, of course, allows the district to retain its most experienced personnel and plan for future hiring. The teachers left out are the ones in the middle or, as it is called, "no man's land." Here the district or the powers that be know that this group has very little to no bargaining power. The higher-ups need new teachers and need to keep their veterans, but this group, the largest in number, cannot afford to leave. At the same time, opportunities outside their field have shrunk—all but vanished from the job market. It is hard to show up with your résumé and work history showing that your only notable experience for the past ten years is as a history or art teacher. Real-world HR department officials will roll their eyes. Also, many teachers have started families and have bought houses with monthly bills that need to be paid and hence cannot afford to start over on the bottom rung. And then there is the comfort factor. After ten years or so of teaching, the instructors have become comfortable with their profession and the demands that go with it. They have developed a style and strategies that work for them. They are comfortable with the subject matter and their delivery style. They now have their own classrooms and parking spots. Don't laugh; we are all creatures of habit, and habits are formed by way of repetition. These veteran teachers are comfortable with their colleagues and superiors. Change is hard, and that is what the district is betting on. These teachers in the middle of their careers have few, if any, options if they choose to leave, hence they get the scraps left after the new teachers and the very senior veterans get their fill. The U-curve or "no man's land." Such is the nature of the beast.

Nick was now very comfortable with teaching. He loved teaching US history, and now, having moved up to teaching Advanced Placement United States History, he was essentially teaching the class he loved, albeit at the college level, for high school. As mentioned previously, he also received a bonus of one hundred dollars for every student who passed the AP exam with a 3, 4, or 5. This reward would get knocked down to seventy-five dollars and then to fifty dollars as the school now received twenty-five bucks and the district twenty-five. Nick never had a problem with the school getting a small portion, but for the life of him he could not see how the district deserved a cut. What had they done or helped with? Such is bureaucracy; it needs to feed on its own because traditional sources of funding for such administrative costs are impossible to find. So, take it from the classroom teacher, which is quite easy, especially if the teacher is at the bottom of the U-shaped curve. Nick was in a routine in almost every way in terms of when he arrived, when and how he taught, and whom he hung out with or socialized with at school. Routine is your friend, and Nick had a comfortable routine about his professional life. Now, his personal life was different, being neither routine nor comfortable. He was at the bottom of the U-shaped curve there as well.

Nick was still very close to his mother. Charlene not only loved her baby son, who now was twenty-eight years old, but also counted on him to do little chores and have conversations with. Charlene had cut her hours at work way down and was considering retiring from the high-energy, stressful job of being an emergency room supervisor. Every day she missed J.W. more and more. She'd had a couple of suitors, but she quickly let it be known that she was not now, nor would ever be, in the market for another man. She already had her man, and sometime soon she would be joining him, hopefully in heaven.

Nick and Charlene still went to church and for breakfast at Greene's Pharmacy on Sundays, and Nick called her almost every night when he could. Now and then he would drop by the TradeWinds condominium on Singer Island, usually unannounced, to check in on her. He noticed she was shrinking in size right before his eyes. She was just not eating much anymore, seeing little need to cook for just one. She needed a whole new wardrobe but refused to pay retail price at Jordan Marsh or Burdines at the Palm Beach Mall, or even higher prices at Worth Avenue on Palm Beach. Instead, she went to the consignment/thrift store on Palm Beach called the Church Mouse run by the church. She would purchase designer clothes there for a fraction of the original price and would be pleased. Nick first commented that she had bought dead people's clothes, to which Charlene quickly retorted, "Well then, they won't need them, will they?" Next, he inquired why she needed new clothes, and she shocked him by saying she needed them because she was about to start traveling again.

Nick was taken aback. "When? Where? And with whom?"

Charlene said that soon she would be leaving and visiting places she always wanted to see but could not travel to because of her duties as a mother and nurse and because of her poor financial situation, the result having put all her money into raising five kids. Now the Finch's had not always been locked down to West Palm Beach and in fact did travel, like many other Palm Beach County residents, to the mountains of North Carolina in the summer. They also went west to visit Charlene's cousin and his family in Bozeman, Montana, where Cousin Dan was the sheriff. They'd also taken shorter trips around Florida, such as to Avon Park to see the kids' grandmother; Fort Myers; the Gulf for some beach time; and of course, Disney World and Busch Gardens. J.W. and Charlene went to the Shriners Hospital in Tampa for fundraisers and events. Nothing exotic or extraordinary—in fact, they never left the country. Charlene was going to change this as she laid out on the table some brochures and booklets of places she intended to visit. On the top of the stack was one for a tour of western Europe. Next was a cruise in the Caribbean. Behind that were the big lights of "sin city" or Las Vegas. Finally came California, starting in San Diego and finishing in the north with the redwoods, with stops in Los Angeles, the Pacific Coast Highway, San Francisco, and the wine country of Napa and Sonoma. Nick was stunned, but also impressed. *Good for her,* he thought. She had reached out to some of the other widows at the church, one at the condo and one being her sister-in-law, and they had formed a group now known as the Widows' Club. The son of one of the members was an attorney and even drew up documents that allowed them corporate rates on travel. This woman who had spent her entire life helping others, starting with her own family, namely, her war veteran husband who privately wrestled with what today we call PTSD, and tending to her five very different children, all while running a city hospital emergency room for more than thirty-five years, was finally going to do what she wanted to do. As Nick's grandmother, Charlene's mother, would say, "Well, bless her heart."

Nick sisters were not as thrilled as they voiced their concerns about her health. Charlene had already had one heart attack and thank goodness that had happened when she was at work, where she immediately received attention and care. Then there was her lifelong battle with asthma, never mind her age. Nick reassured them that their mom was up to the adventure and told them not to worry, saying that he saw her all the time and reminding them that they were tardy in personally visiting their mom, so he would be the judge of whether she was fit to travel. They also voiced concerns about the cost and asked if she had the money. Ah, that was it—they were already looking to see what would be left of the estate. Nick quickly put an end to this line of questioning by saying Charlene was comfortable financially and that it was *her* money, and he hoped that she spent her last dime on the last day of her life.

That did not go over well. The phone became silent on the other end for a few seconds, and Nick broke the uncomfortable dead time with, "Well, I guess that's all. Talk to you later." Even though there were age differences between Nick, who was the youngest, and his three sisters, he was now old enough to speak up for his mother and prevent them from questioning either him or her. Charlene would finally get to see Europe after his father had vetoed such a trip.

While in Europe, Charlene visited American Cemetery in Normandy and later admitted she broke down and cried. It must have been something for her as Nick had never seen his mom cry. The hospital and life in general had hardened her to public displays of emotion. She had a great time in Europe, but complained that the food, the plumbing, and other modern conveniences were much better in the States. Her trip to the Caribbean was eventful. She remarked on the beauty of the water and the islands, and the constant supply of food on the ship, but she also critiqued the work ethic of the islanders and their aggressive selling tactics. Las Vegas intrigued her in that it never slept. She also won two hundred dollars on the slot machines and even got to see Siegfried and Roy, along with Wayne Newton. Also, she got to brag a little bit when Nick's coaching friend and colleague Larry Timmons, whose second job, not a hobby, was professional gambling and who was a frequent visitor to Vegas, called ahead and the "Widows' Club" upgraded to VIP status, with much of their food and entertainment comped.

The California trip was the best of all the trips the widows took. It started in San Diego, with all its beauty, and then went up to LA, including tours of the homes of the rich and famous, along with visits to Santa Barbara, Beverly Hills, and the movie studios. Once again Charlene got to brag when the group went to a Dodgers baseball game—they were playing against the San Francisco Giants—at night at the famous Dodger Stadium. The Dodgers' starting shortstop was a high school team member and classmate of Nick's named Russel Baker. When Nick contacted Russ about his mother and the Widows' Club and their intention to go to the game, the shortstop had their tickets upgraded to box seats behind the Dodger dugout. The skipper, Tommy Lasorda, visited the women and took pictures along with the former Forest Hill shortstop. Because the game was being played at night, the temperature, even though it was summer, dropped much more than it did back in Florida. When returning to the dugout after an inning, Russel Baker, noticing that Charlene was cold, instructed a batboy to go to her, whom he pointed out, and take her a Dodgers jacket. The crowd loved it. As Baker went to bat, he glanced back at the mother of his high school buddy, whom he had known his entire life, and did what baseball players do: tipped his cap to the woman, who was now sporting an official Dodgers jacket. In the seventh inning during the stretch and the singing of "Take Me Out to the Ball Game," the Florida widows looked at the jumbotron and saw their entire group was featured. This was followed by a cheer as they were announced as guests of the Dodgers and shortstop Russel Baker. It is hard to top that.

San Francisco was great. Again and again, Charlene remarked on the flavor of the sourdough bread. She would tell people not to be fooled when other breads were called by that name, because the real thing is exceptionally good and is sweet to the taste. After Charlene had passed away, Nick found the album of photos from her trips. It brought both a tear to his eye and a smile to his face as it made him very happy that his mom had been able to do what she wanted to do after years of doing what others needed or wanted her to do. Good for her.

Now if she would only stop pestering him about when he was going to settle down. She pleaded with him, saying her last request before she left this earth and was reunited with his father was to see him walk down the aisle at their church. She wanted to make sure he had found the right person as she had done and that he would share his life with his new love and maybe even start his own family. Now was that too much to ask? Nick always smiled back and quickly tried to change the subject. Almost all Nick's friends, colleagues, and college classmates were now married, some even married and already divorced, or in serious relationships. Nick was happy, but he knew something was missing. Charlene knew it too. Being married would be much tougher than teaching, so he buried himself in work and coaching. He was constantly being told that he would find the right woman when he least expected it, which he got tired of hearing.

No longer coaching football, Nick now was the head girls' softball coach. About the third week of school, he held an organizational meeting for those who intended to try out for the team or had an interest in becoming a "Lady Falcon". About thirty-five girls showed up at the lunch meeting, which he held in his room. He welcomed them and passed out the necessary paperwork, such as physical forms, proof-of-residency forms, and parental permission documents. Any athletes who would be playing fall or winter sports—volleyball, cross-country running, cheerleading, or basketball—would be exempt as they had already submitted their paperwork. He had them write down their class schedules, phone numbers, and playing experience. The data processor would go through the list and enter the girls' GPAs, then return this information to Nick. He was amazed and impressed by how well these girls performed in the classroom. When he was coaching football, many times players failed to make the grades to continue participating. Not so with these girls. He calculated their team GPA as 3.5—and mostly all upper-level classes. About five of them had Nick as their AP US History teacher or, as it is known, APUSH. If the girls were not playing a fall or winter sport, he expected them to play rec or travel softball at Lake Lytal. Lake Lytal Park is named after the longtime county commissioner Lake Lytal, and in fact there is no lake at this park. The locals called it the Gun Club because it is located just down the road from the county jail. Nick told the girls that if any among them had to work to help with a family situation, they should please talk to him privately. There were no discussions of such. Those who were going to play rec ball were to give him a schedule so he could visit and watch. Next, he had to hire an assistant coach and find a place to play as there were no softball facilities on campus. He found his assistant in Dan Glenndemming, a fellow social studies teacher who had been an assistant baseball coach during the years when Nick was away at Ole Miss. When the baseball coaching job opened, Glenndemming had been passed over. He swore off coaching forever but found himself attracted to the softball program. The only problem was that he had a side job as part owner of and worker at a battery shop that specialized in tractor and semitruck batteries. Nick assured him that he would only need him for games and asked him to just try to make it to practices. Both agreed that this arrangement would work, and it did work well, as the older Coach Glenndemming, the father of a high school daughter himself, had a calming effect on the single and childless head coach.

It was fairly easy to procure a home field, as the Falcons regarded the "A" Street field as their home for softball games. The field was not even in West Palm Beach but in neighboring Lake Worth, but the powers that be for the youth leagues that had custody of the fields welcomed the girls, because in return they were given all the concession rights, and the Lady Falcons drew big crowds. Attendees of home games of course included parents and family, but also boyfriends, classmates, and lots of younger players who looked up to the high school athletes. Title IX, an attempt to equalize the playing field for athletes in terms of gender, was in its infancy but was catching on fast. Just as Nick had done a generation earlier when he wore his youth league football jersey to watch such local stars as future Super Bowl MVP Ottis Anderson and NFL veteran Ken Stone play, these young girls came out in their youth league jerseys to watch their local idols. Title IX was working.

On the first day of school, Mr. Finch was looking over his new roster of students, and one name jumped right off the page: Leon Rawlings Jr. Leon Rawlings Sr. had been a classmate of Nick's going all the way back to kindergarten, through middle school, and on to their graduation from high school. Leon was better known by his nickname "Tater," for "potato." Why he'd been given that name, nobody knew, but it went as far back as the two had known each other, and that was a long time. Teachers called him Tater, as did the PA announcer for high school football games. "Tackle by "Tator" Rawlings would blare across the stadium. You see, Tater was a particularly good but undersized player who knew no fear and loved to hit. The one thing Tater did not hit, however, was the books. He barely graduated, which he was able to do mostly because he had gotten help from classmates and had teachers who looked the other way. One more thing about Leon Rawlings, throughout high school he went to the small regional executive airport in Lantana, where he worked in exchange for flying lessons. Shortly after graduation he got his wings, or his pilot's license. While the rest of the boys went off to college, Tater took to the skies. He piloted small Cessnas to take wealthy people to the Bahamas, then he would put on a cap and goggles and fly a biplane crop duster over the farm fields of the western part of the county, dropping insecticide and herbicide over the crops grown in the Glades. Shortly after that, he married a classmate's sister who was a cocktail waitress at E. R. Bradley's Saloon on Palm Beach. Bradley's was the in place where the beautiful people went and where not only the whiskey flowed, but also the drugs. Pam Rawlings, a beautiful young woman, found herself caught up in that scene. It was Tater who, so to speak, rescued her and got her away from the dark side of the party scene of Palm Beach. They married and soon thereafter welcomed Leon Rawlings Jr. into the world. On the surface, life was good, but underneath there were problems. Money was tight with the recession, and there were fewer trips to the Islands. Upkeep on the plane with general maintenance was expensive and never-ending. A couple of rare deep freezes killed many of the winter vegetable crops, so there was no need for spraying. And Pam, spoiled by her temporary Palm Beach lifestyle, changed her addiction from cocaine to impulse buying. Add to that the cost of a baby boy, and the bills soon outweighed the income. Tater had to do something or he was going to lose everything. He decided to become a pilot for the illegal drug smuggling empires of South Florida.

Tater Rawlings knew some of the well-dressed guys who seemed to appear out of nowhere to exchange briefcases in the airport hangars around the Lantana Airport. They were easy to spot. Some of the movies of the eighties and nineties were not too far off in how they characterized these drug kingpins. Tater would fly at night without lights and low to the ground, with no documented flight plan, traveling to the Bahamas with two passengers who spoke broken

English. Once there, they'd pick up the supply and return, but not to Lantana—to a desolate airstrip isolated out in the Glades marked by lit tiki torches outlining the runway. For six months, Tater did this twice a week and made the kind of cash that professional athletes or entertainers make, until one awful February night.

When Tater landed his plane that night in February, things looked the same as they always did, until he killed the engines. Instead of the contacts meeting his passengers who were waiting to make the exchange, it was the Drug Enforcement Agency. Tater was arrested on the spot and taken to jail. Federal prosecutors offered him a deal: continue to do what he was doing, but now as an informant for the government, and testify. Tater refused, so the feds turned him over to the State's Attorney's Office to stand trial for crimes against the State of Florida rather than face a federal trial. Tater Rawlings was a small fish and uncooperative. But he knew better than to accept the deal, because if he were to do what they wanted, he would end up dead—and, worse, so would his family. Charlene sent Nick the clippings from the *Palm Beach Post* of the arrest and trial in the care packages she sent of small gifts and tokens while he was at Ole Miss. It was a good day when he checked his mailbox at the union and found there was a care package from home, that is, until the day he read about his friend.

During the eighties and early nineties there was the War on Drugs, and the government pulled out all the stops to win it, increasing manpower and funding, even using the US Navy as one of its weapons. They played for keeps, and courts were in on the heavy sentences. *Leon Rawlings v. the State of Florida* was a quick trial because Tater pled guilty. He was sentenced to five to ten years in the Florida correctional system, and he was to have his pilot's license seized and would never again be allowed to fly. His wife Pam, shortly thereafter, filed and was granted a divorce and full custody of their child. Tater Rawlings lost everything, but the most notable of his losses was his son. The former drug pilot was sent to the maximum-security prison in Starke known as the Raiford State Penitentiary. The prison is infamous for its dangerous and almost subhuman conditions and brutality. It also had a death row wing with infamous inmates such as Ted Bundy and Denny Rowling, the latter being the "Gainesville Slasher" who were given the ultimate punishment either by the electric chair, nicknamed "Old Sparky" or lethal injection.

After seven years, Tater was transferred to the state prison in Avon Park, a medium-security facility. On one of Nick's trips to see his elderly grandmother, after having passed the prison many times, he found himself pulling into the visitors' parking lot. He stayed parked for a few moments and then took a deep breath and went to the visitor gate. He signed some papers, showed his identification, went to the visitors' booths, and waited. A guard emerged with Leon Rawlings in a blue prison shirt and blue jeans. The guard directed the inmate to a seat across the table from Nick Finch, informing Tater that he had ten minutes. Nick realized his friend's nickname of Tater had even followed him to incarceration.

Tater sat down. He had aged but overall looked good. The two men stared at each other silently for a moment or two, then Tater bluntly asked, "So, to what do I owe the pleasure of your company today? You, other than my lawyer, are the first person to visit me since I transferred here."

Nick nodded and said, "If you remember, my grandmother lives here, and I just could not pass this place again without stopping." Tater nodded with an expression of gratitude on his face as if saying, *OK*. They both fell silent again. Nick decided to initiate the next bit of conversation by commenting, "Well, this has to be a lot better than Raiford, right?"

The inmate raised his voice a little to reply: "Just a different wing of hell, nothing more, nothing less." They fell silent again. Nick was thinking that maybe this had not been his best idea and that his friend was far more damaged than he had ever imagined.

Tater said he was sorry, thanked the teacher, his lifelong classmate, for visiting him, and apologized for having been short with him. He added he was not used to visitors as both his parents had died, his brother moved to Utah, and Pam had remarried and kept their son from ever visiting him. Nick listened and replied, "Man, I am sorry. Is there anything I can do for you?" Tater asked Nick if by being a teacher he could keep an eye out for his son in the school system, making sure he had the right teachers and such. Without hesitation, Nick looked his friend right in the eye and answered, "Absolutely." Nick felt better after he left the prison and shared the encounter with some of their mutual friends and, of course, Charlene. After that initial trip, the boys each picked a month and visited Tater, who would be getting out in a couple of years. Nick had kicked open the door to the prison for visitors, and now Tater had a supply line of people seeing him. Nick never forgot that, but more importantly, neither did Tater.

Later in that first week of school, Nick called on Leon Jr., asking him to stay after class for a talk. The young boy was handsome, well-dressed, and very smart. He had that same grin as his father, not his stepfather, who was an attorney in the law firm that represented his real father. Are you wondering how Pam and he met? Leon Jr. started the conversation with Nick by stating that he knew that Nick knew that he was friends with his real dad, but Leon himself had nothing to do with his biological father. Nick listened and then explained that it was true that he had known Leon's dad since elementary school and they had been teammates in high school. He also knew his mom. Nick continued by saying how impressed he was with young Leon's grades, his demeanor, and his politeness. Without allowing Jr. to interrupt or jump in, Nick continued by saying that, yes, his father had made a big mistake, but he was paying for it now and soon would be done with his debt to society. And yes, Nick kept in contact with Leon's real dad, who was very proud of his son. He finished by saying it might have been none of Nick's business, but with forgiveness being an honorable trait, Leon should think about forgiving his dad.

About nine months later Leon Rawlings Sr. was released from prison. It was a slow reacquainting of father and son, but the following year at graduation Nick saw the two hug each other. Both had graduated in a way. Nick had never felt so good knowing that he'd had a little something to do with it.

Coaching had been a feature of Nick's life for a very long time. While in high school, he helped when he could with the local youth league teams that he had played on growing up in West Palm Beach. He umpired Little League baseball at the same field he had played on, Phipps Park. It was interesting to him that in the past two years of his stint as head softball coach, games were played in the adjacent field there at Phipps Park located in the south end of West Palm. The field is gone now, replaced by a soccer field and a skateboard park.

When Nick did his internship, or practice teaching, he volunteered and helped with spring football in Mississippi at Pontotoc Central High School. He impressed the veteran coaching staff so much that they did everything in their power to persuade him to stay on. Of course, with his father's declining health, he went back home. And what did he do? Immediately started coaching football at Forest Hill. In fact, he started coaching before he entered the classroom to teach history. The thousands of small children to whom he had given swim lessons in his seven years as a lifeguard and swim instructor in the western communities do not even count, but they too were a version of coaching. Nick Finch had always believed that coaching was the ultimate form of teaching. Unlike in a classroom, where students had to be there and many never saw the need to study dead presidents or understood the importance of the debate on whether to join the League of Nations after World War I, on a sports team, the players chose to be there. They were motivated. Some played for the pure pleasure of competition or being part of a team, and some sought the possible reward of a college scholarship. Some saw sports as a relief valve to ease the pressures of school, work, and home life. They wanted to be there, whereas not all students wanted to be in a classroom. Certain life skills are taught by being involved in organized sports, such as competing, working as part of a team, and relationship building. The same can be said for music, drama, and debate, as well as other after-school activities. Lifelong friendships and memories are made every day on fields, in gyms, on courts, on tracks, and in swimming pools across the country. One does not always remember one's classmates, but one never forgets one's teammates. Other things such as uniforms—a dress code in a way; field trips, which are the team's away games; and learning to win and lose, along with how to deal with both wins and losses, are just some of the positive aspects that come from playing organized sports.

Nick was a young head coach, and unlike many first-time coaches, he was not starting at the bottom of the ladder with a team and program that was marked by losses. Just the opposite. Forest Hill was good, quite good at softball. The previous coaches, who had been two of Nick's high school teachers and coaches, had built a solid program and then, for various reasons, resigned and went on to new challenges. One became a district administrator in human resources—it helped that he was bilingual—but for the rest of his life he would regret leaving coaching and the classroom. The other wanted a new assignment, so he took over SGA, or the student government association, also better known as student council. The one problem was the elephant in the room, or more appropriately the gator in the room, as Forest Hill had to compete against state and national power Palm Beach Gardens. At one time the Gators had won the state championship five out of seven years, and the two years they did not, Forest Hill knocked them out. Two hundred to three hundred people would show up for the Falcon–Gator clashes up on Burns Road in the Gardens or on one of the two fields the Falcons called home. Stressful, but incredibly fun—and that is why you play or coach the game.

Nick Finch would be head coach of the Lady Falcons for only five years, but in that time his girls would rack up an impressive record of one hundred wins versus only twenty-four losses. They would win two conference championships, two district titles, one regional title, and one sectional title, and be runner-up for a state title. Two times Nick would be selected by his peers as Coach of the Year, and once by the *Palm Beach Post* and the *Fort Lauderdale Sun Sentinel* as Coach of the Year. He would be chosen to coach the Palm Beach–Broward County Challenge and one time served as coach for the Florida Athletics Coaches Association in the state North–South All-Star game. Multiple players had been selected for Channel 12's Athlete of the Week and were featured on the evening news. All five years Nick's team had the honor of being selected the Palm Beach Kennel Club / Channel 5 Team of the Week, which also caused them to be featured on the local newscasts. Nick had three players make All-State, and too many to mention were selected All-Conference and/or All-Area. He also helped guide the change from slow pitch to fast pitch in his final year as mandated by the state. Beyond all the accolades and awards, the thing he remained proudest of was that every single one of his players went on to college. While some played ball there, most did not, but all went on to be successful in one way or another. In that area, the Lady Falcons were undefeated, and that is what really counts.

A coach gets to know his players better than he ever gets to know his classroom students. He learns their personality traits, their quirks, and their passions. Hopefully, a coach pushes the right buttons and knows when to figuratively give a pat on the back or a kick in the butt. As with everything, a coach gets better with experience. Luckily, Nick had coached before, but he had never coached girls. For the most part it was the same as coaching boys, but there were some notable differences. Nick Finch was lucky that in many ways he had been raised by his three older sisters. He had a playbook, so to speak. Athletes of both genders want to be on the field, both want to win, and both have natural leaders in the locker room or the dugout. Some are quiet, while some are rah-rah. Among the differences Nick noted between male and female athletes is that boys seemed to take losses harder. Girls moved on to the next game and let it go. Girls were better at prioritizing their goals and responsibilities. Many times, Nick would look into the dugout or on the bus while riding to or away from a contest and find his Lady Falcons with a book out studying. That *never* happened when he was coaching boys in football. The boys could care less about prom, whereas for the girls, the P-word from February through early May was constantly on their lips before, during, and after games and at all practices. Overall, the female athletes were much more mature, but that was also true of females in the classroom. Girls can be seventeen going on twenty-five, for better or for worse, while boys can be seventeen going on twelve. Of course, these are stereotypes built on observation and there are exceptions to every rule.

Nick Finch, as head softball coach of the Forest Hill Lady Falcons, had the pleasure of coaching some seventy-five players, and each one was different. But each was also part of a team that loved to win and hated to lose. Again, Nick did not remember every student he taught, but he remembered every player who played for him. As time marched on, he found that the good memories far outweighed the occasional conflicts. Plus, somehow as the calendar changed each year, he seemed to be a better coach and his players all seemed to be better players. Dwell on the positive.

Some of the personalities, Nick will never forget. There was a talented outfielder by the name of Elizabeth Mary Eagan. She went by both her first and middle name, Elizabeth Mary—not Liz, or Beth, or EM, but Elizabeth Mary, and you had better not forget it. She could run and hit and had a cannon for an arm. Fearless both in the field and on the basepaths, she nevertheless could get under Nick's skin like no other player. Her body language just silently screamed, *why are you wasting my time?* She'd have her hand on her hip and be rolling her eyes as Coach Finch was addressing the team, or she would be looking elsewhere, anywhere except at her coach, when he was trying to get a point across to her. On at least two occasions he just threw her out of practice and sent her home. "Leave. Go. Go now. I'll see you tomorrow!" Abruptly, the left fielder would turn, pick up her stuff, get into her Honda Prelude, and squeal away. The next day there would be a few tense moments between the two, but then things would return to normal as if nothing happened the day before. If you're thinking that probably got old, you're right, but the thing is, nobody played harder or had a shorter memory than Elizabeth Mary. She ran into fences chasing down balls and slid into bases so hard that opposing infielders feared her. And nobody hated to lose more than she did. She hated losing more than she loved the joy of winning. A true competitor. She and Nick run into each other now and then and grin about her ejections from practice and almost everything else. Elizabeth Mary was and is a winner.

Nick also had the opportunity to coach triplets, kind of. He had a set of identical, but mirror image, twins, Lauren, and Lee Redding, on his team. In their senior year, their parents allowed a youth league teammate who was in a very dysfunctional household to move in with them. Forest Hill appealed to the Florida High School Athletics Association for a hardship waiver to allow this girl to both transfer and play for the Falcons. After the state reviewed the documentation discussing her home life, they voted 7–0 in favor, allowing Lori Cooper to join the team. She and the twins were inseparable. In fact, Lori was a stabilizing factor for the two sisters. As mentioned, they were mirror image twins in that they were identical but at the same time completely opposite. One was right-handed and batted righty, while the other was a southpaw and hit from that side. They played completely different positions as the lefty was a pitcher and outfielder and was a singles hitter, whereas Lee was a power-hitting right-handed shortstop. One was kind of prissy, while the other was tomboyish. They parted their hair on different sides. Add to that mix the new stepsister Lori, and it must have been quite a household, as it certainly made for quite a team.

Lauren was a pitcher and, along with her sister, had played in the Palm Beach Gardens youth programs and not at Lake Lytal for some reason, perhaps a falling-out the family had had with the travel summer teams. Nick said he could care less about what had happened in the summer as now it was school ball time. Some of the youth coaches who never missed a game never liked that Nick made sure his players checked their summer allegiances at the first practice. They no longer played for Lytal or Gardens but for Forest Hill. The girls bought in, but some of the adults did not. Again, Nick could care less.

Unfortunately, Lee Redding, the power-hitting shortstop, had hurt her arm badly and could not throw. She had had surgery on her arm and still could hit, however. In one of the wildest and most creative coaching moves ever seen in slow-pitch softball, Nick made Lee a one-armed catcher, but since she could not throw the ball back to the pitcher, who was her sister, she would roll it back! People laughed and were amused at first, but the laughing stopped when Lee came to bat and unleashed her incredible bat speed, hitting a ball harder and farther than should have been possible for a girl all of five foot five. Plus, you had a battery (pitcher–catcher combo) of twin sisters.

There was one time, well, that did not work out. There was a game that Forest Hill should have won in five innings because of the ten-run mercy rule, but instead they were behind after three innings, mostly thanks to overconfidence and the fact that Lauren, the pitcher, was having a hard time finding the strike zone and was uncharacteristically walking batters, which caused the team to fall behind in score. Ultimately, she was forced to grove a pitch that got hit hard. Nick was extremely fortunate to have two outstanding pitchers in Lauren Redding and junior Shelly Benedict. The two played against each other in the summer as Shelly played for Lytal and Lauren for the Gardens. They both could play the outfield as well as anybody, so Coach Finch made sure both were in the lineup. And to their credit, they had no summer rivalry between them. Finally, Nick had seen enough. He went out to the mound to make a pitching change, and Lee the catcher mumbled something to the effect of "Finally," to which her twin responded with a word beginning with the letter *F*, followed by the word *you*. Nick motioned for Shelly to come in from centerfield. The plan was to have Lauren replace her in the outfield—a straight switch. Lauren was not happy. She had never, ever been pulled from the pitching mound, and now it was being done—and in front of everyone. She was pissed. When Nick asked for the ball, Lauren Redding looked right at her coach and dropped the ball to the ground rather than handing it to him. Because the entire infield was surrounding the mound, few in the stands saw the exchange. The players had seen it as the catcher and her twin sister, Lee, went to pick it up off the ground, but Nick shook his head and reached down and got himself.

Lauren Redding trotted out to her place in centerfield and passed Shelly Benedict. The two high fived each other. Everyone around the mound who had witnessed the disrespectful act was in shock. Some looked stunned. Lauren, the adopted girl, was kicking at the dirt and would not look up, while the catcher, Lee, was giving the death stare to her twin sister, who was now in the outfield. Coach Finch gave the ball to Shelly Benedict, who quickly put out the fire and stopped the rally. When Nick returned to the dugout, Coach Glenndemming and the reserves looked at him. A young freshman named Karlee Mildner flat-out asked, "What just happened out there?" Nick shook his head, knowing that how he chose to handle this could either be a teaching moment or else rip the team, and even the girls' family, apart. He turned and looked at the young freshman as if addressing her, but in reality, he was talking to everyone, because when the inning ended, the coaches would go out onto the field to coach the first and third boxes, leaving the players unsupervised. When the inning ended and his players returned to the dugout for their turns at bat, Nick instructed his assistant to stay in the dugout and supervise. He had a reserve player replace him in the first base coaching box. He wanted an adult, another coach, in that dugout just in case. For what, he was not sure.

The Falcons rallied for the expected win and as always, after tidying up the dugout, went out to centerfield for a quick postgame meeting, including a review, maybe a couple of shout-outs, and a reminder of upcoming events on the team schedule. Despite the victory, the team was somber and quiet as the coach went over what he'd seen today and what needed to be worked on. But, as always, he ended with a congratulations, and this time it was for Shelly Benedict. The whole team gave her a loud round of applause. Nick then dismissed the team, except for one player: Lauren Redding. He told her to stay behind. The whole team left for the parking lot, but it was hard for the players to walk away. They kept turning around to see if they could tell what was happening in the private player–coach meeting. What was he going to do, throw her off the team? And if he did so, would the other two quit? Would he suspend her? run her till she dropped? (Softball and baseball players *hate* to run.)

For what seemed like ten minutes but was only about thirty seconds, there was dead silence as the coach looked down at his starting pitcher, who was just staring at the outfield grass and kicking it. Nick broke the silence with a quick and to-the-point question in a voice a couple of octaves lower than usual: "Well, please explain what happened out there today—and it had better be good."

After most postgame meetings when he dismissed the players, they raced to their cars as fast as they could and got the "heck out of Dodge". Not today, as they remained parked and staring out at the meeting taking place in centerfield. Lauren looked up to her coach with eyes full of tears, which were also escaping down her cheeks, and sobbingly blurted out, "I don't know. I really don't, I swear. I have never been taken out of a game, and I went blank. I do not know what to say. If you want my uniform, I understand. If you want to run me, bench me … I will do whatever you want. I cannot believe what I did. I am so sorry." The tears were now flowing freely. *This could go either way,* Nick thought. The coach made sure the players saw their teammate in total breakdown, hoping they would embrace her. She had made a mistake. We all make mistakes. She then placed her head on his chest and continued to cry. She was an eighteen-year-old senior showing the true emotion of remorse, genuine in every way.

Nick said in a comforting voice, "Let's go home." He put his arm around her shoulder as she needed a shoulder to cry on. He added one last thing as the two slowly made their way in from the outfield: "It will never, ever happen again, and we will never talk about it. Deal?" Lauren nodded her head in agreement. And indeed, nothing like it ever happened again and it was never discussed again.

Well, it was close to thirty years later at Nick's retirement party when the triplets showed up and the four of them laughed together at the memories and just enjoyed seeing each other again. Suddenly, Lauren emerged with a softball signed by as many of the girls as she could locate and presented it to Nick on this memorable occasion. Nick was touched and found himself getting a little choked up. When as he reached for the signed ball, Lauren dropped it to the floor, reenacting the incident of thirty years earlier. The difference now was there no crying. Well, Nick cried a little, feeling emotional, but they were tears of laughter as the two of them exchanged a loving hug. Well played, Lauren Redding. Well played indeed.

After the highly successful season, which ended—how else? —with Palm Beach Gardens having lost the district championship, the players would have one more formal meeting, the annual team banquet. The yearly event Nick put together was always held in the private dining room of a legendary West Palm steak house named Manero's. Located on Palm Beach Lakes Boulevard, the place was famous for its gorgonzola tossed salad and top cuts of steak and prime rib, and freshly caught seafood. The adjacent bar made top-shelf mixed drinks for pre- and post-dinner celebrations. The bar itself was kind of an unofficial office for the Atlanta Braves during spring training. After exhibition games, the front office, along with the coaching staff led by Hall of Fame manager Bobby Cox, would leave Municipal Stadium for the three- or four-block trip to the steak house bar and discuss the day's game, player development, and future roster spots. Many players probably never knew that their whole professional careers were discussed, debated, and determined, not in a stadium office or a film room, but at a bar over a mixed drink. Add to this the fact that the Braves were now a national fixture, thanks to Ted Turner's realized vision of cable television and "Superstation" TBS, which broadcasted the Braves every day or night, or so it seemed, from spring right through to fall, the games sandwiched between reruns of *The Andy Griffith Show* and professional wrestling. Early cable was genuine and hokey, but it worked. One could switch from MTV, which then played videos, over to the Braves game, or from Billy Idol to Dale Murphy. Now that is entertainment! There were times when Nick and some of his coaching peers would pop in for a pop or two, and almost every time the skipper of the Braves would wave over to the high school coaches, dismiss himself from his meeting, go over to the high school coaches, and initiate a conversation about how their teams, players, and practices were going. Bobby Cox once shared that his first professional dream had been to become a high school football coach. After a minute or two, the successful manager would go back to his own meeting and then, like clockwork, the bartender, Joey, would notify the high school guys that the Atlanta Braves had picked up the cost of their drinks. A very cool and very classy maneuver by a very classy guy and organization.

Nick had the one and only banquet that the principal and athletic director both wanted to attend. Honestly, seeing as it was banquet season as the school year wound down, they were worn out, but this was a must-be-at event. Great food, a team that was so easy to root for with success both on the field and in the classroom, a strong parent support group, and some lighthearted laughs throughout the evening always made it a success. There were some funny moments, beginning in January with tryouts and ending in early May, that only the players and coaching staff got to be there for that provided plenty of material for choosing a gag gift for each and every player. The banquet was a time to share some of these stories with everyone else. There would be no such joking about the ball dropping incident, but Nick would give Lauren a softball with plastic model airplane wings glued to the side—as Nick explained, the ball that the Palm Beach Gardens player had hit off Lauren Redding and had finally landed. Everyone loved the shtick, even Lauren, as the two could laugh about this one, but not the other incident. Another cool thing was seeing the Lady Falcons dressed up for the occasion. Day in and day out the group saw each other in school clothes—there was not much of a dress code—practice outfits, or game uniforms, but now here they were with their parents dressed in their Sunday best. As the evening ended, Nick wished his seniors only the best. All were going to college, and some would continue playing softball at the college level, having earned scholarships. Then Nick would challenge his returning players to take their respective teams to the next level. They accepted the challenge.

Nick knew that this would be his last year as head coach, as both his personal life and professional life were beginning to overload him. He hoped to go out on top, and he almost met that goal. With a strong team that had lost only four players, the district runner-up team of the year before, a topflight pitcher in Shelly Benedict, and a solid bench with no real weaknesses, he thought this team could go far. And because of declining enrollment with close to nine hundred students having gone to Wellington High once it opened, Forest Hill would drop down a notch in classification and would not be forced to play Palm Beach Gardens. The two teams would play each other, but for regular season only. They split their contests against each other to prepare for the state playoffs. Forest Hill ended up with a regular season of twenty-six wins against only three losses. They breezed through the district playoffs, beating local teams of the same size, and then went north to play a Fort Pierce school for the regional title, then south to play a private Broward County Catholic school for a chance to join Palm Beach Gardens in Gainesville as the other Palm Beach County team competing for the state championship in girls' softball. The Lady Falcons had made it, and now there was only one more game—and maybe a championship ring. One other thing was that their game was to be televised statewide on a new regional cable sports network known as the Sunshine Network.

Facing the Falcons would be traditional power Bartram Trail of the Jacksonville–St. Augustine area. Nick Finch had never seen a team so physically big. They looked like a men's league factory team. He watched them take batting practice during the day before the scheduled one-hour practice time, which each team was afforded. *Oh no,* he thought, *we might simply be overmatched.* The next afternoon, the two teams took the field in Gainesville. Forest Hill lost the coin flip and would be the visitors, batting first. The girls, with their speed and some good base running, were able to squeeze a run across the plate. The Falcons had drawn first blood. When they went out to take the field, Nick instructed his fielders to play real deep. Then what Nick had feared happened: the girls from the "First Coast" crushed the ball. Three runs had crossed the plate before his girls had recorded their first out, when suddenly a ball was crushed right up the middle and ricocheted off the shin of Shelly Benedict. The hit was as hard as any Nick had ever seen, and the ball had hit his All-State pitcher squarely on her lower left leg. She let out a bloodcurdling shriek and collapsed on the mound. Nick raced from the dugout without even asking for permission from the umpires. They understood. The training staff quickly followed him and determined the leg was not broken, but there was a horrible contusion. Immediately, it began to swell and become discolored. Coach Finch literally carried his four-year starter in his arms to the dugout, to a standing ovation from fans in both grandstands. The girl who had hit the screaming line drive now appeared shaken and genuinely concerned about what had just happened. Shelly Benedict was an attractive young woman who resembled the actress Alicia Silverstone of the movie *Clueless*, with stylish blonde hair, who had earlier in the fall been voted to the school's homecoming court—and now she was in the corner of the dugout in tears and in pain with a giant ice bag wrapped around her swollen black, blue, and purple leg that looked as if someone had just taped a golf ball to her shin. One of the younger players actually became ill looking at it. The girl who had hit the ball walked over to the dugout to say how sorry she was. Shelly nodded, indicating she was OK, and said, "Thank you for the concern." Nick thought, *how classy. Adults could learn something from these kids.*

The Trail, which was the team's nickname, pushed a total of ten runs across the plate in that first inning, which came mercifully to an end with the score of 10–1, Bartram Trails leading Forest Hill, who now had to play without their star senior player. Nick looked at the nightmare that was occurring; they were down by nine runs without their star player while being telecast statewide. The game was lost and could really get out of hand, and even though there was a ten-run mercy rule, the contest had to go at least five innings to be official. Nick looked at his players, who were shell-shocked, and told them to go out and leave it all on the field—no matter what the final score was, give it everything that had. At that point, Shelly Benedict hopped over to her teammates, who were standing in a circle, and told them to play as if they had been playing all season. Then she said, "I love you guys so much. Give 'em hell. And remember, Falcons soar!"

Believe it or not, after that they probably played their best ball of the entire season. They held their opponents scoreless for the next six innings, making diving catches, throwing runners out at the plate, and turning four double plays. Unfortunately, they could not score themselves. The final game of the AAA State Championship would go to Bartram Trails, 10–1, but it did last the entire seven innings. No mercy killing here. Not today. But what everyone remembered, other than the horrible line drive injury to Shelly Benedict in the first inning, was what happened in the top of the seventh inning. With two outs and the Trail players beginning to celebrate their championship win, Nick Finch, Shelly Benedict, and the Bartram Trails did something that is still talked about. Because of the injury, Shelly never got to hit in the first inning, and she had pleaded with her coach to allow her to get at least one swing in for her last game. For three innings she would hobble or skip up to Coach and plead for just one at-bat. Before the top of the seventh inning, Nick talked to the trainer and asked if Shelly risked further damage to her leg if she were to stand in the batter's box. The trainer convinced him that she could do no further damage, but any motion would be extremely painful. Nick went over to the Bartram dugout and had a private conversation with their coach before the inning started, and both coaches left nodding in agreement. The opposing coach then had a private one-on-one strategy talk with her pitcher before the inning started. Quickly, Bartram Trails recorded two outs, when Nick Finch called for time. He went to the umpire and announced a reentry for purposes of pinch-hitting. The new batter would be Shelly Benedict. Slowly, and with a pronounced limp, the star pitcher and captain of her team emerged from the dugout. The first baseman, who had hit the shot that had hurt Shelly, dropped her glove and began to clap, as did the entire crowd of spectators, including the Palm Beach Gardens team, who were there because they were going to be playing the nightcap game that followed. Nick came up and warned his player—no, pleaded with her—not to swing and not even to think about running it out. Not to worry, as the opposing pitcher, in a total class act, pitched four straight balls that would have been impossible to hit, earning the senior a walk to first base. Shelly limped to first, where the opposing first baseman gave her a high five. Nick immediately replaced her with a pinch-runner, then Shelly Benedict left the competitive softball field for the last time in her life, but to a standing ovation and cheers from everyone in attendance, including the Sunshine Network announcers, her grit, determination, and sportsmanship fully on display. That would be the last game Nick Finch would coach at his alma mater. Even though they had come up short, what a way to go. He was very proud of his team, his players, and the program.

On Christmas Day, the Sunshine Network ran a loop of the state championships they had covered, and sure enough at two o'clock was the AAA Softball State Championship. Even though some of the parents had recoded it on their VHS players and had given each player and the two coaches copies, Nick could not bring himself to watch. That Christmas Day he did. He shuddered when seeing the line drive that ran his star out of the game. He watched with pride as his team played their hearts out and put everything, they had out there, also found himself getting choked up at Shelly Benedict's final at-bat. To Nick, watching the replay for the first time at Christmas seemed right because he thought it would make a good Christmas Hallmark movie script.

There were two assignments remaining for Nick as head softball coach. One of these was the banquet at Manero's, at the end of which he announced to those in attendance that he was resigning. Most expected it and were not surprised. Instead, they were grateful for his leadership. He felt equally gratified that he had had the opportunity to coach such an outstanding group of young women and to share such memorable experiences. One bit of professional advice that Nick would always give new teachers, interns, or practice teachers was to coach, which he believed was the ultimate teaching experience. He would expand it to include other opportunities, such as drama, music, debate, and service clubs, or endeavors whose purpose was to give back to the school, the student body, or the community.

Such participation, competition, and sharing seldom can be duplicated in the classroom.

The last thing was that Nick Finch had been selected by the Florida Athletic Coaching Association, or FACA, to coach the South team in the annual North–South Senior Softball Classic held in Brooksville, Florida, after the state softball tournament had run its course. This yearly event was for senior players who were nominated and voted onto the team by the local coaches in their respective areas. Shelly Benedict was selected and was also selected first team All-State. There would be two Gardens girls and one from the Catholic school, Cardinal Newman. Nick would be the head coach, assisted by one from Okeechobee High School and another from Vero Beach. Most of the North team was made up of Bartram Trails players. He had seen enough of them. They would be coached by none other than the head coach of the Trails, a woman by the name of Pam Norton. Nick and Pam had a lot of mutual respect with all that had happened a few weeks earlier in Gainesville at the championship game. Their approach to the game differed in that Nick felt it should be fun and was an exhibition, whereas Coach Norton played to win. Whether it be in checkers, card playing, or especially softball, Pam Norton played or coached to win, and this game would be no different.

The place of the All-Star Classic was up for bid each two years. The towns of Brooksville and High Springs combined their resources to be rewarded with hosting the double header, and it would be televised on the Sunshine Network again. The televised game gave the locals the ability to show off their local attractions, such as a 364-day Christmas village and store and the landmark Weeki Wachee Springs, a spring-fed natural tourist attraction marked by crystal-blue waters inhabited by "mermaids". Yes mermaids. Young women wearing fishtails and form-fitting bathing suits, and with ever-present smiles, frolicked under water while secretly sneaking breaths of air from oxygen hoses concealed behind rocks. They would swim in and around each other while flirting with the paying customers who stood behind the observation glass. The two teams would be VIP guests of the attraction and would get a private show, along with a demonstration of the *Birds of Prey* live exhibition—stuffed toy squirrels and such swooping down and being devoured by the different species of hawks and eagles, which would rip the stuffing out, looking for their dinners. The violent demonstration turned most of the girls away in horror, the exception being some of country girls, who ate it up.

The teams would be housed in the local Holiday Inn, which had to have been built in the 1950s in the traditional motor lodge architectural style. There were three wings with outdoor exposed hallways, with ice and vending machines located at the end of each hall. Each hall had two floors. There were maybe one hundred fifty rooms, and despite the teams, coaches, FACA officials, and parents, there was still vacancy. The girls would be on the first wing, with the South team on floor two and the North team on the ground floor. There would be female chaperones on each floor who were actual teachers from the local middle and high schools. One look at these women and one would quickly calculate that the girls would be safe. None of the girls wanted to test them. They could easily have doubled as guards or wardens of a women's penitentiary. There was also a local security guard paid to stay downstairs in case any of the local boys, realizing that there were forty-five or so senior high school girls from around the state right there in their town, tried to give it their best shot. Surely, they wouldn't once they saw the female chaperones.

The middle wing was for the parents and friends of the players. Most of them were well accustomed to motel lodging as they had been following their children all over, not just the state, but also the nation for traveling games. The third wing was for the coaches, the FACA staff, the Sunshine Network personnel, and any tourists passing through who happened to check in during this time. Nick's room was adjacent to Coach Pam Norton's, but there would never be anything between as they played for different social teams, so to speak.

After each team's single allotted practice, they would take the VIP tour of Weeki Wachee Springs, including the *Birds of Prey* and the Mermaids, then return to their rooms and go to dinner at the Golden Corral, which had been reserved for the event. A motivational guest speaker would address the players and invitees about how it was important never to take their freedom for granted. You see, the speaker was a former POW of the Viet Cong who had retired to the area. The girls were polite, but Nick was fascinated by the speaker and made a point of talking to him privately after his speech, explaining that he was not only a American history teacher, but also the son of two World War II veterans.

Pam Ward was too serious as she was constantly going over her potential lineup and strategies with her coaching staff. She did walk by and ask Shelly how her leg was. That was nice. She was all business. Nick, on the other hand, was not. During the mermaid exhibition, he noticed one attractive "fish-woman" who kept smiling and waving at him from the other side of the glass. She would disappear behind some rocks and then reappear, even once tapping on the window and blowing a kiss to the coach from West Palm Beach. He blushed a little as this was most likely part of the act. Shelly Benedict looked down the row of seats at him and blurted out, "You go, Coach. She likes you. Yeah, she does!" Nick just waved his hand and grinned. Then he thought about it. *Well, maybe. Nah. But it would be just my luck that a beautiful woman likes me but is half fish.* He started laughing.

After everybody had returned to the Holiday Inn and the players' hallways were secured for the evening, Nick decided to go downstairs to the motel bar. Once inside, he took a seat on the side of the room with an accordion wall in case more room was needed. It was not. There was a four-member band playing southern rock, and for the most part they were not bad. Pasco, the band's name, apparently named after the neighboring county, covered songs by Lynyrd Skynyrd, the Allman Brothers, and the Marshall Tucker Band. Nick ordered a bourbon and water. There were no top-shelf choices, only Jack Daniel's and Jim Beam, or the well, which was Kentucky Tavern. "Jack", for some reason, turned Nick into not a very nice guy, and Kentucky Tavern was only a small step above polluted wastewater from the Love Canal, so Jim Beam and water it was.

As he settled in to listen to "Ramblin' Man" and then "Sweet Home Alabama," Nick turned his head. Standing right behind him and looking down at him was the mermaid from earlier. She had real legs and feet and not a fish tail! "You're the coach who was at the park today, right?" the young woman asked in a slight southern drawl. Most Floridians have no southern drawl or else a slight one. Nick knew the Dixie twang from his cousins in South Carolina or from his days in northern Mississippi while at Ole Miss.

With a wide grin, Nick moved his tumbler from his lips to the table and said, "I am. And who might you be?" The attractive performer told him her name was Cassidy Gifford, and she asked if she could join him. "Absolutely. Please do." Nick stood up and pulled the empty chair out from under the table as Cassidy took her seat.

The cocktail waitress soon appeared, whom Cassidy knew quite well. The two exchanged hugs. Cassidy explained to Nick that the two of them had graduated together some five years ago from Brooksville High School, where both had been cheerleaders. Cassidy was also on the swim team. Nick thought that made sense with her job qualifications, including performing like a cheerleader and having the ability to move about freely in the water like a swimmer. She might even be too qualified. Nick introduced himself and gave her a quick background, mentioning who he was and a few things about his life, then Cassidy went on to do the same about herself. In five or ten minutes, the two seemed to know each other as they settled into their chairs, enjoying their drinks. Miss Gifford was indeed a mermaid, but she also went to Polk Junior College and was studying to become a paralegal. The mermaid job helped pay the bills. Having married out of high school and then divorced her Polk County deputy sheriff husband, she was in fact starting over. She then asked Nick when he was planning to leave Brooksville to head home to West Palm Beach, and he said, "Right after the game tomorrow, because I have a lot to do back home."

She startled him by taking his hand, standing up, and saying, "Well then, we don't have a lot of time, do we?" Nick paid the bill. As the two left the bar, Cassidy looked back at her high school classmate and waved, sporting a big smile. Then she and Nick went back to his motel room and proceeded to explore each other sexually. Who knew mermaids had such human lovemaking skills? They do, at least Cassidy Gifford did, and she proved it over and over and over again—all night long.

The players and coaches, if they wanted breakfast, had to be in the bar, which now had been transformed into a breakfast buffet, by nine o'clock. Nick was exhausted but well satisfied and had the ear-to-ear grin of a jewel thief who has gotten away with a million-dollar heist. Cassidy was putting herself together, so to speak, getting dressed and borrowing Nick's toothbrush and mouthwash. Suddenly there was a knock on the door. Nick went to the window and pulled the curtain back a touch to see who it was. It was the two team captains, who were the only ones allowed off the first wing. These were the first baseman from Bartram Trails and, of course, Shelly Benedict. They knocked again. Slowly, Nick opened the door barely a crack. "Yes. And what would you want, ladies?" Shelly pushed the door wide open to see her coach in shirtless and shoeless, wearing a pair of gym shorts that were printed on the lower left leg with "Forest Hill PE." Just then Cassidy emerged from the bathroom as if it were a normal day in the neighborhood. She walked right by the coach, gave him a kiss on the cheek, slipped a piece of paper in his hand, and walked right by the players and down the hall past Coach Pam Ward, whose room door was open. Embarrassed and tongue-tied, the head coach of the South team scrambled to find the words to explain what had just happened. Shelly Benedict just stared at her coach with the biggest smile possible.

"All right, Coach, so you hit a home run last night, didn't you? We will see you down in the parking lot for the bus over to the ball field. You are bringing your new squeeze?"

The other player, the one from Jacksonville, was now discussing what she had just seen with her new best friend. She said how lucky Shelly was to have a coach like that because, as she lamented, her coach never seemed to have any fun—softball 24/7/365. Blushing, Shelly said with a laugh, "Well, not my coach."

Pam Ward seemed to be put off by what she saw as a lack of professionalism in her counterpart from Palm Beach County. By carousing, he was disrespecting the game. But not her, no, sir. She played to win, and she was determined to prove that today. Nick, meanwhile, was totally exhausted and could not stop yawning during the pregame meeting with Coach Ward and the umpires. Pam shook her head in disgust. This would be Nick's last game coaching softball. He met with his players with two requests. One, have fun; embrace the whole thing. And two, don't get hurt. As they got ready to break from the huddle, Shelly Benedict added, "Let's go and win. Coach already won last night!" The players roared with laughter as apparently the news of the "love connection" had spread through the South team at lighting speed.

Much to the dismay of Coach Pam Ward, the South team swept both ends of the double header and did so quite easily. Nick made sure everybody played, and in the second game if they wanted to try a different position, well, go for it. They had fun, they won, and no one got hurt. Success.

As the last out was recorded, the players snuck up behind their coach and dumped a large cooler of cold water right down his back. It startled him. As he turned around, he saw not only his players but also Cassidy Gifford cheering. Everyone won that day, well, except Pam Ward. The Sunshine Network, who taped the game, requested a quick postgame interview with the winning coach. The announcer finished the interview with the comment, "Coach Finch, you seemed to be the real winner up here in Brooksville, right?" He then cut the session down and winked because he apparently knew too. Nick and Cassidy would never see each other again, but that was OK. They both had provided, if only for a short amount of time, the companionship that each needed. A home run indeed.

CHAPTER 13

Change Can Be Good, but Too Much Change Can Be Revolutionary

The nineties were an interesting time for the country, the state, and Palm Beach County, and in the life of Nick Finch. The decade saw the end of the "Reagan Revolution" with the defeat of George Herbert Walker Bush in 1992 by a charismatic governor of Arkansas named Bill Clinton. The Cold War was over, and the good guys had won. The economy was skyrocketing toward prosperity as never seen before; for the most part there was peace; the internet and the World Wide Web was unleashed on the American people for better or worse; and cable TV had turned the people into a nation of channel surfers with specialized channels such as MTV, ESPN, and CNN. But there was a dark side. With all the money being made, it seemed only a few were making it as the ranks of the poor and the left behind grew while the middle class continued to shrink. Debt piled up. Crack cocaine became an epidemic like no other drug before, derailing the "American Dream" as the crystallized white rock was everywhere you looked, especially in the inner cities. There was the Rodney King beating, the trial and acquittal of the police officers, and then the Los Angeles riots, as well as the countless scandals, big and small, that rocked the Clinton administration. Monica Lewinsky, an unpaid White House intern, would become a household name and the punch line to countless tasteless jokes. Clinton impeachment would be the second impeachment of a president in US history, and the results of the 2000 election, when all was said and done, came down to Palm Beach County—and everyone learned what a "hanging chad" was. For Nick, there would be new challenges, including getting a new job, finding the woman for him, and settling down, becoming a father, moving schools and homes, and saying heartbreaking final goodbyes.

As softball ended with a splash, so to speak, Athletic Director Jake Carpenter swung by Nick's classroom and asked Nick if he could spare a minute or two before he started teaching. Coach Carpenter never came by his room. In fact, he seldom left his office in the gym unless it was to go to the main office to turn in the previous evening's game receipts or write some checks for officials or vendors. "What's up?" the former and recently resigned head softball coach asked.

Coach Carpenter started out by saying how proud he was of the former student who had turned teacher and coach because of the success of the Lady Falcons softball team, and then he came right out and stated his purpose for having come by: "I am retiring, and I am going to recommend you as my replacement as AD. I took the liberty to schedule a meeting for two o'clock in Mr. Peachstone's office today to discuss it with him. Only four people know this, you, me, my wife, and the boss. No one else. And let's keep it that way. We—well, I—want this to go smoothly and do not want to open the hiring up to outside applicants. Understand?" Nick nodded and walked back into his classroom in somewhat of a daze. Jake Carpenter had been the athletic director for more than twenty-five years and was only the second in school history, as the original one had been Nick's first principal, Bobby Newcombe. Nick would be the third, and the youngest in the state for a major high school.

When they all met later in the afternoon, the principal and AD were already seated and ready to go, as they thought this would be the easiest job interview of all time. When they finally got around to it, they both explained how they had concluded that Nick was the perfect choice and how fortunate they were to have the best applicant right in front of them. They liked that Nick now had head coaching experience; had coached girls' athletics, especially with more and more Title IX mandates coming down; had his master's degree in administration; and was well respected with good relationships with parents, the faculty, and the local press. Also, the fact that he was homegrown and was well-groomed made it all add up to a no-brainer.

"Do you have any questions or requests for us? I guess I should start with, do you want the job?" Joe Peachstone asked.

Nick looked at the two men who had in many ways filled a void in his life after his dad, J.W., had passed away and had given him so many opportunities, both in the classroom and on the coaching field. "Yes, I would be honored. But there is one request. I want to keep teaching along with doing the AD job. I am and will always be a American history teacher. Let me keep, say, my three AP classes and have them all meet in the morning, periods one through three, and the rest of the day can be for athletic administration."

The two were taken aback as most applicants took such a job in part to leave the classroom, and here was one who wanted to stay in his classroom. The principal loved it because now he would neither must advertise for the job nor must hire a new social studies teacher, and he would not have to trade off the athletic director's job in the upcoming budget. The answer was quick and to the point. Joe Peachstone rose from his chair, shook the hand of his new AD, and replied, "Done." Then he said, "We will announce it at the next faculty meeting as there will be loose ends to tie up before we dismiss school for the summer. Thanks, Coach Carpenter. And, Nick, please hang around for a second." Jake Carpenter got up from his seat, nodded to the principal, and shook the hand of the young man replacing him. He would now get to enjoy planning his upcoming retirement.

Nick sat back down and asked, "What's up, boss?"

The principal leaned back in his swivel chair with his hands clasped together behind his head and looked at Nick. "Nick, I am leaving Forest Hill at the end of the school year and transferring to Jupiter. You know I live up there, in the Farms, and my daughters go to school there. The principal up there is opening the new school up, William T. Dwyer High, so there was a vacancy at Jupiter. I decided to grab it before they, the powers to be, changed their minds. My last act was to get you settled and promoted before I left. You earned it and you deserve it. Please keep this between us, as I want to announce it to the staff in person at the faculty meeting." The new AD agreed and left in a complete daze. He kept his word and told no one.

The last faculty meeting was held on the first of June in the chorus room because it had the risers, which made for easier seating and viewing. The staff was restless as they, like the kids, could not wait for summer break. There were the usual announcements about the proper sign-out protocols, followed by special awards and acknowledgments of achievements by the school and staff, then Principal Peachstone announced the retirement of Coach Jake Carpenter, which was followed by a standing ovation. He deserved it. After the proper pause, he then announced the new athletics director, the school's own Nick Finch. There was applause and some well-meaning "cat calls" and remarks that were met with laughter. Then the bombshell was dropped. Joe Peachstone slowly, and with a cracking voice, announced he was leaving Forest Hill for Jupiter. He would be transferring, effective immediately. There was a hush and then a sigh and even some contained sobs. Joe

Peachstone was loved by his faculty, and he loved them. Change is hard.

At that point, after the applause had subsided, a one of the side doors opened. A small, dark-haired man who looked to be of Hispanic descent emerged and walked to the front of the faculty row. Now Joe Peachstone formally announced his successor, Mr. Carlos Martinez. The staff, half in shock from the preceding changes, pulled it together for another standing ovation. Martinez would be the new principal of Forest Hill and Nick's immediate supervisor. Change can be scary, but change can also be good.

The following day, Nick got to work early as he had a lot to do. He had his own office now, which was in the gym. After about three weeks into the following school year, he surrendered the office to his new boys' basketball coach as he felt the head coach of a major sport needed the room more than he did, so he set up a chair for himself in the main office in the school bookkeeper's office. Nick would do more of his work there anyhow. He also moved classrooms from the main campus to one of the four portables that were placed behind the gym and were adjacent to both the football and baseball fields. This would double as his athletic office as it was empty from around ten o'clock in the morning on. There in his new classroom, he was close to the athletic complex, yet he had a work building to teach his AP classes in. It worked out perfectly. Nick also wanted to get to school first so he could have the opportunity to meet his new boss and see what was expected of him. He got there at quarter after six in the morning, and yet during postschool, one was required to sign in before quarter after eight. There was a line outside the new boss's office as people not only had the same thing in mind as Nick had but also wanted to jockey for some early favors or requests.

Nick's timing was perfect. He opened the door to the principal's office and looked at the overflow crowd in the secretary's room just as Mr. Martinez and Joe Peachstone were emerging from the principal's private office with the administrative staff following right behind them. Nick wondered who would be staying, who would be going to Jupiter with Mr. Peachstone, and who would be looking for new jobs or opportunities elsewhere. Teachers in the room leaned forward, hoping to be called next, when the two principals, past and present, motioned for Nick to follow them into the office. There was some grumbling because, like kids in a lunch line, the others were miffed that Nick had skipped ahead and gone straight to the front.

Inside the office there were boxes with personal mementos belonging to both educators. Some of them would be going up the coast about twenty miles to Jupiter, while the others had traveled all the way from Massachusetts, or Nebraska, or even Cuba. These were the major stops on Carlos Martinez's incredible journey of life. Joe Peachstone introduced the new athletic director to his new boss. They shook hands, a very firm handshake, looking each other directly in the eye, but with a smile. Seldom in the four years Nick would work with Martinez would his smile be absent. If it was, watch out, because that Latin temper was about to blow. If there was a smile, you were all right. As Nick's first boss, Bobby Newcombe, had done his imaginary pistol and gunshot, Carlos Martinez had his smile to reassure his audience everything was all right. It was disarming.

Mr. Peachstone explained to Nick that the two principals were going over the staff in an unofficial way—nothing on paper, "Off the record" principal to principal—and talking about whom to trust, whom to look out for, and so forth, along with which staff members would be leaving with him and going to Jupiter. Then Mr. Martinez spoke, saying that athletics was Nick's business, whereas the only two sports he really knew were baseball and jai alai, and the latter was not played on a competitive level at high schools in Florida. He then said to the young AD that he had come highly recommended not only from the two previous principals but also from the highest district level. He said he had only one rule, and that was no surprises. No matter how bad a situation or incident was that night and no matter how late it was or how early in the morning, Nick was to notify the boss of the problem and then they could work together on a strategy to put out the fire. That was fair. Next, he gave Nick one more responsibility: chair of the social studies department at Forest Hill High School.

Joe Peachstone then interjected, saying that Nick was perfect for the job and assuring him it really wasn't that hard and entailed little extra work. Heck, he had even been a chair when he was a teacher earlier in his own career. The current department chair was a nasty biddy of a person who played favorites and was a constant thorn in Peachstone's ass and giving Nick the job was his parting shot. And Carlos Martinez trusted the advice and agreed. Nick would get a stipend of one hundred fifty dollars for every teacher in his department, so around an extra fifteen hundred dollars, which would be nice. Later it turned out that they were right, it didn't entail much extra work, and it sure looked good on his résumé, which was getting better by the year. It was time to update it.

Unfortunately, when a principal transfers, he takes some people with him. Damn good people. Larry Timmons, Nick's football coaching sidekick since his first day at Forest Hill, and a proficient, if not prolific, gambler, would be going to Jupiter to become the athletic director there. Carl James, the talented but troubled English teacher, would also be heading north. He and Nick had taught swim lessons and lifeguarded together for many years. No one, according to Nick, could teach the five-paragraph essay better than Carl James.

The one administrator whom Mr. Peachstone had brought with him was an iconic man named Walker Roberts. An academic scholar and genius from Duke who was reported to be a Mensa member with an IQ of more than two hundred, Mr. Roberts hated the office setting but loved to patrol in his camouflaged golf cart searching for school skippers, trespassers, and smokers. He would climb into trees with binoculars at the neighboring golf course with camera in hand, using a long-range lens to take pictures of the offenders. Kind of laughable, but it worked. Walker Roberts also supplemented his administrative pay by selling merchandize he would procure at garage sales and flea markets, anything from fishing tackle to firearms—and the price could be negotiated. Nick even saw him sell a shotgun to a student, a country kid who loved hunting hogs. A price was agreed upon, including a supply of the wild pork, and then the two shook hands, exchanging the money for the firearm. Done. And this business took place in the school parking lot in front of the gym during a high school basketball game. Just imagine such a thing today. Not possible. Times have changed. With his extraordinary gray matter, Walker Roberts had sat for the Graduate Record Exam (GRE) many times under many names and at different venues. Test security was also different then. Anyway, Roberts would also be leaving.

And then there was the tragic hero Hank Gibbs, who would leaving the classroom and not only starting over at a new school, Jupiter, but also serving as guidance counselor. Nick could not even fathom how Hank Gibbs got up in the morning each and every day after what had happened to him and his family.

It was Valentine's Day Eve in 1990, which also happened to be a teacher workday or professional development day. Whatever. What it really meant was that there would be no kids and they would have an early start to a potential three-day weekend. The purpose was to turn in grades for the progress reports since it was the halfway point of the third quarter. Once they were done, the teachers could take comp time and sign out early. Workdays also offered the opportunity to meet and greet the faculty's own children as many teachers brought their sons and daughters with them to campus. Smaller children brought their coloring books, and the teachers allowed them to draw on their chalkboards or whiteboards. Others did errands or chores, like making photocopies or collating stacks of the freshly printed assignments. Some of the kids even got some free tutoring to learn how to solve complex math or science problems that their parents had no idea how to tackle. Others went to the gym to play basketball or to the weight room for a workout. Many watched videos or found a comfortable couch to relax on while they waited for their parents to finish their assignments.

Nick Finch had a ten o'clock morning softball practice, which meant an early night before, or least he hoped. Hank Gibbs brought his youngest daughter Becky with him for the purpose of allowing her to practice with the high school softball team. Becky Gibbs was an outstanding player for Jupiter Middle School and played traveling softball. Her dad was the girls' track coach at Forest Hill and had been a boys' head basketball coach himself in New York City before deciding to leave the Big Apple with his wife and two daughters and raise them amid the sunshine and safety of Jupiter. The family embraced both sports and Jupiter. Angela, Mrs. Gibbs, was a nurse at the ever-growing Jupiter Medical Center, the town's hospital. The move south seemed like the right idea, and they'd made it for the right reasons. And then came Valentine's Day 1990.

As Nick assembled his team for prepractice and announcements, he told them there would be a new player for today, their English teacher's daughter Becky Gibbs. Becky had arrived at the field after hitching a ride to the park with Nick, who was her dad's friend. At first shy, she soon opened like a "Chatty Cathy". She explained that she was very thankful for the opportunity to practice with the state-ranked Lady Falcons, mentioned how much she loved softball, and said she was very worried about trying out next year to play for Jupiter High School. She talked a million miles an hour but always with a smile, just like her dad. The team welcomed the younger middle schooler with hugs and high fives. At least five of the girls either had had or now had Coach Gibbs as their English teacher, and now they were getting to see the real Rebecca Gibbs, the one and only as their teacher had bragged about her daily as only a dad can. There were at least five, count 'em, five pictures of her on his desk and on the wall behind it, kind of a mini shrine to his baby girl, who was growing up fast, right before his eyes.

Practice was fun and lighthearted as the players, especially the seniors, smothered their honorary teammate in advice and encouragement. Becky Gibbs took her time at the plate and in the cage with batting practice, then took some ground balls, followed by the running of the basepaths. By noon practice was over, and Nick took Becky back to campus to meet up with her dad. They all went through the drive-through at Burger King for some lunch. Becky then began a barrage, telling her dad of what a great time she had had, saying she would love to do it again, and mentioning how nice the girls were, what good softball players they were at, and how hard they hit the ball. She went on, her excitement about her experience that day overflowing. Then she showed her dad the bruise on her shin from having taken a direct hit from the star outfielder Elizabeth Mary. Her dad looked at the contusion and replied with something he often said: "It is what it is.

Apparently, you did not get down on the ball. Oh well." Tough love from a lifetime coach but delivered with a smile. Hank thanked Nick again for the opportunity as the three of them headed to their cars to start the weekend. After all, Valentine's Day was tomorrow, so Hank Gibbs had to stop somewhere between West Palm and Jupiter to get some candy and flowers for his wife and two daughters.

Nick was dateless for the special holiday that he swore had been created by the Hallmark card company. He was all right with that. He was kind of in a dating slump, but that was OK since he was so busy with school and softball. Nando's restaurant called and asked if he would help with the valet service since they would be swamped because it was a Saturday night during season and was also Valentine's Day. Sure, why not? He had no a significant other and could always use the extra money that was all in cash.

Becky Gibbs on that Saturday did what a lot of kids do: went to the beach to hang out with friends. In her case, it was Carlin Park in Jupiter. Her mom dropped her off and told her to be back at the same spot to be picked up at three o'clock sharp as their dad had made dinner plans for the family that night. With her towel in her hand and her Walkman earphones on, Becky ran to the beach. Later that day, when the radio announced the time at five minutes past three o'clock, Becky realized she was late. She knew her mom would be pissed. She grabbed her stuff, said her goodbyes, and raced toward the parking lot, but she made a decision to take a shortcut through a small, wooded area. Unfortunately, there was somebody waiting in the woods. Rebecca Gibbs would be brutally raped and murdered in those woods while her mom was waiting only about two hundred yards away in the parking lot.

The mom began to sense something was wrong and flagged down a Jupiter police officer who was patrolling the parking lot. He agreed to get out of his car and look around. Angela, the mom, went to the lifeguard stand and asked the two guards if they had seen her daughter. They had, but that was at least an hour ago. Suddenly, there was a nightmarish scream. The two guards jumped down from their perch and, along with the police officer, ran to the wooded area. The three stopped, frozen. The officer began hollering into his shoulder mic. Before the three lay Rebecca Gibbs, naked and lifeless with patches of her skin missing. The medical examiner would determine that the missing patches were human bite marks. The bastard had actually torn her skin apart using his own teeth like a rabid animal.

Angela Gibbs then came on the scene. She dropped to her knees and began to wail uncontrollably. Soon police from both the Palm Beach County Sherriff's Office, known simply as the "SO,." and the Jupiter station arrived. They emptied the beach. A mobile crime scene truck pulled up next. Then, of course, came the press, all three local networks—and the *Palm Beach Post* sent reporters.

News of the crime spread fast in the small town of Jupiter. By nightfall the town had mobilized. People showed up at the Gibbs's house. Becky's teammates got together. Parents imposed curfews on their children. There was a madman on the loose, and the cops had better damn well find out who had done this. They never did. The SO and

JPD tripped all over each other, each claiming jurisdiction over the park and hence the crime scene. Later that night, some of the fathers of the upset daughters went back to the crime scene, which for some reason was not secured, and destroyed it with chain saws and fire. Such a thing would never again happen in this place. To a man they thought how lucky they were it was not their daughter. By doing this, they also destroyed any potential evidence. How in the world could the law enforcement officials not have secured or protected the scene? Total incompetence is the answer.

Initially, Nick knew nothing of the incident as he was busy parking cars and collecting tips, then stopping by the Mandarin for a nightcap and maybe a little companionship. No such luck. As he pulled into his apartment at Cotton Bay, located off Summit Boulevard in West Palm, he noticed his answering machine was blinking, but he was too exhausted to hit play, so he decided to check the messages Sunday morning. He was going to bed. When he got up the next morning around seven, he got in the shower to get ready to pick up his mom and go to church. He grabbed his newspaper, which was near his front door wrapped in a clear waterproof sleeve. He kept it in the wrapper because he always saved the paper to read at breakfast after the church service.

When Nick finally got around to hitting the play button on his answering machine, there were seven messages from seven different people, then the tape ran out of space. By listening to these messages is how he found out about the young softball player's demise. Everything became foggy and blurred. A million things went through his mind, but everything was incoherent, as one thought would quickly be replaced by another one. He opened his *Palm Beach Post* and saw the article about the slaying of the Jupiter teen. He was having trouble reading the report because he couldn't concentrate and his eyes were watering.

Nick picked up his mom. She already knew of the murder. Before he could ask, Charlene preempted him, stating, "I have no idea why either. It is terrible. I cannot even imagine if that was one of my children." Nick nodded and said little the rest of the day.

The following Monday, the school was very somber as everyone was hurting for their friend, their colleague, and their teacher. Nick was shocked to his core when he got out of his car in the faculty parking lot and saw Hank Gibbs's car. Nick thought, *He cannot be here. No way.* He walked by the English teacher's room and looked inside, and there he was. Nick was speechless, not knowing what to say to his friend, and just stood there frozen. Hank looked up. He had aged ten years. No sleep will do that to you. Nick finally said in a hushed and pained voice, "I am so damn so sorry. I don't what to say." Hank Gibbs nodded to indicate he understood.

As Nick turned around and headed out, Hank Gibbs said, "I want you to know I have never seen my daughter as happy as she was when she came back from your practice. Thank you, my friend." Nick turned back but was speechless and started to cry. Hank got up from his desk, came over, gave Nick a hug, and said in a reassuring voice, "Now, now, you've got to get yourself together. You have classes to teach and a great team to coach. It is what it is."

Hank Gibbs would deviate from his lesson plans and would introduce "*Our Town*" a play by the American dramatist Thornton Wilder in which one of the main characters, Emily, dies at a young age and is disappointed that people in her town do not embrace the simple joys of life. It was the most courageous teaching moment that Nick Finch had ever seen in his career. Hank Gibbs was the strongest man he had ever encountered in all his years in education.

The pictures of Gibbs's late daughter would soon be hung in his office in the guidance department both as an homage to her and as a teaching or counseling prop. When students would come in and whine or complain, he would point at one of the pictures on the wall or one on his desk and ask the visitor if he or she was familiar with the story of the young girl who smiling in those pictures. He then would tell them about Becky's tragic life and say they needed to live their own lives without second thoughts or complaints because one never knows what might happen. It always worked. It is what it is.

Nick would hold practice, even though some of the girls had come to him and asked him to cancel. No, this would be a teachable moment, and hell, if Dan Gibbs could meet with his classes, then Nick sure as hell could meet with his team. The team went directly to the outfield to stretch and throw. This was their time as Nick seldom interrupted. Most of the time it consisted of lighthearted teasing and laughing, mostly about certain classmates or teachers. Women call it gossiping; men call it bullshitting. Same thing. Today was different; there was no laughing or giggling. Nick went to the outfield where the girls were throwing and had them sit down. He took a seat with them. He said that he hurt bad and that at times in their own lives they would encounter tragedy in one form or another. They had to be strong not just for themselves but also for others who were hurting. He finished the prepractice talk by sharing with them what Hank Gibbs had told him earlier in the day about how much fun Becky had had. She had really enjoyed being a Lady Falcon for at least one day. Then he said there would be no more practice today. The girls were excused but should be ready for Tuesday's game at Boca.

Shelly Benedict spoke up, not just for herself but for all her teammates, and said, "We all want to go to the viewing as a team." She had collected close to seventy-five dollars from her teammates for flowers from the Lady Falcons. Would Nick order them for the team? Nick said he would, then sent them out with, "Please watch out for each other, please."

The viewing would be the next week in Jupiter, a closed casket located in the front of the room but with pictures of a smiling Becky on top, with a Jupiter Middle School Mariners softball jersey strewn across the coffin. Cars were parked all along Military Trail as the town wanted to pay their respects. Jupiter would never be the same. The small fishing and agricultural town had lost one of its own and, with her, had lost its innocence. Hank, Angela, and their older daughter, whom Nick did not know, greeted the well-wishers, and thanked them. Every single one had their hand shaken and or was hugged. This went on for close to four hours.

Three cars pulled up with the Lady Falcons softball team. They gathered in the funeral home's parking lot and then, led by their coach and team captain, Shelly Benedict, walked in. For many this was the first time they had ever been to a viewing, much less a funeral. Nick's parents believed that children should be introduced at the earliest age possible and taught how to act accordingly for such events. Nick was grateful he had been exposed at an early age to the joys of marriage and baby baptism, and even funerals. One by one, the team signed the visitor book. When Hank and Angela noticed the girls from West Palm, they broke free the people they were talking to and came up to Nick and his girls. The mourning parents thanked Nick and the girls, and both once again mentioned how much the practice had meant to their late daughter. Some of the girls forced smiles, others looked down at the floor, and still others locked in on their English teacher, who now was a grieving parent.

Years later, Nick would be reunited with his friend Hank Gibbs when Nick himself transferred to Jupiter from Forest Hill. They never talked about Becky's murder. It was not that Hank was uncomfortable with the subject. In fact, he kept her name in the public sphere, hoping someone would come forward and help solve this crime so the monster who committed it would finally be brought to justice. Years would go by and nothing. SO and JPD detectives, some active and some retired, continued to work the cold case. Maybe they did this because they felt guilty about the substandard police work that allowed a killer to go free. Whatever the case may be, they did try to find the killer, and to this day have not given up on solving the horrible crime. True crime shows on TV would reenact the ordeal. Still nothing. Five years turned into ten and then fifteen, and now more than thirty years later, no one has had to pay for what happened on that Valentine's Day in 1990 at Carlin Park in Jupiter, Florida. No one. Now that is a crime.

Flowers would be left on Becky's grave, not by the perpetrator now filled with remorse for what he had done years before, but by a former middle school teammate who missed her friend and never wanted to forget her. Just last year Hank Gibbs died of a heart attack while jogging. At the same funeral home, they had a viewing, but this time for the father. There was time for an open mic if anyone wished to speak. Angela Gibbs walked over and asked Nick if he would speak because he and her husband back to the old Forest Hill days. Nick agreed. He told the well-wishers that Hank Gibbs was the strongest man he had ever known. He also said there was a silver lining to his death because now he was with his little girl and he now knew who murdered her. Nick ended the short and to-the-point eulogy with Hank's trademark line: "It is what it is," but he added, "God bless Rebecca and Hank Gibbs, together again."

The athletic director's job was part administrator, part ticket taker, part mediator, part referee, part accountant, and part human resources officer. The once proud athletic department that was always at least competitive in football and basketball and dominant in baseball now found themselves as doormats in sports except for baseball and softball. Demographics had a lot to do with this shift. When Wellington High School opened, it took about nine hundred students with it, yet Forest Hill had to wait a year to be reclassified in terms of division since classifications were made every two years. So, Forest Hill was forced to continue to play the largest of schools during this time. What also went with the opening of Wellington were a lot of the financial resources used by the booster clubs. It seemed that at the south end of West Palm Beach, the high school was always lacking in facilities. It was the only high school without a track-and-field facility. The softball team played off campus. The tennis courts were always in disrepair. The gym roof leaked so badly during rainstorms that one game that was stopped because of the rain. Another time, at a Saturday morning freshman game, referees simply put a tall garbage can on the floor to collect the constant drips coming from the ceiling, and the players learned to adjust and play around it. With the decline in enrollment, the teachers had to be reassigned as per the outcome of union negotiations with the school board, which concluded retention would be based mostly on seniority. Most of the coaches at a high school are the youngest on staff, hence these were the ones who were transferred. Nick Finch was protected because he was a department chair, the athletic director, and the head softball coach. Joe Peachstone made sure that he was secure. Nick had his work cut out for him, that's for sure.

When Nick went to talk with the new principal, Carlos Martinez, Carlos said he had some bargaining chips to use with the board, and honestly, he needed them because a lot had to be done or else Forest Hill would become just another casualty of urban "white flight". He explained that he had previously been principal at a school in a tough Boston suburb that catered mostly to minorities and found that athletics were a great unifying tool. "We may be down in a lot of ways, but we will kick your ass on the field or on the court," he said, explaining the mindset. He told Nick to do anything he could to fix the athletic department: come up with a plan, present it to him, and then he would go to the superintendent to get it approved.

Of all the principals Nick Finch would work for in his thirty-seven years as a teacher, Carols Martinez was the most unique and, in many ways, the best. He made more out of less and *always* put the students first. Maybe that was because of his own personal history, as he was a true American success story in so many ways. At the age of seven, he, along with his brother, who was two years older, was put on a raft with others trying to escape the hellhole that was Cuba under the Castro brothers. At one time Cuba had been the jewel of the Caribbean with fancy hotels, casinos, and world-class fishing, but all that disappeared when Fidel came to power in the early sixties. Carlos's father wanted a better life for his boys, so he trusted a group that was going to attempt the dangerous crossing of the Florida Straits to enter the United States in search of freedom and the "O" word, *opportunity*: opportunity to live free and either succeed or fail, but at least be given the chance to try.

The rickety boat made it, but two of the refugees did not; they died on the voyage. Carlos's father would be sentenced to twenty years' hard labor in a brutal prison labor camp for having helped his boys escape. Years later, when he was dying of tuberculosis, the Cuban government, which did want a sick old man on their payroll, released him and allowed him to immigrate to Florida to see his sons and the grandchildren he had never met. Broken and beaten down by the communist regime, the old man moved in with his son Carlos, now the principal of a US high school. The Martinez family called Delray Beach home. Their aged father had never seen such beauty and extravagance, at least since he was a little boy growing up in precommunist Cuba. Shortages were the norm in Cuba, with strict limits on what citizens could buy and how much. Carlos Martinez took his dad shopping one early Saturday morning to Costco, the ultimate big-box store, and it was too much for the old man. Seeing the shelves stacked to the ceiling with all kinds of products one could buy without restrictions, and tables with unlimited free samples, the old man just fell to the floor and began to weep. Carlos helped his father up and took him home. The old man would be dead in a month, but he would die a free man with as much food and drink as he wanted.

Carlos, when he was a young boy, was in a way adopted by Boys Town of Omaha, Nebraska, a religious charity that took in some of the refugee children. Knowing no English at all at first, the young Martinez boy soaked up as much as he possibly could. He was a voracious reader, reading everything from *Reader's Digest* to the *Saturday Evening Post* and, his favorite, *Boys' Life*. There was always a book or magazine in front of him. He also watched TV a lot, his favorite show being the cartoon, *Johnny Quest*. Soon, with his indoctrination into US culture and the structured but loving environment of Boys Town with its caring staff, Carlos had the tools to tackle the challenges ahead of him. His English test scores were so high that he was awarded an academic scholarship to Boston College to further his studies in English. He graduated near the top of his class and put himself through graduate school by teaching English night classes for immigrants who had come to Boston from all over the world seeking opportunity. He moved up through the ranks in the Massachusetts public school system, but he hated the winters and missed things like beaches, sunshine, and palm trees. Then he got married to a local Irish Catholic woman who was a dental hygienist. The two quickly started their own family with the birth of their daughter Madison. At a principals' convention in Atlanta, Carlos met a recruiter from the Palm Beach School District. The wheels were spinning fast now as the family decided to relocate to South Florida. Soon, Carlos Martinez was named Forest Hill High School's fourth principal, and in many ways, he would be their best.

Nick went right to work on the athletic department by first naming a new head football coach to replace a coach who had come from a small private school in North Florida by way of Ohio. This coach had failed in his attempt to turn the Falcons into a pass-happy offense, or maybe the idea was just ahead of its time. Two years later, with a record of 0–20, which followed two 1–9 records back-to-back, the football team was probably the worst high school team in the state. Nick knew exactly whom to go to when seeking a new coach: his high school classmate and teammate Scott Clark. Scott had left Forest Hill as an outstanding high school player and had gone on to start for three years at a small Nebraska college before transferring to the University of Central Florida (UCF) so he could do his practice teaching and coaching in his home state. Quickly snatched up by Palm Beach Gardens, which now had become a powerhouse program, he was immediately named the defensive coordinator for the Gators. While at UCF, he met a fellow education major named Nancy, fell in love with her, and got married. Nancy would move up fast, first as a department chair, then as a principal herself, before becoming a district administrator. *Sharp* and *tough* were words that characterized Nancy more so than Scott. When the new principal at Gardens overlooked Scott, who should have been chosen, and hired an outsider, the timing could not have been any better: now Nick Finch had his coach. Add to this the fact that the Clarks had bought a new house in the Forest Hill District in Lake Clarke Shores and were now raising their two young children, who would accompany the new coach to all the Falcons' games, and it was perfect.

The first game under the new regime, the Falcons upset rival John I. Leonard to break their losing streak. The players and the student body went wild and tried to pull down the goalposts in celebration. They failed. They would win three more times that year. The following year they went 0.500 with a 5–5 record, and by year three they made the state playoffs but lost to a powerful team from the Space Coast named Rockledge High School. Football was one box Nick had gotten to check, and it got checked the old-fashioned way: with hard work. Attendance shot up and pep rallies were fun again.

The new baseball coach was an easy hire. The AD and the principal could not agree more on the choice of Juan Santiago. Coach Santiago was of Cuban descent and had been raised in Belle Glade with its sugar industry, where he excelled at Glades Day High, the local private school. He then attended Palm Beach Community College, which was known as Palm Beach Junior College, where Nick was an adjunct instructor. From there it was to the University of Tampa, where Santiago excelled as a slick-fielding infielder, who then went on to play two years of minor league baseball before that dream ended. Given Forest Hill's large Latino population, particularly Cuban, and with Santiago's baseball background and a boss who could relate to the coach in so many ways, the choice to hire him was a no-brainer. The Falcons, always powerful in hardball, took it up yet another notch. The greatest moment, at least to Nick and the alumni, happened not during a game and was not related to a player, but was the renaming of the baseball field one Saturday morning in early February in honor of the baseball team's longtime legendary head coach Jim Coldwater. Coach Coldwater had retired some five years earlier because of health concerns, mostly a bad heart. He was a lovable man who had never made an enemy and who treated everyone with kindness and respect, even if he could not remember their names. Coach Coldwater was terrible with names, but he was highly effective on the diamond, having retired with a 330–68 record and with five state runner-up trophies. Six of his players went to the major leagues, and he was respected by all in the baseball community near and far. Just as important, Jim Coldwater was respected and loved by the faculty of Forest Hill, fellow coaches, and senior English teachers alike. That was rare. Nick Finch tried his hardest to emulate the man. Coldwater had told Nick when he was new to make a trip to the general faculty lounge just as often as he visited the coaches' office. Nick did just that, and it seemed to work. He got to know the entire staff and not just the coaches.

On that Saturday, the crowd was huge, the stadium overflowing. Even Dodger shortstop Russel Baker had come down from spring training in Vero Beach to speak at the ceremony. The school board had a policy against naming facilities after people who were still alive and therefore had the potential to commit an embarrassing act, with the press able to remind the public that this individual had been honored earlier by school officials. But Nick wanted this done while the coach was still alive because his health was in rapid decline. Mr. Martinez cashed in one of his bargaining chips, but it was an easy decision as even district administrators loved Jim Coldwater. The event was a total success. There weren't many dry eyes during the dedication. Jim Coldwater would die some six months later of heart failure, but he did get to see the new sign under the scoreboard, which read:

Jim Coldwater Field
Home of the Falcons
Pepsi

Box two checked. Now on to basketball. Nick Finch had his eye on the basketball coach at Jupiter named Fred Hughes. Fred had coached the junior varsity team for one year at Forest Hill after recently relocating to Palm Beach County from Wisconsin after a recommendation from his lifelong friend "Boly" Williams, who had also come from Wisconsin and now was the football coach at the newly created Palm Beach Lakes High. In one year, it became obvious that this guy was no junior varsity coach but a head coach. After doing a little research, Nick found out he had accumulated an incredible win–loss record, had won multiple championships, and had earned the respect of all in the upper Midwest. The new Jupiter AD, Larry Timmons, Nick's longtime friend, saw this also and snatched Fred up as he too had made the jump from Forest Hill north to Jupiter. With an undersized and not very athletic team, code for all white, the Jupiter Warriors became instant winners in hoops.

Fred Hughes also knew that there was a limit on what he could do at Jupiter. When he and Nick chatted at the Forest Hill–Jupiter baseball game, Nick saw that they had a mutual interest in the basketball coach's returning to West Palm. The two knew each other from the classroom as Fred Hughes was also a social studies teacher. And the fact that the Falcon AD was also the department chair was just another feather in Nick's cap, increasing his odds of persuading Hughes to make the transfer. Nick assured him that he would teach US history in periods one through five, with six and seven off for planning, and a classroom all to himself in a portable right behind the gym. Nick added he would vacate the AD's office, saying it would be Fred's for the basketball season. Located right in the gym and above the locker rooms, it was perfect for a basketball office.

A week later Nick got a phone call from Fred Hughes. He wanted to come back, but this was to be hush-hush. Nick agreed as he was taking a winning coach from two of his friends, Principal Joe Peachstone and Athletic Director Larry Timmons, and was doing it behind their backs. Not cool. Nick went to Carlos Martinez with the proposal. Without even looking up from the paperwork he was reviewing, Carl, direct and to the point, said, "Make it happen."

The following day, Fred Hughes turned in his transfer papers both to the district and to the front office at Jupiter High. Peachstone and Timmons were not happy, and Nick couldn't blame them. It would take a while for these wounds to heal, but in any event, Nick Finch had his basketball coach.

The athletic department had been rebuilt. All three major sports teams made it to the state playoffs, with basketball and baseball enjoying deep runs in the postseason tournaments. Still, it was not easy as at times, with three egos and professional competition, there were in-house conflicts. Most conflicts were over the recruiting of each other's players during the season. More than twice, Nick had to have sit-downs with the head coaches and have them pledge to play nice in the sandbox. Overall, they did just that, but they still wanted to win. Carlos Martinez was right: it did unite the school with a new sense of pride, but it almost cost Nick two dear friends. If he had to do it over again, he might go in another direction in terms of the basketball team. We will never know.

There were two other things that Nick Finch now had on his plate in terms of athletics. One was that he would be hosting more than Forest Hill home football games, as two other schools would call Kettler Field their home field. Cardinal Newman, the private Roman Catholic school in West Palm Beach, did not have a lighted home field, and their administration had come to both Principal Martinez and Nick Finch with a request to rent Forest Hill facility. Of course, they were permitted, but Forest Hill would get all the money from parking and food concession. Deal. The other was that the newly created Palm Beach Lakes High School off Village Boulevard between Palm Beach Lakes Boulevard and Forty-Fifth Street had not yet completed its home field and came with the same request. Palm Lakes High had been built so the old Twin Lakes and, before that, the old Palm Beach High could be reinvented as a new school for the arts. The TV show *Fame* was quite popular at the time, and the district felt it was time they dove into the realm of magnet schools. This school had some big financial backers who seldom ever heard the word *no*, and they would not here either. Soon the Alex Dreyfoos School of the Performing Arts was born, so gone was the old Twin Lakes, and the new Palm Beach Lakes was created. Nick and Carlos asked for the same rent, except Forest Hill now would be unable to rent the field to actually use it because they were both from the same school district. But again, parking and concession would be Forest Hill's. Financially, it was a big boost to the athletic department, but it did tie the athletic director to campus every Friday, and sometimes Thursdays and Saturday nights too. It also kept Nick from attending the football team's away games, but again, it was good money and the school needed it.

The Palm Beach Lakes football event also brought a new crowd, including staff and faculty from the neighboring school. The school administration came in uniform, so to speak matching maroon blazers. Whatever. Also, in attendance were some of the teachers, including the sponsor of the SGA, or student council, whose name was McKinley Amy Anderson, but she went by Kinley. She was also the department chair for the ESE, or special education department, at her school. Her hair was strawberry blonde, and she was cute. She and Nick were introduced by the athletic director of "Lakes" high school. On the surface it appeared to be a match made in heaven: both were teachers; both had semi administrative roles and were respected on both campuses; both had gone to college in the South and were part of the Greek fraternity–sorority systems; they were similar in age, with only a two-year difference; and both were single and unattached.

The two sparred as best they could as both had assignments at the event. Nick found out that Kinley had gone to Newberry College in South Carolina, not far from Nick's dad's home of Spartanburg. She was a member of the Tri Delt sorority and had earned her master's degree in special education. Her father was an executive for a land development firm but had an engineering background. Her mom stayed at home. The first night Lakes played at Forest Hill, they talked to each other whenever they could, both trying not to make it look obvious, which it was. Nick was going to ask her out for Saturday, but he had to be back at the school as Cardinal Newman would be playing there then. Maybe next week? Nope, Nick had to go to Gainesville because now he was a member of the FHSAA Executive Committee that met once a month on Saturdays to discuss and vote on various issues. It would not have mattered as Nick learned Kinley was also going to be out of town at the state student council convention held at Disney World. He would try a new strategy. On a different day, he found the perfect, albeit hokey, greeting card that in essence was an attempt to make light of the fact that their respective schedules were such that they kept just missing each other. After looking at it and signing it, he placed it in "the Pony."—the in-house district mailing service consisting of a large satchel in the main office—right along with about twenty other folders destined for other places, but mostly the district office. New teachers were often warned that the Pony was for official school district business only. Yeah, right. Birthday cards, invitations, and now even a card serving as a fishing line for possible romance were sent that way. When placing the greeting card in the green satchel and pulling the drawcord tight to close it, Nick was reminded of the best practical joke he had ever seen played. It had made use of the mail—not the "Pony", but the US Postal Service. Nick was the most likely culprit, but he swore he'd had nothing to do with it.

It seemed that the main office kept receiving what can be best described as obscene, or at least indecent, flyers for a commercial charted gay-themed sunset sailboat cruise out of the Port of Key West. A scantily clothed young man seen holding the mainmast in a provocative pose was accompanied by a longhand written message: "We can't wait to see you again. And yes, we can work out a group rate if you bring your team." The flyers were always sent to the baseball coach Juan Santiago. The secretaries, upon opening it, would at first be shocked and then pass the flyer around and giggle, especially when the coach himself entered the main office and checked his mailbox, to find it waiting for him. All eyes were on him when he saw the flyer. He quickly turned around to see the entire staff staring right at him, then made a hasty retreat out the door, mumbling something in Spanish while throwing the flyer in the trash can. The second one came about three weeks later, but this time the first mate was photographed completely naked except for the wineglass strategically placed in front of his nether regions. This time the secretary took it to Principal Martinez. When Coach Santiago came to the main office to check his mail, there was a small note from the principal asking that Juan see him immediately, with *immediately* being underlined and followed by an exclamation point. Nick happened to be up there at the time, depositing the receipts from the day before and about to request checks for the referees and umpires who had worked the previous day's contests. The coach went into the office and, about ten minutes later, exited and walked right out the door, noticing everyone was staring right at him. Carlos Martinez then asked Nick to come in and asked if he knew anything about the flyers. Nope, he knew nothing about it or the source, trying his best not to bust out in laughter. Carlos was trying to be serious as this could be a serious matter. The principal asked if his AD knew who could be behind the practical joke, thinking deep down it was in fact Nick. Nick swore it was not him, but he said that if he found out who it was, he would tell them to stop it. Nick was biting his lip so as not to explode in laughter, then he looked at his boss, who was doing his best to treat this matter as the serious issue it was. The two looked at each other and then just lost it, breaking out in sidesplitting laughter. To this day Nick does not know who had those flyers sent, but it was one hell of a practical joke. One of the best.

Trips to Gainesville were scheduled for once a month. Nick gassed up his Nissan 300Z on Friday afternoon for the four-and-a-half-hour trip to the home of not only the University of Florida but also of the offices of the Florida High School Activities Association (FHSAA). The association would pay his expenses, and he would always book a room at the Cabot Lodge located at the ramp for I-75 and Archer Road. A nice, clean, and convenient rest stop, Cabot Lodge had another drawing point in that from four o'clock to seven o'clock in the lobby, there was a free happy hour and meet and greet. Free drinks and easy conversation flowed in the lobby among everyone from academics, to businesspeople, to tourists on their way to Orlando and the theme parks. All day Saturday the committee would meet with the executive board to discuss a wide range of situations that had come across the director's desk that needed either an approval or a no vote from the committee at large. The committee was made up of mostly high school principals from across the state but seemed to have a North Florida leaning to it. There were three ADs who had been selected, one from the south, Nick; one from the center part of the state; and one from one of the Pensacola schools. Nick was fascinated by the wide range of personalities that made up the committee; it was, in fact, a microcosm of the state itself. The urban representatives had different views from those of the reps from the rural areas, and North and South Florida leaned in different ways, but in the end, after discussion, they would vote yea or nay and move on. There were never hard feelings as the different subgroups respected each other's viewpoints. They gave the kids the benefit of the doubt, and they came down hard on the adults with fines and suspensions. If the discussion dealt with someone or something from a certain member's area, then that member could participate in the discussion but had to recuse himself or herself from voting.

Nick seemed to fit in with both the south and north groups. The reason those from the south liked him was obvious as he hailed from West Palm Beach. The North Florida members liked him because he was a third-generation Floridian with ties also to South Carolina and Mississippi. He usually sat next to a man at the long table who was a principal in the Crestview area, which is about as far north and west as you can go in Florida before you enter Alabama. Heck, it is in a different time zone! Ronald "Red" Burke was his name. He got his nickname, not because of his actions, his behavior, or a stereotype, but apparently because he used to have red hair. Now he was bald as a billiard ball. He would spread out his paperwork and the agenda in front of him and then place a gold-plated spittoon that sported engraving at the base: "Coach Red Burke." Throughout the meeting there was the constant sound of *ping*, which was his spit hitting the inside of the prized possession. Nick understood this, as both his grandfathers chewed tobacco and his dad's father collected the spit and deposited it at the base of his tomato plants. It must have served some good purpose, as his tomatoes grew to the size of small melons when ripe.

The Crestview principal and Nick, separated by a time zone and by forty years in age, would speak during breaks, when Nick himself would sneak a dip of Copenhagen snuff, putting it between his cheek and gum. The two enjoyed each other's company and shared opinions on whatever matter was being discussed at the moment. Add in the fact that they both liked smokeless tobacco, and the "odd couple" was born. Dipping snuff was a horrible habit that Nick's mom, Charlene, despised, so Nick did the best he could to hide it from her. He would find himself reaching for his can after drinking, eating, or doing chores, or whenever was bored. He had started toward the end of his high school days. His mom had hoped it was just a fad but was disappointed when he was obviously addicted to the nicotine. There were always some red Solo cups around Nick's apartment half filled with spit. He would dip snuff throughout the day for close to fifteen years but would quit cold turkey on his wedding night as a wedding gift to both his bride and his mother, never again to chew tobacco. Nick had never smoked as he blamed cigarettes for the death of both his parents, his dad's directly and his mom's by way of secondhand smoke. Deep down he knew he was a hypocrite by using this form of a tobacco that in many ways was just as bad as, if not worse than, smoking. One of his proudest accomplishments was his kicking the habit. He never dipped since. But there had been times when he was very tempted. Still, he hadn't fallen prey ever since that July day in 1993 when he both quit and got married.

The Pony card must have worked because just a few days later, Nick saw that there was a large envelope in his mailbox. Included in the contents was a card in return with a cartoon character saying, "We have to make this happen!" Kinley and Nick would be meeting again this Friday, as Lakes was not only playing at Forest Hill but also would be playing the Falcons, who would be the visiting team for the contest. There was a postgame party planned to be held down the street at a local watering hole named Brandy's Island. Brandy's was a working-class joint that served beer and wine only and stood right by the railroad tracks on Forest Hill Boulevard. When the trains passed, the whole building shook, but nobody cared. They even cheered for the trains because, when they passed by, there were half-price discounts on pitchers of beer and glasses of wine.

This was a Forest Hill coaches' hangout that went by the nickname of Coaches' Office East. The owner and staff loved when the coaches came by, not only because they brought their business but also because they made for good company and conversation. The restaurant bought advertisements in the game programs and had signs adorning the fence lines of both the baseball and football fields. Nick would sign off on some community service hours for some of the staff who got into trouble for drinking and driving. The place was friendly and down to earth. During the game, Nick and Kinley talked when they could as both were busy, agreeing they would meet down at Brandy's after Nick had shut down the stadium and turned off the lights. The stadium itself would be picked up and looked after Saturday morning by the "Breakfast Club," or students who had Saturday morning detention. They were given a choice of four hours with no talking or sleeping in a cold classroom or meeting by the football field under the supervision of the head custodian Mike Gonzalez to clean the place and pick up any garbage, which would take about an hour. Almost to a person they selected stadium duty. It was a win-win.

Kinley took a few of students who had ridden with her home and then swung back to Brandy's Island for her first date with Nick Finch. The Forest Hill group was in a great mood as the Falcons had defeated their crosstown rival in a fantastic game that really showed what high school sports was all about. Hard and clean play, along with spirited bands and cheerleaders. And when all was said and done, Coach Clark and his team, almost winless for four years, squeaked out the victory. Mr. Martinez stopped by the celebration, as did the band director, and of course the entire athletic department came as well. It took Nick a few extra minutes to secure the stadium, clear it, and turn off the lights, then drive by the bank to drop off the receipts from both the gate and the concession stand in the night deposit box. A police officer followed him for the drop-off as recently an AD at another school had been robbed at gunpoint for the money for his school's home football game at a bank's night deposit box. Nick found the tiny parking lot packed, so he was forced to park a block down on Norton Avenue, next to the Fox surfboard factory. When he walked in, there was loud applause for him, followed by, "Speech, speech, speech!"

Nick's reply to the celebrating audience was, "Congratulations to Coach Clark and his staff, and our great band and cheerleaders. And how about that crowd tonight!" Someone handed him a cold bottle of Budweiser. Nick raised it for his signature toast: "Hey, how 'bout it!"

The crowd roared back, "Hey, how 'bout it!" Nick went right over to the main table, where the coaching staff and their wives were all seated. He nodded with approval and grinned at his friend Scott Clark when he noticed there was an open seat that apparently had been saved for him. Right next to the seat was none other than Kinley Anderson.

Nancy Clark and Kinley were in deep conversation. They knew each other from the district meetings for department chairs in their field. Nick sat down, still grinning ear to ear, and before he could say anything to his date, she opened up the conversation by smiling and saying, "Congratulations on the win. It, well, is going to be tough at my school when they find out I went to the victory party here." She then leaned over unprompted and kissed Nick quickly on the cheek. Everyone cheered with approval. They were happy to see Nick had found somebody who maybe, just maybe, would be the one.

The two talked in between interruptions by well-meaning well-wishers who wished to congratulate the head coach, his staff, and the AD. When it was getting time to leave, Nick walked Kinley to her car. She reached for her keys and opened the door, but before she got in, she quickly turned around. The two, finally alone, embraced in a long kiss. Nick made Kinley promise she would call him immediately when she got home to prove she was safe. Kinley liked that. Sure enough, about fifteen minutes after he'd gotten home, the phone rang. It was her. But instead of a quick call to reassure him, the two talked for another hour or so and made plans for dinner, just the two of them, for later that night since it already was Saturday.

Later that day, Nick went to the Top Hat Car Wash on Okeechobee to get the Z washed, vacuumed, and cleaned for the evening. Instead of the usual Nando's for the first date, he decided to mix it up and go to the steak house on Forest Hill not far from school itself, Beefeaters. The hostess, Margret Baldwin, who had been a classmate of his senior homecoming date Annie, smiled with approval and found a booth that was as intimate as possible for the extremely popular steak house, which had a line of people waiting outside for their names to be called once a seat opened. Nick had called Margret earlier that afternoon to reserve his table even though the policy at Beefeaters was no reservations. It is good to be local and know the important people, such as the hostess at Beefeaters. Margret was one of the good ones in every way. She was always helping others, whether it was in high school taking the keys from someone who had had too much to drink or consoling a friend after a painful breakup. She was always there for anyone who needed her assistance. It was not surprising that she was working on her master's degree in adolescent social work and counseling. She would be perfect for it. In a few years, the school district hired her to work in the Safe Schools program for students and families at risk. In this role, she touched countless lives daily, just as she had for the high school group, she called friends. It was a perfect fit.

Kinley and Nick hit it off right from the start. They had very much in common, particularly about their jobs. They would be together as much as possible for the next seven months or so, but their responsibilities many times pulled them away from each other. They tried to combine their activities, such as when Nick helped Kinley by helping to chaperone the Palm Beach Lakes prom held at the downtown Hilton. The event was like most proms, uneventful, except a few students had made bad decisions such as drinking too much before attending, or there was some teenage drama with breakups and jealousy that ended up with raised voices and crying. Some things never change. What impressed Nick was the post prom staff party upstairs at the hotel, which was sponsored by the senior supply and ring company that rented two adjoining rooms and filled the bathtubs with ice and alcoholic drinks. It was their way of saying thanks for allowing them a monopoly on the hugely marked-up class rings, specialized jewelry, and graduation stationery. The door between the two rooms was open, and the beds had been tipped up and were leaning against the wall to make more room for mingling and conversation. Kinley Anderson, as the SGA and senior class sponsor, oversaw both the prom and graduation as the faculty representative, so in a way it was her party. There was no way Carlos Martinez would ever have allowed something like this to happen. What you did in your free time was yours, but this was a school event. Nick thought about his own senior prom, when many of his teachers were arrested but later were found innocent of running a gambling syndicate, but not before the local press had reported it as such. Many of the staff he recognized, and some he even knew either by having grown up there or through coaching, but mostly from the home football games that Palm Beach Lakes played at Forest Hill, which required Nick's setup and supervision. He remembered that all administrators had to wear the official uniform of maroon blazer and gray slacks with matching necktie. He thought they looked as if they worked at the airport. Frank Fletcher, with his wife and Perry Hahn, going stag, were there. Nick knew from parking cars at Nando's that Perry was married. At first the partygoers were polite and respectful, but as the alcohol took effect, the mood changed, and it changed into something not much different from the prom they had just left. Two married administrators, Nick knew because of the blazers and because he had seen them on duty for football games, were on a balcony locked in passionate kissing. Two other staff members were arguing about something Nick could not decipher, but it was heated. The only difference between here and downstairs was the age and the dress. Kinley came up, took Nick's hand, and thanked him for coming and for helping. There were a couple who did not seem to care for the interloper from the rival school. It was just like high school.

Both honestly did not want to go to high school events when they had time off, and both understood. They made time for each other when they could. They introduced each other to their parents. Kinley's mom and dad were respectful, polite, and well-dressed in their perfect PGA National home in Palm Beach Gardens. Nick noticed there seemed to be nothing out of place as Mrs. Anderson showed him around in her Lilly Pulitzer print dress. Mr. Anderson was practicing his golf swing on the back patio, which overlooked one of the golf courses. Kinley's little brother was a sophomore at the University of Miami. Nick had no idea what he was studying and honestly could not care.

Kinley was extremely nervous about meeting Charlene Finch for the first time. And she was right to have been so, as his mom was a tough and to-the-point critic when it came to her baby boy's dates. Charlene was polite as she sized up the teacher who might just become her daughter-in-law. She accepted her nicely and later offered polite reviews that included, "Kinley is polite, well-dressed, cute, and well-spoken. You could have done worse, Nick." Not glowing, but a lot better than previous critiques.

After Kinley and Nick had been dating six months or so, everyone began to wonder if this was the one for him. Some flat-out asked. Nick would respond with a quizzical expression and a shoulder shrug, which was an honest response because he really did not know. Was he in love? Was this the one to become Mrs. Finch and the mother of his children? Would he grow old with her? He was comfortable when around Kinley, and he stopped having a wandering eye for others. *Comfortable* was the perfect word. He even had the nerve to ask his mom when she knew Dad was the one for her. Charlene looked up from her post church service breakfast at Greene's Pharmacy and replied, "So, that's where you are at now with Kinley, is it? Honestly, I knew right when your father asked me out for the first time when we were at Fort Jackson. Granted, there was a lot of other stuff going on with the war and such, but I knew right then and there he was the one. Does she do that for you?"

Nick looked at his mother and said, "I don't know. I guess. Maybe. Could be. I am just not sure." Charlene did not respond but just nodded her head, indicating that she understood without saying so. Breakfast ended quietly.

Two weeks later the relationship ended, and it ended with a thud. Nick never saw it coming. He was over at the apartment his girlfriend shared with a roommate, a townhouse fourplex off Village Boulevard only about half a mile from her school, Palm Beach Lakes. He and Kinley were about to leave to see a movie and enjoy a rare eventless evening, when he noticed her answering machine blinking, which he pointed out to her. He walked over to hit play, and she demanded that he leave it alone because it was private, for her roommate. Nick looked at her in astonishment as he had never heard her raise her voice before, especially at him. He let it go, and they went to the movies. When returning, Kinley said she was very tired and wanted to make an early evening of it, wanting to finish the evening alone. This was code for no sex and *You are to go home to your own place.* The next evening, a Friday, Nick had duty back at the school and went home to change, when the phone rang, and it was Kinley. She started out with, "I need to talk to you. This is not easy to do. Please let me get through this, and do not interrupt me. Nick, you are a great guy, but this is not working out for me. It is not you; it is me, all on me. I am so sorry and hope you can forgive me. I know you will find the right woman because you are a great guy. Please, I need to let this go. And please do not try to understand or try to change my mind. Forgive me. I am sorry. Goodbye." The phone went dead. Stunned, Nick sat down and looked around his small place in total silence for at least ten minutes, before he got up and went back to school. He did his AD duties without saying much. He spent Saturday in a fog and went for a beach walk to see if that would clear his mind. It did not. Why had she ended things? What was wrong? What cue or warning signs had he missed? He felt very alone, but it would get worse.

Sunday, he got up earlier than expected as he had not slept well, even though he'd gone to bed much earlier than usual for a Saturday night. He went to his door and got his Sunday *Palm Beach Post* to read right then as he had time to kill before picking up his mom for church. He usually saved the paper for after church to read at breakfast, but today he had the time to get a head start. He always started with the sports section, followed by the local news, then the headlines and section A. He would finish up with the Accent section, where he'd read about pastimes, leisure activities, and wedding announcements. Today, to mix things up, he started with the Accent section, then the bottom fell out when he came to the wedding announcements. There right in black and white was the announcement of the impending marriage of Miss Kinley Anderson to Mr. Robert Felton of West Palm Beach. The announcement went on to explain that both were teachers at Palm Beach Lakes Community High School. Nick was rocked to his core. As of Thursday, Kinley had been his girlfriend, and just three days after having broken things off with him, she was engaged and planning her wedding to another guy. What in the hell had just happened?

When Nick picked up his mother at the TradeWinds Condo on Singer Island, Charlene was waiting for him outside the front doors, which was unusual. The norm was for him to go upstairs to her place and get her, as a proper woman did not wait outside for a man, even if it was her son. Charlene got into the sports car, which she was not fond of because of its low profile. Already knowing of the announcement, she looked over to her son, who had his eyes covered with his ever-present Ray Ban Aviator sunglasses. Top-of-the-line eyewear designed to keep ultraviolet rays from damaging the eyes, the Ray-Bans were also good at hiding expressions and feelings from spectators—and Nick was an emotional wreck right now. Charlene broke the silence with a comforting, "I am so sorry, Son." She stopped right there and, unlike other times, did not add her two cents regarding what had happened, why it may have happened, and what he should do now. The two went to church, then to breakfast, and then returned to Singer Island. Little was discussed. What was obvious was that Kinley had been cheating on Nick while, the whole time, pretending to be his girlfriend and implying they had a possible future together.

When Nick got back to his apartment, the answering machine was blinking. He looked at it for a moment and then hit play. The voice recording was Kinley. She sounded stressed, almost as if she had been or was still crying. She said, "I am so sorry about the newspaper this morning. I tried to call them to have the announcement pulled, but they said it had already gone to print. I am not getting married to him, and yes, he and I did have something going. I am ashamed, but there is nothing now with Bob, nor will there be in the future. I swear. I do not blame you if you hate me and never speak to me again. I just panicked and got tired of waiting for you to take the next step. It is the worst thing I have ever done in my life. Please forgive me, although I do not expect you to. Goodbye." The machine went silent. For some reason, Nick replayed the message at least three more times.

News of the breakup spread fast, but even faster was the news spread of the wedding announcement. Friends were uncomfortable and didn't know how to approach their buddy. Some showed anger, others, sympathy. Still others just shook their heads in amazement. There was one thing Nick wanted to know, so on Sunday night he drove to Nando's to speak with the two valets who worked with Kinley and were, he thought, his friends. Perry and Frank were outside playing backgammon, waiting on the last few diners to finish up so they could retrieve their cars and pack up and go home themselves. Nick pulled up, not in front of the restaurant, but on the adjacent sidewalk right in front of the establishment. He got out of his car, slammed the door, and looked at his two friends with whom he had worked for many years parking cars, sharing stories, and knocking down a few at the Mandarin in North Palm Beach. He was mad, he was angry, and he was hurt when he looked at the two and just blurted out, "Well, did you know anything about this, these two-playing house while I was being made a fool of? Please tell me you didn't know about it."

Perry spoke for the two of them: "We didn't know about it, but we had suspicions. But they were just that, suspicions. If we had come to you and there was nothing to it, well, how do you think that would have looked?" Nick nodded then jumped into his car and sped off. He went up the street to Flagpole Beach—named for just that, a flagpole standing next to the seawall on Palm Beach—and looked out at the dark sea. It was angry, and so was he. He would not handle this well. He was not sure if the reason was his losing his girlfriend who might have been the one or how the breakup had gone down, being public and in print.

Carlos Martinez called Nick into his office before school that Monday and had a sit-down with the young man who was his athletic director, teacher, coach, and department chairman and, most importantly, his friend. He told Nick he was there for him and said that if he needed to take some time off, he could—Carlos understood. He said he'd heard a rumor that Nick was going to retaliate or react violently toward the male teacher at Lakes. Nick assured him he would not do anything that stupid. As Nick left Carlos's office, he could feel the eyes of everyone in the entire front office on him. Heck, he felt the whole world was staring at him.

For the next few months, Nick buried himself in work, both athletics and the classroom. There was not much else to do: teach his three AP United States History classes, do his paperwork for his department chairmanship, and then get ready for whatever athletics event, doing whatever was necessary, such as going over the prospective athletes' paperwork to ensure the parental permission and residency papers were included, or calculating academic eligibility, or submitting rosters to the state. Then he would check with the coaches to see what was on their plates and what they needed, then he'd move on to do the accounting work—ticket sales and cash from the previous night's gate. After that it was home to change, then back to school for game duty.

In the month of January alone, Nick found himself either back at school for a game, or in Gainesville for meetings, or at a banquet on twenty-eight of the thirty-one days. It was beginning to wear on him. He had gained a few pounds—well, more than a few. In fact, Charlene once commented, as only she could, "You know, it is OK to mix in a salad now and then and maybe eat fewer fries." Ouch, but she did have a point. The problem was that after games, there was little to choose from except fast food, and that is not exactly the menu one wants to be ordering from if one is watching one's weight. Also, Nick did not have a girlfriend since Kinley had dropped him, and because of the way she'd done it, he was a little depressed, which contributed to his poor eating habits. Plus, he'd had no time for the gym. Time to let the belt out another notch.

About two months later, on a Sunday morning, Nick was at his mom's condo getting ready to go to church when the phone rang. Charlene picked it up and listened. She was stunned for a few seconds before regaining command of herself. It was Kinley on the other end. Kinley stated right out of the gate how sorry she was, adding that she was not very proud of her actions and saying she would understand if Charlene hated her and never would forgive her for what she had done to her son. Charlene listened as Kinley continued her apology, but she pointed at Nick and gestured for him to come over to where she was, putting her finger to her lips as a signal for silence. Nick walked over to his mom, and as she was listening to Kinley speak, she wrote Kinley's name on the message pad, underlining it. She then pulled the phone away from her ear so Nick could hear the exchange. Kinley explained that she was wrong, so very wrong, about how things had gone down, adding that not a moment went by when she didn't regret the entire situation that she and she alone had caused. She said that not a minute passed when she didn't wish she could go back in time and start over. There was silence on the Finch side, so Kinley asked kind of sheepishly, "Are you still there?"

Charlene Finch was quick and to the point, with that head ER nurse way of responding: "Yes, I am here, but I will be leaving for church the moment Nick gets here, so please tell me why you called me."

Secretly, Kinley had hoped that Nick was at his mom's house. *I guess not,* she must have thought. But he was there, although she had no idea that he was listening in on their discussion.

Damn, Nick thought, *man, is my mom good or what?* A grin appeared on his face. He had not smiled for a long time. Kinley explained that she had tried to reach out to Nick but he would not return her messages, and most of the time the call went straight to the answering machine. That was true. She also attempted to talk to some of his friends, but they too shunned her. Kinley said this was the hardest phone call she had ever made, but she'd made it because she thought it was her last chance to reconnect with her former boyfriend.

When she finished, there was an awkward silence, before Charlene spoke in a direct and forceful voice, "Listen, young woman, I will tell my son you called when he arrives here for us to go to church. I will also tell him you have tried to reach him through different channels. And yes, I will tell him of the regrets you have shared with me. After that, it is up to him. He is a grown man now, and his decisions are his and his alone. But before I go, let me add this: I will not try to influence him in any way. As I said, he is a grown-up now. But I hope his father and I raised him right and he never gives you the time of day again. Got that? Now you know where I stand. Good luck with your life. I just hope it is not with my son. Never call here again. Goodbye." Charlene hung up, turned to her son, and said it was time for them to go to church or else they would be late, and arriving late to church was plain rude.

Nick was stunned at his mother and her comments, but at least he knew now where she stood on the whole matter.

After about ten minutes into the drive south to Palm Beach, Charlene turned and asked her baby boy, in a caring and sympathetic voice, if he was all right.

Nick turned and smiled, replying, "I am fine, Mom. And thank you. For everything." Mama bear had protected her baby cub one more time. The chapter on Kinley was over for good.

Now Nick had not entered the monastery in any way, and he had taken no vow of celibacy. In fact, just the opposite. Now Nick had to prove to himself and others that he still had it as far as attracting companionship went. He looked at it as a coach holding tryouts for prospective team members after losing his star player. Kinley was gone, so now he needed a replacement: tryouts were needed, and tryouts he conducted. He opened these tryouts to almost anyone interested: younger, older, divorced, single, tall, short, blonde, brunette, redheaded, rich, poor, working, local, or new to the area. Tourists were even invited to the tryouts. Venues for taking prospective players on his team were places like E. R. Bradley's on Palm Beach; the Greenhouse or the Hilton Inn, both on Singer Island or what the boys called "Swinger Island"; and Boston's on the Beach in Delray, where Nick and Larry Timmons had pulled out the live lobsters on display in a tank and freed them from their captivity. As the lobsters raced to freedom across the dining room floor, mayhem ensued. The management frowned on this act and called the police. The two escaped just in time. Thank goodness that back then there were no ever-present security cameras as there are today. Then there were the always reliable places to go on Sunday: Panama Hattie's and the Waterway Cafe on the Intracoastal in Palm Beach Gardens. Going west was good because then you could order the local drink, a Pimm's Cup, and watch professional polo at the Wellington International Polo Club or get a glimpse of Hollywood celebrities in Jupiter at Christine's, which was adjacent to the Burt Reynolds's dinner theater. Nick actually laid eyes on two of the hottest Hollywood actresses of the time at Christine's, Catherine Bach of *Dukes of Hazzard* fame and Farrah Fawcett Majors of *Charlie's Angels*, who were both there working on stage productions being staged right there in Jupiter. Even farther up the coast, in Stuart, was the classic Japanese restaurant and dining show of Benihana. Brian Parker, Nick's best friend and now a full-time lawyer, had gone there together on a double date with two flight attendants from Eastern Airlines. The four of them had a few drinks too many. Brian and Nick became sarcastic, but it was funny to both their dates and the others who were lucky enough to be seated at the same table for the show the master chef was putting on. After slicing and dicing the steak, lobster, and shrimp with explosions of fire, the chef dropped the veggies and rice on the grill. A large cloud of smoke followed this, which caused Nick to ask the performer if it reminded him of Hiroshima or Nagasaki, speaking of the atomic bombings that ended the Second World War that were characterized by large mushroom clouds. Some of the diners laughed, while others shook their heads and blushed at the mean-spirited joke that was delivered in a Don Rickles sort of way. The chef, with a knife in one hand and a cleaver in the other, was not at all amused and began hollering at Nick in Japanese, when the manager, who was also Japanese, raced over to the table and quickly informed Nick, Brian, and their dates that they would have to leave. Brian stated something to the effect of they had been thrown out of better places than this. As a sidenote, there was a retired marine, a veteran of both World War II, where he'd served in the Pacific theater, and the Korean War, at the table who still sported a crew cut who seemed to enjoy the comment more than anyone else. Looking back at the comment now, Nick realized it was wrong to have said it, but you cannot unring a bell. Oh well.

It seemed to many that Nick Finch was enjoying the South Florida singles lifestyle, but Nick knew deep down there was something missing. So did his mother, along with his colleagues and close friends.

There were some festive occasions in the greater Palm Beach County area that draw large crowds of people together for fun and memories, such as the polo and equestrian competitions in Wellington, and spring training in West Palm Beach for the Braves and Expos; Broward County for the Yankees and Rangers; and to the north in St. Lucie County for the Mets. Thanks to complete mismanagement by local officials and the greed of the ball teams, the Orioles are gone from Miami; the Yankees and Texas Rangers are out of Broward; the Cleveland Indians, also because of the damage caused by Hurricane Andrew, never ever made it to Homestead; and the Braves and the

Expos moved from Palm Beach County out to Orlando and Cocoa Beach. Music seemed to be available, but no longer at the West Palm Beach Auditorium—the "leaky teepee" as it was known by the locals—because the city had sold it to a religious organization and it was now off-limits. Municipal Stadium, where spring training had been held and where inexpensive summer minor league baseball games had been played, which sported the iconic street address of 715 Hank Aaron Drive, was now shut down for good with a Home Depot standing in its place. There was now an outdoor music venue out by the fairgrounds that had changed sponsorship names and allowed for music outdoors and headlining acts but remember how hot it is there because of the summer humidity and how wet because of the afternoon downpours that start in late April and run through to October that occur almost daily around four. When the rain stops, the insufferable humidity returns. This is especially true in the western communities, where the rains occur more frequently like in and around the fairgrounds area where the amphitheater is located—and it is at least five degrees hotter there because there is no ocean breeze. These conditions do not make for ideal outdoor listening or concertgoing. To drum up business around the Easter season, the City of West Palm came up with the idea of SunFest, an art and music festival to be held along Flagler Drive in the downtown waterfront district. Easter is traditionally the exit period for the snowbirds, or the temporary residents who return to their native homes, mostly in the Northeast, after having escaped winter there to enjoy South Florida. The original SunFest ran for two weeks and consisted mostly of artwork exhibited by the individual artists in their street-side tents. Nick always wondered just how many ways an artist could paint loggerhead turtles, jumping dolphins, and beach sunrises. Apparently, a lot. And the artwork sold mostly to the condo dwellers, who saw the marine life—turtles and dolphins—in action and the sunrises over the Gulf Stream from their balconies. The interior decor looked perfect next to pictures of their grandchildren on the glass tabletops and the waxy artificial bananas and other false fruits that gave their part-time homes a real Florida look. The music in the early years of SunFest was provided by local acts and some better-known jazz bands. It seemed that the group Spyro Gyra was the unofficial house band as they seemed to play the event yearly. The food and drink were good, but parking was bad. Still, overall, it worked. The event has evolved over the years, with most of the artwork gone, and has moved to the North County—a separate festival known as ArtiGras. There are still the pictures, paintings, and sculptures of turtles, dolphins, pelicans, and sunrises, and now there are a bunch of the Jupiter lighthouse. SunFest has been cut down to less than a week, and the music has expanded to include a genre for most everybody. There is rap, country, contemporary, oldies, and some jazz. Most of the acts are well known, and fireworks open and close the festival. Most the time the weather is perfect as the rainy season has yet to start. People come from all over to listen to the music, eat and drink, and walk along the waterfront of West Palm Beach. Big crowds can also bring the wrong element as there have been documented cases of muggings and assaults, along with the recent stealing of phones from the back pockets of unsuspecting concertgoers mashed together and loving the music, not paying attention to their surroundings. There is another event, both quite local and at the same time European, which is the American German Club's Oktoberfest held in, what else, October in Lantana on the club's grounds. Oktoberfest would change Nick's life profoundly.

It was a Saturday in October when Nick proposed the idea of attending the beer and music festival to two of his single friends, Coach Tim Applewood, who was recently divorced and in the process of leaving Forest Hill for a new start in one of the newer west county high schools, and Perry Hahn, Nick's old parking valet buddy from Nando's. Perry was a confirmed bachelor who had apparently had his heart broken a time or two and now worked parking cars and had a few friends with benefits on the side. Many of the guys went to Perry's apartment/condo to find few hours' escape from the daily commitments of marriage and fatherhood. There they would be welcomed to the HOR, or House of Refuge. They could have a beer and watch a game before returning home to resume their role of both husband and dad.

Both Tim and Perry were ten years older than Nick, but they were good friends and good company. They all drove to John Prince Park, located just a few miles away, where the festivalgoers transferred from their cars to chartered buses to be dropped off at the American German Club. It was quite a scene for South Floridians as they drank authentic dark German beer served by men in lederhosen held up by suspenders, their heads topped off with small green alpine hats; ate bratwurst and other cuisine from the old country; and then if they so dared, danced the chicken dance to a musical accompaniment. A few years earlier, Ray Wade, Brain Parker, and Scott Clark had come in authentic German outfits—the lederhosen, suspenders, hats, and such—and went to one of the concession beer stands, where they notified the workers that they were there for their shift. The actual workers thought the young men were legitimate and surrendered their positions behind the counter. For the next hour, the whole group drank for free, and when others appeared, seeking to buy a beer, the boys informed them that it was a VIP tent and they were not allowed to take their money or serve them. It worked for a while, but about an hour later the official servers made their way back to the tent, accompanied by a Palm Beach County sheriff's deputy. That was when the three ducked out of the tent and into the crowd, blending in as best as possible as they worked their way to the rental lockers where they had stored their regular clothes, which they retrieved. From there it was to the restroom, where they changed back into their everyday wear. The costumes were put into the locker, and off the guys went, the costumes never to be discovered. The risk–reward was not worth it, but the escapade makes for a good story every October.

Tim Applewood noticed someone he knew. She was an attractive woman with blonde hair who had been his marriage counselor when he and his ex-wife attempted counseling before the inevitable dissolution of their marriage. The two talked, and the marriage professional explained that she and a group of her friends had come on a chartered with their condo association. She pointed over to a table of eight or ten young professional people who were drinking and eating, but mostly watching the dancing. Tim asked the young woman if she would like to dance. She said yes. The two went out to the dance floor, where a choreographed dance that looked as if it had come straight out of Munich was on display. Nick shook his head, thinking this should be fun to watch. Nick was not much of a dancer himself, and he presumed Tim Applewood wasn't either. But he was wrong. The former head football coach who had had a tryout for the NFL after a solid college career at Ohio State was fantastic. He seemed to know all the steps, turns, and dips that were required for the European folk dance. He glided across the dance floor right in step. Real German people stepped back in amazement. Nick stood there with his mouth wide open in shock. When the music stopped, the crowd roared. The band immediately began playing the music for the chicken dance. Most stayed on the floor to do the clapping, snapping, and shaking it took to finish the dance. Tim and his partner did not stay. Returning with sweat dripping off his forehead, Tim looked at the table where his two friends were seated, then looked at the table where his dance partner's group was seated, and asked a simple question of the amazed audience: "Not bad, huh?" Then he explained how he had become so proficient on the dance floor, explaining that at Ohio State, the running backs and receivers were required to take a year of dance, both traditional/ethnic and contemporary, as legendary head coach Woody Hayes felt this would help them with flexibility, mobility, and teamwork. It worked. Nick thought this was very cool. It was good to see his friend smile again. The divorce had been hard on Tim. He had found his element again. Not surprisingly, Tim Applewood remarried and retired to the Villages in north central Florida, where he now teaches dance lessons. You cannot make this stuff up.

After Tim Applewood's astonishing display of ability on the dance floor, Nick walked over the table where Tim's dance partner had been sitting. Everyone sitting there looked about the same age, from mid-twenties to mid-thirties. One of the group who appeared bored and disinterested in the whole affair. Nick also noticed she was smoking a cigarette discreetly, holding it in her hand, which she concealed below the table, and turning away from the group when she exhaled. There were two red flags, being a party pooper and smoking, as Nick despised that nasty habit. But there also were some green flags raised by this young woman. To begin with, and most important, she was quite attractive—downright stunning in a natural way. Nothing fancy, but clean and tight with blue jeans and a stylish blouse, finished off with the right amount of makeup and grooming. For Nick, yes, it was important that a woman have the right personality and character traits, but those were things one had to learn about. The first thing that always drew him was physical appearance. This woman checked that box. Next, she did not seem to be caught up in the group conversation, which Nick thought might be a plus. She would be easier to start a conversation with, and he wouldn't have to get involved in all the other discussions that were taking place around the table. The lion always concentrates on the loner of the herd, so to speak, you know, the one that is cut off and isolated from the herd, which this woman seemed to be. So, it was a wash, as the gamblers say, minus two, plus two. The brain works amazingly fast when motivated. For Nick, all these observations, deductions, and conclusions took about ten seconds. He thought, *What the hell? I came with nothing, and maybe I'll leave with nothing. So be it, but on the other hand, time to give it a shot.*

Nick walked over, extended his right hand with a positive, confident look that any fraternity man would be proud of, and introduced himself to the woman, who quickly disposed of her cigarette by discreetly putting it out on the underside of the picnic table and letting it fall to the ground. She thought she was being very stealthy, but Nick noticed the act and appreciated it. The young woman rose to her feet and extended her hand to return the handshake. She was tall, almost as tall as Nick, and had a confident handshake, looking Nick directly in the eye. She introduced herself as Lauren White. Lauren or shadowboxed for the next ten to fifteen minutes, trying to learn as much as they could about each other, yet neither of them giving away. Ah, the mating rituals of the twenty-somethings. Nick learned that Lauren worked in a bank, First National of Palm Beach, the "Yellow Bank," which Nick had spent so much time painting for his dad's company. He also learned she was a night school student during the week and was originally from the Washington, DC, area, and had not grown up locally. Nick countered that he was local but had gone away to college at Ole Miss and was a teacher, coach, and athletic director at the local high school, Forest Hill. Lauren said she was very impressed with his friend's dancing ability, and Nick explained he was shocked at Tim's gracefulness on the floor. Without having to say it, they were each relieved the other did not want to dance. Lauren White also explained she was not very outgoing that night as she was getting over a nagging cold, but she had already paid for the excursion and her friends had all agreed she needed to get out. Nick's earliest summations were that Lauren White was a teller at the bank and was going to one of the local tech schools for either supplemental training in bookkeeping or to learn computer skills. How wrong he would find he was regarding his first impressions of the woman who would later become his wife. They agreed to swap phone numbers. He said he would call her the next day to continue the conversation. Both seemed interested as the evening ended.

That Sunday, Charlene noticed more of a bounce in her son's step before and after church and, in fact, commented on it, noting that his spirits seemed brighter. Nick said everything was the same and never let on about his having met Lori the night before, or his plan to call her later that afternoon, or, if that went as planned, his intention to ask her out on a first date. When he got home and changed out of his Sunday go-to-church clothes, returning to gym shorts and a sweatshirt, his choice of loungewear, he picked up the phone and dialed Miss Lauren White. He was taken aback by how professional the greeting was: "Hello, Lauren White speaking. How may I help you?"

Nick said, "Oh, ah, huh, yeah, I need a loan." Lauren laughed on the other end when she realized quite quickly it was the young teacher whom she had met the night before at Oktoberfest. For the next hour, the two talked like a young couple before high school prom. Nick learned she was indeed going to night school, but to earn her MBA at Florida Atlantic University, and she was not a teller but a graduate of the small prestigious (and expensive) Florida school Rollins College. While at Rollins, she had been the president of her sorority and lettered as a member of the soccer team. She was in fact an executive vice president of the bank and specialized in investments for million-dollar clients. *Wow, how wrong I was,* Nick thought. After an hour or so, Lori brought the conversation to an end. She needed to study for an upcoming exam, and she was confident that with his being a teacher, he understood. He did, but at the same time he'd never had the women be the one to end the phone call. He'd had some dads pick up an extension line and tell him and the girl he was talking to that it was time to wrap things up, but that had happened in high school. Before they hung up, Nick asked if Sandy would like to go out. She said yes, so Nick followed it up with a proposal to go to the Carefree Comedy Corner and see some live stand-up comedy the next Saturday evening. Again, she said yes. He promised to call her back, say, Wednesday, with a more precise pickup time and plans. He finished by wishing her good luck on her upcoming exam.

When Saturday rolled around, Nick could not wait for his first date with the professional banker. But there was one problem, and it was a big problem. Saturday night was the sixth game of the World Series between the Atlanta Braves and the Minnesota Twins, and it was killing Nick to miss this game. Many of his friends were going to the Hooters on Okeechobee to watch, while some others planned to go to the new burger and chicken wing joint named Duffy's on Alt. A1A in North Palm Beach. Nick was really looking forward to his date with Sandy, a nice educated professional woman, which truthfully was a change from some of his recent romantic encounters, yet he still wanted to see this game. The World Series had been so good with many twists and turns that it was already being called a classic. But both teams had performed the worst in their respective divisions the year before, coming in dead last, in fact, causing the series to be nicknamed the "Worst to First" Series.

Nick made reservations to see two comedians do their stand-up acts at a renovated old bowling alley and pool hall that also housed a movie theater. The complex was named the Carefree. It was in the south-central part of West Palm on Dixie Highway, also known as US Highway 1. This had been the main road from Canada to Key West until the Interstate Highway Act led to the creation of I-95. Now the area was in transition. Bowling, billiards, and movies were out, especially because of the competition from the multiplex theaters built in and around the malls. But comedy was thriving, with cable networks like HBO showing uncensored acts, which were now the choice for many for date night. The Carefree offered a small cafe/bar area where you could order an appetizer and a drink and wait for the hall to open. Nick and Lauren decided to have a seat there and do just that. It was killing Nick that on the way to the show, instead of having the game on the radio, music was playing. He was a lifetime Braves fan because they held their spring training in West Palm Beach; they were the closest major league team, located in Atlanta; almost all his Mississippi college friends were fans of the team; and they were broadcast almost nightly on cable's superstation WTBS. Nick had waited for this moment for as long as he could remember. *Wait, there is a God,* he thought, when the two took a seat in the small bar and ordered their drinks and appetizers, because lo and behold, there was a television attached to the wall right above Lori's head that was playing the game. The two made small talk as they had at least a good half hour to kill before being seated. Nick tried his best to concentrate on the conversation and not be rude, but he kept looking over his date's head to watch the game. More than once he let slip a small cheer or a slight groan over a play on the diamond up in Minneapolis.

After about thirty minutes, Lori got up and excused herself from the table. Nick rose too, showing his proper upbringing by acknowledging a woman's exit from the table. He thought it did not matter as he had already blown it by concentrating on the game rather than on his date. No protocol could make up for that. Lori returned. Nick again stood up and waited for her to retake her seat. He expected her to tell him she had called a cab for a ride home, and he wouldn't have blamed her if she'd done so. Instead, Lauren White, DC girl, Rollins grad, soccer player, sorority president, and professional banker, took matters into her own hands by, without asking permission, instead of calling a cab or a friend for a ride home, going up to the hostess and canceling their seats to the show. As she explained to Nick, she had grown up in a house full of sports fanatics—Redskins fans, but you can't have everything—and would rather sit with him right there in the cafe and watch the World Series than go see the stand-up acts. She hoped that was all right with him. She smiled and tilted her head to the side with a facial expression indicating that it is better to ask for forgiveness than permission, waiting for her date's response. Nick was stunned, pleasantly so, and replied with a smile from ear to ear, "Oh, hell yes, it's all right." He nodded with a facial expression that screamed, *Thank you! Thank you very much.*

Nick officially went off the market that night for all intents and purposes. Although he watched his Braves lose a heartbreaker to the Twins—eventually going on to lose in seven games in one of the greatest World Series ever played—he had won something much bigger that night. He won in life. He found his wife and soul mate.

CHAPTER 14

Hello, Goodbye, and Goodbye, Hello

Different cultures and different groups have many ways of saying hello and goodbye. Seeing as the United States is made up of a variety of cultures, it is fascinating to watch Americans say hello and say goodbye. Just think about hello. The greeting is so simple, but it can be expressed in many ways. Take a seat in the airport by a gate where flights are arriving and watch the games begin. There are hugs, handshakes, kisses, fist bumps, high fives, and nods. Certain cultures bow. Others kiss each other on a cheek, or both cheeks, and some kiss straight on the lips. Many cannot get enough of TV news cameras picking up the fantastic scenes of our brave servicemen and servicewomen coming home to their families. The reactions of the family, especially if surprised, are magic moments the cameras love to catch. It melts the heart of even the most stoic of individuals. The ultimate hello is when a mother meets for the first time the baby she just delivered and has carried for the past nine-plus months. No matter how exhausted, the mother is glowing. Not even the best photographer or artist can capture that moment. That hello is God-given.

Goodbyes seem to be more private, but they are every bit as emotional as hellos. Many cry when saying goodbye. Others nod and turn away. Hello, is much easier, as goodbye for many is final. But even it is temporary, such as when dropping off your kids at school or when your spouse is leaving for work, saying goodbye is still an example of showing your love. Some of these goodbyes are taken up a few emotional notches, for example, when dropping your kid off at school for his or her first day of kindergarten or driving away from the campus of your child who is embarking on his or her college years and getting closer to leaving home for good. This latter event is extremely hard on a mom and dad. Then there are the goodbyes on the first day of a new job, with a kiss, most likely followed by a wish for "good luck" wish and a heartfelt wave. Then, of course, there is the ultimate goodbye that comes with the death of a loved one, a family member, a close friend, a colleague or coworker, a neighbor, or even a student. Those are the hardest. Nick was about to experience the best of hellos and the most difficult of goodbyes in the next chapter of his life.

For the next few months Lauren White and Nick Finch were inseparable, well, as inseparable as two people can be with one working for her MBA and the other having school, athletics, and state duties on his respective plate. At least the two-year requirement in Gainesville was coming to an end, but athletics, teaching, and tending to his mom still took up a lot of Nick's attention. Maybe that was what Kinley either could not or would not understand, which caused her to take the exit ramp and end their relationship. Lauren was different from anyone Nick had ever known. She had her own goals and aspirations but kept an even keel when it came to juggling those and her time with Nick. Driven with professional objectives that impressed Nick a great deal, she nevertheless knew when to turn in the time sheet and relax and have fun. She accompanied Nick to his football games and sat at the old, covered barbecue pit located in the northeast corner of Forest Hill's Kettler Field. She watched with a keen eye, but especially the interaction of the various Friday night cliques. The cheerleaders, the band members, the girlfriends, and the parents—she took it all in and seemed to enjoy it. After a few private conversations Nick had had with her, it was obvious to him that her high school years in a Maryland suburb of DC had been pleasant. Lifelong friendships were made there and were still maintained. Her soccer competitions, her experiences managing one of the teams, and even her time as a pom-pom girl were pleasant memories. She enjoyed her high school years—and one can tell almost immediately that a person either loved or hated high school. Lauren White loved her time in high school, and it was obvious Nick had too: after all, he had returned to his alma mater.

When softball season started, Nick informed Lauren that all his home games were in the afternoon at Phipps

Park, located off campus in the south end of West Palm Beach. Nick secretly liked afternoon games as they freed up his evenings for some of his directorship duties, but a four o'clock first pitch also meant a lot of parents had trouble getting there for the whole game. Nick had a love-hate relationship with most of the parents. He loved that they had raised such outstanding young women and had made the time and the sacrifices so they could play. Don't kid yourself, it is a sacrifice that includes money, travel, and putting other family matters on the back burner so that Suzie-Q can play softball. On the other hand, these parents could be the loudest critics in the world, unafraid to voice their displeasure about a coach's strategy or an umpire's call on the field. For the most part Nick ignored their comments, but more than once he'd had to have a private word with a dad. Once he even had one removed. This was a biological father but a man who was not a dad in any way. He did not live in the same house as his daughter and had no parental responsibilities unless you count showing up intoxicated and deriding his own daughter on the field as a parental responsibility. Nick had tried to ignore the man's behavior, but as the evening drew on, it got worse and was affecting his player, as he noticed she was wiping tears from her eyes in the dugout before her turn at bat. Nick called time and looked for Jupiter's administrator. Larry Timmons, his friend, was now the athletic director there, and the principal, Joe Peachstone, was in attendance as it was a home game. Both were there not only because it was the right thing to do, but also because they wanted to see their old friend Nick Finch. And many of the girls remembered their former PE teacher and principal. Nick hollered, "Time!" and walked from the third base coaching box to the left field fence, where the abuse was coming from. He'd had enough. But he didn't have to go far, as Larry Timmons beat him there, along with Joe Peachstone and a Jupiter police officer. The abuse stopped once the father was escorted from the park. Later in that game, the girl who had been the target of the abuse hit a grand slam. Not only did the Forest Hill bench erupt in screams of excitement, but so did the Jupiter bench. They had heard the abuse also. Nick had tears in his eyes when he spotlighted the young woman as Player of the Game. Never had Nick seen both benches applaud in response to such an act. Nick never got tired of telling that story.

With Lauren White being a former standout athlete in her own right, she could not wait to see her boyfriend's team and their games. She worked her schedule at First National, which had gone through various owners after the consolidation of the banking industry. The once private Palm Beach bank had been owned by Southeast, until they went under thanks to the War on Drugs, which took away the free flow of cash, then was owned by other institutions such as Wachovia and First Union, the latter of which became Wells Fargo. Sandy did not have to worry too much about her schedule at work since she was the top performer for the entire nation as a portfolio manager. Not number one in her office, or in Florida, and not the number one female, but number one for the entire country. People noticed that a lot more than they did her changing clothes and leaving to go to a local softball game. Big numbers get big benefits, or so they say. Sometimes she would arrive at the park in her business attire of suit, heels, and hose, and the game would have already started. Other times, especially Fridays, she would be wearing shorts and an official Forest Hill "Lady Falcons Softball" T-shirt that Nick had given her. Whether on time or understandably late, she also brought something else: Charlene Finch, for whom she always made the time to swing by her house and pick her up for the games. The first couple of times they found seats in the lower level of the bleachers that stretched from behind home plate up to the dugouts on both sides. This would change when both Nick's mom and his girlfriend became agitated at the critics and the comments from the spectators. Charlene bit her lower lip, not figuratively, but literally to hold back her response. To this day, when angry or frustrated with a situation or with others, Nick Finch does the same, biting his lower lip until the problem is gone or he has walked away so as not to cause an escalation of the situation. This learned behavior from his mother sometimes kept Nick from making a bad situation worse. Behaviorists call it modeling.

After the first couple of games, Lauren and Charlene now brought folding chairs and a blanket and sat down the left field line, isolated by themselves, to cheer on Nick and his team. The players loved it as they thought it was very cool that the coach's mom still attended games and now, he was bringing a girlfriend—a real girlfriend and not a mermaid! Charlene loved the drive to the games as much as the game itself, as that was when she could size up her son's latest girlfriend in his line of attempts at finding a permanent, solid relationship. Charlene was not getting any younger, and she wanted to leave this earth to join J.W. knowing her son had found happiness. Nick was now thirty years old, and all his friends were married—some married, divorced, and remarried again. Most had started their own families. Not Nick, but maybe this was the one. Charlene hoped.

Charlene also loved Lauren's Acura much better than Nick's 300Z. It was clean and void of softball equipment and papers to grade. And she felt she was not riding right on the road like on a skateboard.

One day, Charlene let her feelings be known to her son as only Charlene Finch could. Straight, direct, and to the point, she pulled her son to the side as Lauren was working her way to the driver's seat and said, "Son, for the love of Pete, do not screw this one up. She is the one." That was that. Then Lauren got into the driver's seat. Charlene rolled down the window and repeated, "She's the one." Then again, Charlene felt that Nick already knew that Lauren White was the one. She sure did know her boy, as it was true that Nick knew that Lauren was the one and had been worth the wait. Now, just do not screw it up.

Nick and Lauren made the rounds with their friends and colleagues. Both groups voiced their pleasure at the new romance. Nick's friends, most of whom were his colleagues, thought Lauren was perfect for him and just the type who could, in a classy way, knock the cocky out of him, bring him down a notch, so to speak, without his even knowing it. And her friends and colleagues thought that he was the perfect guy to get her head out of the books and the briefcase and have some fun. In the past year, Nick had dated what seemed to him to be almost every eligible young woman in town. In fact, he had even been auctioned off by the Cancer Society at a charity event as one the area's "Most Eligible Bachelors" at the in place for thirty-somethings, the Crazy Horse Tavern, located across from the auditorium and the Palm Beach Mall. But on that night, he was worried when he showed up because, as the event organizers had requested that attendees wear clothes that spoke for them, he was wearing starched khakis, a white button down, a collegiate striped tie, a blue blazer, no socks, and Bass tasseled loafers. He felt that if it was good enough for him on Sundays at church and had gotten him through four years at Ole Miss, then it was good enough for a charity event. Other "livestock" ran the gamut in terms of their clothing selections, ranging from bathing suit trunks with tank tops, obviously beachgoers, which showed off their suntans; to tailored customized suits, probably lawyers; to surgical scrubs for one participant who wanted everyone to know he was a doctor. Charlene later filled Nick in on that guy, who apparently was a real tool. Years later he would be indicted and convicted by the feds for prescription abuse, be sent to a minimum-security prison, and lose his medical license. Nick knew what his choice of clothing would be there: most likely orange!

Nick hustled and called a couple of female colleagues who he knew were free, begging them to come, saying he would buy them drinks and asking them to observe the bidding to help him out. If no one was liking what they saw, he asked his friends to bid on him to stave off the humiliation. And if it happened that it was some beast with an open checkbook, would they please outbid that person and he would pay them back? Nick was no Chippindale model, but when he was announced, the females cheered and applauded. That caused him to feel relieved; at least he would not be the lowest-bid-on dude. He walked up and down the bar and felt completely stupid even though he had had a bourbon followed by a kamikaze shot for liquid courage. The bidding started at fifty dollars and soon climbed to more than one hundred dollars—and not one bid from the ringers he had brought in for the event. Because of the brightness of the spotlight, he could not see into the crowd and determine who was doing the bidding, but the gavel swung, and he had sold for two hundred ten dollars. He was not the highest-priced bachelor, more like upper fourth, and thank goodness he was not last, an honor that went to the city manager of West Palm Beach. When Nick went over to the table to meet his date and get the gift certificates to the Raindancer and the Crazy Horse, he finally saw who had purchased him. It was not one date but four! They were all local high school coaches who had coached against him and thought it would be fun to join in on the festivities. Add to this the fact that one of the coaches was a breast cancer survivor, and it made even more sense.

Nick followed them to their table. The women were much more interested in finding real dates, not dating a competitive peer, and Nick got it. He handed over the gift certificates to the women to use how they saw fit. He ordered a drink, took off his blazer and loosened his tie, and relaxed with the group he had previously only seen on the diamond but whom he now saw as friends. Funny thing about the evening, there was a young banker there with her friends who had not bid on Nick or anyone else but enjoyed the show with a scotch and soda. That banker was Lauren White. Nick had forgotten the whole evening until at dinner one night with Lauren, he was explaining that one of the most embarrassing things he had ever volunteered for was the Cancer Society's *Dating Game*–like auction at the Crazy Horse Tavern. Lauren looked at her new boyfriend and confessed that she had been there that night and honestly did not remember Nick and his time on the block. Wow. She did remember the doctor who, she thought, must be a real self-centered jerk, and no, she had not bid on anyone that night, but if she could do it over again, she would have bought Nick. Perfectly placed sarcasm with a dose of humor. They both laughed.

Meeting the parents was next on the big checklist. For the first time, Nick noticed that Lauren was not her usual confident self but was a little uneasy as she was about to introduce Nick to her mom and dad and her brother, who was down from Washington, DC, for the holidays. The Whites lived in a planned Martin County community in Palm City built by one of the most famous developers in the area's history, the firm of Burg and DiVosta. Every home looked the same on the outside, but the new inhabitants had made choices for the interior. Of course, there was a golf course and a country club, and a gated, twenty-four-hour-guarded service booth offering private security for the community. Randy and Grace White had relocated to

South Florida for the last bit of Randy's career with AT&T, first in Plantation in Broward County, and then north to Palm City in Martin County. This happened at the same time Lauren had made her decision to attend Rollins College in Winter Park. Coincidence? The jury is still out on that. Her big brother Geoffrey was a University of Florida graduate who had returned to the DC area to work in one of the cottage industries shadowing the government: lobbying. Lauren had given Nick the background on her family, which was fascinating to him. To begin with, both she and her brother had been adopted because of the condition and age of her mother. Lauren would wrestle with this from time to time throughout her life but always was very grateful for her upbringing and proudly announced Randy and Grace as her mom and dad. The one thing that bothered her was having no family medical history, but later things would become easier with the R & D taking place in the field of genetics.

Lauren was her daddy's girl, and how could she not be? Randy White, not the Dallas Cowboys star, was a caring and loving man who found the good in everyone. As a sidenote, he hated the Cowboys, as he and family were huge Redskins fans. A big man, but very gentle, he had served in the 101st Airborne Division during World War II. Oh, how Nick wished J.W. were still alive so he could watch the two of them talk about their time in Europe and what they had seen and experienced. He wanted this not just as a son and future son-in-law, but also as an American US history teacher. Firsthand accounts cannot be matched. Nick still remembers the day in his first year of teaching when his principal Bobby Newcombe took over his class and gave his students a firsthand account of the war in the Pacific.

Grace White, Lauren's mom, was the perfect match for Randy White, and yet the two were very different from one another. They made it work and were truly in love with each other, as they had been for most of their lives. Theirs was a true love story, even if unconventional at first. Grace White had lived an entire lifetime before she was thirty years old. Born and raised by German immigrants in Appalachia in southwestern Virginia near the college town of Blacksburg, she lost a little brother who had drowned when just a teenager. She had bigger dreams than rural Virginia could fulfill. At age eighteen, she headed north to Washington, DC. A gorgeous young woman who was striking in every way, including in how she carried herself, she found a job with the phone company and signed a lease for a small apartment next to the largest construction project in domestic history right down the street. The Pentagon was being built and war clouds were beginning to form. Grace would soon get caught up in war fever after Pearl Harbor. She married a young serviceman who within months would be killed in action. Burying herself in her work, she moved up through the phone company as fast and as far as a woman could go in those days. She then met and fell in love with a recently divorced executive, and the two were married after a whirlwind courtship. Shortly thereafter, the executive, while on a business trip, found himself on a plane that crashed in the middle of a farm field. There is where no survivors. Grace was a widow again, and this time she had been cut off by her husband's and his previous wife's family, prohibited from ever contacting her stepdaughter. Tragedy followed Grace everywhere, it seemed. She swore off romance and once again went back to work. A trip to the doctor for some discomfort resulted in a diagnosis involving reproductive problems. She would never be able to have children herself. Not that this was a practical option anyway as Grace was nearing forty years old and did not have children on her to-do list anyhow. Then she met Randall White.

Randy had waited the proper time before asking out the drop-dead gorgeous widow who, like him, worked for the phone company. Grace was employed by a "baby bell," the Chesapeake and Potomac Phone Company, which was the firm that handled communications for the DC metro DC. Randy worked for the big Ma Bell, AT&T, which had its corporate offices in downtown Washington. At first, Grace told Randy she would have to think about his offer. Randy was forty-two and had served in Europe for the army, specializing in communications. On his return, he had quickly been hired by the phone company, where he rose through the ranks, thanks to his hard work and the professional way in which he handled himself both in and out of the office. Randy was a son first and foremost. He took care of his elderly parents while his brother and sister went on to live their own lives. Nick could relate. O how he could he relate. Raised in Maryland on the other side of the Potomac River, Randy White was the epitome of a professional southern gentleman. Dapperly dressed and always clean-shaven, he knew his limits on scotch, which he would order regularly, and always pulled out the chair or opened the door for a woman. He was a catch for any woman looking for the perfect companion.

After thinking it over, Grace agreed. For their first date, the two drove to the coastal town of Annapolis for a day of boating. Randy's first love was his boat. The two quickly fell in love and were married on New Year's Eve, with just a few friends in attendance. The boat was soon sold, and a house in the suburbs was purchased. Next, they discussed the option of adopting. Even though they were a little long in the tooth for prospective adopters, their résumé was perfect, and they were granted adoption rights. First, Geoffrey was adopted by these two loving people, and two years later Sandra, born at Georgetown Hospital, rounded out the White family. If you did not know Geoff and Sandy were adopted, you would have never guessed it. They looked like their parents and took on many of their parents' quirks, traits, and characteristics. Nurture vs. nature, and in this case, nurture won out. Grace resigned her position with the phone company and became a stay-at-home mom in every way. The house was spotless and impeccably clean, and dinner was ready at seven o'clock sharp but was preceded by a scotch and soda, always J&B. For the first half an hour it was Grace and Randy time; the children were never allowed to interrupt. Then at dinnertime, family time took over as the day's experiences were shared within the group. To imagine what it was like you do not have to go far. Tune in to a repeat of the "Donna Reed Show" or "Leave it to Beaver" and you got it.

Grace White had done some modeling, which made sense: she looked as if she could have walked off the set of a commercial for a Proctor and Gamble product. Perfectly dressed in excellent makeup and hair, her appearance perfectly complemented her slight southern drawl. On the outside her life looked perfect, and it was perfect now, but very few people knew of her tragic early adulthood experiences. She was comfortable, and Randy really loved her. In fact, he adored her. It was the mid-sixties, and this was suburbia.

The story of Lauren's life was, of course, much different in many ways from Nick's upbringing, and yet there were some similarities. Their fathers were veterans of the war and had the scars to prove it. The wives both cherished their husbands and vice versa. But the major difference between Nick and Sandy—and it wasn't that she had been adopted whereas he had been raised by the people who'd conceived him—was their moms. Charlene, a mother of five, loved nursing, second only to her love for her family. She worked when she did not have to and worked nearly up to the time of her death. The people at the hospital were her second family, and one would do best not to forget this fact. Grace, on the other hand, enjoyed the life of a suburban housewife. Charlene hated cleaning and cooking and other household duties. Grace was never seen with a hair out of place and was always made up as if she were on a print ad for Macy's. Charlene, after a graveyard shift at the hospital, would be in a bathrobe until the afternoon hours.

The two families did share the concept of giving back. The Finch's were churchgoing people, while the Whites were, as they said, "C@E" people, meaning Christmas and Easter only. J.W. Finch was a Mason and a Shriner, and Charlene was a member of the Eastern Star. These were kind of grown-up fraternities and sororities. J.W. loved to dress up as a clown and drive around on a mini motorcycle in parades for the Shriners Hospital in Tampa. The Whites, on the other hand, were members of the phone company's Pioneers, which was the charity arm of the company. Randy was one of the designers of blind softball, a game for those with sight impairment that used beeping sounds for the ball. The joy this game brought to those who just wanted to play ball was indescribable. The two sets of parents, well, they "got it" And it showed. Nick was worried how Charlene would feel when she had the opportunity to meet what was to be his future in-laws. Mrs. White could be quite intimidating with her graceful elegance standing next to her corporate executive husband, hand in hand. The widowed working Florida nurse might feel compromised, but once again Nick underestimated his mother.

Grace and Charlene hit it right off from the beginning as the two, even though different, shared many of the common core values of their generation. First and foremost, they both put their love for their children above anything else—and don't you dare forget that. Privately, Charlene shared with her son that she actually felt sorry for Grace. She went on to explain she had no idea how the woman could marry and bury two husbands—and likely, if statistics proved correct, following them up with a third. She went on to confide to Nick that burying J.W. almost broke her, and she could not even to begin to understand how that woman could have done it twice, and probably would a third time. That was not fair. In fact, it was downright cruel. Charlene would not trade her life for that of any other woman, and she wanted Nick to know that.

Nick was happy that the mothers, once they got to know each other, got along, but the first date to meet the Whites, mom, dad, and brother, could be best described as a disaster. That Nick and Lauren would survive the evening and even laugh about it later proved how strong and grounded their relationship was. When Nick picked up Lauren, there seemed to be something wrong with her. She was not her usual confident, bottom-line, boxes-checked, junior award-winning banking executive self, but was more like a high school girl waiting on her prom date who was about to get the once-over by her parents in the living room. The first thing she did was to suggest that Nick leave his signature blue blazer at her apartment, saying he would not need it for the evening. In fact, it was more than a suggestion; it was a well-placed order. To most that would not be a problem, but to Nick it was. He and his blazer were married in a way and telling him not to bring it was like taking a dog's favorite bone away or taking away a child's security blanket lovingly referred to as his "boo." Both the dog and the child will surrender the object but will question the request and will not be happy about it and be uncomfortable without the item. Nick pleaded his case as he had been raised to always bring his sport coat because he could always take it off and or just leave it in the car, but it he did not have it, then he was shit out of luck.

Nope, leave it there, Lauren said, and it was spoken more as a directive than as a request.

Nick took off his security blanket and put it over a kitchen chair in Lauren's apartment. They climbed into Nick's car. He could smell the scent of cigarettes. Lauren still smoked but never in front of him, knowing how he despised the habit. She certainly lit up when she felt anxious or nervous. He got his point across in a polite way when he offered her a mint after leaving the guard gate on the way to the parents' house. Nick always kept mints in his car for the obvious reason—for good breath, to cleanse his mouth after a dip of snuff—but also to use as a masking agent for alcohol just in case he were to get stopped by law enforcement. Lauren thanked him and took not one, but three, mints. She was nervous, and it showed.

When they arrived and were welcomed in, Nick was very impressed by the clubhouse located on the country club fairway that featured outdoor lighting. It was beautiful, as if it had come out of the latest issue of *Southern Living* magazine. The house was immaculate without, according to his observation, a single thing out of place. It looked like a model house for prospective buyers, much different from the house he'd grown up in with nurse's white stockings hanging over the shower curtain rod and with ashtrays in every room for J.W.'s three-pack-a-day addiction. Randy mixed the drinks as he and Grace made their daughter's beau as comfortable as possible. Peanuts, from Virginia of course, and a chilled silver plate of cheese and crackers were offered. Nick was starved and dug right into both offerings. Mom, dad, and daughter all had J&B and sodas, while Geoff, the brother, made himself a bourbon and Diet Coke. Nick was brought a bourbon and water. He could not help but look at all the framed pictures of the family, thinking that if he hadn't known the children were adopted, he would have never guessed it. The time span for the photographs ran from early childhood, through the school years, including team sports, and culminated with pictures from both high school and college graduation. Nick noticed there were a hell of lot more pictures of this family's life than were displayed in his mom's condo.

Lauren's brother emerged from what must have been a study or office. After extending his hand for a welcoming shake, his first comment to the man who would become his future brother-in-law was, "So, you went to Ole Piss, huh?" A not-so-subtle shot at Nick's alma mater.

Nick answered, "If you are referring to Ole Miss, yes, I did graduate from the University of Mississippi." They both nodded. Geoff retired to a den or TV room, drink in hand, to finish watching the sports event he had been watching before his sister had arrived. Lauren was not upset about her brother's retreat but instead felt relieved. He could be a wiseass. One less stress factor to deal with.

Nick hit it off immediately with Randy, who was a kind gentleman who had the ability to put people at ease almost instantly. The two bantered back and forth about a variety of subjects, but mostly about what Nick did, his duties, and his upbringing. The man just oozed class in every way. Lauren had given Nick a heads-up that her mother's hearing was deteriorating, so she had trouble hearing conversations, and advised him to look right at her when speaking, as she had compensated for her hearing loss by acquiring the skill of lipreading. The son of a nurse more than understood and made every effort possible to look at Lauren's mom when speaking. That would not be a problem. But there was another issue, which to this day is avoided when Lauren and Nick discuss their early dating period.

Dinner was set for seven o'clock sharp at the Monarch Country Club, the social home base for the community the Whites had become part of in Palm City. Randy had suggested there was plenty of room in his spacious Cadillac for the five of them to all ride together to the nearby club. Sure, no problem. And yet there was a problem: the club required its male members and guests to wear a sport coat to be seated in the dining room on Saturdays. Randy asked Nick to go out to his car and retrieve his coat, then they would be on the way. Nick bit his lower lip and mumbled something to the effect that he did not have his jacket with him. He had one, in fact, he had four or five of them in different colors for different occasions and different seasons of the year, but he did not have one with him that evening. He overly explained his wardrobe situation. Oh, that would be a problem, but Grace White had an idea. She asked Geoff to get one his coats for Nick to borrow, just for dinner, of course. Geoff grinned from ear to ear and said there would be no problem. He returned with a bright orange sport coat, obviously worn at University of Florida functions as blue and orange are the colors of the Gators. Nick looked for Lauren and found her peeking out from the kitchen entryway with a horrified, "I am so sorry" look on her face. If Nick had not really fallen for Lauren, he probably would have politely called it an evening, made his way to his car, gone home, let the chips fall where they may, and addressed the fallout the next day. But he really liked her, so despite the humiliation and shame she had been the direct cause of, he plodded forward. The next day he noticed his lip was sore and a little swollen, brought on by the constant pressure of his anxiously biting down on it during the case of the missing blazer and amid the subsequent strategies to find a replacement.

Nick tried on the bright orange coat, and boy, was it bright. It lit up the room—plus it could have fit him and another person at the same time. Geoff was well over six foot two and thick, much bigger than Nick. Nick looked like an orange Kool-Aid Man or a huge M&M, orange of course. The arms of the coat were so long that Nick's hands disappeared beneath the sleeves, and the length reached almost to his thighs and completely covered his ass. He looked like a little kid playing dress-up in his dad's clothes, or a hobo wearing whatever he could find to fend off the cold and the other elements. Geoff let out a big laugh, and who could blame him? He said, "You look great, man. Let's go eat!" Nick looked back at the kitchen entrance, searching for Sandy, and the two locked eyes. She appeared to be sorry for the turn of events, yet it was obvious she was doing everything possible not to explode in laughter. Randy's jackets were out of the question as he was even bigger than Geoff.

There was about a ten-second period of silence, then Nick finally said something. "Ah, no, I cannot do this. I am sorry. It's my fault. I should have brought my jacket.

Should have known better." He fell on the sword, heck, the grenade, for his new girlfriend, as it was her fault. But her parents did not need to know this, at least not now. Geoff made himself another drink as he would not be driving and honestly was loving the whole spectacle. Randy, who had disappeared without notice, returned, and said the maître d', Oscar, said they would make it work and to come on over. Thankfully, Nick took off the orange jacket and handed it back to Geoff, who wanted to be sure and offered it up again. Nick humbly shook his head from side to side and mouthed, "no, thanks".

As they arrived at the club, the valets parked the black El Dorado, and the five went up to the maître d's podium. Randy shook hands with the man who apparently was Oscar, and during the handshake Nick noticed an exchange of money in appreciation for Oscar's having made it work. This Nick understood from all his experience parking cars at Nando's in Palm Beach. For the right amount of money, problems can be fixed, and this one was fixed. The White family and Nick walked through the dining area, where the average age had to be seventy, and that was counting the tables with visiting grandchildren. They kept walking and finally arrived at their table. They would eat in the far corner of the dining room by the swinging kitchen doors. Although they were uncomfortable and embarrassed, the food and drink were good, and the conversation went quite well, considering everything that had led up to the meal itself.

With the meal complete, the family waited for the parking lot attendants to bring the car around. Two of the attendants opened the doors so the diners could get in and finish their evening. Ah, finish the evening. But wait, there would be one more thing as Randy meandered along the curvy roads that led from the country club back to their home at a slow and measured speed of twenty miles per hour. This slow speed limit was better suited for the daytime, when multiple work trucks made their way from house to house for their scheduled jobs, avoiding the many walkers, joggers, and golf carts, and the flocks of grounded mother ducks and their ducklings, who followed close behind. The speed limit probably needed to be slow because of that. But the slow speed along the snakelike road allowed Geoff time to play one more annoying prank, as if the orange jacket had not been enough. The three "kids" were seated in the back seat, which gave big brother the opportunity to exaggerate the twists and turns of the road by violently and aggressively shifting his body back and forth in tandem, thus crushing his sister, who was seated in the middle, and sending her right into her boyfriend's body. Nick could not believe this. It seemed to be the action of a second grader riding with his parents and a friend to the beach or a park. Every few seconds Nick found himself planted up against the back door of the driver's side.

After the five-minute ride that capped off the interesting evening, Lauren and Nick declined the offer to go back into the house and instead decided to head toward Nick's car for the twenty-minute drive back to West Palm Beach. Nick shook Randy's hand and gave a polite peck on the cheek to Grace and thanked them once again for a delightful evening. He promised that next time, he would have his blazer, then looked over at Lauren, who nodded. If they only knew. Geoff was nowhere to be found as he had quickly gone inside after saying something about having to use the bathroom.

The ride home was quiet, noticeably so. Finally, Lauren said she was sorry about the jacket. She was about to make another comment when Nick raised his hand for her to stop. She nodded. Nick popped in a cassette and turned it up very loud without saying a word. He was going to let her think about the problem she had caused, wanting to see how she handled it. Of course, she handled it perfectly.

Nick walked Lauren to her door, gave her a quick kiss on the lips, turned around, and was in his car within seconds and on his way home to his apartment. He would be asleep just fifteen minutes later. Sunday morning, he picked up Charlene for church, but on his way, he called Lauren on his new car phone that had been installed just a few weeks earlier. He'd gotten the idea of getting one from his friend Larry Timmons, who used his for his athletic duties at Jupiter High, but mostly to have access to his bookie. When Lauren answered, Nick started out by saying he hoped he had not wakened her this early Sunday morning. She reassured him that she was already up and studying for an exam later that week, adding that she wanted to get that out of the way early on Sunday. She didn't mention the night before, and asked, "What's up with you?" It was the old Lauren, or least the one Nick had gotten to know in their few months of dating. The tone of the question was pleasant yet confident, just like she was. Nick explained he was on the way to his mother's to pick her up for church and that he had nothing planned for the afternoon. He suggested they go to the movie theater at the Cross County Mall and see the screen adaptation of Tom Clancy's *Patriot Games*, starring Harrison Ford as Jack Ryan. Both had read the novel and enjoyed it. Afterward they would maybe grab some pizza at Zucharelli's, which was particularly good and close to Lauren's apartment. She thought it was a great idea, so Nick agreed to pick her up a little after three. Still nothing about the previous night.

Charlene waited till after church but came right out with it after breakfast. She wanted to know how the date had gone and what the parents were like. Nick didn't bring up the wardrobe malfunction, but he did explain he really liked the family and thought Charlene would too. *Good answer,* she thought.

Nick and Sandy went to the movie without saying much, just offering their opinions on the movie versus the book. When they pulled up to the pizzeria, Nick raced around the car to open Lauren's door, as he always did, and without her noticing, grabbed his blazer from behind his seat. Grinning, he looked at her and said, "Coming prepared today." Promptly the two broke out into laughter. They took each other's hands and went inside for some homemade pizza. This was going to work out after all.

The two began seeing each other even more, as time permitted, yet they kept their own separate addresses as Lauren was against living together because, if nothing else, it would disappoint her parents. Nick understood. This of course did not keep them from staying overnight at each other's places. As summer approached, which meant Nick had a lot of time off coming up, he proposed they go on a vacation together. Lauren agreed, but Grace was not thrilled, feeling that the two of them traveling together when not yet married was not a good look. *Oh well,* Lauren thought. *If she only knew. Well, never mind.*

Nick was adamant about taking his car, the 300Z, for the trip. As he explained, the car was built for the highway. But there was a problem: Lauren could not drive a vehicle with a manual transmission. *Not a problem,* Nick thought. He would teach her. After all, he was a teacher by trade. On a Sunday they went over to Hillcrest cemetery, located only a block or so from Forest Hill High, in the southern end of West Palm—the final resting place of J. W. Finch—for a driving lesson. They pulled up right by J.W.'s headstone. Since they were there, Nick thought, they might as well pay their respects. Two hundred yards down the one-lane road of the cemetery there was a funeral in progress. Friends and family members were paying their last respects to a loved one they had just lost. Nick and Lauren switched seats. The banker settled in the driver's seat, adjusted her mirrors, snapped her seat belt into place, turned the key, and listened for the powerful motor to crank up. Success! That would be the only passing grade of the lesson, though. Lauren White could never get the hang of engaging the clutch, pressing down on the accelerator, and releasing the clutch, then repeating the sequence to engage a higher gear. The car kept jerking forward and then stalling out. She would try again, but she got the same result. Over the course of about ten minutes, they had traveled all of fifteen yards. Nick thought he would be joining his father in the open plot next to his grave that had been already bought for Charlene's final resting place. The funeral goers were noticing the spectacle, and some began to point and laugh. At least the driving lesson brought humor to such a somber occasion. *Must be Irish,* Nick deduced. Finally, Lauren turned to Nick and said in a matter-of-fact voice, "I quit, so it looks like you are doing all the driving." And that was that.

The two decided on an eleven-day journey consisting of two weekends and one full week. The time allotted was, of course, of no concern to Nick as he had most of June, all of July, and about half of August off for vacation. As teachers will say, the three best things about the profession are June, July, and August. Also, seventeen days for Christmas and eleven days in the spring are pretty damn good benefits to count on. Lauren, on the other hand, had to watch her days, not so much for the missed work, but because her clients expected her to be only a phone call away at any time and for anything. Nick's new car phone worked perfectly as the passenger was on call during business hours as they traveled across the eastern half of the United States. From West Palm Beach, they would head north and west up the state of Florida on their way to Oxford to visit Nick's college and his fraternity brothers who lived up there. They would stop for the night in Montgomery, Alabama, and the next day drive to Oxford. The trip took a little longer than it had when Nick had made the same drive solo, as now there were more bathroom and coffee breaks, and Lauren wanted to stop at every farm equipment and tractor showroom because she was doing her own research into the industry. As she explained it so her history teacher / coach boyfriend could understand, it was somewhat possible to predict agribusiness by looking at equipment sales. Nick and Lauren stopped at no fewer than five different places, where Lauren she would investigate sales and the attitudes of the owners and salespeople. Lauren White also opined on the numerous National Guard armories located throughout the states of Alabama and Mississippi. Most had a noncommissioned tank or pieces of artillery on their front lawns for display. Some even had a Vietnam-era Huey helicopter on the property. All these things made them look like mini army bases. Nick explained that in the Deep South, the military had a very large presence because of its heritage, because certain senior members of Congress exercised influence over base locations, because serving in the military part time enabled one to earn extra income, and because the military was often needed when there were natural disasters such as hurricanes and floods. In Florida, the Guard had mostly been called out for riots and other disturbances, mostly in Miami, and of course for hurricanes. Also, many of these armories doubled as community centers for such events as dances, wedding receptions, and professional wrestling matches. Lauren nodded; it made sense. To the Palm Beach banker by way of Washington, DC, the rural countryside of Dixie looked like one farm after another, with many of those homesteads being decorated with yard art. Some southerners liked to accent their front yards with large decorations, not seasonal decorations like at Christmastime but year-round pieces. If one were alert one could see herds of ceramic deer, giant roosters, barn murals, or Nick's favorite: a twelve-foot Elvis on the front side of a house on US Highway 282 in Alabama. Not the later Vegas Elvis, but the young heartthrob from Tupelo and Memphis, from Elvis's *Ed Sullivan* days. Classic.

Lauren was polite, but this area was very different for her. She began to wonder, *where in the hell is this place?* and *What must it be like?* As they pulled off Highway 6 at the exit for Lamar Avenue and downtown Oxford, she quickly pulled her seat up and took notice. It was gorgeous, pristine, and elegant in an Old South antebellum way. One beautiful home after another with large porches and manicured lawns. *Now this is real southern living,* she thought. As they approached University Avenue, Nick made a quick left and drove to the end of Ole Taylor Road. Before it snaked back, he pulled over and announced a quick detour. They got out of the car and walked twenty or so steps. There on the right side was the spectacular residence of the Nobel Prize–winning author William Faulkner that he had named Rowan Oak. With all its splendor, it just stared back as it had done for so many years, even when "Brother Bill" was working on one of his classics on the second floor in his study. Nick was not sure how the economics-inspired traveler from Palm Beach would react. He himself was always in awe of the home, but maybe because he fancied himself a writer someday. Or perhaps it was the history major in him. But how would his girlfriend react to one of his favorite places in the world? She was speechless and awestruck, but she admitted that, like many, she did not care for Faulkner's style of writing. But how beautiful the whole setting was! She wanted to go in. He promised they would return tomorrow for a tour. From there, Nick turned around and got back on Lamar to head north toward the Square, the hub for everything Oxford. Of course, there was the courthouse centered squarely in the middle and guarded by a large statue of a Confederate soldier. Traffic must make its way around in a circular fashion, and the four sides of the square were populated by as many fine clothing and jewelry stores as anywhere, and housed the South's first department store, Nielson's, which first opened its doors in 1839. Lauren's jaw dropped at all the shopping opportunities Oxford was offering her, and most of the windows announced they were having summer sales as most students, especially the coeds, had gone back home for the summer. This was worth the drive, she thought. After a quick spin around the Square, it was off to campus and the Alumni House, which was the official lodging provided by the university located right across from the ten-acre park known to all as the Grove. They would stay in Oxford for the next two days before leaving for the second leg of their journey. The Rollins grad got to see Rowan Oak; took a campus tour, which included Nick's fraternity house and the beautiful house belonging to the Oxford chapter of Lauren's sorority, Phi Mu, located at the top of Sorority Row; and got to shop. Oh, did she shop. Nick had gotten the hell out of the way as she made her way around the Square. He had parked himself on a barstool upstairs at a restaurant named the Downtown Grill. Lauren had made her way to catch up with him and relate her shopping success. The bartender grinned from ear to ear as she explained that this was only half of what she had intended to buy. She was so excited when trying to explain the sales, the name brands, and just how much she was saving that she found herself out of breath as she asked for the keys to put her bags in the trunk of the 300Z. The bartender hoped that Nick had plenty of room on his credit card, as it appeared he would be needing it. Nick laughed and explained she was the money person of this gig. Later, the two hooked up with a couple of Nick's fraternity brothers who lived in Tupelo and Memphis and had come down to Oxford to catch up with the Florida boy and meet "the one." The three couples all got rooms at the Alumni House and, after a night on the town, decided to go swimming in the hotel pool because it was a hot Mississippi night. It was as if they were in college again. All fun. The brothers and their wives really liked Lauren. And what was there not to like? They teased Nick about her height and athletic prowess, compared to Nick's limitations in both categories. All laughed.

The journey would continue after three days in the Deep South as the two, now packed tightly with a whole new wardrobe, headed north out of Oxford to visit Nick's sister Addie, who, now with her husband and daughters, was living in upstate New York. Through Tennessee, then up to Kentucky, and then across into Ohio, the two traveled over the Ohio River, once a waterway west in the nation's early days. It was dark now as they passed a lit-up Riverfront Park, the home of the Cincinnati Reds, who were apparently playing a night game. Nick wanted to stop and see it, but nah, they continued as there was plenty of time to pack on the miles. Nick had acquired so many of Charlene's traits, but he had many that would prove he was J.W.'s son. One was these was, when on vacation, driving on and on without stopping. On one family trip west, the Finches left West Palm and did not stop until Dallas, and the next day Colorado. They would have made it all the way to Montana except for a terrible flood in the Big Thompson Canyon area. As Lauren and Nick traveled, their first real experience with spending an extended amount of time together, they learned a lot about each other, for example, Nick had control issues about driving and stopping, and he was amazed at Lauren's ability to work from the passenger seat as if it were her personal office and desk back in Palm Beach.

Finally, the two made the turn east outside Cleveland, then the copilot asked—well, pleaded—to stop and get a room as they had driven more than twelve hours with only a few stops just for necessities such as snacks, drinks, and bathroom breaks. Lauren had been more than accommodating and now wanted to stop and sleep, and not in the car. Nick agreed. They found a room east of Cleveland right off the interstate. They were lucky, having gotten the last room, as there seemed to be a major summer attraction that had drawn lots of visitors to the area. That attraction ended up being a saltwater aquarium. Nick hated aquariums. After all, he lived close to a real aquarium that did not restrict the stars of the show, who were free to come and go as they pleased, which was the Atlantic Ocean, with all its tropical beauty that it showed off each day off the coast of Palm Beach. Really, dolphins and whales in

Ohio? Added to this fact was that both Nick and Lauren were certified scuba divers, although neither went much anymore. Both had experienced the splendor of visiting aquatic life in its home environment, which had spoiled almost any trip to an aquarium to see a staged show. They both agreed, but during the conversation Nick did find out the guy who had preceded him in the courting of Miss White was a scuba dive instructor. In a tacky example of jealousy, Nick asked Sandy, since she had dated a scuba diving instructor, "What, were all the surfers and pool cleaners taken at the time?" The people of these subcultures are known more for their love of the outdoors than for their responsibility and maturity.

Lauren fired right back, with a smile, "I thought you'd like that since you dated a freakin' mermaid." Well played.

The next morning, they got up early. Nick went down to the lobby to square up at the front desk and to fetch Lauren a tall cup of coffee with two—not one, not three, but two—packets of Sweet 'N Low, no creamer, and take it back to the room. This simple chore would become a routine, continuing for years as the two would be lucky enough to travel most of the world. While Lauren showered and put herself together, Nick would get the hell out the way and yet be productive and feed her addiction to java. It worked, and it had started that day in northeastern Ohio. On the way back to the room, Nick was stopped by a law enforcement official. The cop asked Nick what time he had arrived the night before, and Nick had said it was after midnight but before one o'clock in the morning. Answering the next question, he said he had not seen anything suspicious. Why? Then Nick looked up to the exposed top of the outdoor stairwell between the first floor and the second and saw a mother with her two small children who looked very distraught. He deduced the man whom the other officer was talking to must have been the husband and father. He was correct. It seemed that the family had driven up from Centreville, Ohio, to go to the aquarium for a summer vacation experience, and now their car had been stolen with most of their belongings, apparently including one prized stuffed animal that belonged to the younger daughter. The young girl was crying and was very shaken about losing her baby.

Lauren had now emerged from the room, dressed, and waiting on her coffee, but she too wanted to see what was going on outside the room. Nick and Lauren were both bothered by what they were witnessing. Nick asked the cop if there was anything they could do. Lauren took the two little girls down to lobby for a hot chocolate as the mom and dad worked out a plan B. The father asked, if it were not too much trouble, if Nick could possibly drive him over to the rental dealer near the airport. Absolutely. Lauren took the mom and the two daughters to breakfast at the Bob Evans restaurant across the street. Lauren then talked to the little girl about the loss of her baby and said everything would be all right. Then she slipped a twenty-dollar bill to the mom to allow the little girl to pick out a new baby and, in so many words, adopt it. Lauren understood all about adoption. The mother teared up and thanked the young childless woman from Florida.

Nick returned as Sandy climbed into the Z to continue the trip, but now with an additional story. Nick talked to Lauren about the man he had helped, saying it was the right thing to do and that it just broke his heart to see this hardworking family go through such an ordeal on what was to be a simple feel-good family trip. It was just so wrong. When he finished, it was Lauren's turn. She told of her experiences at breakfast with the mom and the girls, adding that she had given the mom some money so the little girl could adopt a new baby. Nick was in the beginning phases of trying to understand all the complications that Lauren wrestled with in terms of her start on this earth and her own story of adoption. Nick was speechless, almost, when he looked over to his travel companion and said, "That is so cool. Wow, so freakin' cool." Lauren was busy looking out the window, in deep thought, and never even turned around to make eye contact. Maybe, just maybe, the new stuffed baby would be as lucky as she had been. Maybe.

They almost had a terrible accident where northeastern Ohio and New York share a border. Nick was enjoying the drive through the desolate farm country, driving up and down the small hills and along the winding roads, when he took a hill at a high rate of speed and directly on the other side, in the middle of the road, was an Amish family in a horse and buggy. Nick swerved to miss the black-dressed clan and was able to avoid them and a potential accident. He took a deep breath and let out a "Whew." Looking in his rearview mirror, he saw the man who was at the reins was giving the sports-car-driving Floridian the finger, the bird, the ole number one sign. Who knew the Amish were practiced in hand profanity? You learn something new every day, and today Nick saw that people from strict fundamentalist religious sects are also affected by road rage and that the accompanying anger and gestures that immediately follow a road rage incident are universal. Tragedy avoided and lesson learned.

Binghamton, New York, was now the residence of Nick's sister Addie and her family of three young girls. Her husband, Nick's brother-in-law, Henry was an engineer for IBM and had been transferred from the Boca Raton office to the one upstate in Binghamton. It was a promotion and given that it was a field-leading Fortune 500 company, it was a large opportunity for the young family. They quickly moved into what was a company town. IBM employed thousands of employees and ran a 24/7 operation there. There was also Endicott Johnson Shoes and a Singer-Link plant that made plane simulators. The town had flourished after the war as the military-industrial complex supplied the Defense Department and supplementary industries with the new high-tech devices needed for a changing world. Today most of these jobs are gone and have moved overseas, mostly to China and India. It took a while for the Florida girl to adjust to her new environment of the Triple Cities of the Southern Tier.

If you were to dig a hole next to a stream and put your toys, such as Matchbox cars and model trains, into it, you would have a scaled-down version of Binghamton. The city is on the riverfront of the Susquehanna, which in the nineteenth century was both a power source and a transportation source. The city was built next to it, but in a valley surrounded by small mountains or large hills—your choice. This natural setting led to limited sunshine, and with Lake Erie relatively close, winters could be, and were, snowy and brutal. If in Florida there is too much heat and sunshine, there is a definite lack of both in Binghamton. The outgoing young family quickly fit in as they joined and became leaders in the local Episcopal church. Addie opened a women's clothing boutique in an old two-story house on what they called the main drag of the town. Addie's Classic Clothing was a success, and soon thereafter she became interested in politics. At first it was the PTA at her daughters' school and the altar guild at church, but she quickly caught the bug and moved up to city council, then became a county commissioner, and finally was elected as a member of the New York Assembly. Little Addie was a player indeed. Nick was proud of her even though he could not understand her political views, so they avoided political debates. Addie, along with her husband Henry, was a loud and proud member of the liberty Democratic Party and its Kennedy wing. Nick was not.

The Finch house was interesting when it came to politics. J.W. was a southern Democrat, and this was only solidified when Harry Truman decided to drop the atomic bombs on Japan and hence cancel J.W.'s transfer from the European theater to the Pacific theater for an invasion of the island of Japan. The elder Finch drifted even farther away from his registered party after LBJ introduced his Great Society plan, and finally after four years of the Carter experiment, J.W. switched parties and voted for Ronald Reagan. As President Reagan would say—and J.W. would nod in agreement—he did not leave the Democratic Party, the Democratic Party left him. Charlene was a lifelong Republican and would announce with a grin every election night that she had voted so she could cancel out J.W.'s vote. J.W. would shake his head in disbelief. The Finch's were not players in politics, but they *always* voted, especially in local elections, such as for school board and city council. Politics was discussed, but not as passionately as it was in other households. Local anchor Bill Gordon reported the political news of Palm Beach County and the Treasure Coast nightly on the *Bill Gordon Report* on the local NBC affiliate channel 5, WPTV. For the most part, J.W. watched for Tony Glenn, who delivered the weather, and Buck Kinnaird, the sports announcer, especially interested in the results of the race of the night at the Palm Beach Kennel Club. After that it was *The Huntley–Brinkley Report* and the national news. He only half-heartedly paid attention as Charlene was getting busy and dressing for work at St. Mary's.

Nick could be described as moderate leaning right politically. Most of his fraternity brothers were very conservative as the biggest club on the Ole Miss campus was the Young Republicans. If anything, Nick was more libertarian, even though he worked for the government as a teacher, a traditionally left-leaning profession. Nick could care less who married whom and felt the government's role was to provide infrastructure and a military but not much else. As Thomas Jefferson had said, the most important government is the local one. Overall, Nick kept silent on his politics, but most thought he was a card-carrying member of the conservative right. He deplored teachers who pushed their politics on their students. When students would ask him whom he had voted for, he would smile and make it a teachable moment, explaining that one should never ask someone that question. If the person volunteers the information, fine, but one should never ask. He would add, "Never ask a woman her age or her weight." However, he did always wear his "I Voted" sticker on his shirt, and in fact when his own kids were small, he always took them to the poll to let them watch their dad vote, modeling good citizenship. It did not hurt that many times the polling place for his precinct was the school where he worked.

As Nick came to learn about Lauren's politics, he felt the two of them were compatible in this area. She also was a registered Republican, but she was somewhat liberal when it came to financial policy and social issues. Both she and Nick fell somewhere in the middle, but maybe a smidgeon to the right. It depended on the issue or cause.

When they arrived at Nick's sister's split-level ranch-style house, it made Nick think of the *Brady Bunch* house, minus the housekeeper Alice and the big dog. Henry was a cat person. After initial greetings, Addie told Nick that their mom would be there later that week to visit. Charlene would not miss the opportunity to get together with two of her children and three of her grandchildren at the same time. At first Lauren was nervous about the sleeping arrangements with what would be her future mother-in-law arriving, but both Addie and Nick laughed it off as Nick explained that their mother was kind of progressive when it came to matters of love or even lust. Addie thought that once again she would have to share mother time with her little brother. Nick knew that Charlene was going to be there to make sure she would not miss a thing. Nick and Lauren would only spend a day and half there and then head north to the Canadian border to the town of Alexandria Bay on the Saint Lawrence River and the Thousand Islands to get away to Addie's cabin on the river. The others would be joining them later for an old-fashioned clambake on the river.

Driving up I-81 from Binghamton through Syracuse to "Alex Bay," Nick and Lauren found the cabin right on the majestic waterway of the north that connected the United States and Canada, but also connected the Atlantic Ocean to the Great Lakes. Nick also observed that upstate New York was more like Alabama or Georgia with countless farms, pickup trucks, and cafes that advertised early breakfast hours to accommodate the hunters. This was a lot different from his travels to see Michelle Mitchell in Connecticut or New York City. The setting was different and beautiful, but the cabin was, say, primitive. The shower trickled, so one had to bring a cup to fill with water for shampooing and rinsing. Modern conveniences were sparse if existent at all. After the drive, Nick raced to the bedroom and leaped on top of the bed to stretch out and take it all in, but when he hit the bed, he heard something below cracking and then breaking as the bed frame collapsed on the lower right side. He climbed off the bed and got on his knees to look to see what had just happened. Sure enough, the leg on the lower right side of the bed had snapped. Outside, Nick found some stones that were used for a firepit. He took a few of these and used them to prop up the bed. That will work until they could go into town and find a hardware store with the proper materials to fix it before everyone arrived at the cabin in two days.

Nick and Lauren went into the riverfront town of Clayton with several objectives: grocery shopping, finding a liquor store, checking out the local scene, and of course finding the supplies needed to fix the bedpost. The town was quaint and bustling as this was the tourist season. Nearby was the prestigious Saint Lawrence University. Summer tourism and the college provided needed local income. Nick found a hardware store, but no one there seemed to understand his predicament or knew how to fix a bedpost. They looked at him with tilted heads as if he were speaking in a foreign language. Imagine the old *Bob Newhart Show* set in Vermont and the brother characters of Larry, Darryl, and Darryl and you'll get the picture.

Lauren spotted a furniture store. Maybe, just maybe, they would have both the parts and the knowledge to help Nick fix the bed before his sister, her family, and his mother arrived. No luck. Miss White was horrified that of all the things that could break, it had to be the bed. That was not a good look. Nick of course had broken things before when his parents were gone. Most of the time his strategy was simple: lie, lie, and deny. Sometimes it was easy just to move something or glue it, and maybe they would not know the difference or notice the change. The problem here was that it was the bed, the master bed. He knew that his brother-in-law Henry with his engineering background and general handyman skills could evaluate the problem and fix it. Nick, not so much.

The station wagon pulled in. The family exited the car. It seemed Charlene could not wait. She was now used to living alone and without the confusion of a young family, and it showed. Nick's strategy was to come right out with it. Shortly after everyone was gathered, he confessed. Lauren looked on in total embarrassment and quickly retreated to the small kitchen. Not much was said in response, although there was a lot of grinning and blushing. Lauren never looked up as she pretended to be washing dishes in the kitchen.

After the luggage was unloaded, Henry went over to the bed and analyzed the situation. He went out to the small metal shed and came back with some tools and a couple of pieces of wood, mostly 4 × 4's, and within minutes had it fixed. There were a couple of instances of good-natured needling of Nick and Lauren. Charlene stayed quiet, but nothing could wipe away the ear-to-ear grin she was sporting.

The weekend was fun with a trip to Alex Bay to a resort called the Bonnie Castle to see a Vegas-type revue put on by a family group from Buffalo named the Finn Brothers. They were really good as they played a mix of current hits and old-time favorites, such as Frank Sinatra and Dean Martin. The sister of the Finns was a knockout blonde, her striking looks outshined only by her singing voice as she sang tunes from the Carpenters to Whitney Houston and everything in between. The family enjoyed themselves the entire evening, heck, the entire weekend, as Nick now had discovered there was a New York outside the five boroughs, and he liked it. He was quickly informed that summer and winter on the Canadian border was a completely different animal. He asked some locals what they did during those winter months, and almost to a person they explained their strategy as consisting of the three B's: booze, bingo, and baby making, with some opting out and taking extended trips to Florida. Because the resorts were closed during winter, most workers qualified for unemployment benefits, which caused Nick to recall the fact that New York was a high-tax and deficit-spending state. Now he understood why.

On Sunday afternoon, Lauren got a call from her boss, which she took out on the dock next to the river so she could speak in private. When she returned, she informed everyone that she had to book a flight back to West Palm out of Syracuse first thing Monday morning as one of her top clients had suddenly passed away. The family requested—really, demanded—that she be there for all the potential family fallout once the will was read. Lauren apologized to the extended Finch family, but she explained that they paid her—well, the bank—very well for her financial advice, her planning, and her discreet handling of personal matters. Without her telling Nick, he surmised who it was from their discussions about work and the local gossip scene. He thought, *just wait until that will is read and most of the family finds they've been cut out in favor of the man's new wife, a twenty-something former model-turned-socialite who is in line for the bulk of the inheritance, but also with a nice chunk of change going to the local animal rescue league in the name of her never-not-by-her-side miniature Yorkie named*

Buttercup. Lauren's flight would be leaving out of Syracuse at seven o'clock in the morning, so that meant they had to be up and out by five o'clock to get her checked in. She would be back in Palm Beach by noon. How jet travel had changed Florida along with, of course, the invention of the air conditioner. Charlene listened intently to the plans and at the end jumped right in, proposing she would replace the young woman as Nick's copilot for the return trip to Florida. There was one problem in that Nick's car was only two-seater and there would be three of them going to the airport. Not a problem, at least for Nick and Charlene.

The next morning, when it was still pitch-black, the three made their way to the car, while the others in the cabin were still sound asleep. Lauren left a note on the kitchen table thanking the family for their hospitality and saying how sorry she and Nick were about the bed. Nick had made a sort of ditch between the bags and all the clothes that Lauren had bought in Oxford, so now there was a small rectangular space in the middle of the cargo area with a small pillow at the top, bordered by luggage and packages. Lauren would lie flat down with her head nestled right behind the 300Z's center console and gearshift. A small red blanket that sported the name of Delta Airlines covered the determined young banking executive from feet to neck. To the naked eye, it looked like a mother-and-son outlaw team was taking a dead victim out of their hideout to be buried so they could continue with their crime spree. Think Ma Barker and her gang. Lauren took to the arrangement like a real trouper and did not complain at all, instead spending the time reviewing her BlackBerry to see what she would be walking into. When they pulled into the airport's unloading area and Nick hit the button to open the hatch, the porter went to the back of the car to give a hand with the luggage and hopefully earn a tip, but to his surprise a body emerged and climbed out. He was shocked. Lauren nodded to the man and simply said, "Don't ask." She grabbed only one small bag, as Nick could ferry the rest back on his return trip with his mom. After a quick kiss on the cheek between Nick and Lauren, Lauren leaned over to give a kiss to a surprised Charlene, then she was off to her check-in gate, going on to Atlanta, then Palm Beach International, then by taxi straight to Palm Beach and work.

Nick and his mom left the airport and got on I-81 South to head back home. About ten miles south of the city, Charlene turned down the radio and said one more time to her baby boy, "Do not screw this one up. She is the one. And you are an incredibly lucky man to have found her. Don't screw it up. Get what I am saying?" Nick nodded. His mom finished with a simple but forceful, "Good." She then turned the volume back up on the radio and looked out at the New York State farmland, one dairy farm after another, without saying another word for a good two hundred miles. Deep into Pennsylvania, she announced that there was a Cracker Barrel restaurant at the next exit and she would not mind a bite to eat. Nick knew well enough that this was not a request but a polite order. He complied and exited the highway for lunch.

The trip was uneventful but also very informative as Nick and Charlene talked about the past, the present, and the future. Charlene, who had cut her hours way back, was going to retire fully very soon and dedicate a lot of her time to volunteer work. Nick teased her about becoming the world's oldest candy striper. She filled him in on a lot of family secrets, some of which were not all too secret, but Nick feigned shock at the stories of his aunts, uncles, grandparents, and cousins, and even his sisters. The only thing off-limits was J.W. There would be no gossip or stories about his father—and especially from his mother. What was private would stay private. It reminded Nick of the United States' first love story, that of George Washington and Martha Dandridge Custis. Upon the death of the Father of Our Country in December of 1799 at Mount Vernon, Martha retrieved a locked trunk full of what she thought were all the letters between her and her husband, sat in front of the fireplace, reread each and every one of them, and then burned them all. She announced that these were private and were to remain private, just between her and the general. So would be the private lives of J.W. Finch and his wife, Charlene.

After an overnight stay at a Holiday Inn Express off I-95 in North Carolina, the mother and son got up early and hit the road. Other than pit stops for gas and bathroom breaks, it would be a straight shot through the Carolinas, Georgia, and then their home state of Florida. Nick told his mom to drive since it was all downhill. She looked at him as if he were crazy and just shook her head at her grinning son. They did make good time, thanks to light traffic and a new device Nick had purchased for the trip, a "fuzz buster", to help notify him of upcoming speed traps. The game of cat and mouse between the trooper and the driver, the mouse, now was foiled by a secret weapon, namely, a radar detection device. How well it worked was debatable, but Nick escaped any speeding tickets, and his driving record remained spotlessly clean.

They pulled into Palm Beach County in the early evening. Nick dropped Charlene off and made sure she called his sister Addie to tell them of their safe arrival home. Nick, exhausted from the drive, went straight to his apartment. On his way, he called Lauren from the car phone, although he was getting worried about the upcoming mobile phone bill. She was happy and relieved that the two had made it home safe and sound, but she seemed disappointed that Nick would go straight home to his apartment rather than going by her place. He would see her tomorrow as he would swing by the bank to have lunch with her. First National had its own cafeteria that served outstanding food at cost, and he could get her apartment key and drop off all her purchases made on the trip. Nick found out years later that the fact that he had taken his mom home and then went to his apartment rather than hers hurt her a little. It made her feel she was still in second place behind Mama. Nick admitted it had never entered his mind. Maybe it should have, but he was very tired and simply could not wait to get out of that car and go to sleep in his own bed. Sorry. I guess.

The elephant in the room now was not if, but when, Nick was going to pop the question. He and Lauren had survived a trip and travel experience together, not only with extended family, but also with the mother included.

No fights, no realizations that this would not work out, but the opposite: an unspoken agreement that this thing was working and possibly could work out for the long run.

It was back to work for both young professionals as summer ended. Nick still had his duties as AD and taught his three AP United States History classes in the portable behind the gym. He had put together a fantastic coaching staff with his teams, not only winning at the local level but also moving up to the state playoffs in the big three of football, basketball, and baseball. School spirit had rebounded; the pep rallies had life again; and attendance was up at the games. Carlos Martinez ran a tight ship, but was not a dictator, although he did play favorites. And Nick was his favorite. Nick sat in on interviews with potential new teachers as Carlos explained that Nick represented the department chairs, the athletic department, the classroom teachers, the neighborhood, and the alumni. He was right in that Nick was the AD, was the social studies department chair who taught in the classroom, had grown up in the area, and was an alumnus of the school. Nick learned a lot during these interviews, and he tried to be the calming influence as these people came in nervous and anxious, so he tried to convey to them that he too was a teacher and not a boss but a possible colleague. It seemed to work, as to a person smile emerged from the candidate. But the administrators who also there in the office were not smiling, as they could not understand why a classroom teacher was part of the process. Of course, they never said it to the boss or questioned him, but Nick could tell that this was an invasion of their turf. Nick thought how lucky he was in that his first and only interview had consisted of helping the principal with yard work and talking about his dad's declining health, so he wanted to do something to lower the anxiety level of the prospective hires. He always looked for a common denominator, such as college or a listed reference he knew. Carlos said that Nick was a natural at interviewing, and he loved how Nick brought a welcoming spirit to the procedure. Nick also noticed that Carlos Martinez, when he could, hired new teachers right out of college. He explained to Nick that he did like to take in other principals' retreads or the "my way or the highway" teachers. He went on to say that these young teachers were raw clay who, with the right artist, could be molded into great teachers. Sure, they would make mistakes, but those would be the mistakes of youth and the mistakes of burned-out teachers counting the days to summer or, even worse, retirement. Also, since most were single, they had no family duties and could potentially coach and sponsor clubs and organizations. He was, of course, right. He also liked to hire pretty young women for these open positions. The faculty noticed this also. The men liked it, the women, not so much.

At the school Christmas party held next door at the country club, Nick was the one to present the faculty gift to the principal. Most of the staff had no idea what they had selected for their boss, as it was Nick and a few chosen others, mostly coaches, who had come up with idea. Nick had gone to the Palm Beach Mall and picked it out, and then had gone to the embroidery and print shop that did all the school's silk screening and printing work, which was quite extensive because of all the athletic teams, clubs, and organizations, and all the faculty's needs. The shop was more than willing to fill the order—and at no cost. Nick talked to four of the newest members of the faculty, all young and quite attractive women, and asked them to follow him to the front, where he would present Carlos with his gift. The young teachers knew what was in the package and were all in on it. It helped that they had a few drinks in them as there was an open bar provided by the class ring and senior supply company. Carlos himself had already had a few mojitos when he walked to the front of his audience. At least 85 percent of the faculty and staff had no idea what they had bought their leader for a Christmas gift. The fewer people who knew, the better, Nick thought. If it ended up not working out as planned, they could honestly say they'd had nothing to do with it.

The four young female teachers, two math, one English, and one science, split up so there were two on each side of Nick as he, with microphone in hand, got everyone's attention. Of course, that always meant that someone had to holler out, "Can't hear" or "Shh," or just plain "Shut up!" Teachers could be just as rude as their students or even worse when in a group and there was alcohol. Carlos Martinez, the Cuban rafter who as a small boy had taught himself English, and who then became an English professor and later a school principal right here in Florida, who was the poster boy of everything good about the United States and the definition of the word *opportunity*, which came with being an American, carefully took off the wrapping and folded it neatly, explaining that he was doing so just in case he needed to regift what was inside. He opened the box, and out came his present. He looked at it for a second as the crowd hollered out, "What is it? Show us. Can't see." He then took out a red silk bathrobe monogrammed in interlocking script with "CM" on the upper right chest, the exact type of robe *Playboy* magazine founder and editor Hugh Hefner wore around the mansion. Of course, flanking Carlos were four of his "Playmates"—no, teachers of the mansion, no, the campus. The young teachers all at once hugged their new boss as cameras flashed. Most of the tipsy partygoers roared with approval, but there were a few who felt this was misogynist and undignified. What really mattered was what Carlos Martinez thought about his gift.

Nick glanced quickly over to Mrs. Martinez, a dental hygienist from South County by way of Boston, with her Irish roots, and noticed that she loved it. She started to holler out, "Put it on! Put it on!" Carlos now was laughing, grinning, and maybe even blushing as he put on his new bath and bedroom wear. He quickly added two props by pulling out a big Cuban cigar, which he held in one hand, and holding up his mojito in the other. He loved it. A big success. Nick had taken the risk entirely on himself but happily shared the success with everyone, which was easy to do because of the smiles seen everywhere. Lauren, who was of course Nick's date, had been a little apprehensive about the whole idea and had shared that it would never fly in her corporate world.

When Nick returned to his table, where his coaching buddies and the banker were sitting, she looked up at him and said, "That was really cool. I thought I was in college again."

Carlos Martinez continued through the night wearing his prized possession as he made the rounds with his wife from table to table. When he came to Nick's table, he looked upon his AD and department chair, not as an employee, but as a friend. With a wide grin, he mouthed, *Thank you.* Nick nodded back.

When Carlos left to go to another table, his wife turned her head while holding her husband's hand and mouthed, *Thank you*, with a tear in her eye. Years later Nick attended the funeral of his former boss and friend at the same Hillcrest cemetery where his parents were buried. After the service, Mrs. Martinez sought Nick out to thank him for attending. She explained that her husband wanted to be buried here, within a stone's throw from the Forest Hill campus on Parker Avenue. He wanted to be close to his school and all the memories he had made there. She wanted to make sure Nick knew one more thing as the two walked away from the burial site, which was that Carlos had been buried in his bathrobe. He had explained to her when he was packing up his office to move to the district office after he'd been promoted that that one gift given to him at the Christmas party meant that the faculty accepted him for who he was. And the fact that Nick had been the one to present it to him meant so much. Seeing as it was a closed-casket ceremony, the reason for which was that Carlos's body had been damaged by chemotherapy and radiation, few people apart from immediate family knew of Carlos's burial attire. But now Nick knew. He was very familiar with what chemo and radiation did by having watched his own father suffer the effects. Nick got permission from Mrs. Martinez to share the robe story with others. Carlos Martinez was put to rest a few hundred yards from his campus and in his monogrammed bathrobe because that was what he had requested. Request granted.

There was one more gift that Nick had to give, and that was an engagement ring to his girlfriend. He was ready, and he knew she was because of the time at her family's home at Thanksgiving, after dinner and dishes were done, when the two of them were alone, when she looked at Nick and said, "You know, I will not wait forever." She then retreated to the kitchen of her parents' new home in PGA National in Palm Beach Gardens to help slice up the pies for dessert. Point taken. The Whites had sold their former home and moved their residence from the Monarch Country Club in Martin County's Palm City south to PGA National Golf Club and Resort to be closer to their daughter. Randy White also loved the game of buying and selling homes and properties for a profit and wanted a change of scenery. The search, the research, the offer, the counteroffer, and the deal, he just loved it.

Nick had shared his plan to pop the question with some close friends, such as Brian Parker, who would be his best man, and what he got in return was, "It's about time, dude." Nick knew it was time, and he was ready, but still, when it came right down to it, he was a little bit scared. He had been single now thirty-one years and had seen so many people he knew or worked with crash and burn in their attempts at marriage. It seemed after personal injury law;

the next most popular branch of the judicial system was family law. Hell, his one sister was on her third husband. Still, he knew deep down that Lauren was the one and that it was time.

Nick went to the bank and pulled out two thousand dollars from a small passbook account that he'd had since he was little. He had been told never to buy an engagement ring on credit, that it was bad luck to do so. He certainly did not want any bad luck. He went down to the downtown area to Clematis Street to Michael's Fine Jewelry Store to pick out a ring. It helped that Nick's family had known the proprietor's family a long time and Nick had taught their children and helped them with the college admissions process with glowing letters of recommendation. The owner was George Goldberg, not Michael, the latter being George's father and the founder of the store. George took charge of the sale as he dismissed the associate, explaining that the Finch's, and especially Nick, were special customers. Mr. Goldberg brought over a velvet display pillow with a variety of choices. Nick looked them over and pretended he knew exactly what he was looking for, but he had no clue whatsoever how to purchase fine jewelry, much less something forever like an engagement ring. Nick bit his lip and continued to look over the goods until finally Michael Goldberg flat-out asked the man who had taught his children how much he planned to spend. Nick replied, "About two thousand dollars."

The owner responded with an "Oh, OK then." He got up, took the pillow back to his office, returned with five small boxes with rings inside, and informed Nick that these were in his price range. No more velvet pillow treatment. Nick looked them over and selected one. The owner looked at the suggested price of twenty-five hundred dollars and thought it over for a second, then said, "We can make it work, especially if you have cash." Nick did. He peeled off twenty-one hundred-dollars bills. As he handed over the Benjamins, as kids and the movies now described hundred-dollar bills, he thought, *not to worry, Mr. Goldberg is still making money. The governor isn't, but he is.*

Since Nick was downtown, he decided to give Ray Wade a call and ask him if he wanted to meet for a drink at Roxy's, a legendary bar and grill that was generational. Nick had gone there as a small child with his dad to meet the bookie and square up. Ray had finally given up his life as a dive boat captain and scuba diving instructor and had gone into the teaching field. He was now a social studies teacher at a middle school in Royal Palm Beach and seemed to be really enjoying it.

Once at Roxy's, Nick looked around and noticed the small pinball machine that he had played as a young boy while his dad met some shadowy character in a nearby booth. At least they had not completely switched over to video games. Nick ordered up a bourbon and water, and Ray went for a rum and Coke. The two classmates sat down on barstools to catch up on all the local news and share their experiences as teachers in the modern-day classroom. The two reminisced about the time when they were both dating local TV anchors, Ray Wade seeing the weekend news anchorwoman and Nick seeing the young weather girl on channel 5. They laughed at the story of throwing a bucket of water on a pompous weatherman who really thought he was ladies' man when he opened his evening forecast remotely, outside the station, claiming there was little chance of precipitation. The boys hollered, "Hey, Bob, you're wrong, it's raining." Then there was the Ray left a big hickey on the neck of Julie the newscaster only an hour or so before she had to get to the station for the six o'clock Saturday newscast, and Ray and Nick watched with pride as the red mark kept getting bigger and bigger and more visible as the newscast wore on. Breaking news. Funny thing, it was not there at eleven o'clock as makeup responded after a few phone calls to the station. Both romances were short-lived as the young women moved up the TV ladder to New York and Atlanta. Still was funny though. After a good ten minutes of head shaking and laughing, which Raymond Wade was always good for, Nick pulled from his blazer pocket the engagement ring, still in the small box.

Ray Wade looked at Nick and grinned while responding, "Good for you. Knowing you, for goodness' sake, please keep the receipt." He opened the box and looked at the ring and remarked he would be shopping for one shortly as he had fallen for a pharmacist at Good Samaritan Hospital. Then he said, "Well now, you got her the Hope Diamond." After the proper comedic pause, he stated, "If you look close enough, you *hope* to see that there actually is a diamond." Nick laughed. Not bad, not bad at all. In fact, in the future, when comparisons were being made, Nick would refer to his wife's engagement ring as the Hope Diamond. He would never credit Ray Wade because, after all, he had paid twenty-one hundred dollars for that line.

Nick planned on proposing and decided against going to ask Lauren's parents for permission as he felt that was an outdated ritual. He was not some country-ass teenager who had gotten their daughter "in trouble," and honestly, he was still uncomfortable about what was to happen. When he called Lauren and asked what time he should come over that Saturday night, she informed him it was not a good idea that he come over at all because she was sick, either with a bad cold or maybe the flu. He offered to bring over some chicken soup and also offered stop at the pharmacy to pick something up for her if she wanted. She declined the offer. Nick thought about it for a couple of seconds and concluded, *Now or never.* He just blurted out, "I am coming over," then hung before she could protest.

He arrived at her apartment, located off Haverhill Boulevard in the outskirts of West Palm Beach, and knocked, then unlocked the door and opened it. Yes, they both had keys to each other's apartments, a big step. Lauren was not happy as she wanted to be alone. Also, she did want to pass whatever she had to her boyfriend. She was on her couch and looked horrible with the nearby coffee table full of medicines and tissues, some used and some not. Nick could smell the Vick's VapoRub she had rubbed on her chest, just as Charlene had done for him when he was little and had a chest cold. She was wearing a beaten-up robe he had never seen before and had a towel that apparently was about to be placed over her head for the vaporizer, which was about to be turned on. Nick hated that machine as it brought back bad childhood memories of Charlene hooking one up and placing a towel at the bottom of his bedroom door, saying he was not allowed out until morning. It was a jail sentence, and he considered it cruel and unusual punishment and a constitutional infraction. No matter how bad he felt, he would pretend to be healed to escape the POW experience of Nurse Finch.

Sandy looked angrily at Nick and asked, "So, what is so goddamn important that you had to come over? Well?" Nick went over to the small kitchen table, where the two had made a makeshift bar complete with a bottle of J&B scotch and a bottle of Jim Beam. There was a bottle of rum and a couple of bottles of cheap red wine. Of course, there were liter bottles of Coke Classic, Sprite, 7 Up, ginger ale, and club soda. He made a drink and then made his way back to the "living dead" on the couch in the living room, who was sporting the look of, *Why the hell are you here, when are you leaving, and what is your problem?* Nick thought about it for a second. This was not the scene of a groom on one knee in front of the Eiffel Tower, or on a gondola in Venice, or at sunset in Mallory Square in Key West, or even a game day one Saturday in the Grove, but it would have to do. If looks could kill, Nick was not only dead but also now had rigor mortis—and Lauren was digging the shallow grave nearby.

Nick went into his trusty blazer pocket, where he pulled out the ring box and tossed it to her. At first, she looked confused. Maybe it was the NyQuil. You know, the makers, or even Vick himself, will tell you not to operate heavy equipment while on it. The wheel was spinning like on a slot machine, and it came up with all sevens. Lauren White opened the box with her hands trembling. Once again, Nick wasn't sure if that was a side effect of all the over-the-counter meds she was on or if she was coming to the realization of what was really happening. She took the towel off her head; stood up, slightly staggering and weaving, probably from the medicine and lack of food; took the ring from the box; placed it on her left ring finger; and asked if this was what she thought it was. Nick nodded and asked if she would do him the honor of spending the rest of her life with him as his wife.

She shrieked, "Yes!" A miraculous healing was taking place right before his eyes, almost biblical, like with the lepers or the blind. Lauren had fully recovered and did a little dance or jig, the type he imagined she had done when she scored a goal during her soccer career. She hugged and kissed her new fiancé—to hell with it if she was contagious. After all, "in sickness and in health" was part of the sacred vows that she now was going to be able to recite to a full church. She immediately picked up the phone and called her parents. Nick retreated to the kitchen for a celebratory drink and listened in on the call from afar. He heard her say, "Mom, get Dad on the other phone. … Yes, I am feeling better, a lot better. … He did it. He just proposed. I am going to get married!" For the next hour, Lauren Elizabeth White burned up the phone lines of AT&T. The same company that had provided for her and her family was now the communication line of the biggest thing since, well, it was just the biggest thing that had ever happened in this small apartment.

Nick spent the night, but alone on the couch because of health concerns. In the morning he got up and left a small note on the table mentioning that he would never forget the night before, adding a postscript saying he hoped she was feeling better. He raced home and changed, then went to pick up Charlene for church. When the two got into the car and were strapped in, Charlene looked over at her son and picked up on something different about him. Finally, she asked if there was anything up. Nick asked if she had spoken to Lauren. She answered, "No. Why?" Nick had made Lauren promise to allow him to be the one to break the news to his mother, to which reluctantly agreed. Nick told Charlene that she was about to be a mother-in-law again as he had proposed to Lauren last night. She nodded and kept saying the word *yes* repeatedly as if it was the answer to some prayer of hers. After church and during breakfast, she finally put her two cents in, in the Charlene Finch method of getting right to the point and deftly putting in a request in the form of a directive. "Of course, I do hope you two plan to have the ceremony here—of course at Bethesda, right?" Nick replied that the engagement was all of twenty-four hours old and they hadn't even talked about formal plans yet. As Nick dropped his mother off, the phone was ringing. It was the new fiancé wanting to talk to her future mother-in-law. In her message, she notified Charlene that the first thing she was going to do the next morning would be to contact the Accent editors of the *Palm Beach Post* and announce her and Nick's engagement to the reading world of Palm Beach County and the Treasure Coast. Charlene was very happy to hear that as she wanted to make sure that Kinley Anderson would read the announcement. Charlene Finch kept score in the game of life, and her son had just won the big game, with Kinley Anderson having lost, at least in Charlene's opinion. Two weeks later the announcement appeared announcing their engagement, and shortly thereafter Nick received a card sent to him at work. It was from Kinley, wishing him good luck with his engagement and upcoming marriage. He reread it again and never shared and then threw it away, never sharing it with anyone. That was the past, and now he had the future to look forward to.

CHAPTER 15

Playing Catch-Up

In sports, when one falls behind early, one throws the game plan out the window because one must now play catch-up, pull out all the stops in the hopes of evening up the score before the contest ends. In football, a team's offense may switch to the "hurry up two-minute" offense to get in as many plays as possible that offer chances to score. Basketball coaches will order full-court presses and intentional fouling of the opponent, hoping the team will even up the score that way. Baseball coaches who need runs try to get as many baserunners as possible on base with the hope that someone will drive them in and maybe the other team will be forced to change pitchers. Heck, one college team, the University of South Alabama, instructed their players to intentionally try to get hit by the pitch so they would be rewarded first base. Just how many got hit as instructed by their coach Eddie Stankey is the stuff of folklore, but if you have ever been hit by a pitch, you know that it is a true sacrifice, taking one for the team. Wrestlers, if behind, are forced to shoot and try for the pin. Examples in sports go on and on, but the same principle applies to other endeavors. Think of the student who has put off studying and is now forced to pull an all-nighter or, worse, resort to cheating. Businesspeople with deadlines are put under incredible stress. The list of examples is limitless.

Nick, now thirty-one years old, was trying to play catch-up. Almost all his friends were married with children and lived in their own homes. Nick was single and living in an apartment. Lauren White, now twenty-eight years old, had had been to so many weddings of her friends and sorority sisters that the movie *27 Dresses* could have been about her. Lauren and Nick, both separately and as a couple, had a lot of planning, ah, well, catching up to do.

After the initial wedding announcement and all the backslapping and congratulations were over, it was time to set a date, decide on a venue, choose the wedding party, plan a bachelor party, determine a venue for the rehearsal dinner and reception, decide on attire, choose the music, and plan a honeymoon. One can see why rich people hire wedding planners. In this case, the prospective bride and groom were used to making deadlines and making decisions, so they jumped headfirst into the wedding planning pool. Nick at times felt like the previously discussed wheelchair swimmer looking up at all the guests staring at him as he sat helpless at the bottom of the pool, unable to swim or move.

The first order of business was to pick a date for the wedding. Both easily agreed that a summer wedding made all the sense in the world because Nick would be off from work, the season would be over for the banker, venues would be more available, and the cost would be much lower. There were, of course, a couple of drawbacks to the July date they had picked. Front and center was the heat. Most of Nick's invitees had grown up in South Florida and understood it wasn't the heat that got you but the humidity, so they knew to prepare for it, having long ago gotten accustomed to it. Some of the DC guests grumbled a little, but Lauren quickly reminded them that the Beltway area was just as hot, and maybe even hotter, in the summer. Afternoon showers that came with the heat also eliminated any thought of an outdoor wedding. Like canoeing, outdoor weddings seemed like a good idea but seldom worked. Air-conditioning had been invented for a reason, and that chief reason could be Florida in the summer. It was assumed the wedding was to be in Florida as not only did both the bride and groom live there but also the parents and most of the guests did too. Thankfully, a lot of the bride's guests were people she had met and become friends with both from her time in Winter Park and Rollins College and from her time right here in the greater Palm Beach area. Nick was homegrown.

The church, of course, would be the beautiful historic Bethesda-by-the-Sea Episcopal Church on Palm Beach. Surprisingly, the couple needed to clear a few hurdles to be married there. The Finch's were members, but Lauren White was not, so she needed to become a member

ASAP. The clergy helped but still did not rubber-stamp her admission. The bride-to-be was forced to go to a newcomer's class after church services once a week, hosted by a variety of the staff. She learned all the ins and outs of the Episcopal Church, its founding both here and in England, differences and similarities with other faiths, and the rituals. She enjoyed the class. Her parents seemed to be prouder of her membership in the church than they were of her MBA. Randy felt they had dropped the ball when it came to church attendance, and their daughter had now played catch-up. In short, what Lauren found in the Episcopal Church was what one of the priests explained as "Catholicism light, one-third less guilt." This was of course a takeoff on the popular Miller Lite beer commercial theme—and most Episcopalians see nothing wrong with a drink or two. Also, the fact the priests were permitted to marry was reassuring to Miss White given all the sexual problems and scandals that were plaguing the Catholic Church. She learned many of the Episcopal clergy were not only married but also had married a few times over. This, they said, helped in marriage counseling. Speaking of marriage counseling, Nick and Lauren had to take a personality test and go over the results—their similarities and differences, but mostly the differences—to talk about and head off any potential early marriage problems that might arise because of personality conflicts.

Father Theodore "Ted" Bolt, an associate priest, and younger than the rector, would be officiating the ceremony right before his transfer to Colorado. This meant he would be selling and leaving behind his true loves, namely, his thirty-foot sailboat and his waterfront condo. Anglican or Episcopal Church clergy do not necessarily take a vow of poverty, especially Palm Beach priests. Father Bolt was perplexed about Nick and Lauren's personality test results, as they were like none he had ever seen before in all his years of proctoring the exam. Their scores were exactly the same—no difference in any of the questions or the categories tested. None. The two had taken their tests at different times, Lauren at her lunch break and Nick right after school one day. The odds of having the same exact score were virtually zero. Father Ted had the sit-down posttest conference and confessed he never had seen this before, adding that, to his knowledge, no one else had either. Astounded, he congratulated the two but also warned it was good to have different views on things that would certainly come up during their marriage. He was right about that.

Wedding parties, that is, bridesmaids and groomsmen, were selected without much of a hitch, except that Grace White put her foot down and demanded that her son, Geoffrey, be in Nick's wedding party. Nick was not pleased about this, but he submitted. Lauren cleared away the potentially explosive land mine by selecting Nick's sister Addie as a bridesmaid. Nick selected Brian Parker as his best man, and Nick made Brian assure him that the bachelor party would be classy and not a last night of debauchery with strippers and hookers. Brian lived up to the promise, much to the chagrin of the married invitees, and had a closed-door cigar, steak, and open bar dinner in a private room at Beefeaters Restaurant. Margret Baldwin, the hostess, lifelong friend, and previous classmate, made it work. She always did.

It was all coming together with a surprising amount of ease. Charlene went to the "Church Mouse" consignment store to buy the dresses she required. She would need four in total for the two engagement parties, one rehearsal dinner, and of course the wedding itself. She made it there before they closed for the summer, so the sales were even bigger. All four outfits with designer names cost her less than thirty dollars. Grace White went two blocks south to Worth Avenue and picked out her attire. Cost unknown, but rest assured it was more than thirty dollars! Nick's oldest sister had moved up from the Fort Lauderdale area to Palm Beach Gardens, to PGA National. Julia and her husband Dan, a successful stockbroker and golfer with an Ivy League pedigree, asked if they could host a party for Nick and his bride-to-be. Nick was hesitant as he was growing farther and farther away from his siblings, but ultimately, he agreed. Dan saw this also as an opportunity for new clients he could be introduced to and have them move their portfolio to his firm. It also gave the couple a chance to show off their new house right on the fairway of the Jack Nicklaus–designed Champions Course, which now hosts the Honda Classic every spring.

The combination of friends from three different sides enjoyed the evening. One of Julia's friends was a car dealer in the South Hollywood–North Miami area, the patriarch who on TV promised a "million-dollar deal for pennies on the dollar." He approached Nick, drink in hand, to explain just how impressed he was with the young teacher and coach and how he had handled himself the times he had seen him interviewed on TV. Nick smiled and thanked the auto tycoon and wondered where this was going because he definitely was not in the market for a new car. As many car salesmen were wont to do, the man put his arm around Nick and asked him to step outside, saying he had a proposition for him. Nick looked over at the hand now resting on his shoulder. When they got outside, the meeting was gaveled to order. "Son, you are wasting a God-given gift teaching school. You can do so much more. So much. And I assume you and your bride want to start a family soon. Well, let me tell you, kids are not cheap. Let me take you away from all of that. Come work for me and my group. I promise, you will double your salary, not to mention earn side benefits. Well, what do you think?"

Nick did not hesitate. He said, "No, thank you," and was sure of his answer. He was a teacher and would stay a teacher— "But thank you just the same." Lauren had seen the meeting outside. When Nick came back inside, she slid right up beside him and asked him what it was all about. Nick answered, "He offered me a job and said it would pay double what I am making now."

Lauren asked, "Well, what did you say? I mean, you did say you would think about it, right?" Nick looked right back at his fiancée with an expression that few people ever saw. If it must be said, he learned that look from Charlene. It was not an expression that you wanted leveled at you. Occasionally a student got it. Lauren had gotten it when she dropped the ball on Nick during the infamous pitching change, and now was the bride to be getting it.

"No. I told him, 'Thanks, but no thanks. I am a teacher now and will continue teaching.'" Nick continued, "I truly hope you understand that."

Lauren, seeing that this was nonnegotiable with Nick and understanding that she had better get used to the fact she was marrying a teacher, a fact that was not going to change, provided a quick answer: "OK." She walked back into the party.

Charlene asked Nick to set up the rehearsal dinner. Nick knew right where to go: Nando's. Not only had Nick parked cars there off and on for almost ten years, but also, he had been a customer for special occasions, as had Charlene and J.W. Joseph, the maître d', met with Nick that spring as the staff prepared for another night of dinners and drinks on the island. Of course, Nando's would be happy to host the festivities. Joseph could not wait to share the news with Mr. Nando himself, who lived above the restaurant in an apartment-like condo with two European women, most likely Italian and about half his age. Nick selected the menu, giving guests a choice of either steak or the signature dish, shrimp scampi. Of course, Alex would bartend, and Robert would be on the piano providing music before, during, and after the ceremony. Charlene was relieved about the choice, but she did worry a little about the cost. Nick assured her it was within her budget.

Sandy and Randy oversaw the wedding reception. Nick had been to all kinds of receptions since he had been to so many weddings, from "dry" Mississippi Protestant weddings, to which almost everyone brought a flask, to the infamous "Hey, how 'bout it!" debacle in St. Augustine.

The Breakers was out of the question with a cost that even in the summer was prohibitive, and some of the others, such as The Chesterfield and The Colony, were pricey but unfortunately kind of small. Palm Beach was out, but West Palm was in play. Lauren told her dad that live entertainment was not needed, so money could be saved there, but she did want a sit-down dinner and an open bar. Randy agreed, especially when Lauren said the newlyweds would help with the cost of the bar. Nick was worried because he had seen how some of his friends behaved when the booze was free. At a class reunion, Ray Wade snuck under the table of the people selling the tickets to the bar, stole a whole roll of tickets, and handed them out to the group. The Airport Hilton, the venue for the Forest Hill reunion, could not figure out how they had run out of booze yet collected only a fraction of the cash for the tickets that had been redeemed.

The bride's family, really Lauren and Randy, with help from connections at the bank, selected the Governor's Club, which was located at the top of the newest high-rise office building in West Palm Beach, known as Phillips Point. It was built over the area that was once a hangout for Palm Beach High students, with teenagers such as Burt Reynolds and George Hamilton hanging out there. The place was rumored to be the inspiration for the movie *Porky's*. Now it bragged it was the only place in the world that looked down on Palm Beach. Major law and financial firms rented office space there, and at the top, as mentioned, was the private restaurant and club. With the sunset as a backdrop, the venue was perfect.

The honeymoon was the one area where Nick wanted to have some input. He would give Lauren full rein to research potential places, but he made it perfectly clear that the place *they* would select would *not* have palm trees or sand. As Nick explained, he had grown up amid an abundance of both, and he hated cruises to the Caribbean. Lauren went to work, doing her extensive research, which was mostly asking colleagues for ideas. Nothing yet, until the *Sports Illustrated* magazine was delivered to Nick's apartment in one of the late winter months and the cover was adorned with gorgeous models sporting skimpy swim attire in a unique setting. Lauren was looking through the pages that contained photos of Kathy Ireland and other supermodels when she took notice of the setting of the shoot, a place known as Mackinac Island and the Grand Hotel. Quickly she dove into R & D mode, hoping Nick would agree. After hearing the proposal, Nick was sold on it. He did a little research of his own, asking people he knew at the Breakers Hotel, and they explained to him that the Grand Hotel was the Breakers of the North. The funny thing is, when he shared where he and his bride were from with hotel staff in Michigan, they quickly noted that Palm Beach was home to The Breakers, which was the Grand Hotel of the South. It seems there was an outstanding rivalry in terms of who was top dog in the hotel and hospitality business. The cost, which rivaled that of the Breakers during the height of season, made the stay at this gorgeous hotel, which was also the setting for the movie *Somewhere in Time* with Christopher Reeve and Jane Seymour, set in the 1890s and the basis for multiple knockoffs by the Hallmark

Channel, last only three days, and then it was decided to move the party to Chicago for a little big-city fun. It was the perfect choice as the two could celebrate their wedding night at the Breakers, get up the next morning, and fly to Mackinac City, where they would take a ferry to their hotel on an island where no motorized vehicles were allowed and then spend three days at this place that was a throwback in time. For example, coat and tie were required for the dinner hour. Then they would take a small plane, which made three stops in the Upper Peninsula, apparently to retrieve the mail, to Chicago. Perfect. Since Russel Baker would be in the middle of baseball season with the Dodgers and could not attend, he would give one of the most unique wedding presents imaginable to the newlyweds, full VIP access to a Chicago Cubs game at the historic Wrigley Field. Even though the Dodgers would not be in town, Russel made sure everything was taken care of, such as pregame field passes, a meet and greet with legendary announcers Harry Caray and Ron Santo, a chance to witness Hall of Fame Cubs shortstop Ernie Banks hit practice grounders to the Cubs' infielders before the game, box seats right behind the dugout, and a special PA shout-out from the Cubs welcoming the two, and the applause that followed. Memorable and very cool indeed. Nick thought, but maybe not, the two even got a wave from the legendary comic Bill Murray, who was seated in the WGN Cubs announcers' booth next to Harry Caray as the latter was to lead the seventh inning stretch and the singing of "Take Me Out to the Ball Game." What a day. Heck, what a honeymoon. Perfect.

With everything set, it was hurry up and wait, something J.W. said was standard operating procedure in the army, but until the big day, Nick, and Lauren still had to work. The season in Palm Beach runs from about Halloween through to Easter, so Sandy was busy, and she was also finishing up her MBA classwork for a May graduation. Nick still had his classes to attend to, along with his athletic director duties and his department chairman assignments, which meant everything from checking off lesson plans, to working on the schedules for next year, to deciding the assignments his department would teach, who would teach them, and the periods when the classes would be offered. Both had enough on their plates, plus there were little things such as picking out flowers and dress designs, making hotel arrangements for out-of-town visitors, attending tuxedo fittings, choosing church decorations, and deciding on music for the preceremony, the processional march, and the recessional, the last of which Nick called "escape music." It was the week of July 10, 1993.

First up was the picking of the music, which fell on Monday of the week of the wedding. The two showed up promptly at six o'clock with Father Bolt and the music coordinator Hugh Radley. Now Hugh Radley was nationally known for his ability to play the massive organ system at Bethesda, as well as for his arrangements of hymns and carols. Many people came to the church more for his music than for the fellowship and prayer. Parishioners would stay after the recessional just to hear the postlude music he played. Midnight mass for Christmas filled up by ten o'clock with people wanting to listen to the carols sung by the choir with the accompanying organ, strings, and brass, which were also there for the special night. This was true for Easter too.

Lauren had her music already picked out, and truth to be told, she had picked it out long before she met Nick. One of the selections was a song chosen by Lady Diana for her wedding to Prince Charles. Nick grinned when he heard that because he had seen Prince Charles up close a few years back when he was in Wellington for a polo match. The contest drew international coverage because the prince and heir to the throne had been thrown off his mount and, as the tabloids reported, right onto his "royal ass." Another blared, "Prince falls and now has a royal pain in the ass!" Got to love English tabloids. There was another couple there also to pick out their music—a well-connected wealthy couple from Palm Beach and Hyde Park, New York. Jane, who grew up on the island and went to Palm Beach Public before heading north to boarding school and then to Princeton, had met her beau while working for Chanel in New York City. Her father was a well-respected ethical local lawyer, mostly dealing with estates, wills, and trusts. Lauren knew him well as for their paths crossed frequently in their prospective fields. The young man was total prep school from Phillips to Yale and onto Georgetown Law. Nick thought and whispered to Sandy asking her if this was a marriage or a merger of two law firms. Lauren responded with a quick elbow to his ribs. Nick learned he should keep his snarky thoughts to himself from then on. At least he would try. He would ultimately fail, but he would try. He could not help himself.

The groom came from American royalty, which means Gilded Age Captains of Industry stock. His family was mentioned in every history book, and in books about business strategies and business law, especially concerning monopolies and Theodore Roosevelt's implementation of the Sherman Anti-Trust Act.

Hugh looked over Lauren's selection and had one objection because apparently it had come from a famous opera in which the bride murders the groom. Nick looked over at his bride with a cocked eyebrow and asked if there was something he should know now or if he should forever keep his silence. The small group all laughed at the quip. Nick thought that this was an easy crowd to amuse. When Hugh asked if Lauren wanted to reconsider, Father Bolt interjected and instructed the organist to play the music. Nick and Lauren were done, but watching the other couple was priceless as they went back and forth while the father of the bride rolled his eyes in frustration. The big stumbling point was the processional, for which Jane wanted the traditional Bridal Chorus, but the groom had selected a piece that had been written especially for his family back in the nineteenth century by a famous European conductor. The two were excused to go, but Nick said he wanted to stay so he could hear this important family heirloom musical piece. Hugh Radley came to the rescue, explaining that since the wedding party was so big, he could play both. Ah, the art of compromise. And it worked as both agreed to the Hugh Radley cover version of the molded-together wedding processional march.

Nick and his posse got fitted for their tuxedos, so he was all done until Friday and the rehearsal dinner. This event was not only for Nick and the wedding party but also for Charlene Finch. Nick stopped by on Thursday to check if everything was ready, and Joseph the maître d' assured him it was. After all, it was July, so business was slow. Recently there had been a change in tourism as in August many Brits came to holiday on Palm Beach, as did many South Americans and South Africans, escaping the winter months in their countries and spending some time on the island. This provided a nice shot in the arm for the locals. Heck, even the Breakers now stayed open year-round, whereas in the old days before air-conditioning, it would close and be boarded up for the summer months. Many of the employees would head north to resort hotels in the Hamptons, Martha's Vineyard, and Kennebunkport, and even to the Grand Hotel in Mackinac Island, Michigan.

On Friday, both wedding parties met at the church at six o'clock, once again to review the procedure for the wedding the next day. Father Bolt blew right through the whole walk-through as a coach would blow through pregame. He was telling everyone not to worry and saying that if there were any screwups, only the wedding party would know. Next it was off to the dinner, which was right around the corner. Nick's two parking buddies worked the valet service, then came in for a drink and to join the festivities. After all, Perry and Frank would attend the ceremony the next day. The restaurant was closed to the public; the sign on the front door spelled it right out:

NANDO'S CLOSED
PRIVATE PARTY
WHITE–FINCH WEDDING

Charlene liked that when she saw it.

The restaurant looked gorgeous with fresh flowers at every table. Joseph had taken hedge trimmers, clipped off the flowers of the bougainvillea hedge that surrounded the restaurant, and placed them on every table—beautiful blue and purple flowers accenting the tables. Alex made the drinks strong and perfect as Robert played a nice mix of cocktail hour music and post dinner party tunes. As the crowd was enjoying their dinners, most having selected the house specialty of shrimp scampi, Joseph asked to see Nick over by the bar. Nick thought it was time to square up as Charlene, seated next to her son, slipped him her credit card. Nick walked over by the bar. When he looked up, he saw none other than Mr. Nando making his way down the stairs that led from his apartment to the restaurant. On each arm were his two "friends," who were thirty-five to forty-five years of age and wearing formal evening gowns. Nando himself was in a tux. The three took a seat by the bar as Alex quickly made the drinks, they usually requested. Nando whispered something in Joseph's ear that brought a wide smile to the maître d's face. Nando then got up and walked over to the main table, where he leaned forward and gave a polite kiss to Charlene, then one to the bride to be, and proposed a toast that was mostly in Italian. It seemed the only ones who understood it were the waitstaff, but all raised their drinks in honor. The eighty-something-year-old man then hugged Nick and made his way back to his companions at the bar. Nick tried to shake Joseph's hand and discreetly pass him his mom's credit card to pay for the evening. Joseph smiled once again and refused payment, explaining that as a wedding present, Mr. Nando and the restaurant were providing the rehearsal dinner. The entire dinner, including drinks and service, was comped. Free. No charge. Nick was stunned and humbled by the gesture. He looked over at Nando, who now was getting up to go somewhere, and saw him looking back at him, the young man who parked cars for him and who, along with his mother and late father, had often been guests at his establishment. Nando smiled, nodded with approval, and disappeared outside to a waiting car that, once he and his friends were inside, sped off. Nick got back to the table and gave his mother's credit card back to her with a grin, whispering to her what had just happened. Charlene stunned and speechless, then did something that was exceedingly rare for her: she wiped a tear, just one tear, from her cheek. Lauren was giving Nick a perplexed look. He leaned over and told his future wife what had just happened, and she too became a little emotional. She then told her mother. Because of Grace White's hearing impairment, everyone close by now knew of the generous wedding present that the restaurant had given Nick and Lauren. To a person, everyone was stunned by the generosity.

After dinner, Nick went back to the Airport Hilton, where he was staying until the wedding. Brian Parker accompanied Nick back to the hotel as he also had a room there. The two went down to the nearly deserted bar for a nightcap. Brian looked at Nick and said, "You know, I must ask if you want out. It is not too late, and as best man, I will provide the escape if you like."

Nick looked back at his best friend. "Nah, I'm good. I am ready. But thanks anyway."

The young attorney responded, "Good. I was not going to let you anyhow."

Saturday was the big day. The wedding had been planned for six o'clock. Nick and his wedding party would arrive at the church about half past four and wait in an adjoining room out of sight from the actual church. The church was spectacular with candles lit at every pew and fresh flowers throughout. Not clipped shrubs, but real flowers from a real florist. It was hot, real hot, Florida-in-July hot, but at least there was no rain. It was probably raining out in Wellington, but not here next to the beach.

The wedding, just as Father Bolt had predicted, went off without a hitch. After the ceremony, a photographer took some post wedding pictures. Nick had hired the photographer, who was also the photographer for all the sports teams at Forest Hill and the school yearbook. He came at a good price. Mr. and Mrs. Finch then made their way to the Governor's Club for the reception and party. And a party it was. The views were breathtaking. The father–daughter and mother–son dances were special. The best man's toast was perfect and classy, but Brian did conclude it with, "Hey, how 'bout it!"

The crowd, at least Nick's guests, responded with, "Hey, how 'bout it!"

When the DJ announced it was time for the bride and groom's dance and the lights were dimmed, the great Louis Armstrong song "What a Wonderful World" came on. To this day, Nick believes it is the most beautiful song ever sung. Nick glanced over to his mother, who was seated at the first family table with her oldest son and her daughters, remembering what his parents had said was the greatest live show they had ever seen, which took place at the Miami Beach Convention Center: the great "Satchmo," Louis Armstrong. Charlene was nodding in approval. Her youngest was now officially all grown up, and her work was now done. She could move on knowing her baby boy was going to be all right. She had come to that realization on the evening of July 10, 1993, with the great American treasure that was Louis Armstrong telling everyone there that night, but especially Charlene Finch, that it was a wonderful world. Wonderful indeed.

Honeymoons must come to an end, and thank-you cards must be written, and both spouses must get adjusted to married life. With work back in full force, Lauren and Nick went back to their lives with little change. The next big event was to stop renting and to buy their own house. Real estate and house hunting was Randy White's area of expertise. Not only did he volunteer his help, but also, he gracefully put himself front and center. Some people might be put off by that, but not Nick—not at all. He welcomed all the help he could get. With real estate magazines and flyers in hand, Nick and Sandy looked at the homes currently on the market. After finding a few, they circled them and handed the flyers off to Randy. He did the legwork, first by making telephone calls and then by visiting in person and reported back to the working couple which homes they should look at and which they should scratch off their list. One Saturday late in summer at Coach Scott Clark's house in Lake Clarke Shores for a get-together barbecue, the two passed a house with a small For Sale sign on the front lawn about ten houses north of the Clarks' on Pine Tree Lane. Lauren took the number down and immediately called her father on the car phone to relay the address and the information she had gotten from the sign. On the way home from the party, the two stopped, parked the car on a side street, and walked up to the front lawn of the house, when the owners suddenly emerged and gave a friendly wave to the prospective buyers. The four met in the middle of the yard and exchanged handshakes. Nick told them that he and Lauren were in the market for a house, having recently gotten married. The owners then explained that they were intent on retiring to the mountains of North Carolina. The husband explained he was handing in his badge after thirty years on the West Palm Beach Police Force. Nick explained he was a neighbor of former chief Billy Barnhill in the south end of West Palm. The former detective, who had started out on city patrols, asked again what the young man's name was. "Nick Finch, sir."

The man nodded and seemed to be having an aha moment. "Your mom is the nurse at St. Mary's, and your daddy was the painter, right?"

"Yes, sir," Nick answered.

The wife interjected, "You went to Forest Hill with our two daughters. I believe they were a couple of years younger than you. You came back and work there now, correct?"

Nick replied "Yes, ma'am" this time.

Lauren watched the interaction between her husband and the sellers, who all now seemed to be getting along like long-lost friends. would get used to the fact that no matter where they went someone seemed to know her husband Nick. Growing up there helped but even more was the exposure of hundreds which grew into thousands of students he would have the opportunity to teach in his thirty-seven-year career.

The owners then offered a tour of what would be Nick and Lauren's first home. Typical of the period right after World War II, when the house was built, it had small bedrooms, and the kitchen and bathrooms were even smaller. When these homes were built, air-conditioning was new, and if a person had it at all, it was the wall-unit type. Nick called these homes Motel 6's. Central air had not yet been introduced, but when it was, the homes had to be retrofitted to accommodate the modern convenience. In the old days, the hottest rooms were the kitchens and bathrooms; hence, they were small. Also, the tile in the bathrooms was, well, loud in lime green and bright pink. Today these shades are popular, the art deco look of South Beach, Miami. There was no formal dining room, and the three bedrooms had limited closet space. Also, there were no sidewalks and no city water or sewage as Lake Clarke was still using septic systems with drain fields. Those were the drawbacks, but the advantages more than outweighed the age and size of the home. There was a beautiful living room, a large front yard, a large screened-in patio, a beautiful family room or TV room, and an oversized swimming pool that was surrounded by large mature trees. And then came the greatest selling point: the property was directly on Lake Clarke. An oversized seawall bordered the lake beyond the backyard, which sloped down from the house. Boaters went up and back behind the house, fishing and waterskiing, all day long. Nick knew this all too well since he had been one of those water-skiers during his youth.

The sellers knew they had an interested couple, and the young couple was indeed interested, very much so. With all the house's warts, the natural beauty of the lake evened out the minus signs. And some of the defects could be fixed with some remodeling. As Nick's late father used to say, "Putty and paint make the devil a saint." Nick and Sandy set up an appointment for the following day, a Sunday, and invited their professional house hunter, Randy White. Randy went on the same tour his daughter and his son-in-law had gone on, but he took notes and asked questions that never entered Nick's mind, things such as utility costs, city taxes, home schools, age of the roof, and the quality of the utilities and the seawall. He did not say much but nodded and wrote things down. Everyone exchanged handshakes, and Lauren, who had driven, took Randy home to PGA National with Nick in the back seat listening to the banker and phone company executive. He was out of his league and he knew it. Randy told his daughter that she and Nick should get their finances and funding together as soon as possible. The two had an advantage in that they would be first-time home buyers, so they were entitled to various tax advantages the government had legislated to encourage home ownership. Also, Lauren's working at a bank and having the ability to walk down the hall and talk face-to-face with the powers to be about a home loan was a big advantage.

After that the whole affair, which went smoothly, Nick was still shocked at the closing to find that there were so many hidden costs: stamp tax, doc tax, title searches, survey lines. It seemed to go on and on with a different person or organization each time seeking its handout. Nick once remarked, drawing on his knowledge as a history teacher, "We fought a revolution over a stamp tax, which in modern terms is a doc tax." There seemed to be an entire cottage industry made up of individuals and firms that deserved their piece of the pie. After talking to their friends, Nick, and Lauren realized they had gotten lucky in the home buying process because they'd had the helpful Randy, friendly and motivated sellers, and some name recognition. The Finch's had their own home, and it was waterfront!

Of course, the next logical question was "When are you going to have kids?" Some hinted around the question, while others came right out with it. There was no doubt a family was in the planning, and some even warned it was not as easy as ordering a meal through the takeout window at McDonald's as some would have you believe. Nick loved kids and really loved the thought of having his own. Lauren *really* wanted to have her own children and raise them as her own. Being left at a hospital as a newborn had left an unimaginably deep scar that she was going to make right. And Grace, her mother who raised her, would be right there with her to also take in the experience that had eluded her.

There was one more major family function to attend, namely, Lauren's brother Geoffrey's wedding, which was occurring in late August in St. Louis. Now Geoff by family decree had been ordered to be part of Nick's wedding party, but the act was not reciprocated as Nick was not selected to be a groomsman in Geoff's wedding. Sandy would be a bridesmaid in her new sister-in-law's wedding group. Lori, the newest member of the family, was from the St. Louis area and worked with computers at Langley in the DC area. She was a CIA agent who, as she told it, "Followed the money." Jane Bond she was not, but still Nick thought that her job was cool as hell.

Since Nick was not in on any of the prewedding plans, he did what he loved to do: explore. He went to the Gateway Arch of westward expansion, the Lewis & Clark Museum, Bush Stadium, the Mississippi riverfront district, and his favorite, the Anheuser-Busch Brewery. After he'd purchased his ticket for the brewery, he joined one of the groups of twenty for a tour. Nick's group included nineteen Japanese tourists loaded down with cameras. He found them to be polite and friendly as he took pictures for the group and found himself in a few group photo shoots himself. Nick loved the entire tour, which of course included the hospitality room with free samples. Nick was sporting an Ole Miss T-shirt for his day of sightseeing, a practice he would continue when on his many other excursions. The bartender was an Ole Miss junior and this was his summer job, and the tour guide had gone to Mizzou, or the University of Missouri. Wearing his college shirt always seemed to lead to conversations with other alumni, Mississippians, southerners, or supporters of other schools. Someone was always hollering out, "Hottie Toddy" an Ole Miss spirit slogan, or "Roll Tide," or "War Eagle," or "Go, Gators." From Mississippi State and LSU fans, Nick would hear, "Go to hell, Ole Miss. Go to hell!"

When Nick tried to get back to the hotel, he was rerouted in and around what seemed the entire greater St. Louis area because it was the time of the flood of the century, when both the Missouri River and the Mississippi River crested over their banks and St. Louis was in the crosshairs. When Nick finally got back to the room, Lauren asked where the hell he had been. Nick replied in his best Johnny Cash voice, "I've been everywhere, man." Lauren was exhausted from the makeup and hairstyling parties, and she hated the selection of shoes. They hurt her feet. The next day, after the wedding, Nick observed that all the pictures of Lauren at the reception showed her without her shoes on. Because she was barefooted in them, it made it look like a Snuffy Smith Missouri hillbilly wedding.

Close friends of the two back in West Palm were Pat and Dan Glenndemming, both teachers. Dan had been Nick's first assistant softball coach and was his colleague in the social studies department. In fact, Dan had been one of Nick's teachers at Forest Hill as he taught him the now outdated class "A vs. C," which stood for Americanism versus Communism. It was the Cold War after all, and communist Cuba was only ninety miles from the Florida shore. Many Floridians still had fresh memories of the

Cuban Missile Crisis. Nick did not since he was an infant at the time, but he had heard the stories of the immediate closing of the three airports of Miami, Fort Lauderdale, and Palm Beach and turning them into air force bases almost overnight. The railroad tracks were utilized to move supplies south for the possible military invasion of Cuba, and on the man-made Peanut Island, located right where the Palm Beach Inlet, the port, and the Intracoastal Waterway meet, was a protective bomb shelter that had been constructed for President Kennedy. It still stands there today as a monument to a very scary time. Nick had heard the stories about the "duck-and- cover" drills that were practiced in school in case of a nuclear attack, but such drills had now been replaced with tornado drills and drills in case there was a mass shooter on campus. Such were the times, and they were a changing. Until 9/11 and the terrorist attacks on the United States, Nick thought the only two life-changing events he had witnessed were the *Apollo 11* moon landing, especially with the role that Florida played, and the tearing down of the Berlin Wall. The Cold War was over, and the good guys had won without ever having to "duck and cover".

The Glenndemming's gave a recommendation that was so insightful and wise, and brought so much pleasure to the lives of Nick and Sandy, that they could not imagine what their lives had been if not for this suggestion made by Pat and Dan. Simply put, Pat and Dan, who were parents of a middle school daughter, suggested to the two newlyweds that before they start a family, they should first purchase a dog. They said that a puppy was perfect training for the ups and downs of parenting, especially for first-time parents. The two explained that with a puppy, one must get up for feedings and walks, make trips to the vet, and constantly train the creature with praise, rewards, and correction of bad behavior. With a puppy, there would be no more staying out late and no more sleeping in, and the dog's needs had to be budgeted for. It did make sense. Sandy and Nick immediately agreed. On their way home from Beefeaters Restaurant, their topic of discussion was not if they would be getting a dog, but what breed. Neither of them cared for what Nick called "yappy" dogs, or what he sometimes referred to as canine rats. Also, neither cared for the "moving white slippers" that masqueraded as dogs. Both types always seemed to be aggressive, and Nick still remembered the time his uncle's dachshund bit him. Today, Nick and Sandy agreed such breeds had their place with older owners and people with limited space, such as those who lived in condos. Those breeds flourished in those conditions, but they were not for Sandy and Nick. Although Nick had hunted a few times, mostly in Mississippi, he was not very fond of the sport—and not for ethical reasons. He just thought it was kind of boring, and he knew of better ways to spend hours at a time with a bunch of dudes in the woods, or in a farm field or a duck blind. What Nick did like was the work of the sporting dogs. They were trained to assist and seemed to be thankful just to be included in the event. They also seemed to work well not only with hunters but also with families.

After the discussion, the matter was settled: it would be a soft mouth retriever. But what kind or breed? After discussion, the choice was made: the Finch family would search, find, adopt, purchase, register, train, and most of all, love a golden retriever. The clock was ticking because they wanted to find their dog while Nick was still home for summer. Lo and behold, they heard about a litter up in Palm Beach Gardens. The next decision was not if, but which one, as there might not be anything cuter than golden retriever puppies. One kept coming back and nuzzling with Sandy, who was on the floor right in the middle of the litter. Yep, he would be the one. After they paid the owners the fee and left, they stopped by the local Publix supermarket and picked up dog food, treats, and food bowls. The Finches had their first addition to their family, and the name they agreed upon was Clancy. They had selected the name because Tom Clancy, the Cold War writer, was one of their favorite authors.

Clancy the golden retriever was on the reddish side and was big. Ultimately, he would come to weigh more than a hundred pounds. He was a powerful swimmer and, much to the chagrin of Nick, was a spectacular digger. The first night, despite a warm blanket and a ticking clock, which Nick and Sandy had provided because they'd heard it could substitute for the heartbeat of the puppy's mother, Clancy cried and whimpered until Sandy could no longer take it. She pulled him up to bed with them. Soon after, all three fell sound asleep. Clancy would be the first of five golden retrievers the Finch's would have. Each one of them would be a dear family member and, truth be told, would be loved, and respected more than some of the human relatives. Unconditional love they would always bring, and there were times when it was needed during the span of Nick and Sandy's life. Dogs do that. Nick believed it was the greatest deal humankind had ever made to share friendship with a dog. "Man's best friend" is just that. The Finch's now had a home, two respectable jobs, and a golden retriever to share their lives with, which was good because somebody would be leaving very soon. Charlene Finch was going to be called home to be with J.W. forever in the very near future, and it would affect Nick in a great many ways.

CHAPTER

16

Major Changes on The Horizon

It was back to school for Nick and back to the bank for Sandy, but now there was so much going on in their lives. Nick was as busy as ever, and Sandy, not slowly climbing up the corporate ladder but leapfrogging up the rungs, was being recognized not only locally but also nationally. She was the definition of an up-and-comer. Wherever it would take her, Nick was happy to tag along. Some guys might have been intimidated by their spouse's success, but not Nick. He was damn proud. Early that fall, Sandy was recognized for her outstanding numbers and was awarded a VIP pleasure cruise for her achievement. Nick had to decline going because he could not take a whole week off at the height of the football season. Sandy took as a replacement Susan, the wife of Nick's troubled but talented friend Carl James, the English teacher. Susan also worked in the banking industry and could use a break from her crumbling marriage. The only reason it was still going on was that Susan was such a strong and forgiving person. Plus, she had two daughters who needed her. Her nickname among the group was "Saint Susan of Palm Beach," and they regarded her as the patron saint of well-meaning but damaged teachers. She needed the break, and Sandy liked Susan a lot, so the two headed to the Port of Miami that Friday for an eight-day, seven-night cruise with ports of call in the south Caribbean. Nick personally hated cruises, but at the same time he would have liked to go, yet his professional duties called. Thank God he was home.

Sunday afternoon, Nick got a call at his Lake Clarke home. It was Charlene. She had canceled her customary church date earlier that Saturday, which surprised Nick, but he was happy as he had had some of the boys over for a day of watching college football on TV and taking rides on the lake in his new boat. Honestly, he now had a splitting headache and needed a day to recover. He noticed his best friend Brian Parker had spent the night, but not in the house. He'd slept in a hammock out back and never even woke up when he was being drenched by the automatic sprinklers. That must have been quite a sight for the early morning bass fishermen, who loved the angling in the fresh water of Lake Clarke.

Charlene had called not from home but from St. Mary's Hospital—and not as a nurse, as she had retired from full-time nursing about three years ago, but now as a patient. She was having difficulty breathing, and her heart rate was all over the place. At first, she thought it was a temporary condition related to her age and her asthma, but when the symptoms got worse, she got dressed, having struggled to do so, and drove herself early Sunday evening to the hospital, where she checked herself in. She knew exactly where to go, namely, the same emergency room she had run for many years. She even looked at her watch to make sure the shift changes were complete as turnover time could be rough on both the new shift and the one retiring.

She walked through the doors. The nurses on duty took one look and, knowing who it was, rushed to their ailing colleague. Charlene was really struggling now. An orderly raced to get her a wheelchair. There was no customary protocol, such as paperwork and questioning of the prospective patient, as this was Charlene Finch. Everyone knew her and went right to work. The retired nurse nodded to the staff surrounding her but, because of her shortness of breath, was unable to speak. She took a piece of paper and wrote out her symptoms for the nurses. Immediately she was taken to a private room on the third floor, but she did make a request drawing on professional courtesy, more of an order, that was granted, which was not to notify her son or anyone else, and instead let her do it herself the next morning.

Left alone, she got worried and called her baby boy later that evening, explaining where she was and why. Charlene knew she was dying, but she knew she had at least a few days left. That was fine with her, but she needed her boy.

After Charlene had gotten a hold of Nick, he immediately raced to his car and sped off to St. Mary's. He had been there to see or meet his mother so many times, but it was always for some trivial reason, such as bringing her the dinner she had forgotten or jumping her car battery. A couple of times he had gone because she wanted to introduce him to a new nurse or student nurse whom she thought he might like to meet. This was different as he raced north on I-95 to East Forty-Fifth Street and on to the hospital, where he went in the only entrance he knew, the one to the emergency room. The place was busy—must have been a full moon—but the staff all at once rushed over to their peer's son. They told him his mother and their friend was very sick and had been admitted and now was in a room on the third floor. One of the RNs took Nick by the arm and led him directly to the elevator up to the room, explaining the condition his mother was in, which was not good.

They got to the room. Nick was in a fog, a heavy London pea soup fog, and was having trouble with basically all his functions. He was dazed, confused, and scared. The nurse gave him a quick kiss on the cheek and rubbed the tears from her eyes. Nurses are the strongest people on this earth; because they see so much misery and suffering, they grow a very tough outer skin and build high walls to insulate themselves. Nick knew this as he watched his mother, who at first glance could be considered cold and uncaring, but he had grown to realize that was her defense mechanism, her body armor, so to speak. He had just witnessed a nurse thirty- or forty-years Charlene's junior, for a split second shed that protective skin, knock down that wall, or take off that body armor, and he knew right then that his mother was dying. The young nurse's body language gave him all the prognosis he needed to know. He had grown up with it.

When Nick entered the room, Charlene was asleep. She was now seventy-one years old but looked every bit of one hundred. She was hooked up to oxygen and to other machines that provided a variety of information and emitted an array of noises, none of which Nick understood. All he knew was that this mother was right in front of him dying. He pulled a chair up next to the bed and grasped her hand. She squeezed back; opened her blue eyes, which people said were the same as his; and smiled. Nick tried to say something, anything, but nothing would come out. Charlene smiled again and then drifted off to sleep, but she never released her grip on his hand. About an hour later, a young staff doctor entered the room and introduced himself to Nick. He started the conversation off by stating how proud he was to comfort a fellow professional who was respected by everyone he had talked to, from the CEO right down to the custodians, and everyone in between. He looked over the charts, smiled, and then said something about tomorrow working out a plan that would ensure Charlene's dignity and be painless. That, of course, was code for "The hour is near."

Nick regained his composure because he knew he had work to do. He called the school and said he would be out indefinitely because of his mother's circumstances. Carlos Martinez said that was no problem and told Nick that he should take as long as he needed. The next afternoon a beautiful arrangement of flowers came from McLaren's Florist, signed by the whole school and the staff of Forest

Hill High. He knew then that he had to call his brother and sisters, but he wanted more information before doing so. Nick knew right where to go, and it was not to the doctor but to the nurses' station. The nurses looked at each other when Nick asked how long Charlene had left to live. It would have been a breach of official hospital protocol for the nurses to answer as this was the supervising doctor's duty. One of the nurses walked up to the station and introduced herself to Nick. She explained that she not only worked with Charlene but also had done her student nursing under her as a student at Palm Beach Atlantic University. Plus, Charlene was her supervisor on staff at the hospital. She looked over the charts and paperwork and asked Nick, whom she had heard so much about from her mentor, to take a walk down the hall. They stopped at the spot where it was apparent the original hospital had been connected to the new expansion areas. There were large floor-to-ceiling windows that looked over the parking lot. She then said, "Mr. Finch."

Nick immediately interrupted and said, "Ah, Mr. Finch was my dad. I am Nick."

"OK, Nick. Your mom does not have a long time. She is dying as her lungs and heart are both giving out. Combine her asthma and emphysema, probably from secondhand smoke, with the regular wear and tear of motherhood and nursing, and the result is that her time is near. Very near. My guess, maybe a week. But I, I mean we, will do everything to make sure this is as painless as possible. She's one of us, you know." Nick nodded and thanked her for everything, then went back to his mother's room, where the doctor was now repeating what the nurse had just told Nick. Nick pretended as if it were the first time, he was hearing the prognosis, so as not to the get the nurse in trouble. Some doctors, not all, have a God complex and feel it is their duty and their duty alone to break the news. Whatever.

Charlene asked Nick to sit down next to her. She had been told all was good now. She looked at her baby boy and said, "It is your time now, Son. You married the perfect girl, and I will leave here knowing that." She then said it was time for him to call his brother and sisters. She explained that the funeral, to take place at Quattlebaum, was already paid for and that he should just let the church know there would be no special additions, just the traditional Episcopal funeral. She continued saying that last week she had gone through the condo and placed stickers on each item with the names of who was to receive them. She felt she did not have the time to call the lawyer and mention every piece in the will. "Plus, he probably would charge me for a full hour, so I dropped off the list of the items with the corresponding stickers. There is to be no fighting over that old stuff," she said. Then she had one more request, more an order: "Try your best not to let my death break this family up. Good luck on that, but I know you will do just fine. I am so proud." She closed her eyes and fell back to sleep.

Within hours, Nick's oldest sister Julia arrived with her husband the stockbroker. Not much was said between Nick and her, but he was happy to see Charlene smile when she talked with her oldest daughter. J.W. Jr. flew in from

Arizona and was given his inheritance immediately, which was Charlene's Lincoln Continental. Charlene signed over the title and gave him the keys. As before with his dad's death, J.W. Jr. would not be there for the final moments, the funeral, or the burial. He would be on the road back to Arizona. Nick's other two sisters arrived soon after their flights landed at Palm Beach International Airport. There was one person missing, and that was Lauren. Nick was having a difficult time reaching her in the middle of the Caribbean. When he finally reached her, the reception was terrible, but Lauren could make out that her mother-in-law was dying and that here death would happen soon. She also heard Nick say, "Please, if you can, come home." Lauren knew Nick was alone. She needed to be there not only to comfort her husband but also to protect him from the fallout she could see coming. Lauren White Finch worked with family estates all the time, albeit all her dealings were with families in much higher tax brackets and more elevated in social status, but they all had something in common. People got hurt and people felt they deserved more. Some lived to watch their moms or dads die as if a payday or lottery winnings would follow, and Sandy saw this coming for the Finch's. It turned out she would be correct.

Lauren worked her way back to Palm Beach County, flying to three ports of call before she could catch a direct flight from Kingston, Jamaica, to Palm Beach International. She went straight to the hospital. Charlene's eyes lit up when she entered the room. The two hugged. The sisters were taken aback and looked a little envious. Nick was relieved. His support system was there, and he did not feel so alone now. Later that Tuesday afternoon, a hospital administrator entered and explained that the hospital could no longer comp a VIP room and was searching for an alternative. The young man was nervous as he explained the difficult situation, he was in. Nick bit his lip and glared and began to walk over to the administrator. His expression worried Lauren. Right at that point, the CEO of the hospital came in, welcomed everyone, took over the meeting, and excused the very relieved young executive. The well-dressed silver-haired boss reassured the family that the hospital would do everything they possibly could to take care of one of their own. Before the man finished speaking to the room full of people, as now there were family, friends, and clergy in attendance, not to mention a revolving door of nurses who were coming by just to say hello to their dear friend and colleague—Charlene Finch was kind of a big deal, as the Ron Burgundy character, perfectly played by Will Ferrell, in *Anchorman* would describe himself on the silver screen—another team of workers arrived, not dressed like executives, but not dressed as hospital staff either. They whispered something first to the nurse in attendance and then to the CEO, who both smiled. The man introduced himself as Mr. Yardley. He was in charge of Palm Beach County Hospice. Charlene broke into an instant smile. When St. Mary's first inquired about space available at the facility, located right behind the hospital, Mr. Yardley had told them that unfortunately there was no room at the inn. When the hospital changed its request to a demand, explaining that this was no ordinary patient needing comfort, but Charlene Finch, insisting that the hospice find a room, lo and behold a room opened right then and there. Charlene would be moved to hospice for her final days, where she would be given a handheld device to deliver a merciful supply of painkillers, most likely morphine, at no charge. It would be a painless death for her, which she deserved. There would be other problems that would arise and continue to haunt the family, but these were in no way Charlene's fault.

After the move to the hospice, once Charlene had gone to sleep, Nick, Sandy, and his sisters went back to Charlene's condo. Sure enough, the sisters raced around the house checking the stickers on the various pieces of furniture and other objects. There seemed to be more disappointment than grace or dignity as the sisters began to trade what had been given to them for something another sister had been given that they desired. They traded furniture as boys back in the fifties or sixties traded baseball cards. Nick stood by quietly, shaking his head, because the example presented to him was one lacking in dignity and respect. There were a few pieces for Nick, but what he got, he really was thankful for.

In 1826, to commemorate the fifty-year anniversary of the American Revolution, each state and many dignitaries received certified copies of the Declaration of Independence. The Finch's had one of those copies. How it had come to them was never quite explained, but they did know it came from Charlene's side of the family and was given to her mom by her grandmother. If this were true, then the copy dated back almost two hundred years. Years later, Nick took it to a historical art collector, who looked it over and appraised it at fifty thousand dollars. It was indeed an 1826 original. Sweet. Charlene made sure it went to her US-history-teaching son.

The next morning, Lauren pulled Nick aside and said that his mother's limited portfolio of stock was being bought and sold at an alarming rate. She had investigated it herself and explored why. The motive was not to increase the value of Charlene's stock holdings, limit potential losses, or prepare for estate taxes, but to earn commission. Julia's husband was trying to make a few last dollars before his mother-in-law died and make his buy-and-sell quotas for the month. Nick listened and bit his lip. He approached his brother-in-law and quietly asked for an explanation. The broker, becoming nervous, stammered something, and left. Nick was furious. Lauren told him what to do. Since Nick was executor of the estate and his mother was in the final stages at hospice, he had the right to demand a cease-and-desist order and put an immediate end to all stock trades. He did so. He and his brother-in-law have not spoken since.

As he had done with his dad, J.W., Nick asked his mother what she wanted in the box with her. Charlene was feeling no pain thanks to the painkillers, but she was lucid. She wanted to be buried in the dress she had worn to Nick and Lauren's wedding. She also wanted her nursing cap and a copy of the same picture that J.W. had been buried with, the one of the two of them happy together at some social function, probably sponsored by the Masons or Shriners, put in the casket. After his sisters left the room for coffee and most likely to complain about something, Nick found himself all alone with his mother for the last time. He looked down at her. She was the strongest woman, the strongest person, he had ever known up to that point. He could talk to her about anything and everything, and he had done so on many occasions. As Nick looked at her, he asked, "Are you scared, Mom?"

She smiled and replied with a sense of relief, "No, Son. It is beautiful, and I am ready now."

In one their earlier conversations, when Nick was in high school, his mother had suffered a heart attack but thankfully was at work and had been saved by a quick-thinking professional staff. Now that the two were alone in her hospice room, Charlene told Nick something that she had not conveyed to anyone else and would never repeat. She had died that evening in the emergency room at St. Mary's and had been resuscitated. As she explained, during those few moments she visited the afterlife, which she said was very beautiful. She was welcomed by her departed loved ones, many of whom she had not seen in years. The sense of peace and love was everywhere, so no, she was not scared but ready. The reason she had never told anybody else that story was that it was too personal and some might think she was crazy or something. Since she told Nick that story, he had heard of many other after-death experiences that were much like his mom's.

Shortly after this episode, Nick's sisters returned from their walk, and their mom called everyone to come over close to the bed. Lauren stood behind until being ordered by Charlene to join the group. A hospice nurse came in, looked over everything, and said it would be any minute now. Shortly thereafter, Charlene Smith Finch passed away, surrounded by her three daughters, her son, her daughter-in-law, and staff members of both Palm Beach Hospice and her St. Mary's family. The small-town girl from Avon Park who worked tirelessly to save others' lives while raising five children and serving as a faithful wife left for good to be with her soul mate, J. W. Finch. While his sisters cried, Nick smiled because he knew where she was. And unlike most of us, she already knew what to expect on the final journey. Peace, serenity, and love awaited her.

The funeral was quick and dignified and followed the order and rituals of the Episcopal Church as Charlene had requested—er, ordered. Nick had gone to the funeral home to pick out the casket, and the "showroom" reminded him of a car dealership. Models were arranged and accent-lighted to promote the more expensive choices, with the discount ones looking as if they could have been used in the old west on Boot Hill. Some even came with warranties. Nick asked the salesman if anyone ever demanded to redeem the warranty, like maybe having the casket dug up and checked for leaks and malfunctions. The salesman mumbled something but seeing as he was very uncomfortable with the question posed by the prospective client, the two moved on. Nick selected a casket that was middle of the road in terms of price. After the ceremony at the cemetery, Nick announced he would open his home in Lake Clarke for a sort of wake—an open house for conversation and the sharing of memories. And, boy, was it memorable. The Irish seemed to have it right by looking at death as a reason for a party. Southerners bring food, favorite family recipes, to share, and many people of the Jewish faith become very contemplative in their final observations. Charlene Finch's wake was a combination of all three styles.

Nick put out some deli choices with lemonade, juice, soda, and wine. Many people had accepted the invitation, especially the nursing staff from St. Mary's. When they arrived, Nick asked what he could bring them. One immediately responded, while looking over the beverage choices, "Where's the vodka?" Another wanted to know where the cooler was with the cold beer—and that was just from the first carload of nurses. Nick's father-in-law quickly came to the rescue and gave Brian Parker his credit card, telling him to go to the liquor store and stock the bar. "And don't forget the ice."

Pretty soon the bar was open and the drinks were flowing. Nick's friends took turns bartending. As far as food went, there was plenty as each group had brought all kinds of delicious foods to share. As the spirits, both liquid and ethereal, soared, so did the stories straight from the floors of the West Palm Beach hospital. Trade and institutional secrets were spilled, usually followed by laughter and yet another story: who slept with whom, who had to leave the profession or the area and why, which nuns had not taken the vow of celibacy. Still, there were great recollections of absolute miracles of life and death that were followed by head shaking, nods, and tears. The whole afternoon was memorable. Nick knew his mother was looking down and smiling. It was her boy with his new bride and puppy sharing stories of love with family and friends, mostly with laughter. There were some obvious absences as Nick's brother and left after he'd gotten his mom's car keys and started back to Arizona. And Charlene's own brother had failed to show up, having tried to explain why he wasn't there in one of the shortest phone calls Nick had ever had. He listened and answered simply and forcefully, "OK, bye." They have not spoken since. As far as family went, the wake was the last time there was any laughter among them, as shortly afterward, the family imploded. To this day there is very little communication between Nick and his sisters and brother.

On the following Monday after the service and funeral, Nick got a call from his best friend Brian Parker about his mom's estate, saying that he would no longer be allowed any access to the estate or input into the settling of the estate since Nick's sister Julia had gotten a judge to rule there could possibly be a conflict of interest with Nick's best friend overseeing the executor of the estate. The probate judge ordered that Brian's sleazy partner Billy Morgan take over. Nick could not stand Billy Morgan, nor could he understand how an outstanding ethical man like Brian could have gone into business with a person like Billy Morgan. Morgan did bring a book of business, mostly the strip clubs that surrounded the airport. One of the clubs always paid in cash, literally greenbacks, fifties and hundreds, and the club did not use the United States Postal Service, possibly to avoid mail fraud complications, but neither did they use FedEx or UPS. Instead, they had strippers show up at the office on a Friday afternoon with the cash and an offer of personal delivery services. Such is the guy that Billy Morgan was. He had been tied up for a while with some shady land developers. Are there any other kind? And then there were some nursing home abuse scandals where he defended the nursing homes. The partnership between Brian and Billy lasted less than eighteen months. Julia objected not only to Nick's having been named executor but also to the fact that Charlene had signed over an old passbook savings account to Nick so he could pay off any other expenses that might crop up, such as the cleaning of the condo to ready it for resale and old utility bills. Nick capitulated, and once all outstanding bills were paid, he would divide the amount left in the passbook by five and cash out his siblings—and hopefully before Christmas, as a kind of bonus from Charlene. There was not much in the account, only about twenty thousand dollars, yet Julia was not happy that Nick alone had access to it. She was still angry that Nick had shut down her husband's midnight trades and had the portfolio liquidated and divided up equally. Nick thought he was offering a peace pipe in saying that he had to pay a cleaning service to clean their mom's condo, and instead of giving it to a firm or company, he would pay Julia and a friend two times the rate he'd been quoted to clean the place. They agreed, but they did a half-assed job. Nick and Lauren found themselves finishing up the job. What really hurt was finding a scrapbook that Charlene secretly kept on Nick, with everything from report cards to school awards, to pictures and newspaper articles, torn up and thrown in the trash can. That was just plain mean and vindictive. Nick just shook his head in disgust, but Lauren could tell it hurt him deeply.

Then there were legal bills that kept coming in because Julia would call Billy Morgan with some sort of complaint or a strategy, and every time she called, whether they talked for two minutes or an hour, the estate would be billed for an hour. When the estate was finally cleared, Nick took was left in the passbook account and divided it up five ways, sending the money out as a Christmas card from Mom. Lauren worked hard to talk Nick out of sending Julia's share in pennies to her husband at work, using the attorney's strippers as the postal service. Nick still wishes he had done it. For years, his siblings seemed to look down at their little brother as the "oops child" or the "mistake" and many a time referred to him as an only child, all in reference to the ten-year difference. Yes, at times it hurt, but he moved onward and upward with his own life, his hopes, and his dreams. Everything seemed to work out surprisingly well for him, so to hell with them. He had his own family now, and he would not allow his siblings to bring it down. He had now built his own walls of protection against them, and he was finally satisfied with being the oops/mistake/only child because, in a sense, he was free of those hurtful tags. But not a day went by when he did not miss his parents. The rest? To hell with them.

Not all final goodbyes or funerals are sad. Sometimes they can be outright hilarious if you yourself are not the reason for the event. Nick was a firsthand witness to one such hilarious occasion. Raymond Wade slowly but surely had begun to grow up. Maybe this process had started when his mom came home from a weekend away and found that Ray was having a party that had been going on for three days. When she entered the house, she was stunned beyond words, although words eventually did come out when she went out to the backyard and saw that some of her house furniture was in the swimming pool with people sitting on the submerged chairs and couch just as if the items were where they were supposed to be in the living room. She threatened to call the police, but the police were already there because an hour earlier a female sheriff's deputy had come to answer a disturbance call. Ray and the others had promised to quiet down. The deputy was now headed back to her squad car. The boys asked her what time she got off her shift and invited her to return then and take part in the festivities. The attractive law enforcement official smiled at the offer but declined, thanking them just the same.

But then an hour or so later she was back and ready to go. She inhaled three shots and a Big Gulp–size grain alcohol fruit punch that was called rocket fuel, then she was ready. She followed two of the guys to the master bedroom, where she put on a private strip show that featured her nightstick, or Billy club. Soon she was completely naked except for her handcuffs, which were now on her wrists, connected to the master bed's headboard. When Mrs. Wade threatened to call the police, Ray said she did not have to as there was an officer of the law right down the hall in her bedroom. When the matron of the house entered, she could not believe what she saw. According to those who witnessed the scene, it looked as if it were right out of a California porn movie. Mrs. Wade screamed as the boys searched for their clothes. Unfortunately, the cop could not find the key to her cuffs and was stuck cuffed to the bedpost, naked as a jaybird. The embarrassed boys found their clothes, which were on top of the handcuff key and the gun belt. The Billy club was on the nightstand next to the bed. The officer grabbed her uniform and exited as fast as humanly possible.

Mrs. Wade looked at her bedroom, the house, and then her son, and announced to everyone still there that she was very sorry, as it was apparent to her that she had given birth to the Antichrist himself. Satan's child was Raymond Wade, at least that fateful evening, according to the new and modern Rosemary.

Raymond Wade did continue to grow up. He left college with two degrees, one in history and the other in Spanish, which he was fluent in. Upon graduation, he took a job as a dive boat captain and instructor. This allowed him to take a chartered group to Central America for diving, fishing, and surfing. The trip also allowed a side excursion to some of the ancient ruins. It was an overnight camping event, and after a day of exploring the ancient buildings and relics, the group returned to the campground for a night of revelry. There a lot of tequila was drunk. The next morning the group had to take a small plane back to the coast to finish up their Central American vacation. Ray boarded the plane last. He was not feeling very well. And then it happened: he vomited, threw up, "called out Earl"—whatever phrase you might use—right on the floor of the small commuter airplane. The pilot emerged from the cockpit none too happy. The small airline had no ground service crew, so the pilot called out to a man who seemed to be one of the mechanics, who emerged with two of the mangiest dogs imaginable. The tourists were ordered off the plane so the dogs could enter and slurp up the vomit of Raymond Wade. This act, of course, made almost everyone who was witness to it sick.

After the dogs were taken off the plane, the Americans were able to reboard for their quick trip back to the Atlantic coast to finish up their trip. The pilot, who again was none too pleased, ordered Ray to sit next to him in the cockpit in what would have been the copilot's seat. Pretty soon the group was airborne and flying over the lush jungle of Central America, and the pilot and the dive boat captain were having a pleasant conversation in Spanish. Ray asked what happens when you suddenly push down on the steering wheel. Then he pushed down on the wheel in front of him, immediately causing the plane to make a steep dive. Screams could be heard from the passenger cabin behind them. The captain quickly regained control of both the wheel and the plane and restored order. He looked right at his "copilot" and called him a loco Yaqui while shaking his fist at him.

Within a few years, such incidents became few and far between as Raymond Wade was no longer in the dive industry but was a certified social studies teacher and a leader of our young people. He had really cleaned up his act once he was married, shortly after Nick was, to an attractive pharmacist from Pittsburgh who worked at the other big hospital in West Palm, Good Samaritan. Ray had also become quite religious. He had been ordained in the Episcopal Church and had the title of deacon. He was assigned home visitations, hospital trips, and Sunday readings of the Four Gospels—Matthew, Mark, Luke, and John—for the congregation at Bethesda-by-the-Sea. Taking Communion from Reverend Raymond Wade was a miracle of scriptural proportions. Of all his assignments, the one he loved most was helping the community members who made their life by the sea—the fishermen, boat captains, and especially the crews of the both the cruise boats and freighters who called the Port of Palm Beach home. He would visit and consult, give sermons and Communion, and bless both the vessels and the crews. The hours could be rough, but it was his calling. With his captaincy, he also did all the burial-at-sea ceremonies. One of these would lead to one of the most memorable events in Nick's and Ray's life.

Ray called Nick early one Saturday morning and asked if he wanted to go out in his boat *The Mullet* that morning. Seldom did Nick turn down an invitation to go out on a boat, especially if Raymond Wade was the skipper. There was one caveat: Ray asked if Nick, the former acolyte, would assist with a short funeral service on the boat for a family of three, to be concluded by the spreading of the ashes in the Atlantic per the final wishes of the deceased. Sure. After all, it was the Christian thing to do, and Nick had always wondered how a maritime funeral service was conducted.

When Nick arrived at the PGA Marina, Ray was already there, loading the cooler and a supply bag into the hold. The cooler was holding the sacramental wine and bread for the Communion service that would proceed the dispersal of the ashes. Also in the cooler was a twelve-pack of beer and some insulating koozies for the cans.

Also in the beach bag were a couple of towels and a bag of potato chips. The clergy and the crew, who were one in the same, were ready. Nick was asked to pass a metal urn from the side of the dock down to Ray, to be placed in the cockpit of the center-console boat, which urn apparently contained the ashes of the late guest of honor for his final voyage. Ray then opened the bag and pulled out a dark shirt and a white priest's collar and put them on. It looked strange and contrasting with his bathing suit trunks, which sported a design of Hawaiian hula dancers swaying in front of coconut palm trees in mostly the lightest bright blue possible. Flip-flops completed the wardrobe, except for the Maui Jim sunglasses. The deacon was ready.

The deceased was originally from Minnesota, and after his wife's death he'd relocated to Palm Beach and was a regular at the eleven o'clock service, which seemed to cater more to the seasonal islanders, who returned up north after Easter. Mr. Jennesen, whose official first name was Steve but who went by "Swede," had made his money in the logging industry. Not cutting or chopping but speculating on the commodity itself. It paid well. Mr. Jennesen would have three guests for his final sea voyage: his son Steve Jr., who went by Steven, and his twin daughters, Lori, and Lynn. Swede had requested the special service as he had fallen in total love with the South Florida waters and especially the ocean. He had grown up on the lakes of Minnesota, but he much preferred the indigo water of the Gulf Stream and the friendly hand-waving boater community of the Intracoastal Waterway, especially the Sailfish Marina on Singer Island, where he docked his boat, the *Minni Don't Miss*.

The three adult children arrived at the marina about twenty minutes later and were at first taken aback by the sight of the minister and his assistant, who were already drinking beer and listening to the appropriate Jimmy Buffett song "A Pirate Looks at Forty." Steve, or Steven as he liked to be addressed, looked to be in his early forties with thinning blond hair. His body language suggested he was impatient and wanted the whole thing over as soon as possible. The twins were not merely a little overweight but were downright big. They sported matching one-piece bathing suits. Nick extended his hand to help the mourners onto the vessel. The twins immediately went into their travel bag and pulled out some sunscreen that must have had an SPF of at least 100. Full body armor made of aluminum would have let in more sun than the oily substance they coated themselves in from head to toe. The announced they were "not going to get that Florida cancer. No, sir, not us." Steven passed on the chance of using the cancer protection that his sisters demanded each use.

Soon the group was headed for Palm Beach, motoring out past the Lake Worth Inlet. After they passed the Florida Power & Light power station, which company locals had nicknamed Florida Plunder & Loot, then the Port of Palm Beach, passing by Peanut Island, they were now through the inlet, sailing past the pump house and out to the Atlantic Ocean with the sight of endless blue that one never gets tired of after that first look at the open sea. The sea was a little rough in the late morning with swells that made the boat bob up and down a bit. Nick, wondering if his Minnesota guests might get seasick, suggested the old trick of picking a stationary spot on the horizon, mostly back toward landfall, and concentrating on it. That usually that did it. Steven informed the captain/deacon and the first mate / teacher that he had gone through much rougher seas on Lake Superior. Playing dumb, Nick responded, "Ah, the one Gordon Lightfoot sang about."

Steven shook his head in disbelief and said, "No, my friend, that was Lake Superior and the wreck of the *Edmund Fitzgerald*." Nick faked a look of *Oh, OK, thank you, because I am a dumb southern hick redneck who prefers banjo playing accompanied by two bandmates, one playing the washboard and the other playing spoons, over a Canadian folk singer.* Nick loved the folk genre, especially Gordon Lightfoot and Jim Croce, and of course the shrimp boat rock of Jimmy Buffett. Ray grinned in approval of the verbal exchange.

The twins remained in the back of the boat, looking as if they had swum through the *Exxon Valdez* oil spill in Alaska. When the funeral party got between five hundred and one thousand yards off the coast of Singer Island, Ray turned off the radio and quickly went through the Eucharist service and last rites. Usually, the service would take ten minutes or so, but the deacon was done in two, having flown through the ritual at the speed of sound. A small bread wafer was blessed and split into five parts, one for each communicant, and then was passed and eaten. A red Solo cup held the blood of our Lord and Savior Jesus Christ, and each of the five took a sip. Communion was now complete. The boat continued to bob up and down, and at times there was water above the deck line, on three sides at one time. Steven found a life jacket and quietly strapped it on. Ray looked at Nick and winked at the safety precaution the son had taken.

When the last rites had been given, Deacon Raymond Wade went to the bow, or front of the boat, where he opened the urn and turned it upside down to release the ashes that once had been the body of Swede Jennesen into his beloved ocean, but right at that point the boat unexpectedly lifted back up as a gust of wind slapped the front of the boat, which now doubled as a hearse. The gust of wind, Ray later would say, was biblical in nature. It grabbed a hold of the ashes and blew them all over the body of either Lori or Lynn. Nick really had not taken the time to distinguish between the identical twins. Either way, one was covered in ashes, which were stuck to her body because of all the sun protection oil she'd used to protect herself from getting the Florida cancer. (By the way, Swede Jennesen died of cancer, if that matters.) The daughter screamed out and began to shake as if overtaken by a spirit that had inhabited her body. Deacon Ray turned and quickly raced back to the stern, or back of the boat, but he slipped on some of the oil that had been spilled back there and fell. He quickly regained his feet and informed the young mourner, "Apparently, your dad loved you the most!" He then told her not to worry, saying that it wasn't what it looked like; those were not her father's ashes but just some residue that tends to accumulate in older urns. Almost immediately, the young woman regained her composure. Ray announced that they would be heading back to port but would do so by heading north up to the Jupiter Inlet and then going back down to Palm Beach Gardens and to the marina. He gave some excuse about sea conditions. Ray looked over to his friend, who would not return his glance out of fear of bursting into laughter.

Finally, Nick quietly asked his friend, "Residue? To Jupiter because of the seas?"

Ray leaned over and whispered, "No, that *was* her dad's remains covering her." He hoped that the extended trip north might blow some of it off and into the ocean, which was to be Swede's final resting place. No such luck as the oil worked too well as an adhesive, so Dad continued with everyone on his final trip.

After going through the Jupiter Inlet and past the historic lighthouse, Ray pulled in the Canonsport Marina and docked. Located at the docks was a public outdoor shower. The big girl got out of the boat and sprinted straight for the open-air shower. Nick thought for a big person, she had surprisingly good wheels. She made it to the shower in record time and rinsed herself off. The ashes swirled through the drain right into a PVC pipe that fed directly into the Loxahatchee River and then, after the tide change, emptied into the Atlantic. After all the drama and, yes, comedy, Swede had made it to his final resting place, the Atlantic Ocean. And the story of the burial at sea remains part of local folklore: the father who could not say goodbye to his favorite daughter.

Nick and Lauren decided in late fall to start a new family tradition of their own, one that was like an annual going-out-of-business sale, or like Kiss having a fifteenth final farewell tour—but to become a tradition, it would have to have a starting point. This tradition, with a few exceptions, has carried on in December throughout their marriage. It is the annual Finch Christmas party, and 1993 would be the inaugural event. The purpose of the party was not just to provide food and drink and share friendship; the Finches also required a "cover charge," an unwrapped Christmas present to be donated to Lauren's favorite local charity: Families First for Floridians, or FFFF, whose members rolled up their sleeves up and directly immersed themselves in work to help solve the problems faced by local families. In other words, the FFFF knew who needed help, and they did all they could to provide it. The board was made up of professionals from all walks of life, including Lauren the banker, high-ranking members of local law enforcement, judges, elected school board members, lawyers, and politicians. These people on the board met with the field personnel, the people in the trenches who located the trouble and proposed to the board what they could do about it. The FFFF paid the first month's rent, the last month's rent, and the deposit on apartments for families who were homeless or in their cars. They also helped with job recruitment and interviewing skills, including proper dress—in other words, practical strategies to help the underbelly of Palm Beach County, the forgotten people who so often, through no fault of their own, found themselves having fallen through the cracks of one of the nation's wealthiest communities. FFFF kept their expenses to the bare bones minimum, but the love and charity they provided was off the charts. One program Nick thought was very cool was teaching computer skills to the grandparents of children whom the former now had to, for whatever reason, look after, which enabled them to help the little ones with their homework. Once they completed the basic computer skills training, they got to keep the PC as a reward for going the extra mile for their grandchildren.

The Finch Christmas party could now be counted on to provide a toy, a ball, a doll, or a jacket to be placed under the tree for at least some of these children so they could have some sort of Christmas. The food and the drink tasted even better knowing the living room would be overflowing with well-meaning gifts. Many with multiple commitments would stop by just for a second or come by early just to drop off a gift. The party seemed to increase the holiday spirit for everyone.

Like so many firsts—first kiss, first adult drink, first time driving a car—the first annual Finch Christmas party was very memorable, never to be forgotten. We all know about that life-changing first. The first Finch Christmas party was the second big event at the Lake Clarke house after, of course, Charlene's wake, which turned into a nurses' party. The house cleaned up nice with lighting all along the seawall that bordered the lake. A few locals even came by boat, which was cool. One attendee named Valerie, a former student aid of Nick's at Forest Hill who was now married to another former student, who lived down the street, and who was semi famous for being a former Ron Jon Surf Shop bikini model, came by boat. She was now a top-ranking official on the school board. You have probably seen her in a bikini on billboards advertising the store beginning in Georgia along Interstates 10, 4, 75, and 95 and the Florida Turnpike. She turned heads, especially those of the group of bankers Lauren had invited. The invitees ranged from lifelong friends of Nick to members of the faculty and staff at Forest Hill, to people who were part of the Palm Beach banking and investment community. The different groups all got along great. Nick had hired a local bartender, and there was plenty of food for all. Clancy, the Finch's golden retriever puppy, was the hit of the party. Who doesn't love a puppy, especially a golden retriever puppy?

Nick's first principal, Bobby Newcombe, was there, even though he never drank to keep a promise he had made to his late father who, as the county jailer, had seen what alcohol abuse could do to a person, a family, and a community. No matter, storytelling was Bobby's true calling, and he had a crowd surrounding him as he told his various stories. Nick had heard most of them but never got tired of the tales, especially those about the early days of Palm Beach County or of being on the set of one of the many Burt Reynolds redneck movies as an extra. As the former principal was finishing up a story and reloading for another one, he grabbed a potato chip and a glob of dip and began to chew. There was a split-second delay, when Clancy ran his tongue the length of the dip barge, leaving a K-9-made canal. No one noticed except for Nick and Lauren, who had witnessed the occurrence. Both went to grab the long canoe-shaped glass container of clam dip, but before they could get there, Bobby Newcombe dive-bombed into it again. Lauren and Nick both stepped back as if nothing had happened. Something had happened. The next day, Clancy had the runs all morning long, and Bobby

Newcombe had told his fill of tales about Palm Beach. No harm, no foul. This would be Bobby Newcombe's last real public event as shortly into the New Year he fell ill and passed away. A self-made local legend who was a combat Marine, a successful coach, an athletic director, and a topflight principal who helped the county through some difficult times with social changes such as court-ordered integration, Bobby had been there first and foremost for the kids, and Palm Beach County was a better place because of him. Nick would never forget the man who had eschewed protocol and skipped over procedure to reward the grateful twenty-one-year-old with a job.

The party took on a life of its own as it seemed many of the guests had some pent-up party spirit in them that they needed to release. And release it they did. The police came not once, but twice. The first time, they made a plea to keep the noise down and stop parking on the grass. Nick and Lauren were smart and had invited all the immediate neighbors, so there were no complaints from the locals. Lauren offered the officers some of the teddy bears that had been donated so they could put them in their squad cars to help with small children's anxiety when answering domestic calls. The officers were quite grateful. They came back for a second time, and unlike the female sheriff's deputy, they kept their clothes on and did not put on a personal sex show, as had happened about five years ago at Ray Wade's house, an event now known as "the night of the Antichrist." This time, they came back for some honey-glazed baked ham and some Coke and conversation.

It was not until four in the morning when the final guests left. In the future, the invitation would state an ending time of eleven o'clock, more of a suggestion than a rule, but at least it would prevent guests from staying until four in the morning. The parties became a local tradition, and people planned their holiday party season around the Finch party. Even better, many less-fortunate young people would be getting a little something on December 25, while the adults always seemed to have a hell of a time. Is that not what the holiday season is all about? Lauren and Nick thought so. They continue the tradition to this day and have held the party every year, with a few exceptions including when there was a family emergency and when COVID-19 protocols were in place. Merry Christmas from the Finch's.

As the New Year was rung in, it meant that school was reopening, and the season was in full swing for the banking and investment community of Palm Beach. As softball season was getting under way, Nick got a phone call from someone who identified herself as the communications director for the City of West Palm Beach. She asked for—in reality, demanded—an afternoon at the Phipps Park field for a traveling art exhibit sponsored by a prestigious local gallery entitled *Athletes and Art.* The gallery wanted the star of the exhibit, three-hundred-game winner, and first-ballot Hall of Famer Tom Seaver, to stop by the park and throw a few pitches to the mayor, a writer or two from the *Post*, a local anchor, and a few players from Nick's softball team, and for the event to be advertised by the newspapers and TV stations so as to promote the art gallery. Nick said that it would be no problem at all to accommodate the exhibition. After all, this was Tom Seaver, "Tom Terrific" of the Amazin' Mets. Nick had his players wear their uniforms for practice and, never one to waste valuable time, scheduled the yearbook staff to take team pictures for the school yearbook. Sure enough, around four o'clock, a TV news van arrived, along with two writers from the local newspaper, one from the sports section the other from the Arts and Accent section; the mayor; and the star of the afternoon, the great Tom Seaver himself. Seaver brought with him two assistants, who helped set up a table with posters showing him on the pitching mound of some sandlot field, wearing in a T-shirt and sweats, and with a black Labrador retriever at his feet, ready for a game of fetch. Seaver, one of the best pitchers, if not the best pitcher, of his generation signed fifty or so of the posters, then the assistants changed hats and became personal art assistants to the ballplayers as one put on his catcher's equipment and another took a place in the outfield. The three loosened up and played catch before Tom took the mound to pitch a few to the local celebrities. He then would face three of the girls Nick had selected, all of whom were seniors and none of whom knew who he was, but all said he was cute for an old guy. The locals considered it a moral when their bats at least contacted the ball, even though they'd hit a foul. One of the girls did hit a line drive, but it went foul, which brought moans from the onlooking Lady Falcons. Tom Seaver then hollered over to the dugout and asked Nick if he wanted to take a hack at it. Nick looked around in amazement and asked, "Me?" The former Cy Young Award winner teased the coach, saying something to the effect of, "Those who cannot play, coach, right?" Nick answered the challenge, grabbing one of the softball bats and making his way to the plate. The retired hurler picked up his game a little bit and added a little more hair to his fastball as a pitch whistled past Nick and went directly into the glove held by the assistant exhibitor-turned-catcher.

The catcher looked up and said to Nick, "Come, Coach, get the bat off your shoulder and take a hack." The next pitch, Nick Finch got a hold of. He hit what would have been a double down the right field line. He got so caught up in the spirit of the event that he raced down to first and then on to second to the cheers of not only his team of girls but also all the other dignitaries who had struck out.

Tom Seaver gave a death stare to the runner on second. After all, there were no other fielders on the diamond except a guy in center field who jogged over to retrieve the ball. Well, that ought to be about all," Mr. Seaver said into microphone, speaking about having come out to the art museum and saying how much he liked the area. He then gave a few one-on-one interviews, telling everyone not to leave as he wanted another shot at the high school coach who had doubled against him and his phantom team of fielders. Nick was up for it. He grabbed the same bat, hoping it would have lighting in it a second time, and strolled to the batter's box, where he tapped his shoes and dug in. He looked back at the catcher, who was smiling from ear to ear, which was easy to see despite the mask he was sporting.

The catcher gave Nick some advice: "You'd better be loose." Just then, Tom Seaver unleashed his fastball, which struck Nick right where his wallet would have been. In a scorebook it would have been scored HBP or hit by pitch. It stung—hurt like hell.

The star said, "Sorry, it got it away from me. But, hey, you can jog down to first base. You earned it!"

Nick realized immediately that his running out his double had showed up the star—and one should never show up the star. Well, Seaver had gotten his revenge. The crowd booed while Nick sported a grin and tipped his cap in acknowledgment of his earlier screwup. That concluded the afternoon's activities, but the TV stations would show both the double and the HBP during their sports segments on the news. When everyone was cleaning up and Nick was saying a few parting words to his team before sending them home for the evening, Tom Seaver stopped by and said a few words of encouragement, telling Nick not to let things go too fast because these were the best times of their lives. The girls applauded, and the Hall of Famer signed some more stuff, most likely for the girls' dads. Seaver then asked Nick if he wanted to go for a beer or, in his case, a glass of wine. Nick later found out that after he'd retired, Tom Seaver had moved to the wine country of California and bought a few vineyards. The two men agreed to meet at a local Italian restaurant next to the art gallery known as Ambrosia. What a great guy Tom Seaver turned out to be. Nick notified him that he had recently gotten married and had gotten to meet "Mr. Cub" Ernie Banks, and now he could tell his future children, whenever he would any, about facing the great Tom Seaver and reaching base twice!

A few days later, in the morning, Lauren emerged from the bedroom and made her way down the short and narrow hallway of the Lake Clarke home with her trusty sidekick the dog, who in many ways was her first child, by her side. She found Nick reading the sports page of the *Palm Beach Post*. Nick would always start with the sports page and then move on to local news, followed by the Accent section, then finish up with the headlines and the op-eds. He was his father's son, as J.W. had always done the same, but with both the morning and afternoon papers. As J.W. had explained, "Start with the successes and finish with the failures of the day before." The logic worked, and the practice was successfully passed on to his son.

Lauren and Clancy entered the family room. Sandy just stood and grinned down at Nick, waiting patiently for him to put down the paper.

Nick sensed he was being stared at and tried to outwait the two, but finally he lowered the paper and looked up, asking simply, "What?" Lauren White had a grin from ear to ear, and Clancy's tail was wagging so forcefully back and forth that it felt like a wind gust. "Well?" Nick asked.

Sandy produced from her robe pocket a small stick with a strip on it and announced, "I am pregnant. I mean we are pregnant. What I am trying to say is that we are going to have a baby!" She started to jump up and down with excitement.

Nick was stunned, the smooth-talking history teacher and coach being at a loss for words. He put his paper down, stood up, and hugged his wife, who now was crying, but they were tears of joy, not sadness. Nick composed himself and began asking important questions such as, "Are you sure?" and "When?" and "Ah, what do you want me to do?" Usually confident, some would say cocky, Nick was completely overwhelmed. His complete lack of knowledge regarding what to do as the spouse of an expecting woman was quite evident.

Lauren quickly took control and told him not to worry, saying she had an ob-gyn appointment set up for the next day, and from there they would strategize the next nine-plus months. Nick was still in a fog, but it was a late-morning Florida fog that the intense sun was burning off. Nick would, for the next few minutes, walk around with his low beams on as the local TV weather personalities *always* were telling their viewers about the proper safety procedures for driving in Florida fog. Nick was walking in one of those fogs now.

Both were excited, but Lauren especially so. The adopted girl who had been left at a hospital by her biological mother would have her own son or daughter to hold and to love. Lauren's mother was also feeling the joy of becoming a grandparent, probably more than most biological grandmothers would.

Within a few months, the bump began to emerge in Lauren's midsection. It was now obvious to all that the banker would have a new client arriving in the future and the teacher was providing future job security by producing a future student for the rolls of the Palm Beach County school system. Most figured it out early when at social events Lauren declined alcoholic beverages and instead drank water. She must have been very serious because the "java queen" had cut out her all-day habit of drinking coffee. She did experience terrible morning sickness, but it was morning, noon, and night. She never really gained any weight during the pregnancy, probably because she had trouble keeping anything down. The swimming pool provided weightless relief as she floated around in the water with Clancy circling her, proving that golden retrievers are water dogs.

Lauren emerged from the bedroom again as Nick was reading the paper, but this time she made a side trip to the bathroom for her morning vomiting ritual. Unlike eight months earlier, she had no grin or look of excitement, but instead an expression of deep concern. Nick put the paper down and immediately knew there was something wrong. He asked her, "What is the matter?"

Lauren tilted her head slightly and said, "I don't know, but there is something wrong. I cannot explain it, but I can sense it. I have spent the last forty-five minutes poring through all the books we bought, and I just don't know what it is, but I know there is something wrong. I am going to see the doctor this afternoon." Nick asked if she wanted him to come along, but Lauren declined the offer and noted it was probably nothing and that her inexperience with the whole pregnancy thing was leading to anxiety. She also mentioned that Nick had to supervise a game that night. Nick was scatterbrained all day, trying to concentrate on his duties at school. He could not even imagine how Lauren was coping with her work.

Nick got home around three that day and knew that Lauren would be packing up from work to head to the doctor's real soon. At about five thirty, Sandy's black Acura pulled into the driveway on Pine Tree Lane. Nick got up and went to the door. His wife came up to him and hugged him. She had been crying, he could tell. As she fought through a whole new stream of tears, she said to her husband, "I am so sorry, but I lost the baby. I am so sorry."

Nick, stunned, said, "Not to worry. We will try again. The most important thing is that you are OK."

Lauren, looking up at her husband again as more tears flowed, said, "They also had to tie off a tube, so getting pregnant again would be at best a stroke of luck. It probably will not happen. I am so sorry." She disappeared into the bedroom, Clancy following close behind.

Nick, dazed and confused, sat down on the living room couch, and began to tear up himself. What made it worse were the sobbing and wailing sounds coming from the bedroom. Feeling helpless and alone, he looked up to the sky and asked God, "Why?" Then he asked his late mom, Charlene, what to do. There were no responses, at least not now. Three times he went into the bedroom, the first two times asking if there was anything he could do. Lauren replied silently with a labored shake of her head. Clancy's head lay perfectly on Lauren's midsection as she stroked his golden-red coat. As lonely and scared as Nick was, he could not even imagine how his wife was coping with the loss. The feeling was worse than the one he'd had buried his parents.

Nick made a few phone calls to see if anyone could cover and supervise his night game, but all declined. In fairness, he hadn't told them the reason for the request. So, with his hurting wife's permission, he trudged back to the school. Lauren lay curled up in bed with her trusty golden, Clancy, right beside her. Nick, unable to concentrate, buried himself in the office, and when the event was about half over, he broke all the rules and told the coach that he had to leave, adding that the game time coaching staff would have to lock up. He slowly slipped out a side door, got into his car, drove home, and walked straight to the bedroom, where it looked as if nothing had changed since he'd left a few hours earlier. Nick had to tug forcefully at Clancy's collar to get him to leave the bed and go outside for a potty break. Immediately after the canine had done his business, he went straight back to the bedroom and leapt up into the bed and into the waiting arms of Lauren. He sensed the hurt, and his purpose now was to be the comfort she needed. Nick stood and stared, feeling helpless. He should have never gone back to work that evening and left her alone. To this day it is one of his biggest regrets and one of the most unfortunate acts he has ever committed.

Within a few days after the initial shock of the horrible loss, Lauren began to get on her feet again. This woman had won at everything she attempted, and her miscarriage was not going to beat her. She had won the adoption lottery by being snatched up by two of the most loving and caring people a person could ever wish for. She had made captain of her soccer team, both in high school and in college, where she graduated with honors. She was president of her sorority, had earned an MBA, and was one of the highest-ranking women in a male-dominated industry with recognition as a leader in the financial world, not just locally in Palm Beach, but on a national level. She was going to succeed at motherhood come hell or high water. What was having a tube tied off? Heck, a woman had two. And there had been so many advances in reproductive medicine that there was no way she was not going to have her own family.

Lauren did all the research, contacted all the right medical people, and just to be safe had the Episcopal priest from Bethesda provide her with counseling and had her name put on the church prayer list. Everyone was to get on board. Reproductive strategies were introduced to the couple, including fertility drugs, the taking of vaginal temperature, the charting of other factors, and even standing on her head after a baby-making session. Nothing was off the table.

When Nick was in graduate school, he had a professor suggest an assignment for the first day of class or an initial staff meeting: the participants should pick an animal, any animal, they would like to come back as. Nick always loved his own assignment, which he'd used up to his final year in the classroom, of learning the history of one's full name. But this professor apparently had had success with this exercise, and she wanted to share it, hoping her grad students would implement it on their own, when they were either teachers or administrators. You could tell this was her prize baby.

The professor gave the class ten minutes to think about their answers, to write down the animals they had chosen, and to prepare to orally explain their answers. Sure enough, when it came time to share, some students were straining as they raised their hands, wanting to be picked so they could share their responses, obviously proud of their animals. Others like Nick sat quietly. Nick would have to be called on to share, because he sure as hell was not going to volunteer.

As predicted, two students had chosen the eagle because eagles soar to unimaginable heights and symbolize freedom; one had chosen a lion because nobody screws with a lion; one had picked a shark because the student's next step in life was to attend law school and specialize in educational law; and one had chosen a chameleon because of its ability to change colors according to its mood and environment (remember, this was the eighties and mood rings were all the rage). One that brought a chuckle to Nick was a young woman who had picked a kangaroo because she was a mom with a minivan picking up her kids and driving them to the outback. Nick grinned with an approving look. The professor was wrapping up her assignment and was giddy with the responses she had received, when one of the students alerted her that there was one more student who had not shared his answer. Of course, that was Nick. "Ah, so sorry, Coach Finch. Please stand and share your selection with your peers."

Nick reluctantly stood up and looked at his answer, not having known he would have to share it with the class. All eyes were on him now. He said, "All right, you asked for it. If I had to come back as any animal, I would select a horse. Not just any kind of horse, mind you, but a Kentucky stud horse on a breeding farm. And my job would be one of luxury as my only duty would be to produce world-class equines to bet on and cheer on. I would be pampered, bathed, and fed only the best of foods and be cared for by only the best veterinarians in the entire Blue Grass State. They would bring me my partners and then lead them away satisfied." The reaction of the class varied from outright howling to stunned silence. The professor just gazed in disbelief at Nick because of his response to her favorite assignment. The old adage of do not ask a question if you are not prepared for any possible answer was never more fitting.

Now Nick had become Kentucky stud horse who was required to provide the action when demanded by the mare of the Finch house, Sandy. Sandy would check all the variables, and if they added up to an optimal conception opportunity, well then, she'd say to him, "Get in here and do your thing!" This was karma for Nick's having been a smart-ass about the horseplay thing.

Days turned into weeks, and weeks into months, as they tried and tried and tried then Lauren's period would return, along with the disappointment and the tears. She developed a code for it: "That damn painter came to the office [or the house] today." They changed doctors, got second and third opinions, and signed on to the new web portal AOL, or America Online, to search the internet for possible solutions. Nothing seemed to work.

It was fall. Nick and Lauren planned a trip to Oxford to watch his beloved Rebels take on the Alabama Crimson Tide. It would be an October weekend full of good food, friends, football, and the Grove. The fertility doctor instructed Lauren to go off all the drugs for the long weekend and not think about anything other than just going up there and having fun—just get away from all the pressures of work and conception. Nick was all for that, but Lauren was a driven creature who felt it vital to finish all her assignments before taking any leisure time. But this time, unfortunately for her, she had no choice.

Their flight from Palm Beach to Atlanta was delayed, and they missed their connecting flight to Memphis and were rebooked for the last flight out of Hartsfield to Memphis. After picking up the rental car, they drove the hour down to Oxford, arriving around eleven o'clock at night. There would be another snafu as the hotel clerk at the Days Inn of Oxford, unaware of their travel predicament, had sold their room. They could stay in the room Friday and Saturday, but he would have to get them a room at a sister hotel, Days Inn of Tupelo, for tonight. What else could they do but accept the offer? Forty-five minutes later, the two pulled into their new lodgings. After winding down, and without the pressure to perform, Nick initiated the lovemaking session. For the first time he was not on the clock. Sandy agreed. The next day the two slept in and were only awakened by the polite knocking of the maid, who was trying to finish her rounds and clean the rooms for the next set of lodgers.

Leaving US Highway 45 and turning on to Mississippi Highway 6 headed for Oxford, Nick noticed the public information sign declaring Tupelo, Mississippi, as the "Birthplace of the King of Rock and Roll, Elvis Presley."

The weekend went great, with catch-up time with old friends and tailgating at The Grove, which the *New York Times* called the "holy grail of tailgating." The Rebs hung tough for a while, but 'Bama secured another win when a running back raced about seventy yards for a clinching touchdown. It was a great moment when someone in the stands, dressed in Ole Miss navy blue, hollered out, "Run, Forrest, run!" repeating a line from the movie *Forrest Gump*, where Tom Hanks plays a mentally challenged young man who becomes a football star and a graduate of the University of Alabama. You had to laugh and nod in response to this well-placed sarcastic cheer, which reinforced the Ole Miss stereotype of "We may not win every game, but we *never* lose a party!"

Exhausted from the fun and excitement of a much-needed mini vacation, the Finch's returned to Palm Beach County for more work and baby making. At the end of the month, Lauren emerged from the bedroom with a quizzical look on her face as Nick was settling in to watch *Cheers* and *Friends* on NBC's "Must See TV" night of programming. She looked at her husband and said, "I am not sure, but I think I might be pregnant. I will go to the doctor tomorrow." Nick was stunned. He walked outside, looked up to the heavens, and said a quick prayer. He also asked Charlene, if she had any pull up there, if she would please grant their wish for a baby.

The next day Lauren went to the fertility specialist and waited patiently as the doctor pored over the different pages of lab work and such. He looked at her, then put down his folder and said, "Well, I'll be damned. I never thought this could happen with you two, but, Mrs. Finch, you are pregnant. Now be incredibly careful. I will give you strict orders regarding what you can and cannot do and instructions for your diet and your lifestyle that you must follow, at least for the first three months or so. Do not underestimate this, but this child—and, well, your conception—is a small miracle."

Lauren was having trouble concentrating on what he was saying. She began to cry, but not the usual tears that followed her period or her appointments with the battery of doctors. Now they were tears of joy. The doctor narrowed down the conception date to the weekend in Oxford, most likely the night in Tupelo. Lauren went straight to the receptionist's desk and asked to use her phone. She had to call Nick right away. The phone rang and rang until the answering machine picked up. Where the hell could he be? Nick, in fact, was out mowing the lawn and could not hear the phone. Sandy looked around the waiting room and saw two other women waiting to see the doctor. She was speechless but crying and left with a big double thumb-up. The women noticed and smiled as they thought maybe there was hope for them.

Lauren pulled into the driveway of their Lake Clarke home. They had a garage, but they used it for a storage catchall, not for parking cars. Nick was on the south side of the lawn, walking away with headphones on while mowing. He did not notice his wife had pulled in. He turned the mower around to make another lap and saw his wife standing against her car. He turned off the mower and pulled off his one-piece yellow headphones that made him look like he worked on a runway at the airport or on the deck of an aircraft carrier. They locked eyes, and right then he knew it.

Nick raced across the lawn and hugged Lauren. Both began to cry. The fact that he was smelly and sweaty did not matter. Lauren went inside, grabbed her dog by the collar, pulled him close, and cried again, but this time to Clancy. Clancy knew what was happening. His tail wagged back and forth in canine joy. Sandy called her parents and informed them but made them promise not to tell anyone as there was still a long way to go. The husband and wife were speechless for the longest time, until Lauren informed Nick that most likely the conception had happened that night in Tupelo. Nick said, "Hey, we got us a Mississippi child. Hell, we got Elvis! If it's a boy, let's name him Elvis Finch. I like it. Elvis Finch." Lauren did not respond to that request. It would not be granted, but they did hint to a horrified Grace White that Elvis was the leading candidate for the name of her first grandchild. Lauren played right along with it.

After the first three months had passed, along with weekly ob-gyn appointments, things began to look and feel normal. The bump, although small, began to appear, and there was some kicking and feeling in there. The Finch's began to discuss names, but every possible one suggested by one half of the couple seemed to call to mind some ugly history for the other half. A suggested boy's name was met with "He was a jerk"—or a dick, a prick, conceited, arrogant, or a criminal. Girls' names were tagged with things such as ho, tramp, freak, or skank. Lovely, such a name association game. Nick went back to suggesting Elvis, but now he was greeted with the death stare, a sure, veto-proof nay vote from Lauren. They bought a book of names and both pored over suggestions and the origins of the names therein. Nick even brought home his roll book to try to get ideas.

It seemed a red flag was raised with every name. Nick was dead set against having a Nicholas John Finch Jr. or, worse, Nicholas John Finch II. Absolute fingernails on a chalkboard for him was a person who went by his first initial when introduced, such as N. John Finch, or to make it even worse, if such a thing could be possible, N. John Finch II. Stop it. Lauren worked with or around many people on the island of Palm Beach who did such a thing, and almost to a person they were arrogant, conceited jerks. Nick associated the practice with Ivy Leaguers or, worse, Duke graduates. Nick did not want to saddle his son with his own name, whether for good or for bad, and there could be plenty of arguments made on both sides of the aisle. Also, he wanted his son to have a clean slate in life because he had seen from a distance how his older brother never, at least in his own mind, lived up to being J. W. Finch Jr. That sort of thing was not going to happen here.

The two decided to table the motion until they found out the sex of their child. So, they agreed; the motion was passed. Let the record show: no name discussion until the ultrasound discovery.

The trip to the ob-gyn was scheduled with the ultrasound to check not only for the sex of the child but also for a battery of prenatal issues and potential concerns. The nurse smeared the jelly all over Lauren's midsection, then the doctor took a microphone-looking device and began to circle it around the jellied area. There was the sound of a heartbeat, loud and constant with a rough gushing quality, that was very distinctive. The womb apparently was not a quiet, relaxing place but was a place of constant motion and change. Soon an image appeared on the screen located next to the examination table—some sort of moving object. What it was, Nick could not be sure. The screen was showing either a human or some humanlike species out of a science fiction movie. He played along just as if he was seeing what Lauren and the doctor were seeing—and what they were seeing brought smiles and tears of joy to everyone else there. The baby was right on track and doing fine. The procedure continued, then the doctor announced that they would be having a boy, pointing to the penis of the unborn child. My God, it was huge, at least as big as the child's arm. Nick was proud, but then again could the boy have been from Nick's gene pool with such an outstanding member? Nick sheepishly asked about the size, and the three women in the room broke into laughter and said everything was normal.

The dilemma switched back to the name game now that Nick and Lauren knew the child's gender. The two were discussing their situation with Karen, the bartender at Beefeaters Restaurant, along with the hostess and their longtime friend Margret Baldwin, while waiting on friends to join them for drinks and dinner. Sandy was not drinking anything now but water, which made her an excellent designated driver. Karen suggested they look deep into their family tree for names, not the usual brothers and sisters, but aunts, uncles, cousins, and in-laws. Why not?

Something had to jar a positive emotion related to a long-lost relative who happened to have the perfect name. It was worth a try.

Both went home and went to sleep, but first thing in the morning, after Lauren's trip to the bathroom to vomit, which still happened at least three times a day, she joined Nick at the kitchen table. Nick had gotten up earlier to let Clancy out and then grabbed a yellow legal pad and wrote at the top "Mom" and "Dad," underlining each word and then drawing a vertical line separating the two columns. Charlene's family would be easy as it was a small list, but with J.W.'s, who'd had double-digit siblings and countless uncles and cousins, the names flowed. Sone of these relatives, Nick knew little about. In some cases, he had never even met them. Dairy farm families tend to be large—free labor, you know. Then Nick came to the name of a cousin who was much older, the child of one of his dad's oldest brothers, and Nick liked it. The name was Tyler Finch. Trying to remember everything about his distant cousin was becoming difficult. This was before Ancestry.com, so Nick did it the old-fashioned way: he picked up the phone and called a couple of J.W.'s family members whom he still got Christmas cards from. From these people, along with his own sister's recollections, he found out that Tyler Finch was a civil engineer for the State of Alabama and a graduate of Auburn University, where he also played football for the legendary "Shug" Jordan. Nick then went down the hall to the makeshift study, a small bedroom that had shelves of countless books—fiction, nonfiction, and everything else that could be printed—and walked over to the collection of informational books that universities sent the high schools promoting their institutions and athletic programs. Nick loved to go through these, not so much as a fan or coach, but as an historian. He pulled from the shelves the *Auburn Tigers Football Sports Information Guide*. It had to be three hundred pages long, filled with pictures, statistics, and biographies. He went to the index and found "Tyler Finch, Spartanburg, South Carolina, running back 1959–62." He became fascinated with his biography, statistics, and pictures. After doing some more family research by way of the phone, Nick found out that Tyler Finch had gone to college on a football scholarship and played a lot for the Tigers or War Eagles or Plainsmen, or whatever nickname the team was using, as it seemed to the outsider that they used them all. Tyler was an engineering major and had, after graduation, gone to work for the State of Alabama. He made his home outside Montgomery, along with his bride Dorothy, or Dot, and raised a family, all of whom of course went to Auburn and *hated* the University of Alabama. Hate is genetic in that state. Homes that split over such treason were not "houses divided" but "houses divorced." Nick had never met his uncle as the latter had passed away in 1980. He'd had three girls and no boys, so there was no Tyler Finch Jr.

Lauren pulled up a chair and looked at the scribbled list, not tipping her hand as she researched the Finch family tree of names. She came to the name Tyler and noticed her husband had circled it and underlined it twice. If that weren't enough to catch her attention, he'd also used a neon yellow highlighter as part of his lobbying effort.

She looked at the high-pressure suggestion and bit her lip, tossing her head back and forth, not in a yes or a no motion, but in an "I'm thinking about it, so convince me" sort of way. At least it was not a no and there were no comments about a Tyler she had known once who now was doing time for embezzling money from orphanages or some such crime that would lead to a veto. Instead, Lauren asked her husband, "Tell me about him and what you know about his story." Nick showed his wife the Auburn guide and discussed what he had learned about his distant cousin. He admitted he had never actually met the man. She then said, "Tyler Finch. Hmm, Tyler Finch." Finally, as if she were Scarlett O'Hara, she said, "Tyler Finch" in a southern drawl. She looked over and nodded her approval. "I like it. Let's go with it."

It was decided the young boy with the impressive manhood, at least in the womb, would be named Tyler Finch. Now for the middle name. Nick, in a quick move to compromise, suggested Randal after Lauren's father. Lauren thought about it for a second and once again started pronouncing the name out loud. "Tyler Randall Finch. Tyler Randy Finch. Maybe T. R. Finch? Nah, but thanks anyhow." Nick countered with plan B and suggested her maiden name, White, as the middle name. The practice started up again: "Tyler White Finch. Tyler W. Finch. T. W. Finch. I like Tyler White Finch. Let's go with that. That's it." The expecting mom then lowered her voice to a role-playing octave: "Mr. Tyler White Finch, President of the United States. Please welcome superstar Ty Finch to the stage. Now starting in centerfield for the Atlanta Braves, T. W. Finch. Yep, that's it."

Nick nodded in approval but made one counteroffer: "Wait a minute, how about Tyler Elvis Finch? Huh, not bad."

The mom to be gave the simple response she had learned from her years in the world of investment and banking: "No."

With the name game now complete, the first child of Nicholas and Lauren Finch was to be named Tyler White Finch, of West Palm Beach, Florida. Now it was time to get through the whole birthing process, including a discussion of expectations and procedures. They were ready for Ty to join the family, which currently consisted of Lauren, Nick, and Clancy. The last two months were agonizing as they tried to stay busy preparing the baby's room, putting things like cribs and playpens together, and attending multiple baby showers. Soon it was going to be July, and the day was getting close—very close.

Lauren emerged from the bedroom and made her way to the family room, where once again she found Nick watching the Atlanta Braves on the superstation WTBS just as she had almost every night during the summer. The Braves were family as the two had had their first date watching the Braves in the World Series versus the Twins. It was on that night that Nick had fallen in love with his future wife. She looked at her husband sitting in the oversized down-filled green cotton-upholstered easy chair, which was probably too big for the room but which was comfortable as hell, and said, "I think my water just broke.

We need to get to "Good Sam" as soon as possible." Nick quickly got up, grabbed the two overnight bags that were already packed and sitting by the front door, took them outside, and loaded them into the Jeep Cherokee. They were no longer a sports car family since they were starting a family, but both had agreed never to go the minivan route. Clancy had been nervous and jumpy all day as it was apparent to him, what with his instincts and sense of smell, that the big event was on the way.

The two drove to Good Samaritan Hospital with Nick not knowing what in the world to say except, "How are you doing?" After pulling in, they were whisked to the birthing center and maternity ward. The staff quickly came in checked all Lauren's vitals and basically told her and Nick that the baby was coming but was still hours away. It was the early stages of labor. The situation seemed to merit the saying J.W. had learned in the military: "Hurry up and wait." The waiting game was now on. Above the bed facing Nick and Lauren was a TV with a VCR player and twenty or so feel-good tapes that had been selected for such moments, ones with family appeal. Nick brought the tray over, and Lauren picked *Mr. Holland's Opus*, which stars Richard Dreyfuss as a frustrated musician who takes a job as a high school music director. The job turns into a career that he learns to embrace and love. Along the way, there is a shift in emphasis as Mr. Holland and his wife have a baby boy who is discovered to be hearing-impaired, which adds stress to the family and causes confrontations. What started out for the expecting Finch family as a feel-good had become a drama about a teacher's family that maybe was hitting a little too close to home. The doctor stopped by and said they should expect delivery around ten o'clock in the morning, give or take an hour. Upon hearing the doctor's prognosis, Lauren told Nick to go home and stay with Clancy but to be back first thing in the morning. Nick did as he was told.

Nick was extremely excited but also worried. And he was mad at himself for what he thought was his self-centered anxiety. What he was concerned about was the actual act of the birthing of his child and his attendance at the event. Nick kept thinking about tenth grade when, for one week in biology classes, the students were split up by gender for a minicourse on human sexuality. The boys stayed in the classroom, and one of Nick's coaches took over the class and read word for word from a prewritten script with little or no time for questions and answers. The girls were to be instructed by a female coach who, Nick realized now that he was looking back on it, had little chance herself of getting pregnant, if you get the drift. Most of the week was taken up by watching reel-to-reel films, most likely from the mid-sixties. There was a cartoon of Mr. Sperm and Mrs. Egg, who quite noticeably were married, who meet up to produce Junior. There was another film about respect and about how no means no. What the girls saw, Nick did not know. It seemed that both teachers would rather be held in a Vietnamese prison camp or be forced to have a root canal without any anesthesia. You could tell that they had pulled the short straw and were mandated to teach the course that was required by the Florida State Legislature. Nick's coach never looked up as he read the course script without any emotion or variance in tone of voice. He asked if there were any questions after each lesson but never glanced up to see if anyone actually held up their hand. Moving on. Nick forgot almost everything from the course immediately, and although his lovemaking was sloppy and rushed back then, he was not a virgin. Most of his friends weren't either. There were two things that Nick retained from that weeklong class during his sophomore year. One of these things was simple and yet made so much sense. Using the same wording, the teacher wrote two very different sentences on the board:

> women L*ove* sex.
> men love S*ex*.

This showed the difference between how the two genders approached the emotions that lead to lovemaking, and it was spot on.

The second thing was something that haunted Nick: a late fifties or early sixties film of actual childbirth. The film was about twenty minutes long and was narrated by a man who had to have been from the Midwest and probably was a radio announcer or local newsman. In a serious tone of voice, in a baritone, the narrator told the story of the baby traveling through the birth canal and arriving in the world as the next proud citizen of the United States. The soon-to-be mother had a nether region that was more like Canadian beaver in the middle of winter. *So that is where the slang term of* beaver *for a vagina comes from,* Nick thought. The rain forest was sparser than this young woman's pubic hair. And her husband was nowhere to be found. Probably out buying cigars to celebrate with the boys.

Then it happened: the head emerged, and the birth was quickly assisted by the doctor, dressed in a white lab coat, complete with stethoscope around his neck, and three nurses, also all in white, sporting their caps. The nurses reminded Nick of his mom, Charlene. He quickly realized, *never think of your mom during such a moment.* Freud would have had a field day with that thought. Nick started to get fuzzy as he was not enjoying the film about the "most natural act in all of humanity," as the narrator reminded the class.

Then came the afterbirth, or placenta. That almost pushed Nick over the edge, but Ray Wade came to the rescue with much needed and perfectly timed comedy. He announced, "My God, there was a twin and the doctor killed it! Murderer!" The room of boys roared at the star tennis player's commentary. The coach abruptly stopped the film and ordered Ray to the dean's office, where he was not given the option of three whacks or a phone call home. Instead, the dean went straight to the beating. There was to be no joking about such things as childbirth, and punishment for doing so would be quick and painful. It was for Ray, but it allowed Nick the time to regain his composure.

Now the real event was on for Nick, and this was not a 16 mm movie. It was the real thing, a live performance by his wife. And he was expected to be in the room for the holy moment. Nick started to sweat with nervous energy.

The anesthetist arrived too late for the epidural, so Lauren was going to give birth the old-fashioned way, with no drugs. Mr. and Mrs. White were already there, camped right outside the room. What a huge event this was for them, in some ways even bigger for them than for the parents. Grace had never had her own children, and now she was going to be a real grandmother. Randy was stoic as ever. They were worried and more than once raised their concern that Clancy may become jealous of the baby. Nick told them not to worry; the two would be simply fine together. Nick did plan to bring home a blanket belonging to the newborn boy for the golden retriever to smell before bringing Tyler home.

Their priest from Bethesda, Warren Crosby, showed up at the same time as Nick. Warren was great; in fact, he had pulled himself out of a meeting at the National Cathedral in Washington, DC, and flew home immediately after the miscarriage. He provided counseling and was always saying a prayer for the expecting family.

Then the staff took over the coaching, encouraging Sandy to breathe. Lauren had had a very difficult pregnancy, but it turned out her delivery was easy, if that is okay for a man to say. Men have no clue.

The commands were coming now. Nick held Lauren's hand, gripping it so hard that it would bruise. Slowly, Nick found himself moving from the front-row seat to a spot beside his wife and then behind her. He would not be in direct eyeshot of the event. Lauren never noticed his shuffling of places. She had a job to do, and the driven woman was going to get this boy out of her right now!

Then Tyler White Finch emerged into the doctor's hands. After a quick cleaning of both mom and baby, the two were reunited for the first of many times. The sweat of the procedure was sponged away as the first-time mom, who herself had been abandoned as a baby, now held her own child against her chest. The moment was surreal. Nick leaned over and kissed both, having quickly repositioned himself next to his wife and now his son. Within moments, the grandparents and the clergy entered. Father Crosby said a quick prayer, held the child, and anointed him with the sign of the cross on the forehead, the baby being less than ten minutes old. His conception and birth were to Nick an act of God.

Grace came forward. Her daughter passed the child to his grandmother. There now was not a dry eye in the room. Until her death, Grace and Tyler shared a love much closer than she had with her other grandchildren. It was evident. If you had been in that room, you would know why.

A crib was pulled right beside the mother. Nick left the room with his in-laws and Father Crosby as the nurses helped Sandy get it together. On this day, July 3, 1996, Tyler White Finch had been born at Good Samaritan Hospital in West Palm Beach, Florida, making him a fourth-generation Floridian. The fact that his birthday was on the third of July gave the newborn and his parents front-row seats to the fireworks at "Fourth on Flagler" And he would always have the day after his birthday off, which Nick thought was cool.

The new family made it home back to Lake Clarke Shores, changed forever. As J.W. would say, "Parenting is the hardest job you will ever love." The challenges of miscarriage and conception were just chapters 1 and 2 of the Finch family novel as there was so much more on the horizon. Just as they had learned, they introduced the newcomer Tyler to their first son, Clancy. His tail wagged, and he kept sniffing the infant, but he showed no signs aggression, in fact the opposite, as he began to lick the baby's face, much to the horror of Grace White. But Nick and Lauren loved the affection Clancy was showing toward the new arrival. However, there would be crises to emerge.

To begin with, Lauren was unable to breastfeed Tyler. For whatever reason, it just was not working, which was very upsetting to her as a new mom. Almost all journals and publications had articles about how important a mother's milk was to an infant, and she felt bad that she was unable to perform this most intimate act between a mother and her baby. It hurt. Add to that postpartum hormonal dysfunction, and there were a lot of tears around feeding time. Depending on what study you read and what slant the researchers and authors have, statistics range from 2 percent to more than 20 percent of mothers who do not or cannot breastfeed their babies. Nick doubted he had been breastfed, and it had never come up in conversation with Charlene. The doctors at Infants and Children, the pediatric practice the Finches had selected, because that was where Nick had gone as a child, but more importantly because the doctors there were top rated, reassured Lauren it was not a problem and prescribed a newborn formula for feeding. In a way this was good for Lauren as Nick now was on the clock for every other feeding, which gave her a much-needed break and allowed her to get some rest.

On the first night home from the hospital, they laid Tyler in his crib in the bedroom right across the hall from the master bedroom and turned on the baby monitor. Around midnight the two were awakened by the sound of an attacking growling dog and a baby's crying coming from the nursery. The two jumped out of bed and raced the whole three steps across the hall. Had Clancy become jealous and attacked their baby boy as Grace had warned them about? Nope. Just the opposite. What had happened was that one of the helium balloons declaring "It's a Boy!" in blue had begun to lose its lifting power and started to fall into the crib. Clancy would have none of that. Apparently, he jumped and ripped the balloon to shreds. All that beautiful dog had done was to protect his "little brother," making sure nothing or nobody would invade Tyler's space on his watch! When the two parents realized what had happened, they hugged their guard dog and praised him for doing what he had just done. There was another time when the garbage collectors were perturbed at Sandy, who had raced from the house with another bag of trash from the kitchen, so it delayed their route by a whole twenty seconds. The sanitation worker barked his displeasure and went across the lawn to meet Sandy halfway with a raised voice and pissed-off body language. Clancy changed all that when the hundred-pound reddish golden retriever did his own barking and raced from the front door to jump right in front of Sandy with his pearly whites showing and growling his menacing growl. Nobody was going to come across his grass at his woman and talk that way. He had been through so much with her, so this was totally unacceptable. The garbage man realized his mistake and hightailed it back to the truck, where the driver was laughing. Lauren apologized and took her garbage all the way to the roadside, then commanded Clancy to go back inside the house. Once the dog was in the house, the garbage was disposed of into the truck and the sanitation workers continued their route down Pine Tree Lane.

Such an amicable resolution was not always the case, unfortunately. A year or two later, the Finch's were having their kitchen upgraded with a stove and oven from their generation, rather than the 1950s versions that had come with the house. The two workers and a sister had to do some retrofitting, which required new countertops and carpentry work. Nick introduced the workers to Clancy, and the group got along great. Too great. A few days after the job was completed, Nick came home and found the house in disarray. He was perplexed and then realized he had been robbed. He called the Lake Clarke Shores police, who came and took some pictures and did the paperwork for the insurance company, but really little was taken. Looking back on it, Nick believes, his having come home at two thirty, he most likely interrupted the heist as he noticed the back door was ajar. The local police said unfortunately they really could not do much investigative work since the one and only detective was out on maternity leave and would not be back on the job for a couple of months. Maternity leave—O the irony. Two days later, the three workers were arrested trying to use a credit card bearing the name of

Nicholas J. Finch at the K-Mart on Forest Hill and Military Trail. Unfortunately for them, the cashier was a former student of Nick's who quietly called security, who called the sheriff's office, who then called Lake Clarke Shores police, who then notified Nick. It seems the workers/ burglars had used the young girl to crawl through the doggy door and then open the house to them. Clancy did nothing but wag his tail with an approving smile since he knew the carpenters from their work and was comfortable with them. It seems they stole about two hundred dollars in coins that were being collected in a giant water bottle, along with some credit cards and some silver candlesticks, before being interrupted. A criminal record and loss of employment—if we're not counting the work of picking up trash along the interstate, which prisoners do—all for a couple of hundred dollars in coins. What a shame.

There was something else about Tyler that concerned the parents and the pediatricians: his labored breathing. The little guy had an excess of mucus and was often wheezing, so the doctors changed his formula and prescribed some antibiotics in case he had an infection. Still no change, so Doctor Edwards ordered the one-month-old infant into St. Mary's for a battery of tests. That was familiar territory for Nick, and to make it even better, Ray Wade's wife had transferred from Good Samaritan Hospital to St. Mary's and now was their chief pharmacist. What that meant was that they had an insider to give them all the test results even before the doctors even got the information.

To see the baby infant back in the hospital was heartbreaking, and the tests they were doing seemed brutal, such as hitting Tyler on his back to get samples of mucus and the pricking his arms for blood samples and intravenous medicine. Nick more than once found himself leaving the room to go to the Catholic chapel on campus to say some prayers. In his journeys around the complex, he was constantly running into old colleagues of Charlene. They reassured him everything was going to turn out all right because he was in the right place and Tyler's grandmother had a lot of pull up there in heaven.

What the medical staff was worried about was that Tyler might have cystic fibrosis. Nick knew what a tough hill that could be to climb, so he prayed even more. Tests were sent to Shands Hospital at the University of Florida. The Finches had admitted Tyler on a Monday morning. It was now Thursday, and still nothing had come back from Gainesville. Father Crosby came by. He, Nick, and Sandy circled the crib and held hands as the father offered a prayer to the Almighty for his healing powers to touch the infant Episcopalian. After the prayer, Father Crosby took a step back from the crib and announced that he had it on good authority from above that all would be all right because in about five or six years he would need a new acolyte to assist him with church services. When he concluded his pronouncement, Ray Wade's wife, the pharmacist, broke into the room gasping, apparently having run all the way from the pharmacy, to share the news. She later would be the Finch's second child's godmother. Catching her breath, she asked, "I have good news and bad news: which do you want? This just came over my computer. It is Tyler's test results from Gainesville."

The parents looked at each other. Lauren said, "Just give it to us." She and Nick held hands and were joined in the hand holding by Father Crosby as they awaited the news. Lauren looked down at the floor while Nick looked up to the ceiling as if to heaven.

"He does not have cystic fibrosis. He has asthma."

Nick continued looking skyward and said, "Oh, thank you, God." Asthma is tough and there is no cure, but it is treatable. Nick had watched his mother fight it her entire life, and she had done just fine. Now cystic fibrosis was a whole another animal. Doctor Edwards, who was about to retire, but had taken on the young Finch child because he had taken care of the entire Finch clan, came in and announced he had the test results from Gainesville. He looked at everyone in the room, an audience who already knew the punch line to a joke or the final score to a game. Lauren looked at the doctor as the pharmacist snuck out without being noticed; most likely her relaying of the test information was a breach of procedure and policy.

The mother hugged the doctor and said, "We know it's asthma and not cystic fibrosis."

The doctor asked, "How did you find out before me—and so fast?"

Nick looked at Father Crosby and told the pediatrician, "God told us." Father Crosby cracked a smile from ear to ear and concurred. Tyler would be able to go home, but he would be given daily breathing treatments—a steroid from a nebulizer—which was a hell of a lot better than the alternative.

Tyler's other issue was that he was a terrible sleeper and never seemed to sleep through the night. The parents took turns getting up with him. Nick suggested that they cut his formula with a little whiskey. Lauren did not even dignify the idea with a response as she shook her head in bewilderment.

One time when the monitor went off with the crying of their son, Nick elbowed Lauren and asked, "Are you awake?"

She answered without missing a beat, "Nope. I am sound asleep." Nick was stunned at the answer. So quick and right on. Well played. He got up and went to the nursery. Soon it was back to the doctor's office, who concluded that Tyler had an ear infection. In fact, he would go on to have eleven straight ear infections, which culminated with the removal of his tonsils and adenoids. Because of the ear problems, Tyler had trouble lying down flat, which put pressure on his ears. Nightly the parents would take turns sleeping in a chair located in the nursery so the baby could sleep in kind of a standing or vertical position to relieve the pressure on his ears. When it was Nick's turn, he would switch off the baby monitor and then would insert a CD of Pink Floyd's *Dark Side of the Moon* in the player in the baby's room. Since he could not give him whiskey, why not some marijuana music? It worked like a charm; the two would instantly fall into a deep sleep. Later in life, Tyler seemed to enjoy recreational weed, and Nick believed he knew why: because Tyler had been introduced to the culture as an infant with the Pink Floyd music. They say children immediately begin to sense their environment and adapt accordingly throughout their lives. Why not?

The steroidal breathing treatment would accelerate Tyler's heartbeat and at times would make his hands shake, but Nick and Lauren reminded each other that side effect was a hell of a lot better than the alternative they had been warned about at the hospital. Despite having a health-challenged child, the new parents began to adapt to their new lifestyle, even if it meant sleeping in a chair and listening to psychedelic music. The three of them had their first Christmas together, yet Nick and Lauren still threw the annual holiday party. Looking at all the gifts that Tyler had received from family and friends Lauren and Nick were reminded of how important it was to have the party and insist every attendee bring an unwrapped toy for a less fortunate local child.

Tyler's baptism or christening took place at Bethesda with Father Crosby officiating, along with six other children and even two adults. Brian Parker was selected as godfather, and the godmother was one of Sandy's friends who had been a bridesmaid in their wedding. Brian would return the honor and name Nick as his child's godfather. In fact, Nick would be a godfather five times over. Dad, thinking Tyler looked ridiculous in an old traditional English christening gown, whispered in his ear not to worry as he would never let any of his future friends or teammates ever see it. After the baptism, the Whites hosted a brunch at their PGA National home. This was the introduction of Tyler to the church, a church he would lean on for guidance during some rough times and where he also became a youth leader as an acolyte, also serving as a crucifer, leading the processional at the opening, and closing of each service. His first time as crucifer, the youth who holds the cross up high, occurred ten years to the day after he had received the news that he had asthma and not cystic fibrosis. Most had forgotten that event. Nick had not. After the service, he reminded Father Crosby of his spiritual epiphany, when he said that he would be needing Tyler as an acolyte in the future, so everything was going to be all right. When Nick shared this bit of history, the stoic priest got choked up and was visibly moved. It was a great day.

Nick asked his wife what she wanted for Christmas, and without blinking she said, "Sleep!" Nick knew this was not a request but a plea. He nodded in agreement and said he would see what he could do. The next Saturday, Father Nick got Tyler up, dressed him, strapped him into car seat, and loaded the baby stroller into the back of the Cherokee, but not before uttering a string of profanities. Thank goodness most of the neighbors were asleep and therefore were not privy to the cussing. You see, Nick was challenged when it came to basic engineering. To him, it seemed one had to be a NASA engineer to figure how to fold and unfold a stroller. The word *frustrating* does not properly describe the situation.

Once the stroller was folded and, in the Jeep, the father and son duo went into the city of West Palm Beach for a stroll along the Flagler Drive waterfront and the Green Market. Recently the city had opened a sort of farmers market on Saturday mornings, with fresh produce, fruit, flowers, bakery goods, and seafood. Tables were set upside by side, the sellers offering their commodities, some of which included arts and crafts such as jewelry and leather products. A local jazz trio provided the music and had left a straw hat for tips on the stage next to the singer. The Green Market would run starting in the fall, going through the winter, and finishing up in the spring. No summer markets. Too hot, too rainy, and at least half the shopping base would be gone back up north. Nick and Tyler strolled up and down, looking at the different booths and, at times, buying an item or two. Nick also noticed how much more attractive he was to the women there with his son as a prop. Without hesitation they would stop the two, observe the little guy, and ask his name and how old he was, along with other questions usually asked by mothers and hopeful mothers-to-be. More than once, Nick overheard the exiting moms saying how sexy it was to see a man with a baby. Making it even better was that Nick would tell them that he did this for true father–son bonding and because it also allowed his wife to sleep in and get some much-needed rest. "Ah" usually followed that up. If Nick were single and Tyler had been his nephew and not his son, then he would be in the front door, so to speak. Almost as good as a golden retriever puppy for attracting the babes. Occasionally, Nick would stack the deck and not only have Tyler but also bring Clancy. Lauren loved the extra sleep, but not maybe as much as Nick enjoyed bonding with his young son. The two would have their spats and disagreements over the years, as any father and son will do, but they learned to respect each other—and just maybe it started with those early Saturday morning strolls along Flagler Drive at the Green Market.

Tyler quickly went from just lying there to creeping, to crawling, and then to stumble-walking. This led to Lauren's next Christmas request, but Nick could do nothing about this one, as Mom had requested the ability to go to the bathroom by herself. It seemed that Tyler felt his mom needed company in the women's room. Whether she was going number one or number two, he would barge right in unannounced. She was on her own with this problem.

Right after the second Tyler Christmas party, Nick was watching one of the fifty or so college bowl games in the family room when Lauren came in, looked over at her husband, and blurted out, "Well, you are going to be a dad again."

Nick was half listening to his wife and half listening to the call of the Zima Fresno Agricultural Bowl, or some such meaningless game, when what she had just told him registered. "Really? You sure?" was all he could come back with.

Lauren said as a matter of fact, "Yep, pretty sure." After Tyler's birth, the pressure was off, and Lauren had not gone back on the fertility drugs, which she hated for a variety of reasons, but especially because of the side effect of weight gain. She attempted to make an appointment for that next Monday morning, but the ob-gyn was booked till Thursday, so it would be Thursday. If this had been their first rodeo, so to speak, she would have demanded a Monday appointment, but now she was a veteran of the pregnancy wars. In fact, she a medal winner with all the trouble of the first one.

It seemed everything came easier with baby two just because of the experience factor: now everything was no longer the unknown. Looking back at the two baby books, Nick noticed that Tyler's was much bigger as his parents had kept everything as a memento, whereas his sister's—Lauren and Nick soon found out they were to have a girl this time—was noticeably much leaner. Just think how small Nick's baby book was since he was the fifth of five children. There is not one, is the answer. After the trouble, stress, and strife involved in the conception of Tyler, the next one seemed to be much more normal.

The two children would be two years apart. Things were falling into place for the two of them as they should, with a boy and a girl close in age but not too close. And with one boy and one girl, Nick decided he would call for an appointment to get snipped after the birth. Yes, once the baby was born and everyone was declared healthy and fit, he would have a vasectomy. There would not be a third child or, God forbid, an "oops" child as Nick had been. Another plus was that Lauren would never have to use birth control again. It was a no-brainer. As the old southern slogan goes, "Two and a barbecue and we're outta here!"

The name game came back up, but there was a much shorter list this time as the search for a name that had taken place a little more than two years earlier eliminated many potential candidates. Nick and Lauren looked at the family tree again for inspiration, but this time the well had run dry. The problem was that most of the names on Nick's tree had come from farm families and were dated. There was Mildred, Dorothy, Agnes, Betty, and of course his grandmother Sabra. Sorry, it was the twentieth century, so no dice there. The two did agree on the middle name, which had to be Elizabeth. Now for the first name.

During the late eighties and up until the early nineties, ABC ran a popular drama with some comedy that spotlighted the life and times of young urban professionals, or yuppies, called *Thirtysomething*. The ensemble cast was very impressive as most of the group went on to star in other shows and movies. By 1998 the show was off the air, but it ran in syndication on one of the many channels now piped into Nick and Lauren's home by way of the new satellite dish technology used by DirecTV. Mind you, this was not the seventies version of the giant dish one would find outside rural homes throughout the South. Those were so prevalent that they were nicknamed "the state flower of South Carolina." The satellite dish was a staple for countryfolk who could not get cable and wanted more than three stations via antenna. And it worked just fine, thank you very much. The problem was that Nick and Lauren were not very practical for city folk, who depended on the very undependable cable TV companies. Hell, there was even a hit comedy starring Jim Carrey and Matthew Broderick called *Cable Guy* that mocked the service.

Now that *Thirtysomething* was back on the air, there was one character—or the actress who played the character—who always caught Nick's eye because of her striking looks and outstanding personality: Mel Harris. Nick looked over at Lauren and said, "What about her?"

Lauren, who was doing needlepoint, looked back, quizzical, and asked, "Who? What?"

"Her, Mel Harris. How about that name?"

"Mel? Isn't that a man's name?" She put down her needling project and went into deep thought, then said, "I do like Melody or Melanie. Let me think about it. But I think it could work."

The next morning, while seated at a small makeup table in their small bedroom in their small home, next to their extra small bathroom with her son next to her petting his very big dog Lauren looked at her husband and said, "I am good with either Melody or Melanie, so you think about it today and we will discuss it and choose tonight at dinner. Also, we need to think about getting a bigger house. Just saying." Nick nodded in approval and kissed his wife before he made the mile-and-a-half drive to his work at Forest Hill High. He also got to witness how the bank executive handled business proposals from her underlings: listen, ponder it, get input, meet again, and decide.

That night after dinner, while Sandy cleaned the table and took the dishes to rinse and put into the dishwasher, Nick remained at the dining table looking through his recent edition of *Sports Illustrated*. He seldom assisted with the post dinner chores as the kitchen was too small for two people, but also, he cooked about 80 percent of the meals, so it was a fair trade for Lauren to do the dishes. It worked for them. Lauren closed the dishwasher and was planning to turn it on when she turned, looked at Nick, and asked, "Well, which one, Melody or Melanie?"

Nick responded while quickly putting down his magazine. He would finish his article in the little reading room, or bathroom, as this demanded his full attention. "I am good with either one. You pick."

Mom grinned and looked over at her husband. "Me too. Either one." The two looked at each other and began to laugh. She suggested he flip a coin to find out the winner. Heads, Melody, tails Melanie. After all the anguish of selecting Tyler, now it was coming down to a game of chance, a coin flip. They both nodded in agreement as Nick pulled a quarter from his pocket. He also proposed a disclaimer, saying that at any time up to birth of their girl, a new name could be introduced. Lauren approved. "Good idea. And Elizabeth must be the middle name."

Nick flipped the quarter. If George Washington came up, the child's name would be Melody, and if the coin landed on the eagle side, then the girl would be named Melanie. The dad caught the quarter and then closed his hand, turning it over and placing the coin in the palm of his other hand. When he opened his hand, he found the Father of the Country looking right back at him. He produced the winning side for acknowledgment. Lauren and smiled and said, "Melody Elizabeth Finch it is." They both nodded in agreement as Clancy wagged his tail and as Tyler, who was about to have a sister, smiled.

It was getting close to Halloween, and Tyler was getting more and more excited as there would be a costume party at his preschool. Nick was happy because hurricane season was almost over and they had dodged another bullet. Also, it was kind of the unofficial end of summer for the locals.

The heat, but more importantly the humidity, seemed to break right around Halloween, and almost always it rained on October 31. Sure, it would be hot, and there were some Christmas and Thanksgiving celebrations that were downright unseasonably warm, but for the most part the never-ending heat and humidity that started around May 15 and persisted each day and night really did leave around Halloween. Of course, in South Florida there really was no fall or autumn as Nick had discovered when he went to college in northern Mississippi and really saw what fall was about with cool temperatures, pumpkin patches, and the bright and beautiful leaves changing colors in the Grove. But locals will take what they can get when it comes to relief from the endless summer.

Tyler had a purple Barney dinosaur costume ready to go for trick-or-treating. Nick hated that cartoon. *Annoying* is too kind of a word to describe how he felt about having to sit through it with his son. More like tortuous. He did like *Arthur*, the cartoon with the aardvark. Still, it was not *Jonny Quest*, Nick's favorite cartoon growing up. He felt that he had won the lottery when the local Blockbuster video store was going out of business and selling its inventory and he found a collector's edition VHS tape of *Jonny Quest*. He told all his boys about his purchase, and that Saturday they all came over with beer and snacks and watched Jonny, Dr. Quest, Race, and Hadji fight the evil of Dr. Zinn, the dog-sniffing Gila monsters, and the big one-eyed spider that shot out laser beams, the gang talking into their watches and riding personal hovercrafts. Talk about being ahead of your time: *Jonny Quest* was, and it was exciting. Now that was a cartoon, not some freakish weird purple dinosaur. Then again, Nick never really got *Sesame Street* when he was little. We all have our favorites.

A few days before the big fall holiday, Lauren announced it was time to go to the hospital, but this time it would be St. Mary's and not Good Samaritan. Something to do with insurance. But Nick did not mind as it was, in a way, like going home or down memory lane. After all, even though Tyler, as had Nick, had been born at Good Sam, Tyler had been cured at St. Mary's. Add to this the fact that another saint hovered over the place, Saint Charlene, patron saint of the Finch's, and Nick decided that St. Mary's would be just fine, thank you very much.

On October 27, Lauren's water broke. She and Nick went down to the hospital off Forty-Fifth Street with their bags packed and ready. The room was bigger and more comfortable than Tyler's room had been as hospitals were moving toward more of a homey feeling and away from a sterile setting for the new mother and child, also providing extra room for visitors and loved ones. Nick left Tyler at preschool and said he would pick him up after Lauren was situated, at which point he'd take him in to see his mom. Then the Whites would take Tyler home for the night because, if everything went according to plan, the big day would be the following day. A small travel bag with jammies and a change of clothes for his sleepover at Grandmommys was ready to go.

As the father and son walked into the hospital and to the elevator, Nick let Tyler push the button. The lift energized and took them up three floors to their destination. Grace and Randy were already there, spending time with their daughter. Soon after Tyler had been born, Lauren's brother's wife had given birth to their first, a boy also, whom they named Paul. For years, Randy and Grace had been without grandchildren, and now grandchildren were coming like candy out of a Pez dispenser. Soon after Melody's birth, the DC couple would add a daughter, whom they would name Allison. The four offspring now all had cousins.

Nick and Tyler walked down the hall hand in hand. In Tyler's other hand was a small teddy bear and the boy's blankie. Suddenly, Nick stopped in his tracks and looked at the nondescript room adorned by a framed picture of a nurse and a plaque that read, "Charlene Finch Nurses' Room."

Nick was taken aback and for an instant felt embarrassed and ashamed as he had forgotten about the honor that the hospital had paid his mother on her retirement by naming the nurses' break room after her—his mother, Tyler's grandmother. Nick pointed at the picture and asked his little boy if he knew who that was. Tyler looked at the picture. Nick picked him up so he could get a closer look. Tyler said, "No. Sorry, Daddy. Should I?"

"That is your grandmother and my mommy." In a touching moment, Tyler leaned his head down onto Nick's shoulder and smiled.

Nick knocked on the door. A female voice responded from inside with a quick command: "Yes. Come in." Nick opened the door and looked around. He saw three nurses at a table, one with coffee and two with Diet Cokes. They were all sharing a bag of microwave popcorn.

"Can we help you?" one of them asked the visitors.

Just then, a fourth nurse emerged from the women's room. She stopped, looked right back at the father and son, and said, "I know you. You are Mrs. Finch's boy."

Nick responded, "I am, and this is her grandson, Tyler." The black woman then introduced the other nurses and explained that they were taking their break in the room named after their special visitor's mother. They got up and welcomed their guests of honor. Nick looked around the place, which could have doubled as a teachers' lounge on any school campus. There were two restrooms, a bulletin board, two vending machines with snacks, a microwave with a disclaimer about the risk of radiation, and a Coca-Cola machine with a warning taped on the front: "Use at your own risk." The nurse who had recognized Nick came over and spent a little extra time as the other nurses got busy cleaning up to go back on shift. Those three said their goodbyes, then smiled and left. The nurse who recognized Nick explained that she had been a nurse's aide when Charlene worked there but had never given up on her dream of becoming "a nurse just like your mama." She was a proud RN now. She quizzed Nick about what he was doing there, and he explained that his wife was down the hall expecting their second child.

Soon after that meeting, the Finch's became unofficial VIPs and were treated to what seemed like round-the-clock assistance right up to delivery and all the way through the sign-out protocol. This was one of the nurses' own, and they wanted to make sure the Finch's were well taken care of. Charlene would have done the same for them. Thank God for nurses.

Lauren immediately knew something had just happened when her husband and son entered her room. Nick told her what had just taken place down the hall. The Whites smiled, and Randy commented that Nick should be proud. Lauren saw the glow on Nick's face, something that she had not seen in a while because he had been worn down by work, fatherhood, and upcoming life-changing event number two. Seeing that room seemed to have recharged his batteries.

About four or five years later, the family was back at St. Mary's because Tyler was suffering from a serious sinus infection that was awfully close to his developing brain and needed special attention. So, Nick spent three twenty-four-hour periods, night, and day, in the boy's room as he was cared for. Lauren could not be there because she had a different infection and many of the children in the pediatric ward were not allowed to be around sick adults. After seeing all the sick kids, Nick now knew from personal experience why Charlene hated going to the pediatric wing and why St. Jude in Memphis was so special. Same with the Shriners Hospital.

There were two things that really bothered Nick about this visit. One was that the nurses' room named after his mother was gone and had been redesigned as a storage room. When the hospital was sold to a national health-care conglomerate, they needed the space more than a memorial. And the nurses' room could also be a den of discontent. Very few newly designed schools have a teachers' lounge for the same reason. Divide and control. Before the nurses' room had been repurposed, Nick had gotten no notice—nothing. He would have liked to have been given the plaque bearing his mother's name, but no.

The other thing was that there was a little girl about Tyler's age in the adjoining room who seemed to have no visitors. Soon, Nick, once he got permission from the staff, invited the little girl to watch Tyler's new favorite video, which was Disney's *The Fox and the Hound*. Kurt Russell's voice, as he played one of the characters, seemed to be on a constant loop as Tyler and his new friend watched the classic again and again. Nick asked the nurses if the little girl had any visitors or family come see her. The nurses shook their heads and said occasionally her mom would show up and stay, but not for long, because, as the mother explained, she "had a life too." Nick thought, *some people should not be parents*. As Tyler and Nick left the hospital and went to the parking lot, Nick asked Tyler to turn around and wave bye-bye to "Grand mommy's hospital." As they did so, the little girl in the next-door room was looking out her window at them and was waving back. It broke Nick's heart and left a terrible stain on his memory of the stay. No child should be left alone so someone else can "have a life too." He also now knew why Charlene hated pediatric medicine. Heartbreaking.

On October 28, 1998, Melody Elizabeth Finch came into the world. There were no complications, and as deliveries go, it was perfect. At least that is what the male doctor said, and Nick concurred, as if he really knew how perfect it was. Also, once again the epidural had not arrived in time, so Lauren had had a natural, drug-free birth. Once again, Nick had escaped to a spot behind his wife's shoulders to miss the grand reopening of the Lauren store. This time she noticed he had moved, most likely because she had overheard him telling the story of Tyler's birth and his positioning in the room at the time. She could care less. Mom and baby were just fine, and it seemed that the entire nursing staff, but especially the veterans, stopped by with their congratulations.

The Finch's were now complete as a family, but there was so much more to come.

CHAPTER

17

Traveling The Galaxy and Never Leaving The County

The distance between West Palm Beach, the county seat of Palm Beach County, and the North County town of Jupiter is about twenty miles as the crow flies, whereas the distance from the planet Earth to the planet of Jupiter in our galaxy is about three hundred sixty-five million miles, depending on the time of year and the planets' respective positions of rotation around our sun. One is very close, and the other is very far away. The two are different from one another in many ways, but they do have some similarities. In a strange way, the same comparison works for the Palm Beach County towns of West Palm and Jupiter—so close and yet so far.

After the birth of Melody that late October, life tried to get back to normal, if such a thing is possible with a small child and infant in tow. Nick knew one thing: he had to give up being the athletic director of Forest Hill. He was not going to be a part-time father as he had witnessed more than one coach who, because of the hours at night, experienced negative consequences such as divorce and antisocial problem children. Most of all, it just was not fair to Lauren, who worked all day and then would come home only to see her husband leave her to go back to school, thereby leaving her with the brood to tend to all by herself. She told him it was his decision, but Nick knew it was the right thing to do.

Right before the Thanksgiving break, he went to see his boss, Principal Carlos Martinez, and hand in his letter of resignation, effective as soon as possible. Carlos, now a close friend, understood but selfishly held out hope that Nick, with his love for high school sports and for his alma mater, would continue to lead his athletic department. Carlos reluctantly accepted Nick's resignation and surprisingly said that this letter would help him at home as his wife had been nagging him about the hours kept by his AD, saying how unfair it was to a working mom and young family. Maybe she would lay off him now. Carlos made one more counterproposal, suggesting he hire two more assistant athletic directors to relieve Nick from night game duty, but Nick declined, informing his boss he would be there whenever they needed any other sort of help, including with interviewing or serving as a fill-in, but that he could no longer do his duties as AD if he wanted to show good faith to his wife and children.

Nick's last day as athletic director would the Friday before the Christmas break. Carlos hoped to announce his replacement at the annual Christmas—now renamed holiday—party. Nick would be picking up two new classes to return to a full teaching load of five and would remain the chairman of the social studies department.

For purposes of remaining truly objective, Nick recused himself from any interview of a staff member or someone he knew. He secretly wished for certain candidates to get the job, and once during cafeteria duty whispered in Carlos's ear his recommendation of Woodrow "Woody" George. Ten years older than Nick, Woody was also an alumnus of Forest Hill and had served as a lifetime coach for many sports, both female and male. He also sometimes sponsored the senior class and even the student government association or student council. A driver's ed teacher, he did not have to worry about AP exams or grading essays. Nick had gone into his class a couple of times and saw that Woody made driver's ed both interesting and funny. When you think about it, along with first aid, driver's ed makes more practical sense than does teaching how to solve for *x* in algebra or talking about dead presidents in US history. Truth be known, Woody really had wanted the AD job when Nick got it and had been selected by Joe Peachstone, who now was the principal of Jupiter High School. Peachstone had taken a boatload of Falcons up north with him. That hurt Woody.

The week of the big announcement, Carlos pulled Nick aside and showed him a piece of paper on which he had scribbled the name Woody. Nick looked at it expressionlessly and nodded with approval, then the principal tore it up and put it into the cafeteria garbage can, along with all the wrappers, cartons, and other debris. The cafeteria itself, and the school in general, was recovering from two sudden resignations on the first day of school back in August. Both the head custodian and the data processor had quit and left town together in the middle of the night. Apparently the two had secretly been lovebirds and wanted to start their stalled lives over. This was news to both their spouses, and the school was left without the woman who printed up all the schedules and such and the man who kept the building clean. It was a school-centered scandal that had everyone talking. Even the gossip hens had had no clue beforehand. It took about a month for adequate replacements to shore the place up.

Wednesday was the night of the holiday party next door at the country club. The school ring and supply man picked up the bar tab, and the cafeteria women catered the event. Nick picked up Lauren and brought his two children, a breach in protocol, as it was really frowned upon to bring children to the event, even though it was not an official sponsored evening where there was alcohol. The couple would show off their children, but especially the new arrival, as almost no one had yet seen Melody, who now was called Mel by family and friends. Mrs. Martinez doted on the children and told Nick she was very glad of the decision he had made. Lauren concurred. After about twenty minutes at the party, Lauren took the children home for bedtime. Nick remained. He would get a ride home from Coach Scott Clark.

About an hour into the festivities, Mr. Martinez took the microphone in hand, welcomed everyone, said a few other nice things, and called Nick up to the microphone to receive a gift from Carolos and the athletic department. Nick opened it. It was an old-fashioned letterman's jacket with white leather arms, a navy-blue body, and red stitching that read:

> Nick Finch
> Athletic Director
> Forest Hill High Falcons

Nick was stunned and overwhelmed by the selection. It looked as if it had come right out of the late fifties, something that would be worn at the legendary "Hut" Drive-In on Flagler Drive from an earlier, simpler time. Nick was a history teacher, so it was perfect. Now if the weather would just get cold enough so he could wear it. He still has it today. Next, Carlos announced to the staff the new athletic director, "Woody" George. The group gave a round of hearty and polite applause, and then it was back to the bar.

Coming back from Christmas break, Nick learned he now had two senior-level government classes, one of which was mostly made up of his previous year's students from APUSH, or AP US History, and the other of which was a regular class made up of seniors who had beaten many odds and were ready to graduate. These were two different classes, yet each was made up of students who had the same goal of getting out of high school and moving on with their lives, some going to college and some entering the workforce. Nick loved both his new classes. And he thought it was great to get home at three o'clock. He would pick up the baby, while his wife would fetch Tyler, who was right next door to her bank at a special preschool that was started by a group known as the Crippled Children's Society of Palm Beach but now went by a much more inclusive name: the Palm Beach Rehabilitation Center. Island pull had gotten Tyler and the little girl of one of Sandy's secretaries, Molly, into the program, which operated with a fifty-fifty approach: 50 percent of the class had some sort of physical disability, while the other 50 percent were physically fine. The facilities were state of the art and included an indoor swimming pool. Tuition was incredibly low thanks to wealthy Palm Beach Island benefactors and fundraisers. The fact that Lauren was right next door was another incredible benefit. Many times, either she or Tammy went over to the center for lunch, or they brought the two preschoolers back to the office. Tyler and Molly would attend school together every year right up until graduation. The two made the wire services with an impromptu picture in their little caps and gowns at the end-of-year "graduation" ceremony. It was first printed in the "*Shiny Sheet*" more properly known as the *Palm Beach Daily News*. From there it was picked up by the *Post*, and then the Associated Press got a hold of it and it was splashed across the country. That was cool.

A new car or, better yet, a new "truck" which in reality meant a sport utility vehicle, would be the Finch's next purchase. They were moving up in the world and in social circles, especially since Lauren was flying up the corporate ladder. They did their research and settled on a Land Rover, navy blue with captain's seats in the front and with plenty of legroom and cargo space for two adults, two children, and one-hundred-pound dog. It looked great. The Finch's looked as if they had arrived when they pulled in driving the "British Beast as Nick had nicknamed it. The "Beast" would soon earn another nickname. It looked great in the driveway, but it ran like shit. It often broke down. The service manager James knew the Finch's by first name. Hell, he knew their voices on the phone as he took down the address to which to send the tow truck. Everything was under warranty, but the Rover was junk, plain and simple. The breaking point came when Sandy took the children to Lion Country Safari for a "true African adventure right here in western Palm Beach County." Nick had gone once when he was little because his parents had gotten free admission tickets after listening to a real estate agent's pitch on buying land in what would become Wellington. J.W. sneered at the idea, saying there was no way anyone would buy land all the way out there. Oh, how wrong he was. Also, Walt Disney had wanted to buy in the area, seeking a prospective site for his dream of a theme park like Disneyland that he would go on to call Disney World, but the county commissioners turned him down. Orlando and Orange County jumped at the proposal, and as they say, the rest is history.

The idea of Lion Country is that you remain in your car and drive through the park, which is a re-creation of the native habitat of African animals, especially lions. They are the true attraction. The truth is that the lions, especially the male ones, move little and sleep most of the time. There are strict rules and regulations concerning safety and keeping your windows up because "you are now in Africa." As Lauren drove through the park with Tyler, a very small Melody, Molly, and Tammy, the vehicle began to lurch and then just quit. She kept turning the key, but nothing. Cars behind her were beeping and blowing their horns so much that they actually woke a couple of the males of the pride, who yawned and lay back down. The cars drove around and looked angrily at the two moms and three children, but then realized the predicament they were in. One guy rolled down his window and said he would notify the park, while another wished them good luck and Godspeed. The car was completely dead, but the hardwired phone worked, so Lauren called Nick, who had been golfing but now was home. He answered the phone and thought a crazy person had called him and hung up. The phone rang again, and then Nick discovered it was his wife—and she was pissed. Oh, was she pissed. After a stream of profanities, including the seldom-heard "F" word, and a guarantee that this piece of shit would be gotten rid of on Monday morning, she asked for the number of the dealer's service department. Nick thought about how James was really in for it. Nick gave her the number, which was on speed dial, if that tells you anything. James would have a tow truck there ASAP, along with a replacement car.

It was getting hot in the closed-up truck, and Lauren made an executive decision to crack her door, since there were no animals around her, for some fresh air. With no power, the windows were stuck in the up position. Mel now needed her diaper changed. The afternoon was going from bad to worse as the cabin smelled like a jobsite Porta Potty in the middle of summer.

The tow truck got there quickly—it must have come from a western zip code—but when driver first saw the location, he refused to go out because “there are man-eating lions out there.” He reluctantly changed his mind when two members of the staff said they’d follow him in a zebra-stripe-painted open-air jeep. One of the people in the jeep was the driver, and the other was armed with a rifle, providing security. They towed the vehicle back to the parking lot with everyone still inside. Once in the parking lot, the occupants were allowed out as the Land Rover was hoisted onto a flatbed for its trip back to West Palm Beach. Lauren called upon a new Florida law, the lemon law, and was ready to go to war with Land Rover of Palm Beach, but they surrendered when they saw she had kept all the documentation and that it was accompanied by letters from the bank president and Nick’s attorney and friend Brian Parker. A full refund was given later that week.

Nick picked out a “King Ranch” Ford F-150. The pickup truck was a four-door with a really neat interior that included a pop-down TV screen and DVD player for the back seat passengers. Best of all, it had a bed for cargo transportation, which he and Lauren would need as both agreed it was time to make the move to Jupiter. Recently, a neighbor and her dog had been run over and left for dead, so the fact that there were no sidewalks, which had always bothered them, became a more pressing matter. They looked at the positives and negatives of staying in

Lake Clarke Shores and made the decision to head north to the Lighthouse.

The theme park adventures did not end at Lion Country. No, Nick took his last trip to the "Happiest Place on Earth", Walt Disney World, which was also eventful for a couple of reasons. He had first gone to Disney even before it opened as there was a coming attraction building promoting the opening of the theme park located in Orlando J.W. and Charlene had decided to give it a look one summer on the way back from the cool mountains of North Carolina. In the building there was a short film narrated by Walt himself about what was to come to Florida, and it looked really neat. Included were the different sections and themes of the park, and the new rides with artists' renditions of what they would look like when completed. The one that fascinated the young Nick was the submarine adventure *20,000 Leagues.* He could not wait to ride on that. When it did come, it was disappointing as hell, as overrated as teenage sex. You think it is going to be great, but guess what? It is quick, loud, and overpriced, like a prom night. One of Nick's fraternity brothers and Melody's godfather from Mississippi, Paul Watts, would be coming down to Disney, and the Watts' wanted to know if the Finches would like to join them. Sandy knew this might one of the few times she could convince her bah-humbug husband to join her and their kids for a trip to the Magic Kingdom. Nick thought about it and looked back and said, "Sure, why not?"

The kids applauded with a "Yay! And daddy's going to come too!" It was now obvious to Nick that Lauren and Paul's wife, Susan, had been planning on this since last fall in the Grove, when the families tailgated together before and after an Ole Miss football game. At Disney, the two families enjoyed the day riding the rides, meeting the characters, and waiting and waiting and waiting in line. They loved it. Exhausted, they went back to their rooms at the Contemporary Hotel, and after the kids were down, Paul and Nick went down to the Boardwalk section of the park—as Nick put it, "the big boys' theme park." This was where the bars and restaurants were. The wives stayed behind, tired, and exhausted because, really, they'd done all the work and parenting in the July heat of Orlando. In the past Nick would have suggested Church Street Station, which was a myriad of bars in the downtown section of Orlando, the featured places being a throwback saloon named Rosie O'Grady's and a sing-along piano bar called Howl at the Moon. When Disney opened its adult section on the park premises, it was a knockout punch to the downtown area of Orlando. Too bad because it was really fun there.

Nick and Paul spent most of their time at the ESPN club watching the Braves and the Cardinals play baseball. They were getting old—or was it they were getting mature and growing up? Nah, the next morning would prove they weren't. The following day, the moms organized a character breakfast over in the EPCOT section, which was like a year-round World's Fair theme park. Nick had gone to the World's Fair when it was in Knoxville, Tennessee, having decided to do so because of all the stories he had heard about it after his parents had gone to the one in New

York City. Honestly, Nick thought the South Florida Fair, next to the Palm Beach County Prison and Stockade, was better than the Knoxville experience.

The hostess who seated the two families at their table was Mary Poppins; the busboys were the Seven Dwarfs (that has probably changed now given today's climate); and the two waitresses were Snow White and Jasmine, and were of college age, probably students at one of the community colleges or the University of Central Florida. Most likely they were drama or theater majors, but whatever the case may have been, they were extremely attractive and looked just like the characters they were portraying. The entire staff stayed in character, and the busboys even "whistled while they worked" Mary Poppins could have been a voice coach for Julie Andrews. Impressive, but things went downhill fast from there.

The two queens took the table's orders from a limited menu, but they seemed to linger around the two dads with their intoxicating smiles and voices. The two fraternity brothers sat together, as did the wives at the other end of the table, for adult conversation. The kids laughed and cut up like little ones who are excited tend to do. The fathers' conversation became even more adult, and the queens seemed to enjoy it. Jasmine seductively asked Nick if there was anything else she could do, and she did so with a smile, while Snow White, standing beside her, giggled in a cute high-pitched voice. They were either enjoying adult banter or working for a good tip, or most likely both.

Nick said, "Yes, there is something you two could do, and that would be to sit on our laps and kiss each other like you mean it."

Jasmine, without missing a beat, and staying in character, replied, "Oh, I do not think Miss Poppins would like that." She smiled and walked away with the orders. The two queens were laughing out loud, and when they turned around, they both winked. The two moms both saw that. The death stare coming from the other end of the table looked more as if it had come from *Star Wars* than Disney. The children were oblivious to the crude request from the person who was entrusted with other people's children daily, but everyone would find out soon enough.

Mary Poppins came over after talking to her queens, and she was not laughing or giggling. She asked the two men to stand up from the table and told them that they had been "very naughty boys" and they needed to "go to their rooms—right now." Nick looked at Paul and then back at Mary and thought the character thing was going a bit too far now. But she meant it, and the two men had to leave the dining area and wait outside. They were being thrown out of a Disney establishment in front of their families. As the two filed out, the staff, made up to look like characters from various movies and cartoons, were all laughing. Some were giving the two banished dads a thumbs-up. Both Snow White and Jasmine winked and mouthed, "So sorry. Bye." Mary Poppins must have been a real bitch.

Nick and Paul found an empty bench outside the restaurant and looked at each other, wondering what had just happened. Looking at the two disgraced fraternity boys through the window was none other than Mary Poppins, who was shaking both her head and her index finger in disgust. The discipline did not end there as both wives were none too happy and let their husbands know it.

Although this was not a great moment or example of Nick's life or his parenting skills, when he looks back on it, he thinks it makes for a great story to have been disciplined by none other than Mary Poppins after flirting with two fictional queens. It became folklore. "Hey, how 'bout it!"

The other unfortunate event that day could have been much worse if it were not for Lauren. When Nick found out that Paul was renting a car that was just sitting in a parking lot while he was being charged a daily rate, he suggested he take it back to the rental car place at the airport because Disney offered a free shuttle to Orlando International Airport. Why pay a hefty fee for the car to sit idle? Plus, this would allow the two men to leave the park for an hour or so. *Escape* might be a better word. The moms agreed, saying the boys should call them when they returned to meet up to share in more of the "fun". When Nick and Paul returned and had their parking ticket scanned, the attendant immediately told the two to pull over to a special parking place. There, seated in a golf cart, were two security officers, who told the two dads to get into the cart and come with them. Judging by their body language, it seemed a serious situation, and it could have been, but Supermom Lauren saved the day. Apparently while people were boarding a transport bus to go from the hotel to the Magic Kingdom, the bus driver never looked up into his mirror that reflected his passengers in the seating section, because if he had, he would have noticed Mel was not all the way in. She was still waving goodbye to an employee dressed as "Goofy". The driver shut the automatic doors—one in the front and one in the back—and Mel's head got stuck between the two shutting doors in the back. Then the bus pulled away. Passengers screamed and hollered for the driver to stop, but apparently, because he was wearing headphones, the driver could not hear the pleas. "Goofy" broke into a sprint and began to beat on the side of the bus as the little girl's head was still outside, while the rest of her body, including her flailing arms, was all over the place. They say there are documented cases of impossible feats of strength and power performed under duress, and "Supermom" Lauren performed one of these feats. There is no way a housewife, even a past star soccer player turned banker, should have been able to pry those doors apart, but she did. Then Susan Watts grabbed Mel and pulled her back in. The driver, at about the same time, realized the near-tragic event taking place and pulled over. Melody had marks on both sides of her neck and was rattled, but she did not cry a tear. The rest of the riders, after applauding the rescue, began to berate the driver. He was replaced. In an instant, medical personnel and other Disney staff pulled up, along with the two fathers, who had now arrived on the scene. They were filled in on what had happened, and Nick was none too pleased. Lauren was sitting down, exhausted both mentally and physically. A doctor checked Mel out and pronounced her A-OK. Then there was a battery of liability papers to sign off on. As a reward, both families were given Fast Passes to all the rides—no more walking, but personal golf cart transportation with a guide—and were upgraded to the Grand Floridian Hotel with their room being comped. This might have been a precursor to just how tough Nick and Lauren's daughter would grow up to be. A few years later, Mel would enter the world of equestrian competition, and even as a little girl, she showed no fear of the two-thousand-pound animal as it leaped over fences and faux-brick barricades.

Another event that occurred was kind of a combination of the one that occurred in preschool, something from the TV, and in a way the ones that had happened at the theme park. In the time leading up to Tyler's fifth birthday, Lauren came up with an idea for something that would make his day. Both parents noticed how much their young son enjoyed the syndicated children's adventure show *Power Rangers.* Nick liked it—anything had to be better than *Barney*—and in certain ways it was like two of his favorites growing up, *Jonny Quest* and *Speed Racer.* It was exciting and manly, at least according to Nick Finch. Lauren had gotten a phone number from another mother, who had gotten it from yet another mother, for an acting agency that would send an actual thespian to the home or the preschool of a young person and, while in character, help celebrate that young person's birthday. Lauren called and found out the agency did have an actor who could portray the Blue Power Ranger. So, the event was booked and ready to go. On July 3, Tyler's birthday, Nick arrived in the parking lot of the Palm Beach Rehabilitation Center just as Lauren and Tammy were coming from next door with a cake and other supplies in a cooler with wheels. Now whoever it was who came up with the idea of putting wheels on coolers should receive the Presidential Medal of Freedom, as he or she sure as hell deserves it more than some hack retiring politician. Just then, a man pulled up and seemed to be in a rush as he emerged from a beaten-up Toyota Camry. He was wearing blue tights and white boots but was topless, at least until he finished putting on the costume. Nick was seated on the tailgate of his new truck and watched in amazement as the actor prepared for his role. The one thing Nick could not get over was how overweight and out of shape the Ranger was. His stomach was flabby and had rolls. He struggled to put his getup on. He was parked right next to Nick's F-150. The two moms took all the party favors in. What an advantage it was to work right next door. Nick, unable to help being Nick, just had to say something to the actor whom he was paying to perform. Smirking at the guy, Nick said, "Looks like the Power Ranger needs a little more gym time."

The Ranger, now in complete costume except the helmet, never looked up but delivered a comeback that was right to the point. "Fuck you, asshole. And you aren't any Slim Jim yourself."

Nick answered, still smirking, "You are right, my friend. And break a leg." Nick had gained some extra pounds from a combination of no longer coaching, parenting, being exhausted, and consuming beer and chicken wings. Point taken. The actor went into the classroom to the roar of the students and pressed play on his boom box to begin the show's theme song. The kids never noticed the physical shape of their special visitor; what they saw was that the

Blue Power Ranger was there to save the day for any and all. It was one of Tyler's favorite birthdays, and his mom and an out-of-shape actor had made it happen. Bravo!

Once Nick was back at work, Principal Carlos Martinez called him into the office and informed him, after having him agree to a strict rule of confidentiality, that he would be leaving at the end of the school year to take a job as a district administrator in the south end, closer to Boca Raton, where he lived with his wife and daughter. The offer was too good to turn down—less travel, fewer hours, and better pay—but he did say he would miss the students and certain members of his faculty, especially the ones he had hired, mostly young female teachers and, of course, Nick. They were more than colleagues or school site educators but were trusted friends. In fact, Carlos offered Nick a job, inviting him to follow him to the district office, which he said he could make happen. But Carlos knew his former athletic director and department chair did not have a lot of respect for educators who did not work directly with kids. Add to this the fact that Nick was selling his house and moving to the North County, and it was a polite, "No, but thank you for the offer."

Carlos was not finished. He recommended that Nick move on because he was foreseeing a potential personality conflict with the new principal, whose name Carlos was not at liberty to divulge. "Nick, you need to leave here. You have done all you can here, and I don't want to see you get down and become discouraged, which I think you will with the new administration. I have called the North County superintendent, and he has placed calls to Dwyer,

Jupiter, and Gardens high schools. Other than needing to do a formal interview, it is your choice. If you are moving up there, well, that is just another reason for you to leave. Think about it and let me know."

The year 1999 turned into 2000. With the new millennium, the predicted crisis of Y2K never happened. Yet Palm Beach County became the center of the political universe with the presidential election, George Bush vs. Al Gore, from November straight through to January. We all learned about hanging chads, and the recount began in downtown West Palm. Local restaurants and bars loved it as the press, provocateurs, and professional demonstrators from both sides all needed food and drink, especially when the TV cameras were off. Nick felt sorry for the local supervisor of elections, Theresa Lapore, as she seemed to be getting destroyed by both sides. Nick guaranteed at least 75 percent of Palm Beach County residents had no idea who their supervisor was before the election, but now everyone knew her. The Cardinal Newman graduate was front and center, and the outrage was ridiculous. The rent-a-riot crowd and an army of lawyers arrived from out of town to do battle for the right to be the forty-third president of the United States. The Supreme Court would later rule in a 5–4 decision that George Bush of Texas would be the next president. West Palm went back to being normal—well, as much as West Palm can be normal.

After Nick had shared his conversation with Carlos with Lauren, they concurred it was time to move on. Lauren would be leaving First Union, to be named president of Dover Banking and Trust, better known as DBT. Some people wondered if the *D* stood for the capital of Delaware, Dover, or for the power family of the area, the du Ponts. Who cared? Lauren Finch was now one of the highest-ranked females in the entire industry, and her entire family and her many peers were enormously proud of her and her accomplishments once her promotion was announced. She would have offices on the Treasure Coast, in the Gardens, in Boca, and of course on Palm Beach. There would be some travel, but most of it would be car travel, with occasional trips up north. Nick agreed it was time to leave. He called around to the three schools he wanted to look at, and they all recommended Jupiter. For one thing, there was already a contingent of former Forest Hill staff there from when Joe Peachstone had left Forest Hill to become the principal of Jupiter. Hank Gibbs was there as a guidance counselor; Larry Timmons was there, no longer as AD but as a weight room instructor; Walker Roberts was a roving dean of students; Carl James was there teaching English; and Margret Baldwin remained as a North County counselor for troubled youths in the north end—and Jupiter was one of her schools on rotation. An interview was set up with the principal of Jupiter, which was not Joe Peachstone, as he had retired and moved to South Georgia, but was his replacement, a former Spanish teacher turned administrator named Gloria Nunez. Assisting in the interview would be Vice Principal Barbara Benitez.

Nick had always worked for men, so this was new, but he found out a few things about his interviewers. Dr. Nunez was Cuban and was part of the first generation to have fled the island in order to start over in South Florida.

She was no CAP, or Cuban American Princess. She had cut her teeth as a student, teacher, and early administrator at Twin Lakes, which was no walk in the park. Barbara Benitez, despite the fact that her name sounded Latino, was not Latino but Middle Eastern, Lebanese to be exact, and she, like Nick, was a south end West Palm kid who had graduated from Forest Hill. The two would become very good friends as Nick would teach her daughter Angie and host an engagement party for the young woman at his Jupiter home.

Nick thought about his interview, and even though he had been told it was a done deal as the Forest Hill expatriates had all personally put in a good word for him with the principal, he was worried because he had never had a real interview before. Bobby Newcombe "interviewed" him while trimming shrubs at his house, and the jobs of athletic director and department head had simply been handed to him. Nick had always been on the other side of the interview table. This was different and a little uncomfortable. He was a little bit nervous as he walked into the principal's private office. His former boss Joe Peachstone, now retired, had called him to tell him the way to get the job was to go through the principal's office, and the way to get to that office was to go through the principal's secretary Diana Jaymes. Mrs. Jaymes had been Mr. Peachstone's secretary and she protected him and the office better than any guard dog could have. Nick had met her a few times at functions when Forest Hill and Jupiter staffs were together, mostly a happy hour or after a game between the two schools. It was apparent that one simply should not mess with her. She was a fitness freak and, in her fifties, looked to be in her thirties. She taught all kinds of fitness classes at the night school.

Nick arrived fifteen minutes early and reintroduced himself to Mrs. Jaymes, who smiled and asked him to take a seat. One by one, all his former colleagues, now on staff, dropped by the office to say hello and wish him luck. It was a nice gesture, but it was getting embarrassing.

At four o'clock sharp, he was called into the office. He took a seat in front of the big desk behind which Dr. Nunez sat. In a chair with a notepad and pen sat Barbara Benitez. Dr. Nunez opened the meeting with, "I see you know a lot of my staff. And I will say you come well recommended. But tell me a little about yourself." After that came a couple of other questions about what Nick believed were his strengths and what he could bring to the Warriors to make Jupiter Community High School even better.

Barbara Benitez passed on asking any questions. Her comment was, "I already think I know Nick from all I have heard and the fact, though I am not sure he knows it, that he taught three of my nieces and nephews." Nick had not known that, but when she shared their names, he immediately recognized his former students, having had no idea they were related to his future boss and friend. Then came a curveball when the principal asked Nick to stand and give his go-to lesson as if the two administrators were students in his US history class. Nick got up and, after about three seconds, jumped right into the Bay of Pigs fiasco, the Cuban Missile Crisis, the results of US foreign policy, the

Cold War, and the impact on South Florida. One should always know one's audience. Nick explained the bravery of the Cuban freedom fighters; mentioned that the United States had abandoned them in their hour of need against the "Butcher of Cuba," Fidel Castro; discussed how close the world had come to a nuclear Armageddon; and concluded by saying that South Florida had been changed forever because of events just ninety miles from its shores.

The principal and the assistant principal smiled and nodded approvingly. They told Nick they would be in touch with him, but he hadn't even made it to his truck when Barbara Benitez ran to the visitors' parking lot and shouted, "You are hired! Welcome to Jupiter." Barbara would later tell Nick it was a done deal before his interview but that his lesson on Cuban American history hade really impressed the boss. In fact, she had told her that Nick taught it better than a Cuban could.

Oh, hell yeah. He was now a Warrior, but this meant he would have to say goodbye to the place where he had spent more than twenty years as a student, a teacher, a coach, an administrator, and a department chair. And that would not be easy. He had a lot of memories of 6901 Parker Avenue.

Nick announced to his department, his other colleagues, and his students he would be leaving at the end of the year and going to Jupiter. He found himself relating to the two classes of seniors he had since both he and they would be moving on and changing their lives. Packing up each and every day, he was juggling moving jobs and house hunting up in the North County. He was lucky to have Randy doing some house hunting and ground research for him.

Add to this the fact that Nick and Lauren had found a buyer for the Lake Clarke home more quickly than expected. It was a former student from Nick's first year teaching who now was a dad and a veterinarian on Palm Beach. Even though things were moving at warp speed, Nick did find himself, while boxing up yearbooks, taking the time to look through them and see the pictures of his former students and staff. They had all played a part in his life, and he was grateful for them, but he knew it was time to move on.

Two high school names caught his attention, and for completely different reasons. One was one of his best students, and the other was the worst young person he had ever had as a student. Back in the mid-eighties, Nick had a student in his honors US history class named Edward Sean Murphy, or Eddie. Eddie was from Wellington and seemed to have come from a comfortable lifestyle. A transfer or transplant student from the eastern part of Long Island, somewhere near the Hamptons, Eddie had come from privilege. Forest Hill at the time drew from all three socioeconomic groups: the wealthy, who were from the South Flagler area, with a few from Palm Beach Island and Wellington; the middle class, which group made up most of the school, mostly from the south end of West Palm but some from Wellington; and the lower middle class, the majority of whom came from the inner city of West Palm Beach. It really was a perfect bell-shaped curve, and the majority of the students, faculty, and staff made it work. Nick learned to believe that 95 percent of students are created bad or antisocial, but this was because of outside factors such as environment and bad parenting or else no parenting at all. A child brought up in an overcrowded and underfunded foster home surrounded by other troubled teens unfortunately would emerge from his or her teen years troubled. Not all the time, but a lot. The remaining 5 percent, for whatever reason, were split between having some sort of biological or chemical basis for their behavior and being just plain bad, and in the worst case, evil. Eddie Murphy fell into this last group. Upon his retirement, when Nick was asked who his best student had been, he could not name just one but indicated there was an ever-changing "top ten". When he was asked who his worst student had been, he did not hesitate in naming Eddie Murphy. Eddie had not grown-up dodging bullets in Pleasant City, Cherry Hill, or Belle Glade, but living a life of privilege in a wealthy enclave of Long Island. He'd grown up among the people who wintered on Palm Beach, golfed at the exclusive Seminole Country Club in Juno Beach, or competed in either polo or other equestrian sports in Wellington. He'd been raised by his mom because his dad, a hedge fund manager on Wall Street, had divorced the mother of his only child in favor of a new "flavor." Having received a nice settlement, Mrs. Murphy headed to one of her favorite places: Wellington. She was well known among the equine jetsetters and rode every day. She also had a staff to take care of her prize ponies before, during, and after her daily rides. Instead of parenting, Mrs. Murphy bought Eddie anything he wanted, probably failing to give him motherly love. After the move to South Florida, Jordan Murphy enrolled her child at Saint Andrew's in Boca Raton, thinking that if he boarded there, it would free up more time for her. Nope. Eddie was told to leave within two months, so Jordan Murphy took her son to King's Academy, another private school, this one based on strict Protestant discipline. That did not work out as Eddie was expelled this time within a month. If anyone was screaming for help with his antisocial behavior, it was Eddie, but instead of helping him, his mom now tried plan C, which was to enroll him at Riverside Military Academy in Gainesville, Georgia. Military schools fill a need by preparing kids for life in the military, extending a family legacy, or instituting much-needed self-discipline.

The wealthy single mom dropped off her child in north Georgia after telling him, actually tricking him, that they were headed up there for fun at Six Flags, but in reality, she was implementing plan C. As she drove away from the campus, smiling, she looked back at the shell-shocked adolescent, who was giving her the finger with both hands held high. *Their problem now,* she thought. A day later she pulled into her combination home and horse farm in Wellington and waiting for her on the couch was none other than Eddie. Apparently, Eddie had jumped the fence, gone over to the interstate, and gotten himself onto the southbound lane, where he used another finger, this time his thumb, and within minutes had gotten his first ride back home, arriving before she did. Out of options, Mrs. Murphy was left to—gasp—public school, so for Eddie it was off to Crestwood Middle School for his eighth-grade year. His social studies teacher was none other than Mr. Raymond Wade! Ray will tell stories of this uncontrollable and irredeemable student he had. He called him "Son of

Satan." Nick found it hard to believe that Ray, or anyone for that matter, could not handle an eighth grader. Nick would find out for himself in three years.

On the first day of Eddie's junior year, he came into Nick's class five minutes late even though he was not a new student and knew his way around the campus. But he also knew that the policies against tardiness did not kick in until week two of classes. He slithered to the back of the room, where he found an open seat, and immediately put his head down on the desk and went to sleep. Nick walked by and "accidently" kicked Eddie's desk to wake him and explain that sleeping in class would not be tolerated.

One of Nick's softball players in class pleaded with Nick after class, "Please let Eddie sleep. It will be better that way." That was the first day, and it would go downhill from there. Every day there was a different type of confrontation between Nick and Eddie.

Nick tried everything, and nothing worked. Finally, he took the insolent young man outside and, looking up and down the hall to make sure there were no witnesses, grabbed Eddie Murphy by the front of the shirt and pushed him forcefully against the wall. He said, "Listen to me, you arrogant little shit. I cannot do anything here, but I will see you out after school hours, and I swear, your ass is mine. Got it?" The young man had a different look on his face, and it was not the wiseass *You can't do anything to me* expression, but one of fear and shock. This strategy seemed to work, at least for a week or so, but Eddie realized that the teacher really could not do anything and resumed acting like the jerk or prick he really was.

Football star and senior Howard Toney heard that his favorite teacher was in a predicament. Because this teacher, Coach Finch, had always been there for him, he decided to use his brand of "Pleasant City Counseling" one night at a party. The All-American high school football player, waiting until Eddie went outside to the keg, followed him to the patio. The others outside quietly and quickly left the area, going either to the front yard or back inside, so it was just Howard and Eddie. Eddie was not dumb, just the opposite, as his standardized test scores were off-the-charts high and he had passed every high school test with high grades. Homework, he did not do, so most of the grades on his report cards were Cs, with conduct grade of 1. With conduct grades, 1.4 is the highest and 1 indicates that one's behavior is detrimental to one's own and one's peers' ability to learn. C-1 was the grade on Eddie Murphy's annual report card. From what had gotten back to Nick, Howard Toney had taken Eddie Murphy "behind the woodshed" for some "one-on-one peer counseling". This too seemed to work for a few weeks, but as Ray Wade would say, "Satan's child is back, isn't he?" Ray was enjoying the fact that his friend had to go to hell every day with this student. Ray would ask Nick to just imagine what it had been like for him with Eddie's eighth grade hormones factored in. A parent conference was called by the staff of all Eddie's teachers and the principal as it seemed the five other teachers were also sick and tired of the behavior, which was getting worse, if such a thing were possible.

Eddie had a girlfriend for a while. Nick hoped that the beauty could tame the beast, so to speak, but that relationship ended and the girl's parents withdrew her and put her in another school for her own safety.

In the principal's conference room, the participants each took a chair, including Jordan Murphy, her son, and some well-dressed man.

Maybe Mrs. Murphy had a new man who could provide some sort of a fatherly influence? Nah., He introduced himself as the family attorney, saying that any and all questions or inquiries should be addressed to him and him only as he had instructed the mother and son to remain silent. The faculty members and guidance counselor looked at each other in disbelief, the guidance counselor later saying that in her forty years she had never seen anything like that. Mr. Martinez did not take kindly to having his office turned into a lawyer's office for some sort of strange deposition. When he tried to ask the mom something, the lawyer interrupted him and scolded him, adding something about not following directions. That is when the meeting ended. For the remainder of the year, nothing really changed, and for his senior year, Eddie was to be on campus for three morning classes, the minimum permitted by state law, and then leave for a work experience program. Eddie's job was working with the company that took care of his mother's stable and barn, so he never really worked with the spirit of the class. Nobody cared as he was not on campus.

About two years later, Nick opened the *Palm Beach Post* and found in the local section, on page B-1, a headline that read: "Local Wellington Man Charged with First-Degree Murder / Hate Crime." The article went on to say: "Edward Murphy, twenty-one, of Wellington, was arraigned and made his first appearance at the Palm Beach County Courthouse, where he entered a plea of not guilty in the beating death of fifty-one-year-old Ashton "Ash" Simpson of Palm Beach. Mr. Murphy was also charged with an additional felony, a hate crime, as Mr. Simpson was targeted because he was gay." Apparently, Eddie's new job was hustling gay men whom he would target and pick up at some of the local gay bars. He would act interested, leave with them, beat them, and take their money. That answered a lot of questions for Nick as he had always thought that an underlying reason for Eddie's attitude was possibly his conflicted sexuality. Seeing as he was extremely handsome and worked out daily, gay men were attracted to him, no different from older men being attracted to hot-looking younger women, like maybe queens named Snow White or Jasmine. Now if only Jordan Murphy was more like Mary Poppins.

At the hearing was the same lawyer who had come to the parent-teacher conference. What was his retainer fee? The case went to trial, and after only two hours of deliberation, the jury of twelve, made up of six men and six women, found Edward Murphy guilty on all counts. The pictures the prosecutors showed the jury of the beaten man were not of a robbery gone wrong, but the work of a deranged murderer. The judge, also with the jury's input and testimonials from both sides, sentenced Edward Sean Murphy to die in Florida's electric chair ("Old Sparky" to Floridians). The state later switched methods to lethal injection, but Edward Sean Murphy still resides in Starke,

Florida, at the state penitentiary, awaiting the needle thirty-two years later. So sad.

On the opposite side of the spectrum was Jennifer Lapinsky, who was perfect in almost every way. *Smart*, *cute*, *attractive*, *polite*, and *talented* are a small sampling of the adjectives that could be used to describe Jennifer. She was also a student in Nick's US history class at Forest Hill in the early nineties and was lead singer in the award-winning touring choral group "Dimension 20". This group was Forest Hill's pride and joy as they sang for store openings, ribbon cuttings, and inaugurations of both governors and presidents. They were that good. Jennifer, like Eddie, had been raised by a single mother. Her mother had moved to West Palm as a middle school chorus director from the area where New York and Ohio meet, where Nick had almost run over and killed the middle-finger-saluting Amish family. When Nick went to watch the group sing, he was stunned to see the cute ponytail-wearing student, who was dressed in an elegant black evening gown, take the microphone from her male sidekick, and blast out a Broadway show tune. The next morning, a Friday, it was Nick's turn to pick up the doughnuts from the local Dunkin' Donuts for the social studies class, and lo and behold the talented singer was behind the counter in a different uniform. With a smile, she filled the box with a variety of breakfast pastries, including a two extra for her "favorite teacher." After softball games when Nick returned to school to catch the last few innings of the varsity baseball game, Jennifer was always there cheering on her boyfriend, a first baseman and pitcher for the team. She was so good at English and had impeccable office schools that, truth be told, she edited and typed up Nick's master's thesis. When school officials visited from other districts, as required for recertification by the Southern Association of Colleges and Schools, Jennifer Lapinsky was their appointed guide. After they left, she would remain and type up the day's notes and observations. Every one of the visitors was very impressed by her. A couple just could not believe she was student and not an employee of the district. Toward the end of her senior year, Nick asked her if she would be interested in working for a new law firm that his best friend Brian Parker, who had left the State's Attorney's Office for private practice, was starting up. He gave her Brian's number, and sure enough there was no more slinging doughnuts and coffee for Jennifer. She was off to the legal world, even if it was only to file papers and answer phones.

There was not TGI Fridays in Jupiter, where Nick and Brian would hook up for drinks. They no longer went to "Beefeaters" but to a place on Village Boulevard called "John Bull". At first the young lawyer bragged to Nick about how good Jennifer was and how thankful he was for the recommendation. While at his office one day, Nick saw a few pictures of the two together, one where they were deep-sea fishing and the other taken at some social function. Brian became kind of defensive when Nick inquired about the photos. Whatever, as Jennifer was off to Florida State after her two years at Palm Beach Junior College. Nick noticed Brian was going up to "Tally Town," his alma mater, a lot more for football games than he had in the past. Tallahassee is not an easy drive to make, especially a few times a month, but that was what Brian Parker was doing now. Nick began to wonder if there was a little something more there despite the eleven-year age difference between Brian and Jennifer. Nah. Well, maybe. If there was anything, Brian was tight-lipped about it. Nick was busy anyway as he was now courting Sandy. When Nick proposed to Lauren and asked Brian over drinks at "John Bull" to be his best man, Brian obviously replied he would be honored to do so. About a half hour later, Jennifer Lapinsky entered the bar and walked right up to Brian. She kissed him, not on the cheek, but right on the lips like a girlfriend would kiss her boyfriend. "It is time for you to know. And we appreciate you for not pestering me or us, because we both think you already knew."

Nick was speechless and yet incredibly happy for his best man and his best student. He could not stop grinning. All he had to say was, "Son of a bitch." Now that the cat was out of the bag, the four of them—Nick, Lauren, Brian, and Jennifer—were socially inseparable. Nick would be Brian's best man. He gave a much better best man's toast this time, but it still ended with, "Hey, how 'bout it!"

The guests, of course, responded in kind: "Hey, how 'bout it!" Most knew the story. Brian would be Tyler's godfather; the two of them are still close today. Nick would be the Parkers' first child Ellen's godfather, with whom he is still close. The two men were closer than any blood relatives growing up together and witnessing so many things, good and bad, and in one case both, namely, the episode of the Olympic wheelchair swimmer live in Miami.

Nick was finishing up the 1999 school year, preparing to move his professional career up to Jupiter High School as soon as his last official Forest Hill event was over, which was graduation for the Class of 1999. The seniors were already out and were now just waiting on their big day. The ceremony was to be held at the Kravis Center for the Performing Arts, a gorgeous new theater complete with state-of-the-art lighting and acoustics. The three public West Palm schools could use the facility—Forest Hill, Palm Beach Lakes, and the Dreyfoos School of the Arts, the last of which was new and loosely based on the Fame School of New York City, concentrating on the arts. It was public, kind of, but really private with enrollment often determined by a student's talent in the arts. Others seemed to make their way in despite limited art or music skills; instead, they had the right name or address. Now graduation is held for all schools at the Fairgrounds Expo Center in western Palm Beach County next to the stockade.

Graduation was to be held on a Thursday evening in the first week of June. On the preceding Sunday evening, Nick got a call from Carlos Martinez, as this was to be his last event at the school too before moving on to his district administrative job. Nick picked up. To this day he wishes he had not. Carlos started and stopped a good three times trying to deliver his first sentence. Nick could tell that his boss, one of the strongest men he had ever known, was about to break down. He asked, "What is it, boss?"

There was silence, and then Carlos Martinez summoned up the courage to say, "Eddie MacGregor is dead." Just then he broke down and starting sobbing on the other end of the phone line.

"Wait, what? Eddie? When? What happened? How?"

"He was murdered late Saturday night closing up the restaurant. They killed him for fifty dollars, dammit!"

There was silence again as the principal regained his composure. He went on to say that the valedictorian had been asked if he would fill in and close the restaurant as the manager who was scheduled for that shift had to go to a wedding. Eddie had given up his job at the restaurant about two weeks prior to prepare to head off to Harvard, where he had been awarded a full scholarship. Eddie MacGregor had been one of Nick's students. Nick had had the pleasure to teach him two years in a row, both for AP US History and, in his senior year, US government. Nick had written his letter of recommendation for the Harvard committee that would be interviewing him. Eddie was a National Merit Scholarship winner and had won just about every other thing you could think of. At awards night he would need a shopping cart or wheelbarrow to get all his prizes out to the car of his proud parents. He had set up a peer tutoring service for kids having trouble with the new state standardized test called the FACT, which was a requirement for graduation. His tutoring service was called "Skin the Cat". To say that this was all there was to Eddie MacGregor would be to sell him short, as he was one of the most genuine and peaceful people Nick would ever get to know.

Apparently, two desperate teenagers decided to rob the restaurant at a time when most of the employees had left and the manager was counting the cash. They bound

Eddie, who should not have even been there, using duct tape. For some reason, that was not enough for them, so one of the two went behind the future Harvard student and put a 9 mm slug into the back of his head. Both would blame each other at their respective trials, and both would be found guilty, but the damage had been done and the world would be forever deprived of a game changer—for a mere fifty dollars, a senseless act of cruelty.

Nick made his way to the family room, where Lauren was reading a story to both Tyler and Mel. She looked up to see her husband choking up at first and then just breaking down and sobbing like a little boy. "What happened? What is it?" She knew there was a death, but who had died? Nick wiped his tears away. Both children stared at their father as if they had never seen him before.

"Eddie MacGregor was murdered." Then Nick left through the back slider and went out to the dock on the lake, where he sat down and cried his eyes out. Lauren and the kids left him alone. Lauren had known the young man from an interview she had had with him for the Town of Palm Beach Future Leaders Society. After agreeing to recuse herself because of her husband's relationship with the applicant, she stayed and watched the young man wow the dais of questioners.

At graduation, the mood is usually exciting as a new group celebrate the event and get ready for their next step in life, but this night it was very somber. The first student seat where the valedictorian would have sat remained empty except for a class program and a single rose. The salutatorian, or number two in the class, made it through only half her speech before completely breaking down and having to be helped from the podium by Mr. Martinez and escorted to her seat right next to where Eddie would have been seated. Now it was time for the graduates to have their names read aloud, shake hands with the various dignitaries on the stage, get their diplomas, head back to their seats, and wait impatiently for the command to switch their tassels from one side to the other to signify graduation, then be done after the recessional. Cheers from families and friends accompanied the names when announced. Unbeknownst to almost everyone, including Nick, when the first name was read, which was always the valedictorian, it turned out to be Edward James MacGregor's. The crowd rose to their feet and then gasped as a little boy about seven years old in a miniature blue cap and gown emerged from behind the curtain offstage, walked forward, shook the hands, and received the diploma. It was his big brother's, and he was there to take it. There was a mixture of loud applause and sounds of weeping. It was the most emotional moment at a school event that Nick would ever witness.

Funny, those were the three Falcons who had come to mind when Nick was packing up: a fantastic woman who would become Aunt Jennifer to his family and one of his wife's best friends, and the "two Eddies" died, but only one literally. So sad. The recollections solidified for Nick that it was time for him to move to Jupiter High. He needed to buy a house quickly as his house had sold. He was lucky enough to be able to rent it for a few months, but they had to move fast and get a new home.

At the school, the new principal was on campus to meet her new staff. Out of respect for her and the school Nick knew so well, he decided to stop by and wish her luck. Carlos had already cleaned out the office and was already at his new office in Delray. Ms. Belue was behind her desk when Nick walked up to Mrs. Ryles, the principal's secretary, at her desk. The two had worked together for seventeen years and through three principals, Newcombe, Peachstone, and Martinez, and now she had another to break in. Nick said, "Well, Miss Judy, I guess this is it." The two hugged. He asked her, "Maybe I should introduce myself and wish her good luck." She gave him a hesitant look, but Nick walked over to the open door and knocked politely three times on the doorframe. Without going in, remaining at the door's entrance, he said, "Ms. Belue, I am Nick Finch. I know I am leaving to go up to Jupiter High, but I wanted to wish you good luck. This is a great place with great people. If there is anything I can do, please do not hesitate to ask."

She was head down in paperwork. When she got up, Nick noticed she was kind of boxy, square-like, like the kind of cardboard boxes refrigerators arrive in. She walked over to the door, looked up at Nick, and without saying a word shut the door right in his face. Nick stood there stunned with his entire body almost pressed against the closed door. Judy Ryles, who had seen the entire exchange, said, "I am so sorry. I really am."

Nick told her, "Not to worry. It wasn't you. But in a way, it does make it easier to leave." After the awful draining event of the murder and graduation, Nick's Forest

Hill career had ended this way. So be it. He drove over, picked up Mel, went home, hugged an expectant Clancy, and waited on his wife to come home with Tyler as he prepared dinner. He also made a pact with himself that he would never set foot on the Forest Hill campus ever again. Nobody was going to shut a door in his face at his school. It was no longer his school, Jupiter High was, and he swore never to look back. It would almost twenty years before he again stepped foot on the campus he had graduated from, taught at, and coached at. Change can be hard, but it can be good, and Nick would find out Jupiter was good. Very good.

Nick hated house hunting and house buying like he hated a trip to the dentist, but lucky for him he had his father-in-law, who not only was good at it but also enjoyed it. Nick and Lauren put him on a mission to find a new home, selling the idea by saying their new house that would be closer to the Whites' at PGA National and would be a place for their grandchildren to grow up—with sidewalks! Randy White got right on it, doing all the scouting like a soldier dropped behind enemy lines to map out the location for the upcoming battle. Soon he had a couple of options for Nick to look at, then Nick would relay the secret information to General Lauren. Or was it, Admiral Sandy? Nick scratched off a listing in Palm Beach Gardens that bordered on Lake Park. Nope, and for a couple of reasons, one being that it was kind of old and, after having left a house built in the late forties, they both wanted something more up to date. But Nick loved the attic as the owner proudly showed him that he had installed flooring. Nick made a mental note to do the same with whatever house he bought, and he ended up doing just that.

Next it was on to Jupiter. Randy had some listings to show him. Two listings were in a subdivision just north of Indiantown Road, which is the main thoroughfare for east–west travel, starting out west at the Bee Line Highway and ending at the Jupiter Beach Resort, you guessed it, at the beach. The road off Indiantown Road was Central Boulevard, and yes it was centrally located and bisected the town. Geography was not challenging in Jupiter as far as the street names went. The subdivision was called the Shores of Jupiter despite the fact that it was a good three or four miles from the shore and the area was in reality drained swampland, the water having come from the Loxahatchee River. Homes were on the new side. The students who lived there went to good schools, and the subdivision had sidewalks. It also had a homeowner's association, or HOA, which the Finch's had not had in Lake Clarke. The type of HOA and the dues one must pay can be a deal breaker. Horror stories of punitive HOAs with elected boards who get kickbacks from cable TV companies and have muscle-flexing power are legendary throughout the county, from condos on the beach to the South County's "Del Boca" section. The Shores' HOA seemed legit, and the dues one paid in exchange for the services seemed fair. The Shores deserved a visit from Lauren. The other place was also off Central Boulevard, but south of Indiantown, and was called Egret Landing. One thing that jumped out to Randy—and he relayed this fact to Nick, and then Nick relayed it to Lauren, the information moving up the cost-and-control ladder—was that there were at least five different builders and each brought a couple of models to select from so the place did not follow a cookie-cutter format where each house looked the same on the outside, one after another. Randy and Grace had lived in such a place in Palm City at the Monarch Country Club. A variety of shapes and sizes appealed to Nick. Also, good schools and sidewalks and a very fair HOA with relatively low quarterly dues were all pluses. Randy had picked out a couple of homes that were up for sale, but Nick and Lauren y also went to see the builders' model homes. At the end of the day, Nick's father-in-law recommended that the two pick the street and then pick the lot and sit down with the various builders to come up with *their* dream house. Nick agreed, but the time frame between moving out of his old house and into the new one was razor thin. Yet each builder said they could make it work. They lied. Maybe that is too strong a word. They stretched the truth, or as his kids would say, they fibbed. The house would not be completed on time.

That Saturday Nick took the kids and dropped them off with Grace, then Nick, Lauren, and Randy made their way to Jupiter. The first stop was "the Shores of Jupiter" except when pulling into the subdivision, they saw that some of the local teenagers had vandalized the brick-and-mortar welcoming wall, so instead of "the Shores of Jupiter" it read "the hores of Jupiter" as the kids had removed the ***"S"***. Nick laughed, Randy grinned, but Lauren was mortified and quickly let it be known that she was not going to make her home at the "the hores of Jupiter". No way and especially not with a daughter.

Nick sarcastically said, "But then again, Tyler might like it." Death stares as the comment went over, as J.W. used to say, "like a fart in church." So, it was on to Egret Landing—and Egret Landing it would be. The two agreed on a model they liked, but the price was really close to the top of their budget. Randy said not to worry as he and Grace would help with the incidental costs—and there were *always* surprise costs. They signed that afternoon. Lauren's bank connections helped in terms of getting the loan, and she and Nick had some cash from having sold the Pine Tree Lane home. Now for the builders to get going.

The Finch's had picked a lot on a quiet cul-de-sac toward the front of the subdivision across from the large recreational area with basketball and tennis courts, a swimming pool, a workout facility, and a field large enough that any high school would just love to have it for a practice facility. The two walked around as the surveyor marked the spots and staked out the property, but the thing they really noticed was the number of kids outside playing. All seemed to be in the same age group as Tyler and Mel. The Finches would find out that of the more than thirty homes in the subdivision, twelve of them were located on Scrubjay Lane. All the streets seemed to be named after native Florida birds. The *scrubjay*, a bird native to the Everglades and possibly threatened with extinction, would never make it past spell check on the computer, and phone operators up north had difficulty spelling the unique regional word. Nick would have the opportunity to teach at least eight of the children who lived on Scrub Jay Lane in his AP history class. In fact, it seemed a very large number of his students were neighbors from one of the other bird-named streets or lanes in Egret Landing. The Finch's had moved to small-town suburbia, and they liked it. The kids would have birthday parties shared with each other, and for one of Mel's, Lauren had ordered a traveling petting zoo to come to the house, complete with a variety of farm animals such as ponies, rabbits, and goats. One of the goats got loose and scrambled into the house. Most of the moms, donning the unofficial uniform of Egret, which was a tennis skirt outfit, froze or shrieked, but not Sandy's colleague Tammy, who had been raised on a farm in the bootheel of Missouri and now lived west of town in Jupiter Farms. Tammy raced right in, picked the goat up in her arms, and took her back outside. The Egret contingent shook their heads with amazement and in approval of the "farm girl" and her courage. Such is suburbia.

The problem for Nick and Lauren now was getting the builders to get to work on their homesite as there was a building boom in the north area and now contractors, rather than having entire crews working for them, just hired subcontractors to avoid the other costs that came with having employees, such as health insurance. The project fell farther and farther behind schedule, Nick noticed when he was taking a load of things every morning in his truck and transporting them up to a storage garage he had rented out in Jupiter. Every day after leaving Jupiter High, or JHS, he would swing by Scrubjay Lane and, yep, find no workers. Then he would call Lauren and vent. They did catch a break when one of Lauren's friends from the very beginning of her career bought a house in North Palm

Beach and still had three months left on her apartment lease. The apartment was in North Palm and had three very small bedrooms, but it would work. It had to.

So, the Finch's said goodbye to Lake Clarke Shores. Clancy was the first into Lauren 's car as he was making sure he would not be left behind. The family looked back with smiles and good memories, but they also looked forward to a new start twenty or so miles up the road, except for that three-month detour at the Uno Lago Apartment Complex in Juno Beach. That would be a savior. Uno Lago was located right next to the new Florida Power & Light corporate offices, and most of the tenants worked next to the FP&L campus. The power company had moved to northern Palm Beach County a few years earlier from Miami, and after Publix Supermarkets, it was the second-largest private employer in the state. It also seemed to help that the power company's office was located there, because during hurricanes there are a lot of factors concerning the restoration of power. Either way, it sure didn't hurt that such a company charged with electric power was a close neighbor. The Finch's would encounter three or four direct hurricane hits, the number depending later after the fact updates, but they would not be without power for more than four hours. Coincidence? Talking to others who had gone days without power, the Finch's realized they were blessed. One teaching peer went three weeks without power. His wife filed for divorce when the power came back on. Coincidence? The notification of that divorce really rocked Nick because, in the process, the person who was serving the papers had snuck onto campus just as the opening bell was ringing to blend in. After waiting for the halls to clear, he went to the teacher's room and entered, blindsiding the teacher in front of his class, then left smiling like the prick he was, saying sarcastically, "Have a great day." (Note that campus security is much tighter today after the Stoneman Douglas massacre down in Parkland.) It staggered the man, who swore he'd never seen it coming. He went outside his classroom. Nick watched as the grinning server walked past him, with his friend and colleague Ethan standing there shell-shocked. Knowing something was wrong, Nick walked down the hall. The speechless social studies teacher just handed the document to Nick without saying a word. Nick did not have to read far or be a lawyer: the word *divorce* jumped right out at him. Nick told Ethan to go home and call a lawyer, adding that he shouldn't leave his house. He had heard once, although he was not sure if it was true, that one should not leave the house because then one could be charged with abandonment, adding to the reasons for the divorce. Nick asked Ethan to stop by the main office and to call in a sub or arrange coverage for the rest of the day, as Nick said he would sit with Ethan's first-hour class since he was off that period. The class had witnessed the entire exchange, and they were waiting for their teacher to return, but instead it would be Mr. Finch, whom they all knew.

He looked at the class, who was just as shell-shocked, and started with, "I am so sorry you had to see that. Let that be a lesson: adulthood is not easy, especially marriage. But you should have never seen that." He looked at the class of thirty-five or so seniors and observed that they were divided into reactionary subgroups. Some wanted to know exactly what had just happened and just how the law worked. Others took out their books from other classes and got a head start on studying or homework. A few retreated and put their heads down. Obviously, they knew what had just happened because it had happened to them and their parents, and it hurt. It opened old wounds.

Ethan would survive, raise a beautiful, intelligent son who would graduate from Georgetown in DC, get remarried, and be happy, but that day stuck with Nick. That was a private legal matter that should have never been made public, much less on a campus in front of students.

The building of the Finch house seemed to pick up after a strongly worded letter had arrived from the Law Office of Brian Morgan Jr. Suddenly, workers with their subcontractors were pulled off other jobs in the neighborhood and were moved to Scrubjay Lane. The letter also threatened legal action, such as reimbursement for the rent the Finch's were paying at Uno Lago. Lauren, after noticing the uptick in the work, said, "Like or not and ready or not, a moving van will be here on March 1." The work finished on the last day of February and thank goodness it was a leap year. Christmas at the townhouse apartment was tough as Mel was sure that Santa did not know where she lived. Tyler was already skeptical about the whole Santa thing, and Clancy was just along for the ride. To blow off steam, Nick reset his odometer and measured his drive north: 6.6 miles, which he made a mental note of. That Saturday in late January, he jogged to the spot then turned around and jogged back just to see what a half-marathon was like. It was hell, and he would never do it again, but it caused him to gain respect for those who ran half-marathons, never mind complete marathons. That Sunday he felt leg muscles he hadn't know he had; they were sore as hell. Bad idea.

Soon the Finch's were all moved in. For the next academic year, Tyler was enrolled at Jerry Thomas Elementary in Jupiter, and Mel was at the Bluffs Preschool over in Juno Beach. Lauren took her son for his first day, which by all accounts is an exceedingly difficult goodbye. This was true for mom. Her little boy was now school age and on the first step of the academic ladder. Time was moving fast. Tyler would do great throughout his elementary years, so well in fact that he skipped the second grade entirely, going from first grade to the third grade. Academically, it was an easy call as Tyler needed to be challenged, but socially perhaps it hadn't been such a great idea, especially when he was a sixteen-year-old senior and a young seventeen-year-old college freshman. Nick and Lauren had mixed emotions on that decision. Hindsight is 20/20. It seemed that Tyler took after his mother with his intellect. His test scores and IQ score were off the charts. In fact, he was invited to a join very elite "think tank" for young people called the Duke TIPS program that sent him to Durham for the summer, where he was assigned thought-provoking projects. His prize was a suspension bridge he had built based on principles of engineering and laws of physics that had certain load restrictions. He was in the fifth grade! Mel did just fine at the Bluffs School, and then she moved to a school closer to Jerry Thomas, where she did well if she was well supervised and scissors were kept away from her mischievous hands.

One day Lauren went to pick Mel up and was horrified when Mel arrived at the front desk. She had decided to cut her own hair, so there was a chunk missing from her blonde head. Mom was none too happy with the staff. In October, Mel was selected to be Jupiter High's homecoming princess. Her escort was another staff member's child, another five-year-old named Griffin Long, son of teacher and coach Ron Long Jr. Mom and Mel picked out a special red and white dress complete with black patent leather saddle shoes and white pull-up stockings. She looked adorable, but nobody would know the scrambling that had taken place that Friday afternoon as Mel once again had cut her own hair to get ready for the big game. Lauren was now really pissed, but you cannot "un ring the bell" or in this case, reattach the hair. Lauren rushed Mel to a nearby salon and asked the young stylist for a "Dorothy Hammill" cut made popular by the gold medal figure skating star of the mid-seventies. The twenty-something stylist had no idea what a Dorothy Hamill cut was or who Hamill even was and what made her and her hair the craze of the time period. The stylist had not been born yet. Sandy described it the best she could, saying it was a Dutch boy look, then the owner came to the rescue with a book of pictures of different hairstyles. In the book was a "Dorothy Hammill".

That night, Jupiter High's very young version of Dorothy Hamill was introduced. With her tuxedo-wearing escort, she walked onto the midfield of the stadium to applause and awe. Years later, the two, home from college, would meet up at a party and recall the event. They even tried dating each other, but both agreed, "No, it's weird." Nick sent a picture to Mel's "uncle" Paul up in Mississippi, who had witnessed the head-grabbing bus door incident at Disney and had commented, "Mel, honey, you look like you brushed your hair with a hand grenade." Now he looked at the homecoming picture of his goddaughter and said, "That one is going to be framed!" It still hangs proudly in the Watts home in Tupelo, right up there with pictures such as the one of Nick with his godson David, various other family pictures, and pictures of Jesus, Elvis, and Archie Manning. Oh, the South is so very unique. The following Monday, Lauren withdrew Mel from the Bluffs and enrolled her at the Treetops Preschool, which she would attend until her kindergarten year.

Nick started at JHS, the second place he had ever taught, and it was an anxious moment even for the seventeen-year veteran who in a way was starting over. It was strange going from top dog to runt of the litter in a matter of a few days. His schedule of courses included regular US history, one section of honors US history, and one regular US government course. No AP as the department chair taught that, and deservingly so. A sixties liberal flower child in every way, the chairperson was the opposite of Nick, a southern conservative, yet the two were good friends who had spirited but friendly debates ending with laughter. See, it can happen. Just listen well, smile a lot, talk with in even, unemotional tone of voice, and all will be well. Anybody listening?

At the Christmas break the youngest teacher at JHS, who was very talented, decided that teaching was not for him, so he applied for, was accepted to, and enrolled in law school at the University of Florida for the spring semester. So, that left another opening, which went a football and baseball coach and JHS alum who had come down from the district to the north, Martin County. He would be taking over Nick's classes as Nick would be taking on the future barrister's workload. Now Nick had all seniors in his government and economics classes all day, and one honors US history. All in all, Nick taught seven different classes his first year at Jupiter. Both he and the school were lucky that he was a veteran and up to the challenge.

The new teacher moved right across the hall. He and Nick would teach close or next to each other throughout their careers, and they developed a quiet but well-respected friendship. His name was Roman Stoneman, or Ro.

One thing a veteran teacher knows well is trying to defuse a situation before it becomes an office-worthy issue. Keep problems on the reservation. Nick had a potential problem in a student named Bart Michaels. Bart was in his US government class that had forty-plus students who needed the class to graduate. Thirty-five of them were boys, and at least fifteen were members of the varsity baseball team. They could be a handful—they could be downright be wiseasses—but Nick was a veteran who had lived through Eddie Murphy, plus he got along with baseball players because of his background. He'd known the JHS baseball coach, Doug Massey, since the latter's Little League days in West Palm and had been his varsity pitching coach at Forest Hill. If Nick had a problem, he could go to Doug, but that would not happen. The problem was not the class, but Bart, as Bart was very sensitive to sound and was on the autism spectrum. When left alone, he would do outstanding work, but the smallest of sounds would set him off. Nick always had a stack of *Sports Illustrated* magazines that Bart would devour after completing his classwork. He also made sure Bart sat right next to him for protection. One day after an assignment was complete, a couple of the boys starting humming and tapping their pencils in unison, and sure enough, it set Bart off. Nick quickly took control of the situation and removed Bart, sending him outside to regain his composure. Mrs. Michaels, Bart's mom, was a big name in county politics and had made life very difficult for some teachers in the past. Bart's guidance counselor was none other than Hank Gibbs, who kept close tabs on the special student, not because he had to, but because he cared for him. Hank was the one who had made sure Bart was in Nick's class. As Bart composed himself outside, Nick went back inside and gave the class a no-holds-barred locker-room-style ass-chewing that got everyone's attention, especially the athletes in the class. After class, two of the girls stepped up and volunteered to walk Bart to class, but before they left, they informed Nick who the ringleaders were. One was a wrestler, and the other was a baseball player. Instead of dealing with the matter directly, Nick took another approach that would not appear in any books or manuals about teaching. Before class the next day, Nick pulled aside Scott Preston, who was the resident badass of JHS. Scott was the star football player who would be going to the University of Miami next fall on a football scholarship. Nick had already heard some of the legendary stories about Scott Preston, such as the one about his taking on and whipping three college guys at the same time over the previous Christmas break. Scott did his work, but he was not Harvard bound. Let's just say that Scott was fortunate he was a good football player. He was always polite and well-mannered, but you could tell he was one wrong comment or action away from having a new score to settle. He had a floating eye, and in fact the width between his two eyes was noticeably wide. It seemed his eyes ran almost out to his ears. J.W. had once warned about wide-eyed men, saying they tended to be a little crazy. Nick remembered that.

Nick made a proposal to Scott Preston. Scott could be done with any work for the class and could have no more tests. Well, he'd have to fill one out, but it would not be graded, and an "A" would be put into the gradebook. Nick knew not to assign homework to second-semester seniors. In exchange for a free pass, Scott would be Bart's bodyguard, but nobody, not even Bart, should ever know. Scott was to be the Secret Service agent assigned to protect the president's son. It took Scott about two seconds before he said, "Deal. Got it." Smiling, he went back into the room to his seat and pulled out some work for another class now that government was all done.

About a week later, it was time for the one and only test needed to fulfill this special arrangement. Nick stepped outside his room to talk to Roman, when he heard a little commotion coming from inside his classroom. Roman said, "Hey, man, I think you need to get to your room."

Nick smiled and responded with, "Nah, everything's all right." Nick then went into the room and found the class stone quiet. The two troublemakers from before had their heads down on their desks, and Bart was busy reading his *Sports Illustrated.*

Nick looked over to Scott, who nodded, grinned, and said, "All OK here, Teach. So, what is today's lesson?"

Nick responded, "Debate on the death penalty, pros and cons."

One of the troublemakers raised his head just long enough to say, "Figures."

After class, Scott went up to Nick as he was leaving and said, "There will be no more problems for Bart, here or in any other class. I promise."

The same two girls who had informed on the troublemakers earlier came back in the last five minutes of the next class and asked if they could speak to Mr. Finch. The three met out in the hallway, where the girls explained that the two boys had started the humming again and began drumming with their hands on their desks. Suddenly Scott Preston was above them and whispered something in their ears, and immediately both actions ceased. The next day Nick asked Scott what he had said to them, and Scott answered, "You do not want or need to know, but Bart will be OK now. Nobody will mess with him. I should have done this without your prompting. No one should be put through hell like that. But I did make one announcement, saying that if anyone bothered him at any time, not just in this class, I would make things right. Got it?" Apparently, the news spread fast, and Bart Michaels had his Secret Service protection for the remainder of his high school days.

All Nick responded with was, "Thank you for Bart and kids like Bart. I hate bullies."

Nick always wondered what it must have been like to teach after Pearl Harbor as the war years had greatly affected both his parents. An ex-boyfriend of Charlene's had gone down on the USS *Arizona*, so it took a while for her to accept that Nick had bought a Japanese-made Nissan with the money he got from selling his 300Z. Just recently Nick had seen two specialized Florida license plates that made him stop and reflect. One was in the neighboring town of Tequesta, the plate reading "Pearl Harbor Survivor," and the other was in the Publix shopping plaza in Jupiter, reading "Gold Star Family." Both the drivers had stories that very few could relate to. The Pearl Harbor driver was a little man who could barely see over the steering wheel. He had white hair and thick-lensed, black-rimmed glasses. Nick pulled up next to the navy veteran and nodded in appreciation of his service. The old man looked back, smiled, and mouthed, *Thank you.* The light changed green, and the old man, who had a lead foot, sped off, leaving Nick in the dust. Doing the math, Nick figured the man had to be one hundred years old or damn close to it. He thought that this special fraternity had to see dwindling numbers as the years went by, but what they had seen on December 7, 1941, was infamous, in the words of FDR. On that same drive, Nick had pulled into the new Publix

Supermarket, most likely for a couple of lottery tickets, which had parallel parking spaces. One was open right by the sliding entrance/exit doors. Nick pulled in at about the same time a middle-aged woman pulled right in front of him, which was when he noticed the plate indicating that hers was a gold star family—a family who has lost a son or daughter in service to our country, most likely in Iraq or Afghanistan. Nick, having surrendered the spot and parked elsewhere, walked right up to the mother, and said, "I am so sorry for your loss. And thank you for your child's service to our country."

The mother replied with a thank-you, but she did not stop there. She opened her purse and brought out a roll of ten or so pictures in a kind of mini photo album. She explained that her son was a graduate of the United States Air Force Academy and was an F-18 fighter pilot who was shot down in Iraq. The pictures were a true tribute from an enormously proud mom. They ranged from his academy days as a student and baseball player, to his sitting in the cockpit of his fighter jet, to his wedding photo with all the men in uniform, and to his young family together at Christmastime. Nick thanked the mother for sharing, but she was the one to say, "No, son, thank you for your appreciation. I keep these pictures with me, and I share them as much as I can so people can in a way learn the story of my son, so he will not be forgotten. It is I who thanks you." Nick was floored by this woman's grace and dignity. She had suffered the worst type of loss any parent can have and yet still walked around with her head up high and proud.

So, those were Nick's observations about two license plates whose owners had stories to tell, the likes of which most of us will hopefully never know. Then came September 11, 2001, when a new generation of Americans had their own stories to tell and even their own special license plates.

Tuesday, September 11, 2001, started out like any other day for Nick and his classes in his second-floor classroom on the old south campus at Jupiter High. At a little before nine o'clock in the morning, Nick picked up his cell phone, having noticed he was getting a phone call, which was rare during the school day, unless one of the kids was sick or needed something. Because Nick was in Jupiter, he could take of such problems much more easily than Lauren could. It was Lauren on the phone, and she opened with a question: "Do you have a TV in your room?" Nick said he did, and Lauren told him to turn on quickly as something was going down in New York City. Nick had a big, thick, heavy TV atop a wheeled cart that was strapped down to prevent it from falling off, but it may have been one of the most unsafe rigged contraptions ever. With an extremely heavy electronic appliance on an unsteady wheeled cart, it was so top-heavy that when you wheeled it around, it would come close to tipping over onto someone and cause some serious damage. The district clearly had dodged a liability lawsuit. These days, for the most part most, TVs are anchored to the ceilings. Much safer. Nick turned on the TV and turned the channel to CNN to see one of the Twin Towers of the World Trade Center on fire and smoking. A commercial jet had just crashed into it, but it was still too soon to determine why, other than saying it was a terrible accident. It was no accident, though. A few minutes later, a second plane crashed right into the second tower.

The whole class shrieked in horror when watching the events unfolding before their eyes on TV. They looked to the adult in the room for guidance and for an understanding of what was happening. Nick said in the best matter-of-fact voice he could muster up, "Class, we are under attack, and we pray for those people." Nick immediately thought about just a year earlier when he had accompanied his wife to New York for one of her business trips and they'd had drinks at the rooftop bar of The World Trade Center called "Windows on the World" at the Trade Center and how They took a helicopter sightseeing trip around New York flying right up close to one of the towers and how the workers there looked up and waved at the two tourists from Florida. Nick wondered if those workers had survived and gotten out. All they'd done that day was go to work.

Thirty to forty-five minutes later, CNN switched to footage from Washington, DC, as another plane had suicide-crashed, this time into the Pentagon. Nick's classes were glued to the TV as the day went on. They knew as much as their teacher did, and the information coming from reporters was slow, sloppily pieced together, and not always accurate. But the pictures did not lie. As the day went on, it seemed it was all a terrible nightmare and everyone would wake up to find that everything was fine, but no, this was reality TV at its very worst.

Then came the news of another commercial flight having crashed, but this time in a field in rural Pennsylvania. The heroic story of the passengers of Flight 93 would soon be told. Years later, Nick once created a question asking students to compare the defenders of the Alamo to the passengers of Flight 93. Both knew what was to be their outcome, but what would be their legacy to their respective generations?

Nick picked up the kids and waited on Lauren to arrive home. Once she was home, they all hugged. She reminded Nick she was supposed to be in New York today just a few buildings away from the World Trade Center for a business meeting on Wall Street with some Saudi investors, but the Saudis had canceled the Sunday night prior to the Tuesday meeting. Coincidence? Nick Finch would later say those dots were easy to connect. Lauren had colleagues already up there who were preparing for the meeting when the towers were hit. They had to rent a car to drive home as the airlines were grounded for security reasons. Her colleagues did not leave the financial district before they had personally witnessed the "jumpers"—the people who jumped from the Twin Towers and committed suicide, rather than be burned alive by fires started by jet fuel. Those colleagues still have nightmares.

Nick later talked to an old West Palm friend who was a federal prosecutor who had to listen to the black box tapes of Flight 93. It bothered her so much that she left the Justice Department for private practice. The United States changed that awful day, and now Nick kind of knew what it must have been like to be an American on December 7, 1941, when the Japanese Imperial Army attacked Pearl Harbor, or November 22, 1963, the day John F. Kennedy was assassinated in Dallas. Nick now would have students join the military and head off to Afghanistan and/or Iraq. Nick was there for his students on the day of the terrorist attacks on the United States, comforting them, but for the most part he was every bit as rattled as they were and said little, trying to absorb as much information as he could. He found himself staying up late that night, unable to turn off the TV at home, until exhaustion overtook him and forced him to bed. He found himself zombielike, saying little and stunned beyond description. It was a teachable moment, yet the words did not flow as they usually did for the very verbal teacher. Nothing would be the same ever again for him as a history teacher or for this generation of students, who now were going off to war like their grandparents had, whether it was World War II, Korea, or Vietnam. God bless them and all the people who died that awful day, September 11, 1991. Rest in peace.

The correspondence that day between Lauren and Nick would have been impossible were it not for the cell phone. Nick at one time had the hardwired phone in his car, but the technology had improved so much that it now seemed almost everyone from age eight to age eighty had a cell phone. A famous historian reflecting on the impact of Henry Ford's introduction of the Model A and Model T automobiles, which were made in the United States, said, "Mr. Ford, we do not know if you helped us or hurt us, but you sure did change us." And Ford had changed the United States in so many ways, his inventions leading to the creation of new industries. Having created a new method of travel, he indirectly brought about societal change, not just in the United States but really across the world. Most of the subsequent changes have been positive, but some of the consequences—pollution, accidents, and urban decline—have been negative.

Starting with a World War II project, the real first computer, called UNIVAC, was followed up by the realizing of the vision of Mr. Watson at IBM, who, along with others, changed from making adding machines to manufacturing computers. The Apple computer of Steven Jobs and his colleagues made it possible for places other than government institutions, for example, the DMV, schools, and hospitals, to have computers, as they were now smaller and could fit atop desks at the office or even at home. Bill Gates, realizing that people needed an easier software system, unlike FORTRAN, and that not everyone could write their own programs, gave birth to Microsoft, the mouse, and the concept of drag, point, and click. Then, someone—not Al Gore, but the Defense Department and supplemental industries—thought of connecting these computers by way of phone line, so then the internet and companies such as AOL—remember them and that awful dial-up sound? —came into our lives. Next in the sequence came combining the personal computer with the cell phone, and the iPhone fell into our hands. As with Henry Ford's automobiles, most of these inventions helped us, and just as transportation changed forever, so has the act of communication. But still there are some drawbacks from combining computer and telephone, such as texting and driving. Nick swears it has made a whole generation come down with attention deficit disorder or ADD. It has created some mean, insecure people, with the most insecure people of all, adolescents, becoming even meaner and more insecure. Constantly checking and rechecking their phones to see if they have missed out on something and then facing the disappointment of a blank screen adds to the trials and tribulations of one of the most confusing times in a person's life. No more passing notes in lockers. The posting of pictures and events, which can be exploited for all the wrong reasons and by the wrong people, has ruined a generation's trust, reputation, and future. Still the phone has provided so many positives, such as safety and personal security, not to mention that it gives a person access to the entire world and an unlimited bank of knowledge. There is no doubt that small glass and plastic rectangle has definitely changed us.

One of the neat things the iPhone did was to allow the owner to use custom ringtones. Nick and Lauren relented and bought both Tyler and Mel their own phones, and of course the privilege came with strict rules that, as time went on, became less rules and more suggestions. Nick found it more and more difficult to compete against the phone. It unlocked the door to all kinds of possible cheating venues, such as pictures of a test sent on to others and the ability to look up the answers ahead of time. So, Nick came up with an idea one morning in the master bedroom closet he shared with his wife. It was a large closet, probably bigger than three in the Lake Clarke home combined, but about two-thirds was set aside for Lauren 's wardrobe and collection of shoes. There were so many shoes that she had picked up a hanging shoe caddy at Bed Bath & Beyond that had five rows with seven small cubbyholes each to contain them all. The Ben Franklin light bulb of inspiration clicked on in Nick's brain, and that weekend he went to that same store and bought himself one of those hanging shoe caddies. Lauren was perplexed by his purchase as Nick had a total of five pairs of footwear: two pairs of loafers—one penny, one tassel—a pair of white tennis shoes, a pair of leather Topsiders, and a pair of leather flip-flops. Why did he need a caddy? Plus, there was no room for one in the closest. Nick explained his reasoning, and the banker nodded with an approving smile.

Nick's plan was to hang the caddy on the storage door in the back of his classroom, and students were to deposit their phones there at the beginning of the class. At the end of the period, they would be allowed to withdraw their phones from the Finch phone bank. It took about a week for the kids to buy in, but soon they started lining up and depositing their phones. It worked so well that some would forget to take their devices at the bell and would have to come back and get them. On the end-of-year survey Nick gave all his students, almost every student gave the bank high marks, and some commented they liked getting away from their phones for at least an hour. They said it helped them concentrate. Other teachers heard of the strategy Nick was using and began to do the same. Of course, Nick always allowed exceptions, such as if a student had a sick loved one at home or in the hospital. And a few students, diabetics, had a new contraption that they used for monitoring their glucose levels that worked along with their phones. Now that was very cool. Still, at times the phone bank would light up with a call, and sometimes the class would hear a unique ringtone. It was always fun to see who the owner was and if the ringtone matched his or her personality.

Nick had changed his ringtone from the standard one to the "Peanuts theme Linus and Lucy" as a tribute to the American icon Charles Shultz. Another reason for this was that all his students had grown up with that tune, whether it was from "A Charlie Brown Christmas" or "*It's the Great Pumpkin, Charlie Brown*," and. Recognition of the ringtone spanned multiple generations and brought back memories from an earlier time in life, which always brought smiles. Nick then switched to Dave Brubeck's "Take Five" after driving up the Pacific Coast Highway on a family vacation. The tune was just plain cool. Then he switched over to the Ole Miss Band's version of "Dixie." Whatever tune he used depended on the mood of the times. Lauren had a few ringtones of her own, but none like the one she had for just one day, compliments of her son, Tyler. One morning, early, Tyler spotted his mother's phone on the kitchen counter, so he decided to play a harmless joke on her. Like everyone in his generation, he was very comfortable with technology, but especially the phone, so he went into the settings app, located ringtones, and made a few changes.

That day on Palm Beach, President Lauren Finch was having an important staff meeting in her conference room with eight other people in attendance. As she put up her PowerPoint about sales goals, or tendencies, or some sort of banking strategy, the all-important meeting was interrupted with a vulgar hip-hop rap song that made everyone blush. They tried to ignore it, which was impossible to do. The ringtone was the 2 Live Crew song "Me So Horny." Over and over, the meeting attendees heard the moaning of a young Asian woman claiming that she was just that: horny. Apparently, she wanted and needed sex—and now! She let everyone in the conference room know this with her declaration of, "Me so horny." The president ignored the ringtone at first as everyone looked around in embarrassment. She finally commanded, "Will someone get their phone and stop the, well, request of that woman."

One of the attendees who was the most comfortable around his boss since they had worked together at different places, Rob Dodge, said, "I think that is your phone, Lauren."

She said, "No, it's not," but looked down and saw the flashing screen. To her horror, she realized it was hers. She turned it off and then turned three shades of red.

Rob said, "I guess Nick decided to play a joke on you today—and a damn good one."

Lauren shook her head and replied, "No, that was not him. He would not know how to do that. But I do know who the culprit is; I will kill my son tonight." The room exploded in laughter. Lauren tried to be mad that night at dinner, but it was impossible as everyone was grinning from ear to ear. She surrendered and had to acknowledge it was a good practical joke, but she asked Tyler never to do that again. He agreed.

Another neat feature of Nick's iPhone was the iTunes app, which allowed him to download, or is it upload, music to his phone. This feature was more than just for personal use. Nick downloaded mostly music from his college days, especially bands he had seen in person, whether in Florida, in Memphis, or at the Gin in Oxford. But he found that by using one of his Christmas presents, which was a small portable Bluetooth Bose speaker, he could improve the sound quality and could introduce music from each decade, starting with the Jazz Age and moving up to the contemporary period, during the last five minutes or so of class. Mr. Finch knew that because music was such a big part of US culture and history, this new opportunity screamed at him to hit play. Starting with such Jazz Age icons such as Duke Ellington, Count Basie, Ella Fitzgerald, and of course Satchmo himself, Louis Armstrong, the kids could just maybe imagine they had attended the "Cotton Club" in Harlem or a "speakeasy" in another city such as New Orleans. In the thirties, swing music burst upon the scene with musicians such as Benny Goodman and Gene Krupa. During the war years, big band music from people like Glenn Miller got people "In the Mood "with big band music. Rock and roll was born in the era of the sock hop and drive-ins, with Bill Haley & His Comets, Jerry Lee Lewis, Little Richard, and of course the King, the boy from Tupelo, the truck driver from Memphis and Sun Records, Elvis Presley. As the decades got closer, the more familiar the students were with the selected tunes. The sixties included songs by the Beach Boys and music from Motown, along with artist from the psychedelic scene, and some country favorites like the Man in Black, Johnny Cash, all of which blared from Nick's desktop speaker—and the kids loved it. Some songs like Elvis's "Jailhouse Rock" or the Temptations' "My Girl" were instantly recognized by almost everyone, and many joined in and sang along.

There are times when a teacher comes up with an idea that works out beyond his or her wildest dreams. This was one of those occasions for Nick Finch, AP United States History teacher. Somewhat disappointing was the fact that Nick limited the selections to American artists, so no Rolling Stones and "Satisfaction" and no "Let It Be" from the Fab Four. Others like Elton John and the Who were bypassed too, but one must have fences. This was a US history class, and by damn, we had won our independence from the Brits back in 1776! Now the seventies offered a huge variety of music, and Nick would mix it up from class to class, not only to check the reactions of the students, but also so he would not get tired of playing the same songs for five straight periods. He played Jim Croce, the Carpenters, the Eagles, Jimmy Buffett, Grand Funk Railroad, Kiss, and then disco selections such as Florida's own KC and the Sunshine Band, along with punk rock. The 1980s, the era of excess and greed, put out some good music, and add to that MTV, where artists could supplement their songs with visuals and make them even more appealing. One day Nick played Cyndi Lauper's "Girls Just Want to Have Fun" and quickly noticed three of his students smiling at each other with mischievous grins. Then they got up and did a dance, choreographed perfectly. They danced across the classroom and went up to the front, where they continued their routine. At first, they were not sure if this was going to be all right with their teacher, but Nick nodded with approval. The girls finished to a round of applause from their classmates. They bowed, but before they could return to their desks, Nick just had to ask where that routine had come from. They explained that when they were little, around five years old, they were all in the same gymnastics class, and before performances they all ran onto the mat to the music of Lauper's number one song. It was how they began every public performance or competition. Nick was speechless, thinking he had just witnessed a very cool thing. Who knew this little addition during the last five minutes or so of class would have worked out so well? It did, and Nick would continue doing it until the day he retired. If it ain't broke …

Music worked well in the classroom, but it could also work wonders in the real world. A case in point was Rob Rice, a lifelong friend of Nick and the rest of the guys. A year younger, Rob was really part of Nick's class as he participated in their sports and was part of their social environment. Rob had been raised by a single dad, the cool dad for whom rules were more like suggestions, and his house was seen as a house of refuge, much like those built along the coastline of the state in the 1800s to help shipwrecked sailors find refuge and safety. Rob always seemed to have "adopted brothers" as roommates who were in, say, a little difficulty in their own homes and needed a temporary change of scenery. Rob's door was always open. After most of the guys graduated, Rob Rice had to wait a year to follow a lot of them to Tallahassee and Florida State (FSU). Quickly he became a campus leader and a Greek leader and was quite the popular undergraduate. After graduation, it was off to law school at Berry University. He got married to his college sweetheart Elaine and quickly immersed himself in the Palm Beach County legal scene. Seldom was there a Notables section of the *Palm Beach Post* where a picture of him at a charity event was not printed. In fact, most of the time his photo was featured. Moving up fast, Rob and Elaine bought a beautiful home in an exclusive gated country club in the Boynton Beach area. The world was his oyster, so to speak, that is, until the HOA decided to plant mature trees around the green that backed up to his house, which of course destroyed his breathtaking view of not only the green but also the manicured fairway that led to the putting service. Rob loved to entertain in his backyard with that million-dollar view, and inevitably putters would be broken out for a putting contest that was usually accompanied by some sort of drinking game.

Robert Rice had a personality that could best be described as extremely persuasive. He thought he would attend the next board meeting and explain what a bad idea the trees were and why they should come out. He was confident, maybe overconfident, as he entered the venue for the meeting, which was the clubhouse at the golf course. Rob signed in for the HOA board meeting and was told that after a few minutes of association business, he would be allowed to state his case. The board had already heard of the lawyer's displeasure with the new landscaping, and they had come prepared with the oldest trick in the book, stall, and delay.

After Rob introduced himself and thanked the board for allowing him time to state his case, it seemed that each and every member had a question for him even before he stated his position. And sure enough, when it became his time to speak, he found that his allotted time was very short. After about a minute, the chairman banged the gavel and announced, "Mr. Rice, sorry, but you are out of time. But I can speak for the entire board and thank you for your input and assure you we will look over your complaint." For the first time really in Rob's life, he was speechless. He pleaded for more time but was ignored as the board went to the next thing on the agenda, which was the purchase of a new Weedwhacker for the lawn crew. By the way, that motion passed and the new yard maintenance tool was on its way. Meanwhile, the trees stayed.

Rob Rice was a particularly good lawyer, but he would have been spectacular in a sales job as he was by far the most persuasive man of the group who'd grown up together at Forest Hill. Rob would argue any subject and do so persuasively until he got the outcome he wished or won the debate, all while never losing his smile. Nick could see why he was such a good lawyer as he not only had the brains to research the case but also had the personality to argue it. It was a gift, and for the first time it was not working, which frustrated the hell out of him. He opened his mail a few days later and learned his request had been denied. The word *denied* was stamped in large block letters and red ink. Rob then tried to get his neighbors on board, but they respectfully declined, saying they would rather not get involved with board business. Rob was at a dead end, but he decided to go another route. After work, he went to the Boynton Beach Mall and looked near and far, finally finding what he was looking for, which was a man's bathing suit thong. He bought one after making sure it was one size too small. These thongs are horrid selections for beachwear, and they usually scream European or French Canadian. Locals will tell you they can spot a French-Canadian tourist a mile away by the thong the man is wearing and the amount of visible body hair on the woman. Add to this that they are notoriously terrible tippers and you can see why they are not the locals' favorites. Yes, these are stereotypes, but as it is said, stereotypes come from examples observed on a frequent basis. The guys' nickname for the thong, by the way, was "banana hammock."

Next, Rob walked to the other end of the mall to a record store and told the youngest black male salesman there that he was interested in a rap CD and it had to be vulgar and profane. The salesman looked quizzical at first, but Rob explained it was a practical joke he was playing on a friend. The clerk brought him a CD that was not on the everyday shelves but was kept under the counter. It had all types of warning labels on it, one noting that the buyer had to be eighteen to purchase the CD. Last, Rob stopped by the Radio Shack and, after asking for help, bought a digital sound meter. He then went home and began to plan out his outside-the-box rebuttal.

He checked the association newsletter and calendar and determined when the women were scheduled to get together for their weekly game of golf. Most of the women were seasoned or mature, with the average age being seventy to seventy-five. The event was scheduled for the next Tuesday. Rob would be ready and waiting.

Rob figured it would be around ten o'clock in the morning when the women, who were placed in groups of four, would be making their way to the green that bordered his house. Elaine was not privy to her husband's strategy until he emerged from their bedroom in his terry bathrobe and disrobed, to the shock of the mother to his children. Robert Rice, Esquire, stood before her in only his thong and flip-flops. She was stunned and did know whether to laugh or cry as Rob walked proudly, holding a chaise lounge chair and a boom box, attired in a banana hammock that was at least one size too small. He went out to the green area, making sure he was on his own private property and not the club's, opened his lounge chair, set up the boom box right next to one of the new trees, and turned on his sound meter. As the first foursome approached, Rob opened his new CD, inserted it, and hit play. What emerged from the speakers was truly repulsive even to the most open-minded music lover. The song consisted of a stream of profanity, the rapper using every bad word to describe a woman's genital area, sexual acts, and horrible violence—and that was only the first selection. It seemed to get worse as the music played on. Add to that the fact that the DJ was almost totally naked with spiked hair, a fruity frozen cocktail in hand, and a grin from ear to ear. Just imagine the character who plays the quirky Jamie, the foil to Flo, but taller, on the Progressive insurance commercials and you will get an idea of how Rob looked to the women golfers that day. The combination of the vulgar music and the disgusting man was too much for some of them. Others tried to ignore him.

When the second group came around, the music was even worse. The head pro raced out to the green to talk to the resident and plead for him to shut it off. Rob's response was, "Sorry, cannot hear you, my main motherfucker!" in a ghetto-like accent that would have made Eminem proud. By the time the third foursome was showing up, so were the Boynton Beach police. Rob produced documentation of local code pertaining to noise level and then produced his sound meter, which showed he was not violating any local law or code. He also showed the survey markers proving he was on his property and not the club's. The police were taken aback, not having expected a legally prepared subject at the other end of their complaint call. Rob then walked the police back to their squad car, along the way explaining off the record why he was doing this. The two officers doubled over in laughter, much to the chagrin of the golfers who were watching the interaction between the disgusting DJ and law enforcement.

Two more groups got to experience the "Rice factor." Two days later, a member of the board stopped by Rob's house during the dinner hour to discuss what could be done to make everyone happy. Rob's answer was quick and to the point, and that was remove the trees. He then warned, "Just wait and see what I have in store for the next women's golf day, as I am only getting warmed up." In fact, Rob did have another plan, and it involved strippers. But he would not need to implement his plan because as he got up to get ready to go to work that Friday and looked out, he saw some heavy machinery in his backyard area. Workers they were removing the trees. Game, set, and match! Used as a legal and social weapon against a perceived infringement of Rob's rights, music was shown to be a powerful and successful weapon in the battle of the greenside trees. This testifies to the power of music.

CHAPTER

18

The Next Generation of College Students, Dogs, and Travel, and The Ultimate Never-Ending Vacation

Nick began to believe that Harry Chapin really was on to something with his haunting song "Cat's in the Cradle." The song came out in 1974 when Nick was on the island of Palm Beach at the public school there, and he'd never really listened to the lyrics. As years passed, he heard less and less of the song and was so busy with high school, college, teaching, coaching, dating, marriage, and child rearing that he never really had the time to sit down and listen to it. It was not until the move to Jupiter and the kids' promotions up through the grades, from Jerry Thomas to Independence Middle School, then on to Jupiter High, with their sights now on college, that Nick realized he was living the song. This realization was in part made possible by a feature of his new car, a BMW X5, which he'd bought because the truck had done its job of moving the family to Jupiter and, like Charlene, Lauren was not thrilled about arriving somewhere in a pickup truck. The new SUV had satellite radio that featured songs from the different decades, beginning with the fifties, which were on channel 5; moving on to the sixties, which were on channel 6; and progressing to the seventies, music from which was played on—you get the picture—channel 7. Nick mostly listened to the 1980s station, especially since they did not have DJs, but VJs, like the people on MTV when that network actually aired music videos. The eighties music on channel 8 took Nick back to happy times. He also listened to the fifties station, which played the King, and even some sixties, which made him reflect on his times driving around the streets of West Palm Beach with his older sisters. J.W., when alive, had listened to the local news and talk radio of WJNO, but especially Paul Harvey and *The Rest of the Story*. Charlene rarely turned on the car radio when driving but did not mind if her kids did.

Nick would try his best not to become the dad in Harry Chapin's song, but like all dads, he fell short. J.W. had fallen short with him. He also realized it was nobody's fault; it was just the way he was raised. The trait is handed down even if the father does the best he can. It is simply the case that fathers fall short, and it is a shame.

Tyler and Mel sailed through school with few visible distractions but with some interesting memories. Tyler, with a freakish IQ, made academics look easy with his classroom work ethic, although not so much with his grades, but things always seemed to work out fine for him. Math and science seemed to come easy, so Nick realized that Tyler took after his mother. Mel, about two and half years younger but three grades behind, also did well, including when juggling her championship equestrian events and modeling. Very social, she seemed to be in every club and on the student council at all three schools. She loved to write for pleasure and read just as much, so she took after her dad, Nick. There were still some obstacles, such as when the principal of Jerry Thomas Elementary called Nick on his cell and asked if he had a minute to speak about an incident that had happened earlier in the morning on the bus with Tyler. Nick thought, *oh no, what could this be? What the hell did he do?* The principal brought up the name of Ann Labour, who was old school. She took the time to make a professional courtesy call to Nick, a fellow educator who was right down the street, about a half mile away, instead of making a production of whatever had happened. Nick walked out of the portable classroom to which he and most of his friends had been moved because of overcrowding on the traditional campus. They loved the new location for many reasons. They liked the isolation from the main buildings. And the fact that it was the farthest point away from the main office was a plus as it prevented administrators from traveling out to what had been nicknamed by the teachers "the white trash trailer park." A new principal would try her darnedest to rename it "the Villas." Nope, it was the trailer park. Another perk of the location was that one could step outside and really *be* outside and enjoy the sunshine of Florida.

Once Nick got outside, he opened the telephone conference with, "OK, Anne, what did he do?"

The principal could tell by the inflection of Nick's voice that he was concerned and unhappy. Mrs. Labour then took over the conversation. "Nick, not to worry, but it seems that there was a fellow fifth grader harassing and bullying some of the younger kids, kindergartners and first graders, and Tyler took exception and broke a bus rule by getting up, walking up to the bully, and warning him to quit bothering the little ones or, in his words, he was going to beat his ass after school today. The bus driver was just following the regulation against walking when the bus is in motion and objecting to Tyler's use of profanity in choosing the word *ass*. He really did not want to report this, mind you."

After Nick listened, he asked, "What happens now?"

The response was such a throwback: "I just finished talking to Tyler about staying seated when the bus is moving, then I told him I was making his teacher nominate him Student of the Month, which I guaranteed him he would win, telling him that you and your wife will be invited to the presentation at the end of the month. I hope you can make it. I hate bullies, and apparently so does your son. I think that is because of how he was raised. All good here."

"Thank you, Anne. I really appreciate it,". Anne ended the conversation with, "No, I thank you, and I thank Tyler for those little ones, who will not be harassed anymore. Goodbye, Nick." Nick walked back into the classroom, which he had left thinking the worst, but now was returning to as one proud papa.

Tyler's academic challenges were minimal because of the gray matter between his ears, which smarts he had obviously inherited from his mother. He'd taken ten AP classes and passed nine with either a 4 or a 5, winning him college credit, meaning at least one year's tuition free and clear. There was one class where he did not pass the exam and got a 2. That was AP US History, and yes, his teacher was his dad, Mr. Nick Finch. Tyler gravitated toward math and science classes such as statistics, biology, chemistry, environment, and calculus, but he also did quite well in his English-language classes. And then there was history. Now he had passed his other social studies AP classes, such as psychology, taught by his "aunt" Betsy, and world history, as well as geography, but still these were not APUSH. Teaching relatives, especially one's own children, can be a challenge, but it seemed after a couple of days of class that nobody even noticed that Tyler, and later Mel, was Mr. Finch's child, mostly because of how well the Finches handled the situation. The two children never, not once, brought attention to the fact that the man in front of the room was Dad and not Mr. Finch. Nick made a pledge to himself never to coach Tyler, as he had seen firsthand what a train wreck it could be to coach one's own child, but the classroom was different.

Nick's classes always seemed to go from bell to bell as he was a stand-and-deliver sort of teacher reciting the American story, and from what he had been told, his students loved it. After all, the great history teachers were the greatest of storytellers. It was the storytelling of an instructor who not only knew his facts but also loved telling the tales of the people and events that made the United States the greatest country ever to be organized or raise a flag. As Nick would say, "Our country has its faults, but there is only one flag on that moon, and no one has freed more people from misery and suffering than the United States." On day one, he would tell his students about the good, the bad, and the ugly of the United States, but 90 percent of it, he felt, was good and even exceptional.

When the College Board released its results from the May AP exam in late June, both Tyler and Nick went to the organization's website to check out the scores. Going right down to the *F*'s, Nick saw a two next to Tyler Finch's name. He looked at it twice to be sure he was seeing what he thought he saw, and sure enough it was a two. A score of 3, 4, or 5 is a passing grade, and most of the time, the US history AP exam is the toughest with right around a 50 percent pass rate. It is the oldest test offered by the College Board, having first begun in the seventies at New England prep schools. From there, other courses and disciplines were added as Advanced Placement was now a cash cow for the schools and the College Board. And universities loved these exams as they are an excellent predictor of undergraduate success.

That night at dinner in the Finch household, the tension was so thick you could cut it with a knife. Obviously both Lauren and Mel knew about the results, but they were keeping quiet, obviously uncomfortable. Finally, Nick broached the subject: "I got my test results from the College Board today, and for the most part they were what I thought. For the most part."

Tyler quit playing with his food, looked up at his dad, and said, "I know, Dad. I didn't do well. I am sorry." Lauren reached over and held her son's hand for support. Mel was trying to hide a smile, keeping it from becoming too obvious. She was enjoying this as she always seemed to have to live up to her brother's academic success, which was not fair.

Nick put down his fork, leaned back, and asked, "OK, what in the hell happened?"

Tyler responded matter-of-factly: "Dad, I have grown up in this house hearing these stories since I could talk, and we as a family have seemed to visit in person at least half the sites you talked about, so I thought I didn't have to study. I figured I already knew it. I guess I figured wrong. Sorry."

Nick looked at his son, who was looking right back at him, and decided, *no use crying over spilled milk.* There was one thing that Nick wondered: "Well, when did you realize you were in trouble?"

Tyler quickly responded, "About ten minutes in, when I peeked at the entire exam and knew I was screwed." He added, "I tried putting my finger down my throat so I would throw up all over my test so they would have to invalidate it and I could do the retake later. Problem was, I hadn't eaten breakfast and there was nothing in me, so I only gagged a few times. That plan did not work out. So, I decided to give the exam my best shot, and I found out today it was not good enough."

Nick looked stunned. "You did what?" he asked, seeking to confirm what he thought had just heard.

Tyler repeated the story of his failed strategy. Nick shook his head in disbelief for a moment, then he smiled as he looked over at his boy. "You know, that was not a bad idea. Not bad at all. Maybe you do have a little of me in you and not everything comes from your mom."

Academically, Tyler would be just fine with outstanding report cards and college entrance tests such as the SAT and ACT, but he was having trouble with things in the physical realm. Tyler had dreamed of playing football for the Jupiter Warriors as long as he could remember. He had stood next to his dad on Friday nights on the sidelines, up close to the action. He knew head coach Chuck Parsons and JV coach Tyrone Smith almost as family. The problem was that Tyler kept getting hurt, and these were serious injuries. Sure, he was undersized and a little slow, but he did have something all high school football coaches love: no fear of contact. Tyler Finch loved to hit. Kids who realize that football is not a contact sport but a collision sport will always see playing time. First, Tyler suffered a shattered elbow from Little League football, for which a pin had to be permanently placed for reconstruction. Then in his freshman year he tore his meniscus and MCL and ACL, which required a complete knee rebuild using ligaments and tendons from a cadaver. Dr. Frederick Fryman, who had scheduled the surgery for once the swelling went down, was a nationally known orthopedic specialist who helped pioneer techniques such as the "Tommy John" surgery with the legendary Dr. Frank Jobe out in Los Angeles. He was the team surgeon on at least eight professional teams. Nick had gotten to know the famous doctor—who could have been a stand-in for Tom Selleck on "Magnum P.I." because he had had the pleasure of teaching his brilliant son, Shea Fryman. The doctor and teacher got along, maybe because Nick did not fawn over the surgeon but still respected him for who he was—and that was the man who was going to put his son back together. And the doctor respected the dad standing in front of him because of the stories he had heard from his son.

Nick did have one request, and that was if the doctor could a find the cadaver of a male African American athlete for the replacement parts so that Tyler could emerge a better player. The doctor looked up from the paperwork he was doing and said, without missing a beat, "Cannot do that, because then all he would do is run in circles, because the healthy leg would not be able to keep up with the new one." Well played, Dr. Fryman. Well played indeed.

After the surgery, both the doctor and the parents agreed to high doses of Tylenol only and no heavy-duty pain relievers such as oxycodone or OxyContin. Those drugs were ripping the nation apart and ruining families and whole communities. A new contraption was added to the recovery and physical therapy, and it was genius: the ice pack sleeve, which hooked up to a pump that circulated ice-cold water continuously around the repaired area of the leg. Now that machine ate some ice, but it worked wonders. And because Nick had keys to the training room and access to unlimited ice, it worked out perfectly.

For nine months Tyler Finch went to rehab three days a week and then worked out by himself to get himself ready for a doctor's clearance. During the time away, Coach

Parsons stepped down as head football coach and would never coach Tyler, a major disappointment for the boy who was now a junior. He would get ready to play his junior year and his knee would swell up after each and every practice, but he was there. The first game of the year, just about ten plays into the game, it happened again. As he planted himself in position to tackle the ball carrier, he was rolled on by the traffic that happens in football between the tackles, and he heard his knee pop. The training staff and some of the coaches ran onto the field to assess the situation. Even though Nick was not coaching, he was on the sideline. He went out there too. Mom came down from the stands, where she had been sitting with some of the other players' moms. Tyler was clutching his knee and screaming, "It's happened again, Dad! It's happened again! I heard it pop. I can't believe this!" Tyler was assisted to the sidelines, where the training staff elevated the leg and iced it down. It took just four minutes before it was all over—and this time for good.

Lauren called Dr. Fryman on his private cell phone, and they agreed to meet in twenty minutes in the ER at Jupiter Medical Center, the town's hospital. The doctor looked over Tyler's knee and scheduled surgery for Saturday morning at the Jupiter Surgery Center. He gave Tyler a shot of some sort of painkiller and arranged another ice-circulating machine to be delivered to the Finch home ASAP.

Soon after getting their son home, where Nick and Lauren placed him on the downstairs couch so he would not have to navigate the stairs, he fell asleep. The doorbell rang, and Nick went to see who it was. There were about twenty players and cheerleaders, along with two of the coaches, including Coach Tyrone Smith, the former All-SEC tight end from the University of Florida. Nick broke the news and told them Tyler was asleep, saying that surgery was scheduled for first thing in the morning. The players seemed to be choreographed as they all looked down at their shoes, kicked the ground, and shook their heads in disbelief. One by one Nick hugged Tyler's teammates, then collapsed onto one of his front porch chairs, with Tyrone grabbing the other one. Lauren emerged with a glass of wine for herself; a mixed drink of Tito's and cranberry juice, Tyrone Smith's favorite; and a bourbon and water for Nick. She came up behind her husband and rested her hand on his shoulder. Just then Nick broke down and cried like he had not cried since the miscarriage or the death of his mother. He had watched how hard his son had worked just to get on that field again, and then in all of four minutes the bad dream had returned. It was not fair. He hurt for his son because his son was hurting. Life can be cruel.

Tyler would have to go through the rehab sessions again, but now for six months rather than nine to twelve, as the surrounding areas were much stronger thanks to the previous rehab. Tyler stayed away from the heavy painkillers but seemed to be self-medicating with marijuana. Nick himself had never been a fan of the stuff as he felt it made him hungry and lazy, and as he would say, he never needed any help or a boost in those two areas. Tyler was also suffering from depression brought on by the injuries and by the stress not only of being a student but also of being a student whose dad was also his teacher. Weed seemed to relax him. Nick had more than a suspicion that Tyler was smoking because he could smell the residual odor when he came home. More than once, there was a confrontation. Finally, one early evening the Tequesta police. Tyler and some friends had been caught sharing a joint in the beach parking lot after surfing. Dr. Fryman, a surfer himself, really pushed the idea of surfing on Tyler, saying it would build up his leg and also serve as therapeutic mental rehab of a sort.

Nick and Lauren went over to the police station. Sure enough, there was their honor roll student seated in a small room, isolated. The police had split up the boys to interrogate them as to the source of the marijuana. None would name names, and they all said they had found the joint in the parking lot. Nick had arrived feeling angry at his son and surf buddies, but now he was upset with the local police. Finally, one of the officers came out and said to Nick, "You know this cannot be good for you as a teacher at the school. Maybe you can talk some sense into those boys."

Nick responded quickly and to the point: "Those others are not my sons, and as far as my son goes, do what you think you need to do or release him now. One thing I do know from working at the high school is that this is a misdemeanor offense and not a felony, so if you are not going to do anything more, release him to his mother and me now. I will make sure he signs up and takes the diversion class and pays the fee. Are we good?"

It was a quiet ride home. Nick began to soften his stance on marijuana because if the boy's own doctors saw no problem with it, then who was he?

One evening Nick and Lauren were out for dinner with another couple, and they got a call from a neighbor saying that the police were at their home. Mel was up from Florida Atlantic University in Boca, so they called her, and she answered, saying it was just a misunderstanding and "all is good." When they got home, everything looked fine, but Nick would ask the school police officer, a retired New York cop named Kevin O'Malley, to look up why the JPD had been called to his home. This was about three or four days after the Saturday phone call. Kevin came out to Nick's classroom and showed him the report. Apparently, there was a complaint from some new neighbors who had moved in behind them. They were younger, millennials. Nick was not sure where they had moved from, but the license plate frame on their vehicle was embossed with UCLA. Lauren and Nick had tried to introduce themselves but were blown off, as were the other neighbors, who also wanted to extend a welcome.

Nick read the report, and indeed the police had shown up because of a complaint about marijuana use. The paperwork stated that it was on private property and that the twenty-one-year-old woman produced a doctor-signed medical prescription. A classic "nothing to see here" situation. The problem was, for three days afterward, Mel was tormented, fearing that her dad, being a schoolteacher and all, was going to get in trouble and maybe even be fired, and it would be her fault. When the parents finally got a hold of their daughter and told her everything was OK and not to worry. Mel was relieved and came home to hugs and kisses.

Nick went over to his new neighbors' home and knocked on the door to talk things out. He knocked three times. Nobody came to the door, but he could see they were home. On his third attempt, he pounded so hard that he heard the adjacent windows rattle. Finally, the "man of the house" came out, saying that he was sorry he had not heard the knocking. Bullshit. Nick then told him and the wife, who was peeking out from the kitchen, that he did not appreciate the police being called to his home. He said that if the man had a problem, he should just come over and talk it over with Nick personally. He then produced his daughter's prescription for the marijuana. He explained she was concerned that he was going to get into trouble for the police action at their home. Nick then asked where the neighbors had gone to college, because for many, that is where they are exposed to marijuana for the first time. Of course, Nick grew up in South Florida, so he had been introduced to it back in middle school. Nick asked them if they had attended a service academy such as West Point or the United States Naval Academy in Annapolis, or maybe a strict religious school, that made them feel uncomfortable with the scent of marijuana. The resident mumbled something that included the name of California. Nick shook his head and left. The two sets of neighbors have not spoken since.

Both kids would pretty much sail through their high school years with the typical speed bumps, but they really had a big advantage with their dad teaching at the school they attended in that they had the biggest lockers on campus, an on-site ATM (i.e., Dad's wallet), and a network of what were essentially extended family members who took care of them and looked out for them.

Unbeknownst to Nick, Melody was practicing a kind of passive-aggressive rebellion against her first-hour teacher in her student government class, Nick's colleague, and friend Maria Jean McCoy. This was Mel's fourth year in the program. She was a leader in that she not only was a veteran senior but also was well respected by the younger students in the class. Mel had her mentors who helped her, such as Alexandria Landry, who went by Alex, who made sure she was always on her committees and rode with her to district- and state-level meetings and rallies. Alex would become one of Nick's all-time favorites, not only because of her outstanding performance in his class, but also because of the peer nurturing and role modeling she provided for Mel. Today, after having graduated from the University of Florida, where she was a student leader there, both on campus and in her sorority, Alex is an executive with a liquor distributor in the Tampa area.

It seems Mel was "over" the pep talks and the warnings, because now, in her fourth year, she would arrive late every day and with a large—check that, a *Grande*—cup of some exotic coffee concoction from Starbucks. Not occasionally, but daily, which of course was a violation of Jupiter High's policy against unexcused tardiness, which did not pertain to Mel because she always had a pass to go to class signed by one the assistant principals, another teacher, Officer O'Malley, or sometimes even the principal, Dr. Carolyn Esposito. Nick knew of this. He had hoped it would stop immediately, but he had no idea about the resistance movement led by his daughter, much to the delight of the kids who were new to the program. What it did do was put Mrs. McCoy in an awkward position as she was a dear friend of both Nick and Lauren and really liked the work Mel did. Mel's power struggle was turning from rebellion to revolution. And because Mel *always* had a pass signed by one of Mrs. McCoy's superiors, there was really nothing she could do about this. Nick hadn't found out about Mel's serial tardiness until the end-of-year JHS student council banquet, when was Mel recognized as a four-year member who had made contributions to both the class and the school and was awarded, separately from her class, a fifty-dollar gift card to Starbucks with a framed certificate that read: Most Likely to Be Late with Coffee with No Consequences. It was signed by the entire class, all without the prior knowledge of Mrs. McCoy. The revolution was complete. Mel still has the award.

While both Finch kids were still in high school, there was another speed bump, but this time it was with Lauren. One Friday afternoon, she came home early, around two o'clock. Nick arrived shortly thereafter to change out of his shirt and tie and to put on some more comfortable clothes to meet the boys for happy hour. They would normally meet at a local place called the Tabicca Restaurant and Grill. The prefix to the name stood for tavern and bistro. Mel was the hostess there. She usually arrived for work as the group was breaking up to go home and start their weekends with their families. When Nick got home, usually nobody was there except the dog(s), but this time his wife was there at the kitchen table, staring out the back French door facing the back patio, pool, and yard. Intuitively knowing something was wrong, Nick cut right to the chase and said, "I know that look. What is wrong? What happened?"

Lauren looked back at her husband. There were tears in her eyes, and her face was already streaked from teardrops she'd already cried. She said, "I think I am getting fired tonight."

Nick was stunned. "Wait, what? What happened? I mean, just last year you were some kind of employee of the year for Dover. You told me your numbers are great. What is going on?"

Lauren shook her head and replied, "I don't know, except there are some people right above me on the food chain who are very jealous of me and see me as a threat to their existence. That is all I can think of. I am so sorry, especially with Tyler heading out to college next fall. I am so sorry." She started to cry again.

Nick put his hands on her shoulders and said, "No worries. We, and I mean you, will get through this. You are the most talented person I have ever known." For the life of him, Nick could not figure out what had happened. He had always heard of the glass ceiling and workplace discrimination but had kind of looked at that with a cocked eye as perhaps an excuse for failure to meet job expectations. He himself was in a profession where most peers were women, and his last four principals were woman, so maybe he was the last guy they wanted to pass judgment on their predicament.

"I have a seven o'clock meeting at the Gardens Marriot, where I guess I will find out. Two big bosses, along with my two jerk bosses, the one from Miami and the other from Atlanta, will be there. Four of them altogether. And get this: a security guard was told to follow me to my office to watch me clean out my desk and take my keys. I did not do anything wrong. I do not deserve this, Nick. I am so sorry." She was crying again.

Nick said, "Well then, I am going with you."

Immediately she responded forcefully and with the tone of a bank president, "No you are not. It's me and me alone."

Lauren left the house at twenty minutes to seven for the ten-minute drive. When she arrived, she was told by the security guard in the lobby to wait for him to give her all clear and then proceed to a suite on the top level of the hotel. The permission was granted at least half an hour late. When Lauren walked into the room with the Dover Banking and Trust executives, she was instructed to take a seat facing the four men, all dressed in business suits. The security guard stood at the door. One of the men opened with something about this having been a tough decision, but for the good of everyone involved, it had to be done. Then it was explained it was a business decision and nothing personal. At first, Lauren was beaten back, but now she threw her shoulders back and tried to respond. The man cut her off and told her she was there to listen. She then startled the group by producing a small handheld tape recorder and turning it on, saying it was there so she would have a record of the meeting, seeing as this was a professional decision. Nothing personal. The meeting then picked up fast as the executives offered her a onetime severance of three months' salary and the equivalent of a two-week paid vacation, but she would have to sign a nondisclosure form about the severance. And a one-year noncompete clause was added. Lauren Finch looked at the men one by one, who had trouble making eye contact—took the two checks and the agreement, stared the men down, and ripped the documents to shreds, but not before placing the tape recorder right next to the papers as she tore them up so the sound would be recorded for posterity's sake. Once again, she said, this was a business decision. She walked to the door and told the security official she was ready to head over to her office. The men nodded in agreement. Just before she left, she turned around and said in a matter-of-fact tone of voice, with the recorder by her lips, "See you in court."

Lauren got home around nine thirty but stayed in the driveway for a good half hour, talking on the phone. She walked in and hugged her husband. Soon Mel was home from work and found out. Tyler, who was out night fishing for wahoo, had not yet heard the news. He would find out in the morning, or around noon when he got up. Lauren said she was already working on plan for legal action but seeing as Florida was tough because it is a "right to work" state, she would have to go federal. She was already reaching out to contacts and reviewing and updating her résumé. Things might get rough, tough, and tight, but they would make it. She then went upstairs to bed and was asleep, or least pretended to be, when Nick followed her up about thirty minutes later.

Nick thought of another strategy, another coping skill from his upbringing: revenge. He knew two guys he'd gone to high school with who worked in different trades but were mostly cash-only bill collectors and repo men. Nick knew they hung out at Harry's Banana Farm, which was a throwback Key West–style bar and package store in the north end of Lake Worth a few blocks from the C-51 canal separating West Palm Beach from Lake Worth. Harry's opened early for the morning drinkers, many of whom worked night shifts at places like the airport, then in the afternoon, especially on Fridays, it doubled as a check cashing store. If it rained, many of the tradesmen would call it a day and leave their jobsites for a beer and a shot at their friendly drinking site. The evenings brought a strange mix of young people who were getting a head start on the evening at a very reasonable price, while others, mostly regulars, just found the place comfortable. The last group was with whom Nick knew Terry and Tommy would be.

Nick went down to Lake Worth after having explained to his wife he was headed south to see a high school game. Sure enough, Terry and Tommy were both at Harry's. They immediately recognized Nick and waved him over, telling the man seated next to them to beat it, who did as he was told. Come to find out it was one of the two guys' nephews. Which one, Nick was not sure.

Nick ordered a drink, and Tommy opened the conversation by telling Nick he had heard from a mutual friend that maybe Nick could use a friend or two friends, especially two friends who had known him since elementary school. Nick explained what had happened to his wife. The two guys knew her as they had both attended Nick andLauren's wedding. Terry suggested they go out back for a smoke and some privacy. Nick said something to the effect that they would lose their seats at the bar, and the two laughed in unison: their seats would be just fine. Outside, the two explained there were a few different options, ranging from scaring the hell out of the Florida guy to roughing him up a little, or even a lot, if Nick knew what they meant by that. And by the way, this would be free, no charge, what with Nick's being family and all. They explained they usually just collected money, but there were times when they'd had to adjust people's attitudes. Tommy said he loved to do that to divorce lawyers. Nick just listened, then the three returned inside to Harry's, where their seats were just how they'd left them, open but with new drinks on the bar in front of the chairs. Nick thought about the proposition just made to him as he stared at the ice in his bourbon and water. Then he just got up, placed a hand on each of the businessmen's shoulders, and said, "Thanks, guys, but I cannot do it. I would love to pull the trigger, but I keep thinking this asshole, who deserves a world-class ass whipping, has two little kids at home, and I just cannot do it. Thank you. It means a lot you were willing to help me out. I mean that."

Tommy responded, smiling, "I am not surprised. You are a good dude, and what we do is not always good. In a way, I am glad you have not changed, my man. Take care." At times Nick would see the banker's picture taken at some sort of award or charity event and think, *this guy has no idea how close he came to having body parts broken or even worse. Oh well.*

Just as Nick had predicted, Lauren not only landed on her feet but found herself higher up than where she had been before the firing. A local employment lawyer, an Egret Landing neighbor, who was a woman, took an interest in the case and proceeded with legal action against Dover Banking and Trust, who soon wanted to settle before the case ever went to trial. The three months' severance turned into a full year, but Lauren told them not to worry about the two weeks' vacation time since it had been a month, and that was good enough for her. The noncompete clause was laughed off by the plaintiff and her lawyer as Lauren was going to start in her new position as soon as the legal paperwork was signed, sealed, and delivered. Dover folded on every front, and Sandy recorded every minute of the surrender. Once again, it was just a business decision. Financially, it would be one of the best years for the Finch's as Lauren collected from both Dover and her new employer, American Trust & Bank. She would start out as a vice president but was being groomed for the president's role for when the active president retired in about six months. She had been contacted by Rob Dodge, her old colleague, who himself had switched over to ATB about a year earlier. Based out of Chicago, the new firm did some things different, which took Lauren awhile to get used to, but they were much more professional, ethical, and up front and, by the looks of it, were not backstabbers. Midwestern in origin and modeled on such values, it was a refreshing change from the madness of the East Coast banks she had previously worked for. She now was located on Banker's Row on Royal Palm Way in the heart of Palm

Beach and was right across the street from the Palm Beach Public School where Nick had attended junior high.

Sure enough, in only about four months Sandy was promoted to president. A press release was circulated to the financial papers, to the *Post*, and to Palm Beach's own *Palm Beach Daily News*, better known as the "*Shiny Sheet*" because of the high-quality paper it was printed on. Upon hearing the news, Nick went down Harry's Bar in Lake Worth and found his boys sitting at the same seats. He bought a round of drinks and produced the newspaper announcement of Lauren's promotion. The three toasted each other, although Nick still had a little regret that he had okayed the doling out of an old-fashioned lesson. Oh well, things had worked out best in the long run. But still maybe just a little … Nah.

If a teacher is truly honest, he or she will tell you that one of the greatest perks of teaching, well, the three greatest perks, is the period of June, July, and August. Yes, of course it is joy of watching young people grasp a lesson and seeing the light bulb go off when they finally get it or are motivated to take the next step without prompting. Lifelong relationships develop with students, along with camaraderie. These students become like a second family to the teacher. But it is hard to beat summertime and, while we are at it, the seventeen or so days at Christmastime and almost two weeks around Easter. Sweet. And if the teacher belongs to a two-income household and his or her salary is the secondary one, it's even sweeter. Nick was very fortunate and privileged to have the time off he had, but another blessing was Lauren's outstanding salary, which allowed the Finch family to travel. And travel they did. By the time the kids went off to college, they had seen a great portion of the earth and the majority of the United States. Along with their travels, which were pinned on a map in the family den, they made lifelong memories that the children would be able to share with their own significant others and someday their own children. Yes, they were fortunate.

In the United States, the Finches started a tradition of, every third year, renting a lakeside mountain cabin in southwestern North Carolina in a place known as Lake Toxaway. Lake Toxaway was started by some millionaires. Some claim it was John D. Rockefeller himself. Whoever it was, they created a private jewel amid the cool, crisp mountain air of the Smokies. Nestled between the quaint little college town of Brevard and the four-way stop that is Cashiers, which is on the way to the shopper-friendly resort town of Highlands, the place is off the beaten path of the Blue Ridge Parkway and close enough for airport service to either Greenville, South Carolina, or Asheville, North Carolina. And the fact that Asheville has a bohemian flavor to it with a laid-back hippy lifestyle and plenty of microbrews and wineries, along with authentic bluegrass music, amounts to another plus for the grown-ups. Most of all, Lake Toxaway is nearby, providing an escape from the summer heat and hurricanes of South Florida, offering cool mountain air and boating on a crisp private freshwater lake. Nick had first gone there in high school with some friends and later took Sandy there on a return trip from Washington, DC. They loved everything about the area as a young couple and could not wait to share it with their own kids. Add to that the endless trails that always seem to end up at a majestic waterfall, and it is all that South Florida is not. For that reason, it has been an escape for the residents of Palm Beach County for generations. Every third year the Finch children could count on a two-week stay at a rented lakeside cabin. They'd also rent a pontoon boat that served as a nightly booze cruise vessel and, during the day, enabled endless hours of water-skiing and inner-tubing fun and even some fishing. At night, the kids, when young, would chase these magical little insects that were foreign to them called lightning bugs. At least twice the family ventured away from Lake Toxaway toward Highland, where they'd park on the side of the isolated road and take a small hike to a slippery waterfall affectionately known as "Bust Your Butt Falls," where they'd slide down the slick rocks fresh with a constant supply of cool mountain water and a drop off into a pool of cold water at the bottom. It was Mother Nature's own free water park. Everyone there picked up after themselves and left the place as they'd found it. Occasionally, bears would look on at the crazy humans from every age group and listen to the sound of beautiful laughter echoing through the countryside. The kids to this day still talk about Bust Your Butt Falls, and the stories are always told with smiles and laughter. No theme park here, just Mother Nature shared by laughing families. It does not get any better than that. Nick has tried to count the trips to Lake Toxaway, Bust Your Butt, the Brown Trout Restaurant, Crossroads BBQ, and the Old Edwards Inn—at least five separate vacation stays, and all are ingrained in his memory, not to mention that some of Nick and Lauren's most prized photographs that are displayed throughout their house are of these vacation trips. Thank you, Lake Toxaway.

The United States is such a beautiful country with so much to see. Nick never fails to say thank you to our twenty-sixth president, Theodore Roosevelt. You, T.R., created our national park system for generations of people to enjoy. The Finch's would explore this country from one end to the other. One time it was flying into Rapid City, South Dakota, to start a trip westward across the Northern Plains from Mount Rushmore to Yellowstone down to the Grand Tetons, then fly home by way of Salt Lake City, Utah. As had been the case for Nick as a youth in his travels west, the kids also had their breaths taken away by the majesty of the American West. The first sighting of wild buffalo fascinated them, but like Nick, by the end of the trip it was more like, "Will that beast get off the road so we can move on?" White water rafting, when available, was always charted by the family, whether it was in the Smoky Mountains in the East or on the Snake River in Jackson Hole. There was a trip to California where the kids got to go surfing in Santa Cruz and experience true surfing Cali style. They quickly learned that wet suits were a must as the water was much colder than their Gulf Stream–fed Jupiter-area Ocean. They saw the Golden Gate Bridge, rode the famous cable cars, and saw the beautiful rocky coastline of Monterey. Tyler and Mel didn't even complain much about an adult side trip to wine country.

Summer was not the only time for travel. Spring break opened up new opportunities. Unlike the many others who flooded Florida's beaches from Panama City to Daytona, south to Fort Lauderdale and South Beach, and right to the tip, which is of course Key West, the Finches saw it was time for spring skiing. They packed up and went to Jackson Hole and, in the East, to the site of the 1980 Winter Olympics, Lake Placid, New York. Mel turned out to be an excellent skier, just as she had proven her skill on the surfboard in California. Fearless with great balance, most likely from her equestrian training and her time spent in youth gymnastics and tumbling, whether it was hitting the beach or hitting the slopes, she was all in. Lauren had grown up on the icy slopes of Western Maryland and West Virginia and could hold her own on the various ski routes that required different skill levels. Mom and daughter were up to it. Father and son were not. The two males were true Floridians and did not take to winter sports very well. Plus, Tyler's knees had to be considered. Nick was terrible and hated skiing or even ice skating. Nope, not him, and for the most part not for Tyler either, but what they did find appealing was snowmobiling. That they loved. Nick also explored the local historical sites to a point of family contention. He loved the offbeat museums such as the one dedicated to Levi Strauss in San Francisco and the one dedicated to the Olympics in downtown Lake Placid.

Their ultimate trip westward was to Alaska. The family packed up one summer and flew from Palm Beach International Airport, to Atlanta, to Anchorage, where they took a train to the coast to Seward and then took a cruise along the Alaskan coastline to Vancouver, British Columbia. Nick did not like cruises at all, but this one was pretty neat because of the natural beauty that is the great northwest. Whales breaching, grizzlies eating spawning salmon, and the endless sun of summertime were all very memorable, but then there was the time of getting caught in traffic after deplaning in Vancouver and heading to their hotel, finding themselves in the middle of a massive gay pride parade. Mel, who was about seven, asked her parents why the big man with a beard was in a dress and marching with other men, all of them swinging umbrellas in a choreographed march down the street. Tyler, who knew what was going on, chimed in, "Why is that, Dad? And what is exactly going on there?" Tyler knew but wanted to stir the pot.

Nick looked at Lauren, who returned with, "Nick, what is going on? Please share with us."

Nick bit his lip for a second, and then it came to him. "Mel, those men are going to a costume party, like a Halloween party, because it is a holiday or festival up here in Canada." Mel nodded and kept looking at the marchers, whom she was now waving at. Some of them waved right back. The family still talks about the parade.

Although the Finch's stayed in western Canada for only a few days, it did constitute international travel. The kids were to travel to the Bahamas with friends, and there was one family cruise to the southern Caribbean—Martinique and the US Virgin Islands—which Nick hated. If he wanted to go to the Caribbean, he would just go to Key West and never have to leave the country. There was one trip that the family enjoyed and had been forced to take because of the rehab of Tyler's knee. Originally, they were going to go on a Mediterranean cruise, but with his injury, the length of air travel would have been too much for him. Mel would later go on a school trip to England and Italy, and she still swears that the queen, when driving out of Buckingham Palace, looked right at her, and waved to her. Not to the crowd, mind you, but to Melody Finch. Nick asked his daughter if she curtsied, which is protocol, and she replied, "As a matter of fact, I did."

Nick, of course, had been to England, but that was "BL," or before Lauren. He had gone with Michelle Mitchell to be her date at the wedding of some prep school friend of hers or some friend of her parents. Most of those four days were spent drinking in London. But he had been, and Mel had been. Tyler could have cared less for England, and still Lauren has not gone, which is a sore point that she and Nick avoid talking about for obvious reasons. Lauren canceled the European trip but found an alternative that the entire family ended up loving: Bermuda. Pink beaches, lively nightlife, and a polite home team—it was a great time.

The mother of all vacations was also an international one, and it is still the benchmark for all their travels: three weeks "down under" in Australia. This was a chartered group trip guided by Disney, and it was fantastic in every way. First was the brutal plane trip, which started in Miami and went to LA, then on to Australia, for about twenty-five hours total in the air. The worst thing Nick did was to click on the icon on his personal entertainment screen that marked exactly where the plane was when they were right in the middle of the Pacific. Seeing how much time they still had to go was downright depressing. They lost a full day by crossing the International Date Line and finally arrived at the seaside resort town of Cairns and their hotel on the Coral Sea at Palm Cove, where they had some really neat times, including diving around the Great Barrier Reef. One day the kids and Sandy went to a local zoo to see some koala bears, emus, and of course kangaroos, so Nick took that time to explore the local scene. He walked into an establishment known as the "Cairns Surf Club" and sat down to wait for the bartender. The people in the bar were busy watching Australian rules football, a sport that had fascinated Nick since ESPN's early days of programming. Nick ordered a beer and sat quietly, trying to soak in the local flavor. When the bartender returned, he asked Nick if he was a Yank or a Canadian. Nick said he was American and from Florida, adding he had never been called a Yank before. The barkeep laughed and walked back to his group of regulars. In a few minutes he returned and told Nick that the next drink was on him and the mates because it was Nick's birthday. Nick was perplexed. He accepted the brew and thanked the bartender for it, but admitted his birthday was in January, not July. The man responded, "No, mate, where you are from it is the Fourth of July, so it is your birthday. And thanks to you Yanks, we do not speak Japanese." So that was it. Indeed, back in the States it was Independence Day. The United States military, and especially the navy during the early days of World War II, had stopped the imminent Japanese invasion by winning the Battle of the Coral Sea. Nick thanked all the people at the bar and said he wished he could have introduced his two war veteran parents to such outstanding men. Soon they were all seated together swapping stories about their homes. The Aussies are great!

From Palm Coast it was out to the outback, the real center of the Australian continent, not the restaurant chain that had its start in Tampa. The highlight there was riding camels across an arid area that reminded Nick of Arizona around Ayers Rock. Who knew that Australia had more camels than the Arabian Peninsula had? Apparently, they had been brought to Australia to help with construction of a railroad. Because of the heat and the lack of water, it was thought the camel would be the perfect beast of burden. Americans had tried the same thing when attempting to build a southern arm of the Transcontinental Railroad, which was the idea of then Secretary of War Jefferson Davis, who later become the only president of the Confederacy. The camels would have worked, but the local Native tribes felt threatened by what they thought were mutant horses and harassed the workforce until the camels were removed. Then the Civil War soon broke out, and the rest is history.

In the outback, Nick and Mel rode tandem, while Tyler and Lauren teamed up on another camel. Mel and Nick loved it. Mom and son, not so much. From the Outback, it was on to the lovely city of Sydney. Dominated by an opera house, a bridge, and a harbor, the place glistened with beauty. The family decided to treat their guide and take him to a nice dinner on the roof of the Old Government House overlooking the entire harbor. The view was breathtaking, and so was the bill. The dinner for five cost more than one thousand dollars—and that was in 2009! The trip finished up with an excursion down to Melbourne. It was summer, but in Australia it was winter, so the farther south the Finch's went, such as to Melbourne, the colder it got. The high point of the trip for Lauren was taking a bus trip to the very southern tip just a little north of Tasmania. Nick could not get the vision of the cartoon he had watched as a kid on Gregory Road, in West Palm, of the Tasmanian devil out of his head. It brought a grin to his face. But something that his wife got to see in person and up close still sticks with her as one of her favorite memories. When the bus pulled up to the remote destination, the group was led to an observation area where they saw thousands of penguins riding the waves like surfers and going up the beach and up to the hillside, which was kind of like Malibu Beach housing, but for penguins. Lauren had always loved penguins—why, no one knows—and here she had gotten to witness this act of nature right before her eyes. She was thrilled beyond words. The other three Finch's were amused but cold, although they did remain polite because they saw what it meant to the woman of the house.

From Melbourne it was back to the United States by way of LA, then Dallas, and on to Palm Beach. They had left Australia on a Monday morning and arrived home in Florida on a Sunday evening. It would take a few days to get reacclimated, but they'd have a lifetime of memories that would never go away. Traveling was such a gift. The memories never stop giving. They all realized just how fortunate they were.

College was calling to Tyler, and soon it would be calling to Mel. Tyler had told his parents that he wanted to leave Florida and do his own thing out of state. He also wanted to go to a big school, but not too big. Rollins, his mom's alma mater, was out because it was too close, too small, and too expensive. Tyler narrowed his choices to the University of Georgia (UGA) at Athens and Ole Miss. The family went on their college tour and saw there was a lot to like about Georgia: good academics, outstanding sports teams, easy connections for flights out of Atlanta, and a fantastic music scene. What other college town can boast about being the home base of REM and the B-52's? The Finches' former neighbors from across the street, Luke, and Helen McAdams, were graduates of UGA and also decorated athletes. Luke had risen from walk-on to starting linebacker, and Helen had been an All-American gymnast and a finalist for the Olympic team. They were great people. The Finch's were sorry to see them move back to the Atlanta area. Tyler kept his cards close to his vest and did not let on which way he was leaning. Then it was on to Oxford and his father's alma mater. Tyler had in a way grown up on that campus, having gone to The Grove and attended football games since he literally was an infant. The family had traveled to away games and had been in the Champions Club section of Ben Hill Griffin Stadium / Florida Field the day the Rebels upset the eventual national champions the Gators when the defense stopped the legendary Tim Tebow short on a fourth-and-one. Still a great memory for the family. On their last day in Oxford, Tyler looked at both his parents and announced, "This is where I want to go. I want to be an Ole Miss Rebel. I grew up coming here and always wanted to go here. Is that, OK?"

Nick's eyes welled up with tears. He nodded and said, "Of course it is, if that is what you really want."

Tyler looked his dad right in the eye and said, "It is, Dad. Hotty Toddy guys." He would encounter speed bumps, and his grades would rise and fall, but Tyler Finch would remain an Ole Miss Rebel. There is something about legacies, you know.

A few years later it would be Mel's turn, and like her older brother, she selected Ole Miss. Unlike him, she went the Greek route and underwent the process known as rushing. Recently, Ole Miss officials had had to move rush back on account of the number of coeds who transferred out if they were not selected by the sorority, they wanted the most. Mel had a great résumé with her four years of student government, her high grades, her modeling, her equestrian accomplishments, and the fact that she was a legacy (Lauren not only went Greek but also was her sorority's president, the Rollins College chapter of Phi Mu). Phi Mu at Ole Miss is considered a top-tier sorority. They extended an invitation to Mel, and she accepted as a pledge on bid day. Something was off for her and within a few months she had her fill of Ole Miss and wanted to come home. Nick and Lauren notified the University of Mississippi and Phi Mu that she would not be returning for the spring semester. That January she enrolled at Palm Beach State College to rebuild both her transcript and her confidence. It worked. The following fall she enrolled at Florida Atlantic University in Boca Raton. Undecided on a major, she was recently looking into elementary education, thinking maybe she'd become a teacher like her dad, but elementary level. The main thing was that she was slowly returning to her old self the confident model and equestrian.

With the kids out of college now, Nick realized he was on the downward slope of his career. He knew Lauren would work on and on because that was what she did, and she was exceptionally good at it. It would be a long time before she would hang up her banking vocation. Nick was good at what he did, but he figured he had been working in some sort of way since he was ten years old, and now that he was in his late fifties, maybe it was getting to be time to turn in his gradebook. He and Lauren met with district personnel and looked over a special retirement program Florida had called DROP—the Deferred Retirement Option Program. One can declare retirement to become eligible for the program and then retire, yet in a way keep working, while the retirement benefits continue to accumulate in a tax-deferred trust fund. Nick had no idea what it really was, but Lauren was all for it. At the age fifty-four, they signed the papers and Nick had entered the DROP. Now the end was in sight. Nothing really changed as he still got up around five in the morning and hung out with his dogs, then showered, put his shirt and tie on, and drove a little more than a mile to JHS, where he signed in; walked out to his portable classroom, or the trailer park, in the back; taught his AP US History course; hung out with his friends on the fence line, talking mostly sports; and then called it a day. Lather, rinse, repeat for 180 days of the year. He would check in with the kids and maybe plan a trip up to Ole Miss for a game—maybe even a road trip game, like the time when the Rebs played Cal Berkeley out in California. Sandy and Nick had taken fellow teachers and best friends Tyrone Smith and Mike Lynn along. They had never been to the Bay Area, so Lauren served not only as a type of den mother watching out for the boys, but also as a tour guide on trips to Fisherman's Wharf, Alcatraz, and Muir Woods, and a one-day trip to wine country, where Tyrone found the wine for which he claimed he himself was the inspiration, as they had named it after him: "Black Stallion".

With all the changes—moving to Jupiter, having children, starting new jobs, and traveling—there was one constant: the relationship between the Finches and their dogs. Clancy, of course, was the first, and was the crash test dummy for future child-rearing. Clancy had also made the move up to Jupiter after a layover at Uno Lago in Juno Beach. He was never comfortable with the move or, for that matter, Jupiter. He had aged a lot in his last two years, then the massive golden retriever weighing more than a hundred pounds finally had to put down at the grand old age of thirteen. Clancy had been there for almost everything, from the tragedy of a late-term miscarriage and the death of parents to the joyful event of welcoming children into the Finch family, of which Clancy was the bedrock. Both Lauren and Nick later admitted they confided things to him that no one else would ever come to know. Dogs are our therapists, but they do not annoy us by asking over and over, "Just how did that make your feel?" Instead, they listen and cuddle. What more can you ask?

Lauren had to be the one to take him for his last ride as Nick just flat-out said he could not and would not do it. He admitted he was too weak for the final ride. Lauren soldiered on, proving once again just how mentally tough she was. Before Clancy's death at the age of thirteen, Nick and Lauren thought having a puppy around the house might prolong his life, so they brought home Archie, another golden. They had also heard that children who helped raise a family puppy were better adjusted. Clancy was already full grown when the kids were born. Archie was named after the famous Ole Miss quarterback Archie Manning, father of Cooper, Peyton, and Eli. Unfortunately for Archie, he was a hemophiliac and bled to death from internal hemorrhaging. The kids, instead of helping to raise Archie, got to experience the loss of their one-year-old puppy. So next up was Ani, who was brought home on July 10 as an anniversary present to both Nick and Lauren. A female golden, Ani proved to be the smartest of all the Finch canines. She would live to the ripe old age of thirteen and would be accompanied most of her life by a fourth golden, a beautiful, loving, massive dog named Dutch. He was named after Nick and Sandy's favorite president, Ronald "Dutch" Reagan. Dutch, if he were to come back as a person, would be a male model. Gorgeous and with an excellent disposition, he was perfect in every way. The largest framed photo in the Finch household is one of Dutch at Jupiter Beach with a damp coat looking outward to the sea amid a picturesque background. In the photo, the ocean is deep blue and the sky is white and sunny. It has been featured in magazines. Dutch, like Mel, was a model! Both the kids later confided that they, like their parents, shared their trials and tribulations with the dogs, but especially Dutch. As Mel put it, "He's a great listener."

Ani would give out at the age of thirteen, leaving Dutch alone, but not for long, as the next golden to the house on Scrubjay Lane was an English cream, or white, golden named Winston. Dutch would last another two years before giving out and crossing the bridge to heaven—because all dogs go to heaven, you know. The puppy's name came from the great leader of the English Empire during World War II and many-time visitor to Palm Beach, Sir Winston Churchill. Winston was going to be Nick's dog as Nick was slowly preparing for retirement and thought the two could grow old together. Nick's boss, and his favorite of them all, along of with Carlos Martinez, of course, Carolyn Esposito, loved dogs. When Nick proposed that he bring Winston to work with him in the trailer park so the dog could get used to crowds and kids and so the kids could reach out to him, just as he was beginning to talk about the great advantages of having a service dog around kids, Dr. Esposito interrupted, saying, "Yes, of course. But you have to bring him up here to the front so we all can see him." Pretty soon Winston would accompany Nick to class three days a week and would arrive right in Nick's satchel with his white head popping out. He became the class mascot. The students were disappointed when he was not there and were delighted when he was. They loved him. A few minutes after arriving, Winston would crawl under Nick's desk and fall sound asleep. Some of Nick's favorite pictures are of Winston in his portable classroom with his students.

One day Nick's phone rang. He checked the caller ID and saw it was Lauren, so he answered it. She was beside herself, trying to explain she was on the way to the emergency veterinarian because Winston had just been hit by a passing car. Nick was stunned and shocked. The kids immediately picked up on his change of mood. Nick went to the adjoining classrooms and asked if could get someone to cover his class so he could race over to the vet. When he got to the vet's office, Lauren was in the lobby with her head in her hands, sobbing. The vet called the two back to say their goodbyes, explaining that at first, they thought they could save him, but would have to amputate a leg, but now the brain scan was showing that he was brain-dead. So, it was time to say goodbye. Nick could not understand how this could have happened as their backyard was fenced. All Sandy kept saying was that she was very sorry, and to please forgive her. Nick held his puppy, placing his head right against the little guy's white chest, which had streaks of blood on it, and then the dog was gone. Nick's retirement dog had retired before he had. To this day Nick hurts right to the core when he thinks about the loss. He has never gotten over it and likely never will. Dogs are family, you know. And you know how they say you never get over losing a child? Well, Nick lost his baby boy Winston.

Tyler was home from college and had brought home the dog that Mel had gotten him, a rescue from Alabama that was mostly Australian cattle dog but had some Lab. He had basically been raised by five college boys, and it showed. His name was Jackson, after General Thomas "Stonewall" Jackson, and he moved in for the break. But

Nick had noticed a long talk between Tyler and his mother, and shortly thereafter Lauren approached Nick with the idea of keeping Jackson so Tyler could concentrate on his studies. Nick knew by the way Lauren had proposed the idea that it was already a done deal. Jackson was staying, so he had better just get ready and accept it, because her son was struggling academically, trying to juggle upper-level business classes such as accounting and still do the right thing by his dog. So, Jackson became the newest member of the Finch family.

Jackson was very protective of his new house and housemates and let all the other dogs on the street know that. He especially hated small ratty dogs or white "slipper" dogs, which could be aggressive until they were met by Jackson's response, which could be scary. Nick and Sandy took the dog to the vet and explained the situation. Jackson had to be muzzled for the vet's and her staff's own protection. A Finch golden he was not, yet it was very admirable how protective he was. He was protective rather than aggressive—at least that is what Lauren and Nick told the neighbors. He was also much smarter than the lovable retrievers had been. The vet referred the Finch's and Jackson to a renowned dog behaviorist and therapist, basically a dog psychiatrist, named Dr. Anna Roebuck. She was an expert, having published books on the subject. *If only J.W. were alive to see this,* Nick thought. The dog psychiatrist prescribed tranquilizers and mood-altering drugs to reduce some of Jackson's hostility, and it worked somewhat. What really worked was that Jackson's life finally had stability, form, and order. He had been found as a puppy, abandoned by the side of the street, in Alabama, whimpering, and then was raised by five college boys on beer and chicken wings. And now, for the first time, he had scheduled breakfast time and dinnertime, walking-on-a-leash time, and bedtime. He slept at the foot of Lauren and Nick's bed. Many times, he would sleep on his back with his legs wide open like a passed-out college dude. He mellowed a lot and got fat, but, like Santa, he became a little jolly. He still guarded the house as well as any trained guard dog could but was getting more lovable and approachable by the day. He was accepted, but to Nick, who loved him, he was the nephew or cousin who moved in with you and you loved, but who was not one of your own children. Nick's boy had died that morning at a Jupiter emergency animal clinic from injuries after having been struck by an automobile. Jackson helped, but Nick missed his goldens, all of them, from Clancy, to Archie, to Ani, right on to Dutch and, of course, Winston. The Finch's had a small area right outside their back door with field stones that had been etched with their dogs' names as tombstones. It was a final resting place so the dogs would never be forgotten.

The school board, like many employers that offer health-care benefits, now had an enrollment period, but also like many, they added incentives for living a healthier lifestyle, which meant that once a year you had to report to the gym lobby for a series of quick tests and measurements. Height and weight were recorded, blood pressure and pulse were taken, and you were given a quick finger prick for a sample of blood that was analyzed for things such as cholesterol level. Fifteen minutes later you were done and you got your results. If you passed four of the five, you were good to go, but if you failed in more than two categories, you had to see a lifestyle coach once a month to avoid a monetary penalty. Nick was lucky; if this program had started just a few years earlier, he would have been one of the callers. Now he regularly passed four of the five tests, but he could not pass the BMI measurement that showed one's percentage of body fat. Hardly anybody passed that part of the test. In fact, Nick knew only one person who passed that portion of the exam, and that was "Aunt" Betsy Borrowski. Finally, Nick asked what the recommended BMI was for a person his height. He had lost half an inch in height. The answer was 170 pounds. Nick laughed, saying he had not weighed that little since junior high. A few years earlier the results would have been downright embarrassing, that is, until his primary care doctor and his nurse had a real sit-down talk with him about his health.

Nick had never really gone to official doctor visits and checkups for most of his life. If he had some need, he would just swing by the hospital, where Charlene would have one of the physicians there look at him. All Nick's sports physicals were done there, and usually late at night, with a doctor giving him the once-over then signing the official paperwork. Most of the time you simply were not allowed to get sick in the Finch household. As Charlene would say, "I have seen sick people, and you are not one of them. Take a couple of aspirin and go to bed." If you objected to the diagnosis or the treatment prescribed by the emergency room RN, then that proved you were really not very sick.

Dr. Don Surenberg and his nurse Jordan had come into the examination room and looked over the blood test results. Acting as a tag team, the informed Nick that if he did not change his lifestyle, he would be history himself. He needed to drop at least thirty pounds and get his cholesterol numbers to an acceptable level. If not, he was looking at diabetes, stroke, and possible heart disease. It was true that Nick had let himself go and had gained weight, but instead of losing it, he just bought bigger clothes. He knew that he had gotten unhealthy, but it had to be said by somebody he respected. And Dr. Surenberg and Jordan were more than health-care providers; they were trusted friends. Nick agreed and began to change his lifestyle. No one liked buffalo-style chicken wings more than Nick Finch, well, maybe his friend and colleague Coach Mike Lynn, but still Nick decided no more bar food. Little or no beer. Lunch at the school cafeteria was now off-limits as he packed a lunch of fruits and vegetables. Pasta was off the menu, as were most desserts. He began riding his bike for a workout and wore a sweat jacket when he did yard work such as mowing the lawn. Regular Coke was replaced by Diet Coke, and five o'clock trips across the field to the Egret Landing Clubhouse to work out in the gym were now part of his wake-up ritual. It was slow at first, but the weight did start to come off. It was mostly noticed by people he had not seen in a while.

In about two years, Nick had reached all his goals, but he did not stop there, keeping up his routine. He joined an exclusive gym and continued to ride his bike all over Jupiter and added seven-mile beach walks. It worked as he now easily passed four out of five of his insurance requirements, was forced to buy a new wardrobe, and took delight in his yearly physical, where praise was heaped upon him by his doctor and nurse. When it is was all said and done, Nick had lost four inches from his waistline, lost fifty pounds, lowered his blood pressure, and lowered his heart rate and pulse, and his bloodwork was now in the outstanding range. For five years he had been part of a national study sponsored by a prestigious Ivy League school that would match statistical analysis with age. At the end of the study, Nick measured out as a man forty-five years in age. Not bad for a fifty-eight-year-old. Plus, Nick not only eliminated some bad habits but also picked up three good ones that he still practices. He now loves his trips to the gym, the sidewalk above the beach for his walks, and his bike rides around Jupiter. It took a good doctor, Dr. Surenberg and a trusted nurse Jordan to get him to change, and for that he will always be thankful.

One place that Nick, and as he later noticed his own children, hated going was to the dentist. Both kids when young went the orthodontist route with braces and such with Dr. Steve Myers, a very likable and handsome guy who enjoyed life immensely, especially the Jupiter lifestyle that his profitable suburban practice had opened for him. He lived on the waterfront, had an outdoor tiki bar, and owned multiple boats for fishing, booze cruises, and trips over to the Bahamas, not to mention that he was single and he hired like it. The other fathers never minded the ortho trips as the back of the open-air examination area could have passed for a Playboy Mansion party with attractive dental assistants all over the place. Nick never minded going there, but it was his own dental appointments he hated. His original dentist had been convicted of murdering his wife and was sentenced to life in prison, so Nick had to find a new dentist once when he had come back from college. So he went to Nancy Foster, who worked for a dentist whose office was closed on Fridays. That worked out until those two grew apart, so Nick switched to a local guy he had gone to in high school back at Forest Hill. Dr. Kent Estabrook became the new tooth guy. Dr. Estabrook had grown up in West Palm and had gone to Palm Beach High and then the Marine Corps. After his duty was complete, he took advantage of the GI Bill and went to dental school in West Virginia. Dr. Estabrook was a down-to-earth good man, and it helped he had a friendly staff with an office located right in the middle of West Palm. An even bigger plus was that he accepted the mediocre school board's dental insurance, which would cover almost the whole cost. The problem was that Dr. Estabrook was getting older and would retire right about the same time the Finch's moved to Jupiter.

It seemed Nick was on a constant search for a dentist, so instead of finding a new one, he just brushed his teeth more often and, like many did, decided to wait until there was a problem and then ask around. Later, Nick settled on Dr. Craig Cates, a Texas A&M graduate with a military service background. The two hit it off. Nick liked that Dr. Cates always seemed to have students in to observe, so he would not only be taking care of his patient but also teaching and thereby giving back to his profession and trade. Nick admired this, especially because he himself had had seventeen interns and was proud that fifteen of these were still cleaning their chalkboards at the end of the day, meaning they were still teaching locally. The problem Nick had was that it seemed he would come into the dentist's office feeling great, albeit knowing he would be lectured about flossing more, but he would leave either in pain or with a frozen jawline. Add to that the fact that he always left poorer. It was seemed that they always found a problem that had to be dealt sooner rather than later. Sure enough, Nick would go home shaking his head and carrying a lighter wallet.

Nick did like two of the new habits that he had picked up, one being his bike riding. His bike was not fancy one—middle price range—but it did have a drink holder. Nick would fill his water bottle up, put it in the drink holder, and cruise all over Jupiter. Sometimes he would go with Tim O'Shea on what they would call the "tour de pool," where they would ride by at least half a dozen subdivisions' HOA pools, mostly in the Abacoa development of Jupiter. The point of this trip was to observe the sunbathers who were lying out poolside. Nick and Tim would finish up on Main Street in Abacoa at Rooney's Pub, which was owned and operated by the same family who owned the Pittsburgh Steelers and the Palm Beach Kennel Club. Nick would ride all over town, but he would never don the biker's wardrobe, including the tight biker's shorts, the multicolored tight shirt, the spiked shoes, and of course the helmet that made some people look like extras from *Star Trek*. Nope, Nick was not going to be a Lance Armstrong wannabe. Never going to happen. Nor would he join some biking club of ten-plus riders with matching uniforms riding all over the North County as if it were the Champs-Elysées in Paris. Nick cruised and did not bike.

In the previous ten years or so, there was a popular sitcom on NBC that seemed to have more of a following now than it did when it originally aired. It has a great cast with great writers and is set in a place that most people can relate to. The show, now in syndication, is "*The Office.*" The multiple personalities with their numerous quirks all in the same place at the same time every day made for some interesting scripts and character development. Nick noticed the same situation at a dues-paying fitness club. He had joined what was known as the Jupiter Sports Club, and he was pleased to have gotten the family discount, which he'd been given because he had taught the daughter of the owner and her brother was the managing director. Some of Nick's youth coaches used to say Nick had an iron deficiency—not a mineral imbalance but a hatred for lifting weights. Now he kind of liked lifting weights, along with using some of the other machines and apparatuses that were available at the Jupiter Sports Club. What he also noticed was that there were a few different subcultures of people at the gym at the same time almost every day. It was like *The Office*. First there were the meatheads, who wore shorts that were too tight and ripped tank tops that Nick had grown up calling "wifebeaters" because it seemed that with every domestic call on the show *Cops*, the idiot who was going to jail was wearing one. There was another thing about *Cops*; it seemed always to be filmed by the men and women of law enforcement—and all suspects were innocent until proven guilty in a court of law. The meatheads loved to grunt and growl when lifting and finishing their sets, wanting to be noticed. Another group that wanted to be noticed were the women who dressed up, wore makeup, had perfect hair, and wore just a touch of perfume to go to the gym. Peacocks with their tails spread do not garner as much attention as these women did. Funny thing is that they failed to ever sweat. Then there was the older set of gentlemen who liked to sit on the benches that are connected to the different machines that allow for a direct line of sight into the dance studio. They did little lifting but did a lot of looking at the women in the aerobics, Pilates, or yoga classes. These men would tell you that downward dog was the best part of the yoga routine—the same guys who were amazingly comfortable with nudity in the male locker room as they walked around like cast members of *Naked and Afraid*. Swinging and flopping back and forth did not bother them. Modesty was for others. Then there was the younger generation, who could never put down their phones, taking them from machine to machine, constantly looking at their screens in search of something or someone they might have missed. They would sit on a machine just as long as the senior yoga gawkers did, but texting or surfing the Web. Same people, same place, and same interaction each day. Maybe it could be the new *Office* and they could call it *The Gym* or *The Sports Club*. In reality, Nick became very fond of the new group of people he met at the gym. Like the people from the rest of the area, they came from everywhere and had life experiences to share and talk about.

The five years of DROP flew by as every year a new group of juniors would enter Nick's class, gawking and uncomfortable, and end up in late May or early June as mature seniors with their sights set on college and beyond. The eleventh grade is so important to these students as they are usually now in direct competition with their own classmates, and in some cases their best friends, for scholarships, awards, and admittance to their colleges of choice. College Board exams are taken this year, with lifelong rewards or drawbacks, depending on their scores. Juniors are engaged résumé building like no one else, except maybe college seniors or those leaving graduate school. Add to this the extra pressures of high-level classes such as Nick's AP United States History class; or Sheri Williams's AP Biology; or AP Psychology with "Aunt Betsy," Tyler's favorite teacher; or Yearbook with Erica Mook, who could say she was published each and every year with the true memory book, that is, the yearbook. Text messages are fleeting and temporary, but the yearbook stays forever. She also published the school newspaper the *War Cry*. Even with all the new technology, the day of yearbook distribution was one of the most anticipated days of the school year, and Erica never failed to produce a timeless treasure. It was also very cute that she was married to the new baseball coach Andy Muncy. Some kids never added two and two together because of the different last names. Erica and Andy were the first couple of JHS to have produced an award-winning yearbook and won a state championship in baseball. Another class that tied well together with Nick's class was AP Language with Daisy Gilman. Much of the curriculum of these two classes overlapped, as both discussed the culture of the time period, historical events, and the leaders in both politics and literature. Countless times students would say they had just learned about that person, place, or event in either Nick's or Daisy's class. Reinforcement of the content is very helpful, and Nick Finch and Daisy Gilman did such reinforcing as they each not only loved the subject matter they were teaching, but also respected each other. They taught many of the same students, and they got along well and became good friends. It worked out very nicely when Nick taught the exciting time of the Roaring Twenties just as Mrs. Gilman was teaching F. Scott Fitzgerald's *The Great Gatsby*.

The end of Nick's career was nigh as he entered his thirty-seventh and final year as an educator. Actually, he saw it as his final year as a teacher because he had always considered himself a teacher and not an educator. *Educator* was too broad and could be used as a professional tag for one the many overpriced bureaucrats and officials who never had direct contact with the product, which of course was the kids, but who would always list educator as their profession. Nick never could understand that.

Nick also noticed he was beginning to teach legacies, having taught some of his current students' moms or dads, and in some cases both. He had always had siblings, but this was new. That was a flashlight shone right into his eyes indicating that it was time to move on. This was happening more and more as many, like Nick, had migrated from

West Palm and gone to the North County and Jupiter, but also for the simple reason that he had been teaching a long time. The school year of 2019–2020 would be his last and, without a doubt, his most memorable in terms of events inside and outside his classroom.

As the year began, Nick told all his classes that this would be his last year and that the juniors seated in front of him would be his final group of students. He also told the seniors whom he had taught the previous year that they would walk out together across that stage for graduation at the fairgrounds because in a way they were both part of the Class of 2020. Once the school year got started, it was as normal as any year when Nick had taught. Sure, there had been events such as the *Challenger* space shuttle disaster, the 2000 election in Palm Beach County, and of course 9/11, but none of those would compare to the first year of the COVID-19 crisis. Around Christmastime, there were stories coming out of China of some airborne sickness caused by someone eating a bat from a wet market. The concept of wet markets and eating flying rats was almost impossible to comprehend, and it was happening half a world away, so nothing to worry about. Wrong.

Returning from the winter break, Nick noticed the news had stopped calling it "the Chinese virus" and how now renamed it the COVID flu, and the media were reporting that it was becoming more and more prevalent. Unelected people became leaders in the fight against COVID-19. Dr. Anthony Fauci became the most well-known man in the United States. Events were postponed and later were outright canceled. People did not panic, at least most did not, but the directives and list of consequences for not following them changed daily. Not since the Civil War had the individual states differed so much in terms of the programs and strategies their governors adhered to. The difference between Florida and New York was striking and fascinating, never mind that many of the residents of the Sunshine State were transplanted New Yorkers.

Starting at Christmas, Nick began the slow process of tearing down his room and giving away some of the stuff he had accumulated. Some of the keepsakes would be making the journey home with him to Egret Landing. Nick had taken over a downstairs bedroom and transformed into a study, library, and office. He figured he would do a little bit every weekend so that he would not be spending his final days cleaning out his classroom, preferring to spend those moments with his students and friends. Nick had always prided himself on his room decor of mementos and student work. It looked more like a museum than like a high school classroom. A couple of things stood out and were meant to do so. There was a framed picture of an American bison or buffalo with the official adoption papers showing that Nick was the proud papa of an actual buffalo living and protected on a preserve in Wyoming. Nick had always stressed the importance of this American prairie beast, noting the majesty of the animal and just how crucial they were to both the Native Americans and the settlers moving west. Never lost on the story was the importance of Teddy Roosevelt and the actions he had taken to save the species. Obviously, a couple of Nick's students picked up on the fact that Nick had a respect for the animal. One day he opened a package that had arrived for him at the school, and inside was a small stuffed buffalo and an official WWF adoption paper, which Nick framed and hung next to the shelved buffalo he had named Chad after the Saunders boy and JHS grad who was now a defensive back for the University of Colorado Buffalos. That stuffed buffalo was coming home. All in all, there were about seventy-five framed souvenirs that he would place in his new library, each with its own story. These keepsakes in a way tell the story of Nick and his career, but there was one set that garnered the most attention, and it would be coming home.

A neat thing that JHS did for its athletes was, if they had received any postseason awards such as All-Conference, to place their photographs and plaques bearing their names in the gym lobby trophy case for all to see. Many parents would beam with pride and take pictures of their sons and daughters in front of the case, while visiting teams would remark how cool the idea was and why their schools did not do something like that. Nick loved the idea, so he borrowed the concept and used it as motivation for passing the AP exam in May. He went to the Home Depot and purchased an 8' × 2' piece of raw lumber and took it home. He cut the one end into a sharp point and then broke out the paint. The top would be red; next to the red would be silver; the length would be yellow; the bottom areas would be brown; and the tip would be black. What Nick ended up making were some giant no. 2 pencils. Every year after the Christmas break, he would fasten one of these pencils to a wall at the front of his classroom so it was directly facing the students and in their line of sight when they were seated at their desks. He then would place the year of the class across the top and explain that on the first day of their senior year, they should come by his room and sign the pencil for everyone to see that they had passed the national AP exam. He said the pencil would remain hanging in portable no. 4 until Nick retired. It was not only a reward but also a motivation as more than one student remarked that they wanted their names on that damn pencil. This was especially true in cases of sibling rivals. Sure enough, the first day of school the next year there was line of students waiting to sign their names. And soon there would be another blank pencil just waiting for that year's class to write their names on it for posterity. Reward and motivate was the lesson plan, and it seemed to work. Nick would find himself looking at the pencils and grinning when finding the name of an outstanding young person to whom he had had the privilege of teaching the American story. Those pencils were coming home.

It turned out to be a lucky thing that Nick was slowly taking home his things because life as he knew it as a high school teacher would change forever. Schools across the country were closing and going to remote learning. Nick was praying that would not happen to him with his extremely limited tech skills. He began to pick up the pace, taking home more and more stuff, but most importantly his review materials just in case he had to switch to remote learning. He was lucky in that he had a prized gate key, so he could drive right up to his portable at almost any time and load up. He had been entrusted with the key because he would be called upon to open the gate for emergency vehicles or district maintenance people who needed access to the back of the school for repair work. Then he'd close it behind them once they left, which was even more important since the Stoneman Douglas massacre south in Parkland. That event rattled almost everyone even more than 9/11 had. It could have easily been JHS instead of MSD down in Broward County. Nick had always worried a little that something similar would occur in the portables since they were more exposed than the campus classrooms. He hadn't worried about it much at Forest Hill, but he did at JHS as it seemed the pressure these kids were under could push one of them to the breaking point. Nick always pointed out to his students that there were two doors and asked them to please share any concerns they might have, even if there seemed to them that there wasn't much to report. Silence could be deadly. Nick took one more precaution in that he kept a ten-inch knife in his desk. Even though he had a concealed weapons permit, district employees were not allowed to have personal firearms on campus. He understood that decision, so he kept a knife and he made sure that the students saw him use it almost daily. They watched him take the knife and slice oranges or apples, or fix something, so in a way they were so comfortable with it that they did not even notice it. Sure, Nick used it for fruits and vegetables, but he kept it for protection and prayed he would never have to use it to protect his students and himself against any evil that might be lurking.

The main reason Nick had the gate key was that after spring break he would open the back gate and allow his students to park there and meet him for Saturday test prep study sessions. He never got paid for these sessions, but if they were willing to give up a Saturday morning, then he could be there for them. He really enjoyed the sessions as they were much more laid back. Soon the word spread, and students from other schools would show up. Nick never turned anyone away.

Dr. Carolyn Esposito, the JHS principal, had been warning her staff to stay close to the news as the situation was fluid concerning a possible closing and going remote. She made sure everyone had a Chromebook ready to go home with them if the situation warranted it. Nick was lucky that she was his boss; she would become his favorite. Positive, upbeat, and hardworking, a woman who had earned her promotions unlike many of the others who received plum administrative jobs, Dr. Espo was respected because she deserved to be. Nick was glad that he was leaving the profession under the leadership of his favorite principal.

Then the time came. Dr. Espo told everyone on or close to Saint Patrick's Day that they would be going home. "Stay close and check your email as more information will be forthcoming." Nick had taught his last day on the JHS campus. No longer would he see his students face-to-face, wish the graduates good luck and goodbye, or say "See you later" to his friends and the school he loved so much. He had no idea what would be coming next, and it seemed no one else did either.

Proms were canceled. Sports and extracurricular activities were shut down. Senior athletes in the spring sports would not get to play for their schools ever again.

Plays and concerts ceased, and the curtains came down. Yearbooks and, later, diplomas had to be picked up in the parking lot, with the seniors remaining masked in their cars and opening their trunks to a masked school official who would place their rightful items in their trunks. No walking across the stage and hugging one's fellow grads. Many who would go off to college excited about their first time away from home and experience Greek rush and football games had been subjected to mandated closure, a trend that would follow them from high school to college. We may never know the damage we did to these kids, but they answered the bell and made it work somehow.

Nick recorded his final goodbye to the seniors who had been his students just one year earlier, with the signed pencil behind him. He played the recording to the soon-to-be grads as they tried to finish up their crazy last few days within a system gone mad. Nick told them there are three keys to life that come by dividing the twenty-four-hour day into three equal eight-hour segments. For one time period you need a good bed and bedroom for solitude, mood refreshment, and security. After all, one of life's great pleasures is an afternoon nap when it is raining outside. Works every time. For the next eight hours, find a career and not a job, because then you will never merely go to work. Nick explained that is why he never looked at teaching as a job but as a career. Finally, he said, find the right person to share your life with. Never stop looking because there is someone out there for everyone. He had used this same goodbye for years, but this year was different. He added to his seniors that they would be sitting for interviews in the future, and now they had a good answer to the question that seemed to be always asked: "What was your biggest challenge, and how did you overcome it?"

Nick would say, "You are part of the Class of 2020. That should answer it."

Nick went home and finished remodeling the unoccupied downstairs bedroom so that it looked like a mini classroom. This was his portable no. 4. The upcoming Monday would be the first day of Chromebook instruction, and Nick was, as J.W. would say, nervous as a "whore in church". Nick's tech skills were lacking, and to say he had tech skills would be unfair to some of the other people who also were a little deficient in terms of computer skills. All Nick was able to do on the computer was the basic stuff like signing on, replying to emails, and recording grades. For anything else, he had to have people help him or do it for him. One day it might be the tech genius Michael Stunn helping out, and the next it might be the mass media specialist Marilyn Miller. And there was always the standby in portable no. 7, "Aunt Betsy," who really knew her way around a keyboard with a mouse. The fact she and Nick were about the same age and had grown up knowing each other—she had gone to Cardinal Newman and Nick to Forest Hill—made him even more embarrassed that he had never taken the time to learn. Whenever he had to copy and paste, he literally did just that—with scissors and glue. At the house he had three exceptionally reliable advisers in Tyler (when home), Mel, and Lauren, the last of whom was, quite frankly, damn good—and thank goodness, because it was, she who had set everything up for Nick.

That Monday Nick signed on using his confidential class code for his first-hour class, and lo and behold the screen came on but was blank. Suddenly he started hearing beeping sounds, along with a name of the particular student who had signed on, and the screen began to divide up. They were now up and running for the first hour's AP US History class. They all appeared on screen—ah the miracle of the internet and computer. Nick took roll and gently opened his class by saying that he was as nervous as a girl on a prom date, asking his students to be gentle because it was his first time. The class laughed and giggled at the slightly off-color remark, and Nick realized that this group would not get a prom this year or the next because of this thing called COVID. One class after another signed on and then off, and by noon Nick was done—and also surprised at how exhausted he was. He realized he was no longer a stage actor on Broadway, but one on TV. He still dressed up in his signature starched shirt and tie as he tried to keep the class as normal as he could. He was amazed how well the kids behaved, and their attendance was exceptional. At the end of the year, Nick did the basic math and found that his attendance was right around 95 percent, which was the same as he'd had in person. The kids, and to an extent the parents, had made this happen. Once in a while a student would ask if he or she could sign on for another one of Nick's classes because of other school commitments, and his answer was, "Of course you can." Some had technology problems and would email him to let him know they were not skipping but trying to expand their bandwidth, whatever that meant. If there was an assignment, after

Nick called roll, they would present their work right on camera. It was actually working. There were a few who got left behind, and Kelli Floss, the great assistant principal who did some investigating into these situations, said there were problems at home much bigger than Nick's history class. Nick Finch understood and pretty much gave those three or four students a C for the fourth quarter. Miss Floss was the best assistant principal he had ever worked with. Hardworking, competent, and caring—that alone made her better than most. A former social studies teacher herself, she knew what the teachers were going through, and, well, she was quite easy on the eyes. Very pretty indeed. Kelli became friends with Lauren and was a positive influence on Mel. One summer the three of them had a two-day staycation at the Breakers in July, which consisted of beach time, the spa, massages, and wine. It is good when one of your superiors is a family friend, but that was what Jupiter High was all about, one big family that now had the nearly impossible job of making this whole thing work.

Nick would brag to anyone who would listen just how great his kids were and what they were doing. There were a couple of funny things, such as when two of them signed in together because they'd apparently had a sleepover and signed on in bed and in their nighties. Nick was proud that he held his composure and disabled that particular feed. It did produce a grin that no one else got to see. Another time, at the end of a lesson, a mom came into the camera's view and shared with everyone that this time she understood Mr. Finch's lesson, as she had not when he taught her some thirty-five years earlier back at Forest

Hill. It took Nick about three seconds before he realized it was Traci Robbins, whose daughter Hanna was now in his class. She explained that back then she had not spent her nights studying US history but was out on the town at places like the Cruzan Liquor Stand or E. R. Bradley's Saloon. Traci was eighteen but going on twenty-eight back then. She wanted to add more, but her daughter pleaded with her and cut her off. The whole episode was one of Nick's favorite memories from the Chromebook era.

As the days were whittled down to the end, Nick was busy preparing his kids for a revamped College Board AP test that was online. It had a one-question winner-take-all format, but with permanent results. This was now getting crazy, but both the teacher and the students did all they could for the success that would be theirs when the scores were tabulated and it was found that Nick's kids had kicked the national average's ass and hit the proverbial home run. About the same time, the school board needed his final retirement paperwork signed and delivered, along with the official paperwork for the State Department of Education and, most importantly, the Department of Pension Services. Later, Nick was informed of a special time he was to drive down to the district offices and pick up his retirement gifts. Much like the kids at school, he was to remain in his car and open the trunk as the masked district officials placed a cloth shopping bag in it so Nick could drive off and go back home to Jupiter. The end was getting near.

He noticed that the parking lot at the district was a ghost town—desolate and nearly void of parked cars. They worked on a different schedule than the school site people did. Nick was told to tune into the local cable access station for a tribute from the various board members and the superintendent himself. They promised a slide show of the retiring veterans. Some had remarked that there should be something more this year because none of them would get the honor of sitting on the graduation stage and being recognized. Some commented that Nick and some others should further be honored as not only teachers in the district but also graduates of Palm Beach County.

Lauren and Nick tuned in, and sure enough, Nick's name appeared, but as Nick Flinch and not Nick Finch. No picture, nothing. Lauren was disturbed by the lack of effort and professional courtesy, but Nick said it did not surprise him in the least. He then opened his gift bag and found a small etched piece of glass that measured 4.5" × 5" and said, "Congratulations on Retirement." No name and nothing personalized, but there was a spiked plastic cup holder that sported the name of an investment company that the district did business with. It was a gift that was for future use as a beach tool. That was about it. Thirty-seven years and a piece of plastic made in China. Add to that the misspelled name in the slide show, and Nick knew he had made the right decision to retire. He would miss the kids and the on-site people who now were some of his best friends, but he would not miss the bureaucracy of the district. Not in the least.

As the final day drew nearer and nearer, Nick was worried about what he was witnessing going on across the country. He had been very young during the Vietnam protests, but as a history major, he studied the war and the time period with ferocity. What he kept coming back to was two photographs that were etched in his teaching memory that he would show his classes side by side, then ask them what they saw and instruct them to write a list of comparisons and contrasts. The two photographs are still among the most famous in US photographic history, with one being of an anguished coed at Kent State crying out for help for her downed fellow student, and the other being a protester in DC placing a flower into the rifle of an on-duty National Guardsman, with both subjects looking to be about the same age yet appearing to be very different in their beliefs. Nick thought about those people as he now watched the news with nightly images of either protests or riots depending on one's viewpoint. Especially hard hit were the cities in the Upper Midwest like Minneapolis and those in the Pacific Northwest like Portland, Oregon. Nick wondered if they would spread to his area. For the most part they did not, but there was tension, and you could feel it. He wished he were in front of his class in person to make use of this teachable moment in history, but he could not be. and it bothered him to have to lose the opportunity.

Nick was wrapping up his online teaching basically by holding bull sessions with his students. He got to know them more than he'd known his previous students whom he taught in person. They seemed to genuinely miss him, and he sincerely missed them more than they would ever know. Nick Finch had always wondered what it would be like to lock his classroom door for the last time and walk from the outside portables onto campus and down the hall the final time. He kept thinking about the final scene in

Mr. Holland's Opus, where music director Mr. Holland, accompanied by his wife and returning son, attempt to leave together for the last time but swing by the school auditorium, where a surprise celebration is waiting for him, attended by past and present students. Nick never forgot that scene, and he remembered when he saw it for the first time: on July 2, 1996, the eve of Tyler's birth at Good Samaritan Hospital on the Flagler Drive waterfront in West Palm Beach. For years he had replayed that scene over and over in his head when wondering what was going to happen to him on his last day, and now he realized that nothing at all would happen because COVID-19 had stripped him of the chance for a "final goodbye". When he thought about it, he felt a wide range of emotions, such as anger and sadness, but he would quickly snap out of it because then he would think of his students, especially his seniors, who had lost out on their senior year of high school. So, there was no auditorium full of well-wishers for Nick, but for those twelfth graders there was no graduation, no sports, no activities, no prom, and no final goodbyes. That thought put his own life back into perspective. And he did have his school board plastic drink holder to cherish forever and ever. Right.

It was late May and was beginning to get hot, which meant the everlasting summer months were just ahead, which of course would include hurricanes, unforgiving heat and humidity, and daily afternoon torrential downpours. It was a Friday when Nick asked if any of the guys would be going out for a cold one. Mike Lynn, who had grown to become one of Nick's very closest friends, said he was going to swing by the Finch house for a beer there on his front porch. Shortly thereafter, Mike Lombardi, a very gifted teacher whose two daughters Nick had been fortunate enough to teach, one of whom interned with Lauren at the bank before she graduated from the University of Florida and then went on to law school, was coming by too. And then Tyrone Smith heard the happy hour was at the Finch Ranch and said he would be by shortly, but first he needed to know if Nick had any Tito's vodka available. Of course, he did. This could be fun, so Nick picked up around the house and emptied out some chips and peanuts he kept for such occasions, which usually happened late afternoon on Fridays, when the neighbors would stop by the front porch for a toddy to discuss their week's work or how their kids were doing in Nick's class. With it getting hot out, Nick turned down the AC and turned the fans up. He thought it might too hot for the front porch, at least for a couple of hours, especially for Mike Lynn, who always was bitching about the heat—and he had grown up here! Then it was Lauren who called. She informed Nick she would be coming home early because of a planned protest down in the West Palm–Palm Beach area. She wanted to get her people off the island so they would not be caught in the middle of some sort of disturbance. Nick thought Palm Beach would be simply fine because all they had to do was raise the bridges, then the Intracoastal Waterway would act as a protective moat. What happened to Fifth Avenue in New York would not occur on Worth Avenue, Palm Beach's exclusive shopping area. Gucci, Chanel, and Saks would be safe, thank you very much. Lauren asked if

Nick and the boys were going for drinks that afternoon, and Nick said, "They are coming here to the house, so please join us. I think there is an unopened bottle of Cab around here somewhere."

Pretty soon the boys all arrived, along with a couple of the neighbors at about the same time. Then Lauren pulled into the driveway right next to the guys, who had all arrived in the same car. Nick suggested they it take indoors, but the guys and Lauren, who reemerged after changing into leisure wear, all wanted to stay out front. Mike found a Nerf football, which the guys began to toss around, when suddenly things began to change. A car turned down the Scrub Jay Lane cul-de-sac with Stacy Marshall driving her convertible VW and four others from Nick's class hanging out of it with the song "Stacy's Mom" blaring out as they all waved and screamed. Nick noticed their car was covered with streamers and posters proclaiming their love for their history teacher. Then came another car, and another. Each car seemed packed inside like a can of sardines. More cars came with more screaming and waving, but now Rick Springfield was professing his love for his friend Jessie's significant other. Still more cars came, but now the street was getting backed up. But now everyone surely knew the phone number 867-5309 because the volume was off the noise meter.

Nick was stunned and overcome with emotion as his friends slowly made their way up beside him. Lauren took his hand and squeezed it tightly. The cars kept coming and coming. Later, after reviewing the film of the "Thank You, Mr. Finch" parade, Nick discovered the vehicle count was just over forty, and a couple were pickup trucks loaded with students. They had planned all this out, including the eighties music soundtrack, Nick's favorite. Nick now had tears running down his face as the cars stopped. All the parade participants rushed from their cars to hug their teacher. Forget the recommended six feet of social distance; they wanted to show their love for their teacher. Many came with cards and gifts. Some stood back and waited their turn to say goodbye, while others skipped ahead in the line for that last hug. Nick's three colleagues were also choked up, very impressed by the outpouring of love that was demonstrated that Friday afternoon in Egret Landing. For one of the very few times in his life, Nick was speechless. He got his "Mr. Holland" moment, but this was even better. Much better. Slowly, the students climbed back into their cars, never knowing what they had done. Besides the healthy birth of his children and walking down the aisle with Lauren, this was the single greatest moment of Nick's life. Just then, Mike Lynn made some comment about moving the party inside, adding, "Damn, it's hot out here."

Tyrone Smith quickly responded, "No, it's not the heat, it's the humidity, stupid."

Nick turned around and, looking at both of them with tear-streaked cheeks and a million-dollar smile, said, "Nope, it's just perfect."

Printed in the USA
CPSIA information can be obtained
at www.ICGtesting.com
LVHW020521160124
769072LV00004B/37

9 781665 571562